TORCHWOOD
THE ENCYCLOPEDIA

THE DEFINITIVE GUIDE TO THE HIT TV SERIES

GARY RUSSELL

BBC BOOKS

1 3 5 7 9 10 8 6 4 2

Published in 2009 by BBC Books, an imprint of Ebury Publishing.
A Random House Group Company

Torchwood is a BBC Wales production for BBC Television
Executive Producers: Russell T Davies and Julie Gardner
Series Producers: Richard Stokes (Series One and Two)
and Peter Bennett (Children of Earth)
Co-Producer: Chris Chibnall (Series One and Two)

The Random House Group Limited Reg. No. 954009

Addresses for companies within the Random House Group
can be found at www.randomhouse.co.uk

A CIP catalogue record for this book is available from
the British Library.

ISBN 978 1 846 07764 7

The Random House Group Limited supports The Forest
Stewardship Council (FSC), the leading international forest
certification organisation. All our titles that are printed
on Greenpeace approved FSC certified paper carry the
FSC logo. Our paper procurement policy can be found at
www.rbooks.co.uk/environment

Commissioning editor: Albert DePetrillo
Project editor: Steve Tribe
Designer: Richard Atkinson
Production: Phil Spencer

Printed and bound in Germany by Firmengruppe APPL,
aprinta druck, Wemding

To buy books by your favourite authors and register for offers,
visit www.rbooks.co.uk

INTRODUCTION

A couple of years ago, I wrote an encyclopedia to the new series of *Doctor Who*. That was big, and hopefully fairly exhaustive, and a lot of fun.

So when I suggested to BBC Books, 'Hey let's do the same for *Torchwood*' (which at that time had only two seasons, the latter of which I'd been one of the script editors on, so knew it quite well), I thought it'd be a doddle…

And then came a fabulous radio drama. And a marvellous third series. And another three staggeringly brilliant Radio 4 dramas and, suddenly, it was a BIG PROJECT.

And here it is: everything you need to know about *Torchwood*. So far… Can't wait to update it – around the time of *Torchwood* Series Six, I reckon. Or as I call it 'Torchwood: Exhausted Script Editors of Earth'.

Of course, all I've done is compile a list of words and definitions. I didn't even put them in alphabetical order. (Steve Tribe, my editor, did that. With some computer software that Tosh invented, I expect.) And I certainly didn't select the pretty pictures and design it. (That's down to lovely Richard Atkinson.) And, of course, I didn't write the scripts. Or produce, direct, design, or anything else that the geniuses at our Upper Boat studios did.

All I've done is take the hard blood, sweat and tears of a few hundred talented people, type a few words up and take all the credit. And that's unfair. And I'd love to list for you the people who really did make this book – each and every one of the writers, the actors, the directors, designers, etc.

But I can't – because that would be a list as long as this entire book. What I can do – what I must do and I want to do – is thank a few ultra-important people. Firstly, Edward Thomas's art department. Julian, James,

Arwel, Pete, Stephen… and so many other talented and unsung heroes. Marie Doris and her make-up teams; Ray Holman and his costume teams; Neill, Rob and Kate at Millennium FX; Will, Marie and Barney from The Mill – all aspects of their incredible work are seen inside this book. The other script editors – Lindsey Alford, Helen Raynor, and especially Brian Minchin. Our producers, Richard Stokes, Peter Bennett and Chris Chibnall. And of course, our execs, Julie Gardner and the man who gave us the show in the first place – Russell T Davies.

Thanks to all of you for letting me write a book about all your work.

Oh and before you kick off your journey from 'A For Andromeda' through to 'Zenegon Rain', a quick glimpse of some of the things that you won't get to read about, due to script changes, alterations, last-minute cuts and other 'beyond our control' moments… A quick shout-out to George W. Bush (the ex-President was the butt of a joke), Mikey (Carys Fletcher shagged him to death in a car), the Airport Controller (she saw Diane Holmes arrive), David Dickinson (Ianto likened Henry John Parker to him – Parker was an American millionaire at the time with a ghostly wife), Detective Sgt Parry (he was investigating Billy Davis, the serial killer), Stan Spears (Bridget's male alter ego), a Hoix in a Wedding Dress (he'd've looked very fetching, too), Alf the Janitor (the Weevils got him, poor soul), Paul (we would have learned that the child in the 456 tank was Clem's roommate in 1965), the Vardans (*Doctor Who* monsters from the 1970s – one was in the Torchwood cells, apparently), and Sarah Barclay (oh, I wish you could've met Sarah Barclay, maybe one day…).

I love this series. I hope you do too, and I hope you enjoy this book almost as much…

Gary Russell, July 2009

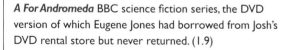

[A]

A For Andromeda BBC science fiction series, the DVD version of which Eugene Jones had borrowed from Josh's DVD rental store but never returned. (1.9)

A&E Doctor Cardiff Royal Infirmary medic who stitched up Gwen's head wound after she and Andy Davidson stopped a pub brawl. (1.1)

A&E Nurse Present at the hospital, in the ICU, where Nettie Williams, the Windsor Café restaurant owner and all of the family in the car were in cataleptic states. She was present when Ianto and Jack managed to revive the young boy by returning his stolen last breath to him. (2.10) (Played by CAROLINE SHEEN)

A470 Trunk road north of Cardiff leading towards the Brecon Beacons. Leighton Reynolds used to meet the Harries & Harries lorries there to pick up the alien meat they were dealing in. (2.4)

A48 Main route between Cardiff and the M4. Eugene Jones ran from the roadside Happy Cook restaurant onto it, where he was hit by a red Vauxhall driven by a drunk driver and killed before he could get all the way across. (1.9)

ABBA Swedish pop stars who won the Eurovision Song Contest in 1974. Jack remembered them fondly. (TDL)

Abaddon Cited in the Bible as the Great Devourer, and called the Son of the Great Beast by Bilis Manger, who also claimed Abaddon had been chained beneath the Rift. Bilis had manipulated the Torchwood team into fully opening the Rift and freeing Abaddon to stalk the world. Everywhere

A

his shadow was cast, death was instantaneous, and he destroyed much of Cardiff before Jack offered himself to Abaddon, who couldn't cope with the life energy of a man that could not die. When Abaddon was destroyed, time was flung back; everyone who had died came back to life and no one other than Torchwood ever remembered the events of the day. (1.13)

Abbey Road Famous music studios in the London road of the same name. When the Rift was opened by Owen, the Beatles were seen performing on its roof. (1.13)

Abergavenny Monmouthshire market town where, Andy Davidson hoped, the Weevils had fled to after they stopped attacking his police station. (2.13)

Aberystwyth University Location of a seminar organised by the North Wales Astronomy Society called 'Black Holes and the Uncertainty Principle', which Eugene Jones and his mate Gary planned to attend. Gary went alone after Eugene's death, but Eugene's 'spirit' form, created by his ingestion of the Dogon Sixth Eye, enabled him to go too, unseen by everyone. (1.9)

Access codes The access code to the Pharm's Records Office was 41040, and the password used by Martha Jones to access the Pharm's medical records was 72zqyfq. (2.6)

Acetone Six per cent of the 456's atmosphere was made up of this. (CoE)

Acid Burn A movie for rent in Josh's DVD store. (1.9)

Africa Continent not yet visited by the fictitious Samantha Jones. (2.6)

Ahab, Captain Fictional sailor obsessed with the great white whale, Moby Dick, in the book of that name. Ianto suggests Jack is as equally obsessed by the alien leviathan that Harries & Harries are cutting up and selling on as edible meat. (2.4)

Alabama 3 South East London music collective whose song 'Mao Tse Tung Said' was playing at Bar Reunion when John Hart entered. (2.1)

Albany Street Location of the police station in Camden where Clement MacDonald was held. (CoE)

Alesha Young girl who befriended Emma Louise Cowell at the hostel. (1.10) (Played by JANINE CARRINGTON)

Alien 1979 science fiction movie featuring British actor John Hurt as a character who was killed when an alien burst out of his chest and stomach. Tosh and Owen discussed it as they examined the skeleton of the nineteenth-century soldier Mary killed. (1.7)

Alien locket Jewellery device that had come through the Rift. When Torchwood Three leader Alex Hopkins opened it, it made him realise that humanity was doomed, so he murdered his team, bequeathing Torchwood Three to Jack and then killing himself. (2.12)

Aliens Unnamed aggressive race that finally attacked the Boeshane Peninsula after the many times they had flown overhead. Jack described them as the most horrible creatures one could imagine, whose howls travelled before them. They killed his father and captured his brother, imprisoning Gray and making him a slave for many years. (2.5, 2.13)

'All Things Will Die' Tennyson poem quoted by Ianto and Jack after they had stopped the alien Ghost Entities invading Earth via the CERN facility. (LS)

Ammonium hydroxide Lethal chemical that Billy Davis injected, via the eyeball, into former Pharm patients to kill them and eliminate any trace of the alien Mayfly larvae they had ingested. (2.6)

Amnesia pill A compound of various mind-altering drugs, coded B67 that Jack created to act as a method of erasing short-term memory. Innocent people who encountered aliens or other Torchwood activity could be given the drug (it came in differing strengths depending on the severity of the experience and length of exposure) to remove any memory of events witnessed. Colloquially referred to as 'Retcon'. Jack gave it to Gwen but she broke through its conditioning. (1.1) Suzie Costello had been repeatedly giving it to Max Tresillian, ostensibly

A

testing its long-term effects, but in reality intending to drive him psychotic – up to that point, Torchwood believed that only 2,008 people had been given the pill. (1.8) Gwen gave it to Rhys and then confessed to her affair with Owen, knowing he would never remember. (1.11) Owen was convinced that Jack would give him such a high dosage if he quit Torchwood that he'd forget everything about his life for the past few years. (1.13) Gwen refused to give the pill to Rhys after he had helped end Harries & Harries's trade in alien meat. (2.4) Jack used it on himself and the rest of the team to remove their memories of the forty-eight hours during which Adam had infiltrated Torchwood. (2.5) Jack used a special Level Six version to knock out and erase the short-term memories of the guests at Gwen and Rhys's wedding. (2.9)

'Amsterdam' Anthemic trance tune by DJ Paul Oakenfold, which was playing in the Nightspot nightclub in Cardiff. (1.2)

Annie Delivery girl from Jubilee Pizza, who knew Ianto quite well. She was murdered by Lisa Hallett, who put her own brain into Annie's skull. Annie's body was destroyed by Torchwood, who shot it to death. (1.4) (Played by BETHAN WALKER)

Antiques Roadshow BBC TV show, which Sean Harris reckoned he might take the Ghost Machine to and discover its worth. (1.3)

Arbroath The Holly Tree Lodge orphanage was about ten miles away from this town in Scotland in 1965. (CoE)

Arcadian Diamond John Hart's lover had one of these and he shot her in the back and killed her in an effort to steal it. She threw it into a Rift storm, and John had been trying to find it ever since. In truth it never existed; it was a ruse set up by the murdered woman to seek revenge on John. (2.1)

A

Arcateenian Alien who took on the form of prostitute Mary. (1.7) Amongst Henry John Parker's alien purchases was an Arcateenian translation of *The Fog* by James Herbert. (2.8)

ARJ27 Login name used by Martha Jones to access the Pharm's medical records. (2.6)

Arkans Chatty liquid life forms who flew tourist craft across the galaxy. A First Generation (collector's item, apparently) Leisure Trawler was flying over Cardigan Bay, and Tosh sent them a polite but firm request to get away from Earth. (1.4)

Arnold, Daniel A mate of Eugene Jones's. (1.9)

Artesia Place where John Hart picked up the trick of apparently swallowing something but in fact keeping it in the throat, enabling him to cough it up later. (2.1)

Arwyn, Alex Estate agent found dead at 96 Oakham Street. Torchwood attempted to use the Resurrection Glove on him to get information on his killer, but he couldn't help them, instead calling for his mum. (1.8) (Played by DANIEL LLEWELLYN-WILLIAMS)

Ashton Down Government military installation where the bodies of Jack and Rupesh Patanjali were taken by Johnson's people. (CoE)

'Assassin' Song by Muse which was playing in the Cube Bar when Mark Lynch and Owen got into a fight with Tommy. (1.11)

Astaire, Fred American dancer, singer and actor. Tosh had watched him in the movie *Easter Parade*. Twice. (2.9)

Astoria Ballroom Dancehall where 17-year-old Estelle Cole met and fell in love with Jack just before Christmas. He also loved her but, because of his immortality, he pretended to go abroad during the Second World War. Years later, he met Estelle again and convinced her he was her Jack's son. (1.5)

ATLAS Biggest of the particle detectors at the CERN facility in Switzerland. (LS)

'Atlas' Track by American band Battles, which Owen listened to whilst clearing out his apartment after his death. (2.8)

Audrey Good-time girl at the Ritz Dance Hall in 1941, who made out with both George and Smiler the day before they were due to fly out on training exercises. (1.12) (Played by NADINE BEATON)

Australia Country Linda at Passmore Telesales told Eugene she had always wanted to visit. He tried to sell his Dogon Sixth Eye on eBay and use the money to send her there. (1.9) The fictitious Samantha Jones had visited Australia. (2.6)

Australia House Diplomatic building in London, which raised a figurative red flag with John Frobisher at the start of the 456 incident. (CoE)

Authorisation codes Security access codes used by Torchwood to access Government files and identify operatives and confirm their status to official authorities. Code 45895 identified Jack when he contacted the UK Prime Minister and later Owen used the same code to access the police files on Operation Lowry. (1.7) Jack used the code 474317 to identify himself to the police. (2.7) Gwen used the code 474317432 to gain access to the secret facility on Flat Holm Island. (2.11)

Automatic, The Band whose song 'Monster' was being played in the car driven by Ellie Johnson when she was abducted and murdered in the Brecon Beacons. (1.6)

[B]

B587 Cardiff road that led to Hedley Point. (1.8)

Bahamas Ianto didn't expect to die there, any more than he did in a freezing tunnel beneath Switzerland. (LS)

Ball, Lee Probable victim of the alien, Mary, who ripped out people's hearts to thrive upon. Ball died in 1976. (1.7)

Banana Boat Rhys's mate and eventually his best man at his wedding to Gwen. He and Rhys were feeling middle age creeping up on them (1.1) and eventually Banana went off to the Canary Islands to sell pirated CDs. He was arrested (2.8) and deported, and got back to Wales in time for the wedding only to be attacked by an alien Nostrovite and trapped in a cocoon with Tosh. Eventually freed, he was given a healthy dose of Retcon. (2.9) (Played by JONATHAN LEWIS OWEN)

Banksy Owner of the Nightspot nightclub in Cardiff. He was watching Carys Fletcher and Matt Stevens have sex in

the women's toilets on his club when he witnessed Matt die in a burst of sexual energy. (1.2) (Played by CERI MEARS)

Bar Reunion Cardiff drinking establishment where John Hart waited for Jack. Once his fellow Time Agent arrived, the two smashed the place up during a fight. (2.1)

Barbara Not, Jack considered, a suitable name for a Weevil. (1.11)

Barmaid Worked in a pub where Clement MacDonald went after fleeing the Duke of York Hospital. She turned him in to the police. (CoE) (Played by LIBBY LIBURD)

Barman (1) Man in the pub where John Ellis and Jack shared a drink who wouldn't let John smoke his pipe. (1.10) (Played by CIARAN DOWD)

Barman (2) Worked in the bar where Owen had a vision of Diane Holmes and disturbed Owen, breaking the vision. (1.13) (Played by PAUL BENNETT)

Barman (3) Served Tommy with drinks in a bar. (2.3)

Barry Seaside town near Cardiff, where a Hoix was once found eating its way through the contents of a Kebab shop. (2.13)

Battersea South London area where the Torchwood Institute had a warehouse that acted as a holding area. The Cardiff Torchwood team used it as a base, naming it Hub 2, during the 456 crisis. (CoE)

Battle of Britain Famous Second World War aerial dogfight, which occurred in 1940. The real Captain Jack Harkness took part. (1.12)

Battles American band, whose first single, 'Atlas', was played by Owen while he cleared out his flat after his death. (2.8)

Baxter, Simon John Frobisher's talkative driver, who took him from home to Whitehall and back regularly. (CoE) (Played by DENZIE PHIPPS)

Baxters, the Family living opposite Rhiannon and Johnny Davies. (CoE)

BBC reporter TV news presenter who reported on the events of the 456's return. (CoE) (Played by LOUISE MINCHIN)

Beatles, The Liverpudlian pop group who disbanded in 1969 but were seen performing atop the Abbey Road studios when Owen opened the Rift. (1.13)

Bedlam Outlands Planet where John Hart found Gray, surrounded by corpses and chained to a ruined building, long abandoned by the savage aliens that had kidnapped him from the Boeshane Peninsula, and driven completely mad by his experiences. (2.13)

Beethoven, Ludwig van German composer and pianist in the late eighteenth and early nineteenth centuries. His *Moonlight Sonata* was playing on the radio that Jack tuned in for John Ellis. (1.10)

'Begging You' Song by the Stone Roses, which was playing in the bar where Owen had a vision of Diane Holmes. (1.13)

Bekaran Deep-Tissue Scanner Alien device Owen had been adapting before he died. Gwen used it on Leon Foiret and revealed that his neutrons were vanishing. (LS)

Bengal Bay Area flown over by Diane Holmes during her four-day flight between England and Australia in 1952. (1.10)

Bennett, Myra Probable victim of the alien, Mary, who ripped out people's hearts to thrive upon. Bennett was a 37-year-old found dead by her daughter in 1970. She was victim number 37. (1.7)

Bennett, Tony Popular singer whose recording of 'The Good Life' was danced to by Diane Holmes and Owen. (1.10)

Bernard Pianist who supplied live musical accompaniment to the 1920s films being shown at the Electro Cinema in Penarth. (2.10) (Played by PETER BLACKWOOD)

Berry, Chuck American musician whose song 'Johnnie B Goode' was included aboard NASA's *Voyager* Golden Records project, remembered by Owen. (2.8)

'Better Do Better' Song by Hard-Fi played at Lynne Pearce and her partner Roy's BBQ to celebrate their fifth anniversary. (1.5)

Bevan, Jonah At the age of 15, while walking home to Penarth one night across the Cardiff Bay Barrage, he was taken by the Rift and deposited on a distant planet that was completely on fire. Badly scarred and burned, he was rescued by a spaceship and, forty years later, was finally returned to Earth and taken into Torchwood's care by Jack.

Disfigured and insane after staring into a dark star, Jonah was placed in a secure safe house on Flat Holm, an island in the Bristol Channel. His disappearance had been vigorously investigated by PC Andy Davidson, and a tiny glimpse of Rift energy on the CCTV was enough to have Andy bring Gwen into the picture. Having found Jonah, Gwen took his mum to meet him, but she was so shocked at how damaged, physically and mentally, Jonah was that she left and never returned. (2.11) (Played by OLIVER FERRIMAN and ROBERT PUGH)

Bevan, Nikki Mother of Jonah, who had gone missing seconds after waving to her from the Cardiff Bay Barrage. She spent seven months and eleven days trying to find him, scouring hours of crowd footage hoping for a glimpse of him. She kept his room immaculate and even slept in his room sometimes, just to breath in his smell. With Andy Davidson's support, she set up a self-

help group for other victims of missing people and, when Gwen came to the inaugural meeting, she was staggered by how many people had gone missing. When Gwen located Jonah, she told Nikki about Torchwood and took her to visit her son, but Nikki was horrified by Jonah's mental state. She begged Gwen never to reveal the truth to anyone else who had lost someone. Shortly afterwards, all hope lost of ever getting her son back, Nikki stripped his room. (2.11) (Played by RUTH JONES)

Big Dave Friend of Rhys's who said that having kids made him feel like his life had ended, although he had said the same thing when his wife Susy made him get rid of his motorcycle. (2.11)

Big House, The Main building in the village of Brynblaidd. The villagers would kill, skin and cook their victims of their cannibalistic rituals in the barn. (1.6)

Big Val Neighbour of Rhiannon and Johnny Davies. (CoE)

Bikini Cops One of the names John Hart thought would be better than Torchwood for Jack's group. (2.1)

Bioxenic Microtron Machine at the Hub which Owen wanted to use on Gwen to remove the Nostrovite egg growing inside her. It wasn't portable and so he took the Singularity Scalpel instead. (2.9)

Birmingham English city. The first bid for Eugene Jones's Dogon Sixth Eye came from there, for £2.50. (1.9)

Black Holes and the Uncertainty Principle A seminar organised by the North Wales Astronomy Society and held at Aberystwyth University. Eugene Jones and his mate Gary had planned to attend it, but Gary went alone after Eugene's death. Eugene's 'spirit' form, created by his ingestion of the Dogon Sixth Eye, enabled him to accompany Gwen there, unseen by everyone. (1.9)

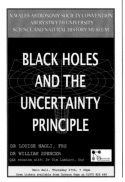

Blackley Suburb of Manchester, where Tommy Brockless was born in 1894. (2.3)

Blackpool Northern football team who beat Bolton Wanderers in the 1953 FA Cup final, which John Ellis had watched on TV with his son Alan. (1.10)

Blackstaff, Mr C. A man who was known on eBay as a buyer of alien ephemera, Beanie Babies and Nazi memorabilia. He was willing to pay £15,000 for Eugene Jones's Dogon Sixth Eye but was jokingly outbid by Josh, who added another £5.50 to the bid. (1.9)

Blaine, Margaret Former Mayor of Cardiff, whose face on a newspaper front page adorned the entrance to Ianto's tourist-shop façade.

Blank Page A document containing a list of names, used by the Government to issue untraceable execution orders. (CoE)

Bletchley Park MOD monitoring base where Tosh's grandfather once worked. (1.7)

Blind patient First World War patient at St Teilo's Military Hospital, in a wheelchair, who cheerfully sung 'I Start My Day Over Again (Clock Song)' to the Nurse. (2.3) (Played by TIM GEBBELS)

Blitz, the Extended period of continuous heavy German bombing raids on British cities including London and Cardiff during the Second World War. (1.1, 1.3, 1.12)

Blizzard One of the names John Hart thought would be better than Torchwood for Jack's group. (2.1)

Bloom, Orlando English actor, of whom Carys Fletcher was something of a fan. (1.2)

Blowfish Colloquial name for a member of a piscine species who have been spotted on Earth a few times. Jack's first freelance assignment for Torchwood was to find one. Another, high on cocaine, took a Cardiff family hostage and was killed by Jack. It was actually a business partner of John Hart. (2.1, 2.12) (Played by PAUL KASEY, voiced by JONATHAN HART)

B

Bob Tosh's boss at Lodmoor Research Facility, who thought she was an excellent worker, unaware she was stealing MoD secrets. (2.12) (Played by SIMON SHACKLTON)

Boeshane Peninsula A fifty-first-century Earth colony where Jack grew up. After an alien attack devastated the colony, Franklin, his father, was killed and his brother Gray was taken prisoner. Jack stayed there, earning a job with the Time Agency, which brought him a degree of fame and a nickname – the Face of Boe – thanks to his image being proudly displayed around the colony. (2.5)

Bolton Wanderers Northern football team who lost 4-3 to Blackpool in the 1953 FA Cup final which John Ellis had watched on TV with his son Alan. (1.10)

Bond, James Fictional spy, whom a man in a street fancied himself to be. (1.7)

'Born to be a Dancer' Song by the Kaiser Chiefs played at Lynne Pearce and her partner Roy's BBQ to celebrate their fifth anniversary. (1.5)

Bosnia Eastern European country which reported its children had become entranced by the 456, causing road traffic accidents. (CoE)

Bouncer (1) Worked in the club where Jack went to visit the Eight-Year-Old Girl and glean the whereabouts of the second Resurrection Glove. (2.7) (Played by BRETT GRIFFITHS)

Bouncer (2) Worked at the Cardiff Bay nightclub, where Torchwood were tracking a Weevil when Martha Jones phoned Jack to ask them to come to Switzerland. (LS) (Played by MARK MEADOWS)

Bouncers Hired help at Bar Reunion who tried to throw John Hart out until the Time Agent revealed some of his weaponry, at which point the bouncers fled along with the staff and customers. (2.1) (Played by ROBERT STONE and JAMES HANNON)

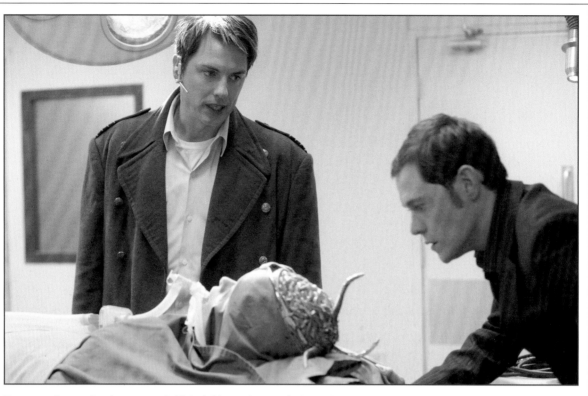

Bowman, Serena Aged patient at St Helen's Hospital who witnessed the entity believed by some to be the embodiment of Death kill everyone in her ward, including her. (2.7) (Played by JANIE BOOTH)

Boy Child seen by Gwen who was briefly put into a trance-like state when being used as a conduit by the 456. When he came out of his trance, he assumed Ianto was filming him to be on television. (CoE) (Played by JORDAN BAKER)

Brain parasite Creature that was living on Katie Russell's brain. It was originally too small to detect, so everyone assumed she had Alzheimer's. When a final MRI scan showed what Doctor Garrett believed to be a tumour, he operated on Katie in an effort to remove it. As soon as it was exposed to the air during surgery, the parasite emitted a toxic gas that killed Katie, Garrett and all the operating-theatre staff. Spent, it was unable to keep Jack from removing it and taking it back to Torchwood. (2.12)

Brecon Beacons South Wales region noted for its natural beauty and secluded areas, including the village of Brynblaidd. (1.6)

Brian Friend of John and Anna Frobisher, who lived in Canada with his wife, Wendy, and their children, who were affected by the 456. (CoE)

Brightman, Sarah, and Hot Gossip Musical dance troupe who had a hit in 1978 with 'I Lost My Heart To A Starship Trooper', which John Hart played in the Hub while waiting for Jack to return. (2.13)

Briscoe, Mark 33-year-old surveyor murdered in his bedroom. Over his and his wife's body was the word 'Torchwood', written in their blood. Torchwood attempted to get information out of him by using the Resurrection Glove on him and he told them they were attacked by a man called Max from Pilgrim and then mentioned Suzie before he died again. (1.8) (Played by GARY PILLAI)

Briscoe, Sarah 33-year-old who worked in education. She and her husband Mark were murdered in their bed by Max Tresillian, who scrawled the word 'Torchwood' above their bodies using their blood. (1.8) (Played by JOANNE MARRIOTT)

Bristol Home town of Emma Louise Cowell, who lived there with her parents. (1.10)

Bristol Channel Waterway separating South Wales from England. Flat Holm island is situated in it. (2.11)

Brittany Holiday destination in north-western France, where Ianto and Lisa Hallett camped on a beach one cold night. A dog relieved itself against their tent. (1.4)

Brockless, Thomas Reginald 24-year-old private in the British Army, suffering from shellshock and sent to St Teilo's Military Hospital in Cardiff during the First World War. His father, Thomas Campbell, died of a heart attack in June 1931, aged 57. His mother, Constance May (née Bassett) died when Tommy was 6 years old. With the modern destruction of the St Teilo's building, a time breach was created and the two time periods were leaking into one another, which would eventually have resulted in the total destruction of Earth. Tommy had been frozen in 1918 by Torchwood because the Tommy of the future told them to take him. Thus, he became the victim of a time paradox. This and the leakage was stopped because Tommy took with him a Rift manipulator built by Tosh, with whom he was having a relationship. As soon as he returned to his own time, however, his mind melded with his original self and he forgot Torchwood and his mission. Tosh entered his mind via psychic projection and reminded

him, and he successfully sealed the leakage and saved the world. Shortly afterwards, he was sent back to the Front, as per Field Marshal Haig's orders, but, like so many, his shellshock quickly resurfaced. He was unable to fight and was branded a coward and executed by firing squad. He was posthumously pardoned in 2006. (2.3) (Played by ANTHONY LEWIS)

Brodsky Gardens Cardiff road where Mike and Beth Halloran lived at number 114. (2.2)

Bromide A chemical compound, often used as a sedative. Gwen suggested introducing it into Cardiff's water supply to lessen the male population's sex drive, but Tosh pointed out that last time Torchwood did that they weren't popular with the local water authority. (1.2)

Brynaeron Terrace Street in Butetown where Thomas Flanagan lived, at number 74. (1.3)

Brynblaidd Welsh village in the Brecon Beacons where every ten years the entire population turned cannibal and kidnapped, murdered, cooked and ate anyone who came near. (1.6)

Bubonic Plague People from the fourteenth century carrying the Black Death arrived in present-day hospitals as a result of Owen fractionally opening the Rift and creating ripples and aftershocks that created Rift splinters. (1.13)

Burglars Two men who broke into the Hallorans' home. After attacking Mike, they were in turn attacked by Beth, via her true form, as a Cell 114 alien. One burglar was killed in

the flat; the other was thrown from a window and landed on an arriving police vehicle. He was taken to hospital but later died after telling Gwen it was Beth who had attacked him. (2.2) (Played by ALEX HARRIES and LUKE RUTHERFORD)

Burton, Amanda English actress who portrayed pathologist Sam Ryan in the BBC series *Silent Witness*. Gwen likened Owen to her. (1.7)

Burton, Jamie 10-year-old boy, dying of leukaemia. After his first bout of chemotherapy had failed, he had returned to St Helen's Hospital for a second course. He was in the loo, playing on a computer game, when the entity believed by some to be the embodiment of Death began stalking the hospital, killing patients and staff. He found the mummified corpse of Amy Carysfort under his bed and then fled from the entity, until rescued by Owen, whom he saw defeat 'Death'. (2.7) (Played by BEN WALKER)

Buster Dog belonging to Freda and her mother in 2069. Dogs generally didn't like 'ghosties'. (A)

Bute Park Grassland area behind Cardiff Castle. Jack was buried alive there in AD 27, remaining there as the city was built around him until he was rescued by Torchwood in 1901.

Butetown Area of Cardiff, near the Bay, where Thomas Flanagan lived. (1.5)

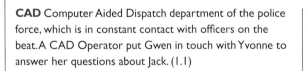

CAD Computer Aided Dispatch department of the police force, which is in constant contact with officers on the beat. A CAD Operator put Gwen in touch with Yvonne to answer her questions about Jack. (1.1)

Caernarfon West Wales city, where the drunk driver of a red Vauxhall was stopped and admitted to accidentally running down and killing Eugene Jones on the A48. (1.9)

Caerwent Monmouthshire town with an abattoir which was where Leighton Reynolds took the alien meat he collected from Harries & Harries to be processed. (2.4)

Calamity Jane Popular musical, loved by Emma Louise Cowell. She later sang a song from it, 'I Just Blew in from the Windy City', to her new friends Jade and Alesha before an angry John Ellis stopped her. (1.10)

Camara, Corporal Officer working at Ashton Down, responsible for the transfer of Rupesh Patanjali's body to Rossiter, the undertaker. Known to his mates as 'Kodak', he unwittingly let Ianto, disguised as a construction worker, into the base. (CoE) (Played by Osi Okerafor)

Camden Area of North London, where Clement MacDonald was held at the local police station. (CoE)

Camera Operator Soldier who entered the 456's tank and discovered the human child hooked up to the alien. (CoE) (Played by Kristian Arthur)

Canada Country whose children had become entranced by the 456. (CoE)

Canary Wharf Location of Torchwood One, the main headquarters of the Torchwood Institute in London. After an invasion by Cybermen and later Daleks centred on Canary Wharf, known colloquially as the Battle of Canary  Wharf, the Institute fell and Torchwood Three became the Government's main contact for Torchwood personnel. Both Ianto and his girlfriend Lisa Hallett worked at Torchwood One before heading to Cardiff. (1.1, 1.4)

'Can't Stand Me Now' Song by The Libertines, which was playing in the pub where Tosh and Owen discussed Edwin Morgan. (1.3)

Capsule Cell An alien device that resembles a small blue pebble but, when activated, emits an energy-based temporary prison cell. It has a short battery life, however. Owen used it to capture Carys Fletcher at her home, and Jack later used it to trap the Gas life form after it left Carys's body, where it remained trapped until it died. (1.2)

Captain Scarlet Fictional puppet, who could not be killed. Rhys likened Jack to him. (TDL) Johnson did the same. (CoE)

Cardiff Capital city of Wales, where Torchwood Three was based.

Cardiff Arms Park Sports ground in Cardiff city centre. Shaun Jones reckoned his son Eugene's brain was the size of it. (1.9)

Cardiff Bay Area south of Cardiff City Centre, reclaimed towards the end of the 1990s and turned into a major tourist attraction, comprising the Wales Millennium Centre, the Water Tower, the moorings and bars, restaurants and shops. The Torchwood Hub was constructed beneath the Oval Basin part of the Bay, close to the WMC.

Cardiff Castle Central castle in Cardiff, which John Hart transported Jack to, where they had a good vantage point to see the destruction of the city. John then transported them back in time, but not space, to AD 27, before the castle was built, believing he was free of Gray's influence and could explain why he was doing what he was doing. Gray, unfortunately, quickly followed them, killed Jack and had John bury him, knowing that in centuries to come, Cardiff would be built on top of him. (2.13)

Cardiff Central Station Railway station where Gwen saw the ghostly image of the young Tom Flanagan when she grabbed part of the Ghost Machine. (1.3)

Cardiff Examiner Local newspaper in the 1950s and 1960s. It reported on the rape and murder of Lizzie Lewis (1.3) and the disappearance of Diane Holmes's aeroplane (1.10).

Cardiff Gas Utilities company for which Owen had a fake ID in his wallet, identifying him as a Supply Services technician. (1.3) Jack and Ianto searched their building looking for the bombs John Hart claimed had been placed there. (2.1)

Cardiff General Hospital Cardiff infirmary where Owen once worked. There one of his earliest cases involved the unexplained death of Lucy Marmer. (1.7)

Cardiff Royal Infirmary Central Cardiff hospital. Gwen went there to have her head stitched after a pub brawl, and saw a Weevil for the first time, when it killed a chatty hospital porter in front of her. (1.1) Owen and Tosh responded to a priority one request from the hospital after its mortality rates went through the roof, where they discovered an outbreak of Bubonic Plague. (1.13) Mike Halloran and the burglars who had broken into his home were all taken there in the aftermath of the burglary. (2.2) Marie Thomas was taken there after Billy Davis's failed attack on her, and died there while Owen and Martha were examining her. (2.6) The victims of the Ghost Maker and Pearl's attacks were taken there. (2.10) Owen and Katie Russell both trained there. (2.12)

Cardiff Water Utilities company. Owen had a fake ID as one of their inspectors in his wallet. (1.3)

Cardigan Bay West Wales coastal area where a UFO was sighted. It was an Arkan Leisure Crawler. (1.4)

Carlisle Cumbrian town, where Harwood's Haulage had offices. (2.4)

Carol Woman who had divorced her husband Neil and was about to marry Lawrence. Neil arrived at her home with a shotgun planning to kill her, their son Danny and then himself, but Tosh stopped him. (1.7) (Played by EIRY THOMAS)

Carrie A guest at Gwen and Rhys's wedding who was presumably killed and replaced by the shape-shifting Nostrovite mother. After eating Mervyn the DJ and cocooning Tosh and Banana Boat for later, she dropped the Carrie disguise because Torchwood arrived in force. (2.9) (Played by COLLETTE BROWN)

Carter, Alice Jack's daughter from a relationship with Torchwood operative Lucia Moretti, born 5 August 1975. Before she married Joe Carter, Jack created a false background for Alice to keep her under the Government's radar. He said her parents were James and Mary Sangster – most likely the name she married Joe under as well. She and Joe had a son, Steven, before their marriage ended in divorce. Jack kept in contact with a reluctant Alice, who had difficulty coping with the fact her father would always look younger than her. She saw through Jack's blatant attempt to take Steven away and examine him after the 456 announced their arrival but was later captured by Johnson and taken prisoner with Steven to Ashton Down where Jack used her son as a conduit to destroy the 456, killing the boy. Afterwards, she would have nothing to do with Jack, which probably led to his decision to leave Earth and the twenty-first century. (CoE) (Played by LUCY COHU)

Carter, Joe Alice Carter's former husband and father of Steven. He moved to Italy and remarried, but was still involved in his son's life. (CoE)

Carter, Steven Son of Alice and Joe Carter, who believed Jack was his uncle and not his grandfather. Steven was briefly used by the 456 to communicate to Earth their imminent arrival and was later kidnapped and arrested by Johnson. Taken to Ashton Down, Steven was used by Jack to channel a destruction frequency. This destroyed the 456 and killed Steven in the process, causing his mother to reject Jack utterly and cut him out of her life. (CoE) (Played by BEAR MCCAUSLAND)

Carysfort, Amy Young nurse at St Helen's Hospital, working in the children's ward. When Torchwood wanted the hospital evacuated so they could defeat the entity believed by some to be the embodiment of Death, Amy remained behind to find a patient called Jamie. The entity killed her before chasing Jamie. (2.7) (Played by JOANNA GRIFFITHS)

Cash cow Nickname given to the alien sea creature that had fallen through the Rift and been beached up in Wales. Harries & Harries, meat suppliers, used it to make a small fortune, due to its ability  to regenerate itself, so each time they sliced part of it off, it grew back. Aided by a vet called Vic, the Harries brothers kept the creature heavily sedated, but it was fully sentient and aware of what was happening to it. Jack tried his best to help it, but Owen realised there was nothing that could be done – it was growing insane through the constant pain and he killed it humanely. (2.4)

Cash in the Attic BBC daytime TV show which Sean Harris cited to Owen as the inspiration for his plan to flog the Ghost Machine. (1.3)

CCTV Cardiff is dotted with CCTV cameras, and Torchwood could easily hack into the system and retrieve images throughout the city.

Cell 114 Aliens who Jack knew to be extremely dangerous. They would infiltrate planets subversively by disguising themselves as locals and going so deep undercover they forgot who they really were until triggered. Four of them were in Cardiff, disguised as Beth Halloran, David, a paramedic and a young mother. After stopping them, Jack was horrified to learn from David that there were more sleepers out there, waiting to be triggered. They could manipulate electronic scans to show what they wanted and had a flexible force field around their bodies, keeping them impervious to infection or medical procedures, unless desired. (2.2)

Central IT Server Building Part of the Cardiff infrastructure attacked by John Hart, acting on Gray's orders, where Tosh and Ianto were attacked by cowled men from the Middle Ages. (2.13)

CERN Swiss scientific establishment, a particle physics laboratory with over 10,000 staff. It had been testing the Large Hadron Collider and unwittingly enabled alien Ghost Entities to come through to Earth, to feed on the neutrons in human bodies. (LS)

Cessna A small plane – Diane Holmes's very first plane had been one and Owen took her to an airfield to try one out, hoping she could take lessons and get a modern pilots' licence, but no teaching slots were available. (1.10)

CF06 FDU
Registration plate of the Torchwood SUV.

CF10 6BY Postcode in Cardiff sent to Dan Hodges' mobile which revealed the location to Torchwood of Mark Lynch's Weevil fight club. (1.11)

Chain Lane Tosh detected the Rift energy surrounding the Ghost Maker and Pearl and sent the SUV to this street in pursuit. (2.10)

Chameleon Circuit Part of a TARDIS. The TARDIS belonging to the Doctor landed in the Oval Basin once and was struck by Rift energy, causing a degree of the energy from its Chameleon Circuit to bleed into the area at the base of the Water Tower. This created a perception filter which enabled Torchwood to use their Invisible Lift with ease as people were instinctively drawn away from the stones when it was in use.

Chandler & Bell A firm, or possibly just two individuals, who were part of an ongoing investigation by Torchwood. Jack asked Owen and Ianto to deal with it/them. (1.1)

Chappel, Sally Probable victim of the alien, Mary, who ripped out people's hearts to thrive upon. She died in 1972. (1.7)

Chara The boat Gwen hired to take her to Flat Holm Island. (2.11)

'Chariot, The' Poem by American writer Emily Dickinson, which Max Tresillian quotes endlessly to place the Hub into a lockdown. (1.8)

Charities Commission UK board who provided a file of information to John Frobisher at the start of the 456 incident. (CoE)

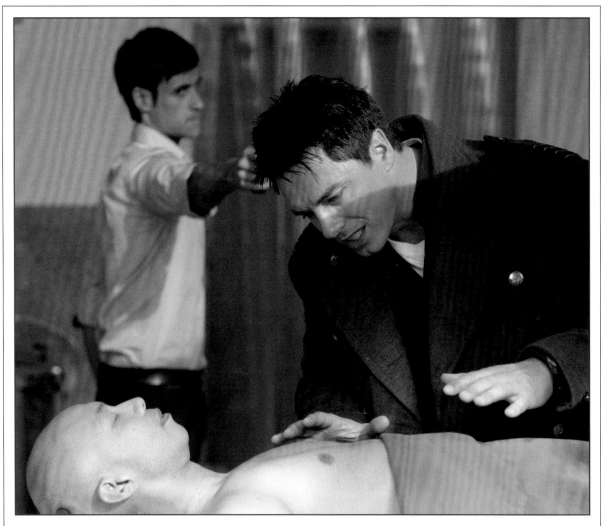

Chesterfield Hometown of Rupesh Patanjali. (CoE)

Chinese girl Young child in Taiwan, being used as a conduit by the 456, so speaking in clear English. (CoE) (Played by JENNIFER CHEW)

'Chocolate' Song by Snow Patrol which was playing in the pub when Torchwood got an alert telling them a UFO was flying over Cardigan Bay. (1.4)

Chosen One Name given by the Fairies to a child to whom they promised immortality and freedom from an unhappy human childhood. In Cardiff, their latest Chosen One was Jasmine Pearce. In 1909, a Chosen One in Lahore was accidentally killed by drunken British soldiers, resulting in their murders by the vengeful Fairies. (1.5)

Chow Lee Jee Chinese man who visited St Helen's Hospital with a nosebleed. Rupesh Patanjali had, as part of his undercover operation at the hospital, created a fictional series of incidents concerning oriental people, to catch Torchwood's attention. Needing to entice Jack back, in order to kill him as per his orders from Johnson, Rupesh killed Chow Lee Jee and showed Jack his body, pretending it was part of the same fiction. (CoE) (Played by JOE LI)

Christina A patient at Providence Park Psychiatric Hospital. When she was a little girl, her parents had been stolen away by the Night Travellers, but she had escaped, and been frightened of any live entertainment ever since. (2.10) (Played by EILEEN ESSELL)

Christopher Schoolboy who was led away by the army to be given to the 456. (CoE) (Played by EDWARD BRESNAN)

Chuckle Brothers Comedic TV double act, beloved by children. Gwen likens Jack and Ianto to them. (CoE)

Church Stretton Shropshire town which the Night Travellers had visited in 1901. (2.10)

Churchill, Winston British Chancellor of the Exchequer who deflated the economy in 1924. The Duchess of Melrose was not a fan. (GA)

CIA American intelligence service, which Ianto believed Jack may have been working for at some point. (1.2) The agency contacted Torchwood to find out what was causing people from history to appear throughout the world. (1.13)

CID Police criminal investigation department that Gwen visited after she had been given a dose of the amnesia pill by Jack Harkness. Seeing DI Jacobs' ongoing investigation and an artist's interpretation of the knife used started to break the amnesia pill's effect on Gwen's memory. (1.1)

CID Officer Policeman who Gwen talked to about the murder spree in Cardiff. (1.1) (Played by DION DAVIES)

City Justice A movie for rent in Josh's DVD store. (1.9)

City Swift Coach firm, which took Emma Louise Cowell to London. (1.10)

Cliffs Rise Nikki and Jonah Bevan lived there, at number 14. (2.11)

Clown Acrobats Some of the Night Travellers. (2.10) (Played by ROSIE MORRISON, DAVE FORD and GAVIN PRIESTLY)

COBRA The British Government's emergency planning room, created as an acronym from Cabinet Office Briefing Room A. (CoE)

'Cocktail Piano' One of the songs played at the Ritz Dance Hall in 1941. (1.12)

Code Four Internal code at St Helen's Hospital for cardiac arrest. (2.7)

Code Nine Manoeuvres Torchwood designation for a manoeuvre in which an opponent would be unable to focus on the group as each officer had moved to a different location, dividing their forces but making them harder to take down. (1.4)

Code Zero Incursion Torchwood designation for when the Hub had been invaded by a single enemy. (1.4)

Cole, Estelle Old flame of Jack's (although she believed she had romanced his now-missing father) who investigated Fairies. She was holding a talk about the Fairy camp in Roundstone Wood when Jack and Gwen showed up to support her. Fervently believing that the creatures were good, even though Jack told her otherwise, she was eventually attacked in her own home by them and drowned, as a warning to Jack to stay away. (1.5) (Played by EVE PEARCE)

Colin Aggressive drunken man who didn't appreciate his girlfriend trying to seduce Owen. Owen then sprayed more alien cologne over himself, Colin inhaled some and immediately wanted to have sex with Owen himself. (1.1) (Played by GWILYM HAVARD DAVIES)

Cologne An alien pheromone in a bottle used by Owen to make himself instantly attractive to other people, thus guaranteeing him a great deal of sex. (1.1)

Colonels, the Selection of men who lived at the Royal Connaught Club in India, all of whom died when the club was destroyed by the exploding Time Store. (GA)

Combination Used to secure the Torchwood alien morgue. The number, known only to Owen until his death, was 231165. (2.7)

'Comfortably Numb' Pink Floyd song re-recorded by Scissor Sisters, which was playing in the bar when Gwen held her hen night party. (2.8)

Commonwealth of Australia John Frobisher told the 456 he represented this when greeting the 456 for the first time. (CoE)

Compound B67 See Amnesia pill.

Connolly, Doctor Angela Physician at St Helen's Hospital who was looking after the aged Martha when the entity that was referred to as 'Death' began killing patients there. She then helped evacuate the hospital. (2.7) She later encountered Owen again when a Hoix was transported to the hospital's basement by John Hart. She aided Owen when he tried to restore power to the hospital after John tried blowing Cardiff up. (2.13) (Played by GOLDA ROSHEUVEL)

Conway Clinic Fertility clinic where Carys Fletcher worked as a receptionist. Once inhabited by the Gas alien, Carys went there on her day off and had sex with a number of men, killing them to feed off the resultant sexual energy. (1.2)

Cooper, Geraint Gwen's father, who was at her wedding. Gwen broke down and told him about Torchwood, because she wanted to explain about the Nostrovite egg she was carrying, but he didn't believe her, assuming it was wedding nerves. However, when Jack arrived and the Nostrovite mother made its presence known, he had to accept his daughter had been telling the truth. He later forgot the events of the day, due to Level 6 Retcon, administered by Jack. (2.9) (Played by WILLIAM THOMAS)

Cooper, Gwen Elizabeth Cardiff Police Officer, number 159, Gwen witnessed John Tucker being brought back to life by Torchwood and began investigating them. This brought her to Jack's attention, and he allowed her into the Hub, planning to drug her and erase her memories. But Gwen's strong-willed determination overcame the Retcon and she found her way back to the Hub, not entirely sure why. There she encountered Suzie Costello who assumed she'd come to arrest her and was about to kill her when Jack tried to stop her. Suzie killed Jack then herself, but Jack came back to life in front of Gwen – she was the only one who knew his secret for a long time. Keeping her new Torchwood job a secret from her boyfriend Rhys and ex-colleague Andy Davidson, Gwen gradually became Jack's new Number Two, although her loyalty was severely tested after Rhys was murdered by Bilis Manger. When Jack

destroyed Abaddon, the recent timeline was erased, and Rhys was brought back to life. Shortly afterwards, Jack temporarily disappeared, so Gwen ran the team until he returned. She eventually married Rhys, not long after he had stumbled into a Torchwood case and learnt the truth about her work. Gwen discovered she was pregnant just as the destruction of the Hub forced her to go on the run with Rhys. Six months after the death of Ianto and the destruction of the 456, she and Rhys met up with a distraught Jack, who left Torchwood in their hands as he returned to space. (1.1–1.13, 2.1–2.13, LS, A, GA, TDL, CoE) (Played by EVE MYLES)

Cooper, Mary Gwen's mother. As he got ready for her 60th birthday, the zipper broke on Rhys's smart trousers; he wanted to wear jeans instead, but Gwen pointed out it was meant to be a smart-dressed evening. (1.3) When Gwen took Emma Louise Cowell into their home, saying she was a step-niece, Rhys checked with Mary and discovered this to be the latest in a number of lies Gwen had told him. (1.10) At Gwen and Rhys's wedding, she spent much of the day trading barbs with Rhys's mother, Brenda. Once the

Nostrovite mother made its presence known, however, she realised her daughter was part of Torchwood. When the Nostrovite disguised itself as Brenda Williams, it took Mary hostage, but Gwen rescued her. She later forgot the events of the day, due to Level 6 Retcon, administered by Jack. (2.9) (Played by SHARON MORGAN)

Copley, Professor Aaron, Bsc, Phd Harvard graduate and professor of molecular pharmacology, who came to the UK to set up the Pharm. Dedicated but utterly amoral, he employed killer Billy Davis to murder the clinical trial patients after his trials involving the use of alien DNA to create the Reset drug began going awry. Torchwood sent Martha in, undercover, posing as a trial patient. But when Copley discovered her unique biochemistry due to her prolonged period of travelling in space and time with the Doctor, he decided to experiment on her. He was furious when Torchwood turned up and began shutting down the Pharm and killing the tortured aliens. After they rescued Martha, Copley threatened to shoot them, and killed Owen. Jack shot him dead in retaliation. (2.6) (Played by ALAN DALE)

Coral, The Liverpudlian band whose song 'Whose Gonna Find Me' was playing when Tommy saw a modern war on TV as he ordered drinks for himself and Tosh at a bar. (2.3)

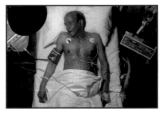

Costello, Mr Suzie's hated father, who she murdered where he lay in his hospital bed, his body riddled with cancer. (1.8) (Played by BADI UZZAMAN)

Costello, Suzie Torchwood investigator and tech specialist, and Jack's trusted Number Two. However, obsessed with her work to extreme lengths, forever testing and re-testing, Suzie was driven to use the Life Knife on a number of victims, just so that she could test the Resurrection Glove. She also experimented with Jack's amnesia pill, repeatedly giving it to a member of the Pilgrim Society called Max Tresillian, and monitoring the psychosis it induced. Aware that she was heading down a self-destructive path, Suzie prepared for death, seeking the immortality that the

Resurrection Glove could potentially offer and set up a trap involving Pilgrim that would ensure she was brought back to life by Jack. She then began draining life energies from Gwen, and murdered her abusive father. When Tosh destroyed the Resurrection Glove, the energies were abruptly cut off, and as Suzie finally died Gwen recovered. (1.1, 1.8) (Played by INDIRA VARMA)

Cottingley British country village which gained notoriety in the early twentieth century after two girls, Frances Griffiths and Elsie Wright claimed to have taken photographs of real fairies. In later years, the girls admitted they had faked the whole thing, but when Gwen discovered one of the fairies was Jasmine Pearce, she was unsure exactly what the truth was. (1.5)

Courtney, Professor Stella Neuroscientist and ex-flame of Jack's, whom she dated for five weeks in the mid 1970s. Torchwood call her in when Jack slips into a coma, brought on by the phone-line effect. She suggests using an MRI at St Helen's Hospital to create an electromagnetic pulse to stop the electrical energy controlling his and all the similar patients' brains. (TDL) (Played by DONA CROLL)

Cowell, Emma Louise 18-year-old travelling to visit her aunt and uncle, Nora and Finn, in Dublin. When the plane she was in, piloted by Diane Holmes, entered the Rift and ended up in modern-day Cardiff, Emma started off in a hostel, and began to enjoy the contemporary lifestyle. She learned that her father had died in 1959 but her mother had lived to the age of 81. She eventually spent Christmas with Gwen and Rhys before accepting a job at a fashion house in London, where her knowledge of 1950s clothing was a huge advantage. History notes that she was reported missing, presumed dead over the Irish Sea in 1953. (1.10) (Played by OLIVIA HALLINAN)

Cowled Leader A scythe-wielding man from the Middle Ages, brought to the Central IT Server Building by John Hart's meddling with the Rift Manipulator. He threatened to kill Ianto and Tosh so they gunned him and his two cohorts down. (2.13) (Played by PAUL MARC DAVIES)

C

CPS PC Andy Davidson wondered how the Crown Prosecution Service would cope with the Latin-speaking Roman Soldier brought through time as a result of Owen fractionally opening the Rift and causing ripples and aftershocks that created Rift splinters. (1.13)

Crazy Frog Ringtone heard on Dan Hodges' mobile phone. (1.11)

CRB As Freda, being from 2069, was not listed in the Criminal Records Bureau, Gwen reminded Andy Davidson that he couldn't hold her. (A)

CrimInt The police Criminal Intelligence database, which Gwen was astonished to discover Torchwood could hack into with ease. (1.2)

Croatian Slavic language which Jack asked Tosh to translate, believing it to be alien in origin. (2.8)

Croft, Lara Video-game and movie character from the *Tomb Raider* series, who Rhys likened Gwen to. (TDL)

Crofton Close Cardiff cul-de-sac where the alien Blowfish took a family hostage. (2.1)

Cromwell Estate The council estate where the Davies family lived. One of the roads in it was called Cromwell Court. (CoE)

Cryochamber A place within the Torchwood Hub where the team kept nameless dead bodies that could be used to cover up deaths caused by Rift activity. Tosh prepared to use one to provide a body for Matt Stevens' family after his true body was turned to ash by the Gas life form. (1.2)

Cube Bar Owen went there for a drink to try and get over Diane Holmes, but instead got chatted up by the barmaid, Laura, and assaulted by her boyfriend, Tommy. He and Mark Lynch returned later and got into another fight with Tommy. (1.11)

Cybermen Intended as the next level of mankind, the Cybermen consisted of a human brain welded directly onto a steel exoskeleton, suspended within a cradle of chemicals. Beneath the chest plate, metal gears and servos were intertwined with human flesh, threaded throughout the suit with strings of tissue to serve as a central nervous system. Emotions were inhibited, and all humanity removed, turning the Cyberform into a simple drone, although the suits themselves could also function without a human subject. Immensely strong and invulnerable to attack, the Cybermen were able to dispense a lethal electrical charge through their hands, and later developed laser weaponry, which they concealed in their forearms. Although impervious to bullets, a Cyber suit could be rendered inoperative by means of an electromagnetic bomb or Dalek gun, and could be destroyed in its entirety by a direct bazooka blast. In the event of a Cyberman's destruction, their knowledge is retained within a central consciousness, and can later be downloaded into another drone if necessary. Created originally on a parallel Earth, they trespassed onto Torchwood's Earth via devices used at the Torchwood Institute in Canary Wharf. They then went out onto the streets, taking people away for upgrading. Later they encountered the Daleks, offering them an alliance, which the Daleks rejected, thus beginning a war between the two alien races, and as the Cybermen fatalities mounted, they began the emergency upgrading of Torchwood One personnel, including Ianto's girlfriend Lisa Hallett. (1.4) One man, Michael Hamilton, still believed he was seeing Cybermen outside his mum's house months later (1.7)

Cyberwoman See Hallett, Lisa.

Cyclist She nearly cycled into Freda as the teenaged asylum-seeker from 2069 escaped Torchwood's safe house in an effort to find her grandmother, Moira Evans. (A) (Played by SARA MCGAUGHEY)

[D]

Dactovian rock shards Eugene Jones had some examples of these in his bedroom. (1.9)

Dad Part of the Cardiff family taken hostage by the Blowfish. He was shot and injured. (2.1) (Played by DAMON JEFFRIES)

Daf One of Rhys's best mates who Rhys had a night playing poker with, planning to stay over, but Daf and his partner Karen rowed so Daf slept on the sofa, meaning Rhys had to go home to Gwen. (1.3) Rhys was out sharing a curry with him when Gwen was trying to stop Lisa Hallett. (1.4) Daf and Karen later separated, and Daf decided to have a Staying Single Stag Night involving a lot of drinking and strip clubs. (1.11) Rhys spoke to him after meeting Torchwood properly for the first time but didn't give away their secret, convincing Gwen not to give him Retcon, despite Jack's orders to the contrary. (2.4) (Played by KODIO TSAKPO)

Dainty Dinah's Toffees that Emma Louise Cowell had with her. (1.10)

Daleks Invaders of planet Earth. Rhiannon Davies was cross with Ianto for being missing when they invaded (in truth, Ianto and Gwen were facing a Dalek in the Hub). (CoE)

Damascene Cluster Area of space where the rarest Arcadian Diamonds are found. (2.1)

Danno One of Johnny Davies' mates on the Cromwell Estate, who was told to get some of the boys on the estate together. (CoE) (Played by GARY DEVONISH)

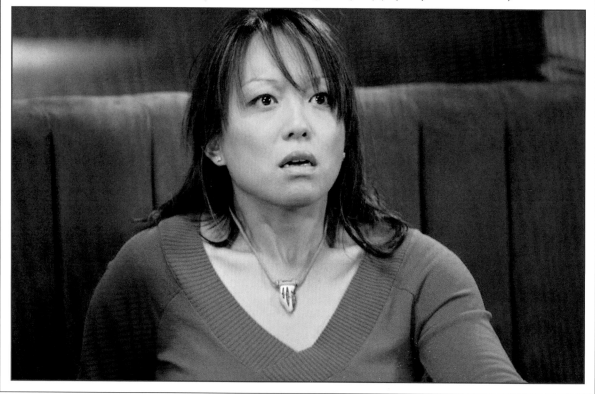

Danny Young son of Neil and Carol. His parents were estranged, and his father planned to murder Danny and his mother but was stopped by Tosh. (1.7) (Played by SHAHEEN JAFARGHOLI)

'Danny Boy' Traditional Irish song of mourning, sung by Shaun Jones at his son Eugene's funeral as a lament. (1.9)

Dark Matter One of the elements that made up the transporter device brought to Earth by the Arcateenian alien that assumed the identity of Mary. (1.7)

Darwin, Charles Robert English naturalist whose theories on evolution shocked Victorian society. Jack reckoned he'd have loved seeing all the different evolutionary avenues species on other planets have taken. (2.9)

Das, Mr Maitre d' at the Royal Connaught Club in Delhi, the base for Torchwood India. He was complicit in the Duchess's Golden Age plan and was responsible for knocking out Gwen and Ianto and placing them in the Time Store. When Jack destroyed the wi-fi mast that was emitting the energy wave, it fed back into the club, destroying Torchwood India and everyone still inside, including Mr Das. (GA) (Played by AMERJIT DEW)

Dave Worker at Harries & Harries who tied up Ianto and Rhys (2.4) (Played by ANDY WATTS)

David Cardiff man who was actually a member of Cell 114. When he was triggered, he killed his human wife and Patrick Grainger before heading to an army base hidden beneath a disued coal mine where nuclear warheads were stored. He intended to set them off but, although he slaughtered the army personnel there, Torchwood were able to decommission his force field. David blew himself up, but not before telling Jack there were more sleeper agents all over the world, ready to carry on. (2.2) (Played by DOUG ROLLINS)

David's wife Killed by her husband, who was actually a member of Cell 114. (2.2) (Played by CLAIRE CAGE)

Davidson, PC Andy Officer number 186. Gwen's former police partner and good friend. Jealous of Rhys, who he had little time for, because Andy was secretly in love with Gwen (which was why he didn't go to their wedding), the two eventually grew to respect one another. Andy never quite understood Torchwood, still believing it was part of the police Special Ops division, but he appreciated that it dealt with 'spooky' things such as the disappearance of Jonah Bevan and the arrival of future asylum seeker Freda. He asked Gwen if he could join – but she said no. When the Government sent agents to destroy Torchwood, Andy tried to convince them that Gwen was no threat. Later, he helped Gwen escape with the Davies' children from the authorities that wished to sacrifice the kids to the 456. (1.1, 1.2, 1.13, 2.1, 2.11, 2.13, A, CoE) (Played by TOM PRICE)

Davies, David Oldest child of Johnny and Rhiannon. He was briefly taken over by the 456 when they used the children of Earth to communicate. (CoE) (Played by LUKE PERRY)

Davies, Johnny Rhiannon's husband and Ianto's brother-in-law. Although he never really understood what Ianto's job entailed, he was very loyal towards Ianto and did everything he could to help stop the army getting Gwen after Ianto's death fighting the 456. (CoE) (Played by RHODRI LEWIS)

Davies, Mica Youngest child of Johnny and Rhiannon. (CoE) (Played by AIMEE DAVIES)

Davies, Rhiannon Sister of Ianto. She and her husband Johnny lived on the Cromwell council estate with their two children David and Mica. Both children were amongst those briefly taken over at various times by the 456. Rhiannon lent Ianto a laptop and car after the Hub was destroyed and, although she never really understood his job, she was devoted to him. When it became clear that children were at risk, Rhiannon set up a crèche at home, for which Johnny charged local parents while they went to work. When the army began rounding kids up, Rhiannon, along with Gwen, went on the run with the kids until the army found them. (CoE) (Played by KATY WIX)

Davis, Billy Killer-for-hire, employed by the Pharm to murder their former clinical trials patients who had been given the supposed miracle drug, Reset. In truth, Reset was a dose  of parasitic alien Mayflies that cured the patients before killing them. He was caught and taken to Torchwood, where Ianto pretended to let Janet the Weevil attack him. Billy had unwittingly inhaled larvae from one of his victims, and a Mayfly grew inside him and attempted to hatch. Owen

D

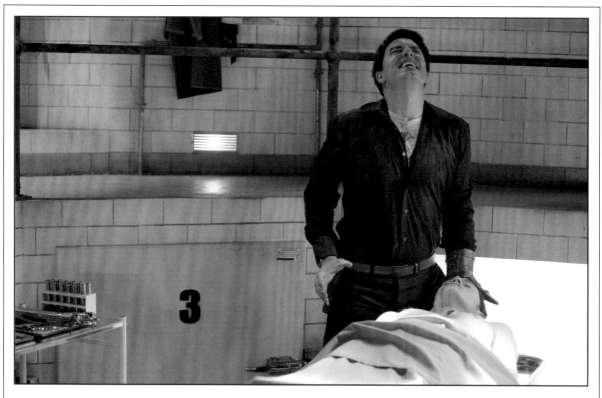

desperately tried to save Billy with the Singularity Scalpel, but it was too late and a mature Mayfly emerged from Billy, killing him instantly. Tosh suggested using his dead body taped to the steering wheel of his car to gain access to the Pharm. (2.6) (Played by RHODRI MILES)

De Havilland Famous aircraft makers. Diane Holmes flew one of their Dragon Rapide planes, which she named *Sky Gypsy* after its engine. (1.10)

'Death' In truth an entity from the Darkness that emerged into reality via the Resurrection Glove. It possessed Owen briefly as he was brought back to life by the Glove, and then left him and began killing, needing thirteen victims to manifest fully, as it had tried to do in 1479. At that time, it was defeated by Faith, a little girl brought back to life by the Glove, which made Owen realise he was the key to defeating

it again. 'Death' tried to feed off Owen as its thirteenth victim but because, like Faith, he was already dead, it was defeated and dissipated back into the Darkness. As the Glove had been destroyed beforehand, whether it possessed any other means to return to reality is unknown. (2.7)

Deb A mate of Eugene Jones's. (1.9)

Debenhams Popular chain department store, where Ianto's father worked for many years in the menswear department. (CoE)

Defence Secretary Part of the British Cabinet, involved in the secret discussions about how Britain would select which children would be donated to the 456. (CoE) (Played by PATRICE NAIAMBANA)

Dekker, Mr Cynical and devious technical expert employed by the Government in 1965 to communicate with the 456. Over the years, he remained essential to Parliament by constantly monitoring the airwaves for their return. By making himself indispensable, he remained the only significant person connected with the 1965 handing over of the orphaned children in Scotland not to be targeted for assassination by Brian Green. He worked with John Frobisher to prepare Thames House for the 456 arrival, but when the 456 began killing everyone in the building, Dekker made sure he survived. He later worked alongside Johnson and Jack at Ashton Down, mainly because Jack had shot him in the leg to prevent him escaping, in finding a way to destroy the 456. (CoE) (Played by IAN GELDER)

Delhi Capital city of India, and location back in the 1920s of Torchwood India, based in the Royal Connaught Club. Torchwood traced time-energy spikes to the city and discovered a Time Store in use by the members of the club, trying to take the world back to how it was in 1924. (GA)

Denmark European country which reported its children had become entranced by the 456, causing road traffic accidents. (CoE)

Derbyshire County that was the original home of Rupesh Patanjali. (CoE)

Derbyshire, Harriet Assisted Gerald Kneale at Torchwood in 1918. She died in 1919, aged 26. (Played by SIOBHAN HEWLETT)

Devlin, Alice One of the people Gwen discovered had been taken by the Rift. She found a cell bearing Alice's name in the Torchwood facility beneath Flat Holm island, which helped her realise Jack had known about the disappearances all along. (2.11)

Diane A mate of Gwen's, presumably from the police force, who Rhys assumed Gwen had gone out and got drunk with. (1.1)

Dickens, Charles Author of *A Tale of Two Cities*, the novel which Tosh transferred to her computer via the alien Reader device. (1.1)

Dickinson, Emily Nineteenth-century American poet favoured by Suzie Costello. She arranged to have Max Tresillian say aloud a portion of 'The Chariot', which resulted in the Hub going into a lockdown. Tosh guessed correctly that the ISBN of the poetry book would undo the lockdown. (1.8)

Digby, Kristian Presenter of the BBC daytime property show *To Buy or Not to Buy*, watched by Owen after his death. (2.8)

Digital frequencies The resistance to the Government's plan to give children to the 456 broadcast across Britain on digital band 141. In 1965, when unidentified aliens took children given to them by the British Government, they communicated via frequency 456. Mr Dekker monitored that frequency from then on, and the Government referred to the aliens by that name because they had no other name for them. (CoE)

DNA bomb Explosive device which the Hologram Woman arranged to find and attach itself to her murderer, John Hart. Owen realised that by pumping into John's heart a cocktail of DNA from the rest of Torchwood, the bomb would be confused and drop off. It did, and exploded alone in the Rift, although it caused an explosion that took time back to the first moment John's DNA appeared on Earth, effectively erasing 24 hours. (2.1)

Docherty, Nira A scientist based at the Turnmill Nuclear Power plant. She had remained at her post, trying to stop the meltdown, but Owen turned up and convinced her to leave him to it, although he warned her that with the Weevils prowling the streets of Cardiff, she might have been safer where she was. (2.13) (Played by SYREETA KUMAR)

Doctor, the Time-travelling Time Lord who was indirectly responsible for Jack's eternal life, after Jack was exterminated by Daleks. Jack wanted to locate the Doctor after all the years he'd spent on Earth and get some answers.

Dog owner Maindy man out with his dog, Samson, when Freda landed in the river. (A) (Played by DICK BRADNUM)

Dogon Sixth Eye Alien eye that usually sat on the back of a head. It had the power to show users their past lives and also give them a degree of perception about their place in the universe. They had become collector's items, and Jack knew of quite a trade in them. One was swallowed by Eugene Jones minutes before he was killed, and its powers enabled him to see his life and put everything in perspective. After it was removed from his dead body, he was momentarily able to return home, save Gwen and say goodbye before he finally passed on for good. (1.9) Henry John Parker had bought one on eBay as well. (2.8)

Doyle, Arthur Conan Author and scientist who believed that the Cottingley fairy photographs were real. (1.5)

'Drag' Song by Placebo which was playing in the bar where Tosh met Mary. (1.7)

Driver Annoyed motorist who yelled at the paramedic from Cell 114 until he realised the sleeper agent was attaching a bomb to his stolen petrol tanker. The motorist ran for his life. (2.2) (Played by MATTHEW ARWEL-PEGRUM)

Dublin Ultimate destination of Diane Holmes, John Ellis and Emma Louise Cowell in 1953, had they not flown into the Rift and ended up in modern-day Cardiff. (1.10)

Duchess of Melrose Eleanor, or Nelly, was an old flame of Jack's who ran Torchwood India from its base in the Royal Connaught Club in Delhi. When Torchwood detected peculiar energy readings from India, they investigated and

D

Jack was astonished to find the Duchess and the club exactly as they had been the last time he saw them in 1924. The Duchess was using alien energy in a Time Store to erase poor members of the local community, using the energy thus created to keep the club powered and entirely unchanged and unchanging. Her plan, which she called Golden Age, was to return the twenty-first century back to 1924. When Jack destroyed the wi-fi mast that was emitting the energy wave, it fed back into the club, destroying Torchwood India and everyone still inside, including the Duchess. (GA) (Played by JASMINE HYDE)

Duke of York Hospital Psychiatric hospital in East Grinstead, where Clement MacDonald was a patient. After seeing a recording of him echoing the words of the children across Earth, Gwen went there to visit him. Government troops, disguised as policemen, later went to the hospital to retrieve Clem once they had worked out who he was, but he had already fled. (CoE)

Duty Sergeant Policeman who locked Jack into Cell 3, next door to Lois Habiba. He later presented Bridget Spears with Lois Habiba's Eye-5 contact lenses. (CoE) (Played by GAVIN YOUNG)

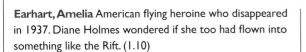

Earhart, Amelia American flying heroine who disappeared in 1937. Diane Holmes wondered if she too had flown into something like the Rift. (1.10)

East Grinstead Sussex town where the Duke of York Hospital was situated. (CoE)

Easter Parade 1948 movie starring Fred Astaire, which Tosh told Owen she had seen. Twice. On late-night TV. (2.9)

eBay Online auction site used by Eugene Jones to sell his Dogon Sixth Eye. (1.9) Also used by Henry John Parkes to buy alien artefacts for his collection. (2.8)

Ebola A disease Owen fears could reassert itself during the crises caused as a result of him fractionally opening the Rift and causing ripples and aftershocks that created Rift splinters. (1.13)

Egypt Country which reported its children had become entranced by the 456, causing road traffic accidents. (CoE)

Eight-Year-Old Girl Exactly what she was, whether she was even human, remained unknown. Jack first got information from her in 1899, when she told him he would not see the Doctor again until two millennia had turned. (2.12) He returned to find her when he wanted to locate the Resurrection Glove to revive Owen. (2.7) (Played by SKYE BENNETT)

Electricity Board Service responsible for the UK's power grid. Jack suggested hacking into them to power Hub 2. (CoE)

E

Electro Cinema Old cinema from the 1920s, situated on Hope Street in Penarth, which in the past had been a known site of Rift activity. Restored by the Penn family and the place where the Night Travellers emerged from their celluloid exile. (2.10)

Eliza One of the children Rhiannon tried to hide from the Government when she set up a crèche. Eliza was lactose intolerant. (CoE)

Ellie Tommy Brockless's former girlfriend. He dated her for two years, but broke up with her whilst on leave from the army because he had changed so much during the First World War. (2.3)

Ellis, Alan Former fireman and John Ellis's son. His father tracked him down after being thrown forward to modern times from 1953, but was unprepared for the young son he had left behind to now

be an old man suffering from Alzheimer's. Alan had a few moments of lucidity but never really grasped that John was his father. Alan's wife Sally had passed away and they had no children. (1.10) (Played by SAM BEAZLEY)

Ellis, John Small businessman from 1953, on his way to Dublin when the plane he was in, piloted by Diane Holmes, entered the Rift and ended up in modern-day

Cardiff. John found it increasingly hard to deal with the new, permissive, loud and fast world and tried to find his place in it by locating his son, Alan. However, Alan was now an old man with Alzheimer's, which was the last straw for John. With Jack at his side, he took his own life by inhaling carbon monoxide from Ianto's car. History notes that he was reported missing, presumed dead, over the Irish Sea in 1953. (1.10) (Played by MARK LEWIS JONES)

Emergency Protocol One Torchwood procedure to fully open the Rift. It required passwords and retinal scans to be activated. (1.13)

Emily Dickinson: The Complete Poems The book which Detective Swanson provided the ISBN for, enabling Toshiko to override the Hub lockdown that Suzie Costello had instigated. (1.8)

Endeavour Terrace Cardiff address where Sandra and Dave Tresillian lived at number 106. (1.8)

Evangelist A religious commentator who described the events surrounding the opening of the Rift as the End of Days. (1.13) (Played by RHIAN WYN JONES)

Evans, Moira Name adopted by an alien refugee who, along with thirteen others, landed on Earth after their homeworld was destroyed by solar flares. 'Moira' became part of society, although she had no National Insurance number, passport or bank account. Her son married a human and together they had a daughter called Freda in 2053. When Freda came back in time, she tried to find her grandmother's house. (A)

Evelyn Street Splott street where Sean Harris's squat was situated and Edwin Morgan killed himself. (1.3)

Evian les Bain French town, from whose hospital Oliver Harrington falsified documentation, implying injured CERN staff had been sent there. (LS)

Evil Dead, The American cult movie series in which the star, Bruce Campbell, spends much of the movie killing zombies with a chainsaw. Jack likened Rhys to him after he tried to use a chainsaw to kill the Nostrovite disguised as his mother. (2.9)

Excalibur One of the names John Hart thought would be better than Torchwood for Jack's group. (2.1)

Eye-5 Software used by Torchwood in the form of smartware contact lenses which could relay images back to the Hub from the wearer and enabled those watching to type messages which could be read by the wearer. Martha wore them to the Pharm. (1.6) Lois Habiba wore an updated version with lip-reading software when trying to find out about the 456. (CoE)

[F]

Fairies Mysterious creatures that came from the start of eternity, from the Lost Lands. They materialised in Roundstone Wood, seeking a new Chosen One to whom they could grant immortality as one of them. They chose Jasmine Pearce. The Fairies could control the elements – fire, earth, air and water – and used these to murder anyone who threatened their Chosen Ones. Each Fairy was once a child who had been selected as a Chosen One. They may or may not have allowed themselves to be photographed in the early twentieth century in Cottingley. (1.5) (Voiced by ZOE THORNE)

Faith A little girl in the parish of St James who, in 1479, was dead but brought back to life by the priest of St Mary's Church, via the Resurrection Glove. The church had been built over the Glove, which brought back into being an entity the locals believed was Death, and it needed to kill thirteen people before it could manifest permanently. Since Faith was already dead when she fought the entity as its thirteenth victim, she defeated it. (2.7)

Farrell, Marcus Man who claimed to have had sex with two lesbians. (1.7)

Farrington, Philip Head of Security for Henry John Parker. Owen confronted him and knocked him out with his own revolver. (2.8) (Played by LOUIS DECOSTA JOHNSON)

Fat man One of the disguises adopted by the shape-shifting male Nostrovite who impregnated Gwen on the eve of her wedding. Gwen tracked him down in a gents' toilet. (2.9) (Played by MIKE HENLEY)

Father (1) While at a car boot sale with his son, he bought some old film cans that may have contained footage of the Night Travellers. (2.10) (Played by STEVE EVANS)

Father (2) Parent of Suzette, the young girl seen in a trance-like state in the street by Gwen. (CoE) (Played by SCOTT BAILEY)

Feeder Welsh group, whose song 'Feeling a Moment' was playing in the pub where Tosh and Owen discussed Edwin Morgan. (1.3)

'Feeling a Moment' Song by Feeder which was playing in the pub where Tosh and Owen discussed Edwin Morgan. (1.3)

Field of Dreams 1989 movie, which Andy Davidson quoted to Nikki Bevan and Gwen. (2.11)

Fiesta One of a number of adult magazines used at the Conway Clinic to help sperm donors get aroused. (1.2)

Filey Area of Cardiff. There was a garage there, on the Filey Road, called Filey Garage, where Shaun Jones worked nights as a cashier. (1.9)

'Filthy Gorgeous' Song by Scissor Sisters, which was playing in the bar when Gwen held her hen night party. (2.8)

Fisherman Owned a boat which Andy Davidson hired to take him and Gwen to Flat Holm island. Gwen doubled the payment to take her alone. (2.11) (Played by PETER CARNEY)

Flanagan, Eleri Daughter of Thomas, who was with her father when Gwen and Owen paid him a visit. (1.3) (Played by LLINOS DANIEL)

Flanagan, Thomas Erasmus Man evacuated to Cardiff during the London Blitz in 1941. He never saw his family again afterwards and stayed in Cardiff for the rest of his life. When she held and activated part of the Ghost Machine, Gwen saw an image of him as he first arrived at Cardiff Railway Station in 1941. (1.3) (Played by CHRISTOPHER GREENE and JOHN NORMINGTON)

Flat Holm Small island in
the Bristol Channel, between
Cardiff and Weston Super Mare.
Torchwood had a holding facility
under it, which Jack used as a
safe house for seventeen victims
of Rift activity, who had been taken by the Rift and later
returned, often irreparably damaged physically and mentally.
He kept on a small staff, including Helen, who were unaware
of the exact origins of their patients. Ianto was aware of
the facility, but Tosh, Owen and Gwen weren't. Jack tried
to curb Gwen's curiosity, and she was furious when she
found out he'd known about the disappearances she was
investigating all along. (2.11)

Fletcher, Carys Cardiff teenager who worked as a
receptionist at the Conway Clinic. She was waiting for her
married boyfriend, Eddie Gwynne, outside the Nightspot
nightclub when the Gas life form entered her body and sent
her on a murderous spree because it could only survive
by ingesting the energy released from a male orgasm.
Gwen investigated Carys, learning that she was born on
13 November 1987, she was a good swimmer, her mother
had died in a car crash when she was 10, and she liked
Orlando Bloom and Heath Ledger. Her father Ivan ran a
builders and decorators firm, and they were reunited after
Torchwood destroyed the Gas life form. (1.2) (Played by
SARA GREGORY)

Fletcher, Ivan Carys Fletcher's
father, who ran his own
building and decorating firm.
His wife had died in a car crash
when Carys was only 10 years
old. (1.2) (Played by BRENDAN
CHARLESON)

Fletcher, Jessica Fictional detective, played by Angela Lansbury, in the long-running television series *Murder She Wrote*. Owen likened Gwen to her. (2.2)

Flight Attendant Alerted passengers heading to Switzerland, including Torchwood, that they would shortly land in Geneva. (LS) (Played by LUCY MONTGOMERY)

Floor manager Member of the TV crew recording Brian Green's speech during the 456 crisis. (CoE) (Played by CLAIRE SKEKEY)

Fluorine Twelve per cent of the 456's atmosphere was made up of this. (CoE)

Flying instructor Having taken Diane Holmes to an airfield, Owen hoped he could arrange flying lessons for her so she could get a modern pilots' licence, but the instructor said the earliest he could fit her in was just before New Year. (1.10) (Played by ANDREW MACBEAN)

Fog, The Horror novel by James Herbert. Henry John Parker owned a copy, translated into Arcateenian. (2.8)

Foiret, Leon CERN technician who encountered the Ghost Entities in the Large Hadron Collider. After he was rescued, he was placed in the care of UNIT medical officer Oliver Harrington. Leon's neutrons were slowly being absorbed by the alien Ghost Entities he had encountered, turning his body a soft golden hue as it began to disintegrate. Once the Ghost Entities in the LHC were destroyed and the portal sealed off, Leon recovered. (LS) (Played by MARK MEADOWS)

Foreman Worked at the demolition site at the old St Teilo's Hospital building. (2.3) (Played by RICKY FEARON)

Fort Apache, The Bronx 1981 movie about a police precinct under attack, to which Rhys likens the predicament he and Andy Davidson found themselves in when Andy's station was besieged by Weevils. (2.13)

456, The In 1965, when unidentified aliens took children given to them by the British Government, they communicated via frequency 456. From then on, the Government referred to the aliens by that name because they had no other name for them. The 456 breathed air consisting of 25 per cent nitrosyl chloride, 22 per cent hydrogen chloride, 20 per cent nitrogen, 12 per cent fluorine, 9 per cent hydrogen cyanide, 6 per cent acetone and 6 per cent phosgene, which was lethal to humans, although, when suckling them, the 456 protected the children's noses and mouths from the toxic air with masks. The 456 wanted the children as a narcotic, a side effect being that the children did not physically age. The 456 and their ship were destroyed when Jack fed back the audio wavelength they had used to kill Clement MacDonald, using his grandson Steven Carter's brain as an amplifier. (CoE) (Voiced by SIMON POLAND)

Fournier, Jacques Coolant expert at CERN, who became a victim of the Ghost Entities. After they were destroyed, he recovered. (LS)

France European country visited by the fictitious Samantha Jones. (2.6) The victims of a strange malady at CERN were allegedly sent there, to the Evian les Bain hospital. (LS) It reported its children had become entranced by the 456 at 9.40am CET, causing road traffic accidents. (CoE)

Frankie (1) Owner of a café round the corner from Josh's DVD rental store, where Eugene Jones regularly ordered two eggs and ham with chips. Frankie had no memory of ever meeting Eugene, however. (1.9) (Played by LEROY LIBURD)

Frankie (2) Carjacker who attacked Paul in a Cardiff car park. John Hart saved Paul by throwing Frankie off the car park to his death, and it was due to their physical contact that Tosh was able to ascertain  Frankie had been close to Rift energy. In all likelihood, these events were erased when a DNA bomb exploded in the Rift, reverting time back to moments before John arrived on Earth. (2.1) (Played by CRISPIN LAYFIELD)

Franklin Jack's father, killed in an alien attack on the Boeshane Peninsula. Jack had a vision of him in a Cardiff sewer and later revisited the day of his death via the alien memory parasite posing as Adam Smith. In revenge for the Torchwood team exorcising him from their memories, the parasite permanently erased all of Jack's memories of his last day with his father. (2.5) (Played by DEMETRI GORITSAS)

Freda Citizen UK818945/CF209B. Teenaged girl from 2069, born 30 May 2053. She was sent back in time through the Rift by the Torchwood of her era. In her own time she was considered a 'ghostie' because she was half-human, half alien (her father was human), and she suffered abuse as a result. Her neighbours burned her house down, killing her mother. Her memories were fragmented when she first arrived in Cardiff, but she knew she had to try and find her grandmother who called herself Moira Evans and lived in Cardiff. After she was caught shoplifting, Andy Davidson arrested her and

called in Torchwood due to the odd nature of her gun-like Universal Remote Control. Gwen and Andy tried to bond with her, which Andy did eventually after stopping her committing suicide. Torchwood realised she was seeking asylum from the future and had to let her stay. (A) (Played by ERIN RICHARDS)

French reporter TV news presenter who reported on the events of the 456's return. (CoE) (Played by ANTHONY DEBAECK)

Frobisher, Anna
John Frobisher's wife, she knew her husband was worried about the 456 incident but she was unprepared for his unexpected return home from work one day whereupon he killed her and their children and then himself. (CoE) (Played by HILARY MACLEAN)

F

Frobisher, Holly Eldest daughter of John and Anna. She died at her father's hand, to prevent her being sacrificed to the 456. (CoE) (Played by JULIA JOYCE)

Frobisher, John Permanent Secretary to the Home Office and the civil servant placed in charge of the 456 incident. Passionate and driven, his job became increasingly difficult when Prime Minister Brian Green refused to put his name to any orders about the potential invasion, leaving Frobisher to carry the can. Assisted by Bridget Spears and Lois Habiba, Frobisher worked with UNIT's Colonel Oduya and made initial contact with the 456, but when the Government acquiesced to the alien's wishes and began selecting children to be donated, Frobisher's daughters were amongst those the Prime Minister chose to sacrifice. Ashamed that he worked for such a Government and terrified at what lay in store for his children, he requisitioned a revolver and went home to his family, where he killed them before turning the gun on himself. (CoE) (Played by PETER CAPALDI)

Frobisher, Lilly Youngest daughter of John and Anna. She died at her father's hand, to prevent her being sacrificed to the 456. (CoE) (Played by MADELAINE RAKIC-PLATT)

Funeral for a Friend Rock group whose song 'Red Is The New Black' was playing in the Wolf Bar when Torchwood tried to find Lucy MacKenzie and Max Tresillian. (1.8)

[G]

Galligaer Welsh town where a Roman Fort once stood around AD 75. Jack speculated that was where the Roman Soldier in PC Andy Davidson's station was originally from. (1.13)

Gandhi, Mohandas Karamchand Political and spiritual leader who wanted to see the British Empire leave India. The Duchess of Melrose was not a fan. (GA)

Garbo, Greta American film actress who famously wanted to be left alone in the movie *Grand Hotel*. Laura cites this to Owen in the Cube Bar. (1.11)

Garrett, Doctor James Senior surgeon at the hospital where Owen and Katie had trained. Initially sceptical, he agreed to another MRI scan and discovered that what he had diagnosed previously as early Alzheimer's was in fact a tumour on her brain. He performed the operation to remove it uncovering not a tumour but a parasitic brain alien, which emitted a poisonous gas that killed him and everyone else in the operating theatre. Torchwood later adjusted the facts to make it appear Doctor Garrett had died in a car crash. (2.12) (Played by RICHARD LLOYD-KING)

Garrett, Mr Maths teacher at Eugene Jones's school. He knew Eugene was a bit of a maths prodigy and was sympathetic when he froze during an interschool competition and cost the school the prize. He gave Eugene a Dogon Sixth Eye which had fallen from the sky one afternoon when Mr Garrett was playing a round of golf. (1.9) (Played by ROGER ASHTON-GRIFFITHS)

G

Gary Best mate of Eugene Jones from Passmore Telesales, where they both worked. They also shared a passion for outer space and science and went to conferences on topics such as black holes. As a joke, he faked a number of eBay IDs in an effort to up the bidding on the Dogon Sixth Eye along with Josh, the guy who ran their local DVD rental

shop. A real bidder took the deal to £15,000, however, and Gary was furious when Josh topped that and won. Unable to pay, Gary and Josh offered just £34. An angry Eugene ran away and was then hit and killed by a speeding car. (1.9) (Played by CELYN JONES)

Gas life form A disembodied alien that could inhabit human bodies, but gradually burned them up. When it got into Carys Fletcher, it began to hunt to survive – which it did through sex, because it thrived off the energy released by a male orgasm. After killing a number of men in Cardiff, and nearly destroying Carys's body, it tried to move into Gwen's body, but Jack trapped it within a Capsule Cell, holding it there until, bereft of a host body, it dispersed and died. (1.2)

Gaskell, Charles Torchwood operative in 1901 who, along with Alice Guppy, located Jack beneath Bute Park where he'd been buried since AD 27 and placed him in hibernation in the Torchwood morgue. (2.13) (Played by CORNELIUS MCCARTHY)

Gavin A parcel courier who regularly delivered to the Fletcher household. Carys attempted to seduce him, to help feed the Gas life form within her, but he was saved by the timely arrival of Torchwood. (1.2) (Played by ROB STORR)

Gemma Friend of Nettie Williams, whose brother was supposed to have driven Nettie home safely, but his car had broken down, meaning Nettie had to take the bus. (2.10)

Geneva Capital of Switzerland. Torchwood flew there to meet Martha Jones at CERN. (LS)

Geoff A football-playing mate of Andy Davidson's who objected to being made goalkeeper. (1.1)

George (1) Short-tempered RAF officer, part of Captain Harkness's group. He was very fond of Audrey but wanted to dance with Tosh as well. (1.12) (Played by GAVIN BROCKER)

George (2) Security guard at the Lodmoor Research Facility who enjoyed flirting harmlessly with Tosh. (2.12) (Played by GARETH JONES)

Germany European country visited by the fictitious Samantha Jones. (2.6) It reported that its children had become entranced by the 456, causing road traffic accidents. (CoE)

Ghosh, Rani Young woman murdered by Suzie Costello as she attempted to understand the Resurrection Glove and its relation to the knife she wielded. (1.1)

Ghost Entities Aliens from a different dimension that used a portal accidentally created within the Large Hadron Collider during a test run. They were first discovered by UNIT medical officer Oliver Harrington, who was still grieving for his dead wife. Believing he was hearing her ghostly voice, Harrington agreed to allow the Ghost Entities access to Earth during the final firing of the LHC. Since the Entities fed off neutrons, they saw mankind as a food source – with their neutrons taken, human bodies began to slowly disintegrate. Learning the truth about them, Harrington tricked the Entities into coming through when the LHC was full of protons and antiprotons, which destroyed the creatures and sealed the portal off for ever. (LS) (Played by LUCY MONTGOMERY)

Ghost Machine An alien device that had fallen through the Rift, which Jack referred to as a quantum transducer. It came in two halves, which enabled the user to witness events of the past or future and feel the emotions of those the user could see (they couldn't see the user). It was found by an old man who collected junk which he kept in a lock-up in Moira Street, Splott. Sean

Harris and a mate burgled the lock-up and Harris took the Ghost Machine. After using it and becoming scared when it seemed to foretell his own death, he decided to sell it. Although he lost one half to Gwen in a struggle he later voluntarily gave Torchwood the second half, wanting to be shot of it. (1.3)

Ghost Maker, The One of the Night Travellers, a travelling circus troupe, whose origins are mysterious and undefined, but who appeared to be alien, or powered by something not of this world. The Ghost Maker operated during the late nineteenth and early twentieth centuries, stealing the last breaths of his victims and keeping them in a silver flask. This created ghost-like after-images of those victims, which would form an audience for the circus. After being captured on film, the Ghost Maker and his assistant Pearl were able to tap into enough Rift energy to emerge from the film and re-enter the real world. He stole the breaths of eight more people, which was enough to power the return to the 3D world of the rest of the Night Travellers. However, Jack and Ianto filmed him, capturing his essence once more, and then exposed the film, hoping to destroy him for good. His last act was to open the silver flask, releasing the last breaths of his victims, and thus killing them, although Ianto managed to save one breath. (2.10) (Played by JULIAN BLEACH)

'Ghostie' Slang term in 2069 for children who had one human and one alien parent. Freda was persecuted for being a 'ghostie', and her house was burned down, killing her mother. (A)

Gibson, Don Probable victim of the alien, Mary, who ripped out people's hearts to thrive upon. Gibson died in 1981. (1.7)

Gillian Was 17 when, as an employee of the Cardiff and West Building Society, she answered a telephone on 24 September 1976, just as a thunderstorm overhead connected with the Rift, creating a strange electrical phenomenon that placed her in a coma. From then on, the Tyler family who owned the building society maintained a private nursing home for her and any of their other employees who were on the phone at the same time and also fell into comas. (TDL)

Girl (1) One of Freda's neighbours and tormentors in 2069. (A) (Played by ISABEL LEWIS)

Girl (2) Child seen by Gwen who was briefly put into a trance-like state when being used as a conduit by the 456. (CoE) (Played by ELLIE RUIZ)

Girl bullies Schoolgirls who regularly tormented Jasmine Pearce, until they were attacked and nearly killed by the Fairies who protected her. (1.5) (Played by SOPHIE DAVIES and VICTORIA GOURLEY)

1941
KISS THE BOYS
GOODBYE
DANCE
Saturday **20th** 7.30 pm
JANUARY
1941
At The Ritz

Girl in park Youngster seen in a trance-like state when being used as a conduit by the 456. (CoE) (Played by COURTNEY BIRD)

'Girl With A Pink Rose' One of the songs played at the Ritz Dance Hall in 1941. (1.12)

Gissing, Colonel George One of the inhabitants of the Royal Connaught Club in Delhi, and the Duchess's right-hand man, who supported her plan to wipe out the present and return the world to how it was in 1924, via an energy wave. When Jack destroyed the wi-fi mast that was emitting the energy wave, it fed back into the club, destroying Torchwood India and everyone still inside, including Colonel Gissing. (GA) (Played by RICHARD MITCHLEY)

Gizmo Nickname Gwen gives the device she used at the Duke of York Hospital to switch off the camera observing her meeting with Clement MacDonald. (CoE)

Glasgow Scottish city and home of Torchwood Two, run solely by a very strange man called Archie. (1.1) Also cited by Gwen as one place where children had gone into a trance-like state shortly before the 456 made contact. (CoE)

Glyn Water-taxi pilot, based in Mermaid Quay, who assured Gwen there were no sea monsters in Cardiff Bay on the morning Earth's children were contacted by the 456. (CoE) (Played by PHYLIP HARRIES)

GMT Greenwich Mean Time. The 456 first made contact via Earth's children at 8.40am GMT, a worldwide event lasting exactly one minute. Their second attempt was witnessed in Cardiff Bay by Gwen and Rupesh Patanjali at exactly 10.30am. (CoE)

Godbole Garment Factory Clothing factory in Delhi where Torchwood saw all the workers vanish when the energy wave from the Duchess's Time Store erased them from existence. (GA)

Godzilla Fictional monster famous for attacking Tokyo in a series of movies. Andy Davidson wondered if that was what the 456 invasion would be like. (CoE)

Gold Command Top-level Cabinet members, involved in the secret discussions regarding which British children would be handed over to the 456. Rick Yates suggested that no children of Gold Command members should be handed over. (CoE)

Golden Age The Duchess's plan to use the Time Store at the heart of Torchwood India to change the whole world back to how it was in 1924. (GA)

Goliath Biblical giant, who, according to the Night Travellers' publicity, could be taken on by their strongman, Stromboli. (2.10)

'Good Life, The' Song performed by Tony Bennett, which Diane Holmes and Owen danced to. (1.10)

Goodson, Mark Business consultant and paedophile who targeted Jasmine Pearce. Before he could get to her, the Fairies she had befriended attacked and stalked him. Desperate for sanctuary, Goodson voluntarily turned himself in to the police. Although he was securely locked in a cell, the Fairies got to him and suffocated him by filling his throat with flower petals. (1.5) (Played by ROGER BARCLAY)

Google Search engine used by Gwen to gain information about the Resurrection Glove's use in the fifteenth century. (2.7)

Gough, Melanie Probable victim of the alien, Mary, who ripped out people's hearts to thrive upon. She died in 1974 and was victim number 40. (1.7)

Graham Worker at the abattoir in Caerwent, who was in on the deal concerning the alien meat with the Harries brothers and Leighton Reynolds. (2.4)

Grainger, Alex Son of Patrick Grainger, he witnessed his father's murder by David from Cell 114. (2.2) (Played by WILLIAM HUGHES)

Grainger, Charlie Daughter of Patrick Grainger, she witnessed her father's murder by David from Cell 114. (2.2) (Played by MILLIE PHILIPPART)

Grainger, Mrs Wife of Patrick Grainger, she witnessed her husband's murder by David from Cell 114. (2.2) (Played by VICTORIA PUGH)

Grainger, Patrick Leader of Cardiff Council and co-ordinator in case of major emergencies, who knew all the security protocols. He was with his wife and children when David from Cell 114 turned up on his doorstep and murdered him. (2.2) (Played by SEAN CARLSEN)

G

Grand Slam Rugby event, which Gwen mentioned to Ianto when trying to arrange a meeting place over a possibly bugged telephone. (CoE)

Grangetown Area of Cardiff, where the Ellis family lived and where John's son Alan was born. (1.10)

Gray Jack's younger brother, who was lost when the Boeshane Peninsula was attacked by aliens and Franklin, their father, was killed. Jack was responsible for Gray's safety but they got separated in the mêlée and Gray was gone. (2.5) Years later, after being held captive, tortured and degraded, Gray held Jack responsible for everything that had happened and sought revenge. He found John Hart, Jack's former lover and used a mind-control device which he embedded in John to make him infiltrate Torchwood and destroy everything Jack held dear. He followed Jack and John to AD 27, before Cardiff was even established, and buried Jack alive. Jack was dug up by Torchwood at the start of the twentieth century, but had himself placed in hibernation until Gray began the destruction of contemporary Cardiff. Revived, Jack captured Gray but was unable to kill his insane brother and instead placed him into hibernation. (2.13) It seems likely that Gray was finally killed, along with everything else in the morgue, when the Torchwood Hub was destroyed by the bomb placed in Jack's stomach by Johnson. (CoE) (Played by ETHAN BROOKE (2.5) and LACHLAN NIEBOER (2.12, 2.13))

Green, Brian The Prime Minister of the UK during the 456 incident. Scheming, devious and self-serving, he was content to let others take the rap for ordering assassinations and, when the 456 arrived and made their demands, he let Britain take charge of the initial negotiations, knowing this would anger the rest of the world. When the Americans arrived, he happily let them take over, calculating that, when it went wrong, they would become the scapegoats, not him. In COBRA meetings, he was quite prepared to let the 456 have the children they needed if it made them leave Earth for a few more years, by which time he'd no longer be in power. He told John Frobisher that John's children were to be given over to the 456. When Bridget Spears recorded him describing his acts of betrayal, his premiership came crashing down, leaving him disgraced and his Home Secretary, Denise Riley, to succeed him. (CoE) (Played by NICHOLAS FARRELL)

Greenleaves Hospital Private hospital where Suzie Costello's father was dying of cancer. Suzie and Gwen went there, and Suzie murdered her father in revenge for something he had done in the past. (1.8)

Griffiths, Frances One of two girls who, in the early twentieth century, claimed to have taken photographs of fairies. Towards the end of their lives, the girls confessed they had faked the images. (1.5)

G

Groove Armada British production duo, whose hit 'I See You Baby' was playing in the bar which Gwen and Rhys took Emma Louise Cowell to. (1.10)

Guard (1) CERN official who checked Torchwood into the facility, believing Ianto was the Ambassador for Wales, Gwen his wife and Jack their personal assistant. (LS) (Played by STEPHEN CRITCHLOW)

Guard (2) Ashton Down trooper who kept an eye on the remains of Jack after the destruction of the Hub. He failed to notice that the body had begun to reassemble itself. (CoE) (Played by QUILL ROBERTS)

Guppy, Alice Scottish Torchwood operative who was with Emily Holroyd when they first found Jack in Cardiff in 1899. (2.12) She tracked an etheric particle signal to Bute Park where she and fellow operative Charles Gaskell dug up a timeline-crossing Jack. They took him back to Torchwood and put him into hibernation. (2.13) (Played by AMY MANSON)

Guyana Country which reported its children had become entranced by the 456, causing road traffic accidents. (CoE)

Gwesty Rhyd-yr-Aur The hotel where Gwen and Rhys got married. (2.9)

Gwynne, Eddie Married to Bethan, he was cheating on his wife with Carys Fletcher and took her virginity. Once inhabited by the Gas life form, Carys seduced Eddie and reduced him to ashes. (1.2) (Played by ALEX PARRY)

[H]

Habiba, Lois Idealistic junior PA and assistant to Bridget Spears, who started working in John Frobisher's Home Office department on the day the 456 made   contact. She discovered the plot to execute Torchwood and later made contact with Gwen and Rhys, believing they were the only people who could stop the aliens. Gwen convinced her to wear the Eye-5 software lenses to let Torchwood see Cabinet gatherings and the meetings with the 456 ambassador. When she revealed she was working for Torchwood, Brian Green had her arrested. She was visited by Bridget Spears, who then took the Eye-5 lenses herself to record the admissions of cowardice and manipulation that eventually brought Brian Green down. Denise Riley had Lois freed shortly afterwards. (CoE) (Played by CUSH JUMBO)

Hafod Street Cardiff street where Mabel Lewis lived with her only daughter, Elizabeth, in 1963. (1.3)

Haig, Field Marshal Douglas Senior Commander of the British armed forces during the First World War, considered by many a hero, but servicemen referred to him as the Butcher of the Somme because of the casualties he ordered. Harriet Derbyshire realised that many of the injured soldiers at St Teilo's Military Hospital would be sent back to the front to die under his direct order. (2.3)

Hall, Caroline One of the people Gwen discovered had been taken by the Rift. She found a cell bearing Caroline's name in the Torchwood facility beneath Flat Holm island, which helped her realise Jack had known about the disappearances all along. (2.11)

MISSING
HAVE YOU SEEN CAROLINE?
Name: CAROLINE HALL
Date of Birth: 14.04.72
Height: 5'5"
Weight: 105 lbs
Build: Average
Hair: Brown
Eye Colour: Brown
Circumstances: Simon was last seen withdrawing large amounts of cash from the bank while talking to himself. Family fear for his mental stability and safety.
IF YOU HAVE SEEN SIMON OR KNOW OF HIS WHEREABOUTS CONTACT THE POLICE'S MISSING DEPARTMENT ON 000-000-0000
Call Freephone
08081-570-980

Hallett, Lisa Former employee of Torchwood One in London and girlfriend of Ianto. She was captured by the invading Cybermen and upgraded to Human Point Two when, desperate for more soldiers, they started grafting Cybertech onto human bodies rather than transplanting brains into pre-existing suits. But the process was halted midway through and Ianto secretly brought her and some of the conversion equipment to Torchwood in Cardiff. Setting the equipment up in one of the basement rooms none of the others ventured near, Ianto kept her alive and brought Japanese cyberneticist Doctor Tanizaki to try and restore her to full humanity. The process instead made her more alien, and she killed Tanizaki and attacked the rest of Torchwood. After fighting off the Pteranodon in the Hub, Lisa concluded the only way to convince Ianto that they should be upgraded together was to look fully human again.

She captured a pizza delivery girl, Annie, and placed her brain in Annie's skull, leaving her own original body to die. Even faced with this brutal revelation, Ianto was unable to hurt Lisa/Annie, so the rest of the team shot her to death. (1.4) Ianto later had a vision of Lisa, as she had been back in their London days, when Bilis Manger was trying to get Torchwood to open up the Rift and enable the demonic Abaddon to enter our dimension. (1.13) The Ghost Entities breaking through into the Large Hadron Collider in the CERN facility imitated Lisa, using her words and memories to try and destroy Ianto's mind. (LS) (Played by CAROLINE CHIKEZIE)

Halloran, Beth Young woman who, when her husband Mike was attacked in their bedroom, unknowingly grew a weapon from her arm and, with superhuman strength, killed one burglar and mortally wounded the other. Beth believed she was a normal person but in truth was Keryehla Janees, an alien from Cell 114, sent to Earth as a sleeper agent, with the intention of providing a spearhead to an invasion. Once Beth learned the truth, she was horrified, but used her alien powers to escape Torchwood and return to Mike, to apologise and explain why she would never be able to see him again. However, her Cell 114 conditioning took over

and she executed Mike. After that, her conditioning was broken sufficiently for Torchwood to use her and her alien physiology, which was now starting to show. With her help, they tracked the others in her local cell. Two of them killed themselves in acts of terrorism, but the third, posing as a man called David, went to a secret army base where nuclear warheads were stored. After Torchwood stopped him detonating them, Beth realised she didn't want to live with the knowledge she had killed Mike and the others, nor of what she might do in the future when the Beth personality was suppressed by her true Cell 114 heritage, so she deliberately provoked Torchwood into gunning her down. (2.2) (Played by NIKKI AMUKA-BIRD)

Halloran, Mike Husband to Beth. He was injured in a burglary at the home they shared, which prematurely triggered Beth's alien DNA as member of Cell 114. Mike remained in hospital, unaware of the truth about Beth, but, when she came to tell him she had to leave him for his own safety, her Cell 114 heritage took over and she killed him. (2.2) (Played by DYFED POTTER)

Hamilton, Michael A man who believed Cybermen were still outside his mother's house. (1.7)

Happy Cook A cheap 'n' cheerful roadside café on the A48, where Eugene Jones believed he was going to meet the buyer of his Dogon Sixth Eye. In fact the deal was a prank by his friends Josh and Gary. Jen, the waitress, told Gwen she remembered the lads getting into a fight shortly before Eugene died outside. (1.9)

Harbour Heights An orphanage in Plymouth where the twelve children from Holly Tree Lodge near Arbroath believed they were going when they were in fact handed over to the 456 in November 1965. (CoE)

Hard-Fi English band whose song 'Better Do Better' was played at Lynne Pearce and her partner Roy's BBQ to celebrate their fifth anniversary. (1.5)

Harkness, Captain Jack A Time Agent from the Boeshane Peninsula in the fifty-first century, who left the Agency shortly after being trapped with John Hart in a time bubble that made two weeks last five years. Both he and Hart became conmen, working independently from one another and, operating on Earth in 1941, he adopted the identity of the real Captain Jack Harkness, who died on 21 January of that year. He befriended the Doctor and travelled with him for a while before being killed by the Daleks and brought back to life by Rose Tyler. However, when he tried to use his Vortex Manipulator to get back to Earth, it shunted him back in time to 1869. Having discovered that he was immortal, Jack came to the attention of Torchwood Cardiff, who employed him on a freelance basis, which continued until near the end of the 1990s, when he joined the staff at Torchwood Three. After the suicide of Alex Hopkins, Jack took over Torchwood Three and created a new team who, after the destruction of the Institute in London, became an independent organisation. Jack tried to keep his immortality a secret from all but Gwen, but this didn't last – when Owen shot him while trying to open the Rift, Jack came back to life, giving much of his life energies to destroy Abaddon, before going into a coma for many days. He awoke and then encountered the Doctor again, leaving Gwen in charge. On returning to Torchwood, he stepped up his relationship with Ianto but was aghast when John Hart returned, with his long-lost brother Gray in tow. In fact, Gray was controlling Hart, and Jack was forced to chloroform his brother and put him in suspended animation. While recruiting for a new medic, Jack was shot and killed by Rupesh Patanjali, and a bomb was placed in his stomach. This went off, destroying Torchwood Three's Hub and everything in it. Jack slowly came back to life at Ashton Down in time to learn that a menace he had been involved with in 1965 had returned – the 456. After losing Ianto in the fight against the aliens, Jack was able to destroy them, but was horrified at how far he had been prepared to go. Having sacrificed his own grandson, Steven Carter, Jack left Earth, leaving Gwen and Rhys to rebuild Torchwood as they saw fit. (1.1–1.13, 2.1–2.13, LS, A, GA, TDL, CoE) (Played by JOHN BARROWMAN)

Harkness, Group Captain Jack On loan to the RAF, 133rd Squadron, from the USAF, he had been awarded a Distinguished Flying Cross medal. On 20 January 1941, he and his men were enjoying a night at the Ritz Dance Hall in Sage Street before flying out on training exercises the next morning. He and Jack met at the Ritz and an attraction formed. But Jack knew this Harkness was the man whose identity he would later steal as the real Harkness was destined to die the next day when their training was ambushed by German planes. Although none of his men would be lost, Harkness himself would be killed. (1.12) (Played by MATT RIPPY)

Harper, Captain James Pseudonym adopted by Jack when he met the real Jack Harkness in 1941. He claimed to be attached to the 71st Squadron. (1.12)

Harper, Jenny Fake name given by Tosh when Mark Lynch rang to check Owen's 'Harper's Jellied Eels' credentials. (1.11)

Harper, Owen Torchwood's cynical, bitter medic originally came to Jack's attention after he refused to accept his fiancée Katie Russell's terminal brain condition. Owen had been proved right to push for extra examinations, as the hospital eventually found what was believed to be a tumour; however, it was an alien creature, which killed Katie and

the medical staff during the operation to remove it. Jack was impressed by Owen's determination to find out the truth. A brilliant medic, Owen's bedside manner was lacking but, when finding something new and unique, he could get swept up in the glory of it all. Seemingly unaware of Tosh's love for him, Owen blatantly played the field, flaunting his conquests and having an affair with Gwen, until he met Diane Holmes, with whom he genuinely fell in love. When she left him, he began a downward spiral of self-destruction that led to him starting a mutiny at Torchwood and Jack firing him. Owen returned and Jack forgave him, and, from

H

then on, Owen's hedonism became a thing of the past. He was shot and killed by Aaron Copley while investigating the Pharm, but Jack used the Resurrection Glove to bring him back, a dead man, living at the moment he breathed his last. Enough breath trapped in his body to speak, but no blood flowing, no need to eat, drink or anything. He was unable to take risks because, if he broke a bone, it would never mend; a cut would never heal. Owen slowly accepted his new life but, attempting to stop a meltdown at the Turnmill nuclear power station, a power surge trapped him inside the building as it was flooded with radioactive waste. He died again, this time for good, his body vaporised by the radiation. (1.1–1.13, 2.1–2.13) (Played by BURN GORMAN)

Harper, Mrs Owen's mother, who packed his bags and threw him out of home when he was 16, saying that, while she had to love him as her son, she didn't like him much. (2.5)

Harper's Jellied Eels Faux company Tosh created as a cover story for Owen to get access to Lynch Frost. (1.11)

Harries & Harries Meat suppliers run by two brothers, Dale and Greg. They had chanced upon an alien creature that had come through the Rift and been beached up in Wales. It could regenerate its flesh each time they sliced

meat off it. Although the meat appeared to have no negative side effects in the humans who consumed it, the brothers were not bothered either way. All they wanted was to make money by selling it off as quickly as they could. When Harries & Harries was infiltrated by Torchwood, they and their staff were given Retcon to wipe their minds of everything concerning the alien. (2.4)

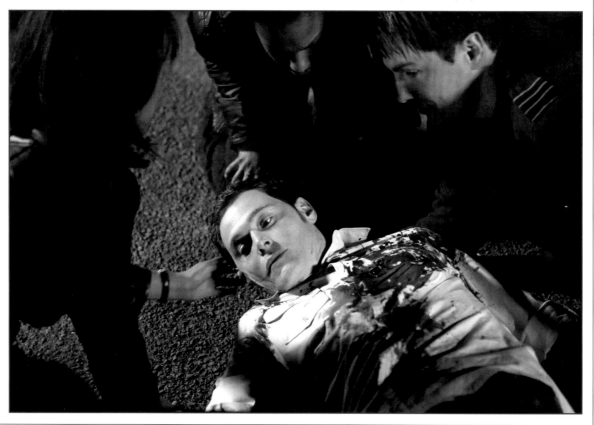

H

Harries, Dale Younger brother of Greg and partner in Harries & Harries. When Harries & Harries was infiltrated by Torchwood, Dale captured Ianto and Gwen and shot and wounded Rhys. He was later knocked out by Ianto and given Retcon to wipe his mind of everything about the alien. (2.4) (Played by MATT RYAN)

Harries, Greg Older brother of Dale and partner in Harries & Harries. When Harries & Harries was infiltrated by Torchwood, he was knocked out by Ianto and given Retcon to wipe his mind of everything about the alien. (2.4) (Played by GERARD CAREY)

Harrington, Doctor Oliver Chief Medical Officer from UNIT, assigned to CERN during the Large Hadron Collider project's lifetime. His wife, Marie, had died and he never really got over it. In the LHC, after a test run, he discovered what he thought was Marie's ghostly voice, and he realised he could bring her back next time the LHC was fired. Unknown to him, the Ghost Entities were aliens from a different dimension, and they began absorbing the neutrons of anyone who came into contact with them. Once he realised the truth, he went into the LHC to distract them while Jack and Professor Johnson sent antiprotons and protons around the LHC, destroying the Ghost Entities,

Harrington and sealing the portal off for good. (LS) (Played by STEPHEN CRITCHLOW)

Harris, Mr The psychiatric counsellor at the hospital where Owen was working when Katie Russell died. He was unaware of the existence of the alien brain parasite, Jack or Torchwood, and he believed surgeon James Garrett had died in a car crash. He told Owen to take three months' leave. (2.12) (Played by SELVA RASALINGHAM)

Harris, Mrs Sean's aggrieved mother, who claimed she had thrown her son out of the family home because he owed her money. (1.3) (Played by JULIE GIBBS)

Harris, Sean 'Bernie' 19-year-old layabout and petty thief who had stolen and used both halves of the alien Ghost Machine. He had witnessed the rape and murder of Lizzie Lewis in 1963 and also

foreseen what he wrongly assumed was his own murder. He also saw a woman drown her baby and, recognising the older version of her from near the Catholic Church in Splott, he successfully blackmailed

her. He was preparing to blackmail Edwin Morgan for the murder of Lizzie. He got his nickname 'Bernie' because he accidentally burned down his neighbour's shed when he was 12 years old. (1.3) (Played by BEN MCKAY)

Harris, Will A client at Mark Lynch's Weevil fight club who ended up in hospital and endured a ten-hour operation to save his life. (1.11) (Played by DAVID GYASI)

Hart, Captain John Neither the rank nor the name is likely to be real. He was another Time Agent and conman, who had had a lengthy relationship with Jack in the past. He veered from witty, warm and friendly to pathologically insane and violent, and the Time Agency had placed John with Jack, hoping Jack could control him. Although John arrived on Earth pretending to be concerned about radiation cluster bombs placed around Cardiff, this was actually part of a ruse to use Jack to help him find a huge Arcadian diamond that had belonged to John's most recent lover, who he had murdered. In fact John soon learned the whole thing was a trap set by his dead partner, and she arranged for a DNA-linked bomb to attach itself to him. Torchwood saved him, and he told Jack he knew where Gray was, before leaving Cardiff through the Rift. (2.1) John

later returned to Cardiff and laid a trap for Torchwood, setting explosive devices in an abandoned building, which detonated and came close to killing Ianto, Tosh and Owen. (2.12) In fact, John had been under Gray's control the whole time, via his Vortex manipulator, which was fused into his flesh. Gray was seeking revenge on Jack for abandoning him as a child; he followed John and Jack back to AD 27, where he ordered John to bury Jack alive. John threw his ring into the grave, ostensibly as a sentimental goodbye but in fact knowing that it would give off an etheric particle signal, enabling Jack to be located and dug up later. After Gray was stopped, John, now freed from his control, set about exploring what Earth had to offer. (2.13) (Played by JAMES MARSTERS)

Harvest, the Name given by the inhabitants of Brynblaidd to their practice that every ten years the newest generation of villagers would turn cannibal and lead the rest of the villagers in a frenzy of capturing, killing and eating strangers. (1.6)

H

Harwood's Haulage Firm that Rhys Williams left Luckley's to become Transport Manager for. (2.1) They had branches in Sheffield, Carlisle and Ipswich as well as Cardiff. Their Cardiff phone number was 02920 180316. One of Harwood's drivers, Leighton Reynolds, was involved with the Harries brothers, who were selling alien meat. When Leighton was killed in a traffic accident, Rhys took his place on behalf of Torchwood and infiltrated the gang. (2.4)

Hastings Used by Bridget Spears as the password to her computer files. (CoE)

Hat and Fire Juggler One of the Night Travellers. (2.10) (Played by ALF)

Hawley, Richard British singer whose song 'Serious' was playing in the café where Gwen and Andy Davidson discussed him joining Torchwood. (2.11)

Hayes, The Cardiff shopping area where the possessed Carys Fletcher saw a number of sex-orientated advertising billboards. (1.2)

Head of Vexor Eleven, the An alien artefact Eugene Jones was gobsmacked to see in the Torchwood Hub. (1.9)

Hedley Point Small bay in South Wales which had a ferry going back and forth to the islands in the Bristol Channel. Suzie was at Hedley Quay when Jack and Owen caught up with her and the dying Gwen. Jack repeatedly shot Suzie but she couldn't die until, back at the Hub, Tosh destroyed the Resurrection Glove. (1.8)

Helen Woman who worked at the Torchwood facility on Flat Holm, looking after what she believed were victims of experiments gone wrong, rather than people who had survived horrific Rift activity. (2.11) (Played by LORNA GAYLE)

Hen night girl Tried to chat up Owen in the Japanese bar where Owen went after being brought back to life with the Resurrection Glove. When she grabbed his groin, Owen realised he was never going to be able to have sex again

and dismissed her, before picking a fight with Jack and being thrown out of the bar. (2.7) (Played by LAUREN PHILLIPS)

Henderson, Detective Inspector Policeman with big hands who contacted Jack about Tosh's saving of Carol and Danny from the murderous Neil. (1.7)

Herbert, James English horror novelist whose novel *The Fog* had been translated into Arcateenian. Henry John Parker owned a copy of this version. (2.8)

Hercules Grecian demigod, who, according to the Night Travellers' publicity, could be taken on by their strongman, Stromboli. (2.10)

Higgs-Boson Particle Scientists at CERN in Switzerland were using the Large Hadron Collider to smash protons together that would ultimately enable them to study the resultant separation of protons and electrons that make up molecules. (LS)

Himalayas Mountain range where Torchwood originally found the Yeti spheres that were amongst the artefacts which Jack removed from their Indian branch in 1924. (GA)

Hitchhiker Pulsating, black alien creature, living within the elderly Mr Williams and pumping harmless endorphins into his bloodstream. It was removed by Jack and Ianto and taken back to Torchwood. (CoE)

Hits From the Musicals A DVD that Emma Louise Cowell bought in the supermarket because she loved show tunes. (1.10)

Hodges, Dan Web software salesman and one of the patrons at Mark Lynch's Weevil fight club. Dissatisfied with his life, despite having a wife and child, Hodges had allowed himself to be killed by the Weevil he

was in a cage with, and his body was dumped. It was later found by Torchwood. (1.11) (Played by MATT KID)

Hoix Alien race frequently seen on Earth, who seem more intent on eating anything and everything than actually causing harm. Torchwood had previously dealt with one that attacked a kebab shop in Barry. Due to John Hart's

misuse of the Rift Manipulator, one had been transported to the basement of St Helen's Hospital, but Owen was able to overcome it with a packet of cigarettes and a syringe of anaesthetic. (2.13) (Played by PAUL KASEY)

'Hole In The Head' Song by Sugababes which was playing in the bar when Gwen held her hen night party. (2.9)

Holly Tree Lodge, the An orphanage, ten miles out of Arbroath in Scotland, where Clement MacDonald lived until the arrival of the 456 in 1965. The children there believed they were being transferred to a similar home in Plymouth when they were handed over to the aliens. (CoE)

Holmes, Diane Pilot from 1953 who accidentally flew her passenger plane through the Rift and ended up in present-day Cardiff. She had completed a flight to Australia in four days in 1952 and had flown planes as ferries during the Second World War. Eventually she realised that the modern world couldn't keep her, even though she and Owen had become lovers, so she flew her plane, the *Sky Gypsy*, back into the Rift on Christmas Eve, leaving Owen heartbroken and unsure of her eventual fate. History notes that she and her passengers were reported missing, presumed dead over the Irish sea in 1953. (1.10) Owen later had a vision of Diane when Bilis Manger was trying to get Torchwood to open up the Rift and enable the demonic Abaddon to enter our dimension. (1.13) (Played by LOUISE DELAMERE)

Hologram woman John Hart's former lover, whom he murdered. She set in motion a plan that would blow him to pieces, in revenge. (2.1) (Played by INIKA LEIGH WRIGHT)

Holroyd, Emily Leader of Torchwood in 1899, and responsible for first employing Jack as a freelance agent. (2.12) (Played by HEATHER CRANEY)

Holy See of Vatican City, the John Frobisher told the 456 he represented this when greeting the 456 for the first time. (CoE)

Home Office Whitehall department where John Frobisher, Bridget Spears, Lois Habiba and others worked during the 456 incident. (CoE)

Hope Street Road in Penarth that ran parallel to Chain Lane. It was the subject of a film show at the Electro Cinema organised by film buff Dave Penn and his family, where they planned to show old film of the street and its residents. Nettie Williams was waiting at a bus stop in Hope Street, and the Windsor Café was on one corner. (2.10)

Hope, Sally-Ann Fake ID created by Tosh for Diane Holmes. (1.10)

Hopkins, Alex Torchwood Three's leader at the end of the twentieth century who told Jack that the twenty-first century would be when everything changed and that humanity wasn't ready. He had

looked into an alien locket that affected his mind, causing him to kill all the other Torchwood staff in the Hub. He bequeathed Torchwood Three to Jack, before killing himself. (2.12) (Played by JULIAN LEWIS JONES)

Hopley, Brian Husband to Maggie, who was killed on his wedding day in a road accident, leaving Maggie distraught enough that a year later, on the anniversary of his death, she prepared to kill herself. (2.8) (Played by GRANT LOCK)

Hopley, Maggie Young woman who, on the anniversary of her wedding, was preparing to commit suicide from the top of a Cardiff building. Brian, her husband, had been killed in a road accident less than an hour after their wedding ceremony and, despite everyone telling her life would get better, she had discovered it hadn't. Owen joined her on the rooftop after a photo of her and Brian she had tossed from the rooftop landed at his feet, and he told her the story of his own death and his gradual realisation that he could move on, but in a different way. He showed her the alien Pulse, in an effort to show her that actually life was worth continuing with. (2.8) (Played by CHRISTINE BOTTOMLEY)

Hospital Porter Worker at Cardiff Royal Infirmary, who was murdered in front of Gwen by a Weevil. Tosh later said she had taken the body and ensured it would wash up

three days later, looking like a suicide. (1.1) (Played by JAMS THOMAS)

Hot Chip British dance band whose song 'Over and Over' was playing in the Cube Bar when Laura was chatting up Owen. (1.11)

Hot Gossip See Brightman, Sarah.

Houdini, Harry Famed escapologist who apparently believed that the Cottingley fairy photographs were real. (1.5)

Hub 2 Nickname given to the former Torchwood Institute holding facility in Battersea, which Gwen, Ianto and Rhys made their base while searching for Jack. (CoE)

Hub, the Originally built in Victorian times when Torchwood Cardiff was first set up by Queen Victoria, the Hub was the vast base located on numerous levels beneath the Oval Basin in Cardiff Bay. A series of basement levels held records, information and flotsam and jetsam retrieved from the Rift over the years. Prisoners, and captive aliens such as Weevils were kept in its Vaults – aka the cells – and, at one time, the Hub contained a submarine bay. There were also tunnels, boardrooms, a hothouse, weapons rooms, offices, games rooms, medical bays, a morgue, etc. After over a century of service to the Torchwood Institute, the Hub and most of its contents were utterly destroyed by the bomb placed in the stomach of Jack Harkness by Government assassin Johnson. Torchwood then used an old Torchwood warehouse in London as a base, ironically dubbed Hub 2 by Rhys. (1.1–1.5, 1.7–1.13, 2.1–2.13, A, TDL, CoE)

Hughes, Howard Robert Jnr Reclusive billionaire who after a lifetime of movie-making, flying and business enterprise, became a recluse, suffering from paranoia and OCD. Gwen likened Henry John Parker's eccentric behaviour to Hughes's. (2.8)

Hula Girl One of the Night Travellers. (2.10) (Played by MERLIN)

Hunstanton Norfolk town which the Night Travellers had visited in March 1911. A local man, Alfred Mace, was left behind, believing his comatose wife could be revived if he could find the flask that contained her last breath. The local paper, the *Chronicle*, thought he was mad. (2.10)

Hunt, Ellen Part of the Government team in 1965 who allowed the 456 to take eleven children from the Holly Tree Lodge children's home in Scotland. Brian Green made John Frobisher issue a Blank Page including Hunt's name, resulting in her assassination. (CoE) (Played by ANN MARIE O'TOOLE)

Hurt, John British actor who played Kane in the movie *Alien*. Tosh and Owen discussed Kane's death scene as they examined the skeleton of the nineteenth-century soldier Mary had killed. (1.7)

Huw Policeman, officer number 620, patrolling the Brecons. Owen and Gwen hoped he'd help them stop the cannibals in Brynblaidd, but it turned out he was the nephew of ringleader Evan Sherman and thus a cannibal himself. He was shot and wounded by Jack, then handed over to the authorities. (1.6) (Played by RHYS AP TREFOR)

Hydrogen chloride Twenty-two per cent of the 456's atmosphere was made up of this. (CoE)

Hydrogen cyanide Nine per cent of the 456's atmosphere was made up of this. (CoE)

Hystrix An alien with detachable spines that Torchwood had to capture at the Wolf Bar. (A)

'I Just Blew In From The Windy City' Song from Emma Louise Cowell's favourite musical *Calamity Jane*, which she sang to Alesha and Jade (1.10)

'I Lost My Heart To A Starship Trooper' Song sung by Sarah Brightman and Hot Gossip which John Hart had blaring through the Hub while waiting for Jack to return. (2.13)

'I See You Baby' Song by Groove Armada, which was playing in the bar that Gwen and Rhys took Emma Louise Cowell to. (1.10)

'I Start My Day Over Again (Clock Song)' Song from the musical revue *The Bing Boys Are Here*, sung by the blind patient at St Teilo's Military Hospital. (2.3)

Ilmenite pyroxene One of the elements that made up the transporter device brought to Earth by the Arcateenian alien who assumed the identity of Mary. (1.7)

Incas Ancient South American civilisation. Owen hoped Tosh wouldn't make him sit through a slideshow about them. (1.7)

India Country which had a branch of Torchwood during the time of the British Empire, based in Delhi. It was closed down in 1924. (GA) It reported its children had become entranced by the 456, causing road traffic accidents. (CoE)

Interschool Maths Competition
The youngest ever entrant, Eugene Jones, being a bit of a maths genius, was expected to win this 1992 competition for his school, but in fact failed, so the winners were Rushmore. (1.9)

EUGENE JONES

Invisible Lift Colloquial name (also referred to as the Service Exit) for an elevator built into a piece of stone surrounding the water tower. It could carry a number of people quickly from the Hub up into the Oval Basin. Anyone standing on the stone remained invisible to others in Roald Dahl Plass. This had been caused by chameleon energy drained from the Doctor's TARDIS into the stonework when the Rift had opened. To passers-by, the stone always seemed present, as a hologram, and a perception filter meant they never noticed Torchwood coming and going and also never stood on that spot. (1.1, 1.4, 2.1, 2.4, CoE)

Ipswich Suffolk city, where Harwood's Haulage had offices. (2.4)

Isherwood, Christopher British-born American novelist, most famous for *Goodbye to Berlin* and the subsequent plays and films it spawned, including *I Am a Camera* and *Cabaret*. Jack and he had a fling in Berlin. (2.6)

Islamic Republic of Iran John Frobisher told the 456 he represented this when greeting the 456 for the first time. (CoE)

Isle of Wight Southern English island where Neil and Carol had holidayed when Danny was a toddler. Their chalet was overrun with spiders until Neil got rid of them. (1.7)

Italy European country to which Joe Carter, Steven's father, moved. (CoE)

Jack's mother As a youth, Jack's mother found him beside the dead body of his father, Franklin, after an alien attack on the Boeshane Peninsula. Jack then had to tell

her he'd become separated from his brother, Gray, during the attack. (2.5) (Played by LAUREN WARD)

Jackson One of Johnson's men ploughing through the wreckage of the Hub. (CoE)

Jacobs, Detective Inspector CID officer in charge of solving the serial killer spree, unaware it was conducted by Torchwood officer Suzie Costello. Jacobs knew of three murders, Sarah Pallister, John Tucker and Rani Ghosh, but was unaware of a fourth – a male, according to Owen. (1.1) (Played by GWYN VAUGHAN-JONES)

Jade Young girl who befriended Emma Louise Cowell at the hostel. (1.10) (Played by RHEA BAILEY)

Janet The name given by Jack to the Weevil who became a long-term resident in the Torchwood cells after her capture in the Cardiff Royal Infirmary, where she killed a porter in front of Gwen. Gwen later saw her in the Vaults on her first day at Torchwood. (1.1) Jack tried to use Janet to lead them to the Weevils taken by Mark Lynch; instead, Lynch's people stole Janet and put her to work in their fight club. Owen was put in a cage with her, and was saved when Jack shot Janet in the arm. Shortly afterwards, Mark Lynch himself went into the cage, and Janet killed him. She was later returned to the Torchwood Vaults. (1.11) She was seen by a confused Beth Halloran. (2.2) Jack was checking up on her when he had

a vision of his long-lost brother, Gray, (2.5) and Ianto used her to frighten Billy Davis into confessing his part in the Pharm-related killings. (2.6) When Owen was possessed by the darkness that emanated from the Resurrection Glove, it gave him power over the Weevils, who remained submissive to him. (2.7) Janet was one of the Weevils released by Gray when he took over the Hub, and she menaced Gwen and Captain John until she was shot and wounded by Ianto and Tosh. (2.13) It seems likely that Janet was finally killed, along with everyone else in the Vaults, when the Torchwood Hub was destroyed by the bomb placed in Jack's stomach by Johnson. (CoE) (Played by PAUL KASEY)

Jason Worker at Passmore Telesales. (1.9)

Jathaa Sun Gliders Spaceships spotted hovering above the Taj Mahal as a result of Owen fractionally opening the Rift and creating ripples and aftershocks that created Rift splinters. (1.13)

Javine One of the children Rhiannon tried to hide from the Government when she set up a crèche. (CoE)

Jen The waitress at the Happy Cook who witnessed the altercation between Eugene Jones and his mates Gary and Josh which

led to his death on the road outside. (1.9) (Played by AMY STARLING)

Jessica According to Charlie Grainger, Jessica was her brother Alex's new girlfriend. Alex strongly denied this. (2.2)

Jodrell Bank Cheshire-based radio telescope establishment. One of its staff, Neil, was known to Jack. (1.4) Prime Minister Brian Green wondered if they had spotted the arrival of the 456. (CoE)

John O'Groats Northernmost part of the UK, and where Rhys thought he and Gwen should go to be safe from Johnson and her troops. (CoE)

Johnson Dedicated enforcer for the Government who was assigned the job of eliminating Torchwood at the start of

the 456 crisis. Ruthless and efficient, she used Rupesh Patanjali who had already been set up by the Government to infiltrate Torchwood some months earlier. He lured Jack to the hospital he worked in, where Johnson killed them both. Expecting that Jack would come back to life, Johnson had an explosive placed inside his stomach, which later detonated, destroying him and the Hub. She then set about trying to round up Ianto and Gwen

J

while waiting for Jack to reassemble before encasing him in concrete. Gwen was eventually able to prove to Johnson that the enemy was not Torchwood but the Government that employed her, and Johnson helped Jack find a way to stop the 456 for good. (CoE) (Played by LIZ MAY BRICE)

Johnson, Ellie Young woman whose car was forcibly stopped near the village of Brynblaidd in the Brecon Beacons. She was kidnapped, slaughtered and prepared for eating by  cannibals. (1.6) (Played by EMILY BOWKER)

Johnson, Professor Catriona In charge of the activation of the Large Hadron Collider in CERN. On the day it was due to be fired, Torchwood informed her that Ghost Entities had been breaking through since an earlier experimental firing, and had already begun feeding off the neutrons in the bodies of various CERN and UNIT staff. Working with Jack, Professor Johnson realised that if she reversed the principles of the LHC, the portal the Ghost Entities were creating would be sealed for good. (LS) (Played by LUCY MONTGOMERY)

Johnson, Sergeant British army officer in charge of the area where the alien meteorite carrying the Gas life form crashed. Sergeant Johnson was not pleased that Torchwood arrived and took over his scene of operations. (1.2) (Played by ROSS O'HENNESSY)

Johnson, Thomas H. The editor of *Emily Dickinson: The Complete Poems*, the book needed by Torchwood to override the Hub lockdown instigated by Suzie Costello. (1.8)

Jones, Bronwen Eugene Jones's mother, who was separated from Eugene's father. After Eugene's funeral, the power of the Dogon Sixth Eye, which had now been removed from his dead body, gave them a chance to see each other one last time. (1.9) (Played by NICOLA DUFFETT)

Jones, Eugene Alien-obsessed lad in his mid-twenties, killed when he was hit by a speeding car on the A48 in Cardiff. He had become interested in alien artefacts when his school teacher Mr Garrett gave him a Dogon Sixth Eye as a consolation prize after Eugene failed an interschool maths competition that he would have won had he not got nervous. Years later, Eugene tried selling the Eye on eBay to raise money to send his co-worker Linda to Australia. The bidding was spoiled by a couple of Eugene's mates as a joke and an angry Eugene swallowed the Eye.

As a result, its powers of perception and inner vision gave him the opportunity to stay invisible on Earth for a short time after his death, to look back over his life. The Eye was removed after Eugene's funeral, and he became briefly visible again, finally saving Gwen from a similar car accident and allowing his family to see him one last time before he faded away for good. (1.9) (Played by PAUL CHEQUER and LUKE BROMLEY)

Jones, Ianto Jack's faithful and loyal assistant at Torchwood ultimately became his lover. Ianto had originally worked at Torchwood One in London with his girlfriend Lisa Hallett but, when the Cybermen attack on Canary Wharf left Lisa semi-Cybernised and the Torchwood Institute destroyed, Ianto went to Cardiff. He first rescued Jack from a Weevil attack and tried to get a job but was turned down. Repeated attempts failed until he led Jack to a pteranodon flying wild in Cardiff. After helping Jack to capture it, Ianto finally joined the team, immersing himself in the minutiae of the organisation, knowing more about its history, cases and operations than even Jack. He was equally infamous for his unique blend of coffee, the secret of which he never shared with anyone. After Lisa was destroyed when her Cyberman programming took over, he slowly began a romance with

Jack, which he eventually confessed to his sister Rhiannon, who was really pleased for him. After the Hub was destroyed, Ianto had to go on the run to London, forced to ask Rhiannon and her family to help his escape, which they loyally did. Reunited after rescuing him from Ashton Down in a JCB, Ianto and Jack went to Thames House to face the 456. The creature filled the building with toxic gas, slaughtering many of the people there, and this included Ianto, who died in Jack's arms. (1.1–1.13, 2.1–2.13, LS, A, GA, TDL, CoE) (Played by GARETH DAVID-LLOYD)

J

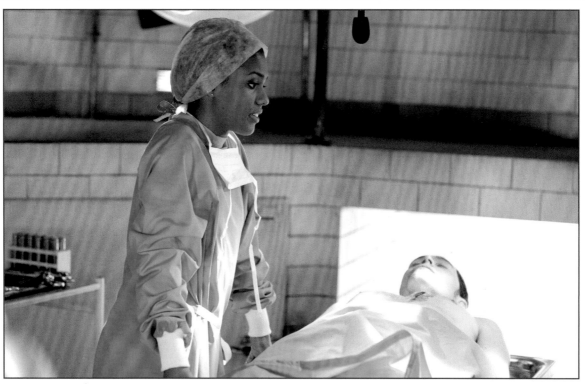

Jones, Martha UNIT medical officer, seconded to Torchwood during their investigation of the Pharm. When Owen was shot and killed, Martha became Torchwood's temporary medic whilst the resurrected Owen was considered too unstable to resume his duties. Martha infiltrated the Pharm, posing as student Samantha Jones, and exposed their work with the Mayfly. She attracted the unwanted attention of Aaron Copley, who was intrigued by her unique body chemistry, affected by her travelling through time with Jack's old friend the Doctor. She was aged to near-death by the Resurrection Glove and, after helping Owen regain some self-respect before his investigation of Henry John Parker's mansion, Martha left Cardiff and headed back to UNIT. She later contacted Jack when working at CERN in Switzerland and asked for his help dealing with the Ghost Entities but, when the 456 returned, Gwen stopped Jack calling her up, because Martha was on her honeymoon. (2.6–2.8, LS) (Played by FREEMA AGYEMAN)

Jones, Mr Ianto and Rhiannon's late father, who once broke his son's leg on the swings at the park (CoE) and used to take him to see Saturday morning films at the Electro Cinema in Penarth. (2.10). Ianto claimed that his father had been a master tailor, (2.9) but Rhiannon later revealed to Gwen that he had in fact worked in the menswear department of Debenhams. (CoE)

Jones, Samantha Pseudonym used by Martha to infiltrate the Pharm as a trial patient. Samantha was a Creative Writing post-graduate student, whose mother was a nurse, and who had travelled the world and once suffered from hepatitis. This made her ideal for the Pharm, although Professor Copley quickly saw through the 'Samantha' ruse. (2.6)

Jones, Shaun Eugene Jones's father, whose disappointment in his eldest son was, Eugene believed, the reason he finally left home for a job in America. In truth, he left because his marriage to Bronwen was already over, and he ended up working as a cashier at a service station in Filey. (1.9) (Played by GARETH POTTER)

Jones, Terry Eugene Jones's younger brother, who was told the truth about their father by Eugene shortly before Eugene's death. After the funeral, Terry finally made up with his absent father. (1.9) (Played by JOSHUA HUGHES)

Josh Guy who ran a DVD rental store which Eugene Jones used. He and Eugene's mate Gary faked a number of eBay IDs in an effort to up the bidding on the Dogon Sixth Eye. When a genuine buyer raised the bidding to £15,000, Josh jokingly topped that and won. Unable to pay, he offered Eugene just £34, and an angry Eugene swallowed the eye and ran away. After Eugene was killed by a speeding car, Gwen interviewed Josh at the DVD store, where he told her he was planning to move to London. (1.9) (Played by STEVEN MEO)

Jubilee Pizza Pizza firm with a branch in Cardiff Bay which regularly delivered to Torchwood. (1.1) Ianto ordered from them for himself and Doctor Tanizaki, but the unfortunate delivery girl, Annie, was murdered by Lisa Hallett. (1.4)

Jules One of the people Gwen discovered had been taken by the Rift. She found a cell bearing Jules's name in the Torchwood facility beneath Flat Holm island. (2.11)

Julia A friend of Owen and Katie Russell's who Katie had stated she didn't want at their wedding after they fell out over a restaurant bill. However, Katie later changed her mind and invited her. (2.12)

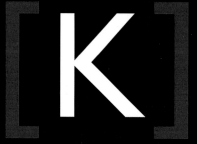

Kado, Toshiko Erroneous name for Tosh, misremembered by Gwen after Jack dosed her with the Amnesia pill. (1.1)

Kaiser Chiefs Yorkshire rock band whose song 'Saturday Night' was playing at the Red Dragon Centre bowling alley where Gwen and Rhys were having a game. (1.2) Their song 'Born To Be A Dancer' was played at Lynne Pearce and her partner Roy's BBQ to celebrate their fifth anniversary. (1.5)

Kaplinsky, Natasha BBC newsreader admired by Owen, who won a *Strictly Come Dancing* final watched by Thomas Flanagan and his daughter. (1.3) She was fronting television coverage of the Millennium Eve celebrations, which Alex Hopkins was watching when Jack returned to the Hub on 31 December 1999. (2.12)

Karen Daf's ex, who once made him sleep on the sofa. (1.3)

Kate Jasmine Pearce's schoolteacher, who witnessed two bullies who had picked on Jasmine being attacked by a tornado conjured up by the Fairies that had sworn to protect Jasmine. (1.5) (Played by HELEDD BASKERVILLE)

Kathmandu Original location of the one-eyed yellow idol that the Duchess claimed was amongst the artefacts which Jack removed from Torchwood India in 1924. (GA)

Keith Park Location where the Cardiff police found the body of Barry Leonard, another victim of Billy Davis. (2.6)

Kelly A friend of Carol's, who gave her a session at a tanning salon as a wedding present. (1.7)

Kendall, Trevor Former boyfriend of Gwen's. She couldn't have sex with him in front of his cat. (1.7)

Kenobi, Obi-Wan Fictional character from the *Star Wars* movies, from whom John Hart, in parodying Princess Leia from the same movies, begged help. (2.1)

Keppoch Street Cardiff road where Leighton and Jen Reynolds lived, at number 54. (2.4)

Kerr, Deborah American actress. Emma Louise Cowell was delighted to note that the fake identity created for her by Torchwood, Deborah Morrison, spelled the first name the same way as the actress. (1.10)

Keryehla Janees The real name of the alien from Cell 114 disguised as Beth Halloran. Its rank was Putaak Graszh and its serial number was ish-nin-fas-du-hap-vac-nal. (2.2)

Ketamine Powerful anaesthetic administered to the alien creature Harries & Harries used to supply their meat. (2.4)

Kevin Worker at Passmore Telesales. (1.9)

Kid in arcade Youngster who Sean Harries blagged cigarettes off and failed to supply a promised iPod to. (1.3) (Played by RYAN CONWAY)

Kieran Teenager who had come to the vicinity of Brynblaidd and been captured by what he thought was a monster but was in fact a group of cannibals. He had escaped and holed up in one the local houses. He shot Gwen, mistaking her for the monster, but later befriended her. However, the cannibals came back and took him and prepared to murder him. He was saved, along with the rest

of Torchwood, by Jack, who gunned down the cannibals. (1.6) (Played by CALLUM CALLAGHAN)

Kingdom of Saudi Arabia John Frobisher told the 456 he represented this when greeting the 456 for the first time. (CoE)

Kipling, Joseph Rudyard Indian-born British author, whose works were amongst those in the library at Torchwood India. (GA)

Kneale, Gerald Torchwood leader in 1918. He and Harriet Derbyshire took Tommy Brockless from his hospital bed in 1918 and froze him, leaving only a few notes for whoever woke him to do whatever was necessary in the future, sealed in a time-locked box. (2.3) (Played by RODERIC CULVER)

Kooks British band whose song 'Ooh La La' was played at Lynne Pearce and her partner Roy's BBQ to celebrate their fifth anniversary. (1.5)

'Kubla Khan' Coleridge poem quoted by Mary as she explored the Torchwood Hub. (1.7)

Lad While at a car boot sale, he and his father bought some old film cans that may have contained footage of the Night Travellers. (2.10) (Played by JOHN O'GARA)

Ladsmag One of a number of adult magazines used at the Conway Clinic to help sperm donors get aroused. (1.2)

Lahore Indian city where Jack, based with the British army, first encountered the malignant Fairies in 1909. (1.5)

Langham House Home of Alice and Steven Carter. (CoE)

Lanzarote Popular holiday resort in the Canary Islands. Banana Boat was arrested there for selling pirated CDs. (2.8)

Large Hadron Collider Main instrument in the CERN facility in Switzerland. It consisted of a massive 25-kilometre circular tunnel 100 metres below ground. Inside this, protons would be sent around at the speed of light, hitting one another and creating the ability to study the Higgs-Boson particle. An earlier testing of it opened a portal to an alien dimension, through which Ghost Entities were gaining access to Earth. By using antiprotons and protons in the Collider, Jack and Professor Johnson sealed the portal and saved the people already affected by the Ghost Entities. (LS)

Laser Saw Equipment used firstly by Jack to remove the Hitchhiker from Mr Williams (and seamlessly reseal the wound afterwards) and later by Johnson on Jack himself when placing the bomb in his stomach. (CoE)

Last Stop Burger van in the Brecons where Ianto bought food for everyone, except Tosh. (1.6)

Latin America The continent of South America, not yet visited by the fictitious Samantha Jones. (2.6)

Laura Barmaid at the Cube Bar, who started a conversation with Owen until her boyfriend Tommy broke it up. (1.11) (Played by ALEXANDRA DUNN)

Lawrence Fiancé of Carol. Neil, who was planning to murder Carol for leaving him, hoped it would be Lawrence who found the bodies of Carol and her son Danny. (1.7)

Lazarus Biblical character who allegedly rose from the dead. Johnson referred to Jack's ability to never die as his 'Lazarus qualities'. (CoE)

Ledger, Heath Australian actor, of whom Carys Fletcher was something of a fan. (1.2)

Leeds West Yorkshire city where Clement MacDonald was found living on the streets aged 11. He stayed there for forty years, in and out of care, before being sectioned and moved to East Grinstead's Duke of York Hospital. (CoE)

Leicester Midlands city where Owen and Katie Russell once shared dinner with a friend called Julia, who refused to pay her share of the bill. (2.12)

Lemnos Mediterranean island where the mythical character Philoctetes was marooned (1.7)

Leonard, Barry Former student who visited the Pharm and, through the ingestion of alien Mayfly larvae, was cured of diabetes. He was subsequently murdered by Billy Davis as  the Pharm attempted to cover up the side effects of their drugs tests. (2.6) (Played by MICHAEL WILLIAMS)

Lewis, Elizabeth 'Lizzie' 17-year-old Cardiff girl raped and murdered by Edwin Morgan in 1963. This event was witnessed separately by Sean Harris and Owen when they used the alien Ghost Machine. (1.3) (Played by EMILY EVANS)

Lewis, Mabel Ann Mother to Lizzie, who left Cardiff – unable to get over the loss of her daughter – and died many years later without ever learning the truth about her daughter's rape and murder. (1.3)

Libertines, The English band whose song 'Can't Stand Me Now' was playing in the pub where Tosh and Owen discussed Edwin Morgan. (1.3)

Lidocaine Anaesthetic drug administered to the alien creature Harries & Harries used to supply their meat. (2.4)

Life Knife Name proposed by Ianto for the ornately carved weapon which, used in conjunction with the Resurrection Glove, could bring the dead back to life. Suzie Costello used the knife to murder people so she could discover the Glove's secrets. (1.1) When Torchwood needed to bring Suzie back to life, her dead body was stabbed with the Life Knife to boost the Glove's energy. (1.8)

L

Linda (1) Owen met her in a bar and, after he had sprayed himself with alien pheromone cologne, she wanted to have sex with him, much to the annoyance of her boyfriend, Colin. (1.1) (Played by CATHRYN DAVIS)

Linda (2) Eugene Jones's co-worker at Passmore Telesales, who specialised in kitchens (she attained the rank of Silver Seller). She was having an affair with her married manager, Craig Telford. Eugene planned to sell the Dogon Sixth Eye on eBay and give Linda the proceeds so she could go to Australia and get away from Craig. (1.9) (Played by ROBYN ISAAC)

Lisa Girl unaware that her male partner was wearing her tights, and stretching them accordingly. (1.7)

Liverpool FC Jonah Bevan was a massive fan. (2.11)

Livescan Police database of fingerprints. Andy Davidson found that Freda was not on it. (A)

Lizzie One of the children Rhiannon tried to hide from the Government when she set up a crèche. (CoE)

Llandow Airfield The place where Diane Holmes landed the *Sky Gypsy* after passing through the Rift. She later returned there and flew the plane back in the direction she had come from, hoping the Rift would take her home or somewhere else entirely. (1.10)

Llangyfelach Lane Cardiff street where John Tucker was murdered and where Gwen first saw Torchwood in action as they brought Tucker back from the dead. (1.1)

Lockbreaker Alien device which Tosh used to escape the Hub during the lockdown instigated by Lisa Hallett. Its

design suggested that it originated from the same place as the alien Reader that Tosh used to scan *A Tale of Two Cities* onto her computer. (1.4)

Lodmoor Research Facility A division of the Ministry of Defence, where Tosh worked. She stole blueprints from them for a Sonic Modulator, which she then built and passed on to a woman called Milton, in exchange for the safe return of her mother. (2.12)

London Capital city of the UK. Torchwood One was based there. (1.1) When the city was bombed in 1941, Thomas Flanagan was evacuated to Cardiff. (1.3) Torchwood One was destroyed by the Cybermen, and Ianto brought the partially Cybernetic Lisa Hallett up to Cardiff. (1.4) Jack met Estelle Cole at the Astoria Ballroom there during the Second World War. (1.5) DVD rental store worker Josh planned to move there after the

death of Eugene Jones. (1.9) Emma Louise Cowell settled there to make a career in fashion. (1.10) Owen pretended to Mark Lynch that his jellied eel business was relocating from London to Cardiff. (1.11) Tosh was heading there to celebrate her grandfather's 80th birthday when she and Jack got sent back to 1941. (1.12) The Torchwood team were all drawn to London – including areas such as Camden, Battersea, Vauxhall and Westminster – after the destruction of the Hub in their search for Jack and the answers to the mystery of the 456. (CoE)

Lorry driver Driver of a truck of potatoes who stopped at Tony's café in Wales, which enabled Gwen and Rhys to hide under his tarpaulin and get a surreptitious lift towards London. (CoE) (Played by ANTHONY HARDWIDGE)

Lost Lands Mythical home of the Fairies. (1.5)

Lotus Nebula Place where John Hart believed he could experience seventeen pleasures simultaneously. (2.13)

Louise Aide at Thames House, responsible for advising on international diplomatic protocols. (CoE)

Luckley's Printing firm that Rhys worked for as Transport Manager. When he went for the job interview, he wore a smart pair of trousers. (1.3)

Luke Aide at Thames House, responsible for coordinating video links between nations. (CoE)

Lundy Street Street in Cardiff, where Moira Evans lived at number 51, and where her daughter and son-in-law and granddaughter lived for a while. (A)

Luxembourg European country which reported its children had become entranced by the 456, causing road traffic accidents. (CoE)

Lynch, Mark Suave, sophisticated and rich estate agent with a philosophy on life similar to Owen's. He believed that life was a struggle, that fighting for supremacy was the ultimate thrill and, when you reached the pinnacle, there was no point in prolonging life – better to go out on top. He had discovered the Weevils and set up a Weevil fight club experience for like-minded people, who would pay a thousand pounds to enter a cage with one of the creatures. The person who stayed the longest took home the night's takings. He quickly realised that Torchwood knew more about the Weevils (without ever knowing who Torchwood were) and sussed that Owen was with them. Moreover, he saw that Owen was tortured by his feelings of loneliness and disassociation and so took him to the fight club. After Jack closed the club, Lynch walked into the cage alone with Janet the Weevil, realising he had nowhere else to go in life, and the Weevil slaughtered him. (1.11) (Played by ALEX HASSELL)

Lynch Frost Cardiff estate agents, run by Mark Lynch. (1.11) The firm continued to trade, as Frost Lynch, after Lynch's death. (CoE)

Lynda The fake name Gwen used to stand bail for Clement MacDonald, and thus free him from Camden Police Station. Lynda was another policewoman she and Andy Davidson had previously worked with. (CoE)

L

[M]

Mac Neighbour of Rhiannon and Johnny Davies, who told Johnny that Ianto was alive. (CoE) (Played by MICHAEL STEWART)

MacDonald, Clement In November 1965, the young orphaned boy believed he was being transferred, along with other kids, from Holly Tree Lodge in Arbroath to another orphanage in Plymouth. However, the bus that carried them stopped in deserted moorland late at night, and the twelve children were handed over to the 456, as part of a deal struck by the British Government. Amongst the handlers on the bus was Jack Harkness; when young Clem asked him if they were going to be safe, Jack lied and said yes. Although Clem fled at the last minute, his senses were permanently affected by his brief exposure to the 456's power: he could smell things out of the range of normal humans, and he developed a strange tick, centred on where Jack had placed a 'comforting' hand on his shoulder. Living rough, Clem fled to

Leeds, adopting the name Timothy White, possibly after the then-famous chain of shops. In and out of care, by the time Torchwood became aware of him, he was forty-five years older and a resident at the Duke of York psychiatric hospital.

When the world's children began speaking with the words of the 456, so did Clem, an incident recorded by a nurse on a mobile phone which drew first Torchwood and later Johnson's interest. When he met Gwen, Clem smelled the child growing in her womb, and when Johnson's men arrived, he smelled the danger on them and fled to London, where he was arrested. Torchwood rescued him and he joined them in Hub 2. He felt safe until Jack returned, and Clem told the others what Jack had done to him. When the 456 sensed Clem's existence, they realised he was the only threat to them on Earth and psychically killed him, but that suggested to Jack that the frequency Clem could sense them on was the way to defeat them. (CoE) (Played by GREGORY FERGUSON and PAUL COPLEY)

Mace, Alfred A man from Hunstanton, whose wife was put in a coma when the Night Travellers stole her last breath in 1911. (2.10)

Mace, Colonel Alan British UNIT commander, posted to Vancouver, leaving Colonel Oduya to oversee UNIT's involvement in the return of the 456. (CoE)

Machynlleth Area in Powys, West Wales where Andy Davidson's cousin lived. He claimed he was abducted by aliens once. (A)

MacKenzie, Lucy Member of Pilgrim and Max Tresillian's next target. She worked at the Wolf Bar, where Torchwood were able to save her from Max. (1.8)

Mahajan, Mr Indian businessman who supplied Torchwood India and the Duchess with all the modern technology needed to put her Golden Age operation into action, just as his family had done for generations, and installed a wireless mast in the grounds of the Royal Connaught Club. He was surprised when she tried to kill him, having deemed him superfluous to her needs and too much of a spiv for her liking. When the Club was destroyed, he fled with Jack, Gwen and Ianto and was therefore the only other survivor. He had a 3-year-old son called Arvind, whose birthdate was part of the code that gave Mahajan access to the wireless mast via his mobile phone. (GA) (Played by RAVIN J. GANATRA)

Mahib, Doctor Doctor at Cardiff Royal Infirmary who told the hospital porter that he believed the police had cordoned off an area of the hospital. (1.1)

Maindy Area of Cardiff where Freda fell out of the Rift and landed in the river. (A)

Man Grangetown passer-by asked by John Ellis if he knew Alan Ellis, John's son. (1.10) (Played by JONNIE CROSS)

Man in bar Person Mary claimed to be trying to avoid when she began chatting to Tosh. (1.7) (Played by TIM PROCTOR)

Man in street Passer-by who Mark Goodson knocked into while fleeing the Fairies. (1.5) (Played by PAUL JONES)

Manchester English city where Tommy Brockless's family were from. (2.3)

Mandarin According to Ianto, the most commonly spoken language on Earth, although the 456 chose to communicate in English. (CoE)

Manger, Bilis Enigmatic time-travelling man with a passion for old timepieces. When Jack and Tosh were sent back to 1941 by the Rift, Bilis was the manager of the Ritz Dance Hall. In modern times, he was the caretaker of the same

building, but looking not a day older than he did in 1941. (1.12) He was manipulating Torchwood into activating the Rift Manipulator and bringing through people from many different time zones – but this was a distraction to occupy Torchwood while he hatched his real plan. He brought the demon Abaddon through the Rift but, even before Jack destroyed Abaddon, Bilis had inexplicably vanished. (1.13) (Played by MURRAY MELVIN)

'Mao Tse Tung Said' Song by Alabama 3 which was playing at Bar Reunion when John Hart entered. (2.1)

Maple, Mrs Admitted to Cardiff General Hospital as Case 4025. (1.7)

Maplin, Sparky Admitted to Cardiff General Hospital as Case 4183. (1.7)

Mara Mythical wraiths believed to suffocate people in their sleep. Jack mused that the Fairies might be part-Mara. (1.5)

Market Street Cardiff street where Gwen first witnessed a couple of children entranced by the forthcoming arrival of the 456. (CoE)

Marmer, Lucy 43-year-old whose heart had been removed prior to her dead body being brought into Cardiff General Hospital in September 2001 as case number 4290. The autopsy results were then placed in the hands of detectives from Scotland Yard as part of their Operation Lowry. It was likely she was a victim of Mary's. (1.7)

Marnie, Tippi Admitted to Cardiff General Hospital as Case 4371. (1.7)

Marrin, David Man brought in by the police and questioned over the rape and murder of Lizzie Lewis in 1963. He was released without charge and never re-questioned. (1.3) Many years later he was admitted to Cardiff General Hospital as case 4472. (1.7)

M

Mars Planet in Earth's solar system. Jack mentioned he'd once been on a flight between Venus and Mars. (LS)

Martin Villager in Brynblaidd who was shot by Jack and tortured into telling him about the Harvest. (1.6) (Played by ROBERT BARTON)

Martin, Aston Person brought in by the police and questioned over the rape and murder of Lizzie Lewis in 1963. He was released without charge and never re-questioned. (1.3)

Martin, Dan A mate of Eugene Jones's. (1.9)

Mary A prostitute from 1812 who was murdered by a crashed Arcateenian. The alien took over her body and survived for almost 200 years by absorbing human hearts. She needed access to Torchwood, knowing that they could re-energise her transporter device, which she had left with the body of her first victim, a young soldier. She eventually met Tosh and seduced her, giving her a pendant with which she could hear the thoughts of others. Jack eventually sent 'Mary' and the transporter into the heart of the sun. (1.7) (Played by DANIELA DENBY-ASHE)

Match Football magazine read by Steven Carter. (CoE)

Matron Senior Nurse at St Teilo's Military Hospital, who did not appreciate her patients singing out loud. (2.3) (Played by HAZEL ATHERTON)

Matthews, Stanley Footballer who played for Blackpool and was responsible for their 1953 FA Cup victory over Bolton Wanderers, as seen by John Ellis. (1.10)

Mayfly Colloquial name given to the parasitical alien insects whose larvae the Pharm were inserting into their clinical trial patients, to form the basis of the Reset drug. The larvae  fed off the damaged cells in the patients' bodies but, when hatched, they killed the patient. (2.6)

McDonald's Fast-food restaurant chain which Ianto offered to take his niece, Mica, to for her birthday, although in reality he was trying to get hold of a child for Torchwood to examine in their investigation into the 456. (CoE)

Mefs Friend of the teenaged shop assistant. (2.5)

Megan Friend of Gwen's who was at her hen night and wedding. Megan was shocked to find the half-digested body of Mervyn the DJ after he'd been attacked by the Nostrovite at the wedding but she was given Retcon afterwards and thus forgot about it. (2.9) (Played by DANIELLE HENRY)

'Melancholy Baby' One of the songs played at the Ritz Dance Hall in 1941. (1.12)

Memory Parasite See Smith, Adam.

Merthyr Tydfil Industrial town north of Cardiff, close to the warehouse Harries & Harries used to store their alien meat. (2.4)

Meteorite The means by which the Gas life form was able to get to Earth. It was damaged by Gwen when she threw a chisel at it, accidentally piercing it and enabling the alien to escape. It was crystalline at its centre. (1.2)

Mezon Energy A strange box that came through the Rift, bringing a memory parasite with it, seemed to be emitting Mezon Energy. (2.5)

MI5 British security service. Carys Fletcher thought it was them, not Torchwood, who had taken her prisoner. (1.2) A policeman joked with Owen that he was from MI5, because he didn't believe Owen's protestations that he was with Torchwood. (2.7) The MI5 building was used to host the 456 on the thirteenth floor of Thames House. (CoE)

Michael, George Pop star whose songs are often played at weddings. When it looked like Gwen and Rhys's wedding was off due to Jack's arrival, Megan decided to tell Mervyn the DJ not to bother with getting any of George Michael's records out. (2.9)

Middle of the Road 1970s folk band whose song 'Soley Soley' came on the radio as Gwen and Suzie drove towards the Greenleaves Hospital. Suzie's mum used to sing along to it. (1.8)

M

Mike Barry Leonard's flatmate, who told Gwen and Ianto about Barry visiting the Pharm. (2.6) (Played by MICHAEL SEWELL)

Millennium Bug Supposed computer virus that many believed would cause a technological meltdown as 1999 gave way to 2000. However, Jack discovered that it could equally apply to an alien creature he encountered that had eighteen legs stacked with poison. (2.12)

Millennium Stadium Sports stadium at the heart of Cardiff. Rhys Williams had a mate who worked there. (1.4)

Millet, Paul Jonah Bevan's absent father. (2.11)

Milton Woman who kidnapped Mrs Sato and held her as collateral to force Tosh to steal the blueprints for a Sonic Modulator being developed at the Lodmoor Research facility where Tosh worked. When Tosh provided a working prototype, Milton activated it but was arrested immediately afterwards when UNIT arrived. (2.12) (Played by CLAIRE CLIFFORD)

Miss B Magazine with saucy sex tips that Emma Louise Cowell found disgusting. (1.10)

Mo Friend of Rhys's, who said that having kids was the best thing he ever did. (2.11)

Moira Street Splott street where an old man who collected junk kept a lock-up. Sean Harris and a mate burgled it and found the Ghost Machine there, along with other things that had fallen through the Rift. (1.3)

'Monster' Song by The Automatic which was being played in the car driven by Ellie Johnson when she was abducted and murdered in the Brecon Beacons. (1.6)

Moonlight Sonata Composition by Ludwig van Beethoven which was playing on the radio that Jack tuned for John Ellis. (1.10)

Morag Worker at Passmore Telesales who used to go out with Eugene Jones. (1.9)

Moretti, Lucia Torchwood operative between 1968 and 1975, who died in 2006 from heart disease, a rare occasion of someone in Torchwood dying after retirement. She and Jack had a relationship, which resulted in the birth of Alice Carter. Lucia warned her grandson, Steven, that one day, presumably because of Torchwood, he would be in trouble if he wasn't careful. (CoE)

Morgan, Cerys Rhys was in love with her once. When he was 12. (2.9)

Morgan, Edwin Cardiff spiv who forced himself on Lizzie Lewis in 1963, raping and murdering her, but was never caught. Many years later, after using the alien Ghost Machine, both Sean Harris and Owen witnessed the event. Harris tried to blackmail Morgan and Owen also revealed he knew what Morgan had done, which caused the old man to have a breakdown. He had been admitted into hospital on 3 December 1989 and diagnosed as suffering from paranoid delusions and violent fantasies due to his agoraphobia and severe depression, but was discharged on 17 January 1990, prescribed with 60mg SSRI tablets. Eventually, he sought Harris out but encountered Torchwood and deliberately threw himself onto a knife held by Gwen. Owen was unable to save his life. (1.3) (Played by CHRISTOPHER ELSON and GARETH THOMAS)

Morgan, Elin Clinical trials patient, born 9 July 1978, who visited the Pharm and was cured of her illness by the ingestion of alien Mayfly larvae. To cover up the subsequent side effects, the Pharm hired Billy Davis to kill her, but Billy failed when Torchwood caught him in the act. (2.6) (Played by NATALIE DANKS-SMITH)

Morgan, Mrs Edwin Morgan's late mother. He inherited her house. (1.3)

Moriarty, Private British soldier who brought Gwen before Sergeant Johnson at the site of the meteorite crash. (1.2) (Played by ADRIAN CHRISTOPHER)

Morrison, Deborah Fake ID created by Tosh for Emma Louise Cowell. (1.10)

Moses Cat belonging to Estelle Cole. The Fairies spooked it and thus used it to lure Estelle out from the safety of her home and into the back garden, where they drowned her in a flash rain storm. (1.5)

Mother (1) Woman who took her 10-year-old daughter to see the travelling circus in 1923, unaware they were the mysterious Night Travellers. Distracted by shadows, when she looked back, the circus had just vanished, taking her daughter with them. (2.10) (Played by LISA WINSTON)

Mother (2) Parent of Tyler, the young boy seen in a trance-like state in the street by Gwen. (CoE) (Played by CRISIAN EMMANUEL)

Mother (3) Parent of two young children seen in a trance-like state in Cardiff Bay. (CoE) (Played by BEVERLY BECK)

Mother in park Parent whose child was seen in a trance-like state when being used as a conduit by the 456. The incident was witnessed by Ianto and his sister Rhiannon. (CoE) (Played by FAY MACDONALD)

Mulder Fictional character from TV series *The X-Files*. PC Andy Davidson likened Jack to him. (1.13, 2.11)

Mum (1) Part of the family taken hostage by the Blowfish. Her husband was shot by it. (2.1) (Played by SANDRA GREENWOOD)

Mum (2) Parent of Sasha, the young girl seen in a trance-like state in Cardiff Bay by Gwen and Rupesh. (CoE) (Played by MELANIE BARKER)

Mum (3) Parent anxious about her son, Christopher, who was led away by the army to be given to the 456. (CoE) (Played by RHIANNON OLIVER)

Mumm-Ra Brirish indie rock band whose song 'She's Got You High' was playing in the bar where Tosh took Tommy Brockless to play pool. (2.3)

Muse British band whose song 'Assassin' was playing in the Cube Bar when Mark Lynch and Owen got into a fight with Tommy. (1.11)

Myakian wings Henry John Parker owned a set of these. (2.8)

M

[N]

Nall, Malcolm Person brought in by the police and questioned over the rape and murder of Lizzie Lewis in 1963. He was released without charge and never re-questioned. (1.3)

Nancy Cardiff girl very much in love with the real Captain Harkness in 1941, although he didn't entirely return her feelings. (1.12) (Played by ELEN RHYS)

NASA National Aeronautics and Space Administration, the American space agency, who launched the *Voyager* Golden Records aboard *Voyager* 1 and *Voyager* 2 in the late 1970s. Owen likened the Pulse to an alien version of these probes, but sent to Earth. (2.8) The British Defence Secretary wondered if NASA would use their 'Star Wars' technology against the 456 threat. (CoE)

National Geographic Journal of world nature. (1.7)

Neil (1) Man who worked at Jodrell Bank whose voice, Jack reckoned, sounded like Sean Connery's. (1.4)

Neil (2) Embittered man who was angry with Carol, his ex, and planned to murder her and his son Danny before killing himself. Having overheard his plan via the alien pendant, Tosh followed him to Carol's home and stopped him. (1.7) (Played by RAVIN J. GANATRA)

Newport South Wales city, which Owen reckoned could have been taken over by aliens in the time it would take him to sort out the seat, mirror, etc after a woman had driven the SUV. (1.4) Ianto joked that maybe Freda came from the Welsh city, because she was a skinny, pale teenaged girl with a gun. (A)

Newsreader Presented television news reports on the UFOs above the Taj Mahal and the random appearances of people in historical costumes attacking police. (1.13) (Played by CARRIE GRACIE)

Neyman, Sybil Relative of Lizzie Lewis, questioned twice by the police over Lizzie's rape and murder in 1963. She was released without charge. (1.3)

Niall Someone Ivan Fletcher was considering using, along with Niall's men, on a job, but Niall was outpricing himself, as Ivan felt he could get Polish workers for a lot less cash. (1.2)

Night Travellers, the A group of circus performers from the late nineteenth and early twentieth centuries, whose origins were mysterious and undefined, but who appeared to be alien or powered by something not of this world. Some time in the 1920s to 1930s, Jack posed as the Man Who Couldn't Die at another circus, because he'd been sent to investigate, most likely by Torchwood, and find some answers but the Night Travellers then vanished. Led by the Ghost Maker, they used the stolen last breaths of their victims to give them power and longevity. For many years they survived as two-dimensional images on film stock,

but after the Ghost Maker re-entered the real world and took more victims, they all had enough energy to rejoin the 3D real world. When the Ghost Maker was apparently destroyed by Jack and Ianto, so were the rest of the Night Travellers. (2.10)

'Nightingale Sang in Berkley Square, A' One of the songs played at the Ritz Dance Hall in 1941. (1.12)

Nightspot Cardiff nightclub outside which Carys Fletcher was taken over by the Gas life form and where she then murdered Matt Stevenson. (1.2)

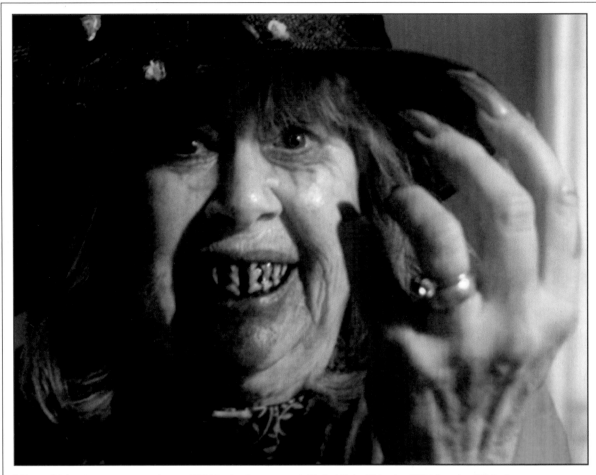

Nilson, Alain Maintenance worker at CERN, who became a victim of the Ghost Entities. After they were destroyed, he recovered. (LS)

Nitrogen Twenty per cent of the 456's atmosphere was made up of this. (CoE)

Nitrosyl chloride Twenty-five per cent of the 456's atmosphere was made up of this. (CoE)

Nobel Prize Won by CERN in the 1980s for creating an antiproton beam to make atoms of antimatter. (LS)

North America Continent visited by the fictitious Samantha Jones. (2.6)

North Wales Astronomy Society Organisation that put on a seminar at Aberystwyth University called 'Black Holes and the Uncertainty Principle'. (1.9)

Norway European country which reported its children had become entranced by the 456, causing road traffic accidents. (CoE)

Nostrovite Fast-moving, shape-shifting aliens who have an exo-biological insemination system for creating their young. The male impregnates a host body (not necessarily a Nostrovite) via biting, which puts a non-sentient blastopheric mass, aka an egg, into the host's bloodstream. There it waits approximately twenty-four hours to hatch, whereupon the female Nostrovite will rip the host apart and free the freshly hatched young. A Nostrovite impregnated Gwen on the night before her wedding to Rhys and was then killed by Jack. The female Nostrovite traced Gwen to the hotel where the wedding was taking place, impersonating a guest called Carrie, then Jack and finally Rhys's mother before Jack obliterated it. The egg was destroyed when Rhys successfully used the Singularity Scalpel on Gwen before it could hatch. (2.9)

Nurse (1) Worked at St Teilo's Hospital during the latter days of the First World War and witnessed strange apparitions – including Gwen, to whom she spoke – that were caused by time breaking through. (2.3) (Played by LIZZIE ROGAN)

Nurse (2) Helping to clear the children from the paediatric ward at St Helen's Hospital, she was asked by Amy Carysfort whether she had seen Jamie Burton. (2.7) (Played by ELEN FLORENCE)

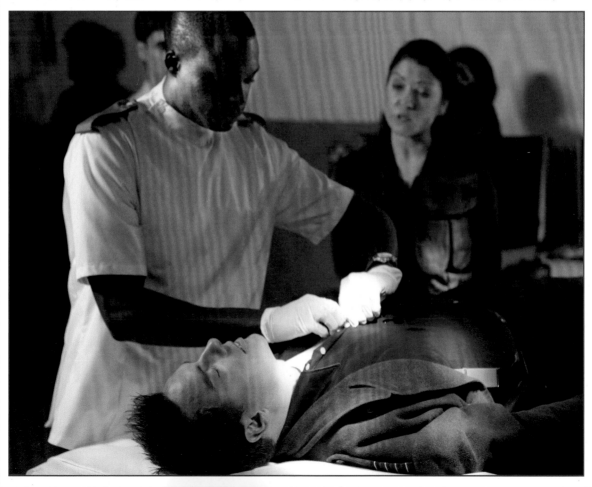

Nurse (3) After Katie Russell died, Jack knocked Owen out and, when he came to, the nurse told him to rest. (2.12) (Played by CATHERINE MORRIS)

Nurse (4) Worked at St Helen's Hospital and showed Professor Courtney to Jack's bed. (TDL) (Played by EIRY THOMAS)

Nurse (5) Woman in charge of the man she knew only as Timothy White at the Duke of York psychiatric hospital in East Grinstead. (CoE) (Played by ANNA LAWSON)

Nurse (6) A male worker at St Helen's Hospital who was part of Rupesh Patanjali's plan to entice Jack there by killing Chow Lee Jee. (CoE) (Played by KWABENA AMPONSA)

N

Oakenfold, Paul English record producer and club DJ whose anthem 'Amsterdam' was playing in the Nightspot nightclub. (1.2)

Oakham Street Residential street where the body of Alex Arwyn was found at number 96 after he had been murdered by Max Tresillian. (1.8)

Oakington Dockside town where failed asylum seekers were held. John Frobisher wondered if children kept there could be offered to the 456. (CoE)

Oduya, Colonel Augustus UNIT officer placed as their representative to the Government during the 456 crisis. He was present when the 456 died. (CoE) (Played by CHARLES OBOMELI)

O'Dwyer, Dan Person brought in by the police and questioned over the rape and murder of Lizzie Lewis in

1963. He was released without charge and never re-questioned. (1.3)

Oestrogen Steroid female hormone, which Jack reckoned he could taste in the Cardiff rain. (1.1)

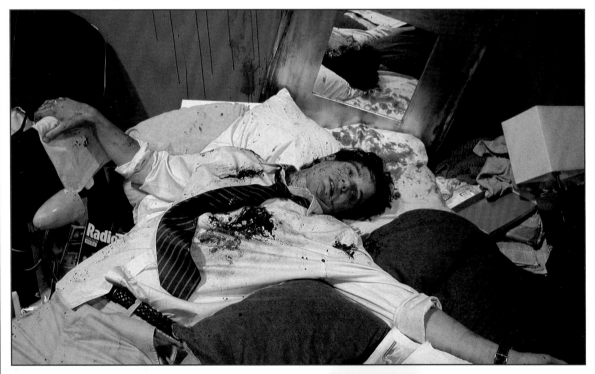

Official Secrets Act Required documentation to be signed by all those working in secure sectors of the Government. Lois Habiba had signed it, but not to condone the murder of Torchwood, which was one of the reasons she made contact with Gwen and Rhys. (CoE)

Okoli, Iffy Probable victim of the alien, Mary, who ripped out people's hearts to thrive upon. Okoli died in 1978. (1.7)

Old Forrest Road Street where Jasmine and Lynne Pearce lived with Lynne's partner, Roy, at number 18. (1.5)

Old lady Woman in her garden, interrupted first by Sean Harris running through it, then by Owen. She told Owen which way Harris had gone. (1.3) (Played by PATRICIA TURNER)

Old woman Cardiff resident who saw a Blowfish, which stopped its car at a pedestrian crossing to let her cross the road. She then saw the Torchwood SUV, and Gwen asked her if she'd seen a Blowfish driving a sports car. (2.1) (Played by MENNA TRUSSLER)

'One O'Clock Jump' Song written by Count Basie played at the Ritz Dance Hall in 1941. (1.12)

One-legged patient First World War soldier at St Teilo's Military Hospital who Gwen tried talking to during one of the time leakages. (2.3) (Played by GWYN WALTERS)

'Ooh La La' Song by The Kooks, played at Lynne Pearce and her partner Roy's BBQ to celebrate their fifth anniversary. (1.5)

Operation Lowry Codename for a 2001 police investigation into women being murdered by having their hearts literally ripped out. An earlier, similar investigation had been called Operation Dogtooth. Before that, in 1970, the investigation was Operation Eleanor. (1.7)

Operative Officer based at Ashton Down who was monitoring communications during the 456 incident and discovered Clement MacDonald was at the Duke of York Hospital. He was later able to locate Torchwood at Hub 2 by tracing Ianto's phone call to his sister Rhiannon. (CoE) (Played by BEN LLOYD HOLMES)

Organa, Princess Leia John Hart mimicked one of her lines from *Star Wars* to attract Jack's attention in a holographic message he left him. (2.1)

Osaka Japanese city to which the Sato family moved when Tosh was 2 years old. She came back to the UK in 1986. (1.7)

Oval Basin Area in front of the Wales Millennium Centre in Cardiff Bay, comprising the Millennium Square, Roald Dahl Plass and the water tower sculpture.

'Over And Over' Song by dance group Hot Chip, which was playing in Cube bar when Laura was chatting up Owen. (1.11)

Pallister, Sarah Old age pensioner who was fatally stabbed in the stomach by Suzie Costello, as she attempted to understand the Resurrection Glove and its relation to the knife she wielded. (1.1)

Paralysing lip-gloss Cosmetic poison which John Hart used on Gwen. He had learned how to use it from Jack. (2.1)

Paramedic Cardiff man who was actually a member of Cell 114. When he was triggered, he abandoned a patient to die, stole a patrol tanker and blew it and himself up by the M4 link road, destroying a military supply pipeline. (2.2) (Played by DEREK LEA)

Paramedics Two fake medical workers employed by the Government to kill any survivors of the destruction of the Torchwood Hub. When they tried to abduct Gwen, she

overpowered them and took their guns. One (played by CURTIS RIVERS) was killed by a sniper, and Gwen forced the other (played by EMMANUEL IGHADARO) to tell her who he was working for. (CoE)

Paris Capital of France, where Gwen and Rhys had once had a romantic weekend. (1.11) A guillotine appeared there due to Owen opening the Rift. (1.13) Gwen and Rhys had another weekend break there before she returned to the Hub and saw Adam for the first time. (2.5)

Park Lido Deserted swimming pool where Pearl absorbed as much water as she could while the Ghost Maker stored the ghostly after-images of his victims in the changing rooms. The victims' real bodies remained in comas in hospital. (2.10)

Park Place Street in Grangetown, where the Ellis family lived at number 14. John Ellis was devastated when he returned to find his old home empty and derelict. He later took his own life in a nearby garage. (1.10)

Parker, Henry John Widowed octogenarian collector of alien artefacts, who was dying after three heart attacks and a failed bypass. After a lifetime of travel, adventure and business, Parker was now living a secluded existence in his big house, with only his armed security guards for company. He remained fascinated with Torchwood and what they did. He had come into possession of a device he called the Pulse, and believed the energy it gave off was keeping him alive. Owen showed him that it wasn't, that the Pulse was entirely different, and it was Parker's amazing force of will that was keeping him alive. Parker, excited

by talking to someone from Torchwood, then had a fourth heart attack. Owen was unable to save him and the old man died. (2.8) (Played by RICHARD BRIERS)

Parliamentary Secretary One of the aides helping John Frobisher at the start of the 456 incident. (CoE) (Played by RACHEL FERJANI)

Passchendaele Famous First World War battle on the Western Front in which a great many soldiers died. (2.3)

Passmore Telesales Company where Eugene Jones worked, alongside Gary, Linda, Pete, Craig Telford, Jason, Kevin and Morag. They sold everything from kitchens and insurance to BBQ sets. (1.9)

Patanjali, Rupesh A doctor, originally from the Midlands, and now working at the A&E department at St Helen's Hospital

P
Q

in Cardiff. Jack and Ianto encountered him while removing an alien Hitchhiker from within the late Mr Williams. His interest in Torchwood piqued, and Jack's in him as well, Rupesh tracked Torchwood down to the Bay and Gwen talked with him at length. In fact, Rupesh was already well aware of Torchwood, having been deliberately placed in the hospital by the Government, who wanted an insider in the organisation. However, when the 456 made contact, the Government decided to destroy Torchwood and Jack in particular. Rupesh was used to draw Jack into a trap but was then killed by Johnson, the freelance operative placed in charge of the Torchwood operation by Whitehall. When Jack

found Rupesh's corpse, it distracted him from Johnson and her troops. Rupesh's body was taken to Ashton Down before being released back to his family. (CoE) (Played by RIK MAKAREM)

Patel, Mr Headmaster at a school where some pupils were led away by the army to be given to the 456. (CoE) (Played by VINOD SONI)

Paul Victim of a carjacking in a multi-storey car park by Frankie. John Hart saved Paul by throwing Frankie off the car park to his death. In all likelihood, these events were erased when a DNA bomb exploded in the Rift, reverting time back to moments before John arrived on Earth. (2.1) (Played by NATHAN RYAN)

Peach Magazine for men on sale in a supermarket. Its cover picture of a scantily clad children's TV presenter shocked John Ellis. (1.10)

Pearce, Jasmine Young girl selected by the Fairies to be their new Chosen One. Jasmine was unhappy at home and school, which made her an ideal and willing recipient of the Fairies' attention. Eventually Jack had to let her go, and she faded into the Fairies' dimension. At the end, examining the so-called faked Cottingley photos, Gwen realised that one of the Fairies was Jasmine. (1.5) (Played by LARA PHILLIPART)

Pearce, Lynn Mother of Jasmine. As well as losing her daughter to the Fairies, Lynne saw Roy, her partner of five years, being murdered by them. (1.5) (Played by ADRIENNE O'SULLIVAN)

Pearl One of the Night Travellers, a travelling circus troupe, whose origins were mysterious and undefined, but who appeared to be alien or powered by something not of this world. The amphibian Pearl operated during the late nineteenth and early twentieth centuries, drinking the tears of her and the Ghost Maker's victims. After being captured on film, Pearl and the Ghost Maker were able to tap into enough Rift energy to emerge from the film and re-enter the real world. Jack and Ianto filmed the Night Travellers, recapturing their essences, and then exposed the film, destroying the Ghost Maker, Pearl and the rest of the Night Travellers, hopefully for good. (2.10) (Played by CAMILLA POWER)

Pearl Harbor US military base in Hawaii that was bombed by the Japanese at the end of 1941, bring America fully into the Second World War. Tosh, trapped in January 1941, worried about this, remembering how badly treated her grandfather had been by the British at the time. (1.12)

Penarth Cardiff area, where a Roman Soldier appeared out of nowhere and stabbed two innocent people to death. (1.13)

Pendant Arcateenian device given to Tosh by Mary. It enabled Tosh to hear the thoughts of people around her. At first she heard everything but gradually learned to filter things out. It was through the pendant that Tosh was able to prevent an estranged husband from murdering his ex-wife and their son. Tosh also began to discover what the rest of Torchwood thought of her, subconsciously, which upset her.

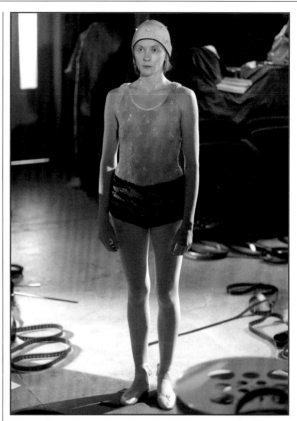

Jack, however, noticed the change in her behaviour and eventually worked out that Mary was exerting some kind of control over her. The pendant was eventually crushed by Tosh after Mary had been destroyed. (1.7)

Penfro Street Road in Cardiff, running under a bridge, where Lizzie Lewis was murdered by Edwin Morgan in 1963. (1.3)

Penn, Dave and Faith Film fanatics, who reopened the old Electro Cinema in Penarth, planning to show the locals old film footage of the local area from the 1920s. Instead, the Night Travellers appeared on the big screen and, unknown to Dave or Faith, two of them escaped and began stealing the last breaths of various people around the local area. While their son, Jonathan, tried to help Torchwood, Dave and Faith were amazed to see the cinema starting to show more film of the Night Travellers. Both Penns were caught by the Ghost Maker and became his final victims. When he was stopped by Jack and Ianto, he opened the flask containing their breaths, which escaped, leaving Dave and Faith dead. (2.10) (Played by STEPHEN MARZELLA and HAZEL WYN WILLIAMS)

Penn, Jonathan Teenaged son of Dave and Faith, he was as in love with old films as his parents were. He was editing together some footage of Hope Street in the 1920s, ready for a viewing at the Electro Cinema, when he noticed unexpected images of the Night Travellers. Although he edited them out, when the film was shown at the Electro, the Travellers were still there, much to the annoyance of his father. After Pearl and the Ghost Maker's emergence from the film, a spike in Rift energy drew Torchwood to the Electro, and Jonathan helped Jack and Ianto investigate further. He later found Pearl in his bath and summoned Jack. As the Ghost Maker brought the rest of the Night travellers back, he killed Jonathan's parents before being stopped, hopefully for good, by Jack and Ianto. (2.10) (Played by CRAIG GALLIVAN)

People's Republic of China John Frobisher said that he represented this when greeting the 456 for the first time. (CoE)

Perry, William Blackpool footballer who scored the winning goal, set up by Stanley Matthews in the 1953 FA Cup Final, watched by John and Alan Ellis. (1.10)

Pete Less than bright worker at Passmore Telesales, who signed the condolence card for Bronwen Jones assuming it was a 'good luck in your new job' card. (1.9) (Played by RYAN CHAPPELL)

Peter Person on the phone to Bridget Spears during the start of the 456 incident. (CoE)

Pharm, the Government-supported pharmaceutical research centre run by Professor Aaron Copley and financed as a private-public partnership with a conglomerate of pharmaceutical companies. They were conducting biotechnology research into finding new cures into diseases and had created Reset, which seemed to revert an ill patient's body back to how it was prior to the infection. This miracle cure was actually

the result of alien 'mayfly' larvae being surgically inserted into the patient's abdomen, which theoretically then lived off the damaged cells in the human body. However, when the Pharm realised their procedure was flawed they set about killing their former patients and, thanks to their governmental access, were able to erase NHS records and the like, covering their tracks. Torchwood sent UNIT medical officer Martha Jones in undercover to get as much information as possible on the Mayflies, but Martha realised the problem was bigger than they thought – Copley had a whole area containing other aliens that he was experimenting on in the name of medical research. Torchwood blew up the Pharm, killing the imprisoned injured aliens as a mercy killing. (2.6)

Pharos Institute Paranormal Research institute who were investigated by the Government during the 456 incident. (CoE)

Philemon Filter Device used to monitor the flow of biochemical energy between a body being revived and the user of the Resurrection Glove. (1.1, 1.8, 2.7)

Philippines South Pacific islands. Gwen jokingly suggested to Rhys that he should adopt a Filipino and get her to sweep their chimneys. (CoE)

Philoctetes Archer in the Trojan war who was marooned on the island of Lemnos. The Arcateenian calling itself Mary likened herself to him. (1.7)

Phosgene Six per cent of the 456's atmosphere was made up of this. (CoE)

Pierce, General Austin Representative of the US Armed Forces, sent to take over the 456 incident from British Prime Minister Brian Green. Initially he failed, but eventually Green acceded to his request, knowing that, if it all went wrong, he would be able to blame Pierce and the Americans and keep his own name clean. (CoE) (Played by COLIN MACFARLANE)

Pilgrim A religious support group run by Mark and Sarah Briscoe. Amongst its members was Max Tresillian who was deliberately overdosed on Retcon by Suzie Costello as an experiment to see what long-term effects it had on people and used as part of her plan to escape Torchwood. Suzie conditioned Max to kill the other Pilgrim members one by one, including Alex Arwyn and the Briscoes themselves. (1.8)

Pilurian currency Eugene Jones had some pre-Gorgon examples of this in his bedroom, which he had authenticated. (1.9)

Pipettes, The Band whose song 'We Are The Pipettes' was being played in the pub where PCs Andy Davidson and Gwen Cooper broke up a fight and Gwen got a head injury. (1.1)

Pixian Aserites Eugene Jones had one of their egg clusters. (1.9)

Pizza lad Youth who worked at Cardiff Bay's branch of Jubilee Pizza and told Gwen where to find Torchwood. (1.1) (Played by GARY SHEPPEARD)

Placebo Rock band whose song 'Drag' was playing in the bar where Tosh met Mary. (1.7)

Plague woman Dying person who brought the bubonic plague to Cardiff after Owen opened the Rift. (1.13) (Played by RHONA JACKSON)

Playboy One of a number of adult magazines used at the Conway Clinic to help sperm donors get aroused. (1.2)

Playle, Richard Probable victim of the alien, Mary, who ripped out people's hearts to thrive upon. Playle died in 1973. He was victim number 39. (1.7)

Plummer, Doctor Aaron Copley's assistant at the Pharm, and complicit in the alien DNA transfers. She was last seen being escorted from the chambers where the aliens were kept in containment before Torchwood blew them up. (2.6) (Played by JACQUELINE BOATSWAIN)

Plymouth The Harbour Heights orphanage was there in 1965. (CoE)

Police officer Lead officer at the Halloran investigation, who was convinced Mike Halloran had killed the burglars. (2.2) (Played by DOMINIC COLEMAN)

Police sergeant Officer in Keith Park who told Torchwood about the discovery of Barry Leonard's body (2.6) (Played by JOHN SAMUEL WORSEY)

Policeman (1) An officer attending the stabbing of John Tucker. (1.1) (Played by GUY LEWIS)

P
Q

Policeman (2) Officer at the hospital where the outbreak of Bubonic Plague started. (1.13) (Played by RUSSELL JONES)

Policeman (3) Attended the accident which killed Harwood's driver Leighton Reynolds and told Rhys that Torchwood were impounding the lorry's cargo of meat and taking over the investigation. (2.4) (Played by COLIN BAXTER)

Policeman (4) Arrested Owen at the Japanese bar after his fight with Jack and didn't believe either of them were connected with Torchwood. (2.7) (Played by RHYS AP WILLIAM)

Polly Friend of Lilly Frobisher. (CoE)

Pollyanna Fictional character created by Eleanor Porter, very much the perfect orphan girl. Rhys referred to Emma Louise Cowell as this when he found out Gwen had been lying to him about who Emma really was. (1.10)

Poppythorne Lane London address where Thomas Flanagan lived, at number 64, prior to being evacuated to Cardiff. (1.3)

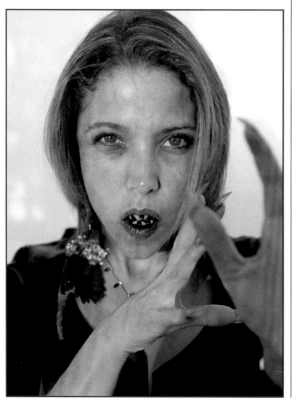

Portugal European country which reported its children had become entranced by the 456, causing road traffic accidents. (CoE)

Pot Noodles Snack food, which Sean Harris was arrested for stealing. (1.3)

Powell, Mervyn The DJ and mate of Banana Boat – also known as the Minister of Sound, the Duke of Disco, the Regent of Rock and the Lord of Love. He was supposed to entertain the guests at Gwen and Rhys's wedding. However, his never-ending quest to get laid brought him to the attention of a guest called Carrie, who took him to her room. In fact, this was the disguise used by the Nostrovite mother waiting for the birth of its young and, feeling hungry, she ate Mervyn for a snack. (2.9) (Played by MORGAN HOPKINS)

Press officer One of the aides helping John Frobisher at the start of the 456 incident. (CoE) (Played by CHRISTOPHER JAMES)

Priest Clergyman at St Mary's Church in the parish town of St James in the fifteenth century. He used the Resurrection Glove to revive Faith, who defeated the entity they believed was Death. (2.7)

Prime Minister Jack telephoned the leader of the British Government to complain that Torchwood's missions were being discussed with the leader of the opposition. (1.7) A later Prime Minister, Brian Green, ordered the destruction of Torchwood to stop them interfering in the 456 situation. (CoE)

Prince of Tides Fake pub name given to Jack by Tosh to explain where she was allegedly doing a pub quiz (1.7)

Probe, the Device with which Jack was able to peel away the fictional life Beth Halloran lived and reveal the truth that she was actually a sleeper agent for Cell 114. It had been used at least once before on an alien whose head had exploded, possibly due to the extraterrestrial's extremely high blood pressure. (2.2)

Proteus gland Organ found in shape-shifting aliens, which enables them to transform their appearance. (2.9)

Proust, Valentin Louis Georges Eugène Marcel French novelist, most famous for the colossal fiction *A La Recherche du Temps Perdu*. Jack claimed he had dated him for a while but found him immature. (2.7)

Providence Park Psychiatric hospital where Christina was a patient. (2.10)

Provinces and Territories of Canada, Japan and the Hellenic Republic John Frobisher said that he represented them all when greeting the 456 for the first time. (CoE)

Pteranodon Prehistoric reptilian bird that lived in the Hub after being captured by Jack and Ianto. (2.12) It was often erroneously identified as a Pterodactyl by the staff. Jack had a special sauce it liked in a canister which he sprayed on Lisa Hallett's Cybernetic body and then heated, causing the Pteranodon to attack her (1.4)

Pulse, the An alien artefact owned by Henry John Parker. Torchwood became aware of it when it started emitting dangerously high levels of energy, which they believed could result in a massive explosion that would take out a significant area of Cardiff. Parker believed the light it gave off was keeping him alive, but it wasn't. Owen discovered it was an alien device sent out to make contact with the universe, likening it to NASA's Golden Records aboard the *Voyager* probes sent into space in the 1970s. He realised the energy was nothing more than its way of communicating, via positive energy. He used it to show Maggie Hopley that there was more to life after the tragic death of her husband. (2.8)

Q19 Warehouse unit where the body of Dan Hodges was dumped by Mark Lynch. (1.11)

Quincy ME American forensic drama series from the 1970s. Jack referred to Owen as the eponymous character when he was examining the soldier's skeleton that contained an alien transporter. (1.7)

[R]

Racing Form, The Paper read by Johnny Davies – Ianto hid a card for Rhiannon inside it. (CoE)

Radiation cluster bombs A series of devices planted around Cardiff which John Hart told Torchwood would destroy the city. They were actually part of a ruse to enable to him to locate a huge Arcadian diamond. (2.1)

Radio actor Took part in an advert for personal injury claims, as heard on Swansea Sound in the SUV when Jack set off Freda's URC. (A) (Played by DICK BRADNUM)

RAF The Royal Air Force, part of the armed services which had employed both of Tosh's parents. (1.7) The real Captain Jack Harkness was attached to the RAF's 133 Squadron as a volunteer from the US Air Force in 1941, when he disappeared. (1.1, 1.12)

Razzle One of a number of adult magazines used at the Conway Clinic to help sperm donors get aroused. (1.2)

Reader An alien device used illicitly by Tosh to scan entire books, such as *A Tale of Two Cities* by Charles Dickens, quickly and accurately onto her computer. Its design suggested that it shared its origins with the alien lockbreaker device that Tosh used to escape the Hub during the lockdown instigated by Lisa Hallett. (1.1)

Receptionist Worker at the Conway Clinic who was surprised to see Carys there on her day off. Carys knocked her unconscious. (1.2) (Played by NAOMI MARTELL)

Recovery worker Helper sifting through the rubble of Roald Dahl Plass who found Jack's severed hand. (CoE) (Played by ASHLEY HUNT)

Red Dragon Centre Cardiff Bay entertainment area where Gwen and Rhys saw a film and went bowling. (1.2)

'Red Is the New Black' Song by Funeral for a Friend, playing in the Wolf Bar when Torchwood tried to find Lucy MacKenzie and Max Tresillian. (1.8)

Registrar Performed the marriage ceremony for Gwen and Rhys. (2.9) (Played by VALERIE MURRAY)

Republic of Iraq Tommy Brockless saw the Iraq war on television and realised things hadn't changed much since 1918. (2.3) John Frobisher said that he represented the Republic of Iraq when greeting the 456 for the first time. (CoE)

Requisition 31 A form John Frobisher requested, which permitted Bridget Spears to recquisition him the revolver that he used to kill his family and himself, to save them from the 456. (CoE)

Reset Name of the drug given to clinical trial patients with incurable illnesses by the Pharm. It literally reset the human body to a pre-illness state, via the insertion of alien Mayfly larvae. When the larvae hatched, they consumed the damaged cells, but this inevitably resulted in the subsequent death of the patient. (2.6)

Restaurant owner Ran the Windsor Café in Penarth and became the Ghost Maker and Pearl's second victim. (2.10) (Played by ANWEN CARLISLE)

Resurrection Glove A metallic gauntlet, found in Cardiff Bay forty years earlier, when it was assumed it had fallen through the Rift. No one knew exactly what it did, but Suzie Costello did the most research on it and discovered that it could briefly reanimate a corpse for up to two minutes, giving them a chance to say goodbye or identify their murderers. It couldn't be used by everyone, just someone with a specific degree

R

of empathy. Jack was unable to use it, but both Suzie and Gwen were. Suzie became addicted to it and, in an effort to learn more, began murdering people with a sculpted knife (referred to as the Life Knife by Ianto) that was found alongside the glove, since the two objects seemed to work in unison. Once Suzie's double life was exposed, she committed suicide and the gauntlet and accompanying knife were locked away. (1.1) After a series of murders pointed directly to Torchwood, all links led to Suzie, so Gwen used the glove to bring her back for questioning. This, though, was just part of a carefully laid plan of Suzie's for immortality – the glove, she had learned, actually stole and transferred its user's life energies. When Gwen used it on her, a symbiotic link was created between them that enabled Suzie to live and grow stronger by draining Gwen's life. Suzie died once and for all and Gwen was restored when Tosh destroyed the glove – although, as Ianto pointed out, gloves tended to come in pairs. (1.8) Jack already knew this and was aware that there was a second glove. When Owen was shot dead by Aaron Copley, Jack recovered this second gauntlet from a group of Weevils in a church and returned him to life to say goodbye and ask for the security code for Torchwood's alien morgue. This backfired when

Owen was returned to permanent existence, but as a dead man, unable to feel, touch, etc. The gauntlet was acting as a conduit for the dark force that had created both gloves and the Life Knife, enabling a Death-like figure to gain a foothold on Earth, just as it had centuries before when the Resurrection Gloves first appeared on Earth. Unable to feed off Owen's already dead body, the Death-like figure was expelled back to the dimension it came from and the second glove was destroyed. (2.7)

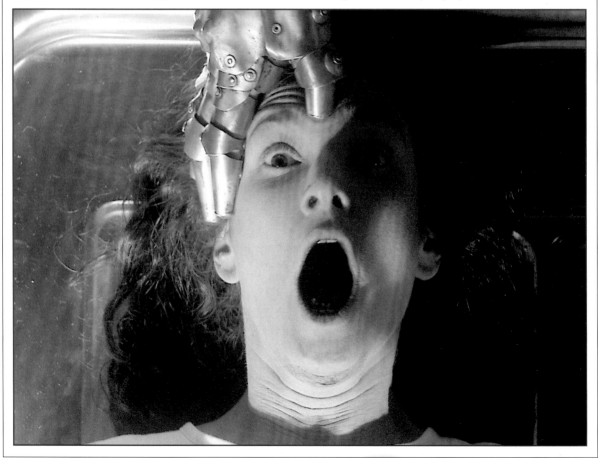

R

'Retcon' See Amnesia pill.

Reynolds, Jennifer Wife of Leighton Reynolds. (2.4)

Reynolds, Leighton 24-year-old driver for Harwood's Haulage, who was taking backhanders from the Harries brothers and helping transport their alien meat. His death in a road traffic accident prompted Rhys to take his place in an effort to find out what Leighton had been doing, and then to go undercover for Torchwood at Harries & Harries. Leighton's wife, Jen, had just had a baby. (2.4) (Played by JAMES SAUNDERS)

Rhea Silva Mythical mother to Romulus and Remus, the founders of Rome. It was Jack's password on his personal safe, where Owen gained access to the missing part of the Rift Manipulator. (1.12) It was also the password to Emergency Protocol One, which opened the Rift completely over Cardiff. (1.13)

Richie Boy who lived on the Cromwell Estate. (CoE)

Rift, the An unexplained phenomenon that crosses through the centre of Cardiff. Its exact start and end points are unknown, although it seems confined to South and West Wales. It has existed for many centuries and emits various kinds of energy, via its red ribbon-like gateways. Much

weaponry and alien technology has also fallen to Earth, which Torchwood Three collected, catalogued and safeguarded against. Many alien races, including the Weevils, are thought to have originally

come through the Rift, as did the alien memory entity that became Adam Smith, and certain beings have been able to manipulate and use it as a deliberate conduit to Earth, as shown by John Hart. The Rift can be partially controlled by devices built into the Hub, although with the Hub's destruction, how safe the Rift now is remains to be seen. Abaddon was allegedly kept prisoner beneath the apex of the Rift; this may have been an allegorical rather than literal imprisonment, although when the Rift was opened, Abaddon was able to escape amid the time leakages this action caused. (1.1–1.13, 2.1–2.13, A, TDL)

Rift Manipulator An integral part of the Hub's machinery, with the potential to open the Rift over Cardiff. When Tosh and Jack were sent back to 1941, Tosh had been working out equations that would give Torchwood greater control over the Rift, and Owen and Ianto argued over whether

R

to open the Rift in the hope of bringing them back. Owen realised that part of the Manipulator was missing, and he located it in Bilis Manger's office at the Ritz Dance Hall. Though Ianto suspected this was part of Bilis's trap for them, Owen searched Jack's office safe for codes to operate the Manipulator, opening the Rift again for long enough for Jack and Tosh to return safely. (1.12) The aftershocks of this caused Rift splinters across the world, through which came people from many different time periods. With the world descending into chaos, Bilis used visions of lost loved ones to persuade Torchwood – except Jack – to reopen the Rift. They activated Emergency Protocol One and fully opened the Rift, which freed Abaddon from beneath the Rift to wreak havoc in Cardiff. (1.13) Jack gave a portable version of the Rift Manipulator to Tommy Brockless to take back to 1918. When activated, it closed the breach between the First World War and the present day, stopping the potentially devastating time leakage that had been triggered by the demolition of St Teilo's Hospital building. (2.3)

Riley, Denise Brian Green's Home Secretary, who proposed giving the 456 society's less successful, intelligent or troubled children rather than a random selection. She was present when Bridget Spears brought Green down by exposing his hypocrisy and planned to take over from him, after ensuring both Bridget and Lois Habiba were cleared of any charges against them. (CoE) (Played by DEBORAH FINDLAY)

'Risen Mitten' One of Ianto's suggestions for an alternative name for the Resurrection Glove. (1.8)

Ritz Dance Hall Built in the 1930s, during the Second World War it was regularly used for dances and stayed in use until the mid 1980s. Jack and Tosh were sent back to 1941, while investigating the Ritz, by its manager, the enigmatic Bilis Manger, who knew all about Torchwood in 1941. (1.12)

Roald Dahl Plass Part of the Oval Basin, leading down from the Water Tower sculpture to Cardiff Bay itself. Along the waterfront from the Plass was the entrance to the Cardiff Tourist Information Office that was really the entrance to the Torchwood Hub.

Roberts, Bob A victim of a strange electrical energy that put him into a coma after he answered his phone then used his comatose brain to call more phones and place more people into comas. (TDL) (Played by MATTHEW GRAVELLE)

Roberts, Jan Woman whose husband, Bob, fell into a coma after answering his phone, which was infected by strange electrical energy that fed off his brainwaves. She spoke to their daughter, Ellie, who was coming down to visit Bob in hospital. (TDL) (Played by EIRY THOMAS)

Roberts, Meredith One of the patients at the Pharm, born 11 January 1962, who later became a victim of hired killer Billy Davis. (2.6) (Played by CHRIS MAHONEY)

Robintree Alley Area of Cardiff where Rani Ghosh's body was found. (1.1)

Rockall Street Cardiff street where a Weevil sighting had been reported, near the sewers. (2.5)

Roman soldier One of many historical figures brought through time to Cardiff as a result of Owen fractionally opening the Rift and creating ripples and aftershocks that created Rift splinters. (1.13) (Played by JAMIE BELTON)

Rossiter, Richard Undertaker charged with collecting Rupesh Patanjali's body from Ashton Down. Rhys took his identity to gain access to Ashton Down and help Gwen find Jack. (CoE) (Played by CHRIS LEE)

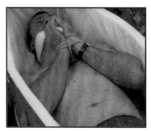

Roundstone Woods Forest area of Cardiff where Estelle Cole witnessed the Fairies playing. The woods, which

backed onto the
garden of their Chosen
One, Jasmine Pearce,
were believed in
ancient times to be a
place of bad luck. (1.5)

Rousseau, Janet
Student on placement
to CERN, who became
a victim of the Ghost Entities. After they were destroyed,
she recovered. (LS)

Roy Long-term boyfriend of Lynn Pearce. He never really
got on with Lynn's daughter Jasmine, finding her sullen and
uncommunicative. In an effort to teach her a lesson, he
fenced off Jasmine's access to Roundstone Wood, where
the Fairies had come through to our world. In revenge, the
Fairies murdered him by suffocating him with flower petals
at a BBQ he and Lynn were holding to celebrate their fifth
anniversary. (1.5) (Played by WILLIAM TRAVIS)

Rushmore School that ultimately won the inter-school
maths competition after Eugene Jones froze and was unable

to answer the question that would have seen his own
school win. (1.9)

Russell, Katie A junior doctor and fiancée to Owen.
She had what was diagnosed as Alzheimer's, possibly the
youngest person ever to get it but, because Owen kept
insisting on more tests, it was discovered that she had
some kind of tumour. She underwent surgery to remove
it, but in fact the tumour was an alien brain parasite. When
threatened by the invasive surgery, the creature released a
toxic gas, killing Katie and all the medical staff in the theatre
with her. (2.12) (Played by ANDREA LOWE)

Russian Federation John Frobisher said that he
represented this when greeting the 456 for the first time.
(CoE)

Ruth (1) Nurse who cared for Alan Ellis, who was suffering
from Alzheimer's, at the rest home where he now lived.
(1.10) (Played by MARION FENNER)

Ruth (2) Rhys's secretary at Harwood's. Bubbly and
efficient, she flirted with Jack. (2.4) According to Rhys, her
tea was like paint stripper. (TDL) (Played by PATTI CLARE)

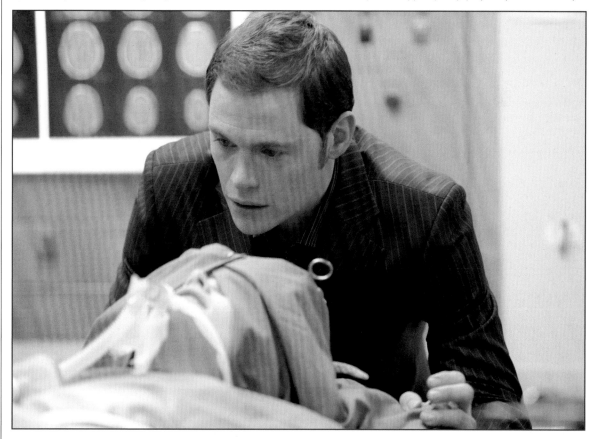

R

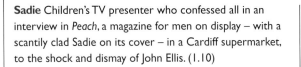

Sadie Children's TV presenter who confessed all in an interview in *Peach*, a magazine for men on display – with a scantily clad Sadie on its cover – in a Cardiff supermarket, to the shock and dismay of John Ellis. (1.10)

Sage Street Cardiff street where the Ritz Dance Hall was situated. (1.12)

Sally Neighbour of Rhiannon and Johnny Davies. (CoE)

Sammy Boy who lived on the Cromwell Estate. (CoE)

Samson (1) Biblical strongman who, according to the Night Travellers' publicity, could be taken on by their strongman, Stromboli. (2.10)

Samson (2) Dog who witnessed Freda falling out of the Rift and into the river at Maindy. (A)

Samuel Aide specialising in Asian policy at Thames House, responsible for advising on international diplomatic protocols. (CoE)

Sand of the East, The Classic movie, a poster for which was displayed in the Electro Cinema in Penarth. (2.10)

Sanders, Colonel Michael, OBE Retired officer who was part of the Government team who allowed the 456 to take eleven children from the Holly Tree Lodge children's home in Scotland in 1965. Brian Green made John Frobisher issue a Blank Page including Sanders' name, resulting in his assassination. (CoE) (Played by JAMES NORTH)

Sandwich shop owner Ran the store where Lois Habiba was buying food. He took a call from Gwen, which he passed over to Lois. (CoE) (Played by PATRICE ETIENNE)

Sangster Maiden name of Alice Carter, although this was a fake, as were her parents, James and Mary Sangster. The names were given to operatives going undercover for the Government in the early 1970s. Alice's real maiden name was Moretti. (CoE)

Sasha Young girl seen by Gwen and Rupesh in Cardiff Bay, who was briefly put into a trance-like state when being used as a conduit by the 456. (CoE) (Played by ANNABEL WILLIAMS)

Sato, Mrs Tosh's mother. Mrs Sato was the bargaining chip used by Milton to force Tosh into building a sonic modulator. When UNIT burst in and arrested Tosh and Milton's team, Mrs Sato was taken away. Jack later gave her an amnesia pill to wipe the memory of the kidnapping from her mind, and Tosh did not see her again. (2.12) When Bilis started manipulating time to convince the Torchwood team to fully open the Rift, he projected an image of Tosh's mother looking exactly as she had been when Tosh had last seen her. (1.13) (Played by NORIKO AIDA)

Sato, Toshiko Japanese technical mastermind who came to Jack's attention when she stole the plans for a top-secret sonic-manipulation device. The plans were flawed, but Tosh instinctively corrected that when she built a prototype, acting on the instructions of a woman called Milton, who was holding Tosh's mother captive. They were all arrested by UNIT, and Tosh was beaten,

S

interrogated and kept prisoner. Jack rescued her on the understanding that she would work for him. Tosh was a computer genius, responsible for much of the reimagining of facts that Torchwood used to cover their tracks. She also built many of the devices they used – often cannibalising alien tech they found – including adapting the Rift Manipulator and building a time lock to keep the Hub inside a time bubble if under threat from outside. In love with Owen Harper from the moment they met, she covered for him during the Slitheen incursion, and always tried to find a way to let him know how she felt, but he was so cynically dismissive, she fell into doomed relationships with the Arcateenian criminal Mary and First World War soldier Tommy Brockless. Eventually, shortly before Owen's death and resurrection, they agreed to go on a date but it never happened because Tosh was shot and mortally wounded by Jack's estranged brother, Gray, in the Hub. Desperately trying to save Owen from a nuclear meltdown, they died talking to one another about their unconsummated relationship. Unlike previous Torchwood operatives, Tosh was granted a traditional funeral service by Jack. (1.1–1.13, 2.1–2.13) (Played by NAOKO MORI)

'Saturday Night' Song by Kaiser Chiefs that was playing at the Red Dragon Centre bowling alley when Gwen and Rhys were having a game. (1.2)

Saturday Night Fever Famous movie about nightclub dancing. Jack reckoned he could dance equally as well as its star, John Travolta. Professor Courtney was less sure of this. (TDL)

Saxon, Harold Former Minister of Defence, running for Prime Minister. (1.12)

Scarlet Pimpernel Elusive English spy who smuggled the French aristocracy out of Paris during the reign of terror in the seventeenth century. Gwen likened the equally hard to track down Sean Harris to him. (1.3)

Scarred woman One of the residents of the Torchwood facility beneath Flat Holm, who was watching TV when Gwen arrived but then moved away. (2.11) (Played by ROSEMARIE-ANNE EASTON)

Scissor Sisters American band whose songs 'Filthy Gorgeous' and 'Comfortably Numb' were playing in the bar where Gwen had her hen night party. (2.9)

Scooby Doo, Where Are You! Cartoon series about a dog, created by Hanna-Barbera in America. Scooby and his gang of teenagers solved mysteries involving ghosts, werewolves, etc. Gwen suggested that allowing Rhys to work for Torchwood meant they were one step away from turning into that TV show. (2.4)

Scott, Captain Robert Falcon Naval explorer who left Cardiff Bay in July 1910 on the Terra Nova Expedition to the Antarctic, during which he died. Tommy Brockless was 16 and remembered reading about it in the newspapers. Tosh took him to the spot in the Bay from which the *Terra Nova* sailed. (2.3)

Scully Fictional character from TV series *The X-Files*. PC Andy Davidson likened Gwen to her. (1.13)

Searchlight The group that Nikki Bevan set up to help people who had friends and relatives go missing. (2.11)

Secret Squirrel 1970s American cartoon series. Rhys referred to Gwen's new job as 'Secret Squirrel stuff'. (1.3)

Security guard (1) Working at the Wales Millennium Centre, he tried to stop Gwen parking her police car on the paved area by the Water Tower. (1.1) (Played by MARK HEAL)

Security guard (2) He captured Freda after she stole supplies from a shop. He sat on her until PC Andy Davidson arrived and arrested her. (A) (Played by MATTHEW GRAVELLE)

Security Level Two Bridget Spears held this clearance rank in the Home Office, but Lois Habiba didn't, so she used Bridget's password to access the files she wanted to read about Torchwood. (CoE)

Security officer Man who tried to stop Ianto and Jack entering Thames House and facing the 456. (CoE) (Played by OSCAR ANDERSON)

Security Visa 45895 Torchwood security code used to access Government files. (1.7)

Senior nurse In charge of the ICU at the hospital where Nettie Williams, the Windsor Café restaurant owner and all of the family in the car were in cataleptic states. When Jack made a comment about the Night Travellers coming from out of the rain, she remembered an old patient called Christina who used exactly the same phrase. (2.10) (Played by YASMIN WILDE)

Sentry Ashton Down guard who let Rhys and Gwen in, believing they were undertakers. (CoE) (Played by ROBERT SHELLEY)

Sergeant Custody officer, number 574, at the station where Mark Goodson was taken. He later discovered Goodson's corpse and called in Torchwood. (1.5) (Played by NATHAN SUSSEX)

'Serious' Song by Richard Hawley which was playing in the café where Gwen and Andy Davidson discussed him joining Torchwood. (2.11)

Severn Bridge Suspension bridge linking Wales to England, which Gwen crossed on her way to East Grinstead. (CoE)

Shaw, Doctor James Houseman trying to cope with the Bubonic Plague in Cardiff. (1.13) (Played by MATTHEW GRAVELLE)

S

Sheffield Yorkshire city, where Harwood's Haulage had offices. (2.4)

'She's Got You High' Song by Mumm-Ra playing in the bar where Tosh took Tommy Brockless to play pool. (2.3)

Sherman, Evan Leader of the cannibalistic villagers of Brynblaidd who every ten years preyed on strangers. Shot and wounded by Jack, he was eventually handed over to the police. When Gwen asked him why he had done it, he just told her it made him happy. (1.6) (Played by OWEN TEALE)

Sherman, Helen A nurse living in Brynblaidd, who pretended to befriend Tosh and Ianto, getting information out of them before revealing that she and her husband Evan were the ringleaders of the cannibal cult in the village. She was shot and wounded by Jack before being arrested by the police. (1.6) (Played by MAXINE EVANS)

Shop assistant (1) Teenaged shop worker who chatting on the phone to his mate Mefs and therefore ignored Rhys's attempts to pay for his shopping, causing one of his traditional rants. (2.5) (Played by LLOYD EVERITT)

Shop assistant (2) Rather tart man working in the wedding-dress shop where Ianto went to buy a new dress for Gwen to accommodate her fuller figure once she was carrying the Nostrovite egg. (2.9) (Played by PETHROW GOODEN)

Sian Friend of Mica Davies, whose parents were lesbians. (CoE)

Silent Witness BBC crime series in which pathologist Sam Ryan was played by actress Amanda Burton. Gwen likened Owen to her. (1.7)

Silicon Valley Northern Californian area, famed for its computer technology industries. A large number of crates were shipped from there to the Royal Connaught Club in Delhi, in the name of Jack Harkness. They were received by Mr Mahajan on behalf of the Duchess. (GA)

Silver flask Small, ornate container in which the Ghost Maker kept the last breaths of his victims, who were left catatonic. Possession of it enabled him to create ghostly after-images of his victims which became the audience for the Night Travellers' shows. Although he and Pearl could never look at the breaths because they would escape, they listened to them sighing over and over again. Just before Ianto and Jack defeated him, the Ghost Maker removed the top and threw the flask away, letting the last breaths float out and killing all his victims bar one, who was saved when Ianto covered the top. (2.10)

'Sing' Song by Travis which was playing in the bar where Tosh met Mary. (1.7)

Singapore Country which reported its children had become entranced by the 456, causing road traffic accidents. (CoE)

Singer One of the band at the Ritz Dance Hall in 1941 whose repertoire included 'Melancholy Baby' and 'A Nightingale Sang in Berkley Square' (1.12) (Played by MELISSA MOORE)

Singh, Mrs Neighbour of Rhiannon and Johnny Davies. (CoE)

Singularity Scalpel Device so-named by Owen, which had come through the Rift. Owen deduced that it was a medical scanner that could also disintegrate an infection or tumour within a patient without affecting the

surrounding tissue, thus eliminating the need for surgical procedures. He used it, after a few unsuccessful attempts, on Martha to destroy the alien Mayfly in her system, injected there by the Pharm (2.6). It was later used at Gwen's wedding to remove the Nostrovite egg from within her, this time operated by Rhys as Owen's broken hand stopped him being able to use it safely. (2.9)

Sky Gypsy The name of Diane Holmes's DeHavilland Dragon Rapide aircraft, registration G-AIDL. (1.10)

Slim man Final disguise adopted by the shape-shifting male Nostrovite who impregnated Gwen on the eve of her wedding. When Jack shot and killed him, he was wearing this disguise. (2.9) (Played by RICHARD HANSEN)

Small girl Watched Sean Harris being chased through her garden by Owen. (1.3) (Played by AMY JENKINS)

Smallpox A disease Owen fears could reassert itself during the crises caused as a result of him fractionally opening the Rift and creating ripples and aftershocks that created Rift splinters. (1.13)

Smiler One of Captain Harkness's RAF officers, who got a snog off Audrey at the Ritz Dance Hall in 1941. (1.12) (Played by CIARAN JOYCE)

Smith, Adam Fake identity created by a parasitical alien which thrived on peoples' memories, feeding off the emotions they brought about in people. Stranded for many years in the void, trapped

within a small box, it was attracted to Earth via the Rift due to the intensity and novelty of Jack's memories, both those present and those suppressed or erased. From there it moved into the rest of Torchwood, manufacturing an illusion of reality just by touching them physically and created a fake Torchwood ID for itself, claiming to have joined Torchwood on 7 July 2005, and that 'Adam' had been born on 16 November 1982. It implanted memories into Tosh that they were in a lengthy relationship, into Owen that he was sweet and geeky, into Ianto that he was a mass murderer. When implanting itself into Gwen, it accidentally erased her memories of Rhys. It took Jack back to his childhood, the loss of his father and the disappearance of Gray. Jack gave his team enough Retcon to erase the forty-eight hours Adam had been in their lives – although they

S

had all believed him to have been in Torchwood for three years. Deprived of their memories, Adam turned to Jack, taking him home one last time and then implanting himself as a boy into Jack's memory. He permanently destroyed Jack's memories of his last day with father, before Jack too passed out from the effects of Retcon, and Adam's physical body faded away, the parasite dying as it did so. (2.5) (Played by BRYAN DICK and RHYS MYERS)

Smoke on the Railway Classic movie, a poster for which was displayed in the Electro Cinema in Penarth. (2.10)

Sniper Gunman working for Johnson, charged with killing any survivors of the Torchwood Hub explosion. His only victim was actually one of Johnson's other operatives disguised as a paramedic (CoE) (Played by MARCUS ELLIOT)

Snooker player Guy at the Snooker Hall who told Torchwood that Sean Harris was banned. (1.3) (Played by IAN KAY)

Snow Patrol Celtic rock band whose song 'Spitting Games' was being played in the bar where Owen met and seduced Linda (1.1) and in the bar where Tosh met Mary. (1.7) Their song 'Chocolate' was playing in the pub when Torchwood got an alert telling them a UFO was flying over Cardigan Bay. (1.4)

SOCO Police Scene of Crime Officers who attend crime scenes to record and examine evidence. One officer, attending the stabbing of John Tucker, was less than pleased to be sent away by Torchwood. (1.1) (Played by JASON MAY) A SOCO team was present after the death of Frankie the carjacker. (2.1) (Played by PAUL AUBREY-REES, JANE HARDING and RICHARD GREATOREX)

Soft Cell British synth-duo whose cover of 'Tainted Love' was played at Gwen and Rhys's wedding. (2.9)

Soldier A young man who was hoping to have sex with local prostitute Mary when she was killed and taken over by an Arcateenian. The alien ripped out the soldier's heart for nourishment. His skeleton was unearthed almost two centuries later, alongside the alien's lost transporter device. (1.7) (Played by TOM ROBERTSON)

'Soley, Soley' Song, by Middle of the Road, which came on the radio as Gwen and Suzie drove towards the Greenleaves Hospital. Suzie's mum used to sing along to it. (1.8)

Somme, the Famous First World War battle which claimed the lives of 1.5 million soldiers. (2.3)

Sonic Modulator A secret device developed at the Lodmoor Research Facility. Tosh stole the blueprints for it and took them home to build a working one,

automatically correcting the plans' flaws. She then handed it over to a woman called Milton who was holding her mother prisoner to ensure Tosh's obedience. Milton used the Modulator, injuring both Tosh and her mother but, when UNIT raided Milton's safehouse and arrested Tosh moments later, they took the Sonic Modulator away with them. (2.12)

Space Invaders Arcade game which Danny had on a portable player and was planning to take on a visit to his estranged father's home. (1.7)

Space pig Augmented by the Family Slitheen, the pig crashed their spaceship into London's River Thames, destroying Big Ben. The pig was taken to Albion Hospital where Tosh was undercover, posing as a medical officer – she was covering for Owen, who was hung over and unreachable, during his second week at Torchwood. (2.13)

Spain European country which reported its children had become entranced by the 456, causing road traffic accidents. (CoE)

Spears, Miss Bridget Personal assistant to Home Office official John Frobisher and immensely devoted to him – they had worked together for thirty years – even when she suspected he was having an affair with Lois Habiba. After the 456 arrived and Frobisher was made a scapegoat by the Prime Minister, Bridget remained loyal. When Lois revealed she was working for Torchwood and was arrested and incarcerated, Bridget went to visit her, while knowing Frobisher was going to kill himself and his family rather than hand them over to the 456. She borrowed Lois's Eye-5 contact lenses and wore them while having a conversation with the Prime Minister, Brian Green, and the home Secretary, in which the Green revealed his duplicity in the 456 incident. She then threatened to use the information gathered via the contact lenses unless Green resigned. (CoE) (Played by SUSAN BROWN)

Special Ops Part of the police force. Nobody in the police or military services was entirely sure who Torchwood answered to, but many assumed they were part of Special Ops.

'Spitting Games' Song by Snow Patrol which was being played in the bar where Owen met and seduced Linda (1.1) and in the bar where Tosh first encountered Mary. (1.7)

Splott Area of Cardiff where Sean Harris lived – originally with his mother but, because she banned him from the house, he now had a small squat in Evelyn Street. (1.3) Gary tried to throw Gwen off the scent of where Eugene Jones was going to sell his Dogon Sixth Eye by telling her the café he was meant to meet his buyer in may have been there. (1.9)

Sport, The One of a number of adult magazines used at the Conway Clinic to help sperm donors get aroused. (1.2)

St Helen's Hospital Cardiff infirmary, where Torchwood took Martha after she was aged nearly to death by the entity that was brought to Earth via Owen and the Resurrection Glove. The entity then began killing patients  there until Owen stopped it. (2.7) When Tosh needed to get Ben Taylor away from Henry John Parker's mansion, she pretended to be calling from St Helen's with news of a car accident involving his wife. (2.8) When John Hart attacked Cardiff, one of his acts was to transport a Hoix to the hospital's basement, where Owen dealt with it. (2.13) Jack and Bob Roberts were amongst the many patients taken there after they fell into comas due to an electrical

pulse that tried to connect people's brains together via telephone lines. (TDL) Rupesh Patanjali was a doctor there. Mr Williams, whose body contained an alien Hitchhiker died there, and Government operative Johnson later shot Rupesh dead in the hospital basement. Jack was fitted with the Hub-destroying bomb in the hospital mortuary. (CoE)

St Ives Cornish town, cited by Gwen as one place where children had gone into a trance-like state shortly before the 456 made contact. (CoE)

St James A small parish town in the fifteenth century that would later form part of Cardiff. St Mary's Church was built there, and the dead girl Faith was brought back to life via the Resurrection Glove used by the church's priest. Because she was already dead, Faith was able to defeat the entity believed to be Death. (2.7)

St Mary Street Cardiff city centre street known for its bars and clubs. Rhys and Gwen saw the alien meteorite zoom overhead while eating at a restaurant there. (1.2) Gwen later told Rhys that even if St Mary Street were full of Weevils it wouldn't stop her marrying him on their appointed wedding day. (2.9)

St Mary's A small church in Cardiff since at least the fifteenth century when it was part of the larger St James Parish. St Mary's Church was built earlier over the Resurrection Glove. The Priest there presumably used the glove to bring a girl called Faith back to life, and she fought and defeated an entity believed to be Death. Weevils, who worshipped the entity, took the Church over, living in it and revering the Glove. (2.7) The Weevils living there were amongst those brought onto the streets of the city by John Hart, and returned there when he sent out a recall signal. (2.13)

St Teilo's Hospital In 1918, it was a military hospital, where the shell-shocked Tommy Brockless was recovering until Torchwood took him away, only for him to be replaced by a time-shifted version of himself. It remained a hospital for many years but its demolition early  in the twenty-first century created a break in time where contemporary events began to collide with 1918. Tommy was able to take a portable Rift manipulator back to 1918 and seal the breach for good. (2.3)

Staines, Captain Andrew A radio operator in the Government team who allowed the 456 to take eleven children from the Holly Tree Lodge children's home in Scotland in 1965. Brian Green made John Frobisher issue a Blank Page including Staines's name, resulting in his assassination. (CoE) (Played by STUART WOODDISSE)

Stallholder At a car boot sale, he sold old film cans to a man and his son which may have contained footage of the Night Travellers. (2.10) (Played by PETER STANNES)

Star Trek American TV series. PC Andy Davidson wondered why Torchwood didn't use transporters like the crew of the USS *Enterprise*. (A)

Stevens, Matt Only son of a Cardiff family who died while having sex with Carys Fletcher in the women's toilets of the Nightspot nightclub. As he orgasmed, the Gas life form inhabiting Carys's body vaporised him to ingest the energy he created. (1.2) (Played by JUSTIN MCDONALD)

Stitch In Time, A The name of the clock shop Bilis Manger appeared to run in Cardiff city centre. (1.13)

'Stolen Child, The' Poem by W.B. Yeats recited by the Fairies as Gwen spotted Jasmine Pearce's face in the Cottingley photos. (1.5)

Stone Roses British group whose song 'Begging You' was playing in the bar where Owen saw a vision of Diane Holmes. (1.13)

Strictly Come Dancing TV show that Thomas Flanagan and his daughter Eleri had been watching when Gwen saw a ghostly image of Thomas as a boy at Cardiff Central Station. (1.5)

Stripper Dressed as a policeman, he demonstrated his prowess at Gwen's hen night. (2.9) (Played by JOHNNY)

S

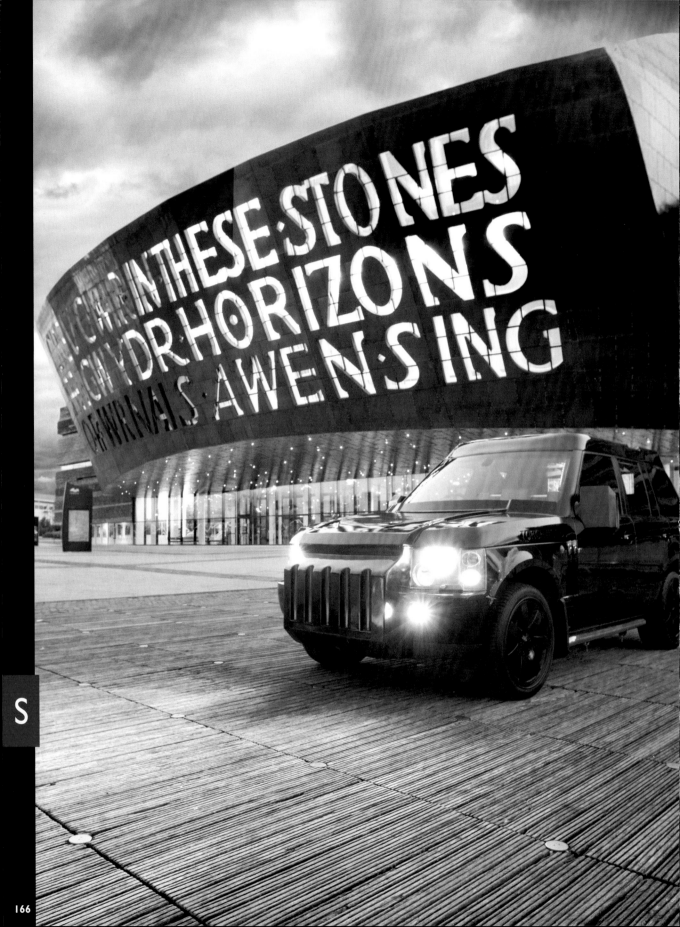

Stromboli the Strongman One of the Night Travellers. (2.10) (Played by SEBASTIAN ABBATIELLO)

Stuart Aide at Thames House, responsible for linguistics, and potentially translating the 456. (CoE)

Sub-Etheric Resonator Torchwood equipment which Ianto insisted should not be sniffed. (2.2)

Sugababes British girl group whose song 'Hole in the Head' was playing in the bar where Gwen held her hen night party. (2.9)

Supplies clerk Government employee who Bridget Spears got a revolver for John Frobisher from, as well as the captured Eye-5 contact lenses Lois Habiba had used on behalf of Torchwood. (CoE) (Played by NICHOLAS CAFFREYS)

Suranium An alien chemical, found within the composition of the Gas life form that came to Earth to feed off sexual energy. (1.2)

Susan Friend of Rhiannon Davies, who witnessed Ianto and Jack having an intimate dinner in a French restaurant in Cardiff. (CoE)

Susy Wife of Rhys's mate Big Dave, who made her husband get rid of his motorcycle. (2.11)

SUV The main vehicle used by Torchwood on missions was a customised bullet-proof multi-person carrier – registration number CF06 FDU – with only a few distinguishing marks, including the name embedded on the side, a parabolic dish inset into the roof, and flashing neon blue lights to alert people and emergency services to Torchwood's presence. It contained a variety of computer consoles, weapons and medical equipment, effectively becoming a portable base for Torchwood personnel. Despite its high-tech capabilities, the vehicle was quite

frequently stolen. After Owen left the keys in it and it was stolen in the Brecon Beacons by the inhabitants of Brynblaidd, it was fitted with a triple deadlock. This, however, was overridden – first by Captain John Hart and later by youths on the Cromwell Estate, who stole it while it was parked outside Rhiannon Davies's home. The car was not seen again. (1.1–1.3, 1.5–1.13, 2.1–2.2, 2.4–2.12, A, TDL, CoE)

Suzanne A secretary present at Ashton Down when Johnson took Alice Carter and her son Steven there. Suzanne looked after Steven until Jack used him to help defeat the 456. (CoE) (Played by CATHERINE OLDING)

Swales, Julia CERN medic and friend of Martha Jones from their training days at the Royal Free Hospital in London. When she realised Martha was there as part of the UNIT medical team, she told her that people had been falling ill and were being transferred to a specialist facility in France yet, when she checked, there was no trace of their arrival. Shortly after this, Julia herself disappeared and Martha called in Torchwood. In fact Julia, like the others, was still at CERN in a secret room, where her neutrons were being absorbed by alien Ghost Entities. Once the aliens were destroyed, Julia recovered. (LS)

Swales, Mr Home Office colleague of Bridget Spears, who had never thought John Frobisher would achieve much. (CoE)

Swansea Gwen's home town in South Wales and home to the DVLA, with which Gwen had the Torchwood SUV's registration plate checked, only to find it did not officially exist. (1.1) Geraint and Mary Cooper, Gwen's parents, still lived there. (2.9) The Cardiff and West Building Society moved there after 1976. (TDL)

Swansea Sound Local radio station, picked up in the SUV when Jack set off Freda's URC. (A)

Swanson, Detective Kathy Police officer investigating a new spate of serial killings in

Cardiff, forced against her will to bring Torchwood in when the evidence pointed to them being involved. She found it greatly amusing when Torchwood got locked in the Hub but agreed to help Jack when he explained that one of his team was in danger. She had the roads cleared so the SUV could easily (and breaking a few speed laws into the bargain) find Gwen and Suzie at Hedley Point. (1.8) (Played by YASMIN BANNERMAN)

Sweden European country which reported its children had become entranced by the 456, causing road traffic accidents. (CoE)

Swipecard What Torchwood used to access the Vaults, and the individual cells inside. Carys Fletcher tricked Owen into giving her access to his, and she escaped the Hub. (1.2)

Switzerland European country, home to CERN. (LS)

Sycorax Race of beings whose spaceship was seen by millions one Christmas but quickly written off as a mass

hallucination. Jack retrieved the Doctor's cauterised right hand after it fell from the Sycorax ship and kept it in a special jar of fluids, waiting for it to become active should the Doctor return to Cardiff, which he did after the defeat of Abaddon. (1.13)

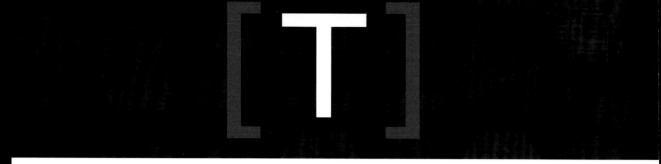

'Tainted Love' Song, much covered but originally written by Ed Cobb. The Soft Cell version was played by Trina at Rhys and Gwen's wedding. (2.9)

Taj Mahal Palace in Dehli over which Jathaa Sun gliders were seen hovering as a result of Owen fractionally opening the Rift and creating ripples and aftershocks that created Rift splinters. (1.13)

Tale of Two Cities, A A novel by Charles Dickens which Tosh transferred to her computer via the alien Reader device. (1.1)

Tanizaki, Doctor Japanese expert in cybernetics, brought to the Hub by Ianto, where he was introduced to Lisa Hallett, who had been partially converted to Cyberform during the Battle of Canary Wharf. Tanizaki tried to modify Lisa and ease her discomfort, but her Cyberman instincts reasserted themselves and she attempted a crude upgrade of him, killing him in the process. (1.4) (Played by TOGO IGAWA)

Tanners Crescent Canton street where Elin Morgan lived, at number 4. (2.6)

Tap House Pub where Gwen, Owen and Jack found more evidence of the cannibals who lived in Brynblaidd. They barricaded themselves in the pub with Kieran, who was eventually caught and taken away by the  cannibals. Jack then found Martin, one of the cannibals, hiding in the pub cellar and tortured him to discover the truth about what was happening in the village. (1.6)

TARDIS Gallifreyan time-travel capsule. The one belonging to the Doctor had once landed in the Oval Basin, where it

was struck by Rift energy, causing a degree of the energy from its chameleon circuit to bleed into the surrounding area at the base of the Water Tower. This created a perception filter which enabled Torchwood to use their Invisible Lift. (1.1) Recovering from the Abaddon assault, Jack heard the sound of the TARDIS arriving in Cardiff Bay and rushed from the Hub up to the Oval Basin, taking with him the Doctor's hand-in-a-jar. (1.13)

Tattooed Man, the One of the Night Travellers. (2.10) (Played by JOHN HERBERT)

Taufeeq, Saeed One of the people Gwen discovered had been taken by the Rift. She found a cell bearing Saeed's name in the Torchwood facility beneath Flat Holm, which helped her realise Jack had known about the disappearances all along. (2.11)

Tavistock Devon town. Gwen eventually found information about the entity believed by some to be the embodiment of Death on the internet by following a link from Tavistock, which led her to an online medical journal. (2.7)

Taylor, Ben Security guard employed by Henry John Parker. He left his post when he got a telephone call purporting to be from St Helen's Hospital, telling him his wife Christine had had a car

accident. In fact this was a ruse by Tosh to get him out of the way to make Owen's entry to Parker's mansion easier. (2.8) (Played by BRETT ALLEN)

Teacher As her pupils, including a boy named Christopher, were led away by the army to be given to the 456, she tried to stop the soldiers taking them. (CoE) (Played by LORNA BENNETT)

Teenage girl Part of the family taken hostage by the Blowfish. It held a gun to her head, constantly threatening to kill her until Jack shot it dead, leaving her unharmed. (2.1) (Played by SARAH WHYTE)

Telecommunications Switching System and Mobile Switching Centre Major communications building destroyed completely by Cell 114, cutting South Wales off from the rest of the world. (2.2)

Telephone number The fake telephone number that Mark Lynch rang to check Owen's 'Harper's Jellied Eels' credentials was 08081570987. (1.11) The Cardiff telephone number for Harwood's Haulage was 02920180316. (2.4) The number for the Cardiff and West Building Society, based at Madoc House in Cardiff in 1976, was 2059. (TDL)

Telford, Craig A manager at Passmore Telesales, who was having an affair with Eugene Jones's co-worker and mate Linda. (1.9) (Played by RHYS THOMAS)

Temple, Superintendent PC Andy Davidson's superior in the police force, and Gwen's until she joined Torchwood. (1.1) Andy used Temple changing the work rota as an excuse not to have gone to Gwen and Rhys's wedding. (2.11)

Tennyson, Alfred English poet and baron, whose poem 'All Things Will Die' was quoted by Ianto and Jack after they had stopped the alien Ghost Entities invading Earth via the CERN facility. (LS)

Ten-year-old daughter Taken by her mother to see the travelling circus during the 1920s, unaware they were the mysterious Night Travellers. She was given a ticket by the Ghost Maker and, as soon as she touched it, she and the circus just melted away and she was separated from her mother for ever. (2.10) (Played by GAIA DAVIES)

Texas Chainsaw Massacre, The Jack told Ianto that he had suggested taking his dates to see that movie in the 1970s. (TDL)

Thames House Home of M15 in London's Vauxhall. A special tank to house the 456 was built on the thirteenth floor. (CoE)

Thomas, Marie Former HIV patient who visited the Pharm and, thanks to the ingestion of alien Mayfly larvae, was cured. To cover up the subsequent side effects, the Pharm hired Billy Davis to kill her, but Billy was interrupted when Marie's dog attacked him to protect her. While she was in hospital, however, the Mayfly larvae hatched, causing a cloud of them to escape her body, killing her in the process. (2.6) (Played by JAN ANDERSON)

Thug Worked for Milton, and brought Tosh's mother to see her daughter. He was present when Milton activated the Sonic Modulator that Tosh had built and was arrested moments later by UNIT. (2.12) (Played by GUY LIST)

Tim RAF navigator, who was good with numbers and so was able to help Tosh in 1941. (1.12) (Played by PETER SANDYS-CLARK)

Time Agency Mysterious organisation that once had a lot of Agents, among them John Hart and Jack. When John arrived on Earth, he told Jack there were only seven of

them now left. (2.1) Rhys briefly believed the Agency was based in Cardiff alongside Torchwood. (2.13)

Time Store Originally an actual storeroom in which Torchwood India kept their alien artefacts. After Jack had removed them in 1924, however, residual alien energy was absorbed by the room and increased in power

exponentially, ultimately becoming an energy wave the Duchess could control, with which she hoped to return the twenty-first century to 1924. (GA)

Times, The English newspaper, popular at the Royal Connaught Club in Delhi if properly ironed. (GA)

Tina (1) Worker at Passmore Telesales. (1.9)

Tina (2) Friend of Rhiannon Davies. (CoE)

Tintin Belgian cartoon character, created by Georges Prosper Remi under the pseudonym Hergé. Owen never liked the character, or his dog, a fact Ianto delighted in telling the rest  of Torchwood. When Owen needed something to protect himself from electrical burns while he fried Henry John Parker's security systems, Jack gave him a Tintin T-shirt to wrap around his hands. (2.8)

To Buy or Not to Buy BBC daytime property show, briefly watched by Owen. (2.8)

Tokyo Japanese city whose subway system was attacked by ancient samurai warriors when Owen opened the Rift (1.13). It reported that its children had become entranced by the 456, causing road traffic accidents. (CoE)

Tom One of Professor Johnson's assistants at CERN. (LS) (Played by MARK MEADOWS)

Tommy Boyfriend to Laura, barmaid at Cube Bar. He picked an argument with Owen and later, when Owen returned with Mark Lynch, he started a full-on brawl. And lost. (1.11) (Played by MATTHEW RAYMOND)

Tony A driver who worked for Ivan Fletcher. (1.2)

Tony's Café Rhys and Gwen stowed away in a lorry carrying potatoes parked near this café. (CoE)

Torchwood Overall name for the Torchwood Institute, originally set up in Aberdeen by Queen Victoria, who took its name from the mansion house in which she encountered the Doctor and a werewolf. Victoria decreed in 1879 that Torchwood would protect the Empire from alien incursion and other unexplained phenomena, and a number of bases were set up, including Torchwood

T

London/Torchwood One in London's Dockland, Torchwood Glasgow/ Torchwood Two in Scotland and Torchwood Cardiff/Torchwood Three in South Wales, which was selected because of  the presence of the Rift. Other smaller Torchwood bases, safe houses and storage areas exist throughout the UK, to store, examine and potentially use alien technology that reaches Earth. At the height of the Empire, there was even a Torchwood India, based in Delhi. After taking over the Cardiff base in 2000, Jack Harkness cut Torchwood Three off, running it by his own rules. The Torchwood Institute fell into disarray after the Battle of Canary Wharf, and Torchwood Three became the main Torchwood base to the Government, although the Glasgow outpost remained active, staffed by one man.

Torchwood India Based within the Royal Connaught Club in Delhi. Established by Queen Victoria but closed down in 1924 when the British Government began winding up the Empire. Although Jack removed what he believed was all of the alien artefacts kept there, a storeroom, which the Duchess termed the Time Store, retained residual alien energy. This grew and sent out an energy wave which fed back into the confines of the Club, keeping everything, including the occupants, exactly as they were in 1924. The Duchess expanded the energy wave via wireless technology, and began erasing sections of India's poorer population, powering Torchwood India up more and more until the point when the Time Store had enough power to take the entire planet back to 1924. (GA)

Towering Inferno, The Movie from 1974 that Jack fondly remembered seeing. (TDL)

Transporter Alien device needed by the Arcateenian posing as Mary in order to get home. She had left it buried with the corpse of a young soldier she murdered in 1812 after first arriving on Earth. Almost two centuries later, the transporter and the soldier's skeleton were unearthed. Jack gave Mary the transporter after adjusting its coordinates, sending her and it into the heart of the sun. (1.7)

Travis British band whose song 'Sing' was playing in the bar where Tosh met Mary. (1.7)

Travolta, John Professor Courtney reminded Jack he was never as good a dancer as the *Saturday Night Fever* actor. (TDL)

Tresillian, Max Large, brutal murderer, driven insane by Suzie Costello, who overdosed him on Retcon, which she later claimed was an experiment to see the long-term effects of the drug on the human psyche. In fact, Max was part of Suzie's plan to be brought back to eternal life via the Resurrection Glove's powers, and she had conditioned him to begin killing fellow members of the Pilgrim group to attract Torchwood's attention. Torchwood apprehended Max at the Wolf Bar and discovered that his murderous rages could be triggered by the word 'Torchwood'. Anticipating his capture and imprisonment in the Hub, Suzie had also conditioned Max to recite an Emily Dickinson poem that would trigger a complete lockdown of the Hub, trapping Torchwood inside for six hours while she escaped. His parents were called Sandra and Dave. (1.8) (Played by CHRIS 'THE SHEND' HARZ)

Trina Friend of Gwen's who was at her hen night and a bridesmaid at her wedding the next day. Trina took over as DJ after the death of Mervyn, but was given Retcon afterwards and thus forgot about the traumatic events of the day. (2.9) (Played by CERI ANN GREGORY)

Trinity Street Road in Cardiff where Gwen and the male Nostrovite fought and she was bitten by it before Jack shot it to death. (2.9)

Tucker, John Final victim of Suzie Costello's serial-killing spree, as she attempted to understand the Resurrection Glove and its relation to the knife she wielded. PC Gwen Cooper witnessed Suzie using the gauntlet to bring Tucker

back to life, which began the journey that led to her joining Torchwood after Suzie's suicide. (1.1) (Played by RHYS SWINBURN)

Tunstall, Mr Man donating sperm at the Conway Clinic. He was killed by Carys Fletcher when she had sex with him. (1.2) (Played by LAWRENCE HAYES)

Turner One of General Pierce's aides, observing the negotiations with the 456. (CoE)

Turnmill Cardiff area which hosted a nuclear power plant which, as a result of John Hart's terror campaign in Cardiff, was in danger of exploding. Although Ianto tried to get there to stop it, he was delayed by Weevils, so Owen ended up going, where he relieved scientist Nira Docherty and took over shutting down the systems

with Tosh's help, from the Hub. However, Tosh was shot and mortally wounded by Gray, and the vital moments she lost before sending the signal to Turnmill allowed a power surge. The safety measures kicked in but caused a lockdown, trapping Owen inside the coolant chamber and killing him, finally, for good. (2.13)

Tyler Young boy seen by Gwen who was briefly put into a trance-like state when being used as a conduit by the 456. (CoE) (Played by OLIVER BUNYAN)

Tyler, Rod Part of the family who set up the Cardiff and West Building Society and, after 1976, a private nursing home to look after their staff who were comatose after a thunderstorm struck Madoc House, where they were based, and switched most of their brains off. (TDL) (Played by BRENDAN CHARLESON)

Tyler, Suzette Young girl seen by Gwen who was briefly put into a trance-like state when being used as a conduit by the 456. (CoE) (Played by MATILDA MATTHEWS)

[U/V]

UCC They provided a file of information to John Frobisher at the start of the 456 incident. (CoE)

UK818954/CF209B Freda's ID number in 2069. (A)

Under the Moonlight Waterfall Classic movie, a poster for which was displayed in the Electro Cinema in Penarth. (2.10)

'Unforgettable You' One of the songs played at the Ritz Dance Hall in 1941. (1.12)

Unicyclist and Fire Juggler One of the Night Travellers. (2.10) (Played by JACK STODDART)

UNIT Unified Intelligence Taskforce which combined military and scientific approaches to dealing with alien invasions. Owen had a fake UNIT Senior Engineer's pass in his wallet. (1.3) UNIT and Torchwood had a fractious relationship but frequently exchanged intelligence and data. (1.7) UNIT contacted Torchwood to find out what was causing the appearance of people from history around the world. (1.13) They had arrested Tosh when she built and passed on a Sonic Modulator to a woman called Milton, and she faced spending the rest of her life in a secret military prison until Jack recruited her for Torchwood. (2.12) They were in charge of security at CERN for the official activation of the Large Hadron Collider. They also had a medical team present, including Doctors Oliver Harrington and Martha Jones. (LS) During the 456 incident, UNIT were represented by Colonel Oduya. (CoE)

United Nations International organisation founded in 1945 to ensure wars between countries ceased and to provide a political platform for the 192 member states. Jack told Gwen that Torchwood operated 'beyond the United Nations'.

Vic Vet employed by Harries & Harries to keep the alien creature they stripped of its meat alive but sedated. He was unhappy about doing this but was too scared of Greg and Dale Harries to walk away. After Torchwood closed the Harries brothers' factory down, Vic was given Retcon and forgot everything that had happened. (2.4) (Played by GARRY LAKE)

Victorian Bride Having cleared up after Gwen and Rhys's wedding, Jack returned to the Hub and opened a drawer in his office desk to look at a photo of him in a Victorian wedding suit with a mysterious bride on their wedding day. (2.9) (Played by SIAN GUNNEY)

Vincent Old friend of Jack's who had a sex-change operation and afterwards became Vanessa. (1.7)

Voice, The Newspaper that Clement MacDonald read about the return of the 456 in. (CoE)

Void, the Area between the dimensions, which the Cybermen crossed and invaded Earth, ultimately destroying the Torchwood Institute and transforming Lisa Hallett into a Cyberwoman. (1.4) The memory parasite that called itself Adam Smith was trapped inside a box in the Void for a very long time. (2.5)

Vorax An alien chemical, found within the composition of the Gas life form that came to Earth to feed off sexual energy. (1.2)

Vortex Manipulator Device used by Jack, worn on his wrist. Originally developed by the Time Agency, it was damaged during his return to Earth in 1869 and he could no longer use it to travel through time. Other functions remained operational though, including an ability to override electrical locks and other components, to scan things and create and transmit holographic messages. Captain John Hart wore a similar wrist-strap device, though Jack claimed his own was bigger.

United States of America Country which reported its children had become entranced by the 456, causing road traffic accidents. John Frobisher said that he represented this when greeting the 456 for the first time. (CoE)

Universal Remote Control (URC) A multipurpose device, resembling a gun, which affected electrical signals. It belonged to Freda and was the only thing she brought back from 2069. (A)

Urban Roast Coffee, popular with the Torchwood team.

Vancouver Canadian city where UNIT's Colonel Mace was seconded during the 456 incident. (CoE)

Vanessa Post-operation name of a man Jack used to know called Vincent who had undergone a sex change. (1.7)

Vegas Galaxies Pleasure worlds, where John Hart reckoned Jack could earn a fortune as the man who couldn't die. (2.1)

Venus Planet in Earth's solar system. Jack mentioned he'd once been on a flight between Venus and Mars. (LS)

Vera A name John Hart said Gwen could call him – he wouldn't complain because he loved Gwen's eyes. (2.1)

[W]

Wales Millennium Centre Cardiff arts and culture centre in Cardiff Bay, built to celebrate the start of the twenty-first century. It stands almost directly over the Torchwood Hub. Gwen used a brochure of events from it to remind herself about the existence of Torchwood (1.1) Jack and Gwen once surveyed Cardiff from its roof. (1.2)

Walking in the Orchard Classic movie, a poster for which was displayed in the Electro Cinema in Penarth. (2.10)

Walking With Dinosaurs BBC natural history series which was playing in Josh's DVD rental store when Gwen returned the late Eugene Jones's rented DVDs. (1.9)

War of the Worlds, The Nineteenth-century fantasy novel by H.G. Wells, adapted into a number of movies and TV shows. John Frobisher tells his wife that the potential invasion by the 456 will not result in the kind of devastation portrayed in the book or films. (CoE)

Ward, David Fake ID created by Tosh for John Ellis. He refused to use it. (1.10)

Washington DC Capital city of the USA, where UNIT had scanned the brains of a couple of children who had, briefly, been entranced by the 456 communication. (CoE)

Water Tower Tall sculpture in Cardiff Bay standing in front of the Wales Millennium Centre. Part of its surrounding frontage houses the 'Invisible Lift' that is the 'scenic route'

into the Torchwood Hub. The Tower was, along with the Hub, obliterated by the bomb placed inside Jack by the British Government.

WC242A Police form which enabled someone to stand bail for a prisoner held on a minor charge. Gwen asked

Andy Davidson to fax one to Camden police station so she could release Clement MacDonald. (CoE)

'We Are The Pipettes' Song by The Pipettes, which was being played in the pub where PCs Andy Davidson and Gwen Cooper broke up a fight, and Gwen got a head injury. (1.1)

Webb, Dave Stocky security guard employed by Henry John Parker. He was confronted and electrocuted by Owen, who was taking out the power to Parker's mansion. (2.8) (Played by GIL KORILIN)

Weeping man One of the residents Gwen saw in the Torchwood facility beneath Flat Holm. (2.11) (Played by MARK FREESTONE)

Weevils Carnivorous, aggressive alien creatures that fell to Earth regularly via the Rift. Man-sized vermin, they lived in the sewers and wastelands of South Wales – their exact origins remain unknown, although it was discovered by the Pharm that their unique biology could be used as pesticides and chemical defoliants. Torchwood would regularly round Weevils up and keep them at the Hub in the Vaults, including a Weevil which Jack named Janet. After he died and was resurrected with the Resurrection Glove, the dark energy that flowed through Owen seemed to be linked to the Weevils. They had guarded the Glove in St Mary's Church for centuries and, when he was briefly taken over by this dark force, the Weevils worshipped him. Indeed, they still considered him to be some kind of messianic figure right up until his final death. (1.1, 1.2, 1.7, 1.11, 1.13, 2.2, 2.5, 2.6, 2.7, 2.12, 2.13, LS)

Weight Watchers Health group who Ianto kept getting linked to when searching on the internet for references to the entity believed by some to be the embodiment of Death. (2.7)

Wellcome Trust Medical research establishment. Gwen had eventually found information about the entity believed by some to be the embodiment of Death on the internet by following up a link she got from Tavistock, which led her to an online medical journal. (2.7)

Weller, Paul A track from his album *Stanley Road*, 'You Do Something To Me', was played at Gwen and Rhys's wedding. (2.9)

Wells, Trinity AMNN TV anchor who reported on the events of the 456's return. (CoE) (Played by LACHELLE CARL)

W

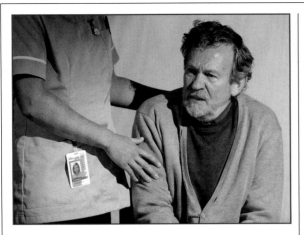

Wellsfield English village which the Night Travellers visited in 1898. (2.10)

Wendy Friend of John and Anna Frobisher, who lived in Canada with her husband Brian. Their children had been affected by the 456. (CoE)

Weston, Mr Gay man donating sperm at the Conway Clinic. He was killed by Carys Fletcher when she had sex with him. (1.2) (Played by DAVID LONGDEN)

'White Cliffs of Dover, The' One of the songs played at the Ritz Dance Hall in 1941. (1.12)

White, Timothy The name used by Clement MacDonald since he was 11 years old to hide involvement with the 456, most likely 'borrowed' from the chain of chemist stores in the UK in the 1960s and 1970s. (CoE)

'Whose Gonna Find Me' Song by The Coral, playing when Tommy saw a modern war on TV in the bar where he sat with Tosh. (2.3)

Wife Swap Television programme which Rhys asked Gwen to tape for him as he was out having a curry with his mate, Daf. (1.4)

Williams, Barry Long-suffering husband to Brenda, and Rhys's dad. He was at his son's wedding to Gwen but sensibly kept his head down when his wife and Gwen's mum Mary started bitching at one another. (2.9) (Played by ROBIN GRIFFITH)

Williams, Brenda Rhys's mother. She often asked Rhys to visit, suggesting he use a company truck to get there.

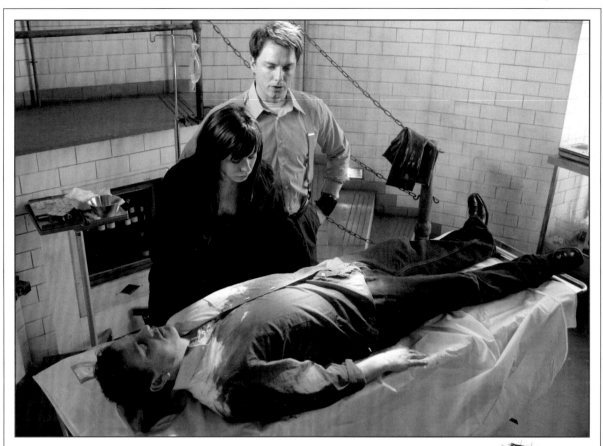

She was unhappy about something that had happened one Christmas, too. (1.1) At the wedding of her son to Gwen (which she didn't really approve of), she and Gwen's mother Mary crossed swords verbally and she was impersonated by the Nostrovite. (2.9) (Played by NERYS HUGHES)

Williams, Mr Elderly man who died from heart failure at St Helen's Hospital. Inside his corpse was an alien Hitchhiker which Jack and Ianto removed before being discovered by Williams's attending physician, Rupesh Patanjali. (CoE) (Played by PHIL SUTTON)

Williams, Nettie Teenaged girl waiting at a bus stop in the rain, talking to her mum on her mobile, when her last breath was stolen by the Ghost Maker and Pearl. She died later when the flask containing the breath was opened. (2.10) (Played by LOWRI SIAN JONES)

Williams, Rhys Alun Gwen's boyfriend, later husband, and father of her child. He started off as a transport coordinator for a small firm of printers but later moved to Harwood's Haulage as their Transport Manager. He first discovered the existence of the Hub during the Abaddon incident, but was murdered by Bilis Manger to torture Gwen. After Abaddon was destroyed, all trace of the death and destruction both the demon and Bilis had created was reversed and Rhys was returned to life, unaware of anything that had transpired. Shortly

after this, he learned exactly what Torchwood did and, although initially suspicious of Jack, the two men grew to like and respect one another, each knowing the other would always look out for Gwen no matter what. (1.1–4, 1.6, 1.10, 1.11, 1.13, 2.1, 2.4, 2.5, 2.7, 2.9, 2.11–13, TDL, CoE) (Played by KAI OWEN)

Wilson, Earl One of the people Gwen discovered had been taken by the Rift. She found a cell bearing his name in the

Torchwood facility beneath Flat Holm, which made her realise Jack had known about the disappearances all along. (2.11)

Windsor Café Restaurant that was closed for the night when the Ghost Maker and Pearl arrived. They convinced the owner to open the door and then stole her last breath. (2.10)

Winters, Vanessa Worked alongside Jack and Mr Dekker when the British Government gave eleven children to the 456 in November 1965. She was actually out on the moorland with Jack and witnessed the children being taken. (CoE) (Played by SOPHIE HUNTER)

Wiregirl One of the Night Travellers. (2.10) (Played by KWABANA LINDSAY)

Wisden Cricketer's Almanack Famous annual tome. Torchwood India had many volumes in its library. (GA)

Wolf Bar Cardiff bar where Lucy MacKenzie worked and where Torchwood captured killer Max Tresillian. (1.8) Torchwood captured a Hystrix there once, and it peppered the ceiling with its spines. (A)

Woman in shop Had very little positive to tell Torchwood about Sean Harris. (1.3) (Played by KATHRYN HOWARD)

Worker I Aggressive Harries & Harries employee who had no concern for the welfare of the alien creature the firm were getting their never-ending meat supply from. He also dealt with Rhys, when he tried to distract the workers and enable Torchwood to get in, and gave the alarm. After Torchwood closed the Harries brothers' factory down, he was given Retcon to forget all about it. (2.4) (Played by MAREK ORAVEC)

Wounded soldier First World War patient at St Teilo's Military Hospital who was waiting to see the medical examiners when the nurse saw Gwen. (2.3) (Played by JONATHAN BURNSIDE)

WPC (1) Young police officer, number 422, who Mark Goodson forced to arrest him and so hide him from the Fairies. She took him to the police station. (1.5) (Played by FFION WILKINS)

WPC (2) Officer at the police station where Freda was taken for questioning. (A) (Played by SARA MCGAUGHEY)

Wright, Elsie One of two girls who, in the early twentieth century, claimed to have taken photographs of fairies. Towards the end of their lives, the girls confessed they had faked the images. (1.5)

[X/Y/Z]

X:IT Bar where Jack stole a customer's credit card from. (CoE)

X74JGF813W The access code Tosh used at the Lodmoor Research Facility to get hold of the blueprints for the flawed Sonic Modulator she later improved upon and built a successful prototype for. (2.12)

X-Files, The PC Andy Davidson likened Jack and Gwen to the TV show's main characters Mulder and Scully. (1.13)

Yates, Rick Adviser to Brian Green during the 456 incident. He had no children to lose. (CoE) (Played by NICHOLAS BRIGGS)

Years In **AD 27**, Jack was buried beneath the future site of Cardiff by his brother Gray and John Hart. (2.13) In **1479**, Faith, a little girl in the parish of St James died but was brought back to life by the Priest of St Mary's Church, via the Resurrection Glove that the church had been built over. The Glove brought back into being an entity the locals believed was Death, which needed to kill thirteen people before it could manifest permanently. With Faith already being dead, she fought the entity as it's thirteenth victim and thus defeated it. (2.7) In **1812**, the spaceship containing the Arcateenian criminal and her captor crashed to Earth. (1.7) Tommy Brockless was born in **1894**. (2.3) In **1898**, the Night Travellers took their victims from Wellsfield. (2.10) In **1899**, Torchwood first made contact with Jack, when he came to Cardiff hoping to find the Doctor using the Rift to power his TARDIS. (2.12) In **1901**, the Night Travellers took their victims from Church Stretton (2.10) and Alice Guppy and Charles Gaskell dug Jack up from under Bute Park, where Gray had left him buried alive in AD 27. (2.13) In **1909**, Jack was based with the British army in Lahore.

(1.5) In **1910**, Captain Scott sailed with his crew on the *Terra Nova* to the Antarctic, which Tommy Brockless read about in the newspapers. (2.3) In **1911**, the Night Travellers took their victims from Hunstanton. (2.10) In **1918**, Torchwood took Tommy Brockless from St Teilo's Hospital and froze him, (2.3) while Jack experienced the ravages of Spanish Flu. (CoE) In **1924**, Jack went to Delhi on 28 February at the behest of the Torchwood Institute to close Torchwood India down and remove all the alien artefacts stored there as the British Empire began to wind up. As a result, it had been 29 February there ever since. (GA) In **1937**, Alan Ellis was born. (1.10) In **1937**, American flying heroine Amelia Earhart disappeared whilst attempting to circumnavigate the globe. (1.10) In **1941**, Thomas Flanagan was evacuated to Cardiff during the London Blitz. (1.3) Tosh and Jack were sent back to 20 January **1941** by the Rift, where they met Bilis Manger and the real Captain Jack Harkness. (1.12) In **1952**, Diane Holmes flew from England to Australia in just four days. (1.10) In **1953**, Diane Holmes, John Ellis and Emma Louise Cowell disappeared, arriving in modern Cardiff on 18 December. (1.10) In November **1965**, Jack, along with other Government personnel including Andrew Staines, Ellen Hunt, Michael Sanders, Mr Dekker and Vanessa Winters, handed eleven children from the Holly Tree Lodge orphanage over to the 456. (CoE) In **1970**, Myra Bennett was murdered by the alien known as Mary. (1.7) In **1972**, Sally Chappel was murdered by the alien known as Mary. (1.7) In **1973**, Richard

Playle was murdered by the alien known as Mary. (1.7) In **1974**, Melanie Gough was murdered by the alien known as Mary (1.7) and Jack had a trimphone. (TDL) Tosh was born in **1975**, as

was Alice Carter. (1.7) In **1976**, Lee Ball was murdered by the alien known as Mary (1.7) and at 3pm on 24 September there was a thunderstorm over Madoc House in Cardiff connected with the Rift, creating a strange electrical phenomena that placed a number of people using telephones into a coma. (TDL) In **1978**, Iffy Okoli was murdered by the alien known as Mary. (1.7) Ianto was born on 19 August **1983**. (2.12) In **1986**, Henry John Parker's wife died, and he became a recluse. (2.8) In **1989**, Edwin Morgan was admitted to hospital, but was released early in **1990**. (1.3) Jonah Bevan was born on 15 February **1993**. (2.11) In **1995**, the Torchwood Institute decommissioned the Battersea warehouse later used as Hub 2 by Torchwood Three. (CoE) Jack returned to the Torchwood Hub on 31 January **1999** to find most of his colleagues shot dead by Torchwood Three's leader, Alex Hopkins. Jack then took charge of Torchwood Three. (2.12) In **2001**, Lucy Marmer was murdered by the alien known as Mary. (1.7) Freda was born in **2053**. (A) In **2069**, Torchwood sent Freda back in time to seek asylum in the past. (A) In **5094**, Jack was voted Rear of the Year. (2.1)

Yellow Alert Level of alert which the UN instructed UNIT to go to after the world's children were first contacted by the 456. (CoE)

'Yes, We Have No Bananas' Song by Silver and Cohn, which was the only thing Jack left behind when clearing out Torchwood India in 1924. The Duchess later tried to get Jack to dance along to the record, but he refused. (GA)

Yeti Spheres Amongst the artefacts Jack removed from Torchwood India in 1924. (GA)

'You Do Something To Me' Track from Paul Weller's *Stanley Road* album, played by Trina at Rhys and Gwen's wedding. (2.9)

Young family Driving through Penarth late at night, the whole family fell victim to the Ghost Maker and Pearl. The mother, father and daughter (played by CATHERINE OLDING, ALASTAIR SILL and MEGAN LANGFORD) all later died, but the son (played by TOM LANGFORD) was the only person to survive the Night Travellers' attacks. (2.10)

Young mother Cardiff woman who was actually a member of Cell 114. When she was triggered, she abandoned her baby in its pram which rolled into moving traffic. Later she entered Cardiff's Telecommunications Switching station, blowing it and herself up, severing all

forms of communication for miles around, effectively cutting South Wales off from the world. (2.2) (Played by RHIANWEN BAILEY)

Young woman Supposed victim of Ianto's killing sprees. In fact she never existed, as these were false memories implanted into Ianto by the memory parasite to confuse him and stop him investigating it. (2.5) (Played by JO MCLAREN)

Yvonne Middle-aged policewoman who investigated the records of one Captain Jack Harkness for Gwen. (1.1) (Played by OLWEN MEDI)

Zenegon Rain A movie for rent in Josh's DVD store. (1.9)

KEY TO REFERENCES

Throughout this book, information pertaining to a specific episode is followed by a bracketed numerical: '(2.9)' after the entry for Brenda Williams indicates that Rhys's mum was in the episode 'Something Borrowed'. As well as the two complete series of *Torchwood* and *Torchwood: Children of Earth*, this book also incorporates references from radio broadcasts 'Lost Souls', 'Asylum', 'Golden Age' and 'The Dead Line'.

1.1	Everything Changes
1.2	Day One
1.3	Ghost Machine
1.4	Cyberwoman
1.5	Small Worlds
1.6	Countrycide
1.7	Greeks Bearing Gifts
1.8	They Keep Killing Suzie
1.9	Random Shoes
1.10	Out of Time
1.11	Combat
1.12	Captain Jack Harkness
1.13	End of Days

2.1	Kiss Kiss, Bang Bang
2.2	Sleeper
2.3	To the Last Man

2.4	Meat
2.5	Adam
2.6	Reset
2.7	Dead Man Walking
2.8	A Day in the Death
2.9	Something Borrowed
2.10	From out of the Rain
2.11	Adrift
2.12	Fragments
2.13	Exit Wounds

LS	Lost Souls
A	Asylum
GA	Golden Age
TDL	The Dead Line

CoE	Children of Earth

August Wilson

August Wilson

A Literary Companion

MARY ELLEN SNODGRASS

McFarland Literary Companions, 1

McFarland & Company, Inc., Publishers
Jefferson, North Carolina, and London

LIBRARY OF CONGRESS CATALOGUING-IN-PUBLICATION DATA

Snodgrass, Mary Ellen.
August Wilson : a literary companion / Mary Ellen Snodgrass.
p.   cm. — (McFarland literary companions ; 1)
Includes bibliographical references and index.

ISBN 0-7864-1903-2 (softcover : 50# alkaline paper) ∞

1. Wilson, August — Criticism and interpretation — Handbooks,
manuals, etc.   2. Historical drama, American — History and criticism —
Handbooks, manuals, etc.   3. African Americans in literature —
Handbooks, manuals, etc.   I. Title.   II. Series.
PS3573.I45677Z89   2004   812'.54 — dc22   2004009594

British Library cataloguing data are available

Cover image: *Foreground:* August Wilson, 1995 *(Photograph by Barbara Penoyar)*
Background ©2004 Photodisc

Manufactured in the United States of America

McFarland & Company, Inc., Publishers
Box 611, Jefferson, North Carolina 28640
www.mcfarlandpub.com

For author and editor Gary Carey,
my colleague and near-brother

Acknowledgments

I owe many thanks to Dena Levitin, August Wilson's secretary, for her assistance in clearing up discrepancies and supplying a working copy of the unpublished play *King Hedley II* and a photograph of the playwright. Also, I appreciate the aid of the reference staff at the Carnegie Library of Pittsburgh for data on the city's history. In addition, I acknowledge the advice and research assistance of the following people and institutions:

John Breglio, literary agent
Paul, Weiss, Rifkin, Wharton & Garrison
New York City

Avis Gachet, book buyer
Wonderland Books
5008 Hickory Boulevard
Hickory, North Carolina 28601

Amy Jew, reference librarian
Catawba County Library
Newton, North Carolina

Susan Keller, reference librarian
Western Piedmont Community College
Morganton, North Carolina

Wanda Rozzelle, reference librarian
Catawba County Library
Newton, North Carolina

Mark Schumacher, reference librarian
Jackson Library
The University of North Carolina at
    Greensboro

Gina Vigna, sales associate
Overlook Press
Woodstock, New York

Contents

To write is to fix language, to get it down and fix it to a spot and have it have meaning and be fat with substance.

August Wilson,
"Where to Begin?" 1991

Preface

For those who have limited knowledge or understanding of August Wilson's literary contributions, *August Wilson: A Literary Companion* is the ideal introduction. It provides the reader, playgoer, student, researcher, teacher, dramaturge, reviewer, and librarian with a source of basic data and analysis on characters, dates, events, allusions, staging strategies, and themes from the canon of one of America's finest playwrights.

The text opens with an annotated chronology of Wilson's life and works followed by his family tree. The 166 entries combine insights from a variety of readings and sources along with generous citations from primary and secondary sources. Each entry concludes with selected bibliography on such subjects as the blues, Malcolm X, irony, roosters, Gothic mode, and the medieval concept of sanctuary. Charts elucidate the genealogies of the Charles, Hedley, and Maxson families and account for weaknesses in Wilson's female characters. Generous cross references point to divergent strands of thought and guide the reader into peripheral territory, e.g., from Troy Maxson to black athletes, character names to Aunt Ester, music to Buddy Bolden, and oral lore to the Parchman Farm, a lethal blot on Southern history.

Back matter is designed to aid the student and researcher. It orients the beginner with a time line of events in Wilson's life and those of his characters, beginning with the first sale of African flesh in the New World. A second appendix provides forty topics for group or individual projects, composition, oral analysis, background material, and theme development. Back matter concludes with an exhaustive bibliography of primary and secondary sources. Many of the latter derive from journal articles and reviews of Wilson's plays in the newspapers of major cities. These secondary sources are particularly useful for study of two unpublished plays, *King Hedley II* and *Gem of the Ocean*, and for references to a proposed tenth decade play set in the 1990s. A comprehensive index directs users of the literary companion to major and minor characters, movements, primary and secondary titles, and issues, e.g., Yoruba, *The Janitor*, John Coltrane, Br'er Rabbit, Nation of Islam, *Porgy and Bess*, and the Pulitzer Prize.

Introduction

Direction for American literature often emerges from unforeseen quarters, as with the soul-delving sea fiction of Herman Melville, the vigorous naturalism of Jack London, the searing stage epiphanies of Arthur Miller and Tennessee Williams, and the feminist revelations of Zora Neale Hurston, Kate Chopin, and Toni Morrison. In a salute to the urban poor, August Wilson's lifetime of drama writing has peeled back layers of misinformation about African Americana by methodically probing the twentieth century decade by decade. Applying an organic rewrite-refine system, he issues polished plays sparkling with the curbside exchanges of realistic characters and startling in the unfolding tragedy of blighted lives. To establish a home base, he has done what other master writers do: anchor himself in his childhood milieu and remain faithful to the voices he absorbed — in his case, the voices of Pittsburgh's Hill District. The authentic ring of black wit, railroad schedule, anecdote, homily, and plaint has convinced a dubious literary hierarchy that a self-educated ghetto boy could grow into a revered conduit for a century of black achievement.

A sure sign of Wilson's acumen surfaces in the debate of literary analysts and drama reviewers as to his purpose and success. Some empty the thesaurus of encomia for the playwright's insights into the human condition; others question his androcentric world view. A few relegate him to the scrap heap of inept whiners who extol criminals and blame black failures on slavery and its aftermath. Of the critics who line up behind yea and nay, none lapses into apathy, for Wilson's vibrant scenarios refuse to be ignored. His cartography of street corner joviality, backyard dicing and whist games, exuberant ritual, somber wakes, and rooming house table talk is well plotted, aligning the daily paths of black citizens with the parallel byways of the outside world. The intersection of a modest cafe with Pittsburgh's urban reclamation and of a Chicago recording session with the oversized dreams of a would-be star of swing erupts in controversies and dilemmas, the stuff of captivating play-acting. Fictional situations arm the powerless ex-con, downtrodden housewife, hotel sweeper, and sidewalk nobody with terrifying and bizarre opportunities for redress. In the evening-up of sides, folk justice grants even the humblest cabbie, street prophet, or handyman his day.

Perhaps the stellar accomplishment of Wilson's decade cycle is a profound, unshakeable humanism. Out of discontent with the status quo for black Americans, Wilson forces readers and audiences to examine at ground level the despair generated by poverty and racism. His championing of small victories—a marriage proposal and diamond ring of dubious origin, a Mother's Day gig at the Blue Goose, rescue on the Underground Railroad, a mortgage sponsored by the G.I. Bill, the birth of a child named Mister—lauds the basics of human striving. In tandem with joys, Wilson sorrows at spirits too easily elated by the gift of discarded plums, a slow dance to Aretha Franklin's croon from the jukebox, new shoes, or the offer of a free fish sandwich, slice of watermelon, or extra breakfast biscuit.

Taken as a whole, Wilson's canon is that treasure of creativity: an honest evaluation of the writer's own turf. Without pretensions toward cosmic truth, the playwright sticks to the verities of couples in love, ribald gossip, families in jeopardy, straight talk between friends, and children absorbing stories of noble grandsires. Wilson's rewards approach overflow with their showering of a citizen writer in superlatives for relating painful realities. Unsatisfied with grimness, he graces his scenarios with hospitality, dreamscapes, jubilant song and dance, and the wondrous prophecies of the seer and shiny man. Balancing out the crookeds with the straights, he combats nihilism with hopeful glimmers that refuse to be extinguished. Such a man deserves to be heard.

Chronology of
Wilson's Life and Works

April 27, 1945   Born in a black ghetto in the Hill district of Pittsburgh, Pennsylvania, Frederick August "Freddie" Kittel (or Kittell) was the first male and fourth
child of poor parents— a heavy-drinking, frequently unemployed, authoritarian Aus-
tro-Hungarian baker, Frederick August Kittel, and Daisy Wilson Kittel, a black
domestic worker who was the daughter of sharecroppers in Spear, North Carolina.
The other children include three sisters— Freda Ellis, Donna Conley, and Linda Jean
Denoya — and two brothers, Edwin and Richard Kittel. After their father deserted
the family following the playwright's birth, his mother reared her three sons and
three daughters at a two-room house behind Bella's three-story mom-and-pop grocery on her janitorial wages and welfare. The building, erected in 1895 at 1727 Bedford Avenue and owned by Jews, was once a jitney station. The setting, which recurs
in *Fences* (1985), had no hot water or toilet, but did provide a pleasant backyard away
from street noise.

   Although the Wilsons lived in the city, they had direct ties to Southern blacks
as far back as the early 1700s through their mother's family. Joining the Great Migration, their maternal grandmother left North Carolina and journeyed on foot to Pittsburgh. The playwright has stated his belief that the African American homeland is
the South, the one place outside of Africa where blacks can be truly self-sufficient.
He told interviewer Wendell Brock, "I always view the South as black America's
ancestral homeland. We spent roughly 250 years there, so there are a lot of my ancestors who are buried there in the South" (Brock, p. E1).

1948   Drawing on her sixth-grade education, Daisy Kittel began teaching Wilson
to read at age three. In addition to letters and words, he learned pride and dignity
from her example. One of his favorite anecdotes describes her rage after winning a
new washer. When the sponsors of the contest realized she was black and a single
mother of mixed race children, they substituted a used washer from the Salvation
Army for the promised prize. Even though she had to heat water and scrub laundry

5

over a washboard at the kitchen sink, she rejected the washer and reminded her son, "Something is not always better than nothing" (Graves, p. D1). She pulled out an empty jar as an impromptu bank, plopped in a coin, and started her savings for a new washer.

A large brood of siblings plus the comforts of Daisy's home were a sanctuary from a biased world in which bi-racial children suffered taunts from blacks and whites. In 1996, Wilson reflected on his mother's importance to his writing: "The content of my mother's life — her myths, her superstitions, her prayers, the contents of her pantry, the smell of her kitchen, the song that escaped from her sometimes parched lips, her thoughtful repose and pregnant laughter — all are worthy of art" (*Seven Guitars*, n. p.).

1950   To assure her children a sense of prosperity, Daisy Kittel always served dessert, even if she only had Jell-O to offer. The early years, though stressful and demanding, set the mold of Wilson's character. A model student, he earned A's at St. Richard's School, obtained his first library card, and delivered newspapers to earn money for the family's milk and bread. Friend Chawley P. Williams credits that sense of cooperative effort for the good of the family with invigorating Wilson's dramas: "His vitality is enormous because he continues to delve within himself and his surroundings to connect with who he is" (O'Mahony).

1952   At home, Wilson remembers seeing Tarzan movies and the joy of sharing radio time: "Like, Monday, at 7 o'clock, the rosary came on the radio, so we said the rosary. On Tuesday, *People Are Funny* came on at 7, and we sat down and listened to that" (Fitzgerald, p. 14). From his earliest years, music was integral to family fun. He told interviewer Sharon Fitzgerald, "They had the Top 40, and we all picked a song. If your song got to be No. 1, you got a nickel. We'd listen and root for our song" (*Ibid.*). One of his favorite singers was Nat King Cole.

Of Wilson's identity with siblings ranging from white to dark, Chawley Williams remarked, "There was a major dilemma within him to resolve his being bi-racial. August will tell you and everybody else that he has always lived in a black world and he has always identified that way, but if you listen to his art, you'll hear the bi-racism" (O'Mahony). Disagreeing with Williams's assertion is Linda Jean Denoya, Wilson's lightest-skinned sibling, who declared that he always identified with his mother's race. Linda attested to feeling pain for her darker brother from racial incidents that never targeted her.

1955   When Wilson wrote his first poems, his mother pondered encouraging him to attend "a nice Catholic college" and become an attorney (Moyers, p. 170). By the fifth grade, he was reading the bible as well as Nancy Drew and Hardy Boys mysteries. His sister, English teacher Freda Wilson Ellis, recalled that literature and composition were Wilson's first priority, "[He] let nothing interfere with that writing. Job, whatever you're supposed to do at various points in life — he wrote instead" (Reynolds, p. E1).

1957   In the seventh grade at Pittsburgh Catholic parochial school, Wilson provoked Sister Mary Eldephonse, who assigned him a non-speaking part of percussionist in the Christmas pageant. His cue was "And, lo, the wise men came unto the manger" (Adcock). Because of a pre-performance kiss shared with classmate Catherine Moran, Wilson imagined an aura around her. Entranced, he failed to clash the cymbals. The mistake did not endear him to Sister Mary Eldephonse.

1958 At age thirteen, the author and his five siblings lived with their mother and black stepfather, David Bedford, a high school football star and would-be physician. When he failed to earn a scholarship to pay his way to medical school, he earned a twenty-three-year sentence in the penitentiary for murder and robbery. He returned to Pittsburgh to work in the sewer department. The family moved to Hazelwood, a mostly white part of the Homestead district embraced by the Monongahela River in southeast Pittsburgh. Neighbors varied in their response to the Kittel children by favoring light-skinned Linda Jean and rejecting August for his darker coloration. Some of the more virulent racists threw bricks through the Wilsons' windows.

1959 Wilson attended college-preparatory courses at Central Catholic High School, an historic landmark founded by the Christian Brothers in 1927 on Fifth Avenue in Pittsburgh. Because he was the only black among fifteen hundred students, Wilson ate alone in the school cafeteria and failed to earn a position on the football team. He withdrew from taunts, hate notes, and fistfights and enrolled at Connelley Vocational School, an uninspiring environment where the budding poet concentrated on sheet-metal class, where he shaped a tin cup. His salvation were the thirty or forty books comprising the Negro section of the Hazelwood Branch of the Carnegie Library, which he discovered one afternoon on his way back from basketball practice. He checked out a collection of the poems of Paul Laurence Dunbar and kept the volume for twenty-eight years.

1960 After Wilson enrolled across the street from his house at Gladstone High School, he ridiculed a wino, Johnson Tidrow. One day, the elderly man handed Wilson a copy of Ralph Ellison's classic polemical novel *The Invisible Man* (1947) and said, "Read this and learn something, fool" (Rousuck, p. 1E). Wilson later discovered that Tidrow was a former professor whom white administrators denied tenure. Daisy Kittel reminded her son that he could learn from all people, even winos. The lesson turned Wilson toward the incorporation of numerous wise fools in his plays, beginning with Gabe Maxson, the half-crazed vegetable seller in *Fences* (1985), and continuing with Bynum Walker, the shaman and sacrificer of pigeons, in *Joe Turner's Come and Gone* (1988), the crazed fence painter Hambone in *Two Trains Running* (1991), the mystic evangelist King Hedley in *Seven Guitars* (1995), the pack rat Stool Pigeon in *King Hedley II* (1999), and Aunt Ester, the prophet and counselor in *Two Trains Running* and *Gem of the Ocean* (2003).

1961 Shortly before his sixteenth birthday, when Wilson was enrolled in the tenth grade, he chose Napoleon as a topic for a research paper because the great military leader was a self-made man. Wilson hoped that a quality paper would get him an invitation to join the College Club. A black history teacher whom he liked falsely charged that the twenty-page paper was actually the work of Wilson's older sister. Wilson refused to prove the paper's originality. In the wake of catcalls and racist remarks, he quit school, but returned to shoot baskets under the principal's window in hopes of being urged back to class. When he was ignored, he gave up permanently on formal education. He hid the dismal affair from his family for months by studying each day at the main branch of the Carnegie Library in Oakland. Ruefully, he recalled, "My mother was terribly disappointed that the child she thought had the most potential dropped out of school and wasn't motivated to do anything" (Plummer & Kahn, p. 64).

With three hundred books of his own choice, Wilson began a four-year self-education in black history, sociology, anthropology, and literature, especially the poems of John Berryman, Dylan Thomas, and Langston Hughes, the prose works of W. E. B. Du Bois and Arna Bontemps, and Booker T. Washington's autobiography *Up from Slavery* (1901). At the pinnacle of the author's reading program was Ralph Ellison's *Invisible Man.* Wilson wrote in the *Pittsburgh Post-Gazette* of the importance of books to his life: "I have often fallen asleep with a book in my arms where there should have been a woman. I have stained the pages of books with coffee, ketchup, water, mustard, bourbon and more than a few times with tears" (Wilson, "Feed"). Of his self-teaching, he feels amply prepared with smatterings of knowledge on a wide range of subjects, but regrets the unhappiness that accompanied poverty, marked by holes in his shoes and small change in his pocket.

Ejected from home after his mother discovered that he had quit school, Wilson resided in the basement and supported himself by cooking, stocking shelves, operating a freight elevator, washing dishes, and mowing lawns. He dreamed of joining the Harlem Renaissance and composed verse, which he submitted to campus journals at the University of Pittsburgh. He deliberately avoided the white canon to favor James Baldwin, Jean Toomer, Paul Laurence Dunbar, and Langston Hughes. When Wilson began publishing, he recalled, "Just the idea that black people could write books. I wanted my book up there too" (O'Mahony).

1962 The military offered little to Wilson, who joined the U.S. Army at age seventeen and ended a three-year hitch in 1964 after a little over one year's service. The failure to thrive in an authoritarian environment preceded his creation of a series of fictional characters who bucked the system or challenged their fathers, either face to face or in mental set-tos long after the parents' deaths. As a result, the authoritarian father-son relationship became an insightful and, at times, violent motif in his plays. As Wilson noted to interviewer Richard Christiansen, "My generation knew very little about their parents. Your parents didn't tell you everything.... Children didn't realize why their parents seemed so cruel at times" (Christiansen, p. 13).

1963 On his own, Wilson worked as a porter and deliveryman, short-order cook, dishwasher, and gardener. He hung out with locals at Pope's Restaurant and Pat's Place, a tobacco shop mentioned in Claude McKay's *Home to Harlem* (1928). Wilson admired boxer Charley Burley, his idol: "I wanted to be like him. And he would get dressed up on a Friday night, real clean, in a Stetson hat, with the Florsheim shoes. And I'd see these men standing on the corner, and I thought, I can't wait to grow up and get dressed up and go stand on the corner of Fullerton and Wylie" (Saltzman & Plett).

Wilson decked himself in raffish corduroy slacks, jacket, and hat and acquired the nickname "Youngblood" from the railroad men who gathered there. According to Sharon Fitzgerald, "Community life represented [to Wilson] a dynamic fusion of struggles, secrets, fantasies, and strengths" (Fitzgerald, p. 14). Content in an intergenerational milieu, he spent his days chain-smoking, jotting down impromptu verse, and gaining the self-confidence to form political opinions about a difficult pass in civil rights history.

Camaraderie with older man stimulated Wilson's imagination, inspiring him with subjects for poems. Among his earliest efforts was "Theme One: The Variations," which speaks of "holy niggers breathing out power" and "the catechism of the spirit" (O'Mahony). When Wilson recited such abstruse works in the street, locals thought him deranged. He got the same brush-off at the Halfway Art Gallery, where he entertained the audience with recitations while musicians set up to play.

1965 Wilson found surrogate father figures in the neighborhood. He reminisced about his community relations at age twenty: "I went down onto Centre Avenue to learn from the community how to be a man. My education comes from the years I spent there" (Davidson, p. F1). He was choosy about men with experiences to share: "Mostly I'd listen to the older guys, because I was impressed. Here was a guy who lived sixty years—and I didn't think I was going to make it to the next year" (*Ibid.*). He toyed with drama by viewing a production of Eugene Ionesco's play *The Rhinoceros* (1958), but felt distanced from stage art because he found nothing in the play to relate to. When the elder Kittel died, the playwright changed his name from Freddie Kittel to August Wilson and settled in a ground-floor flat alongside St. Benedict the Moor Church on Bedford Avenue. Like the transformation of Marguerite Johnson into Maya Angelou, the name change suited the persona Wilson wanted to project through his writings.

April 1, 1965 After resolving to become a poet, Wilson ended his library education. On twenty dollars he earned from his sister Freda for writing her college term paper on Robert Frost and Carl Sandburg, he bought a Royal manual typewriter, lugged it uphill to his room, and set up an office on the kitchen table. He mailed his first three poems to *Harper's* magazine, which promptly rejected them. He recited original poems at Hill District saloons, cafes, jazz clubs, and street corners. From twenty-nine-year-old poet Chawley P. Williams, Wilson received mentoring at regular meetings on Centre Avenue. He began exploring Afrocentrism from literary activism by Nick Flournoy, Gaston Neal, and Rob Penny.

To develop individuality, Wilson joined the Black Power movement and, for five cents each from the St. Vincent de Paul store across from his residence, began buying blues and jazz recordings. His favorite was a bootleg 78 of Bessie Smith's "Nobody in Town Can Bake a Sweet Jelly Roll Like Mine," which he played twenty-two times in succession. Of its meaning to his life and work, he exults, "The universe stuttered and everything fell to a new place" (Wilson, "Where to Begin," p. 2035). To learn about life, he absorbed the strands of local life. He reported to William Plummer, writer for *People Weekly:* "I realized that I had history and connection — the everyday poetry of the people I'd grown up with" (Plummer & Kahn, p. 64). He used Pittsburgh as his spiritual fount, calling it "the fuel and the father for all of my work" (Rawson, "The Power," 1999).

In one of Wilson's favorite anecdotes, he recalls going to jail for breaking and entering his own apartment. Because the landlord padlocked his door for nonpayment of rent, Wilson followed his lawyer's advice and broke in. Wilson served three days because the law disallows breaking into an apartment if it's furnished. The worst of his sentence was trying to sleep in a cell beside a man who continually sang "Ol' Man River."

1967   In a transcendent moment, Wilson and some two hundred local people from the Hill District surrounded Crawford Grill to listen to jazz saxophonist John Coltrane. The music and its powerful rhythms fueled Wilson's drive to express in drama black Americans' emotive culture. He decided that he wanted to create an art so moving that, like Coltrane's blue notes, it would "stun people into silence" (Reynolds, p. E1).

1968   Shaped by the Black Power movement, Wilson dedicated himself to black cultural nationalism. Of his choice of drama as a career, old friend Sala Udin chuckled, "It was cheap and live and relevant and risque and dangerous and radical" (Reynolds, p. E1). Wilson joined scriptwriter and drama teacher Rob Penny in cofounding the Black Horizons Theatre Company, an Afrocentric community outlet that Wilson served as director. To learn his trade, he checked out Alexander Dean and Lawrence Carra's text *The Fundamentals of Play Directing* (1965) from the library and performed the works of Ed Bullins and Amiri Baraka. He recalled, "Doing community theatre was very difficult — rehearsing two hours a night after people got off work, not knowing if the actors were going to show up" (Savran, p. 290). From experience with audiences, he learned the value of drama to ordinary people.

1969   The year of his stepfather's death, Wilson married Brenda Burton, a devotee of the Nation of Islam, a radical Muslim faith that promotes responsibility to home and family through rigid gender roles for male and female followers. He respected the Honorable Elijah Muhammad for promoting self-sufficiency and for supplying black Americans with their own origin myth, the story of Yacoub.

January 22, 1970   Brenda Burton Wilson gave birth to a daughter, Sakina Ansari, who became a Baltimore social worker.

summer 1971   In *Black Lines*, Wilson published two poems, "Morning Song" and "Bessie," a lyric tribute to Bessie Smith.

September 1971   Wilson issued "For Malcolm X and Others" in *Negro Digest*.

1972   After Wilson refused to attend Sunday services or to follow Black Muslim dictates, his first marriage ended in divorce, but his relationship with his daughter continued. He later joined the Nation of Islam, but his actions did not revive love for his former wife.

September 1972   Wilson published "Muhammad Ali," a poetic tribute, in *Black World*.

1973   After seeing a bartender shoot a man dead on the sidewalk outside the bar, Wilson wrote *Recycle*, his first play, an avant-garde experiment that merged verse and dialogue. At the time, he had seen none of the plays of the era's giants—Anton Chekhov, Henrik Ibsen, Eugene O'Neill, Arthur Miller, or Tennessee Williams. The male-female relationship that develops in the plot reflects the collapse of Wilson's own marriage. The language reflects the poet rather than the master of dialogue Wilson later became. For its failings, the play remains unpublished.

1976   Two years after the formation of the Kuntu Repertory Theater as an outgrowth of the Department of Africana Studies at the University of Pittsburgh, Wilson offered for production *The Homecoming*, the story of Blind Willie Johnson, a blues musician who gives his songs away, directed by Vernell Lillie. Wilson and Rob Penny founded a complementary program, the Kuntu Writers Workshop. The sessions, open free to all comers, promoted meaningful discussion among neophyte writers and helped beginners get published and produced. Wilson dedicated his expertise and experience to nourishing talent, including teens from Pittsburgh ghetto gangs.

In longhand, Wilson began writing his first stage success, *Ma Rainey's Black Bottom*, which placed heavy demands on his meager understanding of pacing and dialogue. After lengthy work, he published the play in 1985. Although producers offered him twenty-five thousand dollars for the rights to produce the play as a Broadway musical, he resisted temptation. After keeping the text pure drama, he chose it to initiate his ten-year cycle, which portrays social and spiritual issues and the redemption of black Americans from oppression. His motivation rang true to his credo: "I want the theatergoer to understand that black Americans have their own culture" (Plummer & Kahn, p. 63).

1977   Wilson wrote *The Coldest Day of the Year*, a play about male-female relations inspired by his breakup with a girlfriend. In his fourth play, he followed with *Black Bart and the Sacred Hills*, an encomium to a hero-villain who robbed stagecoaches. The text is a multicultural musical satire composed in verse and set among black settlers of the Old West.

November 1977   At age thirty-three, Wilson left the Black Horizons project in Pittsburgh. Resettled in St. Paul, Minnesota, he volunteered as a part-time cook for the Little Brothers of the Poor on East Lake Street to leave him half days for writing. Among the benefactors he met was actor Marion McClinton, who became his faithful director as well as an actor in two of his plays.

Far from a heavily black population, Wilson began replaying in his mind the dialogue of the blacks he grew up with. He explained, "I came to manhood in Pittsburgh in the '60s. That's still what I know best, and that's what I write about" (Saltzman & Plett). After joining the Playwrights' Center in Minneapolis, he summoned up the lives and voices of Pittsburgh's Hill District and, during Pittsburgh's urban renewal, began writing the two-act play *Jitney*, a realistic dialect drama set at an unlicensed Pittsburgh cab stand, a car service transporting members of the underserved black populace. Director Lloyd Richards was so impressed by the authenticity of the characters' language that he exclaimed, "I recognized them, I knew them from their words, I knew their faces almost" (O'Mahony).

January 1978   In Los Angeles, the Inner City Theater staged a reading of *Black Bart and the Sacred Hills*. The story of former cattle rustler and magician Black Bart, it describes the protagonist's intent to turn water into gold to make it so common that it has no value.

1979   Wilson published *The Homecoming* and *The Coldest Day of the Year*. At the Science Museum of Minnesota on East Tenth Street, he earned his first money for writing Profiles in Science, a series covering the lives of Margaret Mead, William Harvey, and Charles Darwin. He developed scripts to accompany exhibits in the anthropology division, including "An Evening with Margaret Mead," introductions to the work of biologist Charles Darwin and anatomist William Harvey, and two presentations on Northwestern Indian lore, "How Coyote Got His Special Powers" and "The Eskimo Song Duel: The Case of the Borrowed Wife." His texts covered the mythic figures of Peyote and Spiderwoman, who taught literacy to the Navajo.

1980   On a fellowship from the Minneapolis Playwrights' Center, Wilson wrote but did not publish *Fullerton Street*, set in 1941 at the time of the Joe Louis–Billy Conn boxing match. The plot focuses on lynching, alcoholism, welfare, and the Southern black's loss of values while living in the urban North. For the first time, the playwright killed off a character, Mozelle, and wept at the pathos of the experience. *Fullerton Street* was one of his least successful plays, but it encouraged Wilson to return to the unfinished script of *Ma Rainey's Black Bottom*.

1981   Wilson produced *Black Bart and the Sacred Hills* at St. Paul's Penumbra Theatre. He wed his second wife, social worker Judy Oliver Wilson. During summers at the Eugene O'Neill Theatre Center in Waterford, Connecticut, he began submitting dramas to the National Playwrights Conference, his first competition against dramatists of national stature.

summer 1982   Wilson developed a friendship with actor Charles S. Dutton and gained the collaboration of Lloyd Richards, dean and artistic director of the Yale Repertory Theater, by submitting *Ma Rainey's Black Bottom* to the National Playwrights Conference.

October 1982   At the Allegheny Repertory Theater in Pittsburgh, Wilson produced *Jitney*, an uneven effort fraught with the insecurities and false starts of the beginning playwright. Nonetheless, he won a Bush fellowship.

1983 The year that his mother died, Wilson began an annual family reunion and pilgrimage to her grave. He produced *The Mill Hand's Lunch Bucket* in New York, a work bearing the title of the collage "Mill Hand's Lunch" (1978), which Romare Bearden painted on masonite as part of his Mecklenburg County series. Wilson gave an initial reading of *Fences* for the National Playwrights Conference. Of the play's similarity to his life, he clarified that "the cultural context of the play is my life" (Tallmer, p. 28). In another interview, he explained, "I go inside myself and find out what's there. If it's not there, nobody will put it there" (Stern, p. 19A).

1984   In a staged reading at the National Playwrights Conference, Wilson introduced *Joe Turner's Come and Gone*, a drama of ritual purification. He confessed to interviewer Richard Pettengill that it was his favorite play.

April 6, 1984   While Wilson was cooking for the Little Brothers of the Poor for eighty-eight dollars per week, he produced his fourth play and first hit, *Ma Rainey's Black Bottom*, which opened at the Yale Repertory Theatre in New Haven, Connecticut. Directed by Lloyd Richards, it starred Charles S. Dutton as Levee Green and Theresa Merritt as Ma Rainey. In his critique, *New York Times* drama critic Frank Rich dubbed the playwright "a major find" (Rich, p. C13).

October 11, 1984   *Ma Rainey's Black Bottom* advanced to New York's Cort Theatre with Charles S. Dutton in his Broadway debut in the role of Levee Green. The play ran for 275 nights and closed June 9, 1985. It earned Wilson his first New York Drama Critics Circle award for best play of 1984-1985 and won him a Rockefeller fellowship. The progression of time frames from *Jitney* to *Fullerton Street* to *Ma Rainey* intrigued him to continue setting his plays in different eras of African American history as an autobiography of his community and ancestry.

1985   New American Library published *Ma Rainey's Black Bottom*. Wilson completed *The Janitor*, a four-minute play focusing on Sam, the title character, as a frequently ignored source of information. *Jitney* opened at the Penumbra Theatre in Minnesota.

April 30, 1985   To escape the fate of one-shot black playwrights, Wilson immediately completed *Fences*, a domestic drama set in the 1950s highlighting bigotry in professional baseball and failed fatherhood. The play opened at the Yale Repertory Theatre in New Haven, Connecticut, under the direction of Lloyd Richards. It featured Courtney B. Vance as Cory and James Earl Jones in the Tony-winning lead role. Wilson won a McKnight fellowship, Tony nomination, and New York Drama Critics Circle award.

1986   New American library published the definitive version of *Fences*.

April 29, 1986   *Joe Turner's Come and Gone* debuted at the Yale Repertory Theatre in New Haven, Connecticut. For the saga of black migration from the agricultural South, Lloyd Richards directed a superb cast, including Charles S. Dutton as Herald Loomis and Angela Bassett as Herald's estranged wife, Martha Pentecost. Wilson won a third Drama Critics Circle award, American Theatre Critics award, Drama Desk best play award, Guggenheim fellowship, and the Whiting Foundation writer's purse of $250,000 for emerging talent.

1987   *Ma Rainey's Black Bottom* debuted at the Kuntu Repertory Theater in the author's hometown. When Wilson spoke at the Carnegie Library in Pittsburgh, he returned *The Collected Poems of Paul Laurence Dunbar*, which he had checked out twenty-eight years before.

March 26, 1987   Wilson received a first Pulitzer Prize for *Fences*, which debuted at the 56th Street Theatre in New York City starring James Earl Jones as Troy Maxson. Investor Carol Shorenstein attempted to alter the ending of the play and threatened to fire director Lloyd Richards, but Wilson rejected both actions.

October 2, 1987   *Joe Turner's Come and Gone* opened at the Yale Repertory Theatre, featuring Delroy Lindo as Herald Loomis, Angela Bassett as Martha Pentecost, and Ed Hall as Bynum Walker. Although the play ran only three months and closed on June 26, Wilson received a New York Drama Critics Circle best play award, Helen Hayes citation, New York Public Library Literary Lion award, Los Angeles Drama Critics Circle best play award, and an honorary doctorate from Yale University.

November 26, 1987   After an initial reading of *The Piano Lesson* for the National Playwrights Conference at the Eugene O'Neill Theatre Center, the play opened at the Yale Repertory Theatre with Samuel L. Jackson playing Boy Willie Charles. During the production, Wilson met costumer Constanza Romero, his future wife, of Bogota, Colombia. She was educated in textile design at the California College of Arts and Crafts in Oakland, University of California at Santa Cruz, and Yale.

1988   Wilson appeared on PBS-TV on Bill Moyers's *World of Ideas* and issued *Fences* and *Ma Rainey's Black Bottom* from Penguin's London office. His notoriety increased with a lecture on "Blacks, Blues, and Cultural Imperialism" for the Carnegie Library's *Man and Ideas* series.

January 9, 1988   The Yale Repertory Theatre performed *The Piano Lesson*, the fourth major Wilson play directed by Lloyd Richards, starring Charles S. Dutton as Boy Willie.

March 26, 1988   At New York's Barrymore Theatre, Wilson produced *Joe Turner's Come and Gone*, starring Ed Hall, Delroy Lindo, and Angela Bassett from the original cast. Because the play ran in tandem with *Fences*, the opening made August Wilson the first black playwright to have two Broadway shows in production simultaneously.

1989   *Ma Rainey's Black Bottom* opened in London; the Pittsburgh Public Theater produced *Fences*. Wilson won a second American Theatre Critics award.

1990   Wilson contributed to an anthology, *Selected from Contemporary American Plays*, and wrote an introduction to *Romare Bearden: His Life and Art*, by Myron Schwartzman.

March 27, 1990   Wilson completed a fifth major play, *Two Trains Running*, a naturalistic drama about the forced sale of a diner during urban renewal of the 1960s. On its debut at the Yale Repertory Theatre in New Haven, Connecticut, it was directed by Lloyd Richards and starred Samuel L. Jackson as Wolf and Larry Fishburne as Sterling Johnson.

April 16, 1990   *The Piano Lesson* opened in New York City at Broadway's Walter Kerr Theatre to instant acclaim and ran over nine months until January 27, 1991. Directed by Lloyd Richards and costumed by Constanza Romero, it starred Charles S. Dutton as Boy Willie. Wilson, who sat at a bar across the street to observe playgoers, won four Tonys, an Outer Circle award for best Broadway play of the year, John Gassner award for best American playwright, and Chicago *Tribune* artist of the year. The spectacular three-month run of *The Piano Lesson* produced a record for Broadway nonmusicals of eleven million dollars grossed in its first twelve months. Profits enabled Wilson to earn his living from writing. He gained a second Pulitzer Prize, another Drama Critics Circle award, and a third American Theatre Critics award.

November 16, 1990 After a divorce from his second wife, Wilson settled in a century-old house in Seattle's Capitol Hill with portrait painter Constanza Romero, costume designer for *Ma Rainey's Black Bottom, Fences, Seven Guitars,* and *Gem of the Ocean. Joe Turner's Come and Gone* opened in London. Wilson was named Pittsburgher of the year, an honor conferred by *Pittsburgh Magazine.*

1991 Wilson won a fourth American Theatre Critics citation and Black Filmmakers Hall of Fame award. The University of Pittsburgh Press published *August Wilson: Three Plays,* containing *Ma Rainey's Black Bottom, Fences,* and *Joe Turner's Come and Gone. The Piano Lesson* opened at Pittsburgh's Fulton Theater.

spring 1991 Wilson published *Testimonies* in *Antaeus.*

March 10, 1991 Wilson published in the *New York Times* the self-revelatory essay "How to Write a Play like August Wilson," which lauds the influence of collagist Romare Bearden on Wilson's drama cycle.

November 1991 *Two Trains Running* opened at the Kennedy Center in Washington, D.C., starring Roscoe Lee Browne as the storyteller Holloway.

1992 After receiving an honorary doctorate from the University of Pittsburgh, Wilson addressed the honors convocation.

April 13, 1992 *Two Trains Running* opened on Broadway at the Walter Kerr Theatre and ran until August 30. The play, directed by Lloyd Richards, starred Larry Fishburne and Roscoe Lee Browne as Sterling Johnson and Holloway. Wilson won a Drama Critics Circle award for best play of the year, another American Theatre Critics award, Clarence Muse award, and a second Tony nomination for best play.

1993 New American Library/Dutton published *Two Trains Running* featuring a cover drawing of the main characters at the cafe by Constanza Romero. Turner Publications issued *A Game of Passion: The NFL Literary Companion,* an anthology of over forty pieces celebrating football. In addition to an entry by August Wilson were essays by James Dickey, Don DeLillo, Lee Iacocca, Andy Rooney, and Irwin Shaw. *Antaeus* magazine published Wilson's *The Janitor.*

1994 Wilson agreed to the filming of *The Piano Lesson* in Pittsburgh. He married Constanza Romero, his third wife, whom he had met at Yale in 1987 during a production of *The Piano Lesson.*

January 21, 1995 *Seven Guitars,* directed by Walter Dallas, premiered at the Goodman Theatre in Chicago to mixed reviews. Critics declared the play Wilson's most musical polyphony of black voices in concert on universal themes.

February 5, 1995 A shortened screen version of *The Piano Lesson* appeared on CBS-TV *Hallmark Hall of Fame,* starring Alfre Woodard and Charles S. Dutton as the warring Charles siblings. In August, the two-hour film, Wilson's first, earned an Emmy nomination for best television movie, gained nominations of best actor for Dutton and Woodard, and won Wilson induction into the American Academy of Arts and Letters.

September 15, 1995   *Seven Guitars* opened in Boston's Huntington Theatre Company under the direction of Lloyd Richards. *Time* magazine praised the work as "a rich ragout of melodrama and mysticism"; Jack Kroll of *Newsweek* envisioned it as "a jazz cantata for actors … bursting with the balked music of life" ("The Best of 1995," p. 152; Kroll, p. 60).

1996   Wilson was one of thirty contributors to *Speak My Name: Black Men on Masculinity and the American Dream*, a series of essays reflecting on black male identity, fatherhood, violence, and other topics vital to the survival and contentment of African Americans. Dutton published *Seven Guitars*, which the playwright dedicated to his wife, who designed costumes for the play's premiere and a cover for the published edition.

March 28, 1996   After the opening of *Seven Guitars* on Broadway at the Walter Kerr Theatre, it ran until September 8. Wilson won a New York Drama Critics Circle Award, a Tony nomination for best play, and, in April, a William Inge Distinguished Playwright citation. Critics from top publications called the tragi-comedy epic and mesmerizing in its sweep, gritty and bluesy in tone, and heartbreaking in its powerful conclusion.

June 26, 1996   Edward Gilbert, the artistic director of the Pittsburgh Public Theater, advised Wilson to rewrite *Jitney* by lengthening it and evening out rough places in the script. The second version opened at the Pittsburgh Public Theater. That same day at the eleventh biennial National Theatre Conference at Princeton University, Wilson delivered "The Ground on Which I Stand," a landmark speech in which he encouraged the creation of self-sustaining black theaters where artists could express themes and black issues. He called for guidelines and for professional writers and actors to inflame black people with the will to protect and pass on black cultural contributions.

1997   In a turbulent period of his career, Wilson was numbered among the ten Pulitzer-winning playwrights— Larry Gelbart, John Guare, David Mamet, Steve Martin, Elaine May, Terrence McNally, Arthur Miller, Neil Simon, Wendy Wasserstein — writing original teleplays for ABC's "Millennium Project." Wilson rewrote *Jitney*, adding a scene and altering the time frame from 1971 to 1977.

January 17, 1997   Wilson faced his most outspoken critic Robert Brustein in a debate at Manhattan's Town Hall at "On Cultural Power: The August Wilson–Robert Brustein Discussion." Brustein maintained that Wilson was a worthy artist, but denigrated his drama cycle as constrained, boring, and obsessed with victimization. Before a vocal audience, the combatants faced off over the issues of race, funding for the arts, multiculturalism, and black-only casts. Wilson maintained that black-owned theaters are essential educators of people barely conversant with their own heritage. Brustein charged that Wilson was an out-of-date leader of the arts calling for a subsidized cultural separatism and a new form of tribalism. Wilson maintained his faith in black art as a dynamic force for change: "Art doesn't change society. Art changes people. People change the world" (Saltzman & Plett). The debaters' differences ignited a long-lived exchange in print and electronic form that involved *American Theatre* magazine, the *Los Angeles Times*, National Public Radio, *New Republic*, the *New York Times*, and the *Washington Post*.

April 1997   Walter Dallas directed the revised form of *Jitney* at the Crossroads Theatre in New Brunswick, New Jersey.

August 27, 1997   In Seattle, Constanza gave birth to Wilson's second daughter, Azula Carmen, to whom he dedicated *Jitney*.

1998   Wilson won an American Theatre Critics award. To aid neophyte writers, he founded the African Grove Institute of the Arts, which provided resources and support to independent black theaters.

March 1998   While serving as assistant professor of drama and film studies at Dartmouth, Wilson led the National Black Theatre Summit and delivered a speech reiterating his demand for a national black theater.

June 12, 1998   Wilson produced a new revision of *Jitney* at Philadelphia's Freedom Theatre.

August 23, 1998   Wilson accepted the New Frontier Playwright Award at the Edward Albee Theatre Conference in Valdez, Alaska.

October 21, 1998   *Jitney* opened at San Francisco's Hansberry Theater and at the Huntington Theater in Boston a week later.

December 1998   The establishment of the Literary Hall of Fame for Writers of African Descent, a national effort to recognize outstanding black authors, brought more honor to Wilson. For its first induction, the initiators of the hall chose fourteen living writers. Wilson shared glory with Amiri Baraka, Lerone Bennett, Gwendolyn Brooks, Thulani Davis, Ernest Gaines, Nikki Giovanni, and Toni Morrison. Among those recognized posthumously were James Baldwin, Ralph Ellison, Langston Hughes, Zora Neale Hurston, and Dorothy West, some of the groundbreaking writers who influenced Wilson early in his career.

1999   The *Pittsburgh Post-Gazette* labeled Wilson the top Pittsburgh cultural power broker.

January 8, 1999   Twenty years after its debut, the modified version of *Jitney* opened at the Center Stage in Baltimore and moved on in summer to Chicago's Goodman Theatre, in March at the Studio Arena in Buffalo, New York, the next month at the GeVa Theatre in Rochester, New York, and in November at the Huntington Theater at Boston University.

March 18, 1999   The Hill District Branch Library on Dinwiddie Street honored Wilson at its centennial. In a formal address to attendees, he worded a pointed challenge to youth: "If the African who arrived in America chained and malnourished in the hold of a 350-ton Portuguese vessel is still chained and malnourished after 380 years, can it be anybody's fault but ours?" (Rawson, "O'Reilly: Charting," 1999).

May 1999   Steven Winn, drama critic of the *San Francisco Chronicle*, named *Joe Turner's Come and Gone* one of America's top fifty plays of the twentieth century.

May 27, 1999   For Wilson's preservation of black music, at the W. C. Handy Blues Awards ceremony, the Blues Foundation conferred on him the Keeping Blues Alive award for achievement in literature.

June 2, 1999   Wilson received an honorary doctorate from California State University at Northridge.

September 29, 1999   President Bill Clinton awarded Wilson a National Humanities Medal for his epic plays. The citation placed the playwright in company with humorist Garrison Keillor, journalist Jim Lehrer, and moviemaker Steven Spielberg. Wilson remarked, "I'm very pleased, because this is a national honor and I'm most impressed with the company I'm in" (Berson, "Seattle," p. E1).

December 1999   Wilson was mildly disappointed that he was nominated but did not win a third Pulitzer Prize for *King Hedley II*, which debuted at the launching of the Pittsburgh Public Theater at the O'Reilly. The star, Brian Stokes Mitchell, lauded Wilson as "Our Shakespeare. He takes these gigantic, grand themes about humanity and the human experience, and puts them in a small setting with characters and people that we all know and we all live with and we all can relate to, that are very simple … at first glance" (Ifill). In addition to Mitchell's kudos, the playwright received another Drama Critics Circle award and the only high school diploma ever issued by the Carnegie Library of Pittsburgh.

December 31, 1999   Wilson returned to the White House to celebrate the new millennium with President Bill Clinton and first lady Hillary Clinton.

2000   Marion McClinton directed an off–Broadway revival of *Jitney*.

March 2000   *King Hedley II*, the eighth play of Wilson's decade cycle, opened at Seattle's Repertory Theater, starring Tony-winning actor Brian Stokes Mitchell in the title role.

2001   Wilson published *Cultivating the Ground on Which We Stand*. In February, he won the New York Drama Critics Circle Award for best play of the year and claimed six Vivian Robinson Audelco awards, which presented citations to *Jitney* for best play, direction, sets, costuming, lighting, and sound. Wilson also was interviewed for *60 Minutes* and won a Harold Washington Literary Award and a League of Chicago Theaters citation.

April 29, 2001   Wilson received a Tony nomination after *King Hedley II* opened on Broadway at the Virginia Theater. It again starred Brian Stokes Mitchell in the title role and featured Leslie Uggams as a middle-aged Ruby, Hedley's mother. The three-hour play, directed by Marion McClinton and previously performed at Boston's Huntington Theater, the Mark Taper Forum in Los Angeles, Chicago's Goodman Theatre, and the Kennedy Center in Washington, D.C., posed difficulties for audiences and closed on July 1 after twelve weeks in the shortest run of any Wilson production.

May 12, 2001   Wilson received an honorary degree from Clarion University of Pennsylvania and delivered two addresses to the student body.

2002   Wilson earned a Laurence Olivier best play award and the Monte Cristo award, which recognizes distinguished artistic achievement and excellence. The Penumbra Theater in Minneapolis devoted its entire season to Wilson's plays.

May 23, 2002   Seattle's Corporate Council Celebrates the Arts presented Wilson a lifetime achievement award.

October 9, 2002   The Department of Theatre Arts and Dance at the University of Minnesota awarded Wilson an honorary doctorate. At a symposium, he spoke on "The Future of American Art and Politics."

December 2002   *King Hedley II*, produced by the Birmingham Repertory Theatre, premiered in London at the Tricycle Theatre.

2003   In a bid for a film version of *Fences*, Wilson's first Hollywood effort, he rewrote the play, adding a speaking role for Alberta, the unseen mistress of Troy Maxson. Wilson chose Marion McClinton to direct at a Pittsburgh location and picked Alfre Woodard for the part of Rose Maxson and Oprah Winfrey as Alberta. Wilson revealed plans for more works, including dramas, a film version of *Fences*, and a musical, for which he collaborated with jazz great Wynton Marsalis. Wilson also envisioned a novel similar to *Don Quixote*, which would require five years for composition and research.

February 6, 2003   Whoopi Goldberg and Charles S. Dutton starred as Ma Rainey and Levee Green in a new production of *Ma Rainey's Black Bottom*, which opened in New York at the Royale Theatre and ran until April 6.

spring 2003   Wilson published a clarification of his philosophy in *Cultivating the Ground on Which We Stand*.

March 10, 2003   The National Theatre of Uganda presented *Jitney*.

April 28, 2003   Wilson wrote *Gem of the Ocean*, the ninth entry to his ten-play cycle, which debuted at Chicago's Goodman Theatre and in July at the Mark Taper Forum in Los Angeles. Upon its completion, he rejoiced, "It's like you've just given birth. It's painful but it's a joyous process" (O'Mahony). The text focuses on the unmapped road in 1904 from plantation slavery to freedom and the trials of individuals fleeing the tormented past. On thinking about the first generation born after slavery, Wilson mused, "You could walk around and find people who were slaves. I find that incredible" (Reynolds, p. E1). For the first performance, the Goodman Theatre received $60,000, the largest National Endowment for the Arts grant in the Chicago area.

May 13, 2003   The New Dramatists, America's oldest nonprofit workshop, presented Wilson, one of their members, a lifetime achievement award for outstanding artistic contribution to the American theater. His colleagues lauded his ambition and proclaimed him a truly national playwright. In response, he recalled the group's kindness in giving him a place to stay, cash, and access to copier and typewriter. With their help, he dedicated himself to creating a link to the black past and looked ahead to more productions of his plays in Ghana. Of his future success, history teacher Laurence Glasco of the University of Pittsburgh predicted that Wilson would achieve his most important play when he dramatizes black-white relations in his neighborhood.

May 17, 2003 Wilson initiated a one-man stand-up performance, *How I Learned What I Learned*, at the fortieth anniversary of the Seattle Repertory Theater. During a one-hundred-minute freestyle monologue, he wandered from wing-back chair to barstool and commented on his formative years, women, prison, violence, and racism and acted out a killing.

May 22, 2003 For the Seattle International Film Festival, Wilson provided the voiceover for the film *The Naked Proof*, a low-budget romantic comedy from Pinwheel Pictures.

2004 August Wilson intends to open *Gem of the Ocean* on Broadway.

March 3, 2004 Wilson received the Freedom of Speech award at the U.S. Comedy Arts Festival in Aspen, Colorado.

April 2005 Wilson intends to introduce *Radio Golf* at the Yale Repertory Theater, starring Phylicia Rashad as Aunt Ester.

2005–2006 The management of Signature Theatre in New York City plans to dedicate the facility to Wilson's plays.

- *Further Reading*

Adcock, Joe. "A Moment with August Wilson, Playwright." *Seattle Post-Intelligencer*, May 20, 2003.
_____. "Wilson's 'What I Learned' Droll, Thoughtful, Packed with Surprises." *Seattle Post-Intelligencer*, May 27, 2003, p. F5.
Berson, Misha. "August Wilson Makes Leap from Playwright to Thespian." *Seattle Times*, May 18, 2003, p. K3.
_____. "Seattle Playwright Wilson Awarded Humanities Medal." *Seattle Times*, September 22, 1999, p. E1.
"The Best of 1995 Theater." *Time*, Vol. 146, No. 26, December 25, 1995, p. 152.
Brock, Wendell. "Q&A: August Wilson, Pulitzer Prize–winning Playwright: Wilson Sees 'Light at End of Tunnel' for Play Cycle." *Atlanta Journal-Constitution*, September 29, 2003, p. E1.
Christiansen, Richard. "August Wilson: A Powerful Playwright Probes the Meaning of Black Life." *Chicago Tribune*, February 5, 1988, pp. 12–13.
Davidson, Jim. "A Playwright Who Stirs the Imagination: A Dropout from the Hill District, August Wilson Is Now a Hit on Broadway." *Pittsburgh Press*, November 4, 1984, p. F1.
D'Souza, Karen. "Playwrights Dig for Lost History of Blacks." *San Jose Mercury News*, March 17, 2002.
Fishman, Joan. "Developing His Song: August Wilson's *Fences*," in *August Wilson: A Casebook*. New York: Garland, 1994.
Fitzgerald, Sharon. "August Wilson: The People's Playwright." *American Visions*, Vol. 15, No. 14, August 2000, p. 14.
Freedman, Samuel G. "A Voice from the Streets: August Wilson's Plays Portray the Sound and Feel of Black Poverty." *New York Times Magazine*, March 15, 1987, p. 36.
Graves, Jen. "Playwright August Wilson Born to Perform." *Tacoma News Tribune*, May 26, 2003, p. D1.

Hoover, Bob. "Bedford Avenue to Broadway: Childhood in Hill Leads to a Pulitzer for August Wilson." *Pittsburgh Post-Gazette*, June 1, 1987, p. 15.

Ifill, Gwen. "American Shakespeare." *PBS News*, April 6, 2001.

"Interview with August Wilson." *EGG the Arts Show*, http://www.pbs.org/wnet/egg/233/wilson/interview_content_1.html.

Kroll, Jack. "Seven Guitars." *Newsweek*, Vol. 125, No. 6, February 6, 1995, p. 60.

Moyers, Bill. *A World of Ideas*. New York: Doubleday, 1989.

O'Mahony, John. "American Centurion." Manchester *Guardian*, December 14, 2002.

Pettengill, Richard. "The Historical Perspective: An Interview with August Wilson," in *August Wilson: A Casebook*. New York: Garland, 1994.

Plummer, William, and Toby Kahn. "Street Talk." *People Weekly*, Vol. 45, No. 19, May 13, 1996, pp. 63–65.

Rawson, Chris. "August Wilson — A Timeline." *Pittsburgh Post-Gazette*, December 16, 1999.

_____. "O'Reilly Theater: Charting 20th Century Black America." *Pittsburgh Post-Gazette*, December 5, 1999.

_____. "O'Reilly Theater: Wilson Again Proves Home Is Where the Art Is." *Pittsburgh Post-Gazette*, December 5, 1999.

_____. "The Power Behind the Plays." *Pittsburgh Post-Gazette* Special Report, 1999.

Reed, Ishmael. "A Shy Genius Transforms the American Theater." *Connoisseur*, Vol. 127, 1987, pp. 92–97.

Reynolds, Christopher. "Mr. Wilson's Neighborhood: Playwright August Wilson No Longer Lives in Pittsburgh's Hill District, but It Is Consistently at Home in His Work." *Los Angeles Times*, July 27, 2002, p. E1.

Rich, Frank. "A Family Confronts Its History in August Wilson's 'Piano Lesson.'" *New York Times*, April 17, 1990, pp. C13, C15.

Rocha, Mark William. "A Conversation with August Wilson." *Diversity: A Journal of Multicultural Issues*, Vol. 1, Fall 1992, pp. 24–42.

Rousuck, J. Wynn. "People with Vision." *Baltimore Sun*, April 27, 1997, p. 1E.

"The Roving Editor." *The Writer*. Vol. 112, No. 5, May 1999, p. 4.

Saltzman, Simon, and Nicole Plett. "'Jitney' at Crossroads." *U.S. 1 Newspaper*, April 16, 1997.

Savran, David. *In Their Own Words: Contemporary American Playwrights*. New York: Theatre Communications Group, 1988.

Stern, Gary. "Playwrights Agree That the Workshops Process Is a Major Aid in Rewriting." *Backstage*, June 8, 1984, pp. 18A–19A.

Tallmer, Jerry. "Fences: Anguish of Wasted Talent." *New York Post*, March 26, 1987, p. 28.

Wilson, August. "Feed Your Mind, the Rest Will Follow." *Pittsburgh Post-Gazette*, March 28, 1999.

_____. "Living on Mother's Prayer." *New York Times*, May 12, 1996, p. 13.

_____. "Where to Begin," in *Short Pieces from the New Dramatists*. Banbury, Ox.: Orangeberry Books, 1985, pp. 2033–2037.

Winn, Steven. "50 for the Ages: A Critic's List of Great 20th Century American Plays." *San Francisco Chronicle*, May 30, 1999, p. 37.

Wilson's Genealogy

August Wilson's family tree, like those of his characters, reaches back to the South in the 1700s during the slave era and spreads across the United States in the twenty-first century:

August's maternal grandmother
(walked to Pittsburgh
from Spear, North Carolina)
|

Frederick August Kittel=**Daisy Wilson**=**David Bedford**
(d. 1965) | (d. 1983)   (imprisoned for murder
                    | and robbery ca. 1935;
                    | married, 1958)

Freda Ellis (English teacher)	**Donna Conley**	**Linda Jean Denoya**	**Edwin Wilson**	**Richard Wilson**	**August Wilson**=**Brenda Burton** (b. April 17, 1945)

Sakina Ansari
(b. January 22, 1970)
(social worker)

August Wilson=**Judy Oliver** (social worker)
(married 1981;
divorced 1990)

August Wilson=**Constanza Romero**
                          (costumer)
(married 1994)
|

Azula Carmen Wilson
(b. 1997)

August Wilson:
A Literary Companion

achievement

Wilson examines the human need for achievement in all of his dramas. At the beginning of his career, he contemplated reward for labor with Sam's need to support black youth in *The Janitor* (1985). The humble sweeper of a hotel ballroom creates an impromptu homily on worth and reminds his invisible audience, "Ain't nobody innocent. We are all victims of ourselves" (p. 1901). That said, he builds on personal responsibility for achievement until Mr. Collins, his employer, curtails the four-minute speech. The silencing of a humble black sage leaves the audience to contemplate the white world's discounting of African American thought as less valuable than black day labor.

Wilson expanded on the theme of ambition with the immature jazz trumpeter Levee Green's obsession in *Ma Rainey's Black Bottom* (1985) to start his own band and inject new energy and innovation into traditional Southern music. Similar to Levee's yearning are other males seeking achievement: guitarist Jeremy Furlow's desire for a musical career and tinsmith Seth Holly's striving for material gain by manufacturing dust pans and pots and pans in *Joe Turner's Come and Gone* (1988), the title character's eagerness to start a family and launch the Royal Video store in *King Hedley II* (1999), Youngblood's desire for a home in *Jitney* (1982), and Solly Two Kings' dedication to rescuing blacks via the Underground Railroad in *Gem of the Ocean* (2003). The playwright links achievement to poverty in two plays, *Seven Guitars* (1995) and *Two Trains Running* (1991). In the former, Floyd Barton, a rising blues singer, scrounges enough cash to get his guitar out of pawn and for a fifteen-hour Greyhound ride to Chicago, where an appointment with Savoy Records awaits. Equally desperate are Sterling Johnson's gambling and shady dealings in his first weeks out of the penitentiary in *Two Trains Running*, in which he seeks not only a job driving a Cadillac but also the love of diner cook and waitress Risa Thomas. As a foil to Sterling, Memphis Lee, the diner owner, values ownership over profits. After buying his cafe from L. D., because of its intrinsic worth, Memphis spurned West's offer to purchase it at an increase of twenty-five hundred dollars. Memphis exults, "It had come to mean more to me than that. I had found a way to live the rest of my life" (p. 9).

Wilson incorporates achievement in family situations in which members struggle for recognition from their relatives, who are unwitting role models for youth. A tragic example is Booster Becker's need of forgiveness and reclamation by his father in *Jitney*. The hostile reunion of the father with his ex-con son after Booster serves twenty years in the penitentiary for murder comes only a day before Jim Becker is killed in a mill accident. Ironically, Booster is left the heir to an unforgiving father, an ambiguous accomplishment for a man seeking acceptance from his only living family member. In *Fences* (1985), both Lyons and Cory Maxson long for acknowledgement from their father Troy, a failed baseball player who refuses to compliment Lyons's musical ability or Cory's superiority at football. After the father destroys Cory's chance at a college scholarship, the boy accuses him of being "scared I'm gonna be better than you" (p. 58). Nonetheless, Cory practices batting the next morning by mimicking his father's swing, the model that influences his life and ambitions.

A bitter struggle for self-actualization marks a succession of males in the Charles family in *The Piano Lesson* (1990). As the land-based seeker, Boy Willie needs the validation that acreage can bring to his life of toil on Mississippi farms. To boost his self-esteem, he requires property to free him of the racist Jim Crow atmosphere in the South that extends elements of pre–Civil War bondage and disenfranchisement of blacks into the 1930s. Lacking the will or ability to adapt to Pittsburgh's urbanism, he comes north briefly to earn quick money to purchase one hundred acres of the old Sutter plantation. His choice of agriculture as a career elevates him above the enslavement of his great grandfather Willie Boy and his own father, Boy Charles, who sharecropped for Jim Stovall. After grappling with the phantom of Robert Sutter in Doaker's flat, Boy Willie leaves satisfied that he has avenged his clan from the debasement of slavery. His journey south reverses the slave's flight north and sends Boy Willie home to his Mississippi roots.

See also **black athletes, black identity, Avery Brown, Sylvester Brown, opportunity, powerlessness**

- *Further Reading*

Charters, Ann, and Samuel Charters, ed. *Short Pieces from the New Dramatists.* Banbury, Ox.: Orangeberry Books, 1985.
McDonough, Carla J. *Staging Masculinity: Male Identity in Contemporary American Drama.* Jefferson, N.C.: McFarland, 1997.
McKelly, James C. "Hymns of Sedition: Portraits of the Artist in Contemporary African-American Drama." *Arizona Quarterly*, Vol. 48, No. 1, Spring 1992, pp. 87–107.

adaptation

Wilson recognizes that the uneasy separation between Euro-Americans and African Americans derives strictly from skin color and an African heritage. The gap between blacks and white-skinned Germans, Irish, Italians, and Poles defeats the melting pot image. Whites realize that blacks obviously come from different genes, religion, and ethnicity and from a unique world view. Without a shared cultural sensibility, Wilson stated on Swiss television, blacks "can't melt in the pot" (Wang, p. 17).

Despite the devaluation of blacks for the obvious difference in pigmentation and origin, Wilson stresses in his plays the importance of letting go of acrimony toward racism and injustice in the past. His stronger characters— Berniece Charles and her brother Boy Willie Charles, scions of slave woodcarver Willie Boy in *The Piano Lesson* (1990), the conjurer Bynum Walker in *Joe Turner's Come and Gone* (1988), and Risa Thomas, the waitress in *Two Trains Running* (1991) who flees lustful men at age twelve — survive and prevail by adapting to their economic and social environment and by making the most of the economic and cultural opportunities at hand. Less acclimated are characters like Levee Green, who bears the burden of his mother's rape by white men in *Ma Rainey's Black Bottom* (1985); Jeremy Furlow, the bewildered newcomer from South Carolina who is jailed on payday in *Joe Turner's Come and Gone;* and Citizen Barlow, whose theft of a bucket of nails triggers a man's suicide in *Gem of the Ocean* (2003).

More seriously injured by the inability to adapt is the Haitian peddler King Hedley, the machete-wielding poultry slayer in *Seven Guitars* (1995), who mutters apocalyptic warnings and predicts the rise of Ethiopia. His inchoate rage results in two murders, both black males. Symbolically, his machete passes to the title character in *King Hedley II* (1999), an ex-con who believes the elder Hedley is his father. Although there is no blood tie between the men, the pattern of violence and lack of adaptability involves Hedley II in blood-rage, theft, and murder and precipitates his tragic downfall.

See also **Great Migration, opportunity, soul food**

• *Further Reading*

"The Public Stages an Emotionally Explosive 'Seven Guitars.'" *Pittsburgh Post-Gazette,*
        June 14, 1997.
Wang, Qun. *An In-Depth Study of the Major Plays of African American Playwright August
        Wilson: Vernacularizing the Blues on Stage.* Vol. 6 of *Black Studies.* Lewiston, Ont.:
        Edwin Mellen Press, 1999.

African American theater

Initiated from black storytelling, ring chant, pulpit call-and-response, and plantation juba dances, African American theater first developed sophistication through traveling minstrel shows, which survived by actors and viewers passing the hat for donations. The transformation of oral culture to written plays began in the early twentieth century, when blacks first realized the value of written lore as a source of history and strength for a struggling race. Following the theatrical budding of the Harlem Renaissance in the 1920s, black stage presentations burst into full flower with the explosive works of Amiri Baraka and other angry young playwrights of the 1960s, who fought blatant racism in American society. Audiences began sampling black drama for its ties to ancient Africa, its culture, and its issues.

Chief among professional concerns for a lasting theatrical effort was the fact that black people did not support their own dramas enough, either with financial contributions or their presence in the audience. The climate of support for black drama improved after Lorraine Hansberry's Pulitzer Prize for *A Raisin in the Sun* (1958). A decade later, Lonne Elder achieved the first Pulitzer Prize nomination to a black author for *Ceremonies in Dark Old Men* (1968). A new era of acceptance saw the recognition of Charles Gordone, the first black Pulitzer winner for *No Place to Be Somebody* (1970), seven Tonys for the all-black cast of William F. Brown and Charlie Smalls's musical *The Wiz* (1975), and Charles Fuller's Pulitzer for *A Soldier's Play* (1982).

The ensuing success of August Wilson's stage works helped to establish a link in American minds between black lore and meaty, enjoyable stage plays. In 1997, he noted that younger people had turned away from theater: "The hip-hop generation has carved out their own thing; if they saw where the theater could be a viable means of expression then I think more people would get involved [in drama]" ("August Wilson: A Maverick"). He declared that the role of the theater is not to engineer political change but "to make sure the story is told. Write about the history, and the truth will be clear" (Goodale). In his opinion, black Americans deserve their own theater to reflect their otherness from the prevailing white society. Regina Taylor recorded in an article for *American Theatre* Wilson's statement of racial difference: "The fact is, we act differently, we think differently, we face the world differently — and it is our difference that makes us unique. We must embrace our culture or we will lose ourselves and disappear" (Taylor, p. 20).

To keep his race from vanishing into a predominantly European melting pot culture, August Wilson promotes his decade cycle as an element of African American dramatic property, a lasting monument to the struggle for full citizenship and self-worth. His optimism about the evolution of black theater remains high that experience in acting, design, stage technology, and management will push African American efforts to new levels of attainment. As he explained to interviewer Michael J. Bandler, "It's one of the best times. We're coming into our own. There are more black theaters in the country, more playwrights than ever before.... We just need more money. We certainly have the artists" (Bandler).

See also **cultural nationalism, decade cycle, historical milieu**

- *Further Reading*

Ambush, Benny Sato. "Culture Wars." *African American Review*, Vol. 31, No. 4, Winter 1997, pp. 579–586.

"August Wilson: A Maverick Playwright with Unadulterated Wisdom." *New York Amsterdam News*, May 17, 1997.

Bandler, Michael J. "USIA Interview with American Playwright August Wilson." http://usembassy-australia.state.gov/hyper/WF980415/epf308.htm, April 15, 1998.

Goodale, Gloria. "Playwright August Wilson on Race Relations and the Theater." *Christian Science Monitor*, May 15, 1998.

Lowry, Mark. "Still Tasty after All These Years: The 'Chitlin Circuit,' Born in the Era of Segregation, Continues to Tap into African-Americans' Need for a Theater of Their Own." *Fort Worth Star-Telegram*, June 29, 2003, p. 1.

Pressley, Nelson. "D.C. Theater's Uncast Role, Lack of African American Troupe Leaves Nagging Question: Why?" *Washington Post*, October 3, 1999, p. G1.

Renner, Pamela. "Black Theaters in a Fight for Survival." *Variety*, July 10, 2000, p. 35.

Shannon, Sandra G. "Conversing with the Past: *Joe Turner's Come and Gone* and *The Piano Lesson*." *CEA Magazine*, Vol. 4, No. 1, 1991, pp. 33–42.

Taylor, Regina. "That's Why They Call It the Blues." *American Theatre*, Vol. 13, No. 4, April 1996, pp. 18–23.

Baldwin, James

Like blues singers Ma Rainey and Bessie Smith and artist Romare Bearden, eminent black novelist James Baldwin generated a lasting influence on the philosophy of August Wilson. In a eulogy at Baldwin's funeral, Amiri Baraka stated that the novelist "reported, criticized, made beautiful, analyzed, cajoled, lyricized, attacked, sang, made us think, made us better, made us consciously human" (Appiah & Gates, p. 169). Robert Brustein, drama critic for *New Republic*, proclaimed Baldwin's vision as revealed in the essay "Everybody's Protest Novel" (1949). Baldwin urged, "Let us say that truth is meant to imply a devotion to the human being.... It is not to be confused with a devotion to a Cause; and Causes, as we know, are notoriously bloodthirsty" (Brustein, p. 31). The critic exalted Baldwin's philosophy for its devotion to humanity and individual motivation.

Wilson admires Baldwin for establishing parameters by which blacks can articulate the black tradition, particularly the striving for black manhood. Emulating Baldwin's gift for "spirit and texture and substance and grace and elegance," Wilson initiated his own version of black traditions (Wilson, p. 2036). His decade cycle recreates elements of black survival — hope for the younger generation in *The Janitor* (1985), an unincorporated gypsy cab business in *Jitney* (1982), a juba dance in *Joe Turner's Come and Gone* (1988), group singing in *The Piano Lesson* (1990), community mourning in *Two Trains Running* (1991), a lesson in the jump back that dancer Red Carter teaches Vera Dotson in *Seven Guitars* (1995), funeral ritual in *Fences* (1985), respect for religion in *Ma Rainey's Black Bottom* (1985), prophecy and ritual in *King Hedley II* (1999), and griot-style storytelling in *Gem of the Ocean* (2003). By following Baldwin's example, Wilson earned a reputation for professional integrity and historical authenticity.

• *Further Reading*

Appiah, Kwame Anthony, and Henry Louis Gates, Jr., eds. *Africana*. New York: Perseus Books, 1999.

Brustein, Robert. "On Cultural Power." *New Republic*, Vol. 216, No. 9, March 3, 1997, pp. 31–34.

Weisenburger, Steven. "The Shudder and the Silence: James Baldwin on White Terror." *ANQ*, Vol. 15, No. 3, Summer 2002, pp. 3–13.

Wilson, August. "Where to Begin," in *Short Pieces from the New Dramatists*. Banbury, Ox.: Orangeberry Books, 1985, pp. 2033–2037.

Barlow, Citizen

The seeker and confessor in *Gem of the Ocean* (2003), Citizen Barlow, like Boy Willie Charles in *The Piano Lesson* (1990), is the black everyman who journeys from Alabama to Pittsburgh. He bears an unusual Christian name, a gift from his slave mother to a son born free. The story takes place in 1904 in the first decade of Wilson's ten-decade drama cycle, when Southern blacks lived an indentured servitude that was little changed from the plantation era. Of Barlow's confusion, the playwright commented, "What does freedom mean? There were no maps. You had to make it up as you went along" (Reynolds, p. E1). The only way for the ambitious to obtain full citizenship was to flee the powerful white oligarchy and migrate north.

Like others completing the grueling migration north, the young drifter arrives in need of shoes, a symbol of poverty and rootlessness that permeates such classic works as Harriet Beecher Stowe's *Uncle Tom's Cabin* (1852), William H. Armstrong's *Sounder* (1969), and Toni Morrison's *Beloved* (1987). At Aunt Ester's home, he breaks in through a bedroom window rather than wait for her standard audience on Tuesday. He encounters the cynicism of Solly Two Kings and the suspicions of Eli and Black Mary, the major-domo and housekeeper. Ester compares Barlow to a junebug and offers him room and board and a job. To Barlow's dismay, constable Caesar, an obsessive and callous black lawman, stalks Solly Two Kings and Barlow to hold them accountable to the white man's law. The irony of a black oppressor contributes to the despair of blacks who already feel outnumbered by the white majority.

Barlow's intent is to work in a factory, a milieu of the technological world at odds with the Afro-American's rural heritage of farming and herding. After his theft of a bucket of nails results in a tinworker's drowning to avoid false arrest, Barlow insists on an audience to confess his sin of black-against-black violence to Aunt Ester, the long-lived sage who guides him through soul-cleansing. Of the importance of misery in the African American past, Wilson remarked that people like Ester living in early 1900s had direct ties to slavery and its insidious destruction of lives. The penitent's disburdening to her parallels the stories of other confessors in Wilson's plays, including the wanderer Herald Loomis in *Joe Turner's Come and Gone* (1988), the man-destroyer Ruby in *Seven Guitars* (1995) and *King Hedley II* (1999), the adulterer Troy Maxson in *Fences* (1985), and the alcoholic Fielding in *Jitney* (1982). Through talk therapy, the characters purify themselves of past errors in judgment.

In the familiar style of a Wilson play, Barlow acquires serenity and joy through dynamic words. Solly prepares him for the psyche-washing with a stiff drink. As mother confessor, Ester invites him to the parlor and frees him from ignorance of self and race by creating a mesmerizing vision of the Middle Passage from Africa. Her purpose is to assure him that history impinges on his life on the conscious and subconscious levels. His passport to African American roots is her bill of sale into slavery, which she creases into a paper boat called the "Gem of the Ocean," part of the title of a patriotic song that David T. Shaw wrote in 1843. By conveying Barlow to an imaginary undersea kingdom of bones, she enables him to repent and achieve redemption and to discover his relationship to other blacks.

• *Further Reading*

Reynolds, Christopher. "Mr. Wilson's Neighborhood: Playwright August Wilson No Longer Lives in Pittsburgh's Hill District, but It Is Consistently at Home in His Work." *Los Angeles Times*, July 27, 2002, p. E1.

Shirley, Don. "Queen of the Hill: August Wilson's Potent but Ungainly 'Gem of the Ocean' Opens at the Taper." *Los Angeles Times*, August 1, 2003, p. E1.

Weiss, Hedy. "'Ocean' Voyage Proves Rough But Rewarding." *Chicago Sun-Times*, April 29, 2003, p. 34.

Barton, Floyd

Engaging, dynamic blues guitarist and composer Floyd "Schoolboy" Barton suits Wilson's focus on stunted lives and unfulfilled promise. Floyd's funeral in May 1948 is the setting of *Seven Guitars* (1995). Neither hero nor villain, like Levee Green in *Ma Rainey's Black Bottom* (1985), he is the self-destructive narcissist, who deems himself above rules, laws, time limits, even the holy injunctions laid down in scripture. His demise is a brutal and incomprehensible death from a friend's hand. Wilson deliberately avoids a pat conclusion and leaves the reader/viewer to interpret the forces that doom Floyd.

Survivors resurrect a host of memories to sift for clues to Floyd's behaviors and faults. After recording a blues hit, "That's All Right," a song suited to the narcissist's self-exoneration, at age thirty-five, Floyd reaches an impasse when his career stalls because of the control of self-seeking white owners of the recording industry. Lacking sophistication in business matters, he fails to demand royalties rather than a cash settlement, a blunder he shares with Ma Rainey. His song echoes through the opening scenes of the play as his spirit asserts its presence in his friends' lives and influences their conversation and camaraderie. The evergreen melody and lyrics symbolize the historic power of all blues artists, whose words and rhythms infuse succeeding generations with self-knowledge and humanism.

On Floyd's return to Vera Dotson, the woman he wronged, the first flashback pictures him as jumpy and grudge-laden after ninety days in the workhouse. His smooth lover-boy approach to apology prefaces a slow, pelvis-grinding dance, which does little to appease Vera. When she learns the jump back from Red Carter at the end of the Joe Louis–Billy Conn boxing match, the intense lesson angers Floyd, whose flashy good-timing quickly gives way to a lethal temper. Possessive and quick to threaten, he grabs his woman, pulls a .38, and hints at leaving Red D.O.A. (dead on arrival). The test of Floyd's loyalty follows quickly the next morning, when he deserts Vera to squire Ruby about central Pittsburgh and buy her a beer. Louise, the landlady, pegs his character as "the kind of man can do the right thing for a little while. But then that little while run out" (p. 72).

Like Boy Willie in *The Piano Lesson* (1990) and Hop and the title character in *King Hedley II* (1999), Floyd craves a lasting achievement. His mercurial moods hinge on a need to succeed in music. He extols music as the power in his spirit: "It just grab hold of you and hang on" (p. 45). In Act II, Scene 3, time constraints and frustrations accrue in him as he tries to line up guitar and drums for a Mother's Day gig at the Blue Goose. Gnawing at his pride is the impersonal gravesite of his mother, Maude Avery Floyd, and his obligation to pay for a tombstone etched with a pair of roses. The mounting distress causes him to shift blame to Canewell for abandoning the recording session in Chicago the previous year. Floyd vows to live "with" rather than "without" and adds, with considerable self-pity, "It a cold world, let me have a little shelter from it" (p. 82).

Wilson loads his tragic drama with loss. When Floyd aimed his migration north from Pittsburgh to Chicago to establish a music career, he suffered a spiral of defeats. He was returning from his mother's funeral when police arrested him for "worthlessness" (vagrancy), a charge that targeted the homeless and poor and victimized them for having no money or employment (p. 9). They beat him with rubber hoses. During a ninety-day sentence, he worked at the rate of thirty cents a day for a total of twenty-seven dollars, which a clerk denies him because he lacks documentation of his earnings, a situation that Wilson repeats with the lack of a telephone number on a receipt in *King Hedley II*. Like a petulant child, Floyd quibbles, "Paper or no paper, they gonna give me my money" (p. 33). Devoid of hope, he denounces God for being distant and uninvolved in black lives.

In better times, Floyd scored a hit with his first record in August 1947. He depends upon his guitar as a source of esteem. At the crux of *Seven Guitars* is his need for cash to get his guitar out of hock and for a ticket on the Greyhound to Chicago. Destitute and shamed by his mother's burial in the pauper's section of the Greenwood cemetery, Floyd confers with King Hedley, who envisions Floyd's rise to the savior of his people. As though acknowledging a messiah, Hedley bestows on him the honor owed to a king.

Floyd bears the burden of all talented people of allying skill and energies with his peak years, a theme that Wilson depicts as a universal among mortals. Driven to validate a career by making his unique mark on American music, Floyd complains, "Time done got short and it getting shorter every day" (p. 41). As though echoing his struggle, Don Dunphy, the radio announcer, introduces a fight in which Joe Louis defends his world heavyweight boxing title against white Pittsburgh native Billy Conn, a match-up that occurred twice, in 1941 and again in 1946. The next morning, after a frustrating round with a pawnbroker, Floyd voices a hard edge to his ambitions by warning, "I ain't going along but so far" (p. 69). Near desperation, he admits he would take assistance from anybody — Buddy Bolden, High John the Conquerer, Yellow Jack, Br'er Rabbit, or Uncle Ben (p. 70).

Fate offers Floyd his heart's desire — a revival of his career with a gig at the Blue Goose for a Mother's Day dance, an appointment to complete the Chicago recording session on June 10 at 10:00 A.M., and half the money of his next record advanced by his agent, T. L. Hall, a con artist who sells fake insurance. With heavy irony, the playwright places in Floyd's speech a criticism of Hedley's foolhardiness in refusing treatment at the TB sanitarium. As though describing himself, Floyd states that Hedley must decide his own fate and asserts, "Let him find out the error of his ways" (p. 77).

In the play's denouement, tension heightens as Wilson unfolds the last days of Floyd Barton's life in explanation of the funeral that opens Act I. His quiet resolve masks latent outrage and a potential for violence because of poverty and multiple threats to his career. Shoving obstacles out of his way, near the end of his life, he pawns an electric guitar, the source of his income. He proposes to Vera and accepts her hesitation with the title of his hit song, "That's all right" (p. 93). Maddened with frustration and armed with a .38, he robs a finance company in partnership with Williard Ray "Poochie" Tillery, whom a policeman kills with two shots in the back. Floyd completes his gig at the Blue Goose and, flushed with success, is retrieving the buried twelve hundred dollars he stole to make his way north to Chicago. A late-night scuffle with the delusional Hedley ends Floyd's sadly misspent life. Like the neighbor's crowing rooster, he dies a bestial death. The upshot of his murder remains unexplained until Stool Pigeon reports on it in 1985 in *King Hedley II*.

See also **achievement**

• *Further Reading*

Kroll, Jack. "Seven Guitars." *Newsweek*, Vol. 125, No. 6, February 6, 1995, p. 60.
Lahr, John. "Black and Blues: *Seven Guitars*, a New Chapter in August Wilson's Ten-Play Cycle." *New Yorker*, April 15, 1996, p. 100.

Bearden, Romare

Given to seeking father figures, August Wilson revered boxer Charley Burley and claimed as mentors Yale drama school artistic director Lloyd Richards, American novelist James Baldwin, Argentine fantasist Jorge Luis Borges, and folk artist Romare Bearden (1912–1988). The painter, a North Carolina native, spent summers with his grandmother in Pittsburgh. From an ethnic background similar to Wilson's, Bearden, a participant in the Great Migration to the urban North, grew up in Harlem. After service with the 372d Infantry Regiment during World War I, he studied cubism and made friends with Georges Braques and Pablo Picasso. During the Harlem Renaissance, Bearden evolved a unique style from a variety of influences and earned his living by writing songs and producing commercial cover art for the magazine industry.

When the playwright first saw Bearden's oil paintings and collages, he recognized a rich, honest portrayal of everyday black life that ennobled the poor and validated the intent of the Harlem Renaissance. In "Where to Begin?" (1991), Wilson proclaims his connection with Beard's work as "a moment of privilege and exaltation that comes from recognizing yourself as a vital part of a much larger world than you had imagined" (Wilson, "Where," p. 2036). The playwright once approached the artist's door, but lacked the courage to knock. From a study of the immediacy and freshness in Bearden's art and the strands of African ritual that invests the subtexts, Wilson resolved to produce the same earthy realism in his stage plays. He drew on Bearden's imagery and style for *Joe Turner's Come and Gone* (1988), completed the year of the artist's death, and for *The Piano Lesson* (1990), which bears the same title as one of Bearden's paintings.

Essential to the success of Wilson's approach is the layering of collage, a multidimensional art produced from found objects available from the street corners and front-porch conversations that the playwright absorbed from childhood. Using a nondirective method, as he explained in his essay "How to Write Play like August Wilson," he allows his characters to speak their minds and, like a viewer in the front row, awaits the dramatic outcome. As happens in collage, the verbal images allow for distortion by pairing normal speakers with the obsessed and crazed. Characters like Aunt Ester, Bynum Walker, Stool Pigeon, and King Hedley loom out of proportion as their words reverberate among commonplace exchanges. The descant of Wilson's prophets and wise fools discloses the African foundations of black America.

• *Further Reading*

Kelly, Jack. "The Genius of Romare Bearden." *American Legacy: Celebrating African-American History & Culture*, Vol. 7, No. 1, Spring 2001, pp. 66–73.
Wilson, August. "How to Write a Play Like August Wilson." *New York Times*, March 10, 1991.
_____. "Where to Begin," in *Short Pieces from the New Dramatists*. Banbury, Ox.: Orangeberry Books, 1985, pp. 2033–2037.

Becker, Booster

The thirty-nine-year-old ex-con and only child of Coreen and Jim Becker in *Jitney* (1982), Clarence "Booster" Becker is the prodigal son who came to manhood in a jail cell. He is returning from twenty years at the Western State Penitentiary for murdering Susan McKnight, the eighteen-year-old daughter of a wealthy white vice president of Gulf Oil. In boyhood, Booster developed a close relationship with his father while fishing and hunting to the south of Pittsburgh outside Wheeling, West Virginia. A three-time prize-winner at the Buhel [*sic*] Planetarium Science Fair, Booster was set for advanced study on scholarship at the University of Pittsburgh when he ruined his life by beating up McKnight and shooting his daughter for falsely accusing him of rape. After Booster's sentence to the electric chair, he received a commutation, but refused parole at the end of fifteen years because he didn't want to be in debt to the state. The gesture suggests the principles he learned from his father, who lives by a set of inflexible ideals.

The former hero-worshiper of Becker, Booster stands up to his father's charge that "You got a mark on you a foot wide," an accusation that resounds with biblical authority for its suggestion of God's mark on Cain, the bible's first murderer (p. 54). Booster rebuts his father's assertion that the crime and death sentence precipitated Coreen's decline and death. Against his father's railing, Booster tries to explain why he ventured out on his own and refused to be belittled as a rapist of a white girl, the traditional crime for which blacks, whether guilty or innocent, often gave their lives. He expects his father to admire him "for being a warrior. For dealing with the world in ways that [Becker] didn't or couldn't or wouldn't" (p. 57). Their stand-off illustrates the generation gap, a term that came into use during the 1970s to describe a shift in attitudes and morals in the young.

Wilson uses the contretemps as a model of human faults set against the march of time. In retrospect, Booster recalls that his father's rigid ethics kept him from attending the trial with Coreen and from supporting her during an emotional battering by incriminating testimony and condemnation to the electric chair. To Fielding, one of his father's cabbies, Booster rationalizes that "Becker's rules is what got me in the penitentiary" (p. 82). Unfortunately for both father and son, he doesn't breach his father's wall of anger. When Booster learns of his father's accidental death at the mill, his first response is to punch Doub, the bearer of bad news. After the funeral, Booster honors his father's sense of responsibility to family and moves into Becker's old job. Wilson exalts Booster as a flawed, but principled descendent inheriting a flawed world from parents he doesn't understand.

- *Further Reading*

Green, Judith. "Despite Bumps, 'Jitney' a Pleasure Ride." *Atlanta Journal-Constitution*, October 15, 1999, p. R4.

Becker, Coreen

The first wife of Jim Becker and mother of Booster in *Jitney* (1982), Coreen is one of August Wilson's model wives on a par with Mama Ola Charles in *The Piano Lesson* (1990), Maude Avery Barton in *Seven Guitars* (1995), Tonya Hedley in *King Hedley II* (1999), and Aunt Ester, the slave mother in *Gem of the Ocean* (2003). The playwright portrays Coreen as limited by poor health to one child lest she die trying to bear a second. Although weak in body, on a snowy day, she stood by her family at the front door while the landlord, Mr. Rand, swore, threatened, and shouted insults because the Beckers owed him rent. She tried to protect her son by calling him indoors out of earshot. Her instinct was correct that the face-off between father and landlord devastated the young Booster, who lost his idealization of his father.

The playwright characterizes Coreen as a mother who supports her child, just as Berniece Charles refines Maretha in *The Piano Lesson* and Rose Maxson champions sons Lyons and Cory and embraces Raynell in *Fences* (1985). During Booster's trial for rape, Coreen attended court sessions alone. In a bitter reliving of the last time he saw his mother alive, Booster challenges his father, "Anybody could see it was wearing her down.... Where was you" (p. 59)? Coreen fainted in the courtroom when the judge sentenced Booster to the electric chair. In grief, she retreated to bed and refused food for twenty-three days rather than see her son executed at the end of thirty days. She died murmuring his name. In anger at her loss, Becker retorts to Booster, "I was there! Where were you Mr. Murderer? Mr. Unfit to Live Amongst Society" (p. 60).

Wilson uses Coreen's demise as an example of a favorite theme, the constraints of time on human life. Ironically, Booster gained a commutation shortly after her death and was allowed to attend her funeral. In retaliation against his son's crime against family and society, Becker holds so firm a grudge that he shuts Booster from his life and gives up on God for taking Coreen. Because of Becker's unforeseen death in a mill accident, Booster is left parentless with the sour taste of guilt for causing

Coreen's death. Like other of the playwright's survivors, he faces a difficult acclimation to place and time.

See also women

Becker, Jim

The paternal, perennially sad manager of a shabby Pittsburgh cab stand in *Jitney* (1982), Jim Becker, in his sixties, conceals the corrosion around his damaged heart. He has driven cabs for eighteen years and is proud to offer car service to the Hill District. He also takes pride in being a homeowner, husband of second wife Lucille Becker for nearly seventeen years, pensioner of J & L Steel, and church deacon. When Grandma Ada died, he paid for her funeral. He treats his employees kindly and encourages their conversations, ambitions, and checker games. He sticks to business, keeps new tires on his cab, and settles money squabbles. Of his personality, old friend Sala Udin claims that August Wilson modeled the character after him.

On the interpersonal level, Becker embodies the playwright's vision of stalwart urban humanism. He declares his respect for right and truth. To flaws in other people, he takes a live-and-let-live approach. He avoids Turnbo's gossip and advises Youngblood to keep his woman troubles to himself. Becker is lenient with Fielding, an alcoholic, and agrees to help Shealy's troubled nephew Robert get a job at the mill. Unlike the meddling Turnbo, Becker characterizes the Christian virtue of turning the other cheek by choosing to think no evil of others. To stave off violence, he offers Youngblood friendly advice: "You can't go around hitting everybody that don't see eye to eye with you" (p. 46). Pushed to more stringent action, Becker refuses to "put nobody out unless they totally irresponsible" (p. 37).

At the height of Pittsburgh's urban renewal, Becker represents the little man swimming against the tide of history. To keep the cab stand functioning smoothly, he posts five simple rules on a blackboard. He tries to keep the business profitable and deals in person with the Pittsburgh Renewal Council, but feels powerless to rescue his operation, which a highway project threatens to engulf in two weeks. In a private quarrel with God, he abandons his dependence on the almighty for aid. The loss of faith is typical of characters in August Wilson's plays in which a running subtext implies that God shirks his duty toward suffering blacks.

At Becker's low point, the playwright exalts him to an on-the-spot hero. At a powwow with his fellow cabbies, Becker makes a stand that ennobles the American working man: "We already here ... and I don't see no reason to move. City or no city" (p. 85). He chooses to remain open until the bulldozers come and to join Clifford and Hester in hiring a lawyer to press a class-action suit. Becker exults, "Ain't gonna be no boarding up around here! ... We gonna fight them on that" (p. 85). In the meantime, he rallies the men to improve the quality of service with cleaner, safer cabs. Because he fights back against the faceless villainy of the Pittsburgh Renewal Council, he earns the respect of the Hill District.

Even as he arises as a civic hero, Becker's domestic stance weakens because of his stubborn pride. He maintains a tense father-son relationship with his son Booster, who lost personal dignity and sullied his father's reputation in the neighborhood.

After Booster's arrest, Becker bailed him out of jail and hired a lawyer to defend him against Susan McKnight's phony rape charge. Parental animosity results from Booster's murder of Susan, a crime that contributed to Coreen Becker's death a month after Booster landed on death row at the Western State Penitentiary. Becker charges, "You killed her! You know that? You a double murderer" (p. 59). Disappointed that his son isn't "Daniel in the lion's den," Becker retaliates by refusing to talk with him and by spurning him as "just another nigger on the street" (pp. 59, 60). Becker remains so closed-mouthed on the issue that Youngblood isn't aware that his employer has a son.

Becker's enemy is time, the thief of opportunity to renew an acquaintance with his son and settle their differences. After Booster completes a twenty-year sentence, Becker asserts his long-standing grudge and walks out on his boy in mid-sentence. Significantly, Becker also leaves unsaid the last comment he intended for Doub. Following Becker's death in a freak mill accident after a brief return to work, his men honor him with good memories of his management and friendship. With the unforeseen conclusion to his play, Wilson portrays a domestic tragedy that will weigh on Booster. Becker's death emphasizes Wilson's pervasive theme of constant change and also implies that modern technology is an undependable source of succor for the laboring class.

See also **death**

• *Further Reading*

Green, Judith. "Despite Bumps, 'Jitney' a Pleasure Ride." *Atlanta Journal-Constitution,* October 15, 1999, p. R4.
Reynolds, Christopher. "Mr. Wilson's Neighborhood: Playwright August Wilson No Longer Lives in Pittsburgh's Hill District, but It Is Consistently at Home in His Work." *Los Angeles Times,* July 27, 2002, p. E1.

betrayal

August Wilson emphasizes betrayal as a constant of African American experience. More devastating to characters than white racism is the black-on-black treachery that sets African Americans against their own kind. In his drama cycle, human relationships go wrong, often to the point of abandonment, assault, and murder, as with King Hedley's surprising slaughter of Floyd Barton with a machete in *Seven Guitars* (1995) and Neesi's turning state's evidence against her husband in *King Hedley II* (1999). To set the tone of Levee Green's climb above his fellow musicians in *Ma Rainey's Black Bottom* (1985), Wilson speaks of "thirty pieces of silver," the amount Judas earned for betraying Christ (p. xv). The heightened tension in *Two Trains Running* (1991) derives from the trickery of Lutz in paying the retarded handyman Hambone for painting a fence. Parallel to Hambone's demand for his ham are the erratic outbursts of Sterling Johnson, who is armed while he searches for Wolf, the numbers runner, to demand a full return on a winning bet. In *Seven Guitars*, Floyd suffers a comeuppance from Vera for two-timing her with Pearl Brown. In *Gem of the Ocean* (2003), constable Caesar elevates himself to a position of authority by dogging the trail of black felons like Citizen Barlow and Solly Two Kings and earns for himself a soul-shattering isolation from blacks and whites.

Wilson creates his more damning scenarios within families, e.g., Booster Becker's betrayal of his father's principles by committing a revenge murder in *Jitney* (1982) and Ruby's abandonment of her infant son to her aunt Louise in *King Hedley II*. In *The Piano Lesson* (1990), Berniece Charles threatens her brother Boy Willie for involving her husband Crawley in the theft of firewood and leaving him to die in a shootout with law officers. Wilson heats up the inter-familial exchanges in *Fences* (1985) with multiple examples of Troy Maxson's betrayal of his wife and sons. In Troy's concept of marriage, so long as he turns over his pay each Friday night and sleeps at home with his wife, he has fulfilled his commitment as husband, father, and head of household. At a time when his son Cory has the backing of Stawicki, a white football coach; Zellman, manager of the A & P; and a white recruiter from a North Carolina college, it is the father himself who betrays his own. Troy goes behind Cory's back to destroy his chances of playing high school football or of signing with a college sports team. In his free time, Troy frequents the home of Alberta, with whom he can laugh and forget the demands of adulthood. At the play's climax in Act II, Scene 2, Rose halts him at the end of six months of open adultery and confronts him for treachery.

Troy's betrayal is more corrosive to his marriage than he realizes, even though his friend Jim Bono has warned him of the danger. Rose, who is at the breaking point of tolerating a wayward husband, describes his daily visits to Alberta and challenges, "You wanna call that the best you can do" (p. 74)? Not only has he destroyed his son's athletic future and established a lasting loyalty to Alberta and her unborn child, Troy has also signed away his brother Gabe's freedom by committing him to a state hospital in exchange for half his government check. The shambles that remains of the Maxson marriage results in a lengthy stay in purgatory for Troy. After he digests the news that Alberta has died giving birth to a baby girl, Rose reminds him of his marital duty: "I am your wife. Don't push me away" (p. 77). Living loveless and alone, in his last years, Troy obtains little joy from his promotion to driver and, with his back toward his home, dies with bat in hand, as though substituting physical presence for emotional intimacy with his loved ones.

See also **Rena**

• *Further Reading*

Hitchcock, Laura. "King Hedley II." *CurtainUp*, 2000.
Wang, Qun. *An In-Depth Study of the Major Plays of African American Playwright August Wilson: Vernacularizing the Blues on Stage.* Vol. 6 of *Black Studies.* Lewiston, Ont.: Edwin Mellen Press, 1999.

black athletes

Reference to black athletes takes on an iconic significance to black males, who use hero worship as a vicarious taste of success. In *King Hedley II* (1999), Wilson decorates the setting with a faded advertisement for Alaga Syrup picturing Willie

Mays. As the playwright explained, baseball was integral to black neighborhoods: "There you had a league that was self-sufficient, and you had a community of people culturally self-sufficient, and on Sundays they would pay their three dollars, sit in the bleachers and support this league" (Saltzman & Plett). From ghetto spirit came a modicum of prosperity: "Mr. Samuels sold his peanuts, and Mr. Johnson sold his chicken sandwiches, and that gave them income. You had a whole thing going" (*Ibid.*).

More athletic heroes develop as Wilson's plays depict each decade. As demonstrated in *Fences* (1985), a play set up in nine segments like the innings of a baseball game, recognition of black baseball athletes did not occur until the acceptance of Jackie Robinson in the major leagues in the 1950s. The absence of a black model left strivers like James "Cool Papa" Bell, Josh Gibson, Walter "Buck" Leonard, and the fictional Troy Maxson without a path to follow to greatness in their chosen sport. To spare his teenage son Cory the same disappointment, the father spells out inequities that could force the boy some day to haul garbage. Troy commands, "You go on and get your book-learning so you can work yourself up in that A & P or learn how to fix cars or build houses or something, get you a trade" (p. 35). The advice shoves Troy's early yearning under the pile of pragmatic choices for a life's work.

In *Seven Guitars* (1995), set in spring 1948, Floyd announces that there is a Joe Louis match against Billy Conn, which takes place that night at Madison Square Garden. Hedley exults, "The Brown Bomber! Yes! The Mighty Mighty Black Man!" (p. 30). Both men and women rejoice at Louis's victory by laughing and dancing. Puzzling to them is the fact that a black man can TKO a white in the boxing ring, but would go to jail for doing the same thing in private life.

Within a quarter century, the number of black athletes burgeoned as blacks began claiming civil rights and abandoning the dwindling black league to join white teams. In the opening scene of *Jitney* (1982), Youngblood compares his checker-playing to the skills of boxer Muhammad Ali, the hero of the 1970s. Imitating Ali's mouthy self-promotion, Youngblood boasts, "Can't nobody beat me … I'm the greatest" (p. 12)! Shealy follows the pattern of comparing black accomplishments to those of black athletes by congratulating Youngblood for buying a house where some of the Pittsburgh Steelers live. The compliment links a budding family man with the ambitious black athletes who make their name in sports.

See also **Jackie Robinson**

- *Further Reading*

Birdwell, Christine. "Death as a Fastball on the Outside Corner: *Fences*' Troy Maxson and the American Dream." *Aethlon: The Journal of Sport Literature*, No. 1, Fall 1990, pp. 87–96.

Brock, Wendell. "Q&A: August Wilson, Pulitzer Prize-winning Playwright: Wilson Sees 'Light at End of Tunnel' for Play Cycle." *Atlanta Journal-Constitution*, September 29, 2003, E1.

Saltzman, Simon, and Nicole Plett. "'Jitney' at Crossroads." *U.S. 1 Newspaper*, April 16, 1997.

black bottom

A syncopated dance of the 1920s that anticipated the Charleston and modern tap dance, the black bottom developed from the African American neighborhoods of New Orleans. With the aid of blues singer Alberta Hunter, the dance migrated north to Harlem. It may have advanced in popularity from "The Black Bottom Dance" (1919), a song originated by Perry Bradford of Nashville, Tennessee. The vigorous black bottom reached New York's theater district in the stage play *Dinah* (1924) and in the George White Scandals of 1926, which starred performers Ann Pennington and Tom Patricola at Harlem's Apollo Theater. By the slapping of the backside and rotation of the pelvis, the dancer gave a down-and-dirty imitation of exotic solo dancers, but the sway of the knees, pointing of index fingers, rolling eyes, leaps, shuffles, and stomps were typical of standard black minstrels dating to slave times.

• *Further Reading*

Wilson, Charles Reagan, and William Ferris, eds. *Encyclopedia of Southern Culture.* Chapel Hill: University of North Carolina Press, 1989.

black identity

Wilson, who writes primarily from a black male point of view, has characterized himself as the dramatic voice of Afro-Americans. The work grows out of his regard for the survival and creative genius of the black race, particularly its men. To television interviewer Bill Moyers, Wilson extolled the universality of his black characters: "There's no idea in the world that is not contained by black life. I could write forever about the black experience in America" (Moyers, "August," p. 14). He regrets that blacks hide from their past and fail to celebrate the Emancipation Proclamation or derive a credo stating, "This is who we are" (Moyers, *World*, p. 6).

For material, Wilson draws on the Pittsburgh of his boyhood and his own exploration of self. Concerning his re-creation of hometown memories, his sister, Freda Wilson Ellis, an English teacher, remarked, "I think the neighborhood is still in his plays. Because all the plays are grounded in the idea of a person coming into themselves. The process of learning who you are. When you think about all of his plays, the underlying question is: Who are you?" (Reynolds, p. E1).

Under the influence of black novelist James Baldwin and artist Romare Bearden, Wilson is completing a ten-decade play cycle exploring manners and cultural commonalities that strengthen black citizens. Significant to his dramas are characters seeking to know themselves, for example, Wining Boy Charles, the retired pianist in *The Piano Lesson* (1990), who asks "Who am I? Am I me? Or am I the piano player?" (p. 41). Personal struggle is often the source of identity adjustments, as in *Two Trains Running* (1991), where Sterling Johnson needs to get a job, eat soul food, gossip with cafe patrons, romance a black woman, and reestablish himself in free society after a five-year stretch in the penitentiary for robbery. Cory Maxson, the wayward son fleeing a harsh father in *Fences* (1985), finds himself through service in the marines. On his return home, he shuns his father's funeral, but learns from his mother the importance of Troy's behaviors and attitudes, both positive and negative. Similarly, in *Joe Turner's Come and Gone* (1988), in which wanderers from the South share fragmented images of the past, Bynum Walker instructs Herald Loomis on the value of accepting the self after Herald's survival of seven years on a penal plantation.

Wilson's work fleshes out African American values that sustain individuals and families during hard times, such as the title character's insistence on genuine Negro blues in *Ma Rainey's Black Bottom* (1985), Youngblood's establishment of a home and family in *Jitney* (1982), Troy Maxson's insistence on fair workplace treatment by city officials in *Fences*, and the title character's recovery from a serious knife wound that destroys his employability in *King Hedley II* (1999). At the crux of their dilemma is a choice — act like whites and accept their racist laws and codes or retain African American heritage and stand apart for black tradition, ambitions, and dignity. The decision exacerbates identity crises among blacks, who lack the support of their ancestry. Wilson presents an intrafamilial clash over values in *The Piano Lesson*, which poses a carved upright piano as a repository of family pride. The decision about the piano's future pits sister against brother until ghosts of the past intervene and overrule Boy Willie Charles's decision to sell his patrimony.

More universal in scope is *Gem of the Ocean* (2003), in which Wilson presents the accrued memories of the slave era in a fantasy boneyard at the bottom of the sea. To aid Citizen Barlow, a fugitive from justice, Aunt Ester Tyler introduces him to black history through a vision quest to the City of Bones, a mid-ocean cemetery where Barlow encounters the remains of captive blacks who died during the Middle Passage without reaching North America. Through drama, Wilson insists that American blacks return to slave roots and, like Barlow and Boy Willie, retrieve their past. The playwright demands, "If you can't be who you are, who can you be?" (Freedman, p. 36).

Even worse for black self-esteem than loss of African culture is the black's mimicry of whites, a poor excuse for backbone. Confusing the issue of cultural belonging is the double consciousness that W. E. B. Du Bois characterized in *The Souls of Black Folk* (1903) — a duality that binds black Americans to Western homelands and to the fading memories of a pre-industrial African past. As the pianist Toledo points out in *Ma Rainey's Black Bottom*, "We's imitation white men" (p. 94). The statement riles Levee Green, a proud musician who tries to set his own style and destroys his chances by valuing expensive Florsheim over the black worker's clodhoppers.

The most out-of-sync characters in Wilson's plays are those blacks who have abandoned blackness in favor of white behaviors and values, as found in Berniece Charles's cautions to Maretha in *The Piano Lesson* about showing her color to settlement workers and in the despicable hounding of black emigres to Pittsburgh by constable Caesar, a black puppet of white authorities in *Gem of the Ocean*. Wilson stressed in an interview with Yvonne Shafer that, to achieve wholeness, blacks must accept their otherness, from call-and-response worship, burial customs, and the decor of their homes to a delight in verbal agility, blues, folkways, and soul food. In his plays, these cultural elements nurture a spark of Africana in the spirit, offering blacks a retreat from white culture and an internal compass for the future.

See also **blues, music, religion, soul food**

• *Further Reading*

Charters, Ann, and Samuel Charters, ed. *Short Pieces from the New Dramatists.* Banbury, Ox.: Orangeberry Books, 1985.

Freedman, Samuel G. "A Voice from the Streets: August Wilson's Plays Portray the Sound and Feel of Black Poverty." *New York Times Magazine*, March 15, 1987, p. 36.

Moyers, Bill. "August Wilson's America: A Conversation with Bill Moyers." *American Theater*, Vol. 7, No. 6, 1989, p. 14.

_____. *A World of Ideas.* New York: Doubleday, 1989.

Pereira, Kim. *August Wilson and the African-American Odyssey.* Urbana: University of Illinois Press, 1995.

Reynolds, Christopher. "Mr. Wilson's Neighborhood: Playwright August Wilson No Longer Lives in Pittsburgh's Hill District, but It Is Consistently at Home in His Work." *Los Angeles Times*, July 27, 2002, p. El.

Richards, Sandra L. "Yoruba Gods on the American Stage: August Wilson's *Joe Turner's Come and Gone.*" *Research in African Literatures*, Vol. 30, No. 4, Winter 1999, p. 92.

Shafer, Yvonne. *August Wilson: A Research and Production Sourcebook.* Westport, Conn.: Greenwood, 1998.

Black Mary

The protégé of Aunt Ester, the source of wisdom and prophecy in *Gem of the Ocean* (2003), Black Mary exhibits some of the fire and vision of a neophyte African seer. She suffers from kinship with an older brother, constable Caesar, a destructive sociopath who escaped bondage by becoming a cat's paw of whites. In girlhood, she revered him for readying her for school and admired his fortitude in quelling a riot. Once white authorities empowered Caesar to kill a suspect for stealing bread, he became her enemy. After three years of washing clothes at Aunt Ester's Pittsburgh mansion, Black Mary stayed on to learn from her mentor.

In retaliation against lethal males like Caesar, Mary avoids love matches and, like Berniece Charles in *The Piano Lesson* (1990) and Risa Thomas in *Two Trains Running* (1991), actively bashes men for their abuse of power. In a grand speech to Citizen Barlow when he talks romance, Mary vents her contempt: "You got a woman in your hands. Now what? What you got? What you gonna do" (Philips, p. 1)? As implacable as a bulldog, she clings to the argument and makes another sally at Barlow in a stark, melodramatic monologue: "Time ain't long, Mr. Citizen. A woman ain't but so many times filled up. What you gonna do? What you gonna fill me up with? Love? Happiness? Peace? What you got, Mr. Citizen" (*Ibid.*)? Her staccato demands spring from suppressed antagonisms that she no longer controls.

In woman-to-woman dealings, Black Mary sheathes her sharp edge to become less vindictive and more generous. While brewing Ester's tea and supervising her Pittsburgh boarding house in the Hill District, Black Mary willingly serves her and washes her feet in a humble ritual reminiscent of the self-abasement of Mary, sister of Martha, at Bethany during the last days of Christ. By accepting lowly chores, Black Mary tolerates the elderly seer's micromanagement and develops the wisdom and experience to replace the famed counselor, who dies in 1985.

See also **women**

• *Further Reading*

Jaques, Damien. "Dialogue Drives Another Wilson Gem." *Milwaukee Journal Sentinel*, May 1, 2003.

Philips, Michael. "Wilson's 'Gem' a Diamond in the Rough." *Chicago Tribune*, April 30, 2003, p. 1.

Shirley, Don. "Queen of the Hill: August Wilson's Potent But Ungainly 'Gem of the Ocean' Opens at the Taper." *Los Angeles Times*, August 1, 2003, p. E1.

blues

The blues schooled twenty-year-old August Wilson in black culture after his discovery of black singing star Bessie Smith's recordings in 1965. Of the epiphany that resulted from hearing "Nobody in Town Can Bake a Sweet Jellyroll Like Mine," he exclaimed, "It was a birth, a baptism, a resurrection, and a redemption all rolled into one" (Wilson, p. 2035). Unlike classroom lessons, classic songs of the 1920s cut to the heart and soul of blackness, its anguish as well as its glories, and kept them alive. As a black male living in a white-dominated world, Wilson appreciated the success of female blues greats who thrived in the male-controlled music industry. He identified with Smith's lyrics and internalized their message. In 1996, he stated to *American Theatre* writer Regina Taylor his debt to the medium: "All the attitudes of my characters come straight out of the blues. The blues is the bedrock" (Taylor, p. 18).

In an interview with Sandra G. Shannon in 1993, the playwright honored the zest and self-determination of blues musicians, whom he thought of as American troubadours carrying on a sacred task of preserving and disseminating the particolored moods and responses of a marginalized race. As a method, he began internalizing the lyrics:

> When someone sings, "I'm leaving in the morning. I'm going to start walking and take a chance I may ride," I say, "What's driving him? Why is he leaving?" I take a step back and smell the air at 5:30 A.M. Then I just start walking down the road with him, and every step is hard [Plummer & Kahn, p. 63].

Wilson's ability to relive the walker's resolve and to recreate it in stage drama is his key to believable characterization.

The playwright stocks his works with numerous blues references, such as Tonya Hedley's admiration for rhythm and blues queen Aretha Franklin's singing in *King Hedley II* (1999). Tonya's mother-in-law Ruby suffers the resentment of the son she abandoned in infancy to pursue her career as a blues singer with Walter Kelly's band in East St. Louis. Wilson entitled *Joe Turner's Come and Gone* (1988) directly from blues lyrics by naming an historical figure in the South who imprisoned and coerced black males for his personal enrichment. Wilson chose blues great Muddy Waters and Buddy Bolden as models of accomplishment in *Seven Guitars* (1995) and acknowledged that Marvin Gaye's 1971 classic "What's Goin' On" influenced the writing of *Jitney* (1982). Wilson chose James Brown's "Say It Loud: I'm Black and I'm Proud," an ethnic paean from 1968, as a source for *Two Trains Running* (1991). In the action, two characters, Sterling Johnson and Risa Thomas, dance to "Take a Look" (1967), sung by Aretha Franklin. In various other scenes, characters admire Count Basie, Billy Eckstine, Ella Fitzgerald, Lena Horne, and Sarah Vaughan.

Wilson described how a complex blues medium developed from the subtly confrontational chants of fieldhands and railroad workers, the deceptions of West African trickster lore, the wisdom and humor of the storyteller, the ego trips of perennial ramblers and woman-despoiling rakes, and the songs of individual worshippers and sorrowers, all of whom used music as their medium of responding to the world. For African Americans, an embrace of the blues has traditionally repaired and filled in the broken history of a people who lacked opportunities to develop their own culture. In *Seven Guitars*, Floyd Barton is so adept at composing blues lyrics that he produces a belligerent stanza in straight conversation:

> I was up there in the workhouse.
> The captain say hurry...
>   and the sergeant say run.
> I say if I had my thirty-eight
>   I wouldn't do neither one [p. 24].

Of this natural flow of blues, the playwright explained that, if black Americans died out, recordings of the blues would retain for posterity the joys, pain, and beliefs of a distinct body of Americana.

Throughout his plays, Wilson immerses characters in the words and spirit of African American music, which parallels and amplifies dialogue. In the opinion of Bynum Walker in *Joe Turner's Come and Gone* (1988), a man who has lost his song loses contact with purpose and meaning to his earthly travels and discovers that footsteps "bite back at [him]" (p. 71). In a Zen-based explanation of the song, he notes that while he looked for it, he was already singing it. He concludes, "Then I was the song in search of itself" (*Ibid.*). Notably, the blues, a native musical heritage, taps the despair and endurance of black people from the time of their ancestral enslavement and separation from Africa through liberation, Jim Crow lynchings, and economic oppression in the Western Hemisphere. In one example, the falling action of *Seven Guitars*, King Hedley intones his frustration and religious beliefs with repetitions of a personal mantra, "Ain't no grave can hold my body down," a faith-based claim from a Negro spiritual (p. 88).

For the rewriting of *Ma Rainey's Black Bottom* (1985) in 1978, Wilson shut himself in his room with blues recordings of Charlie Patton and Eddie James "Son" House to get the feel of male blues singers. In the play's introduction, he describes in sensual, tactile imagery a blues cadence "that breathes and touches. That connects. That is in itself a way of being, separate and distinct from any other" (p. xvi). Ma exalts her singing of the blues as a form of self-adulation of both her talent and her uniqueness. In Act Two, she presents a personal view of music that fills and balances her and explains the vital role of songs to the African American psyche: "You don't sing to feel better. You sing 'cause that's a way of understanding life" (p. 82). She concludes, "This be an empty world without the blues" (p. 83). Because August Wilson agrees with Ma's declaration, on May 27, 1999, the Blues Foundation conferred on him the Keeping Blues Alive award for achievement in literature.

See also **music, Ma Rainey, Ruby, Joe Turner**

• *Further Reading*

Baker, Houston A. *Blues, Ideology, and Afro-American Literature.* Chicago: University of Chicago Press, 1984.

Gussow, Adam. "'Making My Getaway': The Blues Lives of Black Minstrels in W. C. Handy's Father of the Blues." *African American Review*, Spring 2001.

Lyons, Bonnie. "An Interview with August Wilson." *Contemporary Literature*, Vol. 40, No. 1, Spring 1999, p. 1.

Moyers, Bill. "August Wilson's America: A Conversation with Bill Moyers." *American Theater*, Vol. 7, No. 6, 1989, p. 14.

Pereira, Kim. *August Wilson and the African-American Odyssey.* Urbana: University of Illinois Press, 1995.

Plummer, William, and Toby Kahn. "Street Talk." *People Weekly*, Vol. 45, No. 19, May 13, 1996, pp. 63–65.

Scott, Daniel M. "August Wilson and the African-American Odyssey." *MELUS*, Vol. 24, No. 3, Fall, p. 163.

Taylor, Regina. "That's Why They Call It the Blues." *American Theatre*, Vol. 13, No. 4, April 1996, pp. 18–23.

Wilson, August. "Where to Begin," in *Short Pieces from the New Dramatists.* Banbury, Ox.: Orangeberry Books, 1985, pp. 2033–2037.

Bolden, Buddy

Charles Joseph "Buddy" Bolden (1877–1931), a barber and innovative cornetist from New Orleans, initiated delta jazz in 1895 from a blend of blues with ragtime. A favorite for improvisation and embellishment at parades, military send-offs, saloons, lawn parties, and cotillions, he dubbed himself King Bolden at his head-quarters on the edge of Storyville, the city's black section. He published "Ida" (1903), "St. Louis Tickle" (1904), and "Shoo Skeeter Shoo" (1905), a humorous response to mosquito-borne disease. He taught music and led a successful six-piece band that influenced young Louis Armstrong.

Bolden's tragic end became the stuff of folk legend. At age thirty, he lapsed into alcoholic dementia and assaulted his mother and mother-in-law. He was remanded to the Insane Asylum of Louisiana in Jackson and remained there until his death twenty-four years later. Jelly Roll Morton immortalized him with the song "Buddy Bolden Blues" or "Funky Butt Blues" (1939), which features the line "I thought I heard Buddy Bolden say."

August Wilson uses the musical dialogue in *Seven Guitars* (1995) as a humor-ous colloquy between Floyd Barton and Hedley, whose Haitian father named him "King" after Bolden, his musical idol. Hedley informs Ruby of Bolden's importance to riverboat music and recalls the elder Hedley's joy in describing the musician, whose music made his face light up. Hedley concludes, "It was a thing he love more than my mother" (p. 67).

• *Further Reading*

Appiah, Kwame Anthony, and Henry Louis Gates, Jr., eds. *Africana*. New York: Perseus
    Books, 1999.
Wilson, Charles Reagan, and William Ferris, eds. *Encyclopedia of Southern Culture*.
    Chapel Hill: University of North Carolina Press, 1989.

Bono, Jim

The confidante of the rambunctious, bigger-than-life Troy Maxson in *Fences* (1985), Jim Bono represents the true friend who shares good times and bad. The playwright introduced Jim in the 1970s in *Jitney* (1982), when he is dying of cancer. A decade earlier, a younger Bono works the same garbage route as Troy, his long-term friend, and enjoys payday drinking fests at the Maxson porch. Bono's first line opens the play with "Troy, you ought to stop that lying," an admonition that overhangs the play like an omen (p. 1). Unlike his devious, overbearing, and faithless work mate, Bono remains loyal to his buddy and to wife Lucille and keeps his promise to buy her a refrigerator. Because he lives the example of the promise keeper, he is able to look his friend in the eye and warn about the dangers of juggling time with a wife and a mistress: "Sooner or later you gonna drop one" (p. 63). The advice is both moral and pragmatic, an example of Bono's qualities as worker and family man.

Bono bears a significant load on the falling action of rescuing Troy from total diminution for philandering. Bono succeeds in re-elevating his friend to some semblance of fatherly grace by passing along to Marine Corporal Cory Maxson a posthumous compliment, "Your daddy knew you had it in you" (p. 92). In a more insightful act of generosity, Bono compares the troubled son to his father in Troy's early days, before prison, domestic responsibilities, and self-doubt robbed him of vitality and warmth. Reliant to the last, it is Bono who brings out the best traits in Troy during their working years and it is Bono who comforts his estranged son and lines up pallbearers for Troy's funeral.

• *Further Reading*

Wang, Qun. *An In-Depth Study of the Major Plays of African American Playwright August
    Wilson: Vernacularizing the Blues on Stage*. Vol. 6 of *Black Studies*. Lewiston, Ont.:
    Edwin Mellen Press, 1999.

boundaries

In the volatile staging areas of his plays, August Wilson applies boundaries to the action on several levels, as with the invisible line that Boy Willie draws across Doaker's parlor floor in *The Piano Lesson* (1990) to represent the division of indivisible property, the line that separates a black cat's grave from tender seedlings wrapped in barbed wire in *King Hedley II* (1999), the insulated control booth that secludes white producers from black musicians in *Ma Rainey's Black Bottom* (1985), and the fence that walls off Miss Tillery's grief as she wails for her dead son Poochie in *Seven Guitars* (1995). On the upside of dividing lines, West, the mortician in *Two*

Trains Running (1991), ropes off an aisle to guide viewers to the body of the Prophet Samuel. In a jubilant declaration of boundaries, Bynum Walker, the optimistic binding man in *Joe Turner's Come and Gone* (1988), describes a sailor's search for the horizon: "He know that if you get off the water to go take a look … why, there's a whole world right there" (p. 46).

In Wilson's most boundary conscious play, *Fences* (1985), the backyard fence illuminates numerous themes, especially Troy Maxson's refusal to allow new ideas and points of view to impinge on his stolid opinions. Rose batters in vain at his stodginess: "People change. The world's changing around you and you can't even see it" (p. 40). Begun about the time that he strays from his wife Rose to Alberta, whom he meets at Taylor's bar, the fence represents Rose's too-late bulwark against loss and a meager attempt to hold her frail world in place. At the clothesline, she hums a prayer, "Jesus be a fence all around me every day" (p. 21). Not surprisingly, Troy fails to make the connection between the fence and Rose's fear of loss until Jim Bono explains the picketed circle to the wayward husband. As Bono observes Troy's slide into adultery with Alberta, he realizes that "Rose wants to hold on to you all" (p. 61).

The unfinished fence also plays a major role in the intergenerational tug of war between Troy and Cory, whom his father browbeats to saw planks for the completion of the remaining section. When Cory questions Bono about Rose's desire for a fence, Bono characterizes the emblematic nature of the wooden divider as a protection of family unity. After hostilities with Cory come close to blows with the baseball bat, Troy faces a tough, hard-hitting ego like his own. He uses the fence as the cut-off point in parenting Cory, whose belongings Troy promises to set outside the pale, a gesture of personal rejection and abandonment of parental duties.

Significantly, the concepts of containment and preservation arrive late to Troy, only a few years before his retirement. It is not until he loses Alberta in childbirth that he experiences the need to fence in his loved ones. He challenges Mr. Death to stop stealing and to "stay over there until you're ready for me" (p. 77). By Act II, Scene 4, the fence is complete, but Cory has joined the marines, Lyons is divorced and in jail, and death has taken Troy. Because of his moral decline, it is too late to hold the Maxsons together.

See also **poverty, segregation**

• *Further Reading*

Reed, Ishmael. "A Shy Genius Transforms the American Theater." *Connoisseur*, Vol. 127, 1987, pp. 92–97.
Wang, Qun. *An In-Depth Study of the Major Plays of African American Playwright August Wilson: Vernacularizing the Blues on Stage.* Vol. 6 of *Black Studies.* Lewiston, Ont.: Edwin Mellen Press, 1999.

Brown, Avery

A former farm laborer and settled migrant who came to Pittsburgh from the Mississippi Delta in *The Piano Lesson* (1990), Avery Brown symbolizes the naivete of black seekers from the South expecting great things in the promised land. He once planted cotton on the Willshaw place in Mississippi and, in Pittsburgh, is happy to distance himself from farm labor. A thirty-eight-year-old elevator operator at the Gulf Building, he is easily fooled by the promise of the urban North and overvalues a job that promises a tedious up-and-down motion rather than true advancement. He brags of his raise of a dime on the hour and of the company's annual gift of a turkey.

In addition to his significance as a model of outsized hopes, Avery is a source of biblical faith and strength who serves the playwright as a spokesperson for the black evangelical Christian. Avery reveres a prophetic dream about three hobos traveling by train from Nazareth to Jerusalem. In the dream, a voice from the valley of wolves ordered Avery to lead the people. In response to what he considers a godly call, he replied as did the biblical child Samuel in Isaiah 6:8, "Here I am. Send me" (p. 25). The simple response identifies Avery's faith with a naive belief system that lacks testing.

Avery longs to start a church — the Good Shepherd Church of God in Christ, a name that allies Avery with Christ, who describes himself as the good shepherd in John 10:11, 14. Avery is a devout bible reader who sprinkles his discourse with standard scriptural nuggets, e.g., "Make a joyful noise," "God works in mysterious ways," and "The Lord is my refuge," but mistakes the Twenty-third Psalm for the Lord's Prayer (pp. 69, 70, 71). To fill the pulpit role properly, he yearns for a respectable minister's life. Over two years, he repeatedly proposes to his deaconess Berniece, a thirty-five-year-old widow who rejects a new alliance. Wilson uses Avery as the model of blacks depending on Jewish businessmen by describing Mr. Cohen's offer of a rental building for thirty dollars per month. Overjoyed that his plans are taking shape, Avery suggests that Berniece place the family piano in his church.

Avery's test of faith occurs in the exorcism scene at the end of *The Piano Lesson*. It is his presence that introduces Christian courage in the face of evil. Armed with his bible and a vial of pseudo–holy water, he joins Lymon Jackson and Boy Willie in trying to dislodge the stubborn piano and in facing down Robert Sutter's ghost. When the spirit proves too stubborn for Avery's white-mandated Christian wisdom, he yields to Berniece and Boy Willie, who call on their African American ancestry to defeat the residual power of slave times.

See also **religion**

• *Further Reading*

Vorlicky, Robert. *Act Like a Man: Challenging Masculinities in American Drama.* Ann Arbor: University of Michigan Press, 1995.

Brown, Sylvester

The young Arkansas-born pet and "nephew" of Ma in *Ma Rainey's Black Bottom* (1985), Sylvester Brown follows her to a fateful Chicago recording session at Paramount studios in March 1937. Well-built and muscular, but hampered by impatience and stuttering, he jeopardizes the outflow of love and forbearance in Ma by running a traffic light and precipitating a collision that damages her new car. Her protection saves him from arrest, ostensibly to assure his sexual services as her kept boy. She chides him for sloppy clothes and orders him to remove his hat indoors, stop wandering around the studio, and fetch her a supply of cokes from the corner store. She grooms him to speak the voice-over to "Ma Rainey's Black Bottom" and instructs him to send the money he earns to his mother. After abortive tries, Sylvester speaks his part correctly through an unplugged mike, a dramatic irony that echoes the theme of the black male's frustrations in attaining success.

Brustein, Robert

A columnist for *New Republic* and artistic director for the American Repertory Theatre in Cambridge, Massachusetts, Robert Brustein is August Wilson's most prominent and most damaging critic. Brustein has charged the playwright with writing victim literature and with presenting black Americans *in toto* as objects of white racism. Of the play *Fences* (1985), he mused, "What is remarkable is the way in which audiences sit still for their portion of guilt" (Brustein, *Reimagining*, p. 26). In the opinion of reviewer Hilary DeVries, Brustein interpreted the collaboration of Wilson and director Lloyd Richards as "the cultural equivalent of affirmative action," a pejorative bristling with racial implications (DeVries, p. 46).

Brustein has challenged Wilson's call for a national black theater as a bolster of black pride and vehicle of teaching black history. Following "On Cultural Power: The August Wilson–Robert Brustein Discussion," a public debate between Brustein and Wilson in January 1997, the critic published in a March column his rebuttal of Wilson's belief that black theater is "an avenue to political and cultural power — a medium through which a large disadvantaged class can dramatize its past injustices and, perhaps, find redress through changes in the social or political system" (Brustein, "On Cultural Power," p. 31). Wilson retaliated by labeling the critic "a sniper, a naysayer, and a cultural imperialist" (Saltzman & Plett). In Wilson's view, black experience requires validation and perpetuation through a committed Afrocentric art. The result is a global flashpoint as "art changes individuals, and individuals change society" (Kroll, p. 65).

Brustein refuted Wilson's philosophy with his own declaration that drama is cathartic rather than political, thus highlighting the individual's struggles rather than the collective slights against a particular race or class. Brustein countered implications that he is racist by declaring that he values the "richness of multiculturalism — as long as it is not a pretext for promoting race hatred or generating separatism" (*Ibid.*). To substantiate his claims that Wilson was overly race conscious, the critic remarked on an article in the *New York Times* in 1990 in which Wilson rejected white directors for the filming of *Fences*. Brustein implied that Wilson erred in the belief that he speaks for an entire race and in his intent to divide audiences along strict color lines. In 2003, Brustein further denigrated Wilson by claiming that he has done little more than duplicate past examples of social-protest domestic drama.

See also **"The Ground on Which I Stand"**

• *Further Reading*

Brustein, Robert. "On Cultural Power." *New Republic*, Vol. 216, No. 9, March 3, 1997, pp. 31–34.

_____. *Reimagining American Theater*. New York: Wang, 1991.

DeVries, Hilary. "Drama Lesson." *Boston Globe Magazine*, June 23, 1990, p. 20, 46.

Kroll, Jack. "And in This Corner." *Newsweek*, Vol. 129, No. 6, Feb. 10, 1997, p. 65.

Nunns, Stephen. "Wilson, Brustein & the Press." *American Theatre*, Vol. 14, No. 3, March 1997, pp. 17–19.

Saltzman, Simon, and Nicole Plett. "August Wilson vs. Robert Brustein." *U.S. 1 Newspaper*, January 22, 1997.

Shannon, Sandra G. *The Dramatic Vision of August Wilson*. Washington, D.C.: Howard University Press, 1996.

Caesar

A villainous constable and venal slumlord in *Gem of the Ocean* (2003), Caesar represents the black-face authority who acts and speaks for the white world. He was once the beloved older brother of Black Mary, housekeeper for Aunt Ester at her ramshackle Pittsburgh home in 1904. As a legitimate businessman, he respected and abided by the law until racism twisted his thinking and robbed him of humanity. To escape bondage, he agreed to serve white authorities as law officer, a form of servitude that erodes his spirit. Without conscience he commits arson, a felony that cheats black men of their jobs and casts their families into the streets.

Like the plantation overseers of slave times, Caesar obsesses over capturing felons in flight from the white world's system of justice. One man, a factory worker falsely accused of stealing a bucket of nails from the mill, drowned himself in a river while Caesar calmly watched and did nothing. Because of his relentless pursuit of black fugitives, he subverts the harmony of the Hill District by ignoring truth, mercy, and his own role in the continuum of black history.

Setting Caesar apart from the poor and homeless emigres from the South are his dandyish air and stylish outfit that cloak the tormented soul of a sociopath alienated from both whites and blacks. At Aunt Ester's residence, he dishonors her by sitting in her chair and breaks her heart by arresting the man she loves. His strutting self-assurance and high-yellow superiority express an ego out of sync with the Pittsburgh ghetto during the era of Jim Crow. His name suggests a dangerous edge to his authority, which reviewer Chris Jones compares to the self-righteousness of Supreme Court Judge Clarence Thomas and other blacks who fail to support affirmative action.

See also **injustice, Jim Crow era**

• *Further Reading*

Abarbanel, Jonathan. "Gem of the Ocean," http://ibs.theatermania.com/content/news.cfm?int_news_id=3441, May 1, 2003.

Hodgins, Paul. "Finding the Cost of Freedom: Slavery and Its Aftermath Are Explored in 'Gem of the Ocean.' August Wilson's Latest Play." *Orange County Register*, August 1, 2003, p. 1.

Jones, Chris. "Review: Gem of the Ocean." *Variety*, May 5, 2003, p. 39.

Kendt, Rob. "Review: Gem of the Ocean." *Back Stage West*, August 7, 2003, pp. 19, 20.

call-and-response

Call-and-response is a rhythmic, emotional declamation in counterpoint common to the leader-and-chorus chants of soldiers, chain gangs, field and dock laborers, juke joint performers, protest marchers, tent revivals, choral singers, and black fundamentalist pulpits throughout the South. In *Joe Turner's Come and Gone* (1988), Herald Loomis is surprised to learn that black forms of worship and ritual originated in African animistic religions and gradually allied with Christianity during slave times. Thus, a call on the Holy Spirit applies African folk music rituals to a white-inspired religiosity. When his wife, Martha Pentecost, begs him to commit himself to Jesus, in a rhythmic call-and-response, he repudiates her god for his disinterest in black people and their struggles.

The involvement of a congregation in an emotion-charged sermon provides August Wilson with a method of reviving soul-stirring Southern motifs in *The Piano Lesson* (1990). During a recitation of family history, Wining Boy supports in counterpoint a lengthy slave narrative related by Doaker Charles, the family griot or storyteller. As though citing the familiar episodes as an example to his brother's quarreling children, Doaker concludes, "Berniece ain't gonna sell that piano. Cause her daddy died over it," a reference to the immolation of Boy Charles and four hobos in a boxcar set afire by Robert Sutter's white henchmen on July 4, 1911 (p. 46). The story session serves as a binding of family loyalties through a recitation of a painful truth.

See also **juba, oral lore, religion**

• *Further Reading*

Boan, Devon. "Call-and-Response: Parallel 'Slave Narrative' in August Wilson's 'The Piano Lesson.'" *African American Review*, Vol. 32, No. 2, Summer 1998, pp. 263–272.
Richards, Sandra L. "Yoruba Gods on the American Stage: August Wilson's *Joe Turner's Come and Gone*." *Research in African Literatures*, Vol. 30, No. 4, Winter 1999, p. 92.

Campbell, Mattie

One of the fragmented seekers of *Joe Turner's Come and Gone* (1988), twenty-six-year-old Mattie Campbell bears serious troubles on her shoulders. A native Georgian who migrated to Texas with her mother to pick peaches, Mattie bears a peach-like ripeness paired with vulnerability. She regrets the deaths of her two babies in infancy and clings to faith in love. She arrives in Pittsburgh in search of her wayward lover, Jack Carper, and rooms with him at 1727 Bedford Avenue. After he slips away, to support herself, she irons for Doc Goldblum. Her willingness to work and raise a family contrasts her foil, Molly Cunningham, who intends to be well kept by a man who demands no domestic drudgery or child-bearing.

Mattie complains of uncommitted suitors and, like Risa Thomas in *Two Trains Running* (1991) and Tonya Hedley in *King Hedley II* (1999), refuses to invest in a shaky relationship or to "go through life piecing myself out to different mens" (p. 25). Because Bynum Walker, the finder and uniter of wanderers during the Great Migration, recognizes the harm that Carper will cause, he prefers to guide Mattie to a more compatible mate, who is "searching for your doorstep right now" (p. 23). Her caution about avoiding the wrong male in her love life eases the insult when Jeremy Furlow drops her in favor of Molly. Bertha Holly remarks encouragingly, "You ought to be glad to wash him out of your hair" (p. 75). Wilson indicates that Mattie's first step toward reclamation begins with distancing herself from errors in the past.

The cleansing of the atmosphere leaves Mattie open to Herald Loomis, a more suitable man who offers marital contentment in place of roaming and seeking. For her kind gift of a white ribbon to match Zonia's white outfit, Loomis remarks that Mattie is a "good woman" (p. 87). Bertha Holly encourages her to share love and laughter with Loomis, who acts more civilized when Mattie is around. Peaceable, yet courageous in the play's most violent scene, she does not recoil from him after his self-mutilation. Her rush to catch up with him suggests a willingness to bond with an honest, self-affirming man who needs a dependable wife.

See also **women**

• *Further Reading*

Bogumil, Mary L. *Understanding August Wilson*. Columbia: University of South Carolina Press, 1998.
Pereira, Kim. *August Wilson and the African-American Odyssey*. Urbana: University of Illinois Press, 1995.

Canewell

A good-natured, worldly friend and neighbor in *Seven Guitars* (1995), Canewell serves August Wilson as dramatic chorus to console, affirm, and explain events that puzzle characters. Once the harmonica player for the deceased guitarist Floyd Barton, Canewell harmonizes the dissonance of Floyd, King Hedley, and Red Carter much as Toledo directs and instructs the discourse of the male quartet in *Ma Rainey's Black Bottom* (1985). Canewell refuses to return to Chicago to make more records because of his bad luck on the last trip. He was remanded to the Cook County Jail for thirty days for disturbing the peace by singing on Maxwell Street. Because he placed his hat on the sidewalk for tips, the charge escalated to soliciting, loitering, resisting arrest, and disrespect for the law. Unlike the risk-takers in Wilson's plays, including Booster Becker in *Jitney* (1982), the title character in *King Hedley II* (1999), and Levee Green in *Ma Rainey's Black Bottom*, Canewell espouses caution in his hopes and lifestyle. To protect himself from more injustice, he chooses to remain at his quarters on Clark Street in Little Haiti and keeps his trunk packed.

There is a tender, giving side to Canewell that causes him to present Vera Dotson an RCA Victor radio and a goldenseal plant, gifts offering entertainment and promising health and vigor. The perennial optimist, he counters the doubts and pessimism of Vera and the landlady Louise with a stout faith in love, even an affection that is spurned, as was his for Vera. In his opinion, "Even love that ain't but halfway is still love" (p. 98). He advises Floyd on how to make the most of his fame by demanding a larger percentage of the profits. In the play's falling action, Canewell loses Vera, whom he knows is too quiet to thrive in a noisy city like Chicago. With genial courtesy, he accepts whatever shreds of affection he gleaned from unrequited love by wishing her well in a marriage with Floyd. As though glimpsing himself walking down the street, Canewell objectifies his image as a person "satisfied with life" and a model to others of contentment and self-affirmation (p. 98).

Other forms of adversity spur rather than deflate Canewell. In reference to a neighborhood rooster, he relates a humorous anecdote about the Alabama, Georgia, and Mississippi rooster and concludes that the bird refused to crow during the slave era. In a dialogue with Hedley on Jesus's resurrection of Lazarus, Canewell is certain that a kinder fate would have left Lazarus in the grave rather than force him to relive life's miseries. In token of his caution, he carries a knife and a reputation for using it. To the discussion of Red Carter and Floyd about the assets of a pistol, Canewell remarks, "Cutting don't never go out of style" (p. 43).

After Floyd's hasty uprooting of the goldenseal plant, Canewell hurries to locate a shovel to resettle the roots. The disclosure of Floyd's part in the finance company robbery leads Canewell to a face-off with his rival, who is angry and possessive enough to shoot his old friend and back-up musician. In the aftermath of Floyd's funeral, Wilson awards the coda to Canewell, who ends the play with comic relief that the police didn't charge him with murder. He rounds out the drama with a cheery intonation of Hedley's song, the key to the mystery. Thirty-seven years later, Canewell returns to Wilson's drama suite in *King Hedley II* (1999) as Stool Pigeon, the informer on Hedley for killing Floyd.

See also **goldenseal, humor, Stool Pigeon**

• *Further Reading*

Austin, April. "'Seven Guitars' Makes Sweet, Sweet Music." *Christian Science Monitor*, Vol. 87, Issue 205, September 18, 1995, p. 13.
Clark, Keith. *Black Manhood in James Baldwin, Ernest J. Gaines, and August Wilson.* Urbana: University of Illinois Press, 2002.

Carper, Jack

The tough, unforgiving lover in *Joe Turner's Come and Gone* (1988), Jack Carper is well named for his abusive temper. Mattie Campbell, his former woman, describes him as rough-handed and strong with a tendency to "act mean sometimes" (p. 23). In the three years the couple lived in Pittsburgh after moving north from Texas, they produced two infants who died in the first eight weeks of life. Out of ennui and wanderlust, Jack passes off his disinterest in Mattie as disappointment, a cruel means of compensation for his lack of commitment.

In ridding himself of blame in the failed family, Carper raises the specter of superstition. He accuses Mattie of laboring under a "curse prayer" on her motherhood (*Ibid.*). Using voodoo as justification, he deserts her without a word. His actions compare with those of Wining Boy Charles, a roving piano player in *The Piano Lesson* (1990), the trickster Elmore and Red Carter in *King Hedley II* (1999), Memphis Lee's faithless wife in *Two Trains Running* (1991), the philandering Troy Maxson in

Fences (1985), and Floyd Barton in *Seven Guitars* (1995), who abandons Vera Dotson in favor of Pearl Brown as a companion on a jaunt to Chicago.

See also **Mattie Campbell**

Carter, Red

One of the mourners at Floyd Barton's funeral in May 1948 in *Seven Guitars* (1995), Red Carter is an ambiguous figure in Floyd's circle of friends. After returning from the graveside, Red's first act is a grab for a piece of sweet potato pie, a symbol of the Old South. A native of Opelika, Alabama, he is generous, friendly, and adept at womanizing. In a flashback, he celebrates the birth of WillaMae's baby boy Mister by passing Floyd and Canewell cigars. A congenial spirit prevails as Red joins Floyd and Canewell in reciting silly poems. He complains humorously about his difficulties in scheduling time with girl friends and insults Louise by escorting her to Floyd's performance and ignoring her in the crowd that gathers at the Blue Goose.

Wilson speaks through Red one of the most ironic comments in the play. In an informational exchange with Floyd and Canewell about weapons, Floyd speaks highly of his .38 Smith & Wesson. Canewell replies that he relies on his knife. In a hasty conclusion that precedes King Hedley's slashing of Floyd's throat, Red agrees with Floyd that the pistol is the weapon of choice because "A knife ain't nothing but a piece of history. It's out of style" (p. 43). The playwright returns to Red Carter's role in the community in *King Hedley II* (1999), in which Ruby describes how Red helped her get a job singing with Walter Kelly's band. Mister identifies his father's lover as Edna Stewart, the woman Red Carter claimed when he left Mister and WillaMae behind.

See also **violence**

• *Further Reading*

Papageorge, John. "Train He Rides." *MetroActive*, 1995.

character names

Wilson chooses evocative names for characters, as with Youngblood, the youngest of the cabbies, and Booster, ex-con son of the station manager in *Jitney* (1982), as well as Jesse, the child who bears a revered name from the lineage of David and Jesus. The names display a variety of source and meaning — the real-life blues singer in the title of *Ma Rainey's Black Bottom* (1985); the peddler Rutherford Selig in *Gem of the Ocean* (2003), whose name means "blessed" in German; and the looming, portentous messenger Herald Loomis, Bynum Walker the nomadic binding man, and the Holly family, who, like prickly Christmas decorations, extend hospitality for a price in *Joe Turner's Come and Gone* (1988). Simple ties between names and characters' beliefs and behaviors undergird the flashy temptress Ruby, the truth-telling Vera Dotson, and Canewell and Miss Tillery, agrarian names for the son of a Southern cane cutter and for the neighbor who keeps a rooster in the city limits of Pittsburgh in

Seven Guitars (1995). In *The Piano Lesson* (1990), Wilson turns Willie Boy, the demeaning slave era name of a plantation carpenter, into the source of subsequent names, Boy Charles and Boy Willie Charles. Like the piano Willie Boy carves with faces and events of the clan's past, the elements of family names establish their own nobility into the 1930s. Similarly described by their names are the persistent tracker constable Caesar in *Gem of the Ocean* and the mouthy police informer Stool Pigeon and the self-important thug Mister in *King Hedley II* (1999).

The naming of cast members in *Two Trains Running* (1991) establishes four themes in the heavily symbolic play. August Wilson depicts Wolf as a too-cautious, predatory numbers man, Sterling Johnson as a man governed by a strong set of values, Hambone as the crazed handyman to whom the butcher Lutz owes a ham, and West, the undertaker, who dresses in black and bears a name that suggests sunset in the west, an image of the inevitability of death. Memphis Lee, named for an Egyptian god, is a former Alabama sharecropper and compliant husband who claims to have treated his faithless wife like the Queen of Sheba, an historical figure who once ruled in Ethiopia. Like the Confederate General Robert E. Lee, Memphis fails to hold onto his portion of Tennessee cropland and retreats north.

The playwright's selection of appropriate designations empowers *Fences* (1985), in which he names the protagonist for the fallen city of Troy, a site of Homer's epics *The Iliad* and *The Odyssey*. Troy's brother Gabriel Maxson, the brain-damaged veteran and trumpet player, bears the name of a folkloric archangel who oversees the gate of heaven. Because of his diminished abilities, Gabe associates Rose's name with the flower and refers to Lyons as "King of the Jungle" (p. 48). Troy's second son Cory is the survivor left with the core of his father's philosophy to illuminate his ambitions and guide his decisions. All family members carry the surname Maxson, a two-part emblem suggesting living to the maximum and passing that verve to the males of the next generation. Equally evocative are Bono and Bonnie, bearers of the Latin root meaning "good," and the motherless infant Raynell, the ray of hope in Rose's dwindling family.

See also **Citizen Barlow, Jack Carper, Aunt Ester, humor, Martha Loomis Pentecost, Ruby, Rutherford Selig, West**

• *Further Reading*

King, Bruce. *Contemporary American Theatre*. New York: St. Martin's Press, 1991.
Wolfe, Peter. *August Wilson*. New York: Twayne, 1999.

Charles, Berniece

In *The Piano Lesson* (1990), Berniece Charles represents the black American who clings to the African legacy of phantoms and ancestor worship. One of many Southerners who fled north, she is a thirty-five-year-old widow and mother who left sorrow and racism behind when she moved to Pittsburgh. She serves as maid for a rich white family in Squirrel Hill and as co-owner of the Charles family's carved piano, the only adornment in the flat of her uncle Doaker.

A stubborn, bossy woman, Berniece is developing into the family matriarch. From the moment of her brother's arrival after three years' separation, she suspects him of selling stolen watermelons from a stolen truck. She makes demands on her uncle Wining Boy, sets up stringent rules for her daughter Maretha to obey, ousts Boy Willie and his girl Grace from sexual intimacies in the living room, and rejects both an offer of marriage from would-be preacher Avery Brown and a formal reconciliation with her disruptive brother Boy Willie Charles while she harbors the only palpable link to her grandparents and parents—a piano that she closes and refuses to play to avoid "[waking] them spirits" (p. 70). Her hostility suggests that the ghost that haunts the flat actually dwells in her spirit.

Berniece's sensibilities are paradoxical. She is conservative about parenting and devoted to the memory of her parents. To Boy Willie, she declares, "You can't sell your soul for money" (p. 104). In the privacy of the kitchen before her bath in Act II, Scene 2, she spurns Avery's repeated proposal of marriage. When Lymon dots perfume behind her ear and kisses her, like Black Mary in *Gem of the Ocean* (2003), Berniece displays an arid personality long drained of vigor, affection, and humor. By braiding Maretha's hair with hot comb and hair dressing, Berniece acts out motherly control without undue profession of tenderness. She expresses love for Maretha by forcing her to abandon black mannerisms and to become a sedate, middle-class piano teacher by wearing the mask of the refined white. At the same time, the braiding counterbalances Boy Willie's raving as though negating the chaos he introduces to a calm household.

A symbol of black grudge-bearing, Berniece harbors bitterness toward her teasing brother, the family rogue who, three years earlier, skimmed firewood from supplies belonging to a white man. Because of Boy Willie's thievery, white men shot Crawley, leaving Berniece to rear Maretha, her fatherless daughter. Still livid that her brother allegedly conned Crawley into committing a crime, Berniece slaps Boy Willie and charges that he murdered Robert Sutter. In Boy Willie's estimation, she lacks a personal credo. In his words, "She ain't got nothing to stand on" (p. 35). Avery views her aloofness as a lack of someone to love.

To Berniece, the piano is less a family legacy than an icon of slave sacrifices. The instrument frames the sufferings of her mother, who died in 1928 from the emotional pain of extensive crimes committed by the men in the family. As spokesperson for womanly griefs, Berniece wishes Maretha had been male and mourns the fact that "Mama Ola polished this piano with her tears for seventeen years. She rubbed on it till her hands bled" (p. 52). After studying music under Miss Eula, Berniece used to play the piano at her mother's request. Out of loyalty to her role model, Berniece summarizes the female's legacy by describing the widow's life of "cold nights and an empty bed" (*Ibid.*). After Mama Ola's death, the piano, reduced to a mere "piece of wood," sparked memories of misery, causing Berniece to avoid it (*Ibid.*). She makes no personal investment in the piano, which she silences as a mute gesture of love and respect to Mama Ola.

Without realizing that she is the key to suppressing the hauntings, Berniece quarrels with her brother about keeping the heirloom in the family. Armed with Crawley's .38 pistol, she orders Boy Willie to leave and threatens to add fratricide to

the family's lengthy list of crimes. However, she lacks the authority that her uncle maintains as head of the family. The playwright takes from Avery, a symbol of Christian piety, and Boy Willie, a symbol of commercialism, the power of exorcism, which he bestows on Berniece. By playing the piano and confronting the ghost that emerges from it, she summons her ancestors to help the current generation lay to rest the family's hurtful past under slavery. Her improvised performance summons "a rustle of wind blowing across two continents," an indication that she has bound the two traditions, African and American, into one song (p. 106). Wilson describes the performance as a dynamic force that ends sibling enmity and rids the house of its specter.
See also **supernatural, women**

• *Further Reading*

Blanchard, Jayne M. "An August Tradition." *St. Paul Pioneer Press*, May 4, 1993, p. 10F.
Hodgins, Paul. "A Lesson in Theatrical Greatness: This Ghost Story Will Haunt You with Its Beauty Long After the Lights Go Up." *Orange County Register*, October 25, 1999, p. F3.
Wang, Qun. *An In-Depth Study of the Major Plays of African American Playwright August Wilson: Vernacularizing the Blues on Stage*. Vol. 6 of *Black Studies*. Lewiston, Ont.: Edwin Mellen Press, 1999.

Charles, Boy Willie

The immature, arrogant, blustering protagonist of *The Piano Lesson* (1990), thirty-year-old Boy Willie Charles undergoes a complete change of heart after making a journey echoing the escapes of blacks during the slave era. A restless, landless would-be farmer from Marlin County, Mississippi, he irritates and manipulates his family by keeping them in a state of uproar with his petulant demands. He is a facile liar who quickly blames Lymon for being sleepy and Grace for upsetting a parlor lamp. Like his uncles, Boy Willie is capable of grand theft and makes no attempt to hide his fractious nature, envy of white landowners, and self-aggrandizement, even if they violate Doaker's hospitality and wreck the serenity of his home.

Unlike his great grandfather, the revered carpenter and carver Willie Boy Charles, Boy Willie is a timber cutter in Stoner County and a stealer of wood. The ignoble act, which causes his brother-in-law's death, leaves Boy Willie's ambitions and methods open to question. For skimming lumber from Jim Miller, Boy Willie was waylaid by police and arrested. After serving a prison sentence during which he carried water to inmates on the notorious Parchman Farm, he hauled wood with his friend and fellow inmate Lymon Jackson. With the proceeds, Boy Willie shared the fifty-four-hour, eighteen-hundred-mile drive to Pittsburgh in Lymon's truck, incurring three breakdowns on the way, two in West Virginia. They make their trek ostensibly to sell their load of watermelons on the street. The melons link them to the crude jests of the Jim Crow South, which denigrated blacks as shiftless and easily assuaged by slices of heart-red fruit.

Wilson rescues Boy Willie from the smiley-faced, ingratiating pickaninny stereotype by turning the melon sale into a subterfuge to cloak more serious business. Boy

Willie's real purpose for the journey is a significant shift for the Charles family: he urges his sister Berniece to sell the family piano, thus challenging the female vision of the clan's future. Because Berniece refuses to negotiate, Boy Willie takes a biblical tack. Like Solomon and the divided child in I Kings 3:16–27, Boy Willie jokingly threatens to slice the instrument apart and sell his half. As tenacious and inflexible as his sister, he intends to take his share of the proceeds to buy one hundred acres of land and raise cotton, oats, and tobacco.

Like Memphis Lee in *Two Trains Running* (1991), Boy Willie establishes his fount of life and prosperity in the agrarian South. The plan builds his pride: "I ain't scared of work. I'm going back and farm every acre of that land" (p. 17). The investment will allow him to defy racism, seize control of his destiny, and flourish in the agrarian Mississippi Delta just as whites do. He looks forward to being able to "stand right up to the white man and talk about the price of cotton … the weather, and anything else you want to talk about" (p. 92). The image of a white and black in casual conversation about agriculture encourages Boy Willie to seize the initiative and "[live] at the top of life" (p. 92).

Like his great-grandfather, Boy Willie is a spunky self-starter singing his own "song." He has endured a social and economic form of bondage that engulfed Southern blacks after their emancipation. Because of his experience with white justice, he disrespects the law and honors only an intuitive vision of right and wrong. Symbolically, he longs to purchase not just any land, but specifically the Sutter property, the plantation that Willie Boy and Berniece Charles worked during slavery's last decades and that James Sutter inherited after his brother Robert died three weeks earlier by falling down a well.

Like the field hands who fled vengeful overseers and slave catchers in the antebellum South, Boy Willie eludes the sheriff and Jim Stovall, the farmer for whom Boy Charles sharecropped. Boy Willie flees north to Pittsburgh in search of a stake on the two thousand dollars he needs to finance his start. Boy Willie has only two weeks to clinch the deal to keep the property out of Stovall's hands. He displays hubris by fantasizing the ego trip of paying in cash: "Walk in there. Tip my hat. Lay my money down on the table. Get my deed and walk on out" (pp. 10–11).

At the play's end, the piano retains power over Boy Willie by refusing to move. With considerable ingenuity, he screws casters on a plank to make a dolly. To enforce his will over the object, Boy Willie must climb stairs to do battle with the overbearing spirit of Sutter. As August Wilson explained in an essay for the March 10, 1991, *New York Times*, the confrontation allows Boy Willie to fight "that lingering idea of [Sutter] as the master of slaves" (p. 5). Essentially, the ghost is palpable evidence of the taboo that Berniece places on the instrument as an emblem of her mother's pain. Freed of the mythic burden of the family heirloom, Boy Willie is ready to reverse the escape route to the North, return to the agricultural South, and embrace his great grandfather's lifestyle. To stress this reversal of direction, Wilson gives the characters mirror-image names— Willie Boy and Boy Willie. Leaving the piano intact as a marker of past struggles, Boy Willie perseveres with the energy and vision that has enabled the Charles family to endure.

See also **piano**

• *Further Reading*

Hodgins, Paul. "A Lesson in Theatrical Greatness: This Ghost Story Will Haunt You with Its Beauty Long After the Lights Go Up." *Orange County Register*, October 25, 1999, p. F3.

Wang, Qun. *An In-Depth Study of the Major Plays of African American Playwright August Wilson: Vernacularizing the Blues on Stage.* Vol. 6 of *Black Studies.* Lewiston, Ont.: Edwin Mellen Press, 1999.

Wilson, August. "How to Write a Play Like August Wilson." *New York Times*, March 10, 1991, Sect. 2, p. 5.

Charles, Doaker

In *The Piano Lesson* (1990), forty-seven-year-old Doaker Charles represents one of August Wilson's numerous surrogate fathers. In the absence of his dead brother, the bland, paternal uncle of Berniece Charles and Boy Willie Charles is the patriarch and keeper of the peace in his Pittsburgh flat. A quiet, dignified man, he makes his way in the white world as a twenty-seven-year veteran railroad employee. Ironically, he prefers the settled, predictable life and declares, "If everybody stay in one place I believe this would be a better world" (p. 19). His vision of a stay-put society suggests the sufferings of people who try to avoid pain by physically moving to another locale.

Doaker got his start lining track in Clarksdale and Sunflower, Mississippi, and became a cook. Although servile posts, his employment offered one of the few careers that conferred dignity and a steady living wage on blacks. Like his ancestors, who survived the Middle Passage and enslavement far from Africa in the agrarian South, Doaker must travel the country to earn his living and must return home at intervals at the whim of the rail schedule. After his wife Coreen left him and moved to New York, Doaker stopped thinking about her and steered clear of women. While living with his brother's daughter Berniece and her eleven-year-old daughter Maretha, he attempts to suppress his niece's bossiness and smooths over family outbursts as skillfully as he irons his uniforms.

For his niece and nephew, Doaker is both stabilizer and repository of family history, an antebellum slave narrative of dehumanization and retribution that began with the sale of Grandfather Willie Boy Charles's wife Berniece and nine-year-old son, who was Doaker's grandfather. In Scene Two, by relating the vivid images of how and why his grandfather carved mask-like images on the legs of the family piano, Doaker reintroduces the family circle to past generations. He stresses that Boy Charles, son of Willie Boy and father of Berniece and Boy Willie, died for the theft of the piano, which Doaker and Wining Boy took from the Sutter home to the next county to Mama Ola's family. The purpose of the oral history is a reaffirmation of Willie Boy's defiance of slave owner Robert Sutter and a transmission of the facts to Maretha, a member of the Charles clan's next generation. Berniece contributes to implications of past wrongdoing among the Charles family males by implying that Doaker regrets not staying with Boy Charles to protect him from Sutter.

In Doaker's view, the piano is a visual story of the Charles family's sufferings: "It was the story of our whole family and as long as Sutter had it ... he had us ... we was still in slavery" (p. 45). By corroborating the facts, his older brother Wining Boy illustrates how the older generation maintains a clearer understanding of family history than Berniece and Boy Willie, who are one more generation removed from the hardships of slavery. In fairness to both sides of the argument, Doaker warns his nephew that the cropland he seeks may be worthless. To restore peace, Doaker urges Berniece to relinquish the piano, which hosts a phantom that Doaker saw only three weeks before.

See also **oral lore**

• *Further Reading*

Ching, Mei-Ling. "Wrestling against History." *Theater,* Vol. 20, Summer-Fall 1988, pp. 70–71.

Morales, Michael. "Ghosts on the Piano: August Wilson and the Representation of Black American History," in *May All Your Fences Have Gates: Essays on the Drama of August Wilson.* Iowa City: University of Iowa Press, 1994, pp. 105–114.

Charles, Maretha

The youngest scion of the Charles family, Maretha illuminates the future. After the murder of her father, Crawley, she grows up fatherless in the Hill District of Pittsburgh and basks in the love of her mother Berniece and uncles Doaker, Wining Boy, and Boy Willie. To ready Maretha for a career, Berniece grooms, chides, refines, and smothers her with attention. In addition to public school, she attends the Irene Kaufman Settlement House as a source of white-generated socialization and art classes for ghetto dwellers. Berniece has already foreseen Maretha's profession as a piano teacher, a step up from the humble maid's work by which Berniece supports the family. She relaxes the girl's hair with hot-combing and warns her about "showing your color," an indication that Berniece is rearing her daughter to blend in with citified whites (p. 27).

In contrast to her education from the white world, Maretha has learned nothing about the carvings on the family piano, which her mother keeps to herself. Maretha reads music, but lacks the innate skill of her uncle Boy Willie, who can play boogie-woogie by ear. He opposes the absence of historical truth in Maretha's austere upbringing. He exhorts his sister to "mark down on the calendar the day that Papa Boy Charles brought that piano into the house ... and every year when it come up throw a party. Have a celebration" (p. 91).

The family takes responsibility for Maretha's well being. Uncle Boy Willie offers to escort her upstairs to protect her from Sutter's ghost. When the contretemps between siblings threatens gunfire, Berniece sends her daughter out of range. In the peace of Uncle Doaker's room, she is safer from the family's affray and her mother's .38 pistol. Because Berniece redeems herself from a sterile reverence from the past, Maretha acquires a stronger parent on whom to lean and a believer in Afrocentric lore who can guide Maretha into black selfhood. Boy Willie predicts that his niece will have fewer problems and will be proud of her ancestry.

See also **women**

Charles, Wining Boy

The elder brother of Doaker Charles and uncle of Boy Willie and his sister, Berniece Charles, fifty-six-year-old Wining Boy is a nomad of North and South. A former inmate of Parchman Farm, he once made his living gambling and playing the piano and even recorded a few songs. He gave up professional music because it depersonalized him and left him unfulfilled. Lacking the steady income of his brother, he borrows money and begs for liquor, but refuses to share his sack of money when he's flush. He dislikes visiting Doaker's Pittsburgh flat because of Berniece's bossiness, but the two are similar in their dried-up attitudes toward others.

On arrival from Kansas City on the way south in *The Piano Lesson* (1990), Wining Boy reports to Doaker the death of forty-six-year-old Cleotha Holman Charles, Wining Boy's former wife, on May 1, 1935, from jaundice. He ruined their marriage by rambling and fighting with her. Symbolically, during his stay at Doaker's Pittsburgh flat, Wining Boy plays a song about a roving gambler and another about a hesitating woman, which he wrote in honor of Cleotha. He perpetuates family superstition about ghosts by recalling a time on July 19, 1930, when he stood at the crossing of the Yazoo Delta and Southern railroads and called out the names of the Ghosts of the Yellow Dog. He credits the encounter with a three-year streak of good luck.

See also **piano**

• *Further Reading*

Kramer, Mimi. "Traveling Man and Hesitating Woman." *New Yorker*, April 30, 1990, pp. 82–83.

Charles family

As expressed in facts from *The Piano Lesson* (1990), the genealogy of the Charles family extends over six generations and many human trials from slave times to 1936:

Mama Esther=Papa Boy Charles
|
    Boy Willie Charles=Berniece
    (enslaved carpenter   (pet slave of
    for the Sutters)   Ophelia Sutter)
                    |
        unnamed slave boy
        (transported to Georgia at age
        nine in exchange for a piano)
             |

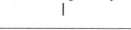

Boy Charles=Mama Ola	**Wining Boy=Cleotha**	**Doaker=Coreen**
(d. July 4, (d. 1928)	**Charles** (d. 1936)	(b. 1889) (fled to
1911 in a	(b. 1880) (railroad	New
burning	(pianist) cook)	York)
boxcar)		

```
                |                                          |
    Berniece Charles=Crawley                   Boy Willie Charles
    (b. 1901;       (d. 1933                   (b. 1906; would-be landowner)
    maid for        in a police
    rich whites)    ambush)
                        |
                    Maretha
                    (b. 1925)
```

City of Bones

August Wilson champions cultural nationalism in his plays by picturing the relationships of decades of African Americans with their enslaved forebears. To envision a mystic connection between the living and dead, he pictures himself standing "on the self-defining ground of the slave quarters. He finds the ground hallowed and made fertile by the blood and bones of the men and women who can be described as warriors on the cultural battlefield that affirmed their self-worth" (Harrison, p. 576). In *Gem of the Ocean* (2003), he creates a mythic monument, an Atlantic burial ground marked by the bones of some 80 percent of potential slaves transported from Africa who didn't survive the hellish Middle Passage. A grand haven rinsed clean of suffering, the spot is marked on a quilt, a graphic representation of cartography to the illiterate, who piece scraps of their heritage together into functional beauty. In the middle of the ocean floor, the undersea boneyard, measuring a half mile on a side, constitutes the world's largest unmarked burial place. It forms a symbolic blacks-only land between capture and sale of natives from West Africa. As Wilson explains, "The flesh of their flesh populates the Americas from Mississippi to Montevideo" (Bloom, p. 10).

The playwright conjures up his Wagnerian bone city to conceptualize an heroic past permeated by suffering and martyrdom. In the safety of her Pittsburgh parlor, Aunt Ester Tyler conducts witnesses on a vision quest to the plantation era that serves as a psyche-altering birth-reenactment. She remarks that the sea's graveyard has caused ships to ground and explains, "They say it's a mystery. It ain't no mystery. It's them bones. In time it will all come to light" (Smiley). She implies that blacks will one day envision their past clearly and proudly and that white people will suffer from the evil inflicted on African captives.

For her patient's enlightenment, Aunt Ester creates immediacy by expressing her own ties with plantation bondage. Using a slave document of her worth to fashion a paper boat, she turns a parlor seance into recovered memory by suggesting a walk through the mid–Atlantic purgatory to cleanse Citizen Barlow's soul. She exalts the slave dead as an enterprising people who built a unique underwater kingdom from bones, the cast-off refuse of human decay. By conferring homage on African forebears, those descendents who experience hurt and despair receive her blessing of wholeness.

The operatic vision of bony remains in the sea recurs seven years later in *Joe Turner's Come and Gone* (1988), in which the down-hearted Herald Loomis experiences a juba-induced trance that causes him to see a march of skeletons that produce a wave that deposits whole people on dry land. The vision strikes such terror in him that he collapses in spontaneous paralysis. As the playwright explained in an interview with Nathan Grant, the event is an epiphany: "[Loomis] is in effect witnessing himself being born. He understands then that his existence is the manifest act of the Creator. Therefore he has to be filled with God's majesty" (Grant).

See also **Aunt Ester, juba**

• *Further Reading*

Bloom, Harold, intro. *August Wilson*. New York: Chelsea House, 2002.
Grant, Nathan L. "Men, Women, and Culture: A Conversation with August Wilson." *American Drama*, Vol. 5, No. 2, Spring 1996, pp. 100–22.
Harrison, Paul Carter. "The Crisis of Black Theatre Identity." *African American Review*, Vol. 31, No. 4, 1997, p. 576.
Smiley, Travis. "Profile: August Wilson's 'Gem of the Ocean,' Starring Phylicia Rashad." *National Public Radio*, August 29, 2003.
Weiss, Hedy. "'Ocean' Voyage Proves Rough But Rewarding." *Chicago Sun-Times*, April 29, 2003, p. 34.

coming of age

August Wilson's concern for stable homes and a sound upbringing for youth dominates his first drama. With examples of good and bad beginnings for children, he invests the ten-play decade cycle with realistic experiences that summarize the socialization of blacks in the twentieth century. Some of his character quandaries suggest the dilemmas he faced in boyhood. With the four-minute scenario *The Janitor* (1985), the playwright expresses a mature man's reflections on youth and its foibles. Of the evanescence and fragility of youth, Sam, a janitor in a hotel ballroom, reminds his invisible hearers, "Don't spend that sweetness too fast! 'Cause you gonna need it" (p. 1901).

Wilson frequently equates the maturing of youth with a face-off between parent and child, as with Ruby's choice of career over child and Red Carter's abandonment of three-year-old Mister in *King Hedley II* (1999). The parenting of eleven-year-old Maretha in *The Piano Lesson* (1990) depicts the coming clashes erupting along with adolescent hormones. Worsening the situation is Berniece Charles's domination of her daughter and an ongoing attempt to eradicate blackness from her family history, behavior, even her hair. In contrast to Berniece's urge to control is Herald Loomis's intent to relinquish his parental duties in *Joe Turner's Come and Gone* (1988). Upon reuniting with his wife, Martha Pentecost, he is glad that their eleven-year-old daughter Zonia will have mothering to guide her into adolescence. Less homey is a fiery motif at the reunion of the jailbird Booster Becker with his angry father in *Jitney* (1982), in which time runs out before the pair can reconcile.

In *Fences* (1985), Troy Maxson recalls a severe whipping with mule harness when his father discovered him playing with a young girl rather than plowing with Greyboy. The pattern of father overpowering a stripling son weighs down on Cory, Troy's son, who bears so heavy a burden of hatred that he refuses to attend his father's funeral. Rose, the family peacemaker, counsels her grown son with a reminder that the shadow that Troy cast over him "wasn't nothing but you growing into yourself" (p. 97).

In *King Hedley II*, the postponement of full identity with parent immures the title character in a protracted state of boyhood. His ambivalence toward self and family results in a crisis for his unborn child, whom his wife Tonya considers aborting. The bloody end of the play costs Hedley his life from one shot of his mother's derringer. Left hanging is the future of Tonya and King's baby, another member of the violent Hedley family. Wilson concludes at this dramatic moment as a model of the 1980s, a decade marred by gangs clashes, drive-by shootings, and random, senseless violence.

See also **Booster Becker, Maretha Crawley, King Hedley II, Zonia Loomis, Cory Maxson, parenthood**

• *Further Reading*

Charters, Ann, and Samuel Charters, ed. *Short Pieces from the New Dramatists*. Banbury, Ox.: Orangeberry Books, 1985.

community

The importance of get-togethers at homes, restaurants, and night clubs fills August Wilson's plays with fun, nostalgia, and bittersweet reflection. Ghetto cohesion, which he recalls from childhood, is a valuable element to character contentment. Of his growing-up years in Pittsburgh's Hill District, he told interviewer Sharon Fitzgerald: "Everybody in the community was your social parent, and everyone knew everyone. I'd come home from school, and the parents would be sitting out on the steps, waiting for the kids to come home. They had gathered at the local store, stood around there and talked for hours and traded recipes" (Fitzgerald, p. 14). The loss of cohesion became one of his repeated dramatic themes and the dominant chord in *King Hedley II* (1999), set in a slum in the hopeless, violent 1980s.

Like the safe house on the Underground Railroad and revival sermons in Toni Morrison's *Beloved* (1987), kitchen tables at the black-operated inn in *Joe Turner's Come and Gone* (1988) and Aunt Ester's home in *Gem of the Ocean* (2003) are the heart of waystations for migrants from the South seeking familiar dialect, food, camaraderie, and consolation for past hurts. The hospitality of Bertha and Seth Holly in *Joe Turner's Come and Gone* includes a Sunday evening juba dance. Its exuberance and welcome unite participants in a tribal act that validates ethnic and racial ties to Africa in the same way that a native American stomp dance binds Indians in an unbroken circle of kinship, belonging, and continuity. In the company of Aunt Ester and Black Mary in *Gem of the Ocean*, outsider Citizen Barlow basks in the welcome and solace that Pittsburgh blacks extend to refugees from hard times.

In *Two Trains Running* (1991), set during the unsettling times of urban rebuilding, Wilson moves from homey kitchen table to neighborhood lunch counter and diner kitchen, operated by Risa Thomas, another soft-hearted female cook. Memphis Lee seeks to preserve his homestyle cafe, a gathering spot where blacks feel at ease to discuss racism, discrimination, unemployment, soul food, women, even the numbers syndicate, which is run by the Alberts, a white family of racketeers. Similarly, in *Jitney* (1982), drivers working out of a cab stand next door to Clifford's make successive trips to wash up and to buy coffee and fish sandwiches as though the eatery were an adjunct of their business. Ironically, Clifford's shares the same fate as the jitney station, which is about to be demolished to accommodate inner-city renewal.

Wilson chooses families as models of the closest form of interpersonal bonding. In an intimate kitchen table setting in *The Piano Lesson* (1990), the arrival of Boy Willie Charles and friend Lymon Jackson from Stoner County, Mississippi, to the Pittsburgh flat of Uncle Doaker Charles reunites Boy Willie with another uncle, the rover Wining Boy, Boy Willie's sister Berniece, and his niece Maretha. Their reminiscing, joking, singing, clapping, eating, and drinking preface the reiteration of details of their ancestry, including deceased great grandparents, grandfather, parents, and a husband as well as two former wives, one living and one dead, who abandoned the Charles family circle. Like a medieval motet, the final scene brings the curtain down on a song fest at the family piano amid family jubilation and triumph over evil.

The embrace of friends and family as a consolation is evident in scenes of grief and mourning. A reunion between Cory and his little sister Raynell in *Fences* (1985) takes place as mourners converge on the front porch of the Maxson house before the funeral of the protagonist. A similar gathering at Memphis Lee's cafe in *Two Trains Running* unites a group of faithful patrons to honor Hambone with a gift of flowers and the ham that he believed he had earned. In *Seven Guitars* (1995), friends gather in a scruffy backyard setting to drink, sing, and dance their post-burial tribute to Floyd Barton, whose recording of "That's All Right" becomes a soothing anthem. The characters use their shared intimacy as a release of shock and grief and a necessary restructuring of their mutual friendship, which is the gelling agent of community.

See also **call-and-response, Hambone, juba, soul food**

• *Further Reading*

Fitzgerald, Sharon. "August Wilson: The People's Playwright." *American Visions*, Vol. 15, No. 14, August 2000, p. 14.
Heilbrunn, Jacob. "Bus Boy." *New Republic*, Vol. 217, No. 17, October 27, 1997, p. 42.
Pereira, Kim. *August Wilson and the African-American Odyssey*. Urbana: University of Illinois Press, 1995.

crime

The sources of crime, according to August Wilson, fester in the black response to bias, unemployment, poverty, self-preservation, disenfranchisement, and white urbanism. In the introduction to *Fences*, he interweaves crime and suffering as the natural reactions to want: "[Blacks] cleaned houses and washed clothes, they shined shoes, and in quiet desperation and vengeful pride, they stole, and lived in pursuit of their own dream" (p. xvii). Of the disproportionate number of black inmates, he mused, "There are approximately a million black men in jail.... When you have somebody in jail that means there is a woman without a husband, there are kids without fathers. So the break-up of the family is part of the continuation of public policies and practices going back to the Emancipation Proclamation" (O'Mahony).

Although sympathetic with ex-cons, Wilson does not shy away from depicting blacks as criminals, particularly Mister and the younger King Hedley, the bumbling jewelry store robbers in *King Hedley II* (1999), who flee in daylight with $3,160 stuffed in a pillowcase. Turnbo, a cabbie in *Jitney* (1982), reports the bold theft of Miss Sarah Bolger's television, which her teenage grandson snatched to pawn for cash. More troubling is the return of Booster Becker, son of the cab stand manager, who must repent for degrading his father and causing his mother's death from grief at hearing him condemned to death row for murdering a white girl. In *Seven Guitars* (1995), Pittsburgh authorities harass citizens with licensing of peanut sellers and street singers, yet harbors Robert Gordon and T. L. Hall, the straw-hatted two-timer who flimflams the public by hawking phony insurance. In Floyd Barton's opinion, the city is a perfect place for frauds and villains to slight the law. He remarks, "Some things you get away with up here you can't get away with down [South]" (p. 68).

The playwright incorporates a range of urban crimes in *Two Trains Running* (1991), in which Wolf runs a serious numbers racket over the phone in Memphis Lee's cafe. In contrast, Sterling Johnson commits ludicrous thefts by taking a gas can he finds unattended in the alley and by stealing flowers from West's funeral parlor meant to honor the passing of the Prophet Samuel. An unknown prowler violates the prophet's dignity even worse by burglarizing the funeral parlor to rob the corpse while the casket is open for viewing. The undertaker remarks that theft of jewelry from corpses is a common occurrence in his business. To protect the cash on Samuel's remains, West glues a hundred-dollar bill to the dead man's hand. In a more poignant example of misdirected crime, Wilson incorporates a fool tale about Bubba Boy, who steals an expensive dress from Surrey's in which to bury his woman, who died of an overdose. Because of his immediate arrest, Bubba Boy is unable to attend her funeral unless community members collect two thousand dollars to bail him out of jail.

On a more serious level, Wilson castigates black crime as a cause of wasted lives and early deaths, as seen in the troubled spirit of the title con man in *King Hedley II*, Booster Becker's murder of Susan McKnight in *Jitney*, the drowning of an innocent millworker for Citizen Barlow's theft of a bucket of nails in *Gem of the Ocean* (2003), and the police shooting of Poochie Tillery for robbing a finance company in *Seven Guitars* (1995). The playwright uses the actions of jazz trumpeter Levee Green, protagonist of *Ma Rainey's Black Bottom* (1985), as proof that blacks burdened by social and economic injustice act out their frustrations and harm other blacks. In *Two Trains Running*, Wilson speaks through West, a former hardened gambler, numbers runner, and bootlegger, a strong indictment of crime: "The only thing you get out of that is an early grave" (p. 63).

In *The Piano Lesson* (1990), Boy Willie's theft of wood proves West right after the situation escalates into a police ambush against his brother-in-law Crawley. He dies of a gunshot wound, leaving a bitter widow. The era's infractions pale beside the hideous crimes of the past, including the separation of great grandfather Willie Boy's family in slave times and the burning death of Boy Charles and four innocent hobos in a boxcar on July 4, 1911. Subsequent retaliation resulted in a series of murders blamed on spirits called the Ghosts of the Yellow Dog. Berniece Charles, a spokesperson for obedience to the law, grows so angry at her autocratic brother Boy Willie that she threatens him with a .38 pistol. Their Uncle Doaker, himself a thief, monitors the argument to "keep you all from killing one another," which is a real possibility as their anger mounts (p. 90).

The playwright justifies his philosophy in *Fences* (1985), in which the burden of frustration attacked Troy Maxson at age fourteen, when he made his way north from Mobile, Alabama, to Pittsburgh and found blacks subsisting wherever they could shelter. He admits that he advanced from pilfering food into stealing money to buy shoes, a symbol of migration. Without justifying his actions, he explains his robbery of a man who was armed with a gun. The resulting match-up left the man dead and Troy sentenced to fifteen years in the penitentiary. The curse of crime passes to his son Lyons, who loses his wife Bonnie, a laundress at Passavant Hospital, because of his shiftlessness. He serves three years in a Pittsburgh workhouse for cashing stolen checks. Wilson injects hope for Lyons in his admiration for his father, who refused to be felled by adversity.

See also **Elmore, gambling, T. L. Hall, injustice, opportunity, violence**

• *Further Reading*

Gutman, Les. "King Hedley II." *CurtainUp*, 2001.
O'Mahony, John. "American Centurion." Manchester *Guardian*, December 14, 2002.
Pereira, Kim. *August Wilson and the African-American Odyssey*. Urbana: University of Illinois Press, 1995.

cultural nationalism

Out of a belief that black talent is wasted, August Wilson has written 90 percent of a ten-play cycle of African American life in the twentieth century as an effort to raise black and white consciousness. He explained to interviewer Sharon Fitzgerald the reason for his efforts: "[Black] culture has not always been valued; it certainly has not been valued by white America. In terms of the value and worth of the humanity of black folks, it has been sometimes very urgently and profoundly denied" (Fitzgerald, p. 14). He fears that, without artistic intervention, the dominant European-based culture will subsume black African traditions and arts. As he commented in an interview, "To assimilate is to adopt the values of another culture. I'm opposed to that idea, because blacks have something of value. To assimilate is to erase yourself, and I don't think that's what we want to do" (Saltzman & Plett).

To halt cultural negation, Wilson writes dramas that inform viewers about the black past, present, and future through instructive theater experiences, as with the fable of the African stew that Toledo relates in *Ma Rainey's Black Bottom* (1985), a recipe for greens in *Seven Guitars* (1995), a juba dance and blood baptism in *Joe Turner's Come and Gone* (1988), and the seance of Aunt Ester in *Gem of the Ocean* (2003) that informs Citizen Barlow of the sacrifice of black Africans during the Middle Passage. In *King Hedley II* (1999), Stool Pigeon, who is both griot and prophet, mourns the dissociative power of ignorance: "The people wandering all over the place. They got lost. They don't even know the story of how they got from tit to tat" (p. 1). Wilson typifies these narratives as a form of cultural nationalism. His intent is to uplift the poorest, least actualized element of society: "When you look at black America, yes we have Colin Powell, we got Clarence Thomas and we got the head of Time Warner. That comes to about ten people out of 35 million" (O'Mahony). Wilson complained that "The majority live in dire poverty in housing projects without any avenues for participation in the society" (*Ibid.*).

Wilson's African American drama decade unifies the cultural chronicle with lyric dialogue, humorous repartee, unsettling acts of rage and violence, and revealing moments of animistic ritual and self-knowledge that hearten and empower black people. The characters in *Two Trains Running* (1991) embrace belonging and community at Memphis Lee's cafe, where they can relax, eat soul food, and discuss community events. A similar gathering in *Seven Guitars* shares memories and consolation for the violence and unexplained death of Floyd Barton, an admired guitarist. In the final moments of *Fences* (1985), Gabe, the half-witted war veteran, overcomes frustration with his imperfect trumpet and gives way to dance in movements "eerie and life giving. A dance of atavistic signature and ritual" (p. 101). The occasion concludes with Gabe's wordless howl that ushers his brother Troy through heaven's gates, one of Wilson's transcendent acts of cultural viability.

See also **religion, soul food, superstition**

• *Further Reading*

Brantley, Ben. "'King Hedley II': The Agonized Arias of Everyman in Poverty and Pain." *New York Times*, May 2, 2001.

Fitzgerald, Sharon. "August Wilson: The People's Playwright." *American Visions*, Vol. 15, No. 14, August 2000, p. 14.

Fulani, Lenora B. "Black Empowerment: Playwright August Wilson Less Known by Blacks." *New Pittsburgh Courier*, March 5, 1997.

Harris, Trudier. "August Wilson's Folk Traditions," in *August Wilson: A Casebook*. New York: Garland, 1994.

Metzger, Linda, et al., eds. *Black Writers: A Selection of Sketches from Contemporary Authors*. Detroit: Gale Research, 1989.

O'Mahony, John. "American Centurion." Manchester *Guardian*, December 14, 2002.

Saltzman, Simon, and Nicole Plett. "'Jitney' at Crossroads." *U.S. 1 Newspaper*, April 16, 1997.

Cunningham, Molly

Molly Cunningham, a twenty-six-year-old newcomer to the Hollys' rooming house in *Joe Turner's Come and Gone* (1988), impacts the text with self-centered independence. After Bynum Walker advises Jeremy Furlow on respect and appreciation for women, her appearance onstage seems prophetic of a love match. Fashionable and appealing, she immediately catches Jeremy's eye, but appears scatter-brained and irresponsible by mentioning that she missed the train to Cincinnati. After the Sunday evening juba dance, she confides to Bynum that her father was a malcontent.

In reaction against his grumblings, she avoids stress and "just [takes] life as it come" (p. 61). One of Wilson's few characters who has cut all ties with the South, Molly seems ready to embrace new experiences that have no relationship to the past.

As though speaking from past wounds, Molly hoists a combative attitude bristling with pessimism and suspicion of everybody but her mother. To Mattie Campbell's job ironing for Doc Goldblum, Molly spurns domestic chores: "That's something I don't never wanna do. Iron no clothes…. Not Molly Cunningham" (p. 62). To avoid childbearing, she learned birth control from her mother and warns Mattie about trusting men. A female version of the philanderer Floyd Barton in *Seven Guitars* (1995) and womanizer Levee Green in *Ma Rainey's Black Bottom* (1985), Molly smirks, "One's just as good as the other if you ask me" (*Ibid.*). To Jeremy's offer to travel the road with him in Act II, Scene 2, she warns that she doesn't work, prostitute her body, or go south.

See also women

• *Further Reading*

Bandler, Michael J. "USIA Interview with American Playwright August Wilson." http:// usembassy-australia.state.gov/hyper/WF980415/epf308.htm, April 15, 1998.

Cutler

The guitarist, trombonist, and dutiful, rock-steady bandleader for the title character in *Ma Rainey's Black Bottom* (1985), Cutler is one of August Wilson's reliable father figures. Like Bynum Walker in *Joe Turner's Come and Gone* (1988) and Doaker Charles in *The Piano Lesson* (1990), Cutler displays a maturity lacking in Ma's twenty-something trumpeter Levee Green and in her pet duo, Dussie Mae and Sylvester Brown. A traditional musician in his mid-fifties, Cutler relies on religion, the blues, and a long-time relationship with Ma to steady his difficult job of backing up her singing and maintaining the output of squabbling, discontented musicians. By controlling his temper and mediating difficulties, Cutler endures chain-of-command blowups with Irvin, Ma's manager, over the list of titles that the band will record during the session.

Least effective in rattling Cutler is Levee Green, a self-important climber whose jive talk the older man debunks for its illogic. To Levee's derision of Ma's style, Cutler informs him of the pecking order: Levee plays accompaniment, not the lead, and must adhere to the group's style. Cutler is fair about refusing Levee time to improvise when the group is waiting to rehearse. When Levee belittles Slow Drag's manhood, Cutler comes to his defense with a tale of Slow Drag's sensual dance with another man's girl. Although Levee's blasphemy goads Cutler to bloody his nose and mouth in defense of his religion and to raise a chair to ward off Levee's advance with a blade, the bandleader remains even-handed. He intercedes with Ma's decision to fire Levee by reminding her, "He plays good music when he puts his mind to it" (p. 78).

• *Further Reading*

Clark, Keith. *Black Manhood in James Baldwin, Ernest J. Gaines, and August Wilson.* Urbana: University of Illinois Press, 2002.
Crawford, Eileen. "The B Burden: The Invisibility of Ma Rainey's Black Bottom," in *August Wilson: A Casebook.* New York: Garland, 1994.
Pereira, Kim. *August Wilson and the African-American Odyssey.* Urbana: University of Illinois Press, 1995.

death

August Wilson invests his plays with regular references to the inevitable passage of time, a reminder of missed opportunities and human mortality. As the cabbie Doub notes in *Jitney* (1982), "Time go along and it come around" (p. 17). His workmate Shealy echoes, "It don't never stop" (*Ibid.*). Later, Turnbo, an older driver, speaks of time as an impatient entity that "don't wait on nobody. Everything change" (p. 30). Youngblood, who perceives time from a young adult perspective, complains that urban renewal is ruining his chance of buying a house. He recalls that, on his return from the Vietnam War, Ace's death left a job vacancy that Youngblood filled at the cab stand. The latter comment is prophetic of the shift in management at the play's end, when Booster takes over after his father dies unexpectedly in a mill accident.

A more fearful reminder of evanescence than the passage of days, death overwhelms characters with its finality, as Boy Willie comments in *The Piano Lesson* (1990), Reuben Mercer regrets in *Joe Turner's Come and Gone* (1988), and Solly Two Kings states in *Gem of the Ocean* (2003). In the opening scene of *King Hedley II* (1999), the title character laments the failure of a police investigation of the drive-by shooting that killed Little Buddy Will, whose mother later avenges him by shooting his attacker. Mattie Campbell, a mournful mother in *Joe Turner's Come and Gone*, repines over the deaths of her two infants, who didn't live to eight weeks. To Vera Dotson in *Seven Guitars* (1995), the intersection of life and death is a mystic phenomenon: "[Scripture] say you know neither the day nor the hour when death come" (p. 5). To Doub, his nine-month corpse detail during the Korean War left horrifying memories. Wilson's choice of time span links the vision of soldiers maimed in combat with the term of human pregnancy, a balance to the frequent deaths in his plays. By referring to WillaMae's birthing of the baby boy Mister in *Seven Guitars*, Tonya Hedley's pregnancy in *King Hedley II*, and Alberta's infant daughter in *Fences* (1985), the playwright retrieves the theme of death from blatant morbidity to the normal yin and yang of earthly existence.

Humor and wisdom humanize Wilson's quips about dying. Levee Green, a respecter of death in *Ma Rainey's Black Bottom* (1985), asserts, "Death got some style. Death will kick your ass and make you wish you never been born" (p. 92). When West, the widowed mortician, describes his undertaking experiences in *Two Trains Running* (1991), he remarks on the fragility of life, which "you can blow … away with a blink of an eye" (p. 75). Later in the play, Holloway, the local philosopher, summarizes the extremes of life as love at one end and death at the other. He advises,

"Death will find you ... it's up to you to find love" (p. 102). The one character who appears to elude the stalker is the pervasive figure of Aunt Ester, the mythic black seer who manages to survive to age 366. According to Holloway, a devotee of the prophet, death fears Ester. When death tries to nab her, her holiness repulses the unearthly cold hands. In *King Hedley II*, her stout avoidance of death results in a squabble between the coroner and her butler Eli, who refuses a request for an autopsy, an ignoble dissection that would rob her being of mystery and uniqueness.

Throughout Wilson's drama cycle, permanent loss restructures relationships and alters family power alliances. Following the 1928 death of Mama Ola Charles, a beloved parent in *The Piano Lesson*, her daughter Berniece hardens toward the family heirloom, a piano that her mother polished and cared for in widowhood for over seventeen years. In *Seven Guitars*, Canewell, a mourner, comments on the personal touch of throwing dirt on the grave of his friend Floyd Barton. The rightness of the ritual prompts Canewell to declare that he would rather do the covering of the casket than have a stranger from the funeral home fill the grave. The somber statement precedes Canewell's wry acknowledgement to the corpse, "You was a good old boy ... but you dead and gone" (p. 4). Later, he mutters, "I wonder when's my time. Seem like I'm lucky to still be alive" (p. 21).

The playwright comments frequently through his characters that time and change are human constants. He insists that death is so conjoined with life that it is as undeniable as King Hedley's success at killing poultry and selling chicken sandwiches following George Butler's funeral in *Seven Guitars*. Hedley remarks darkly, "Everybody got a time coming. Nobody can't say that they don't have a time coming" (p. 19). In the title of *Two Trains Running*, Wilson implies that life and death are the two opposing forces of the title image. In the playbill, he clarified with a brief homily: "There are always and only two trains running. There is life and there is death. Each of us rides them both" (cover). His sermon concludes with a reminder to individuals to live responsibly and nobly and to celebrate their allotted time on earth.

Supporting the image of death in the midst of life is the play's setting, which Wilson characterizes as a diner "across the street from West's Funeral Home and Lutz's Meat Market" (n.p.). The community gathering place shares space with two venues of death, one human and one animal. Risa Thomas, the cook and waitress at Memphis Lee's diner, grieves for days over the demise of the Prophet Samuel, but retreats from viewing the man's remains, even though Wolf taunts her with "Ain't nothing to be scared of" (p. 15). The undertaker notes the number and variety of items that people tuck into the casket to add a touch of familiarity. From experience comes his understanding that the mementos—"Bibles, canes, crutches, guitars, radios, baby dolls," even tomatoes from a sister's garden — are important to the family, not the deceased (p. 37). He adds with a pragmatic touch, "I don't mind putting anything in there with anybody as long as the casket close" (*Ibid.*). Countering the gloom at the funeral home and the fastidious white gloves of the mortician is the diner itself, which takes on the humanity of a character in a dying urban setting.

With *Fences* (1985), Wilson creates an odd familiarity with death in the defiance of Troy Maxson. The malcontented garbage collector is unable to express honest emotions to his wife and sons, but turns to converse with Mr. Death, whom he describes as though his adversary were palpable and human. Troy claims to have wrestled the personified Death for three days and nights on their first encounter in mid–July 1941 at Mercy Hospital, where Troy was being treated for pneumonia. Like Jacob, the biblical patriarch in Genesis 32:22–31, Troy exhibits epic fortitude by seizing Death's sickle and tossing it away. In Troy's view of the inevitable end of life, he must remain strong and vigilant and must fight for survival. Thus, his nearness to Mr. Death makes him appreciate what life is left to him.

In contrast to Troy, his mentally handicapped brother Gabe speaks familiarly of St. Peter as though they were companions sharing biscuits. Gabe prattles on about having died already, a comment that suggests the suffering and loss he sustained from a skull wound during World War II. To Troy's annoyance, Gabe claims that St. Peter has marked Troy's name for judgment. Unlike his older brother, Gabe exhibits no dread of death and saves money for a new trumpet to summon St. Peter "when it's time to open the gates [of heaven]" (p. 27).

Death proves to be a wily adversary in *Fences*. It returns unexpectedly at the play's climax in 1959 with the loss of Alberta in giving birth to Troy's daughter. He takes the loss as a personal affront, a side-door method by which Mr. Death waylays his victims. Troy rages openly at Death, challenging him to bring his army and renew their metaphoric wrestling match man to man rather than through the theft of a tender loved one. Truculent in grief, Troy challenges, "Ain't nobody else got nothing to do with this" (p. 77).

In his last months, loss saps Troy's vitality. Rose abandons their failed marriage and takes up the church; his old friend Jim Bono plays dominoes each Friday night with Skinner. Left to drink alone on payday, Troy sings a mournful verse to his dog song: "Old Blue died and I dig his grave/Let him down with a golden chain" (p. 84). Cory, more man than boy, refuses to treat his father courteously. After years of devaluing his wife and sons, Troy tastes the same discounting when Cory calls him "just an old man" (p. 87). The symbolic taker of life is Troy's final visitor in 1965 on the day that he swings the baseball bat and collapses from a heart attack. Typical of Troy's refusal to be cowed by death, he died grinning. His children, Cory and Raynell, join voices for four verses of Troy's song about Old Blue, concluding on a positive note — his delight in the Promised Land "where the good dogs go" (p. 99).

See also **Floyd Barton, Gabe Maxson, Troy Maxson,** *Seven Guitars,* **West**

• *Further Reading*

Monaco, Pamela Jean. "Father, Son, and Holy Ghost: From the Local to the Mythical in August Wilson," in *August Wilson: A Casebook.* New York: Garland, 1994.

Wang, Qun. *An In-Depth Study of the Major Plays of African American Playwright August Wilson: Vernacularizing the Blues on Stage.* Vol. 6 of *Black Studies.* Lewiston, Ont.: Edwin Mellen Press, 1999.

decade cycle

Wilson has completed 90 percent of an ambitious career-long project — the writing of a decade cycle, an interconnected series of plays that has been compared to a graph. *New Yorker* drama critic John Lahr acclaimed the project's importance to stage history: "No other theatrical testament to African American life has been so popular or so poetic or so penetrating" (Charters & Charters, p. 1900). The ten segments depict black Americans living in each decade of the twentieth century in a form of spotlighting that critic John Lowe of Louisiana State University calls "foci of racial memory" (Lowe, p. 250).

The lineup so far of plays by historical milieu and publication date extends to the 1980s:

era	title	publication	time frame
1900s	*Gem of the Ocean*	2003	1904
1910s	*Joe Turner's Come and Gone*	1988	August, 1911
1920s	*Ma Rainey's Black Bottom*	1985	1927
1930s	*The Piano Lesson*	1990	1936
1940s	*Seven Guitars*	1995	mid–May, 1948
1950s	*Fences*	1985	1957
1960s	*Two Trains Running*	1991	mid–May, 1969
1970s	*Jitney*	1982	1977
1980s	*King Hedley II*	1999	1985

The cycle began with *Jitney* (1982), a conversational working class drama set in Pittsburgh during urban renewal. Three years later, Wilson continued his decalogue with *Ma Rainey's Black Bottom* (1985), which takes place in Chicago a half century earlier. Completing two plays in the same year, he added *Fences* (1985), which takes shape outside the main character's ragged two-story brick residence. Three years later, Wilson published *Joe Turner's Come and Gone* (1988), which captures the milieu of a Pittsburgh boardinghouse during the generation that sought a stake in American freedoms in the aftermath of the Civil War.

Wilson maintained his literary momentum with a fifth play, *The Piano Lesson* (1990), written two years later, which describes family life in a simple urban flat in 1936, the late Depression era. Within a year, Wilson wrote the sixth, *Two Trains Running* (1991), which pictures Pittsburgh in the tense era of Black Power and the failed promises of President Lyndon Johnson's Great Society. The seventh, *Seven Guitars* (1995), takes place in the post–World War II era that buoyed white industry and investments, but offered limited prosperity to blacks; the eighth, *King Hedley II* (1999), carries the characters thirty-seven years ahead to a time when the son of the original King Hedley faces his own manhood crisis while unwittingly welcoming his father's murderer. The text refers to Aunt Ester, a mystically long-lived sage mentioned in *Two Trains Running*. She materializes in the flesh as rescuer of Citizen Barlow in the ninth play, *Gem of the Ocean* (2003), which Wilson placed in the first decade of the twentieth century, within memory of slavery, runaways on the Underground Railroad, and emancipation. Lacking from the century of plays is a tenth covering the 1990s, in which Wilson intends to depict the black professional serving the black underclass. The character, an attorney educated at Harvard, restores a sense of wholeness in the ghetto by retrieving the corpse of Aunt Ester in a *pro bono* court case. While involved in the case, the protagonist realizes that he is her nephew, a blood kinship that suggests the interrelations of all members of Afro-America.

Like Thomas Hardy's characters living in fictional Wessex, England, Ernest Gaines's made-up microcosm of Bayonne, Louisiana, and William Faulkner's novels and stories set in Yoknapatawpha County, Mississippi, Wilson's plays draw on some recurring characters, places, events, and motifs, including stores, cafes, and Pittsburgh's Irene Kaufman Settlement House. Aunt Ester, Ruby, Elmore, Stovall, Jim Bono, Louise, and King Hedley are significant in multiple plays, as is the unseen community businessman Hertzberger or Hartzberger. Seefus's night spot, alternately spelled "Sefus" and "Cephus," flourishes across the time span of Wilson's decade cycle, as do the Crawford Grill and other black landmarks on or near Pittsburgh's Wylie Avenue. The motif of betting on the number 651 crops up in *Fences* and *Two Trains Running* as testimony to the endurance of the numbers racket in black society, a symbol of the human need to believe in good luck and better times.

See also **historical milieu, Pittsburgh**

• *Further Reading*

Charters, Ann, and Samuel Charters, ed. *Short Pieces from the New Dramatists.* Banbury, Ox.: Orangeberry Books, 1985.
Lowe, John. "Wake-up Call From Watts." *World & I*, Vol. 13, No. 5, May 1998, p. 250.
Rawson, Chris. "O'Reilly Theater: Charting 20th Century Black America." *Pittsburgh Post-Gazette*, December 5, 1999.

dialect

Like the poetry of Paul Laurence Dunbar, August Wilson's selection of language for stage presentation reproduces the exchanges of real people he has known or observed. By employing robust, colorful, sometimes ribald African American dialect, the language peculiar to a limited population in a small geographical area, the playwright shows preference for the street talk or patois of a heavily localized and poorly educated segment of a ghetto population. One brief example, *The Janitor* (1985), allows Sam, a humble sweeper of a hotel ballroom, to ascend to the microphone and address unseen hearers on the joys of youth. He warns about the rapid passage of the early years and, from personal experience, admits "I's fifty-six years old and I done found that out" (p. 1901). Unschooled black syntax endears Sam to his audience and expresses the importance of wisdom spoken from the commoner's point of view.

Language also delineates the changes in black culture when people make the Great Migration from South to North. The country-boy repartee between Lymon Jackson and Boy Willie Charles in *The Piano Lesson* (1990), makes the two easily identifiable by Pittsburgh's urban blacks of 1936. Three decades later, Memphis Lee, the diner owner in *Two Trains Running* (1991), is able to differentiate between the language of Pittsburgh blacks and those newly arrived who are still under the influence of "that old backward Southern mentality" (p. 30). He ridicules their plantation-era posturing before white males and their ingratiating "Yessir, Captain," "How do, Major," a necessary form of black obsequiousness during the unpredictable Jim Crow era (p. 30).

The use of dialect in Wilson's dramas establishes the authenticity of the characters' speech, particularly the Haitian patois of King Hedley in *Seven Guitars* (1995) where he boasts before George Butler's funeral, "Hedley sell plenty plenty chicken sandwiches tonight" (p. 18). In *The Piano Lesson*, Boy Willie's pulsing, provocative vocal patterns slyly negate Berniece's arguments and accusations with his own perception of family history and meaning. Berniece and Maretha, who ally with the urban North, avoid the slang and agrarian expressions of Mississippi that set Boy Willie apart from Uncle Doaker's northern wing of the Charles clan. The energy and fire of the Charleses' verbal clashes attest to the potential for growth in a dynasty scarred by slavery and a long-term cross-country separation.

In less localized drama, Wilson's skill at recreating black street vernacular conveys the salty tang, vigor, and phrasing of African American thought. Examples are plentiful in Toledo's fable of the African stew in *Ma Rainey's Black Bottom* (1985), Herald Loomis's renunciation of white religion in *Joe Turner's Come and Gone* (1988), Hambone's demented yelps for his ham in *Two Trains Running*, Elmore's courtship tale in *King Hedley II* (1999), and Solly Two Kings's collection and sale of dog dung in *Gem of the Ocean* (2003). In *Jitney* (1982), Fielding frames aphorism with black grammar in his advice to Booster about being in the treetop: "Did you climb up to get some apples or was you run up by a bear?" (p. 80). The authenticity of cadence and rhythm accounts for audience reception and critical acclaim that has boosted the playwright to preeminence on the American stage.

Wilson's accuracy has roused the censor's anger. In March 1995, Cissy Lacks, a twenty-five-year veteran white teacher at predominantly black Berkeley High School in St. Louis, was fired in March 1995 from the Ferguson Florissant School District for having her creative writing students emulate Wilson's *Fences* in a composition exercise. After she videotaped their plays, the school board dismissed her for allowing coarse and unsettling ghetto vernacular. Two years later, she was rehired and received a court settlement of $750,000. Her reinstatement acknowledged that the firing was race-based and exonerated her stand on uncensored language. At the same time, the case recognized the importance of Wilson's dialogue to young students as genuine communication methods within the black milieu. In June 1998, an appeal overturned the ruling. The Supreme Court refused to rule on the case.

Dialect drama earned the regard of Nilo Cruz, a Cuban playwright, who applies the lingual patterning of Athol Fugard and Wilson to his own plays, including *Two Sisters and a Piano* (1999). Nilo works from his childhood memories of Cuba much as Wilson draws on his growing-up years in Pittsburgh. Of the impact of Wilson's writing, Nilo declared that the success of such works as *Jitney* "gave me permission to write about my own people and to embrace inflections and embrace politics" (Breslauer, p. 42).

• *Further Reading*

Appiah, Kwame Anthony, and Henry Louis Gates, Jr., eds. *Africana*. New York: Perseus Books, 1999.
Breslauer, Jan. "Theater Lifting an Embargo on the Past Writing about His Native Cuba Did not Come Easily to Playwright Nilo Cruz, But Once He Started, He Quickly Found Familiar Territory." *Los Angeles Times*, April 25, 1999, p. 42.

Charters, Ann, and Samuel Charters, ed. *Short Pieces from the New Dramatists.* Banbury, Ox.: Orangeberry Books, 1985.

McCracken, Nancy. "When the YA Authors Are the Students: Learning from Cissy Lacks." *ALAN Review,* Vol. 23, No. 2, Winter 1996.

"The Roving Editor." *The Writer,* Vol. 110, No. 6, June 1997, p. 4.

diaspora

Diaspora, a term for the separation of people from their traditional homes, typically refers to ethnic groups—Jews and gypsies forced out of Europe by pogroms, American Indians herded off ancestral lands and onto reservations, and blacks ripped from their motherland in West Africa to serve white masters in the Western Hemisphere. A unifying force in black relations is a shared legacy from the descendents of bondage—the forcible separation from culture and religion, the journey across the Atlantic Ocean on the deadly Middle Passage, and the enslavement and sale of black survivors in a vigorous white economy. After emancipation, blacks found no place to call home in the South and attempted a self-directed diaspora to the industrial cities of the North, where the money and power of white males rechained them in a new form of serfdom. Marginalized, they lived on the fringes, enjoyed limited civil rights, encountered frequent unemployment, and worked for low wages, all sources of frustration in August Wilson's plays, particularly *King Hedley II* (1999) and *Gem of the Ocean* (2003).

On March 10, 1991, Wilson wrote for the *New York Times* his concern for the loss of continuity caused by the diaspora: "We as black Americans need to go back and make the connection we allowed to be severed when we moved from the South to the North, the great migration starting in 1915" (p. 5). By abandoning Southern culture, blacks began producing generations of youth with no tie to their grandsires or to political and social history. Through the character of Boy Willie Charles in *The Piano Lesson* (1990), Wilson presents the fervid, proud black male who rejects flight to the North as senseless. By sending him briefly to Pittsburgh to retrieve the family piano, the playwright revalues the South as the appropriate homeland for folk reared in an agrarian milieu. Blacks like Boy Willie are comfortable with the South's African American qualities, e.g., oral traditions, superstitions, love of the land and the earthy diet it produces, and a strong sense of kinship and clan survival. Symbolically, Boy Willie reverses the pattern of the plantation runaway on the Underground Railroad by planning to return to Mississippi immediately by train.

August Wilson's *Joe Turner's Come and Gone* (1988) echoes with the bewilderment of displaced residents at a rooming house who have made individual journeys from the South to Pittsburgh in an effort to develop social, familial, religious, and economic wholeness in their lives. The controlling theme presents the black search for identity and self-empowerment in the staged pilgrimage of ex-con Herald Loomis, who seeks to reunite himself and his daughter Zonia with his wife Martha. Guiding the way is Bynum Walker, the healer designated by a mystic "shiny man." He points out a path and bolsters courage as seekers make the transition from familiar rural districts to the perplexing urban setting in Pittsburgh.

Wilson's fictional diaspora is a test of human endurance and adaptability. Some

of his Southern blacks acclimate well to the North and its urban industrial ethic, particularly Jim Becker, who retires from J & L Steel in *Jitney* (1982) and establishes a gypsy car service for Pittsburgh's Hill District. In *Two Trains Running* (1991), Memphis Lee, who fled Jackson, Mississippi, in 1931, applies hard work and frugality toward achieving his goals in the same area. In a humorous exchange with Wolf and Holloway, he describes wanting to buy a V-8 Ford so he can drive by the Henry Ford mansion and blow the horn. Memphis adds, "It took me thirteen years to get the Ford. Six years later I traded that in on a Cadillac," a symbol of the next rung of the ladder of prosperity (p. 31). He makes no concrete plans to return to Mississippi, yet keeps tucked into his thoughts the fact that "They got two trains running every day" (*Ibid.*).

See also **City of Bones, displacement, Great Migration, railroads, Rutherford Selig, shiny man, Solly Two Kings**

• *Further Reading*

Elkins, Marilyn, ed. *August Wilson: A Casebook*. New York: Garland, 1994.
Harrison, Paul Carter, Victor Leo Walker, and Gus Edwards, eds. *Black Theatre: Ritual Performance in the African Diaspora*. Philadelphia: Temple University Press, 2002.
Wilson, August. "How to Write a Play Like August Wilson." *New York Times*, March 10, 1991, Sect. 2, p. 5.

displacement

August Wilson applies the psychological principle of displacement to dramatic events and themes characterizing the dispersal of blacks in the diaspora. In interviews, he has asserted the importance of the South to the descendents of former slaves. With a subtextual nod toward Jesus's parable of the sower and seeds, the playwright noted the failure of ethnic seeds in unreceptive soil: "We attempted to plant what in essence was an emerging culture, a culture that had grown out of our experience of two hundred years as slaves in the South" (Charters & Charters, p. 1899). He spoke from experience when he added, "The cities of the urban North have not been hospitable. If we had stayed in the South, we could have strengthened the culture" (*Ibid.*).

In *Gem of the Ocean*, set in 1904, when Citizen Barlow arrives from Alabama to Pittsburgh, he inadvertently causes an innocent man's death over a stolen bucket of nails, an ironic symbol of permanence as well as crucifixion. The onus of sin and guilt forces Barlow to search out the prophet Aunt Ester to aid him in understanding and correcting a serious character flaw. In 1927, the Florsheim shoes in *Ma Rainey's Black Bottom* (1985) represent the status-seeking hopes and intentions of Levee Green, a blues trumpeter eager to abandon the clodhopping brogans and sharecropping of Fat Back, Arkansas, as he seeks fame and success in the Chicago music industry. The strength of his resolve surfaces after Toledo soils the shoes, precipitating a backlash in which Levee knifes Toledo in the back. In both instances, Citizen Barlow and Levee victimize themselves by allowing personal frustration to erupt into crime.

More significant to the theme of displacement, in *The Piano Lesson* (1990), set in 1936, Wilson employs a carved piano as a repository of the Charles family's pride. The displacement of strong emotion onto the instrument results in a clash between a rural brother and urban sister. To Berniece, the piano is the well-polished heirloom on which Mama Ola lavished daily labors and a widow's tears. To Boy Willie, the piano is a valuable object that he can sell for $1,150 cash and apply his half to the purchase of cropland in the rich Mississippi Delta, where the racist Jim Crow laws extend elements of slavery seven decades after Abraham Lincoln issued the Emancipation Proclamation. Thus, property ownership becomes the capitalistic symbol of the black man's rise from underling to self-actualized landed gentry.

Still combating the down side of the diaspora, blacks in *Seven Guitars* (1995) live lonely, disconnected lives in a Pittsburgh boarding house in 1948, the height of the post–World War II boom. Significantly set on Mother's Day, a revered family holiday, the plot pictures boarders and travelers getting together for makeshift intimacy as card players, blues singers, celebraters, and short-term lovers. Ruby, a new arrival from Birmingham, settles in just as Floyd Barton, freed from a ninety-day sentence to the workhouse, attempts to woo Vera Dotson, his former girl friend, and settle with her in Chicago. Canewell, a failed suitor for Vera, bunks in temporarily with a woman on Clark Street in Little Haiti. King Hedley, the darkest and least understood of the play's septet, lives in a private world of rebellion and apocalypse that he brought with him from the West Indies. Adding to character dislocation are a guitar, harmonica, and drums at the pawn shop and a crowing rooster deemed out of place in Pittsburgh's Hill District. Wilson ends the strivings of Floyd, one of his most alienated characters, at the Greenwood cemetery, a burial site for the poor that receives too many of the city's dispossessed blacks.

See also **Citizen Barlow, diaspora, Dussie Mae, Great Migration, railroad**

• *Further Reading*

Charters, Ann, and Samuel Charters, ed. *Short Pieces from the New Dramatists*. Banbury, Ox.: Orangeberry Books, 1985.
Pereira, Kim. *August Wilson and the African-American Odyssey*. Urbana: University of Illinois Press, 1995.

Dotson, Vera

August Wilson creates a palpable, appealing female character in Vera Dotson, the subdued almost-wife and pious mourner in the opening scene of the character-driven play *Seven Guitars* (1995). Likeable and accommodating like Risa Thomas in *Two Trains Running* (1991), Ruby in *King Hedley II* (1999), Bertha Holly in *Joe Turner's Come and Gone* (1988), and Rose Maxson in *Fences* (1985), Vera deserves better than being the wronged girlfriend of the blues guitarist and singer Floyd Barton, but, like moth to flame, can't resist his passion and charm. In Act I, Scene 2, the first flashback of Vera's failed romance, she thrusts Floyd aside and reminds him "my feet ain't on backwards," a spunky metaphor indicating that she intends to abandon their one-sided romance (p. 8).

Wilson characterizes Floyd as a man drawn to women's appearance. The Barton-

Dotson relationship began with eye contact and the appeal of a blue dress on Vera's size nine body. Newly mustered out of the army, Floyd was drawn to her comeliness, but Vera had just left home to be on her own in Pittsburgh and recognized that a brief sexual fling was his main objective. After he wronged her and left for Chicago with Pearl Brown, Vera, like Risa Thomas, hardened toward men because of their inability to pledge a lasting love to one woman. In Act I, Scene 3, Vera rebukes Canewell for his short-lived "understanding" with a woman on Clark Street and stereotypes such uncommitted men as faithless: "Time you put two and two together and try and come up with four ... they out the door" (p. 28).

Wilson places the stirrings of insight in Vera, the model of wisdom gained the hard way. Although she delivers a sharp line in her dealings with Barton, in private discussion with Louise, the landlady, Vera charitably defends her former beau as meaning well, but inept at everything he attempts. By Act II, Scene 2, she considers following him to Chicago. Unable to sever her tie to a two-timing man, she sits up until 3:45 A.M. worrying that he hasn't come home. Floyd's offhand proposal of marriage and purchase of a bus ticket to Chicago are insufficient inducements to Vera. For good reason, she ponders, "What am I saying yeah to?" (p. 92). His love is powerful enough to accept her, even with a precautionary return-trip bus ticket in her shoe. After his burial, she envisions his spirit hurrying off and leaving her behind, much as he did in life in his obsession with a big-city music career.

See also **betrayal, women**

Doub

A veteran of the Korean War and a railroad pensioner, Doub is a long-time cab driver in *Jitney* (1982), one of the worthy common men whom the playwright honors. Because Doub is single, he is free with money and advice. Out of camaraderie with other cabbies, he lends four dollars to Fielding to buy liquor, buys him a fish sandwich, and speaks charitably of Youngblood as "just young. Got a lot to learn" (p. 24). Like the bobbing pointer on a balance beam scale, Doug tries to maintain social equilibrium. To Turnbo's constant intrusion on other people's lives, Doub retorts, "Ain't nobody told you what you need" (*Ibid.*).

Just as William Shakespeare groomed Malcolm and Fortinbras as replacements for the tragic heroes in *Hamlet* and *Macbeth*, August Wilson elevates Doub to replace the station manager at a crucial time in the jitney station's history. After twelve years under Jim Becker's management, at a crucial point in the city's development, Doub charges his faithful manager with letting the station deteriorate. Doub cites as evidence Jim's tolerance of Fielding's drinking on the job and allowing others to violate the rules about overcharging. Doub is astounded that their gypsy cab stand is closing because of urban renewal. His only choices are to rally the drivers to "figure out one way or another what we gonna do" or to fall back on driving a bus until he can claim his retirement money (p. 38).

While discussing the injustice of the military draft with Youngblood, Doub recalls the corpse detail that required him to heap combat casualties for nine months in 1950 during the Korean War. He was sickened by exacting work calling for five corpses per stack and was disappointed that he didn't learn a trade. Because he recognizes more opportunities for blacks in the 1970s, he encourages Youngblood to go to school rather than depend on cab-driving as a career. After Becker's sudden death, Doub becomes his employer's unofficial replacement by trying to keep order and stop the daily bickering among the disgruntled staff. Less defensive than other blacks, Doub is a good choice of stabilizer for his belief that the "White folks is against me" tack is detrimental to black advancement (p. 65).

See also **white-black relations**

• *Further Reading*

Bowen, Joseph. "Jitney." http://centerstage.net/theatre/articles/jitney.html.
Rawson, Chris. "Stage Review: Wilson Polishes 'Jitney' in Richer, Longer Production." *Pittsburgh Post-Gazette*, November 22, 1998.

Dussie Mae

Ma Rainey's female lover and rival of Sylvester Brown in *Ma Rainey's Black Bottom* (1985), Dussie Mae becomes a battle trophy sought by two generations of musicians. On her initial appearance, she exemplifies a form of disorientation in the big city. She seems diffident and out of place in the multi-level Chicago recording studio in which the play takes place. She wanders the room and peers about in search of the toilet. The sexually venturesome Ma dresses Dussie Mae in big-city styles "to look nice for me," advises her to wear comfortable shoes, and promises to buy whatever Dussie Mae needs (p. 60). Unfortunately for the younger girl, she has little to trade on beyond looks and sex.

Though secure with Ma, Dussie Mae falls victim to big-city amorality and allure. In defiance of Ma's orders, in Act Two, Dussie Mae enters the studio and bares her thighs for Ma's rival, Levee Green, who tried to impress her at the club the night before. Dussie Mae speaks for the independent black female by refusing sexual favors to a would-be music star who makes empty promises of getting his own band. She asserts, "I don't need nobody wanna get something for nothing and leave me standing in my door," but she risks Ma's reproach and continues to snuggle up to Levee so long as Ma isn't looking (p. 81). Dussie Mae's willingness to risk a cozy, lucrative arrangement with Ma implies that belonging to a man is more gratifying.

See also **women**

• *Further Reading*

Clark, Keith. *Black Manhood in James Baldwin, Ernest J. Gaines, and August Wilson.* Urbana: University of Illinois Press, 2002.
Elam, Harry J. "*Ma Rainey's Black Bottom:* Singing Wilson's Blues." *American Drama*, Vol. 5, No. 2, Spring 1996, pp. 76–99.
Pereira, Kim. *August Wilson and the African-American Odyssey.* Urbana: University of Illinois Press, 1995.

Eli

The militant and highly competent caretaker of Aunt Ester at her Pittsburgh rooming house in *Gem of the Ocean* (2003), Eli is one of the witnesses to the guilt and self-castigation in Citizen Barlow. In contrast to blacks living disconnected lives on the run, Eli is steady and reliable, a rock bearing the biblical name of an Old Testament priest and mentor to young Samuel. Chief among Eli's duties is to maintain peace and serenity in the residence to preserve its value as a sanctuary. On a daily basis, Eli keeps Aunt Ester's stove in working order for heating pots of tea and questions any symptoms of ill health in her.

Eli's placidity contrasts his younger days, when he and the formidable Solly Two Kings once retrieved slaves from the South on the Underground Railroad. To Solly's incessant reminiscing about their deeds of blood and thunder, Eli urges him to exit the mental battlefield and live in the present. Apparently, Eli's good advice keeps him alive an abnormal length of time, as indicated by mention of him in *Jitney* (1982), set in 1977. In *King Hedley II* (1999), set eight years later, Eli maintains order at Aunt Ester's house after her death, names Stool Pigeon as one of her pallbearers, and hires Hedley again as yard man. After the coroner proposes an autopsy to explain Ester's longevity, Eli puts up a fight as though protecting the dignity of his beloved mistress.

- *Further Reading*

"Gem of the Ocean." *New York Times*, April 27, 2003, p. 26.
Hodgins, Paul. "Finding the Cost of Freedom: Slavery and Its Aftermath Are Explored in 'Gem of the Ocean.' August Wilson's Latest Play." *Orange County Register*, August 1, 2003, p. 1.

Elmore

The on-and-off lover of Ruby and vengeful killer of his rival Leroy Slater in *Seven Guitars* (1995), Elmore is the returning suitor in *King Hedley II* (1999) who values "traveling light" (p. 32). At age sixty-six, he is still playing the part of the blustery trickster-assassin and credits his oldest son Robert with liking guns, a family trait. When Ruby arrives in Pittsburgh from Birmingham in the earlier play, she reveals to her aunt Louise how Elmore and Leroy romanced her. After Elmore knifed Leroy and went to prison, Ruby, pregnant with Leroy's child, fled north to escape man trouble, which she reveals after receiving Elmore's letter.

Like the resurgent bad penny, Elmore visits Ruby every four or five years to "talk sugar but give salt" (p. 15). Like the snake in Eden, his emergence on stage in old age reveals the slick, lethal deceiver in the form of an affable dandy and gambler. Elmore charms the audience with a tale of courting a woman with a dollar sixty-seven cents in pocket change, a one-hundred dollar Stetson on his head, a pint of gin, and a razor in his pocket. He cajoles Ruby with cheap jewelry. To King, he rationalizes the sale of a worthless watch as a valuable lesson and offers to abet him in crime by helping him and Mister sell stolen refrigerators. Elmore's willingness to aid criminals and his frequent disappearances on "business" in Cincinnati suggest a career criminal who zigs and zags just ahead of the law.

As the dubious father figure of the title character, an ex-con just returning from jail, Elmore becomes his sage and mentor. The pairing proves deadly. Elmore admits to knifing two people and to serving five years in an Alabama prison, but conceals that one of his victims was Hedley's biological father. On the way to retrieve Ruby once more, Elmore sells Mister a pearl-handled derringer and fleeces him and Hedley on the purchase of a refrigerator for Ruby. The amorality of Hedley's deals reflects a self-centered hustler who cares little about hurting those closest to him.

Up to his usual tricks, Elmore talks Ruby into marriage and buys a stolen ring from Hedley. Against her wishes, it is Elmore who reveals to Hedley the details of his pouring five shots into Leroy Slater's head and who divulges to Hedley the truth about his parentage. In the final scene, Elmore retreats from shooting Leroy's son. The final waver of his gun hand exemplifies the legacy of the mid–1900s passing to a younger, deadlier generation.

• *Further Reading*

Fisher, Philip. "King Hedley II." *British Theatre Guide*, 2002.
Hitchcock, Laura. "King Hedley II. *CurtainUp*, 2000.
Papatola, Dominic P. "Thunder, Lightning Pierce 'Hedley' Storm." *St. Paul Pioneer Press*, May 31, 2003, p. B6.
Preston, Rohan. "Hudson Returns in 'King'-size Role." *Minneapolis Star Tribune*, June 1, 2003.

Ester, Aunt

The long-lived matriarch, conjurer, and visionary of Pittsburgh's Hill district, Aunt Ester is August Wilson's first dominant female character. Her name suggests both Easter, the holiest day of the Christian calendar, and the biblical character Esther, Ahasureus's queen and the heroine of Purim, a Jewish holiday honoring her for saving the Hebrew people. Aunt Ester speaks resonant monologues that express the playwright's humanism. Through her, he claims that God listens to all people's voices. When Greta Oglesby played the role, she confided, "When I first read this script, I knew this woman is ancient and wise. I went back to my aunt and grandmother for that kind of wisdom" (Preston, p. 4F).

Divinely blessed, after crossing many waters, both real and allegorical, Aunt Ester inherits a woman-to-woman mantle of grace and restoration to become the eternal mother of Wilson's fictional black Americans. A saintly beacon who has survived slavery and outlived four husbands, she dotes on her many children, whom she named for stars as a token of stability in an impermanent world. The astral symbols comfort a woman laden with the memories of black history back to the beginning of America's sale of imported Africans. According to Wilson, she is "the most significant persona of the cycle" (Gener).

An element of magical realism, Ester is the one black character who cheats death, the stalker who figures in each of Wilson's plays. As seer and voodoo priestess who was sold into bondage at age twelve, she derives from a pre–Christian literary convention that dates to such universal wisewomen as the African juju sage and Virgil's Cumaean sybil in *The Aeneid* (19 B.C.). Ester, who finally appears in the flesh in *Gem of the Ocean* (2003), trains her housekeeper Black Mary as her successor, and, in 1904 at age 287, receives the wanderer Citizen Barlow at her Pittsburgh parlor for a mystic redemption ceremony. In her off hours, Ester enjoys a feisty give-and-take with Solly Two Kings, an old flame and former conductor on the Underground Railroad.

A living conscience for Wilson's cycle, Ester is the voice of Africa, the culture-keeper of America's black residents. Her advanced age links her to the birth of slavery in colonial North America, which began in 1617, two years before she was born. The first twenty Africans to arrive among English colonies reached Jamestown, Virginia, aboard a Dutch frigate bound from the West Indies. In the initial act of objectifying humans for their cash value, the Dutch crew exchanged human captives for food and supplies. Aunt Ester herself, who was sold into bondage at age twelve, possesses a document declaring her worth at $607.

In *Two Trains Running* (1991), at an estimated age of 322 years, Ester lives behind a red door at 1839 Wylie Avenue, sharing the ordinary milieu of West's burgeoning funeral parlor and Memphis Lee's declining diner. Amid the commonplaces of a vibrant black community, she supposedly possesses the extraordinary, a predictive power and acumen for counseling that she developed during her long life. Holloway believes she has the power to restore serenity; he declares that "Aunt Ester give you more than money. She make you right with yourself" (p. 22). To assure humility and faith in her counselees she makes demands, rejecting the greedy seeking get-rich-quick answers and requiring Sterling Johnson to try three times before obtaining an audience with her.

Ester stands at the far end of the continuum from the grifters and users of Wilson's drama cycle. Rather than accept cash, she instructs seekers to throw the money into the Monongahela River, from which the cash mystically returns to her. Holloway comments on her effect on counselees, who visit her residence at the back of the house for the laying on of hands, a humbling, uplifting Judaeo-Christian method of conferring blessing. Instead of encouraging superstition, she offers spiritual peace and comfort by solacing inner grief and confusion. Her method is obviously effective because she and her caretakers want for nothing.

Aunt Ester provides continuity in the final two plays of Wilson's drama cycle. In *Gem of the Ocean*, she stocks her pocket with candy, casually spurns an arrest warrant, and confers solace and absolution on Citizen Barlow for causing another man's death over the theft of a bucket of nails. Through a parlor seance, she sends Barlow to the City of Bones, a slave graveyard in the Atlantic Ocean and site of past deaths from torture and disease. At a significant moment in the drama, she holds a document declaring her worth, which she fashions into a paper boat called the "Gem of the Ocean." Wilson stresses the importance of her early history for assisting future generations to smooth sailing.

Aunt Ester's passing in *King Hedley II* (1999) is a momentous event in Wilson's decalogue. In the opening scene, Stool Pigeon muses over the lack of interest in history and the metaphoric weeds on the path leading to her door. Her subsequent demise symbolizes the loss of connection between American blacks and their African ancestry. Stool Pigeon, one of the playwright's wise fools, regrets that she "knew all the secrets of life but that's all gone now. She took all that with her" (p. 19). He reports from Eli that she died of grief with her head bowed on her hand. The undergrowth outside her door implies that blacks long before stopped returning to her for solace and wisdom. Ruby acknowledges that, in 1948, Aunt Ester helped Ruby decide between keeping and aborting her unborn son by claiming, "God got three hands. Two for that baby and one for the rest of us" (p. 46). In Wilson's last cycle play, an unnamed drama set in 1990, the loss of the gentle old lady results in a court fight for her corpse. The attorney who accepts the *pro bono* case discovers his kinship with Ester, a symbol of the kinship of all blacks.

See also **Marion McClinton, supernatural**

• *Further Reading*

Gener, Randy. "Salvation in the City of Bones: Ma Rainey and Aunt Ester Sing Their Own Songs in August Wilson's Grand Cycle of Blues Dramas." *American Theatre*, Vol. 20, No. 5, May-June 2003, pp. 20–28.

Henerson, Evan. "A 'Gem' to Behold." *Los Angeles Daily News*, August 1, 2003.

Preston, Rohan. "Oglesby Sparkles in Wilson's 'Gem.'" *Minneapolis Star Tribune*, May 4, 2003, p. 4F.

Rocha, Mark William. "American History as 'Loud Talking' in *Two Trains Running*," in *May All Your Fences Have Gates: Essays on the Drama of August Wilson*. Iowa City: University of Iowa Press, 1994, pp. 116–132.

Shirley, Don. "Queen of the Hill: August Wilson's Potent But Ungainly 'Gem of the Ocean' Opens at the Taper." *Los Angeles Times*, August 1, 2003, p. E1.

Fences

Set in a ramshackle two-story brick residence and yard in Pittsburgh around 1957, *Fences* (1985), Wilson's most popular play, is an elegy based on multiple failures of the American dream. Some critics refer to the text as a black version of Arthur Miller's *Death of a Salesman* (1949) because of the motif of father-son disillusion and the death of an average American head of household. Joseph H. Wessling of Xavier University categorized Wilson's blend of anguish and joy as metacomedy, a form of drama that moves beyond the strictures of traditional comedy and tragedy. Unlike standard comedy, the text concludes amicably with a funeral and hope for the future. The protagonist, an outsized loser often compared to William Shakespeare's Othello and Eugene O'Neill's Emperor Jones, enacts the tragedy of the black man who overreaches and suffers the consequences. Although Paramount Studios offered to film the play, Wilson refused to allow white director Barry Levinson to manage a project so devoted to the quandaries of the black male. The studio scrapped plans for the movie.

The play's content focuses on black urban life, yet speaks directly to all American families. Turmoil in the multigenerational Maxson household derives from the father, Troy Maxson, a loudmouth bully whose discontent with life and work causes him to tyrannize his wife and son Cory, discount the accomplishments of Cory and his older half-brother Lyons, and inflict pain through a flaunted affair with Alberta. The abiding virtue of a much-flawed protagonist is Troy's spunk. In three soliloquys with Mr. Death, he refuses to go willingly and challenges his old nemesis to face him for the final wrestling match.

Because Troy's anti-authoritarianism and rancor cause him to destroy rather than build, the unfinished backyard fence stands as a condemnation of his neglect of family in favor of a mistress who is much younger than his wife Rose. In peevish displacement of blame, he accuses Cory of failing to finish the sawing of planks for the final segment. The real source of work slowdown is Troy, who reneges on his Saturday project by watching baseball at Taylor's bar and romancing his new woman. More eager to fight battles from the past rather than guide his two sons and nourish his failing marriage, Troy salves his discontent by massaging old wounds and by pursuing sexual pleasure with a woman he doesn't have to support or join in mundane domestic chores. Applying a child's logic to his choices, he contends, "I ain't sorry for nothing I done. It felt right in my heart" (p. 79).

Wilson establishes the price of perpetual malcontent and marital disloyalty by depicting Troy as a loner cut off from friends and family. After Troy's advancement to driver, Jim Bono shares less off-duty time with Troy, who must continue his payday drinking alone without the sustaining camaraderie of his work buddy. Troy's son knocks him to the ground for manhandling Rose and disclaims his fatherhood with a telling accusation, "You don't count around here no more" (p. 85). Rose withdraws from the toxic home environment into church work, taking with her Raynell, who cares more for her surrogate mother than for her biological father. To his shame, Troy relinquishes care of Gabe to a state institution as a way to reclaim half of his government check. The arrangement portrays Troy as heartless and mercenary.

Demeaned by difficult choices and self-aggrandizement, Troy seems unworthy of the reunited family that gathers for his funeral and burial or of the blessing that Gabe confers with his howl of farewell and primitive dance. Wilson exalts Rose to head of the household and faithful nurturer as she shepherds the Maxson men to the church. To Cory, who battles internally much as his father did, she redeems the father figure posthumously: "I do know he meant to do more good than he meant to do harm" (p. 97). Her magnanimous gesture to a man who brought her grief relieves Cory of some of his anguish. Because of her nobility and Christian charity and forgiveness, she tears down the symbolic fencing that separates her family into isolated cells. The noble act bodes well for Cory, who appears to relax his grudge.

See also **Jim Bono, boundaries, Cory Maxson, Gabriel Maxson, Lyons Maxson, Rose Maxson, Troy Maxson, parenthood**

• *Further Reading*

Awkward, Michael. "'The Crookeds with the Straights': *Fences*, Race, and the Politics of Adaptation," in *May All Your Fences Have Gates: Essays on the Drama of August Wilson*. Iowa City: University of Iowa Press, 1994, pp. 205–229.

Wessling, Joseph H. "Wilson's *Fences*." *Explicator*, Vol. 57, No. 2, Winter 1999, pp. 123–127.

Fielding

An alcoholic and former tailor, Fielding is dependent on an informal community. He is an eight-year veteran cabbie in *Jitney* (1982) who survives on the good will of his work partners. He clings to love for an unnamed wife he separated from twenty-two years earlier. To Booster Becker, he confides, "I ain't never loved nobody the way I loved that woman" (p. 52). Her loss turns him to liquor, which he guzzles straight from the bottle. In a dream, he pictures her reaching out to help him hold his place on the last rung of a gold ladder leading to heaven. Significant to the motif is the apathy of the other celestial residents, who remain aloof from Fielding's strivings.

Wilson uses Fielding as a model of self-reclamation. In the opening scene, Fielding panics upon finding his pint liquor bottle empty and scrounges four dollars from Youngblood and Turnbo. His demand of a four-dollar fare from the next client suggests that, in violation of Jim Becker's cab stand rules, Fielding sets the rates based on the price of booze at the State Store. When Fielding gets brave about sipping from his stash at the cab stand, Becker fires him and, a half hour later, relents, a pattern reflecting the manager's concern for his men's failings. To Booster, Fielding admits that the bottle "tore a whole lot of things apart" (p. 81). After attending Becker's meeting of drivers, which fires up the communal spirit of drivers, Fielding chooses not to take a drink and admits, "A little lemonade never killed nobody" (p. 87).

See also **reclamation**

Furlow, Jeremy

A bedeviled North Carolinian from Raleigh transplanted to Pittsburgh in *Joe Turner's Come and Gone* (1988), twenty-five-year-old Jeremy Furlow carries his guitar on the way north. In the opening scene, boardinghouse owner Seth Holly comments on Jeremy's arrest for drunkenness the night before. Bynum Walker recognizes that, after only two weeks away from the South, "That boy got a lot of country in him" (p. 5). He is easy pickings for predatory police. When he arrives for breakfast, he smiles readily and tells about his arrest by "Piney's boys," who fined him and his drinking buddy Roper Lee two dollars each (p. 13). After winning cash at Seefus's place by playing the guitar, Jeremy gloats, "I got a whole dollar here" (p. 44).

Jeremy is one of Wilson's low-key seekers. Naive and soft-spoken, he suffered one failed romance and took to the roads as a solace. Like Floyd Barton and friends in *Seven Guitars* (1995), the title character in *Ma Rainey's Black Bottom* (1985), Doaker and Wining Boy Charles in *The Piano Lesson* (1990), Ruby in *King Hedley II* (1999), and Lyons Maxson in *Fences* (1985), Jeremy takes comfort in music and claims to "play guitar like I'm born to it" (p. 26). A self-proclaimed gambler, he looks forward to wide horizons because he "don't want to miss nothing" (p. 66).

Because of his boyish outlook, Jeremy proves unstable in love matters. He appeals to fellow roomer Mattie Campbell and makes a hasty overture within minutes of meeting her. In crude macho language, he claims to have "a ten-pound hammer and I knows how to drive it down" (p. 26). On a more gentlemanly note, he invites her to Sunday dinner at the inn and persuades her to move in with him, ostensibly to help her save money.

In a matter of days, Jeremy proves the stereotype of the disloyal black male by dropping Mattie in favor of Molly Cunningham, a newly arrived roomer who shares his wanderlust. He admires her for being independent, "the kind that know what she want and how to get it" (p. 65). A struggling road builder, Jeremy rails against the white man who extorts a half dollar per week from black workers by threatening them with firing. In defiance, Jeremy refuses to ante up and loses his position. Without funds, he must beg on the streets and shelter under a bridge abutment, a symbol of the disconnect between ideal race relations and the reality of discrimination. The business dynamics of his precarious situation illustrate the vulnerability of black laborers in a capitalistic system run by whites.

See also **poverty**

• *Further Reading*

Üsekes, Ciggdem. "'We's the Leftovers': Whiteness as Economic Power and Exploitation in August Wilson's Twentieth-Century Cycle of Plays." *African American Review*, Vol. 37, No. 1, Spring 2003, pp. 115–125.

gambling

Wilson characterizes black urbanites as victims of the frail hope of a mystic stroke of good fortune in the future. He expands on superstition and reliance on luck with frequent mentions of blackjack, a raffle, and the numbers racket, which pays a jackpot to the person who predicts a multi-digit number published in a common source. Selecting a number offers several possibilities of a win: by playing straight, the bettor wins only if the digits match the exact order of the winning number. By making a boxed bet, the bettor receives a smaller payout by naming the correct digits in any order.

Easy wins are seldom, a fact that Elmore attests to after losing seven dollars at dollar tonk in *King Hedley II* (1999). In *Jitney* (1982), Shealy's son Pope hits the numbers big and buys a Buick Riviera. Red Carter, a flashy gambler in *Seven Guitars* (1995), blames a broken mirror for a stream of bad luck and fails to blame himself for the loss of forty dollars at the gaming tables at Seefus's nightclub. In *Fences* (1985), both Lyons and Rose Maxson pursue an easy win on the numbers. Rose comments on the luck of Pope, who won enough to buy a restaurant, and of Miss Pearl, who won a dollar by betting on 651, a number that recurs twice in 1969 in *Two Trains Running* (1991). Discouraged with her own paltry winnings, Rose concludes, "Poor folks can't get nothing" (*Fences*, p. 21).

Wilson establishes that settled, family-minded people like Jim Becker in *Jitney* take no stock in gambling. In *Fences*, Troy greets his son Lyons with an accusation of guilt by association for frequenting Sefus's place (with spelling varying from the above), a seedy lounge and casino named as the site of a police raid in the *Pittsburgh Courier*, a black-owned newspaper founded in 1910. Troy dismisses all of Sefus's patrons as "rogues" (p. 45). His intent is less superiority over gamblers than a subtextual swipe at his ambitious son, who prefers being an out-of-work musician to collecting garbage like his father.

The playwright depicts a paradoxical attitude in Memphis Lee, the upright operator of a Pittsburgh diner in *Two Trains Running*. He warns the predatory Wolf about "tying up my phone with them numbers," yet Memphis is all too willing to "get a dollar on seven sixty-four" (pp. 2, 11). His logic is typical of cynical black urbanites—because the economy is controlled by white capitalists, the only way to defeat their extortion is through the illegal means of playing the numbers. Ironically, Wolf is much more careful with his own cash and refuses to contribute to the pool to bail Bubba Boy out of jail for his girlfriend's funeral. In a cafe-counter discussion of the ex-con Sterling Johnson, the philosopher Holloway refutes Memphis's belief in hard work for steady wages by suggesting that Sterling gamble for much higher stakes. Holloway rationalizes the hustler's fleecing of gullible blacks of their money: "If he don't, somebody else will get it.... I got it today and you got it tomorrow" (p. 33).

See also **superstition, Wolf**

• *Further Reading*

Üsekes, Ciggdem. "'We's the Leftovers': Whiteness as Economic Power and Exploitation in August Wilson's Twentieth-Century Cycle of Plays." *African American Review*, Vol. 37, No. 1, Spring 2003, pp. 115–125.
Wilde, Lisa. "Reclaiming the Past: Narrative and Memory in August Wilson's *Two Trains Running*." *Theater*, Vol. 22, No. 1, Fall/winter 1990-1991, pp. 73–74.

Gem of the Ocean

Returning to the first decade of the twentieth century, Wilson added to his ten-play cycle a glimpse of 1904 in *Gem of the Ocean* (2003), the ninth of his decalogue. For the debut of his most allegorical work, Marion McClinton directed the two-act play at Chicago's Goodman Theatre in May 2003 and in the West Coast premiere at the Mark Taper Forum in Los Angeles the following July, starring Phylicia Rashad as the elderly Aunt Ester. In admiration of Wilson's grandly operatic melodrama, critic Hedy Weiss labeled the play a "tale of inheritance," a reference to the black world's burden of inherited sufferings and wrongs (Weiss, p. 34). Wilson summarized the action as a situation where "Blacks wanted to leave the South and go north to seek their fortune, but the South was trying to hold on to its cheap labor and wouldn't let them go. Despite emancipation, you essentially have a situation that is like slavery" (O'Mahony).

The Great Migration developed its own momentum. In an overview by reviewer Jonathan Abarbanel, "The rural poor flock to the city seeking the freedom and equality promised to them by the Civil War" (Abarbanel). The title resonates with dissonance: the promise of America, extolled in the anthem "Columbia, the Gem of the Ocean," in conflict with the Reconstruction era white backlash of deception, legal maneuvering, and intimidation of blacks who provide cheap labor for Northern manufacturers. In flight from Ku Klux Klan violence and lychings, gullible newcomers from the South run afoul of the bleeding of tin mill workers through extravagant nickel and diming by the company store — a dollar and a half for housing and a dollar for food leaving them owing fifty cents above their weekly earnings of two dollars.

Wilson's play melds spiritualism and biblical authority with melodrama. Abarbanel says of the characters' verbal contributions, "The telling — the testimony, if you will — is just as important as the tale" (Abarbanel). The protagonist, a millworker named Citizen Barlow, steals cash from a man owing him money and robs the factory of a bucket of nails. A laborer who is wrongly blamed for heisting the nails drowns himself in the river to escape branding as a felon. Wracked with guilt, Barlow flees the implacable constable Caesar, a vicious slumlord, and seeks sanctuary and redemption from mortal sin. To confess and cleanse himself, Barlow makes a spiritual journey to a boardinghouse in Pittsburgh's Hill district on Aunt Ester's 287th birthday. He arrives at what Weiss calls "ground zero," the kitchen table, the hearth-like focus of *Joe Turner's Come and Gone* (1988) and *The Piano Lesson* (1990) (Weiss, p. 34). Because of his unmannerly entrance through a bedroom window, he encounters the fiery Black Mary and somber Eli, Ester's housekeeper and steward. With the aid of the long-lived black sage, he acquires food, lodging, and work and redirects his life by reclaiming the past. In the process, Ester spouts wisdom and pauses to mourn her dead son.

The mystic drama features a number of historic touches, notably, the ex-slave Solly Two Kings, a former Union Army scout and pilot on the Underground Railroad who collects dog excrement from the sidewalk for use in the tanning industry, and the magical-realistic voyage of the paper boat "Gem of the Ocean" that Ester creases out of her slave era bill of sale. The vessel carries Barlow to an Atlantic anomaly, a city of bones where slaving vessels once ran aground. The gatekeeper is the man who died in Citizen Barlow's place. The tableau elevates the play with an historic grandeur and pathos.

At the play's climax, Ester reunites Barlow with slave times at a seance that projects him to the Atlantic graveyard. Gothic engineering enhances the site with a claustrophobic slave hold, chains around Barlow's neck, the hiss of the lash, and a rocking slave vessel beset by thunderclaps and torrents of rain. Solly's vengeance against political and emotional slavery takes the form of arson at a Pittsburgh mill and at the city jail. Barlow achieves wholeness by merging with the lengthy past of the black race.

See also **Citizen Barlow, Caesar, Eli, Aunt Ester, Black Mary, supernatural, Solly Two Kings**

• *Further Reading*

Abarbanel, Jonathan. "Gem of the Ocean." http://ibs.theatermania.com/content/news.cfm?int_news_id=3441, May 1, 2003.
Kendt, Rob. "Review: Gem of the Ocean." *Back Stage West*, August 7, 2003, pp. 19, 20.
O'Mahony, John. "American Centurion." Manchester *Guardian*, December 14, 2002.
Philips, Michael. "Wilson's 'Gem' a Diamond in the Rough." *Chicago Tribune*, April 30, 2003, p. 1.
Weiss, Hedy. "'Ocean' Voyage Proves Rough But Rewarding." *Chicago Sun-Times*, April 29, 2003, p. 34.

goldenseal

In *Seven Guitars* (1995), the goldenseal plant *(Hydrastis canadenis)* that Vera Dotson receives from the sweet-natured Canewell has a long history of value as folk medicine. A versatile perennial with a name suggesting the motherland on the Gold Coast of Africa, the plant grows in shady woodlands, sending long roots into moist loam, especially in the rich forests of the Carolinas, Georgia, Alabama, and Arkansas. Among Cherokee healers and American pioneers, the herb, also called eyebalm and eyeroot, soothes inflammation of the eyes and gums. The shaman prescribed the plant for control of bleeding, and promoting the healing of gastric, respiratory, vaginal, and urinary disorders. Some twenty-first-century herbalists value goldenseal in combination with echinacea for restoring the immune system.

Canewell's gift of the herb is a protective gesture. The giving precedes Vera's move to Chicago with guitarist Floyd Barton, her faithless boyfriend. Suited to the gentle Canewell, the plant is a stroke of grace, a gift that doesn't have to be deserved. Hedley attests to the power of the leaves, which his West Indian grandmother used as a tea or a chest rub. Intended as a curative, the plant requires careful tending and watering to keep its roots from shriveling, a symbol of the immense cultural loss that blacks suffered when they migrated from the rural South to hostile Northern industrial centers. Floyd's destruction of the roots while he caches twelve hundred dollars in loot from the finance company robbery suggests the loss of a cultural foundation, the spiritual anchor that Floyd lacks in his yearning toward the idealized mecca of Chicago. Ironically, he falls dead on the curative plant.

• *Further Reading*

Dobelis, Inge N., project ed. *Magic and Medicine of Plants*. Pleasantville, N.Y.: Reader's Digest Association, 1986.

Gothic mode

A literary style based on themes, settings, and motifs from the barbarous Middle Ages, Gothic mode gains energy from the incorporation of blood feuds, piety, mystery, and magic as well as elements of terror, dreams and illusions, the grotesque, dissipation, and perversity. In revolt against cold rationalism, Gothic works encourage crude folkways, ignorance, disorder, and licentiousness, all elements found in August Wilson's plays. The Gothic genre arouses interest by depicting heroism, thwarted love, variety, and danger from the unexpected, the common strands of American ballads, bluegrass, country music, and stage drama. The resulting texts allow the intellect free play with fancy and insight.

Wilson gives full reign to Gothic conventions, as with the intuition of Bynum Walker in *Joe Turner's Come and Gone* (1988), the exuberance of jazz trumpeter Levee Green in *Ma Rainey's Black Bottom* (1985), the melancholy of cab drivers in a declining city in *Jitney* (1982), the uncouth behaviors of Boy Willie and the presence of a ghost in *The Piano Lesson* (1990), the sexual allure of Ruby and the madness in the machete murderer King Hedley in *Seven Guitars* (1995), the younger King Hedley's descriptions of Pernell Sims's gory death in *King Hedley II* (1999), and the other-worldliness of Aunt Ester's seance in *Gem of the Ocean* (2003). To enhance contrast, Wilson focuses on the uninitiated naif, e.g., Cory Maxson, who hopes for a football career in *Fences* (1985), the motherless Zonia Loomis in *Joe Turner's Come and Gone*, and Lymon Jackson, who searches for a likely wife in *The Piano Lesson*. The decade cycle ornaments stagecraft with exoticism, as with the slash marks on Risa Thomas's legs and the laying out of the Prophet Samuel with hundred-dollar bills in *Two Trains Running* (1991), the peculiarities of animal sacrifice in King Hedley's poultry slaying in *Seven Guitars*, and Stool Pigeon's ritual burial of Aunt Ester's black cat in *King Hedley II*. To accommodate twentieth-century demands, Wilson resets claustro-phobia from traditional Gothic castles and crypts to the encroaching city that iso-lates the inn in *Joe Turner's Come and Gone*, devours the diner in *Two Trains Running*, and engulfs the cab stand and its environs in *Jitney*.

Recurrent motifs of the Gothic mode enliven Wilson's decalogue. He creates despicable villainy in the black constable Caesar in *Gem of the Ocean* and in Jim Sto-vall, a white exploiter of blacks whose name recurs in *The Piano Lesson* and *Two Trains Running*. Bleak, forbidding settings and costumes are essential to Aunt Ester's mysticism and Solly Two Kings's tattered lifestyle in *Gem of the Ocean;* unsettling sounds erupt from Miss Tillery's roosters in *Seven Guitars*, in which a morbid con-templation of death motivates the gathering of mourners after Floyd Barton's funeral. An indulgence in paganism results in the juba dance in *Joe Turner's Come and Gone*, which incorporates talking wind and concludes with the blood baptism of Herald Loomis. The New World version of Gothic mode emphasizes macabre terrors (Sut-ter's fall down a well in *The Piano Lesson*), horror (an impromptu knifing in *Ma Rainey's Black Bottom* and *Seven Guitars*), eeriness (an exorcism of a poltergeist in *The Piano Lesson* and the mystic angels hovering above Floyd Barton's grave in *Seven Guitars*), mystery (the long life of Aunt Ester in *Gem of the Ocean* and *Two Trains Running* and Floyd Barton's unfathomable murder in *Seven Guitars*), dissipation (Wining Boy's begging for drinks in *The Piano Lesson* and Fielding's boozing on the job in *Jitney*), the *femme fatale* (Ruby in *Seven Guitars*), the hovering phantasm of death (Miss Mabel Holly in *Joe Turner's Come and Gone* and Troy Maxson's argu-ments with Mr. Death in *Fences*), surreality (Citizen Barlow's descent to the City of Bones in *Gem of the Ocean*), doom-laden melodrama (Alberta's death in childbirth in *Fences* and the dice game that ends *King Hedley II*), raffish criminal-heroism (Floyd Barton in *Seven Guitars* and Elmore in *King Hedley II*), and subconscious impulses (Levee Green's to-the-death protection of his Florsheims in *Ma Rainey's Black Bot-tom* and the title character's impetus to crime in *King Hedley II*).

• *Further Reading*

Auerbach, Nina. *Our Vampires, Ourselves*. Chicago: University of Chicago Press, 1995.

Gamer, Michael. *Romanticism and the Gothic: Genre, Reception, and Canon Formation.* Cambridge: Cambridge University Press, 2000.

Goddu, Teresa A. "Blood Daggers and Lonesome Graveyards: The Gothic and Country Music." *South Atlantic Quarterly*, Vol. 94, No. 1, 1995, pp. 57–80.

Monaco, Pamela Jean. "Father, Son, and Holy Ghost: From the Local to the Mythical in August Wilson," in *August Wilson: A Casebook*. New York: Garland, 1994.

Great Migration

The Great Migration refers to the departure of largely agrarian blacks from the South to urban and industrial areas in the North, notably, Chicago, Cleveland, Detroit, New York, and Pittsburgh, August Wilson's hometown. According to Kim Pereira's *August Wilson and the Great American Odyssey* (1995), the mass move was an attempt to reunite family members who fled or were sold off. It resulted from painful emotions—"a yearning to return to the lost community from which they were originally severed" (Pereira, p. 2). The exodus spread over three decades, beginning at the end of World War I and continuing into the post–World War II boom years.

In *Seven Guitars* (1995), set in 1948, Red Carter claims that more rural blacks live in Chicago than in Pittsburgh because Highway 61, the world's longest stretch, runs straight from the South to Chicago, like the Underground Railroad, carrying many black emigres toward the promise of opportunity. In reality, Route 61 reached from New Orleans through Natchez and up western Mississippi to Memphis, where the number changed to Route 51. The road continued in a northeasterly direction through Bloomington, Illinois, west of Chicago and into Wisconsin before ending on the shores of Lake Superior in sight of Canada, the free land that runaway slaves sought as an end to servitude.

Driving desperate blacks out of the South were poverty on tenant farms, voter disenfranchisement, injustices from the white-dominated court system, and the insidious lawlessness of the Ku Klux Klan. Begun during the invasion of the boll weevil in cotton fields and the subsequent decline in cotton as a money crop and after serious flooding of Mississippi Valley bottom lands in 1915, the mass move derived from a quest for stable jobs in the boom years of World War I. Nomads sought the security of property ownership and hope for beleaguered families, both themes of *The Piano Lesson* (1990).

In the introduction to *Joe Turner's Come and Gone* (1988), a preview sets the tone:

> Isolated, cut off from memory, having forgotten the names of the gods and only guessing at their faces, they arrive dazed and stunned, their hearts kicking in their chest with a song worth singing. They arrive carrying bibles and guitars, their pockets lined with dust and fresh hope [n.p.].

Like immigrants landing at Ellis Island, men like Jeremy Furlow test their feet on new soil and listen and learn from those who preceded them on the Great Migration. While acclimating, they encounter the scorn of citified blacks like Seth Holly, who disdains "niggers coming up here from the backwoods" (p. 6). His sneer echoes throughout American history with the settled American's contempt for Irish fleeing the potato famine, boat people escaping the fall of Southeast Asia to communism, and wetbacks braving the Rio Grande to escape the chaos and despair of Mexico.

One naysayer, Floyd Barton, indicates that not all newcomers to the industrialized North are capable of thriving. A rising blues guitarist and composer in *Seven Guitars*, he cautions that, to make the most of big cities, people have to know how to grasp opportunity. His alarum refers to the situation in *Gem of the Ocean* (2003), set in 1904, when Citizen Barlow and other emigres were like lambs to slaughter in the grasp of greedy white mill owners and dishonest businessmen and civic authorities. A similar restraint of talent and ambition in *Ma Rainey's Black Bottom* (1985) causes the title character to scramble for her rightful place in the music industry.

In Wilson's estimation, the mass transplantation of blacks from South to North failed because it further dispersed to the city a people grounded in African values and culture based on herding and farming. By moving north, wanderers abandoned their homes and adopted citified mannerisms and language by abandoning folk expressions and oral traditions. They left behind the structure of community to huddle alone and isolated from the foods, worship, and rituals that gave their lives meaning. From the restraints of Southern group identity, the boldest voyagers sought the freedom of ambition and individuality, but at a price. The heavy cost was a shedding of an African past with its traditions and knowledge of folk healing for the wounded soul.

One of the most poignant wanderers is Floyd, the recently famous blues guitarist who lives here and there, in Chicago with Pearl, then "around the corner somewhere" in Pittsburgh (p. 3). After his funeral, Vera Dotson, his soulful former lover and mourner, cites scripture, a foundation of morality, hope, and consolation that blacks like Floyd abandoned when they exited the Bible Belt. In *The Piano Lesson*, the outsider Lymon Jackson, a naive farm boy from Mississippi, views Pittsburgh as a source of attractive women and a land of opportunity far from a stalking sheriff and the oppression of white Southern landowners like Jim Stovall. In contrast to his naive friend, Boy Willie, a spokesman for the rural South and for the playwright, mutters sarcastically, "You think this the land of milk and honey" (p. 17). Corroborating Boy Willie's disillusion with Pittsburgh is Troy Maxson in *Fences* (1985). When Troy left home in 1918 at age fourteen, he found blacks living on the river banks, under an urban bridge, and in thin-walled tarpaper shacks.

Through his drama cycle, Wilson sets out to prove that Boy Willie is right in doubting tales of financial independence and instant happiness in Pittsburgh. Travel north from Mississippi ruins Wining Boy's relationship with his wife Cleotha and ends Doaker's marriage to Coreen. Similarly, the North bears no soul satisfaction for the taxi drivers in *Jitney* (1982), displaced musicians in *Ma Rainey's Black Bottom*, the victims of drive-by shootings in *King Hedley II*, the unemployed musician Lyons Maxson in *Fences*, or the ex-con Sterling Johnson in *Two Trains Running* (1991). In the latter play, cafe owner Memphis Lee attests to the availability of trains going south twice a day. He comments that unsophisticated blacks arrive in Pittsburgh clinging to extremes of courtesy to white males, "that old backward Southern mentality" that retains them in a state of thralldom (p. 30).

Wilson declared the decades of migration another blow to black self-esteem from cultural rejection, ghetto living conditions, increased violence and threats to young blacks, and loss of contact with the land. His ten-play cycle stresses the curse that migration placed on rambling black characters, who suffer a number of losses and setbacks:

- imprisonment (Booster Becker, Jim Bono, Boy Willie Charles, Doaker Charles, Wining Boy Charles, Elmore, King Hedley II, Lymon Jackson, Sterling Johnson, Herald Loomis, Troy Maxson)

- parental abandonment (King Hedley II, Zonia Loomis, Natasha)

- rape (Levee Green's mother)

- discrimination and disappointment (Floyd Barton, Levee Green, Herald Loomis, Troy Maxson, Ma Rainey, Youngblood, Mister)

- disillusion (Berniece Charles, Wining Boy Charles, Eli, Levee Green, King Hedley II, Tonya Hedley, Seth Holly, Lymon Jackson, Louise, Ma Rainey)

- isolation and loneliness (Jim Becker, Caesar, Canewell, Berniece Charles, Doaker Charles, Mama Ola Charles, Fielding, Louise, Bynum Walker, West)

- mental and emotional disturbance (Citizen Barlow, King Hedley, Herald Loomis, Gabe Maxson, Stool Pigeon)

- depression (Canewell, Wining Boy Charles, Tonya Hedley, Ruby)

- obsessions (Hambone, King Hedley, Martha Pentecost, Stool Pigeon)

- faithless lovers and mates (Mattie Campbell, Vera Dotson, Jeremy Furlow, Memphis Lee, Leroy, Bonnie Maxson, Rose Maxson, Bynum Walker, Wolf)

- disjointed families (Berniece Charles, Doaker Charles, Wining Boy Charles, Fielding, King Hedley II, Tonya Hedley, Sterling Johnson, Herald and Zonia Loomis, Maretha, Cory Maxson, Lyons and Bonnie Maxson, Rose and Troy Maxson, Martha Pentecost)

- fraud (buyers of phony insurance, Jeremy Furlow, Hambone, King Hedley II, Mister)

- loss of livelihood (Memphis Lee, Jeremy Furlow, Lyons Maxson, King Hedley II, Robert Shealy)

- loss of life (Alberta, Floyd Barton, Coreen Becker, Jim Becker, Mama Ola Charles, Cleotha, Crawley, Eugene, Neesi Hedley, Leroy Slater, Poochie Tillery).

To echo the pain of displacement, Wilson returns repeatedly to blues songs as a vehicle for black despair and an expression of cultural strangulation and individual failures.

See also **diaspora, displacement, opportunity, railroad, soul food, Jim Stovall**

- *Further Reading*

Foner, Eric. *Reconstruction: America's Unfinished Revolution.* New York: Harper & Row, 1988.

Lorant, Stefan, et al. *Pittsburgh, the Story of an American City.* Pittsburgh: Esselmont Books, 1999.

Pereira, Kim. *August Wilson and the African-American Odyssey.* Urbana: University of Illinois Press, 1995.

Shannon, Sandra G. "A Transplant That Did Not Take: August Wilson's Views on the Great Migration." *African American Review*, Vol. 31, No. 4, 1997, pp. 659–666.

Green, Levee

An able, but stubborn, defensive jazz trumpeter in *Ma Rainey's Black Bottom* (1985), Levee Green is his own worst enemy. In his early thirties, he is an over-confident improviser and climber — a naive upstart who convinces himself that racial obstacles will not hinder him as they have his black colleagues, even Ma Rainey herself. After witnessing eight or nine white men rape his mother on their fifty acres in Jefferson County, Tennessee, when Levee was eight, he recalls how his father bided his time, played the accommodator, then settled the score with four of the attackers before he was captured, hanged, and burned. From his parent, Levee acquired what drama critic Elyse Gardner called a "fake smile and a thirst for vengeance" (Gardner, p. 5D). An emotional cripple, he is unable to control a rage that victimizes a black friend rather than a white exploiter.

Displaying a knife scar on his chest from the attack, Levee bears a miserable paranoia that causes him to blame the plotting of his downfall on God. After the burden and unfairness of black farm life, he chooses the pose of the cool dude and combative antagonist who refuses to be drawn into a therapeutic male bull session. True to his instrument, his voice brays like a trumpet. Like the dog in Aesop's Fables that would rather have a bad reputation than to be ignored, Levee ridicules the country ways of Fat Back, Arkansas, and the clodhoppers of bassist Slow Drag and pianist Toledo. By elevating himself and denigrating God, Levee becomes a version of the apostate Faust for his bold talk about signing on with Satan.

Levee's struggle assails obstacles of race and gender as he battles the control of a white producer and a female employer, symbols of the power of white males and of the legendary black matriarchy. He thrusts himself beyond the role of Ma's side-man to rival soloist, the source of her frustration with his brilliant, but inappropriate trumpet riffs added to her most prominent song "Ma Rainey's Black Bottom." By showcasing an individual style, Levee intends to escape the stigma of the backward sharecropping South and to write original music and lyrics a grade above Ma's "old jug band" style and "barn dance" tunes, which he later insults as "that old circus bullshit" and "tent-show nonsense" (pp. 64, 65). To outflank Slow Drag, Levee ridicules a musician who hasn't been to New Orleans, a blues Mecca to true aficionados.

Levee's opportunism emerges in even the smallest act, including nabbing more than his share of deli sandwiches intended to feed Ma Rainey's back-up band. Lacking Ma's experience and savvy, he becomes the exhibitionist in the combo and apes her diva behavior by declaring that he will "tell the white man what to do" (p. 94). More damning is the repudiation of his African heritage to throw in with white producer Mel Sturdyvant, but Levee never gets that far with his dream career. The inescapable clash with Ma produces the classic face-off between old with young, mother figure with rebellious son, experienced professional with brash, over-confident tyro. Like a petulant brat sassing his elders, he excuses his variant playing as an act of will: "I was playing it the way I felt it" (p. 101).

Failure precipitates Levee's sulky, peevish behavior, which lurks beneath the smiley-faced, white-pleasing persona he beams at Sturdyvant after Irvin accuses him of kicking out Sylvester's microphone plug and ruining a recording take. Both band leader Cutler and Slow Drag accuse Levee of playing the subservient Step 'n Fetchit, the stereotypical houseboy in thrall to the "man." More detrimental to group solidarity is Levee's attack on religion, which precipitates a thrashing, ably administered by Cutler. Because of a string of painful setbacks—a white producer for Paramount discounts the work of Ma Rainey's group and offers them a token twenty-five dollars, Sturdyvant refuses to further Levee's career, and Ma Rainey fires him for trying to revamp her own style with his innovations—the trumpeter displaces his frustration and anger.

Levee's downfall results from multiple attacks on his manhood. The playwright's description warns that "All the weight in the world suddenly falls on Levee" (p. 110). Instead of retaliating against Ma Rainey or Sturdyvant, he releases pent-up anguish at the closest victim and stabs Toledo in the back. The detonator of the time bomb is pathetically trumped up — Levee murders a fellow musician for stepping on Levee's newly purchased eleven-dollar Florsheim shoes, a flashy status symbol representing a week's pay and a means of impressing a woman. Behind the immediate motivation lie years of struggle against the men who raped his mother, against white exploiters of black musicians, and against Ma herself, the source of his income and of his fight for full acknowledgement of masculinity.

See also **violence**

• *Further Reading*

Gardner, Elysa. "'Bottom' Sings Blues with Bounce, Charm." *USA Today*, February 10, 2003, p. 5D.

Majors, Richard, and Janet Mancini Billson. *Cool Pose: The Dilemmas of Black Manhood in America*. New York: Lexington Books, 1992.

McDonough, Carla J. *Staging Masculinity: Male Identity in Contemporary American Drama*. Jefferson, N.C.: McFarland, 1997.

Smith, Philip E. "Ma Rainey's Black Bottom: Playing the Blues as Equipment for Living," in *Within the Dramatic Spectrum*. New York: University Press of America, 1986, pp. 177–186.

"The Ground on Which I Stand"

At a pivotal moment in his professional evolution, on June 26, 1996, playwright August Wilson addressed the eleventh biennial National Theatre Conference at Princeton University on the need for black people to seize cultural sovereignty by creating and supporting a black national theater effort. Of black culture, Wilson declared:

> Growing up in my mother's house at 1727 Bedford Avenue in Pittsburgh, Pennsylvania, I learned the language, the eating habits, the religious beliefs, the gestures, the

notions of common sense, attitudes towards sex, concepts of beauty and justice, and
the responses to pleasure and pain, that my mother had learned from her mother,
and which you could trace back to the first African who set foot on the continent.
It is this culture that stands solidly on these shores today as a testament to the
resiliency of the African American spirit [p. 14].

He stated that to be a black American is to share a race, social and economic condition, and the results of enslavement, social segregation, and absence of opportunity.

Wilson's ground-breaking speech encouraged the creation of self-sustaining
black theaters where artists could express ethnic themes and issues. He demanded
artists who understand black sensibilities and called for guidelines and for professional writers and actors to inflame black people with the will to protect and pass on
black cultural contributions. The "call" he issued shocked and surprised some whites
in the audience and instigated commitment in blacks who agreed with his point of
view. The text was so vital to the times and their needs that *American Theatre* magazine published the entire speech in its September 1996 issue.

Wilson's bold, race-based demands alienated Robert Brustein, a white-Jewish
humanities scholar and critic and artistic director of Boston's American Repertory
Theatre. His columns in *New Republic* on July 19 and 26, 1996, led to a public forum
to thrash out the issues of black-only vs. multicultural theater. On January 27, 1997,
Wilson faced Brustein at Manhattan's Town Hall at a formal debate entitled "On
Cultural Power." The event was organized and moderated by actress-playwright Anna
Deavere Smith.

Before an audience of fifteen hundred, Wilson affirmed the need for a black
national theater for specific reasons:

- to correct distortions of black history
- to reclaim a collective black mindset
- to restore black spirits crushed by white oppressors
- to rebuild black dignity and self-esteem
- to state black issues in vernacular terms
- to provide a venue and source of income for black talent
- to showcase black tastes, values, and autonomy
- to present characters and stories that uplift the black self-image
- to celebrate the endurance of a black minority in an overwhelmingly white
  society
- to legitimize black ethics, pride, and values in theatricals that are uniquely
  African American.

Wilson's strongly pro-black philosophy intimidated and angered some whites who
described his views as elitist, insular, and potentially harmful to American unity. The

next month, Brustein retaliated in the *New Republic* with renewed charges that August Wilson rejected assimilation into American society and championed self-segregation, singularity, and the beginning of a new era of divisiveness, race consciousness, and exclusion.

- *Further Reading*

Ambush, Benny Sato. "Culture Wars." *African American Review*, Vol. 31, No. 4, Winter 1997, pp. 579–586.
Barnett, Douglas O. "Up for the Challenge." *American Theater*, Vol. 13, No. 10, 1996, pp. 60.
Gates, Henry Louis. "The Chitlin Circuit." *New Yorker*, Vol. 72, No. 45, February 3, 1997, pp. 44–55.
Powell, Jason. "August Wilson: The Playwright Versus the Politician." *Knox College Common Room*, Vol. 4, No. 1, May 29, 2000.
Wilson, August. "The Ground on Which I Stand." *American Theatre*, Vol. 13, September 1996, pp. 14–15, 71–74.

Hall, T. L.

The con artist in *Seven Guitars* (1995), T. L. Hall is one of August Wilson's many white exploiters of blacks. Hall fits the stereotype of the impressive, but shady deceiver. Canewell connects Hall with a status symbol, a "black shiny Ford," a metaphor for his slick exterior (p. 84). Louise, the landlady, recalls how, winter and summer, he wore a nasty straw hat pushed back, a suggestion of cockiness. With bold insouience, he mismanages Floyd Barton's music career and, abetted by accomplice Robert Gordon, sells phony insurance to poor blacks.

Like the rationalizer Sterling Johnson in *Two Trains Running* (1991), Robert Sutter in *The Piano Lesson* (1990), and the title figure, Mister, and Elmore in *King Hedley II* (1999), Hall appears to lack a conscience. In addition to stealing Floyd's advance money for the Mother's Day gig at the Blue Goose, Hall cheats local blacks by signing up fifty thousand dollars' worth of phony policies "for the Security Mutual something or another" (p. 81). Red Carter reads from the newspaper an article on Hall's arrest along with his partner Gordon. The collaring of the two con artists is a rare example in an August Wilson play where the law forces dishonest whites to pay for bilking blacks.

See also **crime**

Hambone

A mentally impaired handyman and house painter in his late forties in *Two Trains Running* (1991), Hambone is the butt of white treachery against blacks. Bearing the name of a Jim Crow stereotype named in minstrel repartee, he is an Alabama native with no known relatives or even a surname. Like a gentle, beloved street dog begging from door to door, he survives on handouts. Similar in lacklogic to the deranged trumpeter Gabriel Maxson in *Fences* (1985), Hambone has difficulty communicating in adult-level sentences and flourishes in a climate of kindness, acceptance, and loving gestures. His symbiotic relationship with Hill District people portrays August Wilson's concept of the altruistic community as an essential of civilization.

When Hambone appears at the beginning of the play, he is so obsessed over being cheated by Lutz, the white butcher, that he mutters repeatedly about his ham. According to Holloway's version of the disagreement, the butcher promised Hambone a ham around 1959 for painting a fence down the side and across the back of Lutz's Meat Market. Because his employer reneged on the original deal and offered only a chicken, for nearly a decade, Hambone waits at his store each morning to demand a ham. The diner owner, Memphis Lee, restates the offer in two stages—a chicken for painting the fence and a ham for a good job. From his own dealings with whites, Memphis concludes that Lutz "quite naturally ... gonna say it ain't worth the higher price" (p. 23). The concept epitomizes a view of business lacking in fairness and compassion.

Just as Memphis maintains his intent to return south to reclaim his land, Hambone holds firm to his demand for full payment. By standing vigil outside Lutz's store, Hambone shames the cheater before the whole neighborhood. Although Hambone appears to deteriorate mentally and emotionally during his adamant stance, Holloway, the philosopher of Memphis's diner, sees Hambone's method as worthy of pride. Holloway chortles, "If Lutz ever break down and give it to him ... he gonna have a big thing. He gonna have something he be proud to tell everybody" (p. 30). The nurturing mother figure, Risa Thomas, rejects the community belief that Hambone lacks reason. She insists that "he understand everything what's going on around him. Most of the time he understand better than they do," a foreshadowing of Memphis's successful fight with white authorities by using Hambone's methods (p. 45).

A more telling pairing of characters involves the teaming of Hambone with Sterling Johnson, a similarly disenfranchised black male who demands that society accept him and offer him work without a lot of union interference. Sterling considers interceding with Lutz for Hambone, but recognizes that an end to the argument would leave the handyman no reason "to get up out of the bed in the morning" (p. 50). Instead, Sterling tries to teach Hambone about pride by making him memorize "Black is beautiful" and "United we stand, divided we fall" (pp. 62–64). The playwright uses the tutorial session as a satire of the senselessness of polemics to blacks who are more concerned with finding jobs and putting food on the table.

Wilson uses Hambone's death as a commentary on life and luck. The poignance of his peaceful passing in bed at his room on Herron Avenue contrasts West's finding that the handyman's body was badly scarred, a symbol of the undisclosed hurts that blacks carry from the past. The friends the handyman made in his lifetime rally around him at the funeral home. Risa expresses her fondness for him by asking the cost of a metal casket. Memphis, the character who regularly spurned the retarded man and denied him free meals, softens at Hambone's death and spends fifty dollars on flowers from "everybody who ever dropped the ball and went back to pick it up" (p. 110). Sterling adds the final touch of grace by stealing a ham from Lutz's store window for West to tuck into the casket. The gesture reminds the audience of the Christian contention that there are no throwaway people.

See also **Marion McClinton**

• *Further Reading*

Wang, Qun. *An In-Depth Study of the Major Plays of African American Playwright August Wilson: Vernacularizing the Blues on Stage.* Vol. 6 of *Black Studies.* Lewiston, Ont.: Edwin Mellen Press, 1999.

Handy, W. C.

The father of the blues, songwriter and cornetist William Christopher Handy (1873–1958) of Florence, Alabama, was the nation's first male professional blues artist, a spotlight he shared with Ma Rainey. He made his mark on American music by publishing Negro spirituals and blues and by melding the blues with ragtime. He played in minstrel shows, led his own band, and conducted an orchestra from 1903 to 1921. For his own publishing house, Pace and Handy Music Company, he composed two collections—*Blues: An Anthology* (1926) and *Book of Negro Spirituals* (1938)—plus marches, spirituals, and hymns. He is best known for distributing sheet music for forty memorable singles, including the prototype, "Memphis Blues" (1911). To popularize the blues idiom, he followed with "Yellow Dog Blues" (1914), "St. Louis Blues" (1914), "Joe Turner Blues" (1915), "Beale Street Blues" (1917), "Harlem Blues" (1923), "Atlanta Blues" (1924), and "Careless Love" (1925). His variation on the Joe Turner persona, "Joe Turner's Come and Gone," is a title that Wilson chose for a play about identity and selfhood.

See also **blues**

• *Further Reading*

Baker, Houston A. *Blues, Ideology, and Afro-American Literature: A Vernacular Theory.* Chicago: University of Chicago Press, 1984.
Gussow, Adam. "'Making My Getaway': The Blues Lives of Black Minstrels in W. C. Handy's Father of the Blues." *African American Review,* Spring 2001.

Hedley, King

August Wilson creates two vehicles for seriously disturbed characters named Hedley. In *Seven Guitars* (1995), the first King Hedley, a fifty-nine-year-old West Indian slaughterer of crated poultry at a makeshift backyard abattoir, lives in a dark emotional state caused by a "plot-against-the-black-man" illusion (p. 77). Oddly prescient in his delusions, he is marked by the print of his father's boot heel on his mouth in childhood, an event that evokes Hedley's constant verbal aggression, even when he is talking to himself. Speaking through his friend Vera Dotson, the playwright declares that Hedley "living too far in the past" (*Ibid.*). Wilson chose a Caribbean background for Hedley because he reflects the revolutionary spirit of the Jamaican maroons, the fugitive Africans who challenged British colonialism.

Wilson exonerates Hedley for his faults by making him the bearer of history: "I've encountered people like that in the black community who were encouraging me as a young man" (Rousuck, p. 1E). Wilson had his own awakening to the past in 1968 when he worked at a Pittsburgh theater. "I was totally unaware of anything that existed in theater prior to me. I was talking to a guy who owns a record store — he said, 'Oh yeah, we had a Negro theater in 1952'" (*Ibid.*). The casual acquaintance with a literary landmark proved worthwhile: "I thought how valuable and important that would have been to me. We thought we were the only ones who had the idea. That's when I began to recognize the importance of history" (*Ibid.*).

Mentally turbulent with dreams and wheeling visions, like Gabe in *Fences* (1985) and Hambone in *Two Trains Running* (1991), the old islander spouts wisdom veiled in gibberish. He bears the ironic name King because his evil-tempered father was enamored of New Orleans trumpeter King Buddy Bolden. Long after the father's death from medical neglect, his son sings a jingle about Bolden. It refers to a dream in which the father promised that Bolden would appear with the funds for Hedley to invest in his goal, a plantation, where he can grow oats and tobacco. The playwright depicts him as rural and backward in his thinking about tuberculosis, which he treats with Miss Sarah Degree's root tea. The physical malady symbolizes the emotional miasma that clouds his thinking. Ironically, Hedley dismisses the coughing up of blood by refusing medical attention, thus precipitating the same physical peril that killed his father.

As an inchoate shaman, Hedley is a curious blend of Bible reciter, militant Afrocentrist, killer of chickens, peddler of sandwiches, and imbiber of moonshine. In recitations that rumble with Old Testament prophecy stated in West Indian patois, he takes literally scriptural promises that persecutors shall be brought low. He interprets biblical injunctions as a diatribe against racism and looks forward to becoming a big man and landowner. Womanless and lonely, he pursues the landlady Louise, to whom he owes a month's rent, and longs to have a son. Like the biblical patriarch Abraham, Hedley's quasi-fatherhood comes late in his life when "[his] time is running out" (p. 68).

In a play filled with neighborly conversation, Hedley's responses are the brief and enigmatic mouthings of a fanatic. He makes limited music on a single wire nailed into a two-by-four, a symbol of his obsessive rants and apocalyptic mutterings about the rise of Ethiopia, the philosophy of Jamaican activist Marcus Garvey, and the majesty of freedom fighter François Toussaint L'Ouverture, who led Haitians in freeing slaves and establishing a black government of the French island. Hedley's attempt at music derives from a desire to commune with his great grandmother. During Floyd Barton's game of reciting "I thought I heard Buddy Bolden say," Hedley carries the repartee to a prophetic ending by promising to knife the person who owes him money (p. 39).

Hedley's acts appear to lack rational motivation. At the conclusion of Act I, he surprises the card-playing characters by stalking off into the night to grab Miss Tillery's rooster, a symbol of the masculinity that Hedley doubts in his own makeup. His incoherent opinions about God's call and the inevitability of death conclude with a quick knife slice to the bird's throat. As though re-enacting a voodoo ritual, he bloodies a circle, tosses the carcass on the ground, and warns the startled card players, "Your black ass be dead like the rooster now" (p. 64). Floyd puzzles over the eerie ceremony, about which Vera Dotson confides, "He ain't right" (*Ibid.*).

Hedley's mental vagaries suggest a blend of fantasy and deep-seated paranoia. To stop a man for ridiculing the name "King," Hedley beat him to death with a stick.

He bears the burden of murder, but declares he has no sorrow for taking another man's life. To Ruby, an outsider from Alabama, he claims that the killing was an act of pride. In a confused flow of need and longing, Hedley links his relation with his father to the biblical hierarchy of God the father and Christ the son. Garbling his thoughts on the rise of Ethiopia, Hedley sees himself as the "Lion of Judah," the title that Nation of Islam adherents accord to Ethiopia's Emperor Haile Selassie. Hedley anticipates the birth of a great black messiah and informs Ruby that she may be the mother of a great child, "the flesh of my flesh, my seven generations" (p. 89). Wilson creates additional irony in *King Hedley II* (1999) in the strivings of Hedley's namesake to establish a family. Although King Hedley II is burdened by the first Hedley's dynastic urge, he must face the fact that Ruby deceived the first Hedley about the fathering of her unborn child.

In Act II, Scene 2, at an electric moment shared with Floyd, Hedley goes into a delusional state, which seems to give him a vision of the future. He confers on Floyd both kingship and a death warrant. The delusions of an approaching messiah cause Hedley to elevate Floyd at the same time that he warns him that whites will not allow the rise of a black savior. Hedley urges, "Watch your back! The white man got a big plan against you" (p. 71). Ironically, both times that Hedley strikes, he kills a black male. The second time, he kills Floyd.

The resolution of the play hinges in Hedley's delusion about the promised money from Buddy Bolden. In Scene 5, Hedley returns from a chat with Joe Roberts and brandishes a machete wrapped in burlap. His musings grow more jangled and laced with omens of death and destruction and promise of seven generations. He prates, "I wag my tail. Look, I stirreth the nest. I am a hurricane to you, when you look at me you will see the house falling on your head. Its roof and its shutters and all the windows broken" (p. 88). Boozed up on rotgut, Hedley misperceives Floyd as Buddy Bolden with a handful of money and rejoices that Father Hedley has sent a legacy just as the dream promised. The quick slice of Hedley's machete that ends Floyd's life negates one man's dream while fulfilling that of his killer.

When the character recurs in Ruby's memories in *King Hedley II* (1999), she describes him as Haitian and honors his experience with horticulture and his knowledge of good soil. Metaphorically, he knew a good planting medium from ordinary dirt, a reference to the ghetto milieu that won't nurture seeds. The title character, who considers himself the elder Hedley's son, recalls that he was only three in 1951 when Hedley died. The reminiscence highlights one of Wilson's frequent depictions of sons looking for fathers.

See also **Buddy Bolden, Marion McClinton**

• *Further Reading*

Clark, Keith. *Black Manhood in James Baldwin, Ernest J. Gaines, and August Wilson.* Urbana: University of Illinois Press, 2002.

Preston, Rohan. "Hudson Returns in 'King'-size Role." *Minneapolis Star Tribune*, June 1, 2003.

"The Public Stages an Emotionally Explosive 'Seven Guitars.'" *Pittsburgh Post-Gazette*, June 14, 1997.

Rousuck, J. Wynn. "People with Vision." *Baltimore Sun*, April 27, 1997, p. 1E.
Tynan, William. "Death and the Blues." *Time*, Vol. 145, No. 5, February 6, 1995, p. 71.

Hedley, King, II

The fierce dreamer of *King Hedley II* (1999), the younger Hedley is an enigmatic character. Marked by his fifth-grade teacher's prediction that he would never rise above the level of janitor, he reveals a touch of energetic altruism by claiming to have mowed Aunt Ester's grass and delivered her prescriptions in boyhood. She gave him a gold key ring, a symbol of promise if he can supply the key. At age thirty-six, he exits a seven-year prison term for manslaughter. He contends that the next murder "ain't gonna cost me nothing," an indication that he doesn't plan to be at fault (p. 91). The prediction is ironic in that he pays for the final shooting with his own blood rather than in years in a cell.

A somber, grudge-bearing patriarch, Hedley II served time for pumping fourteen bullets into Pernell Sims, a known sneak from a sneaky family. Their fight erupted because the attacker repeatedly mocked Hedley as "Champ," the type of insult that roused the first Hedley to murder (p. 88). Returning home from Western Penn to his mother's residence, he bears the scar of his victim's blade up the left side of his face from cheek to forehead. In the opinion of critic Rohan Preston, "He looks like a bogeyman at the crossroads — a bad character like Stagger Lee" (Preston, "Cast," p. 5B). Curiously, the horribly defaced Hedley dreams of being an angel.

Contrasting Hedley's belligerent approach to ghetto survival is an almost boyish question, "Do I have a halo around my head?," a question he repeats in Act II (p. 9). Vigorous and demanding, he reprises the labors of Troy Maxson in *Fences* (1995), Sterling Johnson in *Seven Guitars* (1995), Lymon Jackson and Boy Willie Charles in *The Piano Lesson* (1990), and Herald Loomis in *Joe Turner's Come and Gone* (1988), all ex-cons attempting to return to normal life and establish a viable identity. Wilson's friend and former mentor, Pittsburgh Hill District poet Chawley P. Williams, claims that his is the troubled life on which Hedley is based.

Wilson burdens his protagonist with regrets and old scores to settle. Hedley grieves for his dead wife Neesi and dismays his new wife Tonya by visiting the grave of the mate who turned states evidence against him. For Tonya, he clutches at a sterile patch of ground as a symbol of ownership: "This the only dirt I got. This is me, right here" (p. 4). When Hedley interviews for jobs, he receives immediate turndowns. To himself he muses, "I could dance all night if the music's right. Ain't nothing I can't do" (p. 64). He lists his talents — to build railroads, create metalwork, run Andrew Mellon's bank, even hold the office of mayor or governor. His boasts balloon into self-pity when he asserts, "I ain't got no limits. I know right from wrong. I know which way the wind blows too. It don't blow my way!" (*Ibid.*).

From repeated rejection, rage threatens to destroy Hedley, who charges that whites have all the money. He thunders his discontent with the world: "They set up the rules, and then they don't want to follow them themselves" (p. 3). In his jaundiced view, blacks were in some ways better off under slave masters. He laments, "I used to be worth twelve hundred dollars during slavery, now I'm worth $3.35 an hour" (p. 65). He later complains, "I ain't bothering nobody. I got to feel right about myself" (*Ibid.*). His train of thought illustrates the playwright's belief that lack of opportunity is the cause of black discontent and crime.

In an era of romanticized visions of black heavyweight champ Joe Louis, high unemployment and despair target urban blacks. In the view of Stool Pigeon, Hedley is the wingless eagle who yearns to mount to a precipice. He maintains outsized ideals as he builds a new future, but his thoughts return to the past to his faithless mother Ruby, who abandoned him to her aunt Louise. Because he faces serious problems with locating a job and controlling his anger, he allows a hustler named Mister, a childhood companion and son of Red Carter and WillaMae from *Seven Guitars*, to join him in a scheme to sell GE refrigerators stolen by one of Hedley's fellow prisoners. Hedley and Mister get two hundred dollars each for them and stockpile the cash while telling themselves that, once they have enough, they will turn from felonious business to operating a legitimate video rental store. Their rationalizing is unconvincing.

At the heart of Hedley's plan is a goal to raise ten thousand dollars to open Royal Videos and become his own man. Bedeviled by comparisons to King Hedley I, a West Indian peddler and his alleged father, Hedley II develops into an inflated inner-city warrior. To extend his family line, he wants to father King Hedley III. He harangues his thirty-five-year-old wife Tonya to abandon plans to abort their unborn child, which will be younger than her grandchild and will grow up in a violent, economically fragile milieu. To build his dynasty and secure the only immortality he is capable of, he woos Tonya with seeds planted in her garden. He admits, "I'm living for you. That's what I told you when we got married" (p. 42). The trampled results at the center of the bare ghetto lot prove Tonya's misgivings and Hedley's baseless hopes, which he destroys by joining Mister in robbing a jewelry store.

• *Further Reading*

Brantley, Ben. "'King Hedley II': The Agonized Arias of Everyman in Poverty and Pain." *New York Times*, May 2, 2001.

Cohen, Robert. "In Los Angeles." http://drama.arts.uci.edu/cohen/jitney.htm.

Cummings, Scott. "King Hedley II." *Boston Phoenix*, May 18-25, 2000.

Gardner, Elysa. "It's Good to Be Wilson's 'King.'" *USA Today*, May 3, 2001.

Gutman, Les. "King Hedley II." *CurtainUp*, 2001.

Ifill, Gwen. "American Shakespeare." *PBS News*, April 6, 2001.

Keating, Douglas J. "A 'King' with Majesty Sadly Thwarted." *Philadelphia Inquirer*, January 31, 2003.

Preston, Rohan. "Cast Gives Lift to Heavy 'King Hedley.'" *Minneapolis Star Tribune*, May 31, 2003, p. 5B.

_____. "Hudson Returns in 'King'-size Role." *Minneapolis Star Tribune*, June 1, 2003.

Rawson, Chris. "Stage Review: Wilson's Hedley a Thrilling Ride." *Pittsburgh Post-Gazette*, December 16, 1999.

Robb, J. Cooper. "August Tidings." *Philadelphia Weekly*, January 22, 2003.

Hedley, Tonya

The pivotal female in the life of August Wilson's monumental title figure in *King Hedley II* (1999) is his thirty-five-year-old bride, who creates some of the play's intense moments. A fully employed insurance office worker, she takes responsibility for household finances. Nonetheless, as the widowed mother of Natasha, a seventeen-year-old mother of a newborn, Tonya is wracked by defeatism. Her depression stems from the jailing of J. C., Natasha's father, and from the girl's materialism. Like the downtrodden and devalued Rose Maxson in *Fences* (1985) and the self-effacing Risa Thomas in *Two Trains Running* (1982), Tonya is loyal and virtuous without exuding self-righteousness. When Hedley begins to self-destruct, she vows, "I ain't visiting any more jailhouses" (p. 95).

Tonya wrestles with the idea of bearing Hedley's child, who will be younger than her grandchild. Upon examining the violent, failing Hill District, in Act I, Scene 2, she makes one of the powerful statements the playwright allots to his female characters: "Why I want to bring another life into this world that don't respect life? I don't want to raise no more babies when you got to fight to keep them alive" (p. 43). She fears betrayal by both friends and police, either of whom could extinguish her child's life. She uses as an example of womanly grief the suffering of Little Buddy Will's mother on Bryn Mawr Road, who must identify a corpse marked with a toe tag labeled "John Doe number four" (p. 44). Tonya's empathy for the mother fills her with the chill of a future day when that same generic marker may encircle her own child's toe.

- *Further Reading*

  Brantley, Ben. "'King Hedley II': The Agonized Arias of Everyman in Poverty and Pain." *New York Times*, May 2, 2001.
  Gardner, Elysa. "It's Good to Be Wilson's 'King.'" *USA Today*, May 3, 2001.
  Ifill, Gwen. "American Shakespeare." *PBS News*, April 6, 2001.
  Keating, Douglas J. "A 'King' with Majesty Sadly Thwarted." *Philadelphia Inquirer*, January 31, 2003.
  Preston, Rohan. "Cast Gives Lift to Heavy 'King Hedley.'" *Minneapolis Star Tribune*, May 31, 2003, p. 5B.
  _____. "Hudson Returns in 'King'-size Role." *Minneapolis Star Tribune*, June 1, 2003.

Hedley genealogy

As described in *Seven Guitars* (1995) and *King Hedley II* (1999), the line of the Hedley family illustrates the Great Migration as members move from the West Indies and from Birmingham, Alabama, to Pittsburgh in the urban North:

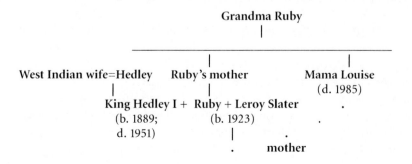

| | |
Neesi Hedley=King Hedley II=Tonya=J. C.
(killed in a   (b. 1949 of uncertain   (jailed)
car crash)   parentage and reared
                 by his great-aunt Louise;
                 d. 1985 from a bullet
                 to the throat)

                              | |
                         unborn child   Natasha
                         (1985)   (b. 1968)
                                        |
                                        infant
                                        (b. 1985)

historical milieu

August Wilson's cycle of ten dramas about African Americans sets each play in a real period of history. His ninth play, *Gem of the Ocean* (2003), which opens in 1904, places a guilt-ridden protagonist, Citizen Barlow, in the presence of the phenomenal Aunt Ester on her 287th birthday. In flight from constable Caesar, Barlow takes refuge with the beloved Pittsburgh sage while he begins making sense of his life. His confusion typifies the unsettling effects of the Civil War and Emancipation Proclamation, which resolved the slavery issue, but left blacks ill-equipped to manage employment, money management, housing, education, and obedience to the law. In an interview, Wilson explained, "All of a sudden black men had to ask themselves things like, 'What is money?' 'What is marriage?' ... What were black men supposed to do to make a living?" (Rocha, p. 38).

For *Joe Turner's Come and Gone* (1988), set in a Pittsburgh boardinghouse in 1911, the playwright sounds an alarm that echoes through the remainder of the century and into the new millennium. Wilson depicts an ex-con attempting to reassemble his family from the wreckage of a life destroyed by crime and imprisonment. Like others of the first black generation born free of slavery, Herald Loomis flees a chain gang and searches for identity and self-empowerment by joining the early stage of the Great Migration north. At a loss for coping skills outside the rural South, the characters work at low-paying manual labor and live on society's fringes. Comforting and uplifting men like Loomis are Afrocentric dances, music, and animistic religion and superstitions, the shreds of culture that survived the Middle Passage as his ancestors were hustled from Africa to auction blocks in the plantation South.

Wilson moved to the 1920s for *Ma Rainey's Black Bottom* (1985), a recreation of the post–World War I era that saw the rise of the first Afro-American blues stars while most blacks lived little better than their enslaved ancestors. Although a few like Ma Rainey flourished in the biased music industry, most blacks struggled against the injustices of Jim Crow laws, which relegated non-white citizens to subservience, blacks-only hotels, and back-door entrances at eateries. The lyrics of songs reprised the hardships of tolerating daily indignities directed by whites at non-whites, particularly the bleak existence of black sharecroppers in the rural South.

With *The Piano Lesson* (1990), set in 1936, Wilson moved on to the stirrings of self-determination among the first generations born out of direct memory of slavery. To improve opportunities for her daughter Maretha, Berniece Charles enrolls her at the Irene Kaufman Settlement House, an arts and educational outreach established by philanthropic Jews in Pittsburgh's poor, mostly black Hill District. The house offers free socialization programs as a means of uplifting residents of the black ghetto. Children like Maretha learned about diet and health care as well as proper English and etiquette. In the second half of the twentieth century, the center falls victim to urban renewal.

Perhaps more touching than the privations of the Great Depression were dreams such as Boy Willie's attempt to own and farm the Mississippi Delta land that his grandparents worked as slaves. As the Great Migration took blacks out of the share-cropping South and away from the Ku Klux Klan, capricious arrest, prison camps, and chain gangs, in the years following World War II, the flight to industrial cities in the North and its honky-tonks and saloons produced a new round of regrets and disappointments, the subject of *Seven Guitars* (1995), set in 1948. Exacerbating the restlessness and yearnings were the war years, when black soldiers enjoyed more respect and public accommodation in France than they received on their return home.

The stirrings of the civil rights movement were already apparent in Wilson's *Fences* (1985), an outgrowth of the 1950s, when the Supreme Court ended segregation in public facilities and schools. Black families were learning to cope with big industry and powerful trade unions, buying permanent dwellings, and achieving financial security while pushing their children beyond the struggles of the first half of the twentieth century. The Negro Baseball League turned up native talent like Troy Maxson, who might have flourished as professional athletes, but who lacked the chance until Joe Louis and Jackie Robinson made the first dents in racist sports leagues. Maxson's memories spanned four decades, back to his flight to Mobile, Alabama, in 1918, when he wandered homeless among blacks who resided in tarpaper shacks. To shield his son Cory from illusions of championship sports and a dead-end job, Troy and others of his milieu groomed their children for the trades and steady work. Troy declares, "The white man ain't gonna let him get nowhere with that football" (p. 8). His wife Rose counters his gloomy outlook by reminding him that times have changed since World War II.

The turmoil of the 1960s, Wilson's backdrop for *Two Trains Running* (1991), left inner-city blacks immured in burned-out, going-nowhere ghettos. Racial unrest forged the Black Is Beautiful concept of emerging black authors and artists, the powerful preaching of Malcolm X for the Nation of Islam, and the sweeping promises proffered by President Lyndon Johnson and the Great Society. In a vast reshaping of neighborhoods with high-rise projects, urban renewal attempted to rid cities of crime and social deterioration. In Wilson's fictional setting, the brutality of the wrecking ball strikes at the cultural enclaves of small markets, night clubs, a dime store and pharmacy, grocery, medical and dental offices, and diners such as Memphis Lee's cafe, where black patrons gather to share their accomplishments and batter the obstacles to their dreams.

The 1970s saw blacks like the gypsy cabbies of Wilson's *Jitney* (1982) improvising means of surviving the canker that ate at the foundations of urban America. Returning Vietnam veterans, family men, and would-be entrepreneurs fought the ongoing collapse of black communities as urban renewal chewed at their storefront efforts. The stress of Northern city life from alcohol, drugs, and crime destroyed men like the alcoholic Fielding and ate at families, creating gulfs like the one that incites distrust in Youngblood's girl Rena and separates Jim Becker from his ex-con son Booster.

The title character and protagonist in Wilson's *King Hedley II* (1999), set in 1985, portrays the disproportionate burden that blacks pay for crime, a cancer that favors the male population. Upon return from prison, ex-cons like the title character located few worthy jobs and made little headway in distancing themselves from past mistakes. The playwright delineates hopelessness and blight by depicting withered yards and the dispirited Tonya Hedley, King's wife, who prefers to abort her unborn child rather than to breathe promise into yet another member of the black underclass.

See also **decade cycle, Pittsburgh, Time Line of Hill District Residents and Events (Appendix A)**

• *Further Reading*

McDonough, Carla J. *Staging Masculinity: Male Identity in Contemporary American Drama*. Jefferson, N.C.: McFarland, 1997.
Rocha, Mark William. "A Conversation with August Wilson." *Diversity: A Journal of Multicultural Issues*, Vol. 1, Fall 1992, pp. 24–42.

Holloway

A sixty-five-year-old gambler and former house painter as well as storyteller and philosopher in *Two Trains Running* (1991), Holloway adds street wisdom at Memphis Lee's cafe to balance customers' discussions of money and women. A keen observer of the neighborhood, Holloway supports Aunt Ester, the 322-year-old prophet, and makes regular visits to her to keep his life in sync. He understands why Risa Thomas mutilates her legs with a razor to keep men from pursuing her and why she chastises ex-con Sterling Johnson for not working to buy what he wants. To a discussion of Sterling's return to society from imprisonment for bank robbery, Holloway counters Memphis's suggestion that a steady job is the best beginning of a new life. To Holloway, blacks are in constant competition with whites for money. The best way for blacks to rise from poverty to wealth is through gambling. He sneers at a salary of ten dollars a day by admiring the black man in Squirrel Hill carrying big money in his pocket.

In an eloquent summation of the black experience, Holloway describes the black role in American history. His well thought-out philosophy refers to the principle of "stacking," an image of captive Africans layered in slaving vessels during the Middle Passage (p. 35). With a wry quip, he muses, "It's lucky the boat didn't sink with all them niggers they had stacked up there" (*Ibid.*). He summarizes three hundred years of slavery as working for free to enrich whites and uses the railroad as an example of blacks laboring for minimal pay to enrich white entrepreneurs.

Rather than lambaste blacks for laziness, Holloway characterizes them as "the most hard-working people in the world" (p. 34). He visualizes the tyranny of wealthy whites as "standing on top of you," his image of exploitation by the ruling class (*Ibid.*). He charges that, after slavery, whites stopped working blacks because the government required payment for labor. Thus, unemployment and idleness followed an era of unending toil in cotton fields as black Americans became expendable.

Holloway spits bile in his comments on crime. He recognizes the potential for violence in Sterling, particularly after he arms himself with a pistol. In reference to blacks and guns, Holloway identifies a pervasive fear in whites of armed blacks. He describes whites as wielders of guns and the atomic bomb, but they are terrorized by the first mention of blacks brandishing firearms. He charges that white police immediately escalate the situation by inflaming the public with talk of "sabotage, disturbing the peace, inciting a riot, plotting to overthrow the government" (p. 86). Wilson allows Holloway's ranting to escalate beyond dialogue to an ill-concealed mouthpiece for the playwright himself.

See also **injustice**

• *Further Reading*

Rocha, Mark William. "American History as 'Loud Talking' in *Two Trains Running*," in *May All Your Fences Have Gates: Essays on the Drama of August Wilson*. Iowa City: University of Iowa Press, 1994, pp. 116–132.

Holly, Bertha

The fryer of chicken and maker of coffee, grits and gravy, and biscuits at a Pittsburgh boardinghouse in *Joe Turner's Come and Gone* (1988), Bertha Holly is a female shaman in the African tradition. In her late forties, she salves the spirits of demoralized transients with generosity, acceptance, good humor, and down-home meals served in her kitchen, the nexus of social interaction. Even though she is childless, she is the rare female in August Wilson's drama cycle to enjoy a stable home and a twenty-five-year marriage to a responsible husband, Seth Holly, who is willing to work three jobs and still offer a hand around their inn.

Like her husband, Bertha is dutiful. She demands pay for room and board, yet is amenable to an arrangement by which Herald Loomis receives a 50-percent discount in exchange for his daughter Zonia's domestic service. She reminds Jeremy Furlow to change his sheets. In gratitude for her exceptional cooking, he awards her a compliment: "I thought my mama could fry some chicken. But she can't do half as good as you" (p. 50).

Bertha's credo is a simple ideal: "To have love in one hand and laughter in the other" (p. 87). The antithesis of Joe Turner, enslaver and dehumanizer of men, she displays welcome and charity and turns domesticity into a life celebration. Of herself, she claims, "I ain't no trouble to get along with" (p. 50). She looks for positives rather than negatives, particularly in the suitability of the love-lorn Mattie Campbell for the questing Herald Loomis. In Bertha's rosy philosophy of love, a woman who exerts her energies to be herself is bound to find the right man.

See also **women**

• *Further Reading*

Kubitschek, Missy Dehn. "August Wilson's Gender Lesson," in *May All Your Fences Have Gates: Essays on the Drama of August Wilson*. Iowa City: University of Iowa Press, 1994.

Holly, Seth

The self-actualized tinsmith in *Joe Turner's Come and Gone* (1988), Seth Holly stands out as the rare North-born black whose roots reach back to free ancestors. Married for a quarter century to the same woman, in his early fifties, he manages to work nights for Mr. Olowski at a factory job, shape pots and pans, mentally tot up sums, and aid his wife Bertha in myriad chores at their boardinghouse. Seth's skills come from his father, who trained him in metalwork and in operating the family inn. A combination of farmer and Yankee engineer, he blends the talents of both the South and the North —cultivating a vegetable plot and managing a home smithy. He looks ahead to the next year, where he plans to get a vine cutting from Butera to grow his own grapes, a suggestion of the biblical lore of Christ as the vine (John 15:5) and of communion (Matthew 26:28).

Seth's faults include a too-literal view of nature and religion and an eagerness to judge agrarian immigrants from the South and to ridicule the mystic shaman Bynum Walker for conducting African rituals. Seth suspected the intent of Moses Houser, the suicide who leaped from the Brady Street Bridge, and disdains Herald Loomis on the basis of his bedraggled appearance. To Bynum, Seth confides that Loomis is "mean-looking ... like he done killed somebody gambling over a quarter" (p. 20). In contrast to Bynum's humanism, Seth's tendency to expect the worst in people compels him to rebuke Zonia Loomis about where she can play and to suspect Loomis of eyeing Bertha and plotting to rob the church and harm Martha Pentecost.

In contrast to the transients at the inn, Seth is the consummate conformist. Because he has embraced the values and objectives of the North, he retains no African beliefs and rejects Walker's superstitions and Herald Loomis's peculiarities. In Seth's opinion, "These niggers coming up here with that old backward country style of living. It's hard enough now without all that ignorant kind of acting. Ever since slavery got over with there ain't been nothing but foolish-acting niggers" (p. 6). After he evicts Loomis for going into a trance during the juba dance, Bertha sends Seth to his workshop with the comment, "That's the only time you satisfied is when you out there" (p. 60).

To assure that mercantile aims don't jeopardize what he already owns, Seth remains skeptical of risky business dealings. He states the offerings of the boarding house, the cost, and his expectations that visitors respect their lodgings. In mutually beneficial dealings with his white associate, Rutherford Selig, Seth is above board in exchanges, generous in offering food and hospitality, and willing to help Selig stock the wagon.

• *Further Reading*

McDonough, Carla J. *Staging Masculinity: Male Identity in Contemporary American Drama.* Jefferson, N.C.: McFarland, 1997.

humor

August Wilson depicts normal human life as a blend of reward and loss, the straights with the crookeds, as exhibited in *King Hedley II* (1999), in which Mister nets a period of solitary confinement for requesting a copy of his police mugshots as gifts for the family, Rose's banishment of Troy Maxson "so the marrying kind could find me" in *Fences* (1985), and, in *The Piano Lesson* (1990), Boy Willie's interruption of Avery Brown's biblical exorcism by a mocking display of throwing water around the room and banishing the ghost of Robert Sutter. In *Two Trains Running* (1991), Holloway tells a favorite anecdote about partying females who arrived in eleven Cadillacs from Las Vegas and joined other mourners in drinking and dumping dice and playing cards over the freshly dug grave of Patchneck Red. Ex-con Sterling Johnson creates humor at his own expense by joking about being born with seven cents in his hands and by describing the no-win situation of needing a job to join the union and needing to join the union before applying for work. Memphis Lee adds to the drollery with his garbled accounting of Risa's pay and his explanation of the statue of blind justice. He interprets the blindfold on her eyes as proof that there "Ain't no justice" (p. 42).

With *Jitney* (1982), Wilson hones his humor to suit the situation, ranging from an argument over Lena Horne's beauty to a dig at Aunt Lil, a self-appointed expert on scripture since she joined the Jehovah's Witnesses. Wilson manages to honor the average man's struggles at the same time that he gets laughs from common predicaments and failed aspirations. Shealy, the numbers runner who hangs out at the cab stand, presents a lengthy monologue about losing Rosie, the only woman whose face still haunts him. He describes giving her 99 percent of his cash and losing her love when his largesse ran out. Since she barred the door, Shealy comforts himself with "that little yellow gal used to work down at Pope's [restaurant]," but strikes out once more (p. 16). He visits his new flame's home to retrieve the key from the mailbox and finds three rivals already in attendance. Shealy mutters, "I don't know who had the key" (p. 17).

Humor extends from domestic imbroglios to lethal situations in Wilson's dramas, as with the shooting over two fish sandwiches in *King Hedley II* that "was a surprise to God" (p. 37). Herald Loomis, the seeker in *Joe Turner's Come and Gone* (1988), claims to have traveled so far in search of his wife Martha that "You'd have thought I was a missionary spreading the gospel" (p. 42). In *Ma Rainey's Black Bottom* (1985), Toledo tells an illustrative joke about a man who quotes the familiar child's bedtime prayer "Now I Lay Me Down to Sleep" as though it were the Lord's Prayer. In token of the black man's ability to recycle loss into gain, Solly Two Kings, the dog dung collector in *Gem of the Ocean* (2003), quips about his search for "great dane pure" (Preston). In *Jitney*, Turnbo creates a hypothetical case of two men courting Betty Jean and Betty Sue. When jealousy leads to violence, one possessive male kills the other. Turnbo extemporizes, "Here lie Bubba Boo. Was caught with Betty Jean instead of Betty Sue" (p. 63).

Frequent jolts of wry wit, coarse snickers, and belly laughs relieve anguish, e.g., Elmore's claim to "make a pit bull shit bricks" in *King Hedley II* (p. 39). In *Seven Guitars* (1995), humor is homespun, particularly Hedley's explanation of why pawn shops have three gold balls painted out front and Canewell's comparison of roosters from Alabama, Georgia, and Mississippi. According to the explanation of his surname, it derives from a Louisiana grandfather who was expert at cutting sugarcane. Canewell adds, "Otherwise my name would be Cottonwell" (p. 25). A major source of drollery, Canewell remarks that the fraudulant insurance that T. L. Hall sells to poor people is a natural act of self-sufficiency. In Canewell's generous view, cheating people "might have been [Hall's] only chance not to be poor" (p. 85).

Described as Wilson's funniest play, *Seven Guitars* picks up the dramatic pace with frequent laughs, including lengthy recitations of doggerel, Floyd Barton's reenactment of his arrest for vagrancy, Red Carter's woman troubles, sexual innuendo about roosters, and Ruby's suggestion during intercourse that her oversexed lover Elmore "look in the mirror and count that as twice" (p. 73). In a scene between quarreling lovers, Wilson lightens the exchange with humor by describing Floyd's employ of a Pittsburgh workhouse letter-writer to concoct a romantic statement that sounds out of character from the real man. Floyd is so impressed that he pays a quarter and considers tipping the scribe an extra twenty-five cents, then decides to wait to see how effective the florid words are on Vera Dotson, his angry former girlfriend.

• *Further Reading*

Preston, Rohan. "Oglesby Sparkles in Wilson's 'Gem.'" *Minneapolis Star Tribune*, May 4, 2003, p. 4F.
Wang, Qun. *An In-Depth Study of the Major Plays of African American Playwright August Wilson: Vernacularizing the Blues on Stage.* Vol. 6 of *Black Studies.* Lewiston, Ont.: Edwin Mellen Press, 1999.

injustice

In his decade cycle, August Wilson stresses both everyday unfairness and outright connivance, such as Susan McKnight's fabricated rape charge against Booster and Turnbo's slander of Youngblood and Peaches in *Jitney* (1982). Examples range from the false jailing of Wolf and the charging of mourners waiting to view the remains of the Prophet Samuel in *Two Trains Running* (1991) and constable Caesar's fierce recriminations against black felons in *Gem of the Ocean* (2003) to the white-on-black injustices that have historically denied African Americans the full benefits of liberty. In *Two Trains Running*, Memphis Lee, the cafe owner, warns about the undertaker West, the kind of cheat who robs corpses of gold and jewels and dumps the remains from the casket into a raw grave. Memphis further denigrates West's ethics by ridiculing the clients who demand a twenty-year guarantee that the caskets they buy are waterproof. A galling form of black-on-black injustice appears later in the play when characters discuss Chauncey Ward's father, Pittsburgh's first black judge. Memphis notes that Ward typically comes down hard on black criminals, sentencing one felon to five hundred years.

Ironically, justice in *Two Trains Running* brings triumph from an unlikely source. Lutz, the butcher, who deliberately tricks Hambone, discovers the intransigence of the retarded handyman, who paints Lutz's fence in exchange for a ham. Lutz promises a chicken for a lesser job and judges the paint job as worthy of only a chicken. For nine and a half years, Hambone carries his complaint to the streets and stands outside the meat market demanding just compensation for good work. After his sudden death, Sterling Johnson, a bank robber and ex-con, smashes Lutz's plate glass window and snatches a ham to place in Hambone's coffin. The ambiguous act honors Hambone at the same time that it calls into question Johnson's willingness to risk another jail term for an empty gesture to a corpse.

Wilson's characters disagree on the nature and source of justice, for example, the series of killings attributed to the Ghosts of the Yellow Dog in *The Piano Lesson* (1990) and the venality of a judge in *Fences* (1985) who palms fifty dollars from Troy Maxson before releasing Gabe into his brother's custody. In a lengthy cafe-counter discussion of freedom and justice, Memphis refutes the basic premises of Black Power advocates and holds forth on the individual's responsibility to secure human rights. In a folksy reference to the New Testament, he comments, "Jesus Christ didn't get justice. What makes you think you gonna get it?" (p. 42). In Memphis's version, the only way to hang onto possessions is with a shotgun, a sign of force that potential usurpers understand.

The more insidious type of injustice — white-on-black unfairness— receives the playwright's harshest denunciation, particularly in *King Hedley II* (1999) in which Hop submits the lowest bid to tear down a hotel in East Liberty but doesn't get the contract until he takes the matter to court. In another offstage imbroglio, Hedley causes a scene at Sears when the photographer can't locate his pictures with just the receipt. In *Two Trains Running*, a disturbing miscarriage of justice occurs after white officers wrongfully arrested Wolf for obstruction of justice after he collided with a fleeing suspect. A more serious incident involved the racist Jim Stovall, who ordered the killing and emasculation of Memphis's mule and drove Memphis off his land in Jackson, Mississippi. In Wolf's estimation, in a racist world, "You always under attack" (p. 54). Holloway describes how Meyer burned his own drugstore to claim the insurance money and predicts that the white justice system will be obligated to sentence an innocent black to jail for arson. In response to decades of whites scapegoating blacks for crimes, Memphis blames blacks for failing to take action against the police who shot Begaboo. After three weeks of rallies at the mayor's office, protesters gave up and returned to everyday activities. Outraged, Memphis complains, "When it comes time for action these niggers sit down and scratch their heads" (p. 85).

Because of many occasions when whites turn the law against blacks, Wilson's characters become paranoid about guarantees of justice for all, a theme in humorous discussions of arrest in *Seven Guitars* (1995). Blacks tend to rely on deception, flight, or native intelligence to help them cope with white-controlled justice, such as the arrest of Floyd Barton for having no money and of Red Carter for having too much. More dramatic is the type of mob rule in *The Piano Lesson* that resulted in the burning death of Boy Charles and four vagrants in a boxcar of the Yellow Dog, the folk designation for the Yazoo Delta railroad. As the mistrustful Wining Boy Charles summarizes, "The colored man can't fix nothing with the law" (p. 38).

Injustice permeates the blues, the oral lore that records and muses upon the inequities of black life. In *Joe Turner's Come and Gone* (1988), the protagonist, Herald Loomis, labors on a chain gang after being jailed on a false charge. Working for the governor's brother, Loomis loses heart and complains, "Great big old white man ... your Mr. Jesus Christ. Standing there with a whip in one hand and tote board in another, and them niggers swimming in a sea of cotton" (p. 92). Female singers in the drama intone in blues style:

> Got my man and gone
> Come with forty links of chain
> Ohhh Lordy [p. 67]

The song implants on black culture an oral record of injustice to men whom bigots like Turner exploit for personal gain. The subversion of the Bill of Rights results in the displacement of blacks, as demonstrated by men separated from their homes and families to serve sentences in prison and on the chain gang.

See also **blues, crime, opportunity, Parchman Farm, racism, violence**

• *Further Reading*

Gates, Henry Louis, Jr. "Department of Disputation: The Chitlin' Circuit." *New Yorker*, February 3, 1997, pp. 44–55.
McDonough, Carla J. *Staging Masculinity: Male Identity in Contemporary American Drama.* Jefferson, N.C.: McFarland, 1997.

irony

Wilson excels at irony, a literary device implying a discrepancy between what is said and done and what the author means, as with the blood sacrifice of the title character in *King Hedley II* (1999), who dies on the black cat's grave in lieu of a sacrificial goat or fatted calf. In *The Piano Lesson* (1990), the playwright describes the recovery of a slave-era heirloom on Independence Day, 1911, and depicts a domestic fracas between Boy Willie and Berniece Charles over an inheritance from their grandsires, for whom both characters are named. Despite the siblings' ties to beloved ancestors from the slave-holding past, they differ diametrically on how to honor their patrimony and how to apply its noble examples to their own lives in the mid–1930s. In *Two Trains Running* (1991), Memphis Lee, the cafe owner, ridicules Hambone's persistent demand that Lutz, the butcher, give him a ham as payment for painting a fence. Wilson turns the situation to dramatic irony by demonstrating how Hambone's example replicates Memphis's demand that city authorities reimburse him completely for his property. Other models of dramatic incongruence appear in *King Hedley II* when the title character unknowingly takes as mentor his father's killer, and in *Jitney* (1982), in which Jim Becker rejects Booster Becker, his son and heir, only days before Jim dies, leaving his cab service and car to Booster.

Wilson also uses irony as a means of defeating stereotypes. In *Jitney*, he plays directly to white beliefs that blacks are philanderers and drunks. By the drama's end, he has redeemed Fielding from alcoholism and Youngblood from destructive gossip about his relationship with Peaches, his wife's sister. Wilson rewards Youngblood with a stronger commitment and the purchase of a home for Rena and for Jesse, their son. In the words of critic Gene Lichtenstein, "Indeed, Wilson goes out of his way to invest all his characters with middle-class virtues" rather than the slum world values that whites theorize as a standard (Lichtenstein).

In *Joe Turner's Come and Gone* (1988), Wilson reveals self-defeating acts in Herald Loomis and his estranged wife Martha Pentecost. Ironically, both turn from a husband-wife relationship to their own forms of worship. Loomis enshrines Martha's face during his years of imprisonment and launches a pilgrimage to her as though she were a saint. On her own pilgrimage, Martha joins the Reverend Tolliver in a religious trek north to rescue the church from Southern racists. Before locating Martha, Loomis ridicules Pentecost, her chosen name, as "tongues of fire to burn up your wooly heads" (p. 93). When husband and wife reunite at the Hollys' boarding house, they have lost the original glue that bound them into a couple, a fact made known to them by Bynum, the binding man. In the end, Martha continues to embrace Christianity; Loomis rediscovers the African strands of manhood. In search of opposing icons, the couple must part permanently and follow paths more appropriate to their individual longings. In being tossed from father to mother, their daughter Zonia feels like excess baggage.

In *Fences* (1985), the playwright holds up his foils, Jim Bono and Troy Maxson, to emphasize the value of a wholesome marriage to peace of mind. As Troy juggles a deteriorating home life while concealing high times with his mistress Alberta, Bono strains to comprehend how his friend can stray so far from fidelity. Wilson gives him a revealing speech: "You done learned me a lot of things. You showed me how to not make the same mistakes ... to take life as it comes along and keep putting one foot in front of the other" (p. 62). Ironically, Bono is the husband who has set the example of devotion. Troy fails to follow his friend's example and ends a pattern of camaraderie and hero worship that dismays Bono. A more dramatic irony is the death of Troy's lively mistress Alberta during childbirth. The limited affair leaves him with another mouth to feed and more home responsibilities than he had before escaping from home to indulge in sexual misconduct.

See also **goldenseal, Red Carter**

• *Further Reading*

Lichtenstein, Gene. "An Evening with August Wilson." *Jewish Journal of Greater Los Angeles*, February 11, 2000.
Wang, Qun. *An In-Depth Study of the Major Plays of African American Playwright August Wilson: Vernacularizing the Blues on Stage*. Vol. 6 of *Black Studies*. Lewiston, Ont.: Edwin Mellen Press, 1999.

Irvin

The manager of the title character in *Ma Rainey's Black Bottom* (1985), Irvin is a money-driven exploiter of talent and ameliorator of kinks in the production schedule. In the opening scene, he tests the mike and promises Mel Sturdyvant, the seedy producer, that he will stop Ma from acting like "Royal Highness ... Queen of the Blues" (p. 18). Irvin is the peacemaker who must keep the singing group on schedule and Ma from sniping at Sturdyvant, a police officer, and Levee Green, Ma's cocky trumpeter. To settle a traffic accident, Irvin passes money to the investigating officer, Wilson's symbolic representation of white venality and disrespect for law.

Like a well-trained flunky and placater, Irvin provides deli sandwiches for the performers and suffers Ma's demands and late arrival. He keeps her humble by inviting her to sing for white dinner guests, but not to join them at the table. He eases into the changing of musical styles by reminding her that "Levee's arrangement gives the people what they want. It gets them excited ... makes them forget about their troubles" (p. 62). He later tries to deliver harsh news from Sturdyvant that Ma must pay her nephew, Sylvester Brown, out of her own proceeds. Irvin takes the blame for making a mistake and coerces Ma into signing forms, a task that demeans him by forcing him to beg and wheedle while she keeps him waiting. The power struggle exhibits the psychological games that both sides play to retain the upper hand.

• *Further Reading*

Adell, Sandra. "Speaking of Ma Rainey/Talking about the Blues," in *May All Your Fences Have Gates: Essays on the Drama of August Wilson*. Iowa City: University of Iowa Press, 1994.
Wang, Qun. *An In-Depth Study of the Major Plays of African American Playwright August Wilson: Vernacularizing the Blues on Stage*. Vol. 6 of *Black Studies*. Lewiston, Ont.: Edwin Mellen Press, 1999.

Jackson, Lymon

The fellow inmate and business associate of Boy Willie Charles in *The Piano Lesson* (1990), twenty-nine-year-old Lymon Jackson projects a complex image of a Southern rube blessed with humor, common sense, and honor. He is a sensitive, gentle man who left home at age sixteen to reduce his mother's responsibilities. Wining Boy describes Lymon's mother in the same candid, unfeigned innocence by narrating how he paid fifty dollars to bail L. D. Jackson out of jail, then slept with L. D.'s wife as a reward. The anecdote offers a brief hint that Lymon's tie to the Charles family may lie deeper than mere friendship.

In an appealing example of manhood, Lymon is tough without wearing the bravado that coats Boy Willie. Lymon survived a bullet to the stomach for stealing wood and served a three-year sentence at Parchman Farm in Mississippi. He aided Boy Willie in finding work cutting timber off Lymon's cousin's property. Boy Willie and Lymon paired up to buy watermelons from Pitterford and drive them to Pittsburgh to sell in Squirrel Hill out of the back of Lymon's ramshackle truck. A model of the easy mark come North from rural Mississippi, Lymon accedes to Wining Boy's sales talk and buys his outdated silk suit, shirt, and shoes. Lymon is so gullible that he expects his spiffy outfit to impress women and believes the salesman who declares that the perfume he stocks is the same type worn by the queen of France.

As partners, Lymon and Boy Willie differ in outlook and behavior. Steady and family-minded, Lymon saved one hundred twenty dollars from his wood-hauling job to buy the second-hand truck. He needed transportation to take him away from Mississippi to satisfy his curiosity about the North and to look for a wife. He dresses neatly, takes Dolly and Grace out for drinks, and tries to romance Berniece. To support himself, he considers finding work unloading rail cars. In contrast, Boy Willie tries to bed down on Doaker's sofa with Grace, who shares her residence with Leroy. Boy Willie wants to return home as his own boss rather than work for a paycheck in Pittsburgh. Lymon urges him to stay, but his partner prefers to risk two thousand dollars on a stake in Southern farm life. Unlike his partner and foil, Lymon respects Berniece's share in the piano and suggests that Boy Willie not sell it.

- *Further Reading*

Bissiri, Amadou. "Aspects of Africanness in August Wilson's Drama: Reading *The Piano Lesson* through Wole Soyinka's Drama." *African American Review*, Vol. 30, No. 1, 1996, pp. 99–113.

The Janitor

A one-act, four-minute play, *The Janitor* (1985) demonstrates August Wilson's ability to observe common human actions and transform them into stage drama. He wrote the play to raise funds for the New Dramatists, the nation's oldest nonprofit workshop. The title character, fifty-six-year-old Sam, sweeps a ballroom only hours before a gathering of youth. In the empty room, the menial domestic takes the rostrum and, citing William Shakespeare and Popeye, improvises a speech worthy of a paid orator for its relevance and truth.

Wilson's insightful text rejoices in the ability of young people to be themselves. Above all, Sam urges them to retain their individuality and to value each moment of their unfolding lives as a prologue to adulthood. With a fatherly concern, he consoles, "If you down and out and things ain't going right for you ... you can bet you done put a down payment on your troubles" (pp. 1901–1902). The bark of Mr. Collins, Sam's employer, cuts short the testimonial and forces the janitor back to his broom, a symbol of stereotypical low-paying jobs reserved for non-whites whom the dominant class devalues and ignores. The ironic situation characterizes black philosophy as largely unheard because the white world relegates blacks to low social, educational, and economic status and discounts their experiences as worthless.

- *Further Reading*

Charters, Ann, and Samuel Charters, ed. *Short Pieces from the New Dramatists*. Banbury, Ox.: Orangeberry Books, 1985.

Jim Crow era

In the decades followed the emancipation of slaves, whites, especially share-croppers who lived on a par with poor blacks, resented federal edicts encouraging black recovery from servitude. The "rebby" backlash led to violation of rights to public transportation, housing, and education. White disappointment in losing the Civil War and ownership of slaves resulted in the emergence of the Ku Klux Klan, which ex–Confederate General Nathan Bedford Forrest and other former Confeder-ate soldiers organized. As a result of secret plotting, the South was awash in night riders' horrendous acts— assault, arson, rape, genital mutilation, lynching, butchery of livestock, and general terror. White lawmen, who were often Klansmen them-selves, tended to investigate few of these lawless acts. Southern blacks avoided white troublemakers and kept out of the sight of white law officers, who often allow racists to roughhouse blacks on public streets.

The Jim Crow era turned the struggle for black survival into a cat and mouse game. Blacks avoided run-ins with bigots by cultivating the smiling darky face and the obsequious bowing and shuffling ridiculed in minstrel shows as Jim Crow. Cutler's story in *Ma Rainey's Black Bottom* (1985) about the Reverend Gates portrays the need to think quick and swallow humiliation to weather white hooliganism. After whites surround and hector the minister, they make him dance. While he cavorts, they des-ecrate his cross and tear up his bible. Toledo legitimizes the image: "You don't even have to tell me no more. I know the facts of it. I done heard the same story a hundred times" (p. 97). Gates's name suggests the role that ex-slaves played in advancing black Americans by swallowing their pride and holding back from violent retaliation.

• *Further Reading*

Harris, J. William. *Deep Souths: Delta, Piedmont, and Sea Island Society in the Age of Segregation*. Baltimore: Johns Hopkins University Press, 2001.

Tolnay, Stewart E., and E. M. Beck. *A Festival of Violence: An Analysis of Southern Lynch-ings, 1882–1930*. Urbana: University of Illinois, 1995.

Wang, Qun. *An In-Depth Study of the Major Plays of African American Playwright August Wilson: Vernacularizing the Blues on Stage*. Vol. 6 of *Black Studies*. Lewiston, Ont.: Edwin Mellen Press, 1999.

Jitney

A two-act urban dialect melodrama set at an abandoned storefront-turned-gypsy-cab station in 1977 in the Hill district of Pittsburgh, *Jitney* (1982) is one of August Wilson's familiar human tapestries. Reviewer Joseph Bowen characterized the text as "a quiet character study, a comic, touching and engrossing portrait of life" (Bowen). *Jitney* is the only play in August Wilson's decade cycle that he wrote dur-ing the era he was describing. For that reason, critics laud its immediacy and the cumulative effect of its truth-telling situations and characters in a period marked by arbitrary, ham-handed government projects that threatened the fiber of black com-munities. In the text, hard times in the area call for the city's razing of Pope's restau-rant to comply with urban renewal, the abstract villain of the play.

The two-act drama earned several rejections before its debut in Pittsburgh. It won critical acclaim for faithful recreation of black speech, ribald humor, and attitudes, three elements of August Wilson's mastery of African American drama. In reference to the doom-laden tone, Sala Udin, a Pittsburgh city councilman and old friend of the playwright, promised, "The scene [on the Hill] is changing, but the struggles are the same. And what August has captured is the timelessness of these struggles" (Reynolds, p. E1).

Wilson creates drama from the interaction of the men who provide a community car service. The worn setting is heated by a prominent pot-bellied stove, a symbol of the fairness and encouragement of Jim Becker, the warm-hearted manager. A blackboard offers policy numbers, cab rates, and Becker's simple slate of five rules, which require courtesy and sobriety, cleanliness, fair rates, and replacement of borrowed tools. The atmosphere hums with frequent phone calls to Court 1-9802 and demands for rides. Because the company has no logo, drivers identify their cars by color and make. Wilson uses the in-and-out of taxis to establish the importance of public transportation to clients at the Giant Eagle grocery store, bus station, Ellis Hotel, and beauty shop and to residents traveling to and from East Liberty and the Francis Street Projects.

Central to the play's core is its view of survival among the underclass — the cooperative effort of cabbies who drive their own cars and contribute fifteen dollars a month to a communal pot to nourish the makeshift business. Candid dialogue reveals the slim securities of men like Doub, a widower, father of two sons, and twenty-seven-year veteran of railroad work, who clings to the hope of retiring on a railroad pension. The main emotional crisis results when the owner's son, Booster Becker, returns from a twenty-year prison term to reunite with his father. In lesser clashes, Fielding uses the circle of men as a sounding board for his troubles with alcohol and the wife who left him; Youngblood, a Vietnam veteran, vents his anguish over a complicated application for a mortgage; Turnbo seeks attention by spreading rumors and stirring up enmity against Youngblood, whom he accuses of betraying Rena by seeing her sister Peaches on the sly.

Personal conflicts aside, the main threat to the drivers' common cause is urban renewal, which will destroy the building as well as Pope's restaurant and Clifford's next-door eatery in two weeks. The loss will force the drivers to seek new quarters and reorganize their business or else disband. For his own reasons, Becker conceals the news until Act I, Scene 2. When Doub reminds him that each driver depends on the station for his livelihood, the manager is too worried and weary to argue. He repeats the playwright's mantra about time and life, "Every day cost you something and you don't all the time realize it" (p. 36). The sad truism foreshadows Becker's sudden death and his son's arrival on the scene as his replacement. Wilson uses the events of the play to exalt the laboring class. Of their nobility, he explained, "These are men who, not having the opportunities for jobs, created jobs. [The play's] about the ability of black people in America to find a ways and means to survive and prosper" (Saltzman & Plett).

See also **Booster Becker, Coreen Becker, Jim Becker, Doub, Philmore, Rena, Turnbo, Youngblood**

• *Further Reading*

Bowen, Joseph. "Jitney." http://centerstage.net/theatre/articles/jitney.html.
Jones, Chris. "Homeward Bound." *American Theatre*, Vol. 16, No. 9, November 1999.
Rawson, Christopher. "Stage Review: Wilson Polishes 'Jitney' in Richer, Longer Pro-
    duction." *Pittsburgh Post-Gazette*, November 22, 1998.
_____. "Stage Reviews: Wilson's 'Jitney,' 'King Hedley II' Have Become Clearer, Tighter
    Since Leaving Pittsburgh." *Pittsburgh Post-Gazette*, June 25, 2000.
Reynolds, Christopher. "Mr. Wilson's Neighborhood: Playwright August Wilson No
    Longer Lives in Pittsburgh's Hill District, But It Is Consistently at Home in His
    Work." *Los Angeles Times*, July 27, 2002, p. E1.
Saltzman, Simon, and Nicole Plett. "'Jitney' at Crossroads." *U.S. 1 Newspaper*, April 16, 1997.

Joe Turner's Come and Gone

The third of August Wilson's decade cycle and one of his most complex and
critically debated plays, *Joe Turner's Come and Gone* (1988) is a story of itinerant folk
in the big city. The playwright compiles data collage style from varying voices and
overlays all with a mystic African element. The materials are allegorical — Seth Holly,
the seeker of manhood through industry and thrift; Jeremy Furlow, the seeker of self
through music; and Bynum Walker, the seeker of identity through mysticism. The
action takes place in August 1911 at a Pittsburgh rooming house during the Great
Migration where it seems that "everybody looking for something" (p. 70). Seth stresses
responsibility to his roomers by demanding two dollars per week up front in payment for a room, two meals a day, and the promise of fried chicken on Sundays. Tow-
els are twenty-five cents extra. To Molly Cunningham, he states that he will issue
her a key to the front door and won't pry into her business, but he warns that he
doesn't condone prostitution in his house.

To set the tone of the second decade of the twentieth century, Wilson portrays
blacks who have abandoned rural life in the South to seek better lives in the North
during a period of growth in the American urban economy. The playwright identifies
them as "foreigners in a strange land" laden with baggage and weary hearts (n.p.).
Seth remarks: "Niggers coming up here from the backwoods ... looking for freedom.
They got a rude awakening" (p. 6). Cut off from the agrarian milieu that shaped their
ancestry, newcomers to the North like the wanderer Jeremy Furlow learn through
failure that the promise of American industry does not guarantee them acceptance
and reward in white-controlled cities. Relief from spiritual disruption comes only
from reclaiming a sustaining African tradition.

The controlling theme presents the black search for identity and self-empowerment in the staged pilgrimage of an ex-con looking for his wife. Among rootless
fellow boarders arriving "dazed and stunned" at the waystation operated by Bertha
Holly, Herald Loomis stands out in perplexity and intensity (n.p.). An energetic
rebel, he pulses with life and raw selfhood and denies the power of the Christian God
and the sanctity of the Holy Spirit. Like an allegory of everyman seeking his destiny,
the events picture him reaching toward black sages for advice, then turning inward
for a coalescing vision. The risk is considerable, leaving him stricken and immobile
halfway through the play.

To round out his most spiritual play, Wilson turns to stark melodrama. With the aid of Bynum Walker, the African spirit man, Loomis finds his legs again, both physically and spiritually. Agitated by his wife Martha's biblical injunctions, he must divest her of hopes to evangelize him. A slice of the knife to the chest releases his blood, freeing him of devotion to his missionary wife and of reliance on the white man's Christ. Joyful in the self-anointing in blood, he can exult, "I'm standing now!" (p. 93). The startling ending tends to leave reviewers puzzled as to a neat interpretation of Wilson's intent.

See also **Mattie Campbell, Jeremy Furlow, W. C. Handy, Bertha Holly, Seth Holly, juba, Herald Loomis, Reuben Mercer, Martha Loomis Pentecost, Rutherford Selig, shiny man, Bynum Walker**

• *Further Reading*

Marshall, Michael. "Spiritual Odyssey: August Wilson's *Joe Turner's Come and Gone*." *World and I*, December 1987.

McDonough, Carla J. *Staging Masculinity: Male Identity in Contemporary American Drama*. Jefferson, N.C.: McFarland, 1997.

Powers, Kim. "An Interview with August Wilson." *Theatre*, Vol. 16, No. 1, 1984, pp. 50–55.

Rocha, Mark William. "A Conversation with August Wilson." *Diversity: A Journal of Multicultural Issues*, Vol. 1, Fall 1992, pp. 24–42.

Savran, David, ed. *In Their Own Words: Contemporary American Playwrights*. New York: Theatre Communications Group, 1988.

Wang, Qun. *An In-Depth Study of the Major Plays of African American Playwright August Wilson: Vernacularizing the Blues on Stage*. Vol. 6 of *Black Studies*. Lewiston, Ont.: Edwin Mellen Press, 1999.

Johnson, Sterling

A thirty-year-old sweet-talking lady's man and former driver of a getaway car, Sterling Johnson, the ex-con in *Two Trains Running* (1991), is a prize example of the immature wastrel. His inflated self-image prompts him to consider opening a nightclub and to boast that he can do most things better than more educated whites. His amorality extends to heisting a five-gallon can of gas, breaking a store window, and filching flowers from a funeral bouquet to give to a girl. Ironically, when he describes how he would replace a judge, he claims an instinctive knowledge of right and wrong. Preferring gambling to honest work, he pictures himself as the luckless individual who encounters adversity from birth. His birth mother gave him away in infancy to Mrs. Johnson, who taught him to protect his sister. Johnson develops a feeling of strength and importance by shielding women from harm, metaphorically described as King Kong or Mighty Joe Young, two massive gorillas in Hollywood movies.

Sterling's past appears to have deprived him of a normal conscience. After his foster mother died, he passed to Toner Institute, a Pittsburgh orphanage, where he came under the mentorship of Mr. Lewis, a father figure who taught him how to wash the grille of a car. At thirteen, Sterling witnessed the suicide of Eddie Langston, a fellow orphan who died in bed after cutting his wrists. By age eighteen, when Sterling began caring for himself, he was certain that suicide was not a suitable answer to his problems, yet declares in adulthood, "The world done gone crazy. I'm sorry I was ever born into it" (p. 52).

Sterling's choplogic rationalizing indicates the absence of the work ethic in his makeup. After carrying bricks for Hendricks's construction company for a week, he quits the sweaty job, but claims he was laid off. His self-pity limits his success in a neighborhood where West the undertaker, Memphis Lee the cafe owner, Risa Thomas the waitress and cook, even Hambone the painter and handyman put their faith in hard work. Sterling's flowers, slow dancing, and soft kisses fail to dazzle Risa, who classes him with other slackers and good-timers who "want what everybody else want" (p. 100).

Like Lymon Jackson and Boy Willie Charles in *The Piano Lesson* (1990) and Booster Beck in *Jitney* (1982), Sterling is guileless about acknowledging that he served five years for robbing a bank. He rationalized the need for cash, which overwhelmed him after Lewis died. Sterling describes desperation as an ever-deepening hole. Because of his unwise spending of stolen money only ten minutes after its theft, he was an easy nab for police. Only one week out of the penitentiary, he chooses idle flirtation with Risa, community gossip, and purchases of soul food and a pistol as the means of restoring himself to life on the outside. When he seeks work, he is surprised that people are unaware that he has been away serving a prison term. To right a wrong committed by Mr. Albert, the racketeer who halved the numbers payout, Sterling foolishly goes armed to his headquarters.

Memphis and Holloway reveal much about their own personalities by discussing Sterling's return to society. Memphis contrasts Sterling to his grandfather, a hard worker willing to labor for three dollars a day. Holloway exonerates Sterling for rejecting wages of a dollar and a quarter per hour hauling bricks when he could make as much as three hundred dollars per day gambling. The cafe owner predicts either Sterling's death or a return to prison within three weeks. His embrace of shady dealings casts a pall over his weeks of freedom, but adds a touch of humor to the text. In his twisted discussion of career plans, he asks himself what he likes to do and decides that his ambition is to drive a Cadillac. In the viewer's last glimpse of him, bleeding from smashing the butcher shop window, Sterling, the headstrong man-child, returns to the stage with ham in hand to speak his obeisance to Hambone in tandem with the wail of a burglar alarm.

• *Further Reading*

Harrison, Paul Carter. "August Wilson's Blues Poetics," in *Three Plays*. Pittsburgh: University of Pittsburgh Press, 1991.

Launer, Pat. "'Two Trains Running' at the Old Globe Theatre." *KPBS Radio*, March 21, 1991.

Wang, Qun. *An In-Depth Study of the Major Plays of African American Playwright August Wilson: Vernacularizing the Blues on Stage*. Vol. 6 of *Black Studies*. Lewiston, Ont.: Edwin Mellen Press, 1999.

juba

A spontaneous circle dance performed counterclockwise to complex percussion rhythms, clapping, and foot taps, the juba translates from the Yoruban tongue as "homage." The ritual of the ring shout, which survived on American plantations until the end of slavery, enlivened black African communities during ancestor worship and other celebratory moments free from labor and the control of a master or overseer. The joyous steps, drumming, clapping, sing-song chanting, and gestures of open arms and hands were an invitation to ecstatic trance in the presence of spirit gods called orishas. These African deities included the creation god Obatala, the handycrafter Ogun, the warrior god Oshosi, the messenger and trickster Eshu, the weather god Shango, the love goddess Oshun, and the underworld protector Oya. The last two in the West African pantheon were Yemoja or Yemaya, the goddess of the family, and the wise Orunmila, a counterpart of the classic Apollo, the Greek sun deity and god of prophecy and healing.

The experience of the juba became a vehicle for improvisational folk interaction and expression of common emotions, doubts, fears, and triumphs. Because slaves were often unable to communicate with those who spoke different African languages, dance encouraged unified expression without words. The triumphant tones often enabled singers and shouters to connect with slaves on a distant plantation. After rooming house owner Seth Holly proposes playing his harmonica for a traditional post–Sunday dinner dance and shout in Act I, Scene 4 of *Joe Turner's Come and Gone* (1988), Bynum Walker and Jeremy Furlow hammer on the table in preparation. Dropping the mask of the proper, citified black, participants release tensions in a lively African American spiritual catharsis akin to a religious revival. Critic Jack Kroll declares that "Freedom becomes visible in a shared juba dance, a signal that these blacks will never be free until they accept and build on their African heritage" (Kroll, p. 82).

Free in form and substance, the communal dance inspires Jeremy to abandon his guitar and encourages Bertha Holly to leave the dishes in the sink while she joins in the shuffling, frenzy, and calls on the Holy Ghost. Herald Loomis, in a moment of deranged anguish, confronts the others for exalting the Christian spirit. He unzips his fly, speaks in tongues, and circles the table. His unsettling gestures allow him to testify to "some things he ain't got words to tell" (p. 53). At the height of trance, he sinks down by the front door in terror of "bones walking on top of the water" (*Ibid.*). Like a psychoanalyst, Bynum encourages him to talk out bad memories, but Loomis is too weak to stand up. His collapse suggests the need of the beginner for a guide in ordering and interpreting history from slave times.

Juba dancing serves both spontaneous and planned occasions, as Toni Morrison portrays with Grandma Baby's group-healing sessions in the grove in *Beloved* (1987), during which ex-slaves rid themselves of self-hatred and learn to love their bodies part by part. In *The Piano Lesson* (1990), Doaker Charles refers to another ritual celebration when he relates how Boy Charles and Mama Berniece wed in an unofficial union called "jumping the broom" (p. 44). In lieu of legal union, slaves made up a ritual to sanctify and legalize a relationship. The ceremony concluded with a juba dance. With joyous shouts and call-and-response outbursts, dancers twirled and postured in African style as a means of reuniting body and spirit with their ancestry and culture left behind in the motherland.

• *Further Reading*

Appiah, Kwame Anthony. *In My Father's House: Africa in the Philosophy of Culture*. New York: Oxford University Press, 1992.

Keller, James R. "The Shaman's Apprentice: Ecstasy and Economy in Wilson's Joe Turner." *African American Review*, Vol. 35, No. 3, Fall 2001, p. 471.

Kroll, Jack. "August Wilson's Come to Stay." *Newsweek*, April 11, 1988, p. 82.

Richards, Sandra L. "Yoruba Gods on the American Stage: August Wilson's *Joe Turner's Come and Gone*." *Research in African Literatures*, Vol. 30, No. 4, Winter 1999, p. 92.

Robinson, Beverly J. "Africanisms and the Study of Folklore," in *Africanisms in American Culture*. Bloomington: Indiana University Press, 1990.

Stuckey, Sterling. *Slave Culture: Nationalist Theory and the Foundations of Black America*. New York: Oxford University Press, 1987.

King Hedley II

An angry dramatic rumble, the weighty socio-political tragedy *King Hedley II* (1999) is the playwright's first sequel play. Wilson sets the action in 1985 in Pittsburgh's Hill district, where he lived in early youth. The grim, unwieldy cycle of recriminations and bloodletting coincides with the death of the black seer Aunt Ester, a beloved constant in ghetto life who expires at the play's climax. According to reviewer Philip Fisher, the dark themes and momentum are Shakespearean in power. In the words of director Marion McClinton, "Sometimes it feels like Muhammad Ali fighting Joe Frazier — [Wilson] keeps coming at you!" ("Sharing").

The era recalls the drug-related drive-by shootings, broken families, theft, homelessness, and vainglorious Reaganomics that promised trickle-down profits as the nation's wealth accumulated in the hands of the rich while inner cities crumbled. The action focuses on ex-con King Hedley II, who returns from prison both physically scarred and emotionally impaired. The setting, like *Jitney* (1982) and *Two Trains Running* (1991), bears its own burden of defunct dwellings, crumbling plaster, and urban despair, enhanced in menace by the cousin of Pernell Sims, Hedley's victim, who lurks in the background in search of revenge. The cast reprises from *Seven Guitars* (1995) the characters Canewell (called Stool Pigeon) and sixty-two-year-old Ruby, the title character's mother, who was a nubile beauty in the earlier drama. Of the assembly's turgid dialogue, Stefan Kanfer, critic for *The New Leader*, complained that "Hedley II should have been cut by a third, and its lengthy speeches hammered into dialogue" (Kanfer, p. 45).

Much of the play involves the complex exchanges of angry males, the star speakers in Wilson's drama cycle. Elmore, a rehabilitated murderer who knifed Leroy Slater over Ruby in *Seven Guitars*, is a dying man who voices the smoldering anger of the dispossessed male. Externally, he is a cool hand and snappy dresser who bears hard truths, including memories of his breakup with Ruby, loss of his woman to Leroy, and the secret of Hedley II's siring. Like the brightly patterned snake, Elmore draws the unwary to him, then strikes.

Like Elmore, King Hedley II follows the playwright's pattern of rage-filled ex-cons. An embryo in *Seven Guitars*, he was nurtured in a muddle after Ruby deceived the first King Hedley into believing that her unborn infant was his. Released from Western Pen with a formidable facial scar as the token of a violent life, Hedley II takes comfort in a friend, Mister, the son of Red Carter and WillaMae born in May 1948, shortly after Hedley was conceived. Partners in crime, the contemporaries try to open Royal Videos by saving their take on the sale of stolen GE refrigerators, a subtextual metaphor suggesting the rise of American commerce on the backs of black slaves stolen from Africa. To increase their wealth, the two team up to rob a jewelry store, the kind of spur-of-the-moment daylight crime that caused Poochie Tillery's death in *Seven Guitars*.

Wilson appears to recycle a motif from *A Raisin in the Sun* (1958) by revisiting the quandary of whether or not to abort a child. Hedley II and his proud, down-to-earth wife Tonya anticipate the birth of their first baby at the same time that the father seeks the truth about his own siring. To reassure her about the possibility of giving birth to King Hedley III, he claims, "I'm living for you" (p. 42). Uncertain about the future with a violent, emotional mate, she is ambivalent about motherhood and regrets an era in which girls like her daughter Natasha are too soon parents and in which the mortuary business flourishes in black corpses. Unlike his wife's internal debate, the source of Hedley's truth must come from Ruby and Elmore, a self-knowledge that will ease Hedley's restlessness.

As portentous as Greek tragedy, *King Hedley II* reverberates with the clash of ambition and defeat, themes that fueled the seven August Wright plays preceding it. In the estimation of McClinton:

> It operates in the language of August Wilson, the blues idiom, the gospel idiom, the idiom of the black church, it operates out of classic Western theater — the Greeks, in particular *Oedipus*. And it operates in the land of Yoruba myth and religion, which is the hardest one to actualize but the one that gave the play its bed to ground it ["Sharing"].

To portray the West African myth of Ogun, the iron god, as well as Christ's crown of thorns, Wilson has the title character surround Tonya's garden with a stretch of barbed wire, a symbol of his prickly relationship with the Sears photographer and with a woman who isn't convinced that the world needs more tender children. More ominous is the adjacent burial spot of Aunt Ester's black cat, a metaphor of African ritual and a prediction of doom for the black man. Castigating himself for failure, Hedley stomps his seedlings, crushing tendrils of spiritual nourishment and hope. The conclusion of the play with a duel of crap shooters over dead plants weights the finale with the chancy lifestyle of black males during the 1980s, when personal hurts and longings erupt into senseless killings.

See also **Elmore, King Hedley, Tonya Hedley, Mister, Ruby, Stool Pigeon**

• *Further Reading*

Billington, Michael. "King Hedley II." *Guardian Unlimited*, December 12, 2002.
Brantley, Ben. "'King Hedley II': The Agonized Arias of Everyman in Poverty and Pain." *New York Times*, May 2, 2001.
Fisher, Philip. "King Hedley II." *British Theatre Guide*, 2002.
Ifill, Gwen. "American Shakespeare." *PBS News*, April 6, 2001.
Jones, Chris. "Homeward Bound." *American Theatre*, Vol. 16, No. 9, November 1999, pp. 14–19.
Kanfer, Stefan. "Kings and Commoners." *New Leader*, Vol. 84, No. 4, July 2001, p. 45.
Mckanic, Arlene. "Wilson's 'Jitney' Drives Home." *New York Amsterdam News*, pp. 21, 22.
Papatola, Dominic P. "Thunder, Lightning Pierce 'Hedley' Storm." *St. Paul Pioneer Press*, May 31, 2003, p. B6.
Rawson, Christopher. "Stage Review: Wilson's Hedley a Thrilling Ride." *Pittsburgh Post-Gazette*, December 16, 1999.
_____. "Stage Reviews: Wilson's 'Jitney,' 'King Hedley II' Have Become Clearer, Tighter Since Leaving Pittsburgh." *Pittsburgh Post-Gazette*, June 25, 2000.
"Sharing the Stage with August Wilson." http://www.donshewey.com/theater_articles/marion_mcclinton.htm, April 29, 2001.

Lee, Memphis

The owner of a rundown homestyle diner at 1621 Wylie Avenue in *Two Trains Running* (1991), Memphis Lee is a pragmatist who steers a survival course through discrimination by whites and blacks. He wisely left Jackson, Mississippi, in 1931 after racists hired by Jim Stovall knifed his mule in the belly and emasculated it, burned his crops, and forced Memphis off his land by voiding his deed. He migrated to Pittsburgh. When his mother died in 1954, he felt free of responsibility. After hitting the numbers in 1960 or 1961, he won enough to change clothes daily, a mark of distinction not shared by poorer blacks. With some of the cash, he bought a small diner from L. D. for fifty-five hundred dollars, an investment both shrewd and demanding. According to the author, Memphis's battles against city authorities exalt him to the stature of "a warrior with ethics and integrity" (Blanchard, p. 10F).

Memphis Lee is a steady worker. He earns his living by renting out his upstairs room and by turning four cases of chicken into two days' worth of diner meals. He explains his business logic: "Everybody got to eat and everybody got to sleep. Some people don't have stoves" (p. 10). He enlarges on loss with a comment on the failure of marriages and other assaults on family life: "Some people don't have nobody to cook for them. Men whose wives done died and left them. Cook for them thirty years and lay down and die. Who's gonna cook for them now? Somebody got to do it" (*Ibid.*). To fulfill the diner's promise of becoming the people's eatery, Memphis develops a martinet personality by constantly nagging at Risa Thomas, his waitress and cook, to fry chicken, refrigerate the bread, and buy supplies. He ousts the witless Hambone, the neighborhood handyman, for wearying customers with complaints about being cheated by Lutz, the meat dealer. Lee insists on careful management of goods, especially sugar, a representation of the absence of sweet contentment in his life.

By intense management of his diner, Memphis fights low self-worth. After twenty-two years of marriage and the birth of four children, his wife left him. To bolster achievement in an unforgiving economy, he works hard, rags his waitress for incompetence, and, over a period of nineteen years, saves his money to buy first a V-8 Ford, then a Cadillac. He spurns the "Black Is Beautiful" movement as proof that blacks believe themselves ugly and reiterate the slogan to convince themselves otherwise. Of himself he says, "I know I look nice. Got good manners and everything" (p. 43).

Memphis maintains a tenuous hold on old grudges. He keeps in the back of his mind the possibility of riding the train south to confront white persecutors and reclaim his land. He mutters defensively, "I still got the deed" (p. 31). The effects of unsettled disputes are detrimental to his state of mind. In his dealings with cafe patrons, he displays an acid-tinged cynicism about signs of the end-time, a poster announcing a rally honoring Malcolm X, the gullability of the followers of the Prophet Samuel, and the likelihood that Sterling Johnson will remain out of trouble with the law.

As urban renewal encroaches on his part of Pittsburgh, Memphis dickers over a decent price for his investment. He rejects a low figure that the city housing authority offers him for his residence and refuses the counteroffers that the hustling undertaker proposes. Memphis explains, "I ain't greedy. But if they wanna tear it down they gonna have to meet my price" (p. 10). He puzzles over the city's claim about a clause in the deed that allows them to set their own price for the property and fires his black attorney, Chauncey Ward III, for concurring with white bureaucrats. Ironically, Memphis learns from Hambone, a retardate, how to evade victimization and demand his rights. To his surprise, Memphis salvages his investment through the assistance of a white attorney, Joseph Bartoromo, and a white-dominated court system.

The city's unexpected offer of $35,000 frees Memphis from his worries and allows him an opportunity to return to his hometown to settle with Jim Stovall and to return to Centre Avenue in Pittsburgh to open a big restaurant. Memphis has a second chance with his wife, but he moves out after she returns to their house. His main ambition is to build a new, larger restaurant offering sit-down meals and a take-out window. A decade later, his example is a model to Turnbo, a cabbie at a threatened stand in *Jitney* (1982), who recalls how the city high-handedly tried to run Memphis out of business.

See also **achievement**

• *Further Reading*

Blanchard, Jayne M. "An August Tradition." *St. Paul Pioneer Press*, May 4, 1993, p. 10F.
Üsekes, Ciggdem. "'We's the Leftovers': Whiteness as Economic Power and Exploitation in August Wilson's Twentieth-Century Cycle of Plays." *African American Review*, Vol. 37, No. 1, Spring 2003, pp. 115–125.

Loomis, Herald

The disoriented nomad of *Joe Turner's Come and Gone* (1988), thirty-two-year-old Herald Loomis, a model of the alienated black male on a quest for self, ushers in a new generation of seekers. Wilson extracted the dejected figure from Romare Bearden's painting "Mill Hand's Lunch" (1978), part of the Mecklenburg County series. In the play, Loomis's physical trek north is a metaphor for his internal pilgrimage. As though cocooned, he travels from Ohio to a Pittsburgh boarding house in August 1911 wearing a long wool coat, a symbol of the layers of need that encase his wounded spirit. His clodhoppers attest to his long months on the road; his worries about his eleven-year-old daughter Zonia's rapid growth indicate an urgency to find a female role model for his preteen.

Loomis's arrival resets the tone of the first scene from Bynum Walker's glorious expectations of a shiny man to the doldrums of a man out of harmony with the world. Loomis bears the scars of what critic Qun Wang calls "physical incarceration and spiritual enslavement that has plagued African Americans long after the ending of the Civil War" (Wang, p. 38). On arrival, Loomis is a model of the disillusioned Christian, a former sharecropper for Henry Thompson and a deacon of the Abundant Life Church who once evangelized gamblers. The choice of church name echoes Christ's promise in John 10:10, "I am come that they might have life and have it more abundantly." By alluding to biblical promise, Wilson stresses the spiritual deprivation of the early 1900s and hints at the prosperity due to Loomis for his pain and isolation.

At sea in a personal and spiritual maelstrom, Loomis seeks his song, the satisfying personhood he has lost after seven years at debilitating labor on a Tennessee chain gang that works Joe Turner's fields. When Loomis regains his freedom on Turner's birthday in 1908, he needs a means of harmonizing his longings with a world he hasn't seen or interacted with in seven years. Still symbolically shadowed by Turner, Loomis seeks his wife Martha, who left a decade before, and reunites with Zonia, who lives with her maternal grandmother. For two years, father and daughter seek the family matriarch, his "starting place in the world. Find me a world I can fit in" (p. 76). Father and daughter travel north to reshape the Loomis household, a microcosm of wholeness that gives their lives direction.

In addition to searching for family, Loomis is a marked man, an ex-con who longs for personal contentment. He tries to escape bad memories by objecting to Bynum's singing "Joe Turner's Come and Gone." In Bynum's estimation, "You a man who done forgot his song," Wilson's metaphor for soul (p. 71). Bynum characterizes the song as the key to identity and purpose. Fragmented by loss of humanity, home, and ambition, Loomis carries the internal burden of spite against the white Joe Turners of the world who inflict wrongful punishments against blacks or who deprive them of their human rights.

In rejecting white ways, Loomis abandons white religion in favor of the ecstatic black shamanism of West Africa. By whirling juba style, speaking in tongues, and reliving biblical images of Ezekiel's vision of the dry bones (Ezekiel 37:1–28), Loomis experiences a liberating purge of negative energy and a rebirth of strength that threatens to topple him. According to interviews, Loomis's speech so pleased the playwright that he considered it a pinnacle of his artistic development. Wilson exulted, "The bones rising out of the ocean — when I wrote that I thought, 'OK, that's it, if I die tomorrow I'll be satisfied and fulfilled as an artist that I wrote that scene" (Shirley,

p. E1). In token of his approval of the character, the playwright awards the rejuvenated Loomis a new woman, Mattie Campbell, whom Loomis reaches out to touch with awkward hands and sniffs at like a feral beast seeking a mate. His tentative, dog-like appraisal signifies the depth of dehumanization at Joe Turner's prison farm and the distance that Loomis must go to retrieve manhood.

Loomis's reemergence from the wreckage of his past uplifts the falling action. In Act II, Scene 5, he seizes a knife and challenges everything that hinders him, including Martha's Jesus. To her recitation of the Twenty-Third Psalm, he shouts in call-and-response his negation of white religion. He envisions "Mr. Jesus Christ" as an overseer waving a whip over "niggers swimming in a sea of cotton" (p. 92). In a testimonial to his self-reclamation, he experiences an epiphany, slices his chest, and rubs blood over his face.

Loomis's symbolic act of self-salvation breaks the bindings of the past. Consecrated in a new faith that ritual has freed from his subconscious, Loomis exults, "My legs stood up!" (p. 93). As a spokesman for Afrocentric faith, Loomis rejects the white interpretation of Christ's blood sacrifice by asserting, "I don't need nobody to bleed for me! I can bleed for myself" (*Ibid.*). Through a painful self-salvation and blood baptism, he cuts himself free of worthlessness and despair to reclaim his humanity. The final view of Loomis leaves a tenuous after-image of a man adrift from family and community, but willing to abandon security to forge a new identity.

• *Further Reading*

Grant, Nathan L. "Men, Women, and Culture: A Conversation with August Wilson." *American Drama*, Vol. 5, No. 2, Spring 1996, pp. 100–22.

Keller, James R. "The Shaman's Apprentice: Ecstasy and Economy in Wilson's Joe Turner." *African American Review*, Vol. 35, No. 3, Fall 2001, p. 471.

Shirley, Don. "Queen of the Hill: August Wilson's Potent But Ungainly 'Gem of the Ocean' Opens at the Taper." *Los Angeles Times*, August 1, 2003, p. E1.

Wang, Qun. *An In-Depth Study of the Major Plays of African American Playwright August Wilson: Vernacularizing the Blues on Stage*. Vol. 6 of *Black Studies*. Lewiston, Ont.: Edwin Mellen Press, 1999.

Wilde, Lisa. "Reclaiming the Past: Narrative and Memory in August Wilson's *Two Trains Running*." *Theater*, Vol. 22, No. 1, Fall/winter 1990-1991, pp. 73–74.

Loomis, Zonia

The motherless child of *Joe Turner's Come and Gone* (1988), eleven-year-old Zonia Loomis, like her father Herald, sings her own song of waiting for belonging. She shares Herald's rootlessness in seeking his wife Martha. An obligation to the penniless seeker, Zonia observes her father's bargaining for her room and board at the Hollys' boardinghouse. Without a word, she hears innkeeper Seth Holly offer her only a half portion of food and his wife Bertha accept her as domestic help. Zonia's silence at the offer of half an adult's daily sustenance introduces her willingness to be a little girl if staying small will please her father.

Zonia's song "Just a pullin' the skiff" suggests a woman's burden shouldered by a pre-adolescent girl (pp. 26–27). Her resemblance to her mother is Holly's clue to the missing woman, who changed her surname from Loomis to Pentecost. Zonia's sketchy awareness of her runaway mother's whereabouts and of the crime of Joe Turner, who "did something bad" to her father, indicates her immaturity and vulnerability within a scattered family (p. 28). To a contemporary, Reuben Mercer, she confides, "We never stay too long nowhere," a hint at the insecurity she has weathered (p. 29). When the family reunites in Act II, she fears losing her father and disavows puberty by promising not to grow any larger. Her Alice in Wonderland approach to security suggests the price exacted from children for family rootlessness during the Great Migration.

• *Further Reading*

Bogumil, Mary L. *Understanding August Wilson*. Columbia: University of South Carolina Press, 1998.

Louise

In *Seven Guitars* (1995), August Wilson reserves some of the most humorous, poignant, and revealing lines for the landlady Louise, the forty-eight-year-old aunt of the flirtatious Ruby, an Alabama relative. Louise manages Bella's boardinghouse and encourages community while maintaining order and decorum. She expresses egocentrism by demanding that King Hedley, the West Indian sandwich seller, not only supply her with cigarettes, but that he give up his brand to buy her favorite, Old Golds. In mercenary remarks about Vera Dotson's love life, Louise votes against the womanizing Floyd Barton in favor of the iceman, "as ugly as he is" (p. 17). The image suggests that a man who is cold and ugly is less destructive than a charming, two-timing heartbreaker like Floyd.

Louise speaks of love from experience. Once involved in a twelve-year relationship with the faithless Henry, like the scarred waitress Risa Thomas in *Two Trains Running* (1991), abandoned Mattie Campbell in *Joe Turner's Come and Gone* (1988), and wounded widow Berniece Charles in *The Piano Lesson* (1990), Louise guards her heart from further bruising. She allows only a glimmer of romance into her life from a mostly verbal relationship with King Hedley, whose tuberculosis worries her. Out of true concern for Vera, Louise warns her not to let a lover "use you up" (p. 32). Rather than watch Floyd walk away, Louise counsels Vera, "Shoot him first" (*Ibid.*). Her advice is more peaceable in Act I, Scene 5, when Floyd threatens Red for dancing with Vera. Like a placating mother, Louise interrupts the argument and substitutes the non-violent competition of whist.

In matters of the heart, Louise is the wise sage. As Vera gradually talks herself into following Floyd to Chicago to become a different person, Louise reminds her that "Wherever you go you got to carry you with you," a restatement of the Aesopian moral that to change place is not to change one's nature (p. 72). To Ruby, who dislikes the controlling nature of her jailed lover Elmore, Louise cuts to a simple truism: "All men are jealous" (p. 73). She adds that women worsen the situation by encouraging their lovers' possessiveness, a veiled charge that Ruby caused Elmore to knife Leroy to death out of jealous rage.

From dealing with life logically and realistically, Louise has difficulty taking in Ruby's success in getting Hedley to seek medical treatment. After learning that Ruby intends to pass off her unborn child as Hedley's, Louise takes an interest that carries over to *King Hedley II* (1999), in which Ruby abandons Hedley II at age three for "Mama Louise" to raise. At Louise's death from leukemia two months before the play opens in 1985, Ruby returns too late to reclaim the maternal role that Louise aptly filled. By accusing Ruby of scheming to gain title to Louise's house, Hedley implies that his foster mother did a better job than his greedy, self-serving birth mother.

See also women

Ma Rainey's Black Bottom

Ma Rainey's Black Bottom (1985) was quick to draw attention to August Wilson's skill. Brendan Gill, reviewer for the *New Yorker*, noted that the play, "a genuine work of art, … mingled farce and tragedy in oddly unequal proportions" (Gill). He looked forward to more of the playwright's works. Set in the basement band room and studio of a Chicago recording studio in March 1927, the play is the rare Wilson drama not divided into scenes and not located in Pittsburgh. He struggled with the writing of the satiric play, which opened at the Yale Repertory Theater in New Haven, Connecticut, on April 6, 1984.

The play's milieu saw the emergence of the big-band sound and swing, accompanied by the rise in fame of Count Basie, Duke Ellington, and Louis Armstrong. The text, one of the "volatile, hyperbolic word games" that caught the attention of critic Ishmael Reed, defines the ambitions of black musicians (Reed, p. 95). They must steer their course at the direction of white promoters, who calculate artistry by how many records sell in New York. The themes of competition, frustration, and interpersonal strife lock in tragic combat black strivers advancing their careers. Upsetting Ma's attempts to maintain control is a shift in the zeitgeist, the spirit of the times that moves away from old-style blues to exuberant dance tunes like boogie woogie, which dominated music into the 1940s.

The tenor of the play is fretful and nervous as manager Mel Sturdyvant demands to know why Ma is late and threatens to drop her if she leaves before completing the recording session. As the band waits in the basement rehearsal room, the men feel free to disclose personal concerns and to articulate philosophies of achievement. Their anticipation serves as an introit to her cumbrous arrival and settling in. Cutler complains to Toledo that the chosen songs—"Prove It on Me," "Hear Me Talking to You," "Ma Rainey's Black Bottom," and "Moonshine Blues"—are not Ma's original list. The last song belongs to Bessie Smith, Ma's historic protégé. Against the rhythm of the music business is an undercurrent of godlessness and blasphemy, which causes Toledo to admit that blacks have sold out to white materialism.

The drama's driving power is the desperation of jazz trumpeter Levee Green, who recognizes that he must seize any opportunity if he wants to succeed in the cut-throat music business. His last-ditch effort to steal and revise Ma Rainey's signature song crashes head-on with Ma's autocratic personality. To her, the song is a personal statement, unsuited to the voice and style of other performers. After narrating a knifing scene at Lula White's brothel in New Orleans, Levee, before withdrawing in a pout, warns ominously, "You all don't know me. You don't know what I'll do" (p. 65). In a review of the 2003 Broadway version of the play, drama critic Elysa Gardner admired its "visceral potency and jazzy charm," two qualities that Wilson accentuates in depicting black history (Gardner, p. 5D).

See also **Sylvester Brown, Cutler, Dussie Mae, Levee Green, Irvin, Gertrude Malissa Nix Pridgett "Ma" Rainey, Ma Rainey (fictional), Slow Drag, Mel Sturdyvant, Toledo**

• *Further Reading*

Gardner, Elysa. "'Bottom' Sings Blues with Bounce, Charm." *USA Today*, February 10, 2003, p. 5D.

Gener, Randy. "Salvation in the City of Bones: Ma Rainey and Aunt Ester Sing Their Own Songs in August Wilson's Grand Cycle of Blues Dramas." *American Theatre*, Vol. 20, No. 5, May-June 2003, pp. 20–28.

Gill, Brendan. "Hard Times." *New Yorker*, October 22, 1984.

Powers, Kim. "An Interview with August Wilson." *Theatre*, Vol. 16, No. 1, 1984, pp. 50–55.

Reed, Ishmael. "A Shy Genius Transforms the American Theater." *Connoisseur*, Vol. 127, 1987, pp. 92–97.

Shannon, Sandra G. *The Dramatic Vision of August Wilson*. Washington, D.C.: Howard University Press, 1996.

Malcolm X

In *Two Trains Running* (1991), Sterling Johnson distributes flyers announcing a rally at the Savoy Ballroom celebrating the May 19th birthday of Malcolm X (1925–1965), a patriarchal religious leader for the Nation of Islam and spokesman for pan–Africanism and the subjugation of women. Holloway recalls the preacher's discipleship under Elijah Muhammad and Malcolm's incautious rise to fame among an initial clutch of twelve followers. Sterling admires the way that Malcolm X told the truth. Of the outpouring of public interest in the preacher's message, Memphis comments that anybody could see that "the only place he was going was to the graveyard" (p. 41). Memphis's statement refers to the bold shooting of Malcolm X in a Harlem ballroom on February 21, 1965.

Wilson portrays the divergence of opinion about Malcolm X through his characters' response to a holiday honoring his birthday. In Memphis's view, the most disturbing fact about the preacher's martyrdom is that he was shot by blacks. Holloway explains, "When you get to be a saint there ain't nothing else you can do but die" (*Ibid.*). Thus, the assassination resulted from the generation of a hero so big that he had no future. The men compare Malcolm X to other saintly martyrs— the apostle Peter, the missionary Paul, and Dr. Martin Luther King, Jr., all of whom died for their beliefs.

• *Further Reading*

Appiah, Kwame Anthony, and Henry Louis Gates, Jr., eds. *Africana*. New York: Perseus
    Books, 1999.

Maxson, Cory

The fictional Cory is the troubled, indignant son of Rose and Troy Maxson, an
unhappy couple in *Fences* (1985). While coping with their son's adolescent troubles,
the duo is torn by Troy's infidelity and personal recriminations. Cory is the typically
busy, self-absorbed teenager who works at the A & P, attends Saturday football practice, and ponders recruitment for a North Carolina college sports team. He is the
victim of his father's bitter rejection of Cory's athletic scholarship. The father's ploy
is intended to ward off disappointment in a white-dominated sport; he counters the
thinking of Rose, who believes that the recruiter has honored Cory. Stressing the
positive side, she suggests that the boy might have a chance because of the easing of
racial discrimination since World War II, but Troy clings to the caution of blacks
who grew up in the early twentieth-century with suspicion of promises from the
white world.

Cory experiences a tug of war from conflicting loyalties. He owes allegiance to
his boss, Mr. Stawicki, who keeps his job open during football season; to Coach Zellman, who coordinates the offer of a college scholarship; to Rose, who tempers his
task of scrubbing the steps with the offer of a meat loaf sandwich; and to Troy, who
overrides Cory's loyalty to the team by ordering him to "get your book-learning" (p.
35). Cory translates his father's hard-line advice into personal rejection. In Act I,
Scene 3, Rose pinpoints what Cory needs most — his father's approval. Family tensions spill over after Troy admits to siring an illegitimate child and suffers a blow
from Cory for hurting his mother.

The widening gulf between father and son prefaces Troy's death. In the same
style and accusatory tone as his father's didactic stories of duty and responsibility,
Cory becomes his father's judge and jury by blaming him for Rose's flight to the
church and for Troy's abandonment of Gabe in a state institution. The man-to-man
tussle over a baseball bat reduces Cory once more to defeat and humiliation. Before
Troy's decline and death from heart disease in 1965, Cory flees the emotional battleground at home and takes refuge in the marines. After six years of service and
promotion to corporal, he continues to flounder emotionally.

Cory owes much to the past, a recurring subtext in Wilson's drama cycle, like
his stubborn, obstructive father, Cory, in his mid-twenties, deliberately arrives late
on the day of the funeral and refuses to share breakfast with the family. In the same
yard in which the playwright staged son-against-father forays, Cory hears from Jim
Bono how much the son looks like the father and how earnestly Troy admired him
in boyhood. With a nod toward Raynell, the innocent daughter born of Troy's philandering, Cory agrees to honor his father by attending the funeral. Like much of
Wilson's subtle voicing of change in the human heart, the gesture toward forgiveness is small, but powerful.

• *Further Reading*

Blumenthal, Anna S. "More Stories Than the Devil Got Sinners: Troy's Stories in August Wilson's *Fences*." *American Drama*, Vol. 9, No. 2, Spring 2000, pp. 74–96.
Wessling, Joseph H. "Wilson's *Fences*." *Explicator*, Vol. 57, No. 2, Winter 1999, pp. 123–127.

Maxson, Gabriel

In *Fences* (1985), Troy Maxson's thirty-six-year-old handicapped brother Gabe poses constant troubles to the family. After suffering cranial trauma from combat in the Pacific during World War II, he survived the fitting of a metal plate to his skull. He remains unmarried and childlike and lives out the fantasy that he is the Archangel Gabriel. When he makes too much noise by singing and playing his trumpet to chase away hellhounds in Act II, the police arrest him for disturbing the peace. It is the sixth or seventh episode requiring Troy to bail him out of jail and leads to a new wrinkle for the caretaker, who may have to defend Gabe from commitment to a state institution.

Wilson describes Gabe as a simple-witted scavenger subsisting on the sale of discarded fruit and vegetables that he gleans in the strip district, an act that identifies him as a redeemer. In the style of street arabs like those in the American jazz opera *Porgy and Bess* (1935), by Dubose Heyward and George Gershwin, Gabe sings out his prices for plums and warns good-naturedly, "Come and buy now/'Cause I'm here today/And tomorrow I'll be gone" (p. 24). The line becomes a wry commentary on the brevity of life, which permeates all of Wilson's cycle plays. Gabe follows with a reference to St. Peter, the keeper of the gates of heaven who "[opens] the gates for the judgment" (p. 26).

Gabe's desire for autonomy causes Troy concern. The elder brother mutters "messin' around with them Japs, get half his head blown off" and repines, "I can't make him get well" (pp. 27, 28). With familial concern, Troy worries that Gabe can't take care of himself after he gets a job and moves into two rented rooms at Miss Pearl's house. The departure from Troy's care also shifts Gabe's disability check from Troy's control, a financial loss that deepens the rift in the economically strapped Maxson household.

To Gabe, the move is a mark of maturity. He proudly displays his door key as a significant advancement. As the family's inspired fool, he turns a mental handicap into the fount of an intuitive wisdom. His impromptu observations enable him to celebrate his doomed brother's release from earthly discontent and his arrival into heaven. As Christ commands in Matthew 18:3, Gabe functions with the outlook and simplicity of a little child. For him, there are no words appropriate to Troy's departure, only an atavistic howl in salute to his brother's transformation.

In the analysis of Joseph H. Wessling of Xavier University, Gabe balances the cast "because he is valued as a teller, even if his story seems as inexplicable as the one a tribal African might receive from the god Esu" (Wessling, p. 126). Gabe's innate values extend beyond money and position to a joy in individuality and inclusion in a family. As Wilson explains Gabe's instinctive grasp of belonging, "It's not a question of going back to Africa. It's to understand the Africa that's in you" (Moyers, p. 14). Thus, Gabe functions as the mystic savant, the wise fool, a universal character found in Miguel de Cervantes's *Don Quixote* (1615) and William Shakespeare's *King Lear* (ca. 1603) as well as in the folkways and storytelling of native Americans, who revere mental defectives as beings endowed with godly blessing.

Gabe precedes other of Wilson's wise fools—the binding man and shaman Bynum Walker in *Joe Turner's Come and Gone* (1988), Hambone, seeker of justice in *Two Trains Running* (1991), the chicken slayer King Hedley in *Seven Guitars* (1995), and the prophet Stool Pigeon in *King Hedley II* (1999). Wilson noted, "The play is not complete unless it has that character. If you wanted to write about black culture and were an anthropologist or sociologist, you would have to write about that character—the mystical aspect of black American life" (Rousuck, p. 1E). Despite his enthusiasm for Gabe's intuitive grasp of suffering, critics have found the inchoate celebration of life in the play's final moments disturbingly bizarre.

See also **Hambone, King Hedley, Marion McClinton, Bynum Walker**

• *Further Reading*

Moyers, Bill. "August Wilson's America: A Conversation with Bill Moyers." *American Theater*, Vol. 7, No. 6, 1989, p. 14.
Rousuck, J. Wynn. "People with Vision." *Baltimore Sun*, April 27, 1997, p. 1E.
Wessling, Joseph H. "Wilson's *Fences*." *Explicator*, Vol. 57, No. 2, Winter 1999, pp. 123–127.

Maxson, Lyons

In *Fences* (1985), Lyons, the thirty-four-year-old half-brother of Cory and Raynell Maxson, is the son of Troy Maxson from an early marriage to an unnamed wife. Lyons is bitter that his father went to prison and thus took no part in rearing him. A foil to the conscientious, hard-working Cory, Lyons cultivates the pose of the musician with sporty dress and a meticulous goatee, but seeks shortcuts to a professional career. He remains unemployed because he refuses to punch a time clock and "don't wanna be carrying nobody's rubbish" (p. 17). His father recognizes a pattern to Lyons's behavior of casually drifting into the Maxson yard on payday to beg a loan, which he attempts to repay in Act III, Scene 4. Troy scolds his son for being a mooch.

Through frequent interactions between Lyons and Troy, Wilson expresses how a selfish, implacable father alienates his son by withholding love and encouragement. Troy scolds Lyons for frequenting Sefus's place, a night spot that the police raid, and summarizes Lyons's profligacy as "living the fast life … wannabe a musician … running around in them clubs and things" (p. 18). Lyons repeatedly asks his father to come to a performance and hear him play. Troy further destroys Lyons's spirit by labeling his efforts "Chinese music" (p. 68). Ironically, it is Lyons who recognizes the growth pangs in Cory and informs Troy that the boy is "just busting at the seams trying to fill out your shoes" (p. 50). In the final lines of Act II, it is Lyons playing the part of adviser to Cory and bearer of honor to their dead father.

• *Further Reading*

Blumenthal, Anna S. "More Stories Than the Devil Got Sinners: Troy's Stories in August Wilson's *Fences*." *American Drama*, Vol. 9, No. 2, Spring 2000, pp. 74–96.

Maxson, Rose Lee

A loving, but frustrated and long-suffering wife of Troy Maxson in *Fences* (1985), forty-eight-year-old Rose Lee Maxson is a silenced female freighted with an explosive mix of suppressed regrets and anger. At age thirty, eighteen years before the play begins, she married Troy, a thirty-five-year-old ex-con, in Pittsburgh and established a home for the couple and their son Cory. At their meeting, she refused his advances and chose to remain free for "the marrying kind" (p. 6). Because she ignores or forgives his faults, she is capable of overlooking his Friday night indulgence in a pint of gin and a stream of lies. The unrelieved assault on her good nature reaches a breaking point when Troy strays into blatant philandering. Wilson indicates that women like Rose endanger male spirits from a constant whittling down of the men they purport to love.

Early on, domesticity envelops Rose. Devoted to courtesy and goodness, she sings about Jesus's protection while attending to the family wash. As family mediator, she passes ten dollars to Troy's son Lyons, encourages him to bring Bonnie for a visit, and bakes biscuits to please Troy's brain-damaged brother Gabe. When Troy misstates the source of the family furniture, she quietly reminds him it was Glickman, not Hertzberger, who sold them household goods and refutes Troy's claim about making ten dollar payments each month for the past fifteen years. When he berates Pope the restaurant owner for giving preferential treatment to white patrons, Rose intuitively recognizes that her husband is still displacing his fear of a summons to the commissioner's office by attacking others.

In a preview of the women's movement, Wilson reveals Rose's stirrings of individualism, which Troy trounces with hard-edged tyranny. The seedlings of hope and autonomy serve her well as she struggles to endure an unfulfilling marriage and counters her husband's bellowing summons with "I ain't no dog" (p. 43). When Troy admits to impregnating Alberta, Rose voices her unexpressed wants and needs. Realizing that she has cheated herself of wholeness, she charges, "I been right here with you, Troy. I got a life too" (p. 70). At Alberta's death in childbirth, Rose displays her true stature by offering the innocent infant Raynell a home, yet declares that Troy is a "womanless man" for his selfishness and betrayal of their union (p. 79). As the child's name suggests, Raynell admits a ray of hope into Rose's occluded heart.

Wilson allows Rose a late-in-life triumph after her investment in love pays off. In widowhood seven years later, in her mid-fifties, Rose draws around her the people who form the family circle — her birth son Cory and adopted daughter Raynell, the half-witted brother-in-law Gabe, Troy's old friend Jim Bono, and Lyons, Troy's firstborn by his first wife. Rose consoles Cory with wisdom born of years of compensating for a bitter mate and by balancing the pains of marriage with its joys. She compares Cory's strong will to that of his father and explains how Cory must shape Troy's example to fit his own life. Wilson's delineation of the dutiful wife elevates her to near-sainthood, a stance that leaves in doubt whether her piety and goodness may have lessened her appeal to Troy. His desire for a jolly bedmate suggests that marriage to Rose left him unfulfilled and shamed him for not matching her devotion to home and family.

See also women

• *Further Reading*

Elam, Harry J., ed. *Colored Contradictions: An Anthology of Contemporary African-American Plays.* New York: Plume, 1996.
Wang, Qun. *An In-Depth Study of the Major Plays of African American Playwright August Wilson: Vernacularizing the Blues on Stage.* Vol. 6 of *Black Studies.* Lewiston, Ont.: Edwin Mellen Press, 1999.

Maxson, Troy

A fierce rebel and self-promoter, Troy Maxson, the protagonist of *Fences* (1985), is the outgrowth of August Wilson's observation of his stepfather, David Bedford, and of middleweight boxer Charley Burley (1917–1992), who lived across from the Kittel family in Pittsburgh. Over a fifteen-year career that began when Burley was eighteen, he flourished in the Pittsburgh Fight Club and survived ninety-eight matches, including bouts with Ezzard Charles and Archie Moore. Underrated and forgotten, he won eighty-three matches, but no world titles. When his career flagged, he collected garbage for the city of Pittsburgh. When Wilson pictured the man as a character in *Fences*, he envisioned the barrel-chested, deep-toned James Earl Jones originating the role.

The fictional Maxson, a combative fifty-three-year-old garbage collector, suffers an ailment common to late middle age — he has failed to keep up with changing times and mores and is thus out of step with the educational and career opportunities available to his two sons and to the liberation of restless women like his wife Rose. Troy is a complex, seriously flawed braggart and bluff whom the playwright describes as "crude and almost vulgar, though ... capable of rising to profound heights of expression" (p. 1). An illiterate family man dressed in a burlap apron and trapped in the tedium of work and a domestic rut, he earns a weekly salary of $76.42, which he turns over to his wife for paying their bills in exchange for six dollars in pocket money. For a role model against whom to measure his own progress, he recalls growing up on forty-two acres of Lubin's cotton farm two hundred miles from Mobile, Alabama, and reflects on his own abusive father, a downtrodden, womanizing sharecropper who didn't spare the strap and always ate before his eleven children were served. Like other nomadic characters in Wilson's dramas, Troy fled north in 1918 during the Great Migration and, within a year, was remanded to prison for manslaughter, the result of lack of guidance and education in his youth.

The more recent past hangs like a daily burden on Troy Maxson's shoulders. He once batted for the American Negro Baseball League, but failed to launch a career in sports. Claiming he "come along too early," he bitterly lashes out at others in frustration that he spent fifteen years in prison for robbery and for fatally knifing an assailant (p. 10). Most grievous is the fact that Troy never achieved his athletic potential. He blames racial prejudice against black players. His more realistic wife reminds him that he was too old to play after he got out of prison, but Troy chooses to tell life stories as they suit him, even if he must bend the truth. In his self-pitying view, "Everything lined up against you. What you gonna do" (p. 71).

Whatever the reason for Troy's lapsed baseball career, he impresses his best friend Jim Bono with powerful batting and a will to win. Even with Bono's steadfast friendship, Troy hangs suspended in late middle age like the rag ball dangling from a tree limb in the yard. Within the toxic home atmosphere that his own waywardness poisoned, he bounces obliquely with each blow of the bat and gradually recenters himself, ready for the next swing. It is not surprising that the hardest hitter is Cory, a child developing into manhood without a proper male authority figure to model himself after. Ironically, Troy constantly berates his son for irresponsibility, a failing more prevalent in the father than in the teenager.

Troy admits to his share of human faults, which haunt him with regrets and self-recrimination. He is humiliated by the knowledge that he bought a home with his brother Gabriel's disability payment of three thousand dollars, the government compensation for an injury in combat in the Pacific theater during World War II. Troy's prime failure is in negating the hopes of the coming generation. To salve a wounded ego and halt the stream of would-have-beens that haunt his waking hours, he turns stern eyes on Cory. Troy mismanages parenthood by snooping into the boy's daily goings and comings, coercing him to work at the A & P, and forbidding him to accept an athletic scholarship. For stop-gap solace, Troy tyrannizes his wife Rose and, fleeing the house for long afternoons at Taylor's bar, engages in an obvious affair that wounds his wife and children and destroys their homelife.

Beyond his mistakes in the past, Troy belittles himself in the present by crass, bullying, and unloving behaviors. Like his brutal father and absent mother, he fails at parenthood. He takes responsibility but no pride in the position of head of household. He spouts orders to Cory to learn a trade, blames his older son Lyons for frequenting a gambling den that has been raided by the police, and coarsely grabs Rose from behind as an overture to marital intimacy. In contrast to his gruff, offhand, and impenitent treatment of family members, Troy easily states his love for Bono, the old friend and fellow garbage worker who claims "I knew you when" (p. 4).

To his credit, at work, Troy is a bold renegade and champion of justice who courageously challenges the system. In the opening scene of Act I, he admits to Bono the posing of a brazen question to the boss, Mr. Rand: "Why you got the white mens driving and the colored lifting?" (p. 2). At Rand's passing the buck to the union, Troy carries his complaint to labor officials, but comes up against an unspecified "pack of lies," the rejection of his generalized grievance, and a summons to appear before the commissioner the next Friday (p. 3). Like a warrior facing an escalating enemy, Troy swaggers before Bono, claiming that he does not fear being fired when he keeps the end-of-week appointment with the commissioner.

Stubborn, pessimistic, and deliberately self-limiting, Troy maintains a philosophy that "Life don't owe you nothing" (p. 18). He snatches at fleeting physical pleasures, beginning each payday with a pint of gin shared on the back steps with Bono and including frequent sexual encounters with his paramour Alberta, a strapping newcomer from Florida whom Troy describes as part Indian. Mentally, he kicks himself for ruining his first marriage, but makes no headway in changing his self-defeating attitudes or behaviors, which threaten the vitality and warmth of his second marriage. He exonerates adultery as stealing second base, an act of male chutzpah and athletic prowess.

As the play progresses, work continues to define Troy's sense of accomplishment in his last seven years. When he receives a promotion as Pittsburgh's first black garbage truck driver, he mars the achievement by admitting that he has no driver's license. The advancement limits Troy's self-sustaining friendship with Bono, whom he rarely sees during the work day. Three years after becoming a driver, Troy retires. Spiraling downward through wrong-headedness and self-will, he dies in an idiosyncratic pose, swinging a baseball bat, a dominant symbol of the outlet that both Troy and his younger son use to vent anger and frustration. A scrapper to the end against the status quo, like William Shakespeare's Macbeth, Troy faces his adversaries— social injustice, human failings, and the inevitability of a losing bout with Mr. Death.

Through attendees at Troy's funeral, August Wilson reflects on the memorable qualities of the deceased as a husband, father, and friend. Rose, who is generous to her husband's memory, encourages the seething Cory to accept the best that Troy had to offer. She acknowledges a motif that the playwright implies is normal to human families— the sins of the parents recurring in their offspring. Just as Troy lamented over his father's harsh lashings and his theft of Troy's young girlfriend, he must face a hostile son who blames his father for stealing opportunity from Cory and for depriving Rose of a loving marriage and stable home. Gracing the moment are encouragement of Bono, the kind words of Lyons, the family song about Old Blue that Troy once sang, and a touch of grace, an ennobling send-off from the feeble-minded brother Gabriel, who dances and wails a salute to Troy's memory.

See also **betrayal, Jim Bono**

• *Further Reading*

Bogumil, Mary L. *Understanding August Wilson*. Columbia: University of South Carolina Press, 1998.
Jones, James Earl. "August Wilson." *Time*, Vol. 158, No. 1, July 9, 2001, p. 84.
Oliver, Edith. "Interlude 1987: 'Fences.'" *New Yorker*, May 31, 1993, p. 136.
Vaughan, Peter. "Mending 'Fences.'" *Minneapolis Star Tribune*, May 11, 1997, p. 1F.
Wang, Qun. *An In-Depth Study of the Major Plays of African American Playwright August Wilson: Vernacularizing the Blues on Stage*. Vol. 6 of *Black Studies*. Lewiston, Ont.: Edwin Mellen Press, 1999.
Wessling, Joseph H. "Wilson's *Fences*." *Explicator*, Vol. 57, No. 2, Winter 1999, pp. 123– 127.

Maxson genealogy

As expressed in facts from *Fences* (1990), the genealogy of the Maxson family includes Troy's legitimate and extra-marital alliances:

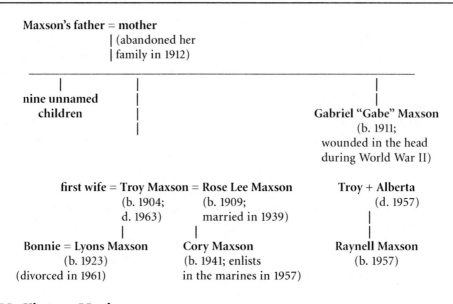

Maxson's father = mother
| (abandoned her
| family in 1912)

| nine unnamed children | | Gabriel "Gabe" Maxson (b. 1911; wounded in the head during World War II) |

first wife = Troy Maxson = Rose Lee Maxson   Troy + Alberta
(b. 1904;   (b. 1909;   (d. 1957)
d. 1963)   married in 1939)

Bonnie = Lyons Maxson   Cory Maxson   Raynell Maxson
(b. 1923)   (b. 1941; enlists   (b. 1957)
(divorced in 1961)   in the marines in 1957)

McClinton, Marion

Prize-winning playwright, actor, and director Marion Isaac McClinton has been a friend and colleague of August Wilson for some thirty years. A resident of St. Paul, Minnesota, McClinton decided on his future in childhood from watching two film actors— Marlon Brando in *Streetcar Named Desire* (1951) and *On the Waterfront* (1954) and Sidney Poitier in *Lilies of the Field* (1963). In 1978, McClinton linked up with Wilson, who lived near him during McClinton's studies at the University of Minnesota. The two found a professional sanctuary among other young black players at the Penumbra Theater.

From a long kinship with the stage, McClinton is well versed in the works of William Shakespeare, Samuel Beckett, and Jean Genet. Of Wilson, his colleague, McClinton claims, "It's August's language, the rhythm of hurt, of pain, of ecstasy, the rhythm of family sets him apart" (O'Mahony). McClinton staged Lorraine Hansberry's *A Raisin in the Sun* (1959) and shares much of Wilson's professional history and outlook, particularly a belief that black theater requires a black director and players. McClinton narrated *Black Bart and the Sacred Hills* (1978) and played the alcoholic driver Fielding in *Jitney* (1982) and has directed productions of *Jitney*, *Fences* (1985), *The Piano Lesson* (1990), *Two Trains Running* (1991), *Seven Guitars* (1995), and *Gem of the Ocean* (2003). After the retirement of Lloyd Richards, Wilson's most prominent director, McClinton debuted on Broadway at the helm of *King Hedley II* (1999) and took *Jitney* off Broadway and on the road in October 2001 to London's Lyttelton Theatre. His reason for staying with Wilson reveals much about both men: "[Wilson] is constantly in pursuit of truth. He writes about the truth of a people, the truth of a decade, with great poetry" (Ifill).

As dramatic collaborator, McClinton highlights Wilson's intent to enmesh his plays in multiple voices, a strategy that benefited *Seven Guitars* by pairing an eerily off-kilter King Hedley with the flashy singer Floyd Barton, his victim, backed by a chorus of friends. The director is also responsible for softening the portrayal of

Wilson's females and with modulating interaction from normal exchange to climactic flashpoint. Of his role in shaping Wilson's plays, the director accords the highest praise to the playwright: "History will prove me out on this, but I think he's the most significant figure American theater has created" (Preston, p. 4F).

Of Wilson's wise fools— Gabe Maxson in *Fences*, Hambone in *Two Trains Running*, Bynum Walker in *Joe Turner's Come and Gone* (1988), King Hedley in *Seven Guitars*, Aunt Ester in *Gem of the Ocean*, and Stool Pigeon in *King Hedley II*— McClinton explains, "Sometimes [these characters] are mistakenly called the idiot savants, but in actuality, in August's plays they're visionaries" (Rousuck, "People," p. 1E). Hedley is a case in point: "[He] sees a great future coming. He can almost see the coming of the '60s. He's a revolutionary" (*Ibid.*). McClinton's perception of Hedley's importance helped to arouse audiences to his value as a seer and storyteller.

See also **Aunt Ester, Hambone, King Hedley, Gabriel Maxson, Stool Pigeon, Bynum Walker**

• *Further Reading*

Ifill, Gwen. "American Shakespeare." *PBS News*, April 6, 2001.
O'Mahony, John. "American Centurion." Manchester *Guardian*, December 14, 2002.
Preston, Rohan. "Oglesby Sparkles in Wilson's 'Gem.'" *Minneapolis Star Tribune*, May 4, 2003, p. 4F.
Rousuck, J. Wynn. "Everyone Wants to Get into the Act." *Baltimore Sun*, May 2, 1997, p. 1E.
_____. "People with Vision." *Baltimore Sun*, April 27, 1997, p. 1E.
"Sharing the Stage with August Wilson." http://www.donshewey.com/theater_articles/marion_mcclinton.htm, April 29, 2001.

Mellon, Andrew

For background material for Pittsburgh in *Two Trains Running* (1991) and briefly in *King Hedley II* (1999), August Wilson incorporates an historical figure, financier Andrew William Mellon (1855–1937), the son of Irish immigrants who advanced from selling apples and potatoes at age nine to ownership of Gulf Oil. A construction magnate, he founded Union Trust and Union Savings Bank of Pittsburgh and helped to launch Alcoa and Union Steel. As a symbol of the white world of money, materialism, and entrepreneurial power, in Wilson's play, Mellon operates his bank with an eye toward profits rather than helping lenders. In contrast to numbers running, Wolf comments, "You might take out more than you put in ... but Mellon ain't gonna let you do that. The numbers give you an opportunity" (p. 3).

As a model of the white male power structure, Mellon continues to crop up in the text and in *King Hedley II*. According to an anecdote, the Prophet Samuel, a street evangelist, once involved the famed Pittsburgh-born industrialist and innovative money man in Samuel's confrontation with the mayor. At the time, Mellon had risen from bank builder to Secretary of the Treasury under presidents Calvin Coolidge and Herbert Hoover. At the end of World War I, Mellon earned regard for negotiating a schedule of repayment of Europe's war debts to the United States.

To end police harassment of Samuel's evangelism, according to an anecdote in

Act I, Scene 1, the prophet ordered the arrest of Mellon and threatened a heavenly sign if the mayor refused. When the stock market fell the next day, the mayor dropped charges against Samuel. Because Gulf Oil stock rose, Mellon donated five hundred dollars to Samuel's ministry and offered financial advice. The prophet's connection with one of America's most influential moneymen brought Samuel a photo opportunity with Mellon and no more police harassment.

• *Further Reading*

Jackson, Kerry. "Industrialist Andrew W. Mellon His Focus Helped Him Become One of History's Most Prosperous." *Investor's Business Daily*, March 8, 2001.

Mercer, Reuben

A young boy living next door to the Hollys' boarding house in *Joe Turner's Come and Gone* (1988), Reuben Mercer presents local matters from a child's point of view. He gossips about Seth Holly and teases Zonia Loomis about her father's "mean-looking eyes" (p. 30). Lacking courtesy and decorum, Reuben noses into the Loomises' business by asking about Zonia's unusual name and the family's homelessness. In a neighborhood with few children, his prying stems from boredom and loneliness. He regrets the death of Eugene, his best friend, but violates the boy's deathbed wish that Reuben free Eugene's pigeons. By having Reuben prefer to sell the birds to Bynum for sacrifice, Wilson emphasizes a budding willfulness that echoes the faults of the play's grown-ups.

In Act II, Scene 4, Reuben fills in offstage after he returns to the yard with Zonia and reports on Bynum's unusual activities the previous night. As Wilson's storyteller, Reuben freely accepts the supernatural, revealed by a wind that talked back to the rootworker. The next morning, Reuben experiences a visit from the ghost of Miss Mabel, Seth's mother, who canes him for breaking a promise to liberate Eugene's pigeons. The haunting precipitates Reuben's rapid opening of the coop door, a subtextual suggestion of the sins of slavery visiting the slave master. In the aftermath, his childish courtship of Zonia retrieves him from bad behaviors to a promise of worthy manhood.

• *Further Reading*

Gantt, Patricia. "Ghosts from 'Down There': The Southernness of August Wilson," in *August Wilson: A Casebook*. New York: Garland, 1994.
Shannon, Sandra G. *The Dramatic Vision of August Wilson*. Washington, D.C.: Howard University Press, 1996.

Mister

A recurring figure in August Wilson's sequel plays, *Seven Guitars* (1995) and *King Hedley II* (1999), Mister advances from baby boy to abettor in crime. The son of WillaMae and Red Carter, Mister, born in May 1948, bears a name intended to make white people respect him. When he appears in the second play at age thirty-seven, he maintains his principles on the job and quits when his employer reneges on a promised raise. Mister's outsized vision of wealth colors a dream in which he is so wealthy he must be transported in a wheelbarrow. He encourages King Hedley to take the easy way out on their partnership in Royal Videos, which will cost them ten thousand dollars. When selling stolen GE refrigerators nets only eight thousand, the two buddies team up in Act II to rob a nearby jewelry store in daylight. Their spur-of-the-moment plan is amateurish and deadly.

Mister combines lethal menace with the standard elements of the foolish side-kick. He allows the gambler Elmore to con him into purchasing a balky pearl-handled derringer with no bullets and inflates the value from fifty-five dollars to five hundred when Mister offers the gun to Hedley. At the robbery, after King deviates from the simple plan by demanding that the victim open the safe, Mister flees out the door. As though acting out a set piece, Mister comments, "The way it supposed to work is he see the gun and give you the money. It ain't supposed to go past that" (p. 80). In his simplicity, Mister arms Ruby with his new pistol, the weapon that snuffs out Hedley's life.

See also **crime**

Mordecai, Ben

August Wilson's production partner, Ben Mordecai, controller of marketing and promotion, devised a series of interlinking regional theater productions. Unique to the system is the playwright's organic method of refining and upgrading the original script along the way, a technique he first applied to *The Piano Lesson* (1990). Wilson observes his plays in rehearsal and learns from director and cast response what needs adjusting. He explains, "Some things you simply can't tell unless you see it staged. On paper you could read it a hundred times and not tell" (Stern, p. 18A).

The system works for Wilson. In the style of a screenwriter, he adds and deletes dialogue overnight for the actors to perform the next day. The system sent *King Hedley II* (1999) on a series of big-city productions and numerous cast changes before the launching of a final version on Broadway, a refinement method also intended for *Gem of the Ocean* (2003). Because critics have access to the progression of versions, they are able to analyze the process by which Wilson rethinks and revises his work.

• *Further Reading*

Heard, Elisabeth J. "August Wilson on Playwriting." *African American Review*, Vol. 35, No. 1, Spring 2001, p. 93.
Stern, Gary. "Playwrights Agree That the Workshops Process Is a Major Aid in Rewriting." *Backstage*, June 8, 1984, pp. 18A–19A.

music

As a dramatic medium and evidence of shared culture, Wilson repeatedly laces dialogue with music, both spontaneous and professionally rendered. In *Fences* (1985), the playwright balances the Maxsons' despair with Troy's rollicking "Blue was a good old dog" and his wife Rose's gospel singing at the clothesline. In a description of her choice of a future, Rose opted for "a house that I could sing in." Additional singing in the text incorporates her brother-in-law Gabe's spiritual and Troy's lullaby to three-day-old Raynell, his motherless infant (p. 44). When Corey Maxson returns from six years in the marines, he joins his sister Raynell in singing a second-hand tribute to their deceased father:

> Blue laid down and died like a man
> Now he's treeing possums in the Promised Land
> I'm gonna tell you this to let you know
> Blue's gone where the good dogs go [p. 100].

The implication is that Troy, for all his faults, was human and deserving of forgiveness and redemption.

Wilson uses music and musical instruments as a rejuvenating motif for black characters to apply to everyday experiences. The songs they sing and play amplify a unique creativity interweaving oral traditions, jazz, hymns, Negro spirituals, work tunes, and blues. In *Seven Guitars* (1996), an abrupt segue from death to song occurs in the opening lines, when Louise returns from a burial singing a suggestive call, "Anybody here wanna try my cabbage/Just step this way," a universal juncture of death and sex that links the end of one life with the libido of another (p. 1). Canewell, a fellow mourner, redirects the conversation from carnality back to life's impermanence by calling death "a thief in the night" and singing a gloomy verse about the snatching of a mother from her bed (p. 5).

In terms of the impact of music on his drama, Wilson validates varying musical styles, but extols the blues above other genres. In *Ma Rainey's Black Bottom* (1985), set in a professional studio in Chicago, the making of traditional black music assures Ma's earnings, by which she provides a living for herself and the back-up band. Ironically, differences over style and control create a disharmony that results in trumpeter Levee Green's stabbing of Toledo. Conversely, in the first flashback of two lovers in *Seven Guitars,* thirty-five-year-old Floyd Barton and Vera Dotson, who is eight years his junior, restore harmony to their relationship by dancing pelvis to pelvis to his hit recording of "That's All Right." The sweet-sad lyrics speak of betrayal in a foreshadowing of Floyd's jilting of Vera. As the drama progresses, a replaying of Floyd's record turns "That's All Right" into a mantra expressing confidence in the progress of blacks who, like Ruby, flee the South for better times in the industrialized North. After Floyd's savage murder, the song implies exoneration for his faults, including the embroiling of Poochie Tillery in a finance company robbery that leads to his death.

As is obvious from these examples, Wilson creates from song multiple opportunities to comment on the complexities of human relations. In *Joe Turner's Come and Gone* (1988), the playwright explains the duality of African American music, which expresses both the joy of their unique culture and the sorrow of the diaspora that spread black African slaves across the Western Hemisphere. In *The Piano Lesson*

(1990), Berniece plays the family piano to exorcise the ghosts of slave times; Lymon Jackson and the males of the Charles family chime in on "O Lord Berta Berta," a recreation of the insecurities in male prisoners. In *Two Trains Running* (1991), Sterling Johnson courts Risa Thomas with a sweet morning song after Zanelli's rental jukebox, a sure moneymaker, stood silent at Memphis Lee's diner for a year during the turmoil of the civil rights era. Music also supplies Memphis a means of celebrating sale of his property when he returns from a successful negotiation with city authorities to sing a sassy "We don't care what Mama don't allow/We gonna barrelhouse anyhow" (p. 108). As an inchoate tribute to Troy Maxson in *Fences* (1985), Gabe, the trumpet-blowing war veteran, attempts to blast his brother into heaven with notes from his horn. Undaunted by failure, Gabe improvises a dance to express a wordless farewell.

Whatever their circumstances, Wilson's characters extol music as life-enhancing, as with Ruby's crooning to her dying son in *King Hedley II* (1999) the wistful ballad "Red Sails in the Sunset," popularized by Bing Crosby in 1935. Ruby comments about her career with Walter Kelly's band, "I always did like to sing. Seem like that was a better way of talking. You could put more meaning to it" (p. 95). In the words of Lyons Maxson in *Fences*, music is an essential because it gives him a sense of belonging and provides "the only way I can find to live in the world," a subtextual comment on the spiritual uplift of music to a disenfranchised people (p. 18).

Most telling of Wilson's acclamation of black music comes in *The Piano Lesson* when Boy Willie pounds out a percussive boogie-woogie, a popular dance rhythm from around 1928, and sings Lymon's song, encouraging both Lymon and Doaker to join in with rhythmic clapping and enjoyment. The unity and harmony of their participation in music and oral culture communicate their feelings of black history, belonging, and identity. Just as Doaker's telling the story of the carved piano keeps the Charles family and their martyred ancestors alive, Berniece's playing the piano unites the surviving relatives in a festival of song that defeats the ghost of slavery.

See also **black bottom, blues, Buddy Bolden, community, Gertrude Malissa Pridgett "Ma" Rainey**

- *Further Reading*

Plum, Jay. "Blues, History, and the Dramaturgy of August Wilson." *African American Review*, Vol. 27, No. 4, Winter 1993, pp. 561–567.
Shannon, Sandra G. "Blues, History, and Dramaturgy." *African American Review*, Vol. 27, No. 4, Winter 1993, pp. 539–559.
Wang, Qun. *An In-Depth Study of the Major Plays of African American Playwright August Wilson: Vernacularizing the Blues on Stage*. Vol. 6 of *Black Studies*. Lewiston, Ont.: Edwin Mellen Press, 1999.

opportunity

A rankling theme in Wilson's plays involves a pervasive tension in characters between their missed opportunities in the past and more promising options to come. In an example from *King Hedley II* (1999), Stool Pigeon opens Act I, Scene 1, with a metaphoric complaint that the neighborhood "done got broke up. Pieces flying every-where" (p. 1). In *Gem of the Ocean* (2003), the action focuses on the vast underwater burial ground of black Africans who died on the treacherous Middle Passage without reaching North America. The playwright uses a private moment in the life of Sam, a hotel ballroom sweeper in *The Janitor* (1985), to speak the wisdom of an older man on the sweetness of youthful promise. With optimism for the next generation, he reminds young people, "What you are now ain't what you gonna become" (p. 1901). The abrupt scolding of Mr. Collins deprives Sam of his podium and thrusts him back into manual labor, an ominous sign of a low-end job with no future.

Wilson uses subsequent promises of opportunity as pivotal points prefacing struggle and loss. In *Seven Guitars* (1995), possibilities crop up for Floyd Barton's second recording session with the Savoy Record Company in Chicago and for treatment of King Hedley's tuberculosis at the recently opened black sanitarium on Bedford Street in Pittsburgh. Ironically, one cancels the other after Hedley slays his friend and grasps his cache of stolen money out of the delusion that Hedley's dream of mystic enrichment has come true. One of the strong-willed survivors of Wilson's drama cycle, Memphis Lee, the business owner in *Two Trains Running* (1991), makes his own luck by setting goals, playing the numbers, and saving money from his rental property and diner to buy what he wants. By play's end, his persistence in seeking full value for his investment and his willingness to trust a white attorney, Joseph Bartoromo, to press his case pays off in a surprise settlement with the city for thirty-five thousand dollars.

The interpretation of opportunity is a complex issue in Wilson's decade cycle, for example, the harsh realities innkeeper Seth Holly faces in borrowing from banks in *Joe Turner's Come and Gone* (1988), the shady dealings by which Mister and the title character hopes to open Royal Videos in *King Hedley II*, and the sudden rise of Booster Becker from jobless ex-con to heir after a mill accident kills Jim Becker in *Jitney* (1982). None of these instances offers something for nothing. In *The Piano Lesson* (1990), a longstanding animosity between Boy Willie Charles and his sister Berniece derives from her clinging to the past and refusing to sell a piano that could finance improvements to both their lives. The play ends with a new accounting of assets after Boy Willie wrestles the avenging ghost of Robert Sutter, which Berniece exorcises by playing the contested piano and calling on ancestors. In *Fences* (1985), Troy Maxson stews over lost hopes for a baseball career while discarding chances to love his wife and foster the dreams of sons Cory and Lyons. Similarly, the fleeting nature of opportunity in *Seven Guitars* pictures Canewell and Red Carter without instruments and missing opportunity because they have hocked guitar, harmonica, and drums at the pawnshop. Floyd intends to get his guitar by fair means or foul and to record a hit in Chicago. In his philosophy, "You got to take the opportunity while it's there" (p. 47).

The assessment of opportunity in these instances requires intricate accounting of costs and losses. Seth could lose the Holly family boardinghouse by offering it to the bank as collateral for a tinware shop. King Hedley II risks a return to prison by clinging to illegal methods of supporting his family. Booster Becker gains a failing car service, but loses the opportunity to settle animosities with his father. Boy Willie accepts Berniece's demand for the piano and returns south without enough cash to buy his own farm. Troy Maxson retreats into self-indulgent sex with Alberta and loses the respect of his wife and family. Floyd Barton, a puzzling victim of success, confuses Hedley by claiming a stash of money and riling Hedley into a murderous rage. Floyd's death leaves his friends with an inexplicable crime to solve and a single pop song as a memorial to his fleeting stardom.

See also **Floyd Barton, black athletes, Levee Green, Troy Maxson, powerlessness, racism, Ma Rainey**

- *Further Reading*

Charters, Ann, and Samuel Charters, ed. *Short Pieces from the New Dramatists.* Banbury, Ox.: Orangeberry Books, 1985.
Majors, Richard, and Janet Mancini Billson. *Cool Pose: The Dilemmas of Black Manhood in America.* New York: Lexington Books, 1992.

oral lore

In 1965, August Wilson realized the precious cargo that oral lore bears. He embraced the black races's history recorded in stories and the blues and recreated it in dramatic scenarios, such as Elmore's witty tale of outrunning a bullet in *King Hedley II* (1999) and Ma Rainey's dedication to traditional blues in *Ma Rainey's Black Bottom* (1985). In *12 Million Black Voices* (1941), author Richard Wright depicted black lore as recollections of black forebears dating back to Africa. In the opinion of Lawrence W. Levine, black storytelling was originally both "wish-fulfillment" and "painfully realistic stories which taught the art of surviving and even triumphing in the face of a hostile environment" (Levine, p. 115). His description of the black milieu fits all of Wilson's cycle plays.

Of the importance of the verbal arts to uneducated people, the playwright extolled black cultural nationalism for the truths it contains of a preliterate African people attempting to preserve ties with their pre-slavery past. In the essay "Where to Begin" (1985), he acknowledges that, for centuries, the non-black world tried to mimic white success by degrading and dismissing the roots of blackness as ignorant and worthless. Growing up in Pittsburgh's Hill District, he saw around him "a world that did not recognize their gods, their manners, their mores. It despised their ethos and refused to even recognize their humanity" (Wilson, "Where," p. 2035). Overcoming the diminution of black culture became his ambition.

To validate oral forms of black self-definition, in his essay "How to Write a Play Like August Wilson" (1991) for the *New York Times*, Wilson intended to define and affirm what James Baldwin called "that field of manners and ritual of intercourse that will sustain a man once he's left his father's house" (p. 5). Wilson's dramatic cycle stresses music, call-and-response, humorous anecdotes, family histories, Aunt Ester's seance, familiar adages, ribald quips, and other forms of storytelling as elements of African American orality. In an early example, Slow Drag, the bassist in *Ma Rainey's Black Bottom*, contributes to oral religious wisdom a cautionary tale about how Eliza Cotter sold his soul to Satan. In *Fences* (1985), Jim Bono describes storytelling as an innate characteristic in Troy Maxson. Of Troy's colorful story about wrestling Mr. Death, Bono remarks, "I know you got some Uncle Remus in your blood," a reference to the black plantation griot in the story cycle of white Georgian journalist and raconteur Joel Chandler Harris (p. 13). Troy later gives a spirited account of a coming-of-age confrontation with his father when Troy was fourteen. He characterizes the arrival of manhood as a time when "the world suddenly got big" (p. 53). He reinterprets his story by recognizing self-will as a legacy from an otherwise reprehensible parent. His ability to separate wisdom from ignoble acts recurs in the last scene as Troy's son Cory makes the same effort to embrace the good in his flawed father.

In *The Piano Lesson* (1990), Wilson turns to pulpit oratory for an in-house exorcism. Avery Brown, a self-proclaimed minister of the Good Shepherd Church of God in Christ, counters Robert Sutter's ghost by summoning the power of God the Father. Wilson characterizes the sermonizing of the semi-literate storefront preacher by having Avery botch a recitation of the Twenty-third Psalm as "Our Father taught us how to pray," a reference to the preface to the Lord's Prayer in Luke 11:1 (p. 104). In citing from Jesus's confrontation with Satan in the wilderness, Avery forms a mishmash of phrases into "Get thee behind the face of Righteousness as we Glorify His Holy Name!" (p. 105). The failure of Avery's religion is typical of Wilson's characters, who take greater stock in the pagan underpinnings of West African culture than in the white man's Christianity.

More valuable wisdom tales and sing-song stories permeate Wilson's plays, as with the philosopher Toledo's description of culture formation in *Ma Rainey's Black Bottom* (1985), which initiates the young into the black social order:

> Everybody come from different places in Africa, right? Come from different tribes and things. Soonawhile they began to make one big stew. You had the carrots, the peas, and potatoes and whatnot over here. And over there you had the meat, the nuts, the okra, corn … and then you mix it up and let it cook right through to get the flavors flowing together … then you got one thing. You got a stew [p. 57].

At other times, a short, insightful witticism is often the method of expressing the value of black lives in America. In *Two Trains Running* (1991), Holloway, the retired painter and pragmatist, smirks, "Niggers is the hardest-working people in the world, worked 300 years for free and didn't take no lunch hour" (p. 34). Unlike Toledo's graceful fable, the ironic quip stings with its wit and hard-hitting truth.

As Ma Rainey explains in *Ma Rainey's Black Bottom* (1985), oral nuggets like blues lyrics fill up the inexplicable voids and help blacks overcome hardships, validate their longings, and understand their lives. In *The Piano Lesson*, precise oral expression balances the circular arguments that get nowhere. Doaker Charles, the griot or family storyteller, demonstrates the value of rhythmic jingles as a memory device for recording the train schedule on the Jackson to Memphis route:

> Gonna leave Jackson Mississippi
> and go to Memphis
> and double back to Jackson [p. 54]

In more meaningful example of oral lore, Doaker preserves episodes in compelling oral form to impress on his niece, nephew, and great-niece the value of the carved piano to family members. These oral lessons become an enabling device for a people to whom white education systems have denied their share of cultural accomplishment and pride.

See also **blues, call-and-response, juba, music, Parchman Farm, wisdom**

• *Further Reading*

Hobsbawm, Eric, and Terence Ranger. *The Invention of Tradition*. New York: Cambridge University Press, 1983.
Levine, Lawrence W. *Black Culture and Black Consciousness: Afro-American Folk Thought from Slavery to Freedom*. New York: Oxford University Press, 1977.
Wilson, August. "How to Write a Play Like August Wilson." *New York Times*, March 10, 1991, Sect. 2, p. 5.
_____. "Where to Begin," in *Short Pieces from the New Dramatists*. Banbury, Ox.: Orangeberry Books, 1985, pp. 2033–2037.

Parchman Farm

To enable listeners and readers to visualize his themes, Wilson cleverly pairs abstracts such as Jim Crow oppression with palpable images, such as the slave-era ankle chain that Solly Two Kings retains for good luck in *Gem of the Ocean* (2003). In *The Piano Lesson* (1990), Boy Willie Charles tries to forget his three-year sentence to Parchman Farm, an historic two-thousand-acre penal plantation created by Governor James Kimble Vardaman and operated by inmate labor. According to David M. Oshinsky, a history professor at Rutgers University and author of *"Worse Than Slavery": Parchman Farm and the Ordeal of Jim Crow Justice* (1997), winner of the Robert F. Kennedy Book Award, in the post–Civil War justice system, convict leasing was the South's answer to prisons and jails overcrowded with unruly blacks incarcerated under the infamous Black Code system for misdemeanors and felonies. When populist pressures ended the merchandizing of prison labor, penal farming, a form of convict bondage similar to medieval fiefdoms, took its place.

The history of prison farming survives in state archives and penitentiary records, legislative minutes, court proceedings, folk tales, and dramatic monologues from blues lyrics by Mose Allison (1927–   ) and Booker T. Washington "Bukka" White (1906–1977). White served time at Parchman Farm from 1937 to 1940 for shooting a white man and recorded his Delta blues from a cell in 1939 for Alan and John Lomax, folk collectors for the Library of Congress. Near the Gordon Station railroad spur in Sunflower County, Mississippi, prisoners at Parchman Farm tended and slaughtered cattle, raised vegetables, and harvested cotton on forty-six square miles of prime delta cropland. To the observer, the complex mimicked the well-kept plantations of the antebellum South. Skilled and unskilled labor, which was 90 percent black and mostly male, ran a sawmill, brickyard, cotton gin, and fruit and vegetables cannery. Threatening the health and lives of inmates were heat, insect-borne disease, exhaustion, and accidents as well as chaining and caging, filth, bread-and-water diet, strip searches, dog bite, shooting, haltering and pillorying, branding, ear cropping, and lashings with a yard-long leather strap known as Black Annie, a holdover from slave days.

Each public whipping involved two to four guards holding the culprit, stripped to the waist and spread-eagled on the floor, for punishment issued by a sergeant for infractions such as laziness, breaking tools, fighting, pilfering, or bad-mouthing or cursing the prison staff. More serious penalties involved lashing palms, soles of the feet, calves, and buttocks over a period of several days, sometimes resulting in death. From 1905 until the federal courts ended convict farming in 1972 for "cruel and unusual punishment," the brutal farm system spawned breakouts, protests, and a whole subset of prison blues lyrics and horror stories. Because of the informal cataloguing of the farm system's crimes against humanity, singers of prison blues kept alive eyewitness accounts of black history for the edification of subsequent generations.

See also **Jim Crow era, powerlessness, racism**

- *Further Reading*

Oshinsky, David M. *"Worse Than Slavery": Parchman Farm and the Ordeal of Jim Crow Justice*. New York: Free Press, 1997.
Plum, Jay. "Blues, History, and the Dramaturgy of August Wilson." *African American Review*, Vol. 27, No. 4, Winter 1993, pp. 561–567.
Taylor, William Banks. *Down on Parchman Farm: The Great Prison in the Mississippi Delta*. Columbus: Ohio State University Press, 1999.
Yardley, Jonathan. "In the Fields of Despair." *Washington Post*, March 31, 1996.

parenthood

August Wilson creates scenarios that laud the value of good parents, for example, the loving mother Ester who named her children for stars in *Gem of the Ocean* (2003); Coreen Becker, Booster's mother, who attends his murder trial and dies of despair while he sits on death row in *Jitney* (1982); Berniece Charles's concern for her daughter Maretha's future in *The Piano Lesson* (1990); and the loyal father Herald Loomis, who returns for his daughter Zonia after he left a Tennessee chain gang in *Joe Turner's Come and Gone* (1988). Critics are quick to surmise that the patterns of disrupted father-and-son relationships in Wilson's plays derive from his own complex response to an alcoholic white biological father and a black ex-con stepfather. Bynum Walker, the binding man speaks of his own daddy, who gave Bynum identity through song. Because the burden of selfhood was laborious, he tried to locate his father to return the song. The realization that he couldn't abandon so personal a thing causes Bynum to acknowledge, "I looked long back in memory and gathered up pieces and snatches of things to make that song. I was making it up out of myself" (p. 71). Eventually Bynum and his song merge into an inseparable whole, much as rivers run to the sea and lose themselves in its immensity.

Parenthood dominates the subtext in *Seven Guitars* (1995) in Hedley's reflection on the ingratitude of whites whose horses his father tended, Red Carter's dread of the day he must wear a white flower to denote his mother's passing, Canewell's delight in WillaMae's newborn boy Mister, and the melodramatic recitation of the Lord's Prayer that causes Floyd Barton to state how much he misses his recently deceased mother, Maude Avery Barton. In token of Floyd's fond memories of Maude, he spends the last of his few dollars for a gray marble headstone flanked by two carved roses and arranges for the monument to be delivered by Mother's Day, 1948. From a negative stance, Troy Maxson in *Fences* (1985) recalls the humiliation of a punitive father who beat him bloody with mule harness and stole his teenage girlfriend. Wilson contrasts the bitter pugnacity in Maxson with the gentle good nature of his wife Rose, a devout mother who disciplines and consoles her son Cory, uplifts and encourages her stepson Lyons, and treats her retarded brother-in-law Gabe to snacks. Rose's generosity emergers during her most trying time, when she welcomes into her heart Troy's illegitimate daughter Raynell as a substitute for the other babies that she wanted but didn't produce.

Wilson describes the result of varying degrees of responsible parenthood. Although Sterling Johnson had a kind foster mother and male mentor at the Toner Institute, an orphanage in *Two Trains Running* (1991), he grew up lacking in mature, sensible values. On his first weeks out of the penitentiary, like a spoiled teenager, he declares, "All a man need is a pocketful of money, a Cadillac, and a good woman," then makes an offhand remark about "that other part of satisfaction" (p. 93). Holloway, the cafe's philosopher-in-residence, had such bad memories of his grandfather, an accommodator of whites, that he wanted to murder him. In reference to positive role models, the playwright describes West, the undertaker, who recognizes the wisdom of his father about finding the right woman, and Memphis Lee, the cafe owner, has fond memories of his grandfather, a role model who taught him how to locate water underground. The male-to-male transfer of knowledge strengthens character and provides confidence in nature, a quality that blacks lost after their abrupt departure from Africa.

Not all characters look forward to children. Three male characters— Sterling and Wolf in *Two Trains Running* and Jim Bono in *Fences*—choose not to father children, a stance echoed by the self-centered Molly Cunningham in *Joe Turner's Come and Gone*. In *The Piano Lesson*, Boy Willie explains his hesitance: "If I was Rockefeller I'd have forty or fifty. I'd make one every day. Cause they gonna start out in life with all the advantages. I ain't got no advantages to offer nobody" (p. 91). In contrast, King Hedley in *Seven Guitars* (1995) wants a family so much that he romances the youthful, vibrant Ruby and attempts to sire a child by her. Because she lies about the father of her unborn child, in *King Hedley II* (1999), the second King Hedley grows up lawless and confused, but still aching to see his line continue with the birth of King Hedley III.

See also **Berniece Charles, King Hedley, King Hedley II, Tonya Hedley, Rose Maxson, Troy Maxson, Ruby**

- *Further Reading*

Lichtenstein, Gene. "An Evening with August Wilson." *Jewish Journal of Greater Los Angeles*, February 11, 2000.

Rawson, Chris. "Playwright August Wilson Still Has Miles to Go." *Pittsburgh Post-Gazette*, July 5, 2001.

_____. "Stage Review: Wilson's Hedley a Thrilling Ride." *Pittsburgh Post-Gazette*, December 16, 1999.

Pentecost, Martha Loomis

The wife bereft of her husband during his seven-year imprisonment on a Tennessee chain gang in *Joe Turner's Come and Gone* (1988), Martha tells a brief story of loneliness and disillusion. Like Troy Maxson's Rose in *Fences* (1984), Martha is the person in whom Herald Loomis invests his search for continuity. He remembers her as pretty and describes her as five feet tall and brown-skinned with long hair. She was seventeen years old when he began a seven-year sentence on Joe Turner's chain gang, leaving her with a daughter to rear without help. During his first two months apart from the family, Henry Thompson evicted her from his land. After five years of waiting at her mother's house, Martha joined an evangelical sect, left her child behind, and moved north with Reverend Tolliver to settle at Rankin southeast of Pittsburgh. Seth indicates that she is a respected Christian who once roomed at the Hollys' boarding house and cleaned and sewed for Doc Goldblum.

During the long, arduous imprisonment, Loomis turns his wife into an icon on which he fixes his love and hopes. He honors and adores Martha as the anchor of his being and explains, "I just wanted to see your face to know that the world was still there. Make sure everything still in its place so I could reconnect myself together" (p. 89). She describes the separation of their family as a splitting of the universe, a shattering of her life. She explains to Loomis that, after five years of misery, she abandoned her marriage and began a new existence among fellow Christians. She placed Zonia with Martha's mother "so she be safe" (p. 89). A symbol of newness of life is Martha's adoption of the surname "Pentecost," a Christian holy day marking the post–Resurrection coming of the Holy Spirit to Jesus's disciples as recorded in Acts 2:1. Because of the profound change in Martha, she becomes the catalyst of change in Loomis. She interacts with the world through white-formulated Christian dogma, which she recites in counterpoint to her husband's blasphemies. When Loomis attempts to reclaim his fragmented self, she chants Psalm 23, invokes Jesus, and begs her husband to lay down his knife. The alliance is a powerful inducement — the gentle shepherd poet and Jesus the teacher and healer against an armed and irate black man. In her world view, the blood of the lamb is the only power that can redeem and restore. She realizes that her husband is lost to her and charges, "You done gone over to the devil" (p. 91). By embracing Jesus over her husband, she gives up on the world and looks to the hereafter. After directing him toward her version of a meaningful life, she leaves him free to seek his own salvation.

• *Further Reading*

Bandler, Michael J. "USIA Interview with American Playwright August Wilson." http://usembassy-australia.state.gov/hyper/WF980415/epf308.htm, April 15, 1998.

Keller, James R. "The Shaman's Apprentice: Ecstasy and Economy in Wilson's Joe Turner." *African American Review*, Vol. 35, No. 3, Fall 2001, p. 471.

Wang, Qun. *An In-Depth Study of the Major Plays of African American Playwright August Wilson: Vernacularizing the Blues on Stage*. Vol. 6 of *Black Studies*. Lewiston, Ont.: Edwin Mellen Press, 1999.

Philmore

As Wilson's model of John Q. Citizen, Philmore patronizes the Hill District cab stand in *Jitney* (1982). He is named briefly in *Two Trains Running* (1990) as a property owner in 1969 who sells out to West, the mortician, after urban renewal encroaches on the neighborhood. West remarks that the sale was an act of desperation because "He know the city wasn't gonna give him what it's worth" (p. 39). In *Jitney*, set eight years later, the playwright depicts Philmore as an ordinary resident and flawed human being. In the gloom that follows Jim Becker's death, Philmore pays his respects to the other drivers and offers to get off work to serve as a pallbearer.

A doorman at the William Penn Hotel for six years, Philmore is a steady, dependable worker who takes pride in perfect attendance and the promise of a raise. Because he stays out all night listening to music at the Working Men's Club, his wife ejects him from their home above the Frankstown Bar. He jokes about the domestic tiff by stacking dollar bills and blowing them over. The stunt lends truth to his claim that "I been out blowing my money" (p. 19). By maintaining his character's genial nature, Wilson stresses the role of humor in enabling harried, misunderstood people to survive.

See also **humor**

• *Further Reading*

Wang, Qun. *An In-Depth Study of the Major Plays of African American Playwright August Wilson: Vernacularizing the Blues on Stage*. Vol. 6 of *Black Studies*. Lewiston, Ont.: Edwin Mellen Press, 1999.

piano

The family heirloom in *The Piano Lesson* (1990), the old upright piano is a psychologically charged bas relief illustrating the Charles clan's progression from servitude to the Robert Sutter family to a hardy, enduring extended family surviving the Great Depression. While his own limbs were held in bondage, Boy Charles carved the piano legs with a free-wheeling human montage — an unofficial plantation marriage, birth, funeral, and the removal of two slaves from Mississippi to Georgia. Textured in wood as dark as the skin of African slaves, the figures form a keepsake album, a sacred relic and symbol of clan continuity. As critic Paul Hodgins notes, "It sits in the corner of Berniece's living room like a silent elder" (Hodgins, p. F3). When Doaker Charles, the repository of family lore, tells about his own father's death, he legitimizes the sacrifice of Boy Charles, whose brothers, Doaker and Wining Boy, raided the Sutter farm during the county picnic celebrating Independence Day, 1911. In a noble act costing Boy Charles's life, the two men repossessed the piano.

Set a quarter century later in 1936, the play focuses on the piano's value to the current generation. To a white buyer, the instrument is worth $1,150. To Boy Willie, who plays boogie woogie by ear, the piano is a source of impromptu amusement, but is not worth preserving when it could provide him cash to buy land. To Wining Boy Charles, the itinerant musician, playing the keys allows him to demonstrate a professional skill and relieves his sorrow over the demise of his ex-wife Cleotha Holman Charles, who died on May 1. For Doaker, the piano was once worth stealing from Sutter's house in Mississippi and transporting to Pittsburgh, but it is not worth a family ruckus.

An ironic battleground with a violent history, the piano is the source of potentially explosive sibling rivalry. Berniece Charles, whose mother died as a result of enmity aroused by ownership of the piano, chooses to retain the instrument as though it were a relic in a shrine. Her ambitious brother Boy Willie demands that they sell the piano and divide the proceeds. In his opinion, "I ain't gonna be no fool about no sentimental value" (p. 51). The vitriolic argument between sister and brother turns on their conflict over the piano's value: to Berniece, it is an artifact, a priceless family icon. To Boy Willie, it is a useless object that he wants to liquidate into dollars. The resolution of their enmity requires Lymon, the outsider, to invoke family and community harmony as the end to the disagreement. He declares, "It's going to take more than me and you to move this piano" (p. 83).

In the falling action, the piano transcends wood and wire to become a ritual object capable of reuniting the living with the dead. Berniece's improvised ceremonial chant and accompaniment produce a liberating doxology that frees the family from corrosive anger and resentment. Appropriately, she voices gratitude. When Boy Willie resolves to retain his Southern identity and farm in Mississippi, he abandons his quest and leaves the piano behind with his sister and niece. Thus, a significant relic of Southern violence and demand for recognition remains in the industrialized North. Carved with ancestor figures, it bears for posterity the events and African values of an enslaved people and lifestyle that no longer exist.

See also **irony, supernatural**

• *Further Reading*

Christiansen, Richard. "Artist of the Year: August Wilson's Plays Reveal What It Means to Be Black in This Century." *Chicago Tribune*, December 27, 1987.

Glover, Margaret E. "Two Notes on August Wilson: The Songs of a Marked Man." *Theater*, Vol. 19, No. 3, Summer-Fall, 1988, pp. 69–70.

Hodgins, Paul. "A Lesson in Theatrical Greatness: This Ghost Story Will Haunt You with Its Beauty Long After the Lights Go Up." *Orange County Register*, October 25, 1999, p. F3.

The Piano Lesson

Named for a painting by artist Romare Bearden and set in 1936 late in the Great Depression in Pittsburgh, Wilson's *The Piano Lesson* (1990) presents a provocative view of the African American's burden of ancestry. In discussions with Bill Moyers, the author expressed his admiration for people who began resisting white coercion as early as the black African's arrival in the Western Hemisphere. At stake was the value of self. Wilson insisted that "If, in order to participate in American society, in order to accomplish some of the things which the black middle class has accomplished, if you have had to give up that self in order to accomplish that, then you are not making an affirmation of the value of the African being" (Moyers, p. 7).

To express the struggle for wholeness, the playwright structures *The Piano Lesson* like a folk tale that reviewer Jayne Blanchard described as "letting go of the past and reinventing yourself" (Blanchard, p. 5C). The action opens at dawn in a kitchen and parlor, an auspicious time in the heart of an urban home. The flat becomes a crucible in which unforeseen events test the Charles family's unity and endurance. More peaceful than the parlor with its ornate piano are the kitchen and unseen bedroom, Doaker's domain. In the former, he quietly cooks and grills bread, irons a uniform, plays solitaire, and shares good quality liquor with his brother while narrating family history. While Berniece heats water for her bath at Doaker's stove, she is less volatile and more amenable to discussion than when she approaches the piano, which brings out the edgy, demanding side of her personality.

The action centers on inhumane captivity — the Charles clan's mistreatment by the slave-holding Robert Sutter family, who owned them during the mid–1800s. Critic Craig Hansen Werner describes the uproar that follows as "the disruption of the surface of family life by repressed or buried secrets" (Werner, p. 278). As though trading livestock or inanimate property, Sutter swapped slaves for a piano as an anniversary present for his wife Ophelia. In lieu of cash, he offered Joel Nolander and his brother two slaves, Berniece and a nine-year-old, the wife and son of Willie Boy Charles, a plantation carpenter, the grandfather and great-grandfather of the drama's main characters. To appease Ophelia, who pined for Berniece, Willie Boy carved the piano legs with the family's history in a montage of scenes comprising a slave narrative celebrating the life of his scattered clan.

Like the insurance money bequeathed by Big Walter to his family in Lorraine Hansberry's *A Raisin in the Sun* (1958), Willie Boy's legacy to his family is a valued but problematic gift. To claim the family's heritage, Willie Boy's grandsons, Doaker and Wining Boy, stole the piano on Independence Day in 1911 and took it by wagon across the Sunflower County line. The instrument's unlawful removal set off a chain of crimes, including arson and seven deaths. Sutter chased the wrong brother, Boy Charles, whom pursuing whites immolated along with four hobos by burning a boxcar of the Yellow Dog or Yazoo Delta railroad. Ed Saunders, a suspect, died two months later from a fall down a well; Sutter's grandson and namesake fell or was pushed down a well three weeks before the play begins. The power of the instrument over the Charles family survives in Robert Sutter's ghost, which inhabits the piano in its current place of honor in Doaker's parlor and forces them to comprehend its haunting through more frequent appearances to family members. Wilson's repetition of events involving the piano and the similarity of family names compresses the action and implies an immediacy that unites the Sutter and Charles families from the mid–1800s into the 1930s.

In 1936, Boy Willie Charles arrives at Doaker's Pittsburgh flat at 5:00 A.M. to demand the piano. Berniece, who lacks the farm boy's familiarity with arising before sunup, appears in a snarly mood and fights her brother for possession of the heirloom. Rather than anguish over the piano as a burden of the past, the brother wants to use the instrument as a positive means of financial and personal betterment. After Berniece improvises a prayer and plea to ancestral spirits, the settlement of the sibling squabble results in an epiphany of forgiveness, exorcism of a slave-era ghost, and a reevaluation of the family inheritance. The sibling quarrel is mooted, with neither party forcing the hand of the other. To reviewer Mervyn Rothstein, Wilson explained, "I didn't want to make a choice between Boy Willie and Berniece because I thought there was validity in both their arguments" (Rothstein, p. 1).

See also **Berniece Charles, Boy Willie Charles, Doaker Charles, Wining Boy Charles, Charles genealogy, Maretha, piano, Robert Sutter**

• *Further Reading*

Bissiri, Amadou. "Aspects of Africanness in August Wilson's Drama: Reading *The Piano Lesson* through Wole Soyinka's Drama." *African American Review*, Vol. 30, No. 1, 1996, pp. 99–113.

Blanchard, Jayne M. "This 'Piano' Found the Key for Great Theater." *St. Paul Pioneer Press*, May 4, 1992, p. 5C.

Brustein, Robert. "The Piano Lesson." *New Republic*, Vol. 202, No. 21, May 21, 1990, pp. 28–30.

Moyers, Bill. *A World of Ideas.* New York: Doubleday, 1989.

Rich, Frank. "A Family Confronts Its History in August Wilson's 'Piano Lesson.'" *New York Times*, April 17, 1990, pp. C13, C15.

Rothstein, Mervyn. "Round Five for a Theatrical Heavyweight." *New York Times*, April 15, 1990, pp. 1, 8.

Werner, Craig Hansen. *Playing the Changes: From Afro-Modernism to the Jazz Impulse.* Urbana: University of Illinois Press, 1994.

Pittsburgh

August Wilson's epic decade cycle reflects the interrelated histories of black urbanites and the city of Pittsburgh. In the 1890s, the city profited from European immigration. In the words of scholar Regina Naasirah Blackburn, "They swelled its belly until it burst into a thousand furnaces and sewing machines, a thousand butcher shops and bakers' ovens, a thousand churches and hospitals and funeral parlors and money-lenders" (Blackburn). The demand for labor enticed black Southerners, who saw little chance of thriving among bigoted landowners who were the sons and daughters of slavers. Blackburn noted the disparity of welcome to nonwhites: "The city rejected them and they fled and settled along the riverbanks and under bridges in shallow, ramshackle houses made of sticks and tar-paper. They collected rags and wood. They sold the use of their muscles and their bodies. They cleaned houses and washed clothes, they shined shoes, and in quiet desperation and vengeful pride, they stole, and lived in pursuit of their own dreams. That they could breathe free, finally, and stand to meet life with the force of dignity and whatever eloquence the heart could call upon" (*Ibid.*).

In Blackburn's assessment, Wilson is a playwright-historian whose "memory embraces the Middle Passage, enslavement, torture, economic deprivation, pseudo-freedom, and human ability to endure" (*Ibid.*). He concentrates on the milieu of the 1.4 square mile Hill District, the city's first residential neighborhood near the juncture of the Allegheny and Monongahela rivers, where he spent his first twelve years. He mentions numerous architectural landmarks, including the Mayview State Hospital, which opened in 1818 as an almshouse for the poor. It developed into an insane asylum, which, according to *King Hedley II* (1999), was still in operation in 1985. Another Hill District landmark, the Ellis Hotel, once offered its hospitality to Kareem Abdul-Jabbar, Ray Charles, Miles Davis, Duke Ellington, Jackie Robinson, and Nina Simone. Damaged in fires in 1993 and 1995, the structure was demolished in 2002.

In the first years of the twentieth century, various characters in Wilson's play *Gem of the Ocean* (2003) search out the home of Aunt Ester, the district's African guru, who offers compassion and hope for forgiveness. A decade later in *Joe Turner's Come and Gone* (1988), Southern blacks converge on the city during a period of feverish expansion of steel mills, tunnels, roads, and bridges. In spite of ready employment, dispossessed blacks like Jeremy Furlow huddle under bridge spans in tarpaper shacks. In *The Piano Lesson* (1990), set in 1936 at the end of the Great Depression, Boy Willie Charles and Lymon Jackson attempt to sell a truckload of watermelons to well-heeled white residents of Squirrel Hill, an area southeast of the Hill District. After their truck breaks down, they must sleep in it to guard their melons from looters.

During the post–World War II boom, Pittsburgh's black community continues to grow. In 1948, Floyd Barton, a musician in *Seven Guitars* (1995), takes Ruby on a tour of the North Side and Workingmen's Club, a social center and fraternal lodge built in Homestead in the 1890s. When his friends look for him, they scour a variety of dives, pool rooms, and clubs. In *Fences* (1985), set in 1957, Lyons Maxson plays in a band at the Crawford Grill, a famous jazz lounge and Pittsburgh landmark that opened in 1943 at 2141 Wylie Avenue and, according to *King Hedley II*, was still hiring local singers in 1985. Lyons reports that his wife Bonnie is a laundress at Passavant Hospital twelve miles north of the city. Troy, who played baseball at Homestead Field and once faced death from pneumonia at Mercy Hospital, gets a promotion to driver and hauls garbage from Greentree, a white suburb southwest of the city center that develops across the Monongahela River out of range of blacks on the Hill.

Wilson reflects on the Hill District of his childhood, when it was "a mixed neighborhood. It was a lot of Syrians, Jews and other people who had not made their way into American society yet. They were sort of outcasts themselves, and so they lived in the community with the black folks" (Fitzgerald, p. 14). After whites fled to the suburbs, center city was 95 percent black and powerless against civic authorities, who took a from-the-top-down attitude toward decision making. Under vigorous plans for revitalizing the area, the old neighborhood was disintegrating from urban renewal and the wrecking ball. In the words of journalist Michael A. Fuoco in a special feature for the *Pittsburgh Post-Gazette:* "In essence, the heart had been torn out of the community. Longtime residents were ripped from the only neighborhood they had known…. Some likened it to a nonsurgical amputation that threatens the rest of the body" (Fuoco).

Precipitating the end of the Hill District's vitality were three days of looting and violence on April 4–6, 1968, following the murder of Dr. Martin Luther King, Jr. Wilson regretted the loss of eighty blocks and the uprooting of four hundred businesses and eight thousand residents. With a touch of nostalgia, he mourned, "I remember walking up that avenue when it would just shimmer with activity" (Reynolds, p. E1). He later surmised, "If [the Hill] had been allowed to continue to develop economically and culturally, separate from the mainstream, blacks would be in a much stronger position today. But that was destroyed, and I'm not sure if it wasn't purposeful" (O'Mahony).

Even in the area's serious decline, young Wilson found in its personal relationships and from interaction with the urban scene the strands that he eventually wove into a ten-play cycle about black American life. In *Two Trains Running* (1991), he describes the Hill District of 1969 as the property of white Jews like Hartzberger and Meyer and black entrepreneurs like West, the local mortician. Memphis Lee, the cafe owner, remarks that business has dropped off from four cases of chicken per week to less than one case. He describes his trip to the courthouse and nearby Brass Rail bar and explains how he stood on the Brady Street Bridge and dropped twenty dollars tied around a rock into the Monongahela River. After the loss of doctor, dentist, grocer, drugstores, dime store, and shoe store, he contrasts the lifeless, denuded block with Squirrel Hill, a wealthy white district too ritzy for him to open a new restaurant. Ex-con Sterling Johnson adds that he grew up in Toner Institute, a boys' orphanage operated by Capuchin fathers that fell to urban renewal. Cook and waitress Risa Thomas wonders if Hambone, a local retarded handyman, moved to East Liberty or Homestead, a black community southwest of town on the north bank of the Monongahela. Wolf runs numbers as far away as Beltz-Hoover, which lies south of town near the University of Pennsylvania. These shreds of information point to further dislocation of a once-thriving inner city population.

In *Jitney* (1982), set in 1977 at the height of urban renewal, the city appears more eager to destroy than build. There is much worth salvaging in the heart of Pittsburgh, including the Henry Buhl Planetarium and Observatory on Allegheny Avenue. After the construction of a senior citizen highrise on Bedford, a street bearing the name of a surgeon at Fort Pitt, Turnbo complains about losses to the Hill District. Authorities eagerly tear down the block, but their promise of new houses and a hospital on Logan Street go unfulfilled. Turnbo adds that the city tore down but failed to replace a section of the five-story brick Irene Kaufman Settlement House, a non-sectarian education center established in 1908 at 1835 Centre Avenue to honor the daughter of a Jewish couple, Mr. and Mrs. Henry Kaufman. The outreach offered visiting nurse care, a well baby clinic, maternity and pre-school clinics, milk stations, night classes for adults, scholarship programs, legal aid, after-school clubs, swimming lessons, and access to Emma Farm, a summer camp for underprivileged children.

The outlook for these neighborhood amenities grew dim as Pittsburgh's white leadership discounted or ignored the needs and feelings of black citizens. In *Jitney*, Jim Becker warns, "You ain't gonna see nothing but the tear-down. That's all I ever seen" (p. 84). His prediction comes true in *King Hedley II*, a bleak play set in 1985, when a collar of barbed wire fails to save the Hedley family seedbed from tension and violence. By 2000, subsequent looting and loss of population reduced the district to around 22 percent its original size and left its windows boarded and its grounds weedy and unkempt. In Wilson's last two plays, the demise of a former lively neighborhood culminates in the death of Aunt Ester, his dreamer and forecaster of the future.

See also **historical milieu**

• *Further Reading*

Barbour, David. "The Mysteries of Pittsburgh." *Entertainment Design*, Vol. 34, No. 7, July 2000.

Blackburn, Regina Naasirah. "Erupting Thunder: Race and Class in the 20th Century Plays of August Wilson." *Socialism and Democracy*, Vol. 17, No. 2.

Fitzgerald, Sharon. "August Wilson: The People's Playwright." *American Visions*, Vol. 15, No. 14, August 2000, p. 14.

Fuoco, Michael A. "Hill District Determined to Regain Lost Greatness." *Pittsburgh Post-Gazette*, April 11, 1999.

Margolis, Lynn. "Black Artists Who Defied Stereotypes." *Christian Science Monitor*, October 3, 2003, p. 19.

Norman, Tony. "Demolition Leaves Artist Scavenging for Answers." *Pittsburgh Post-Gazette*, September 24, 2002.

O'Mahony, John. "American Centurion." Manchester *Guardian*, December 14, 2002.

Power, Edward M. "Our Wonder of the Hill District." *Greater Pittsburgh* [a publication of the Chamber of Commerce], February 1932.

Reynolds, Christopher. "Mr. Wilson's Neighborhood: Playwright August Wilson No Longer Lives in Pittsburgh's Hill District, But It Is Consistently at Home in His Work." *Los Angeles Times*, July 27, 2002, p. E1.

poverty

Wilson demonstrates in his plays the direct connection between limited opportunity and poverty. The post-slavery generation requires versatile answers to money problems, for example, in 1904, Solly Two Kings's business in dog dung in *Gem of the Ocean* (2003); in *Jitney* (1982), set during the insecure urban renewal era, Doub recalls a poor man who sought a free taxi ride and meal until he could scrounge the money to pay for them. In *Joe Turner's Come and Gone* (1988), set in 1911, Seth Holly, a tinsmith and truck gardener, operates a Pittsburgh rooming house with his wife Bertha. To rise financially, he learns he must pledge their property as collateral if he is to secure a loan to open a separate business. More tenuous than Seth's financial state is that of Jeremy Furlow, a young guitarist and roomer with the Hollys. While employed as a road builder at eight dollars per week, Jeremy loses his job because he refused to kick back fifty cents, over 6 percent of his wages. Reduced to beggary, he withdraws to a hovel under a city bridge.

Lack of money for funerals and burials in 1948 fills the pauper section of Greenwood cemetery with seven friends and relatives of characters in *Seven Guitars* (1995). Among the unfortunate dead is protagonist Floyd Barton's recently departed mother,

Maude Avery Barton, who lies "in the poor-people part" (p. 50). In a quiet speech in the denouement, he seethes with frustration and anger that his ambition for a good life collapses to nothing. He states his belief that "I'm supposed to have. Whatever it is. Have something" (p. 81). He asks that the cold world supply him "a little shelter from it" (*Ibid.*). In 1969 in *Two Trains Running* (1991), the situation remains unchanged. Poverty and community losses deprive Hambone of a worthy casket, rob Cigar Annie of a residence, and cause Bubba Boy to steal a dress from Surrey's in which to bury his girlfriend, who died from a drug overdose.

In 1957, need entraps Jim and Lucille Bono and the Maxson family in *Fences* (1985), a title symbolic of the walling off of the Hill District from the city's prosperity. Working as a garbage collector, Troy Maxson, like Sam in *The Janitor* (1985), puts a face to the featureless dray laborer who disposes of the city's detritus. Summing up his situation with a familiar adage, he worries about a leaking roof, claims to have a bank balance of only $73.22, and exaggerates his cashless situation with an old folk saying, "Ain't got a pot to piss in or a window to throw it out of" (p. 9). Troy surmises that, if he had achieved his dream of becoming a professional baseball player, he might have lived more comfortably and enjoyed the luxuries common to white homes. Corroborating Troy's yearnings for a better home are his friend Bono's memories of a residence on Logan Street, comprised of "two rooms with the outhouse in the back" (p. 7). He recalls cold wind in winter and ponders why he "stayed down there for six long years" (*Ibid.*).

In an effort to rescue his characters from victimization, Wilson portrays downtrodden ghetto dwellers as ingenious survivors, a drive that fuels *Ma Rainey's Black Bottom* (1985), set in Chicago in 1927. Her backup musicians battle Jim Crow inequities and butt up against the stone wall of white-owned business, yet continue to ply their trade and vie for the best gigs. Two decades later, King Hedley, the resilient old chicken slaughterer in *Seven Guitars*, makes his living peddling candy, cigarettes, and homemade chicken sandwiches from a wire basket. His friend Vera makes and sells Mother's Day flowers constructed from red and white crepe paper. *Jitney*, set in 1977, reveals blacks living in an integrated society, yet being no better off financially. To survive, the main characters, a brotherhood of cabbies, form and operate their own gypsy cab service. By 1985 in *King Hedley II* (1999), the title character has only a janitor's job to aim for. He deals in stolen GE refrigerators and robs a jewelry store to start him on the way to a legitimate business in video rentals, an escapist amusement that offers blacks a respite from poverty.

See also **achievement, blues, Great Migration, humor, injustice, opportunity, powerlessness, racism, victimization, violence**

• *Further Reading*

Lowe, John. "Wake-up Call from Watts." *World & I*, Vol. 13, No. 5, May 1998, p. 250.
McCord, Keryl E. "The Challenge of Change." *African American Review*, Vol. 31, No. 4, Winter 1997, pp. 601–609.

powerlessness

The theme of powerlessness permeates Wilson's plays as black characters attempt to overcome the losses caused by enslavement and by prejudice that relegates African Americans to manual labor and low economic and social status. Legal hassles precipitate the flight of Citizen Barlow, Solly Two Kings, and other blacks from the relentless constable Caesar in *Gem of the Ocean* (2003). A contemporary, Jeremy Furlow, rejects workplace graft and loses his job building roads. Wining Boy Charles, the piano player in *The Piano Lesson* (1990), comprehends the corrupt workings of law that favor whites. He grumbles, "Now that's the difference between the colored man and the white man. The colored man can't fix nothing with the law" (p. 38).

Memphis Lee, the cafe owner in *Two Trains Running* (1991), is one of Wilson's survivors of black disenfranchisement by more powerful Southern whites. Memphis narrates his ouster from Jackson, Mississippi, after Jim Stovall hired men to knife and emasculate Memphis's mule, burn his fields, and force him to flee. After prospering in the cafe business in Pittsburgh, he challenges urban renewal, a faceless enemy that gradually wears down the resilience of Hill District residents. Although Memphis holds a deed to his land and retains the train schedule listing the times that he can return and reclaim his acreage, he takes no action on exiting from Pittsburgh and reestablishing his old life in the racist South.

Lacking the power and sophistication of the entrenched white society, blacks feel not much better off than they did before the emancipation of slaves. An overwhelming obstacle is the rapid growth of cities, which threatens Jim Becker, Youngblood's employer and the owner of a doomed Pittsburgh car service that stands in the way of a highway project. Because of the ramshackle businesses and low quality housing in which blacks subsist, city planners offhandedly mark them for destruction as eyesores and obstacles to progress. The economic impasse of white-controlled business in *Ma Rainey's Black Bottom* (1985) leaves Levee Green no room to negotiate the price of his compositions with Mel Sturdyvant, an elitist music magnate. The disillusion that robs Levee of an outlet for his talents crushes his dreams, causing him to lash out and murder Toledo, an innocent bystander, with a plunge of Levee's knife into his back. Youngblood, the family man and cabbie in *Jitney* (1982), carries on a telephone conversation with Harper, a loan officer who hampers the purchase of a home under the GI Bill. He demands a title search, paperwork that raises the price of Youngblood's down payment on a house. Another legal impediment of modern enslavement is incarceration in the workhouse or jail, in an asylum, and on the chain gang, which victimizes Floyd Barton in *Seven Guitars* (1995), Gabe and Lyons Maxson in *Fences* (1985), Herald Loomis in *Joe Turner's Come and Gone* (1988), the title figure in *King Hedley II* (1999), and Boy Willie Charles and Lymon Jackson, both former inmates of Parchman Farm in *The Piano Lesson*.

The effect of control by the outside world impacts domestic scenarios. Work for a white bureaucracy causes a negative reaction in *Fences*, in which the protagonist, Troy Maxson, develops into a hard master. Like the overseers in the antebellum South, he uses fear for his son Cory's future as a reason for dominating the boy's free time, forcing him to answer "yessir" rather than "yeah," and overriding his career decision to accept a football scholarship to college. As an explanation for outright tyranny, Troy thunders, "I'm the boss around here. I do the only saying what counts" (p. 36). The coercion of family offers Troy an outlet for his frustrations, but places his wife and children in a similar stranglehold. To the detriment of marriage and the family, the vicious cycle perpetuates a subtext of survival of the fittest.

See also **Ma Rainey, victimization, violence**

- *Further Reading*

Maufort, Marc, ed. *Staging Difference: Cultural Pluralism in American Theatre and Drama*. New York: Peter Lang, 1995.
McDonough, Carla J. *Staging Masculinity: Male Identity in Contemporary American Drama*. Jefferson, N.C.: McFarland, 1997.
Vorlicky, Robert. *Act Like a Man: Challenging Masculinities in American Drama*. Ann Arbor: University of Michigan Press, 1995.

promiscuity

In August Wilson's fictional milieu, the merchandizing of sex is common knowledge. In the Hill District of Pittsburgh, women peddle their bodies as a means of earning a living. Unlike the casual attitude toward coupling exhibited by Grace and Lymon Jackson's mother in *The Piano Lesson* (1990), Alberta in *Fences* (1985), Ruby and WillaMae in *Seven Guitars* (1995), Molly Cunningham and Jeremy Furlow's woman in *Joe Turner's Come and Gone* (1988), Dussie Mae in *Ma Rainey's Black Bottom* (1985), Wolf's greedy woman in *Two Trains Running* (1991), Rosie and Susan McKnight in *Jitney* (1982), and Ruby in *King Hedley II* (1999), outright prostitution is a business that offers women more opportunities to turn youth and beauty into profit. Seth Holly, a conservative innkeeper in *Joe Turner's Come and Gone*, rejects prostitutes from his boardinghouse, a family business with a solid reputation built over two generations. In *Jitney*, Cigar Annie is dispossessed after the building she lives in is condemned. Two years later, when authorities move her furniture out to the sidewalk, she stops traffic on Robert Street by cussing and raising her dress at passing cars. She claims that sex has been her only commodity since age twelve. After several examinations at Mayview State Hospital, an almshouse for the poor and asylum for the insane, she proved herself sane. Turnbo quips that nobody is interested in Annie's sexual favors, but if Pearline offered her body, "That be another thing" (p. 23). In fairness to Annie's predicament, Turnbo describes her peculiar behavior as "sending out an S. O. S.," a metaphor that pictures her flapping dress tail as a semaphore flag (*Ibid.*).

Other arrangements are more pragmatic than entrepreneurial. In a straightforward exchange of sex for companionship and additional income, an unnamed woman in *Seven Guitars* shares her Clark Street residence with Canewell, who accepts the arrangement day by day and keeps his trunk packed in case a better offer crops up. Troy Maxson, the protagonist of *Fences*, maintains a polygamous lifestyle by supporting his wife Rose and son Cory while spending his free time with Alberta, mother of his infant daughter Raynell. When Alberta's unforeseen death in childbirth ends the adulterous relationship, Troy has little choice but to merge his illicit offspring with his legal family. Ironically, for his affront to Rose's sense of decency, she welcomes the baby girl and ousts Troy from her bed.

See also **women**

• *Further Reading*

Bennett, Weyman. "Hill District Blues." *Socialist Review*, January 2003.

racism

Wilson's characters experience bigotry and prejudicial treatment that often results in economic oppression, injustice, and subsistence in bleak social and familial settings, as with constable Caesar's stalking of black felons in *Gem of the Ocean* (2003) and Herald Loomis's flight from a Southern chain gang to a nomadic existence in *Joe Turner's Come and Gone* (1988). In *The Piano Lesson* (1990), Wining Boy Charles, a former itinerant pianist, sings about six months of work for "the rascal Joe Herrin":

> He fed me old corn dodgers
> They was hard as any rock
> My tooth is all got loosened
> And my knees begin to knock
> That was the kind of hash I got
> In the state of Arkansas [p. 47].

The life of the blues star is no better. For the vainglorious title character in *Ma Rainey's Black Bottom* (1985), a white cab driver's refusal to rescue her from a traffic collision sparks out-of-control anger. After Ma knocks him to the ground, her white manager Irvin must smooth over the legalities of public affray with a sop to the ruffled investigating officer. The use of a bribe to obtain justice discloses that whites advance from racism to other forms of moral and ethical malfeasance.

Wilson freights *Seven Guitars* (1995) with repeated accusations of police corruption and scapegoating of blacks. Canewell, who doubts that the Jim Crow era will end, regrets visiting Chicago, where police lodged him in the Cook County Jail for thirty days for playing the harmonica and soliciting on the street without a license. When he tried to extricate himself from arrest, the charge escalated to disturbing the peace, loitering, resisting arrest, and disrespect for the law. In commentary on retribution for prejudice against blacks, King Hedley states with the authority of the prophet Isaiah, "Every abomination shall be brought low," a veiled threat to white persecutors (p. 24). Near the play's end, Louise interprets the disappearance of the loot stolen from Metro Finance as a police trick: "They shoot the man in the back. Take the money out his hand and put it in their pocket" (p. 97).

Racism is the source of long-nursed acrimony and plans for reprisals. In *Two Trains Running* (1991), Memphis Lee, the likable owner of a Pittsburgh eatery, summarizes his flight north as the result of racist persecution. Twice he states that "they"— henchmen of Jim Stovall — ran him out of Jackson, Mississippi, in 1931. The attackers, who killed and emasculated his mule and burned his crops, forced Memphis to abandon his acreage. He describes living in Natchez for a few years, then leaving the South behind. Still stoking resentment, he plots the purchase of a rifle for a foray against Stovall, who plotted Memphis's ouster. Although Memphis gives no sign of settling the old grudge, his memories and occasional mention of his plan offer him everyday release from the pain of racial injustice.

Balancing repeated examples of white-on-black bias are signs that times are changing and racism easing, notably, Cory Maxson's rise in *Fences* (1985) from son of a wannabe baseball player and nobody garbage collector to high school football athlete scouted by a North Carolina recruiter. Louise, the landlady in *Seven Guitars*, adds to Wilson's commentary on improvements to African American life by urging King Hedley to seek medical help for tuberculosis at the newly integrated sanitarium rather than die without proper treatment. Another example of the decline in overt racism taps Floyd Barton, the doomed blues musician, who rejoices in a letter from the white-owned Savoy Record Company urging him to return to Chicago on March 10, 1948, to issue a second disk. To Floyd, the envelope is an ego booster for its address beginning with "Mr. Floyd Barton," a mundane gesture of respect from a white typist who may not have been aware of the singer's race (p. 10). Floyd exults to his girlfriend Vera Dotson, "You get you a hit record and the white folks call you Mister" (*Ibid.*).

See also **Jim Stovall, Mel Sturdyvant**

• *Further Reading*

Maufort, Marc, ed. *Staging Difference: Cultural Pluralism in American Theatre and Drama.* New York: Peter Lang, 1995.

McDonough, Carla J. *Staging Masculinity: Male Identity in Contemporary American Drama.* Jefferson, N.C.: McFarland, 1997.

Vorlicky, Robert. *Act Like a Man: Challenging Masculinities in American Drama.* Ann Arbor: University of Michigan Press, 1995.

railroad

The value of the railroad to blacks is a common element in August Wilson's plays, in which iron rails symbolize freedom and a life's journey. He depicts trains as cheap and reliable transportation, a ready egress from difficult situations, a source of jobs, and a standard element of storytelling and blues lyrics, such as Bynum Walker's song about the Illinois Central in *Joe Turner's Come and Gone* (1988). To Doaker Charles in *The Piano Lesson* (1990), a twenty-seven-year veteran of track labor and dining car cooking, and to Doub, a widower and another rail worker with twenty-seven years of service in *Jitney* (1982), trains offer steady employment and the promise of a pension. Doaker summarizes the needs of travelers to visit the sick, avoid trouble, meet someone, or find a more satisfying life. He sings out the route that takes him on a regular sweep of points between Pittsburgh, Mississippi, and the return loop north. He exults, "It's going to get where it's going…. The train don't never stop. It'll come back every time" (p. 19). When Doaker's nephew Boy Willie decides to return to Mississippi, his friend Lymon Jackson suggests the train rather than Lymon's unreliable truck.

Rail service and the Greyhound bus became the main modes of transportation during the Great Migration of blacks to the North, but the bus never achieved the panache of the train. A pervasive legend in *The Piano Lesson*, the railroad once represented a source of hard manual labor and a means of fleeing the slave-owning South and its post-slavery cruelties. Doaker describes the hardship of laying track for the Yazoo Delta link between Clarksdale and Sunflower County, Mississippi, and takes pride in his and Wining Boy's contribution to making the Yellow Dog a reality. The Charles men sing:

> When you marry, marry a railroad man, oh-ah
> When you marry, marry a railroad man, well
> Everyday Sunday, dollar in your hand oh-ah
> Everyday Sunday, dollar in your hand well [p. 40].

Like the sacred piano of the Charles family, the iron rails continue to bear the ghosts of men who died attempting to flee Mississippi's racism. The story of those lives given for black dignity and emancipation empower future generations. Contrasting their admiration of a reliable mode of travel are the words of Holloway, the hard-edged philosopher in *Two Trains Running* (1991), who contends that the railroad is just another example of exploitation of black labor for a utility owned and managed by whites.

Wilson also chooses rail travel as a significant image. In reference to human life, he summed up his philosophy in *Two Trains Running* in terms of parallel trains, symbols of life and death. One character, Memphis Lee, the owner of the declining cafe, exits Mississippi after the racist Jim Stovall slew and emasculated Memphis's mule and torched his crops. Memphis comforts himself on his flight to Natchez and north to Pittsburgh by recalling that he only has to access the depot for one of two daily rail journeys back home. The connection between his new life and the old steadies and reassures him that, until the time that he is able to return and reclaim his old farmland, the train will continue to make the life-sustaining circuit.

- *Further Reading*

Thompson, Maxine. "Writer's Watershed." *The Writer*, Vol. 110, No. 11, November 1997, pp. 5–6.

Wang, Qun. *An In-Depth Study of the Major Plays of African American Playwright August Wilson: Vernacularizing the Blues on Stage*. Vol. 6 of *Black Studies*. Lewiston, Ont.: Edwin Mellen Press, 1999.

Willis, John C. *Forgotten Time: The Yazoo-Mississippi Delta after the Civil War*. Charlottesville: University Press of Virginia, 2000.

Wolfe, Peter. *August Wilson*. New York: Twayne, 1999.

Rainey, Gertrude Malissa Nix Pridgett "Ma"

Renowned contralto blues artist Ma Rainey (1886–1939), the legendary "Mother of the Blues," serves Wilson as an example of a talented black singer whom whites exploit. The daughter of minstrels from Columbus, Georgia, she liberated blues from chain gangs and rural cotton fields. She got her start in 1900 with the "Bunch of Blackberries" performing at the Springer Opera House and, two years later, incorporated blues into her repertory as leader of the Rabbit Foot Minstrels. At age eighteen, she and husband William Rainey launched a cabaret act as Ma and Pa Rainey, a favorite with Southern audiences. Backing up her raspy-voiced stage performances of ribald lyrics and folk blues were makeshift combos, including slide guitar and jug bands, a link to rural black amusements.

Ma divorced Pa Rainey and, in 1923, continued her rise to become one of the first African American blues stars to snag a recording contract. She spread her influence over American stage music as the prime female performer for Paramount Records, which sold her ninety-two recorded songs by mail and in music stores managed by blacks, a growing venue for the white-owned music industry. Backed by the Theater Owners' Booking Association, she toured large cities by private bus and appeared on the vaudeville stage in the South and Midwest. At a height of stardom in 1926, she popularized "Moonshine Blues," "Bo-Weevil Blues," and "See See Rider," models of rural Southern themes and style. Her stage act flourished until her retirement at the height of the Great Depression. She was responsible for the discovery and coaching of jazz star Bessie Smith.

See also **blues**

• *Further Reading*

Hine, Darlene Clark, et al., eds. *Black Women in America: An Historical Encyclopedia.* Bloomington: Indiana University Press, 1993.
Reich, Howard. "The Real Ma Rainey the Mother of the Blues Was More Than a Flashy Character." *Chicago Tribune,* June 30, 1997, p. 1.
Rich, Frank. "Theater: 'Ma Rainey's Black Bottom.'" *New York Times,* April 11, 1984.

Rainey, Ma (fictional)

August Wilson's version of Ma Rainey in *Ma Rainey's Black Bottom* (1985) exalts the Mother of the Blues for remaining faithful to her black supporters. He pictures her from two points of view: as the first female professional blues artist preserving the integrity of black music and as a self-important bisexual diva flanked by a coterie of flunkies and hangers-on, particularly Sylvester and Dussie Mae, the lovers she treats like children. At the head of the aging troupe is Cutler, the guitarist, trombonist, and bandleader, who acquiesces to Ma's autocracy by declaring, "It's what Ma say that counts" (p. 37). In the midst of her concert schedule in the South, she abruptly ended the tour to appear at the Paramount recording studio in Chicago, where she anticipates a session in March 1927 at 1:00 P.M.

The playwright characterizes Ma as a paradox of power and powerlessness. A renowned African American blues artist, she is an abusive, self-important star. Although short and heavy and bothered by sore feet, she remains regal in posture and manner and in her insistence on being called "Madame Rainey" (p. 49). Within a single scene, Ma can be dynamic and willful, yet victimized by whites. She browbeats her back-up musicians and refuses to kowtow to a white producer and white agent. Her message is straightforward: "What you all say don't count with me. You understand?" (p. 63). Past experience with the dismissive white world keeps her wary and on edge. She synthesizes in one line the gist of white-on-black exploitation: "As soon as they get my voice down on them recording machines, then it's just like if I'd be some whore and they roll over and put their pants on. Ain't got no use for me then" (p. 79). To prevent future steamrolling, she strikes first and hard.

Ma's imperious persona rules the drama. She dislikes the North and demands from whites a list of personal services that include a heated studio, bottled Coca-Cola from a deli, and a microphone for the stuttering Sylvester Brown, who speaks the introduction to her recording. Balancing her tantrums are soothing words to the stammerer, whom she coaxes, mother-like, with "You take your time, you'll get it right" (p. 76). In reference to her intuitive skill, she declares, "Ma listens to her heart. Ma listens to the voice inside her" (p. 63). In contrast to these moments of motherliness, Wilson posits that the climate of discord that follows Ma like a black cloud is detrimental to all who serve her. Her extended clashes with music promoters leave the four-man back-up band with nothing to do but amuse themselves in conversation that escalates to jazz trumpeter Levee Green's arguments with the pianist Toledo, whom he stabs in the back.

Wilson bases the plot on an actual recording session at Chicago's Paramount studios. Wearied by the constant undercurrent, Ma knows that both whites and blacks can and will undermine her stardom. To Levee, she's what critic Keith Clark calls "a Mammy figure, an operative of the white power structure" (Clark, p. 110). To recording companies, she's just the incumbent voice they record and peddle. She can entertain at the manager's dinner party, but not sit at the table with his white guests. With her own race, she fights the classic battle of older savant with Levee, an up-and-coming black contender. Personally galling to Ma is his flirtation with her favorite, Dussie Mae. On the professional level, when he offers her theme song, "Ma Rainey's Black Bottom," some hot licks from the latest dance band music, she knows that she will someday pall on the ears of the audience and that egotistical comers like Levee will jockey into her vacated spot.

See also **blues, Gertrude Malissa Nix Pridgett "Ma" Rainey, women**

• *Further Reading*

Adell, Sandra. "Speaking of Ma Rainey/Talking about the Blues," in *May All Your Fences Have Gates: Essays on the Drama of August Wilson.* Iowa City: University of Iowa Press, 1994.

Bigsby, C. W. E., ed. *Modern American Drama, 1945–1990.* Cambridge: Cambridge University Press, 1992.

Clark, Keith. *Black Manhood in James Baldwin, Ernest J. Gaines, and August Wilson.* Urbana: University of Illinois Press, 2002.

Wang, Qun. *An In-Depth Study of the Major Plays of African American Playwright August Wilson: Vernacularizing the Blues on Stage.* Vol. 6 of *Black Studies.* Lewiston, Ont.: Edwin Mellen Press, 1999.

Willis, Susan. *Specifying: Black Women Writing the American Experience.* Racine: University of Wisconsin Press, 1989.

reclamation

Reclamation is a resonant theme in August Wilson's ten-play cycle on African Americana. Characters who have lost home, family, belongings, and self-respect through financial struggle and injustice retain their hopes of returning to their roots. Examples permeate the playwright's decade cycle — Citizen Barlow, a petitioner for redemption in *Gem of the Ocean* (2003), the ex-con Booster Becker and the alcoholic Fielding in *Jitney* (1982), and Herald Loomis, the seeker of his wife Martha in *Joe Turner's Come and Gone* (1988), who redeems himself with an act of self-mutilation. In 1936, the possibility of reclamation offers the Charles family of *The Piano Lesson* (1990) a viable hope through an embrace of spirituality and family and community history. Two decades later in *Fences* (1985), Troy Maxson continues to shape his life around his job as a garbage collector, the kind of job an ex-con can expect to hold. The pattern of rehabilitated felons toting the city's refuse continues to hold true in 1985 in *King Hedley II*, in which the title ex-con struggles to locate a post-prison job, even janitor.

The return of prisoners to normal life is a recurring motif in Wilson's plays, as with Booster Becker's failed reunion with his father in *Jitney* after Booster serves a twenty-year sentence for murder. In *Two Trains Running* (1991), Sterling Johnson leaves the penitentiary with his manhood and ambition intact. While dining on soul food in Memphis Lee's center-city cafe, Sterling flirts with the cook and waitress Risa Thomas, catches up on gossip in the black community, and ponders driving a Cadillac, buying a pistol, and landing a job that will preface eventual ownership of a night club. With a more sensible outlook, Memphis has thrived on hard work and frugality. He maintains the option to return to Jackson, Mississippi, to reclaim the acreage he fled after Jim Stovall had his hirelings slice the belly of Memphis's mule and set fire to his farmland. In the safety of Pittsburgh, Memphis was content to buy a building that allows him to rent out living quarters and to run a popular diner.

One of the most enigmatic of Wilson's reclaimed characters is King Hedley, the oversized Haitian poultry-killer in *Seven Guitars* (1995). As the name suggests, the character is a physically violent brute whose thinking is misdirected by paradoxical scriptures. Relegated to confused sermons and food selling on the street, he labors to elevate himself from the bottom rung of the social order to a "big man" (p. 86). Hampering his reclamation of self-esteem are the harsh criticism of his teacher, Miss Manning, to "you little black-as-sin niggers" and the sudden death of Hedley's abusive father (*Ibid.*). Without an opportunity to make up to the old man for filial shortcomings, Hedley "dragged him with me these years across an ocean" and arrives in Pittsburgh laden with regret (p. 87).

Lacking a sane hold on the present, Hedley mutters loosely about his evil-tempered father and clutches at shreds of promise in the lives of black leaders Toussaint L'Ouverture and Marcus Garvey and boxer Joe Louis. Hedley's grand vision of the future comes late in his life, when his hopes of siring a messiah cling to the sexual promise of the temptress Ruby. Out of charity for the lonely old sandwich peddler, she couples with him and plans to deceive him that her unborn infant is the child of his seed. As though making restitution to God for past lapses, Hedley returns to church, agrees to be tested for tuberculosis, then, drunk on moonshine, sinks into Sunday afternoon escapism. His brief reclamation ends in a delusional machete swinging by which he murders Floyd Barton, an unsuspecting friend. The explosive conclusion to the play gave the playwright ample loose ends to tie in the sequel, *King Hedley II* (1999), in which the man who thinks of himself as the elder Hedley's son inherits his machete and relives his confusion and violence.

See also **Fielding, Herald Loomis, parenthood**

• *Further Reading*

McDonough, Carla J. *Staging Masculinity: Male Identity in Contemporary American Drama*. Jefferson, N.C.: McFarland, 1997.
Taylor, Regina. "That's Why They Call It the Blues." *American Theatre*, Vol. 13, No. 4, April 1996, pp. 18–23.
Weber, Bruce. "Sculpturing a Play into Existence." *New York Times*, March 24, 1996, p. H7.

religion

August Wilson notes in his plays the importance of folk religion as a refuge for troubled, frustrated people. As Eugene D. Genovese explains in *Roll, Jordan, Roll* (1976), adaptation of blacks in the Western Hemisphere required the "developing of a religion within a religion in a nation within a nation" (Genovese, p. 281). Worship became a normal part of existence, notably to Citizen Barlow, a seeker of Aunt Ester's wisdom in a Pittsburgh rooming house in *Gem of the Ocean* (2003), and to the boarders who shout and dance at Seth and Bertha Holly's rooming house in *Joe Turner's Come and Gone* (1988). Against a social backdrop interwoven with differing opinions on godhood and sanctity, the characters in these plays manage to forge a workable alternative to white Christian dogma, which the German scholar Friedrich Nietzsche typified as a self-mocking, self-mutilating philosophy that rid slaves of hatred and the urge to revolt.

Sin pricks the consciences of characters and causes them to think on God, as with the title character's observations on the godlessness of murderers in *King Hedley II* (1999). In *Gem of the Ocean*, Aunt Ester's seance directs Barlow to purify himself of wrong by living out the myth of an undersea graveyard of black captives who did not survive transportation to the Atlantic Coast. In *Joe Turner's Come and Gone*, the performance of the juba dance releases dissension and personal griefs by allowing each participant to frolic and shout while embracing self and an individual vision of deity. Through the success of worshippers at adapting to their African roots, Wilson implies the failure of Christianity to nurture and satisfy black Americans, particularly males. The theme of religious alienation reaches bold expression in *Ma Rainey's Black Bottom* (1985), in which jazz trumpeter Levee Green claims: "God hate niggers! Hate them with all the fury in his heart" (p. 98). Levee declares that God listens only to the prayers of whites, a charge that echoes through Wilson's personal credo.

Wilson's characters find humor in demythologizing religion. In *The Piano Lesson*

(1990), Wining Boy Charles makes fun of an exhibitionist in Spear, North Carolina, who aggrandizes himself by reliving Christ's final meal and ride into Jerusalem on a mule, then gives up role-playing before being nailed to a cross. In *Seven Guitars* (1995), characters ridicule the venality of white religion. The landlady Louise returns from a funeral to sing about offering her "cabbage" to the parson, who expresses his thanks by giving her the church collection (p. 1). Characters agree that the minister, Reverend Thompson, spoke pretty words over the deceased, blues guitarist Floyd Barton. In a blend of humor and commentary on pulpit ministers, Red Carter observes that Thompson "makes it where you want to die just to have somebody talk over you like that" (p. 2). Canewell replies that Thompson's oratory "sounds like he reading from the Bible even when he ain't" (*Ibid.*). Later, Canewell remarks on his own call to preach, but defends his secular life with a humorous truism, "God speak in a whisper and the devil shout" (p. 45). Because of his shaping of a wry metaphor, Canewell appears less blasphemous and self-damning than Levee and Herald Loomis.

Religion is the source of heated discussion among characters, who frequently debate the strength of Satan, adversary of the almighty. In a distortion of scripture syncretized with voodoo and African animism, King Hedley, the Haitian sandwich seller in *Seven Guitars* (1995), explains to Canewell that Jesus was a copper-skinned man with wooly hair who inherited his traits from Mary, his Moabite mother. Canewell, exasperated with outlandish historical revisionism, reminds Hedley that the original exchange was about Jesus's questionable decision to raise Lazarus from the dead, not about racial identity. The gentle humor of their dialogue attests to the oral nature of black theology, primarily because of the speakers' limited education and experience with bible reading and formal worship. The scene also stresses the unanswered questions about ethnic identity that override quibbles over the nature of good and evil.

Wilson incorporates church-going with escapism from domestic misery. In *Fences* (1985), religion becomes the late-in-life bastion for Rose Lee Maxson, who loses heart after her husband Troy absorbs himself in blatant adultery. A patient, but wronged wife after eighteen years of marriage, she accepts his illegitimate daughter Raynell to rear. Near the play's end, Rose carries Raynell toward the church bake sale. As though abdicating her role as woman of the house, Rose refuses to divulge the time when she will return. Long bereft of love for his wife, Troy interprets the abandonment in monetary terms. He confides snidely to Jim Bono of Rose's embrace of religion as just another congregation member fattening the wallets of preachers.

See also **biblical allusions, King Hedley, juba, Prophet Samuel, supernatural, Bynum Walker**

• *Further Reading*

Clark, Keith. *Black Manhood in James Baldwin, Ernest J. Gaines, and August Wilson.* Urbana: University of Illinois Press, 2002.
Genovese, Eugene D. *Roll, Jordan, Roll.* New York: Vintage, 1976.
Pereira, Kim. *August Wilson and the African-American Odyssey.* Urbana: University of Illinois Press, 1995.
Shannon, Sandra G. "The Good Christian's Come and Gone: The Shifting Role of Christianity in August Wilson's Plays." *MELUS*, Vol. 16, No. 3, 1989, pp. 127–142.

Wang, Qun. *An In-Depth Study of the Major Plays of African American Playwright August Wilson: Vernacularizing the Blues on Stage.* Vol. 6 of *Black Studies.* Lewiston, Ont.: Edwin Mellen Press, 1999.

Rena

A restaurant employee, accounting student, and the unmarried mother of two-year-old Jesse, Rena echoes the female version of work-related challenges shared by male cabbies in *Jitney* (1982). The playwright depicts her frustration from assuming too many responsibilities, a nod to females that he repeats in the portrayal of Rose Lee Maxson, the embittered housewife in *Fences* (1985), Berniece Charles, the hard-working widow and single mother in *The Piano Lesson* (1990), and Tonya Hedley, the despairing pregnant wife of the title figure in *King Hedley II* (1999). Rena is the girlfriend of Youngblood, a Vietnam veteran and jitney driver, and the sister of Peaches, whom Youngblood appears to court. Rena violates his rule about bothering him at work for a one-on-one settlement of rumors of betrayal. In her own defense, she asserts that she spends money only on the family rather than on whims such as "some nail polish or some Afro Sheen" (p. 34). To justify her suspicions, she charges, "It ain't like you ain't got no track record," but she refrains from airing past animosities (p. 73).

As described by the meddling, eavesdropping driver Turnbo, Rena is a classy woman who deserves the respect and love of a steady man. She quarrels with her lover because she wants an honest relationship. From a mature perspective, she can say, "I'm not seventeen no more. I have responsibilities" (p. 75). Their rocky domestic arrangement comes close to foundering because he perceives the responsibility of buying a home for his family as man's work. In the vacuum that surrounds his mysterious car trips with Peaches to Penn Hills, Rena's imagination, goaded by Turnbo's intrusive gossip, builds rumor into unfounded suspicions of disloyalty and adultery. The text implies that women, who exist out of the loop of neighborhood events by staying home and tending to family matters, are less capable of sifting truth from falsehood.

See also **women, Youngblood**

• *Further Reading*

Jones, Chris. "Homeward Bound." *American Theatre*, Vol. 16, No. 9, November 1999.
Rawson, Christopher. "Stage Review: Wilson Polishes 'Jitney' in Richer, Longer Production." *Pittsburgh Post-Gazette*, November 22, 1998.
Saltzman, Simon, and Nicole Plett. "'Jitney' at Crossroads." *U.S. 1 Newspaper*, April 16, 1997.

Richards, Lloyd

The head of the Yale School of Drama, director of the Eugene O'Neill Center, and mentor to August Wilson, Lloyd Richards (1924–   ) is a behind-the-scenes enabler of African American drama. He was the revered black mentor of Lorraine

Hansberry and the first black to direct a Broadway play. In 1959, he helped her groom *A Raisin in the Sun* (1958) for its Broadway debut. The play won the first New York Drama Critics' Circle award presented to a black dramatist. A quarter century later, he refined and tightened the action and stagecraft of Wilson's first five plays.

Richards's role was largely psychological—"to stimulate, provoke, and to get [Wilson] to function at the top of his ability" (Pettingill, p. 199). As a result, Wilson and Richards's collaboration strengthened the decade cycle's dramatic structure while maintaining the playwright's lyric gifts. In enthusiasm for Wilson's skill, Richards stated, "There has been a lack of material on the library shelves on black theatre and a lack of theatre by blacks. All that is beginning to change. Having August's body of work in there leads people to an examination of theatre and an examination of themselves in theatre" (O'Mahoney).

With Richards's aid, in 1984, Wilson began retuning his original script of *Ma Rainey's Black Bottom* (1985) into a major breakthrough in black stagecraft, the first in a quarter century. The director summarized his role in the text: "Sometimes people think they know things that they don't consciously articulate. And so my job becomes to get all of that out of him" (Backalenick, p. 18). The synergy of writer and director proved profitable for both men. When Richards began rehearsals, his empathy for Wilson's characters seemed intuitive enough for the playwright to relax and let the director do his job. As a result of high quality direction, critics lauded Wilson for his blend of wisdom, wit, and emotional power with raucous political and sexual gibes.

Wilson grew so fond of his mentor that he thought of him not only as a trainer but also as "Pop," a father figure. He values his colleague for his empathy: "It's Lloyd's understanding of the characters that lets me trust him. At times he knows the characters better than I do" (Freedman, p. 80). Richards returned the compliment by lauding Wilson's freshness and freedom from literary rules and scholarly expectations. Richards directed *Fences* (1985), *The Piano Lesson* (1990), and *Two Trains Running* (1991), the year he resigned as director of Yale Repertory Theatre. In 1995, he also directed the filming of *The Piano Lesson* for CBS-TV, but health problems forced him to surrender the stage direction of *Seven Guitars* (1995) to Walter Dallas.

See also **Chronology of Life and Works, August Wilson**

• *Further Reading*

Backalenick, Irene. "A Lesson from Lloyd Richards." *Theater Week*, April 15, 1990, pp. 16–19.

Fitzgerald, Sharon. "Lloyd Richards: The Griot Wears a Watch." *American Visions*, Vol. 13, No. 4, August-September 1998.

Fleming, John. "A Casting Call." *St. Petersburg Times*, March 7, 1997, pp. D1–D2.

Freedman, Samuel G. "Wilson's New Fences Nurtures a Partnership." *New York Times*, May 5, 1985, p. 80.

Ifill, Gwen. "American Shakespeare." *PBS News*, April 6, 2001.

O'Mahony, John. "American Centurion." Manchester *Guardian*, December 14, 2002.

Pettengill, Richard. "Alternatives … Opposites … Convergences: An Interview with Lloyd Richards," in *August Wilson: A Casebook*. New York: Garland, 1994.

Shannon, Sandra G. "From Lorraine Hanasberry to August Wilson: An Interview with Lloyd Richards." *Callaloo*, Vol. 14, No. 1, 1991, pp. 124–135.
Sheward, David. "Seven Guitars." *Back Stage*, Vol. 37, No. 14, April 5, 1996, p. 5.

Robinson, Jackie

Like Ma Rainey, black baseball star Jackie Robinson (1919–1972), the son of California sharecroppers, is a real hero of African American history whose example inspired other budding athletes to compete with whites. After becoming the first black athlete to letter in baseball, football, and track and field at UCLA, he led protests against military racism while serving in the army during World War II. From the Negro American League, he advanced to the Brooklyn Dodgers in 1945 and, four years later, was named the National League Most Valuable Player. To Troy Maxson, protagonist of *Fences* (1985), Robinson's entry into baseball's major leagues in 1947 rankles rather than uplifts because his break into professional sports came too late to help Maxson achieve his own athletic ambitions.

See also **black athletes**

• *Further Reading*

Appiah, Kwame Anthony, and Henry Louis Gates, Jr., eds. *Africana*. New York: Perseus Books, 1999.

rooster

Wilson makes numerous references to roosters as the irrepressible egotists of the barnyard and symbols of masculinity, for example, in jazz trumpeter Levee Green's strutting, self-adulatory crowing, and sexual overtures of his "red rooster" to Dussie Mae's "brown hen" in *Ma Rainey's Black Bottom* (1985) (p. 82). In *Fences* (1985), Troy Maxson recalls courting Rose and deciding to place a banty rooster in his backyard to watch for men threatening his possession and control of a new and beautiful wife. The strongly male behavior of a watch bird flapping his wings while sounding his call epitomizes the territorial male attitude toward their women as possessions to be locked up and watched. Troy turns the statement into a joke by admitting that the newlyweds had no yard. The comment suits the motif of the fence and Troy's domination of Rose. Wilson turns his repressive treatment of Rose into irony after Troy, like a bird wandering from the pen, strays to Alberta, abandoning Rose to housework and the church.

As is common in Wilson's plays, male behavior dominates *Seven Guitars* (1995), a verbal polyphony of local voices discussing matters they hold in common. In the presence of three women, the men who play cards and converse in the Pittsburgh backyard behave like strutting roosters. After the arrival of the seductive Ruby from Birmingham, like feisty gamecocks, Canewell and Red Carter glare at each other while grabbing for her suitcase. The male characters' exchanges, soliloquys, and comebacks form a human version of rooster talk with precipitate breaks, posturing, pecking orders, and swaggering ego. In Act II, Scene 4, Wilson acknowledges the motet of voices with Red Carter's counting of seven birds on the fence.

Miss Tillery's rooster, which seems out of place in the city, suggests the farm culture that blacks abandon in their rush to resettle in the industrialized North. She suffers a second outrage from the dog catcher, who insists she get a license for her pet. In reference to the strictures of Pittsburgh's big-city life, Red Carter declares, "Once upon a time in America it used to be all right to have a rooster in your yard.... Seem like everything broke down" (p. 82). Characters take both sides of the issue of using a rooster as a morning call: the bird is both a symbol of citizens' rights to own poultry and a throwback to a time when people preferred waking up to the rooster's crow than to the jangle of a wind-up alarm clock. The bird also represents an unabashed embrace of nature and traditions, which it perpetuates despite laws forbidding livestock in the city limits.

Wilson stresses transience and sudden death in a makeshift slaughter pen where King Hedley houses, then kills poultry. Like an impersonal god who chooses victims by whim, Hedley selects, then beheads the chickens that will provide meat for his sandwich business. The abrupt crow of a rooster that interrupts singing and dancing to Floyd Barton's hit record "That's All Right" suggests the unpredictability of fate, which violates human attainment. A symbol of death's unforeseen call, the noise is intermittent and unexpected, like the hard luck that ends Floyd's relationship with Vera Dotson and the stroke of Hedley's machete that stills Floyd's voice and lops off his life at a promising era in his career. The playwright balances the terror of the omen with a saucy retort from Vera, who asserts that the rooster's lusty male call "sounds just like [Floyd]" (p. 6).

Hedley's on-stage bird-slaying adds another layer of meaning by linking the atavistic act with the ritual bird-killing of voodoo, an animistic religion that originated in West Africa. Critics interpret the act as a wake-up alarm to blacks who have jettisoned both African and Southern connections during their search for higher pay in Northern factories. Despite the rooster's insistent male libido, Hedley foresees the gradual decrease of the number of roosters as an omen that America's black men will also decline in viability and number. As though speaking for death, he warns, "You hear this rooster you know you alive. You be glad to see the sun cause there come a time sure enough when you see your last day and this rooster you don't hear no more" (p. 64).

Like the resilient life forces in the playwright's characters, the rooster refuses to yield, even to death. A model of old-time country folk who migrate to Pittsburgh and maintain their rustic ways, Miss Tillery refuses to give in to senseless violence or to live without a rooster. In the last scenes, her rooster sounds a new call, leading Vera Dotson to muse that their neighbor must have bought a replacement bird. Wilson uses the old lady's spunk as a gesture to the survival instincts of tough women like Louise, Ruby, WillaMae, and Vera, all of whom reach for a life that will satisfy their wants.

See also **slavery**

• *Further Reading*

Wolfe, Peter. *August Wilson*. New York: Twayne, 1999.

rootlessness

Wilson's plays extol the value of home and parents and epitomize the harm done to people who lack continuity by living in fleeting moments of amusement and contentment. He stresses the rupture of human safety nets and the loss of hope with the loosening of interpersonal bonds, for example, the drifter Citizen Barlow who flees constable Caesar and breaks into Aunt Ester's home to confess his sins in *Gem of the Ocean* (2003), the unsatisfying migrations of Wining Boy Charles in *The Piano Lesson* (1990), the lack of family and the insubstantial living arrangements of Canewell in *Seven Guitars* (1995), the tours that keep musicians on the road in *Ma Rainey's Black Bottom* (1985), the unemployability of Hambone in *Two Trains Running* (1991), and the destructiveness of drive-by shootings of the 1980s that the philosopher Stool Pigeon laments in *King Hedley II* (1999). In *Fences* (1985), Jim Bono comments on a difficult childhood because his father was a rambler with "the walking blues … searching out the New Land" (pp. 51, 50). Similarly, other men choose to "walk out their front door and just take on down one road or another and keep on walking" rather than assume the role of head of household (p. 51). Because of the family's lack of a father figure, Bono did not develop a sense of parenthood and elects not to have children. Of the need of blacks to avoid entanglements and extra baggage, the white salesman Rutherford Selig in *Joe Turner's Come and Gone* (1988) claims, "It's not an easy job keeping up with you Nigras the way you move about so" (p. 41).

In *The Piano Lesson*, Wilson creates a more balanced life in the professional travels of the railroad worker. Doaker Charles maintains a respectable home and sanctuary for his extended family in Pittsburgh while leaving regularly to cook on the train. He knows every stop of the circuit and has no fear of returning to the South or leaving it behind on the train's dependable circuits. His steady strokes at the ironing board over his uniform form a metaphor of the loyal railroad worker accepting his duty by smoothing out the wrinkles.

In another view of uprooting, Wilson characterizes family disruptions in *Jitney* (1982). Jim Becker, a steady, dependable business manager and husband of Lucille, gives the impression of surviving the sufferings common to black families. His facade gives way upon the return of his son Booster, who served twenty years in prison for murdering a white girl. Tumbling out of Jim's past come the grudges against his only child for precipitating the death of Jim's first wife Coreen and for reducing Jim's standing among his peers as the father of a felon. Tragically, Jim dies in an accident without resolving the dissolution of family or conciliating the hurt and need in Booster. Wilson pairs Booster with Youngblood, a young man who works two jobs and maps out his finances to assure his young family of a home. The contrast suggests that, while Youngblood will continue to work toward stability for his wife and son, Booster has no family to maintain as an anchor in an uncertain period of Pittsburgh history.

See also **community, Great Migration, slavery**

• *Further Reading*

Elam, Harry J., ed. *Colored Contradictions: An Anthology of Contemporary African-American Plays*. New York: Plume, 1996.
West, Cornel. *Race Matters*. Boston: Beacon Press, 1993.

Ruby

August Wilson makes triple use of the character Ruby, whose name suggests worth as well as fire and sensuality. In *Seven Guitars* (1995), Louise's twenty-five-year-old niece Ruby, named for Grandma Ruby, sashays on stage following a robust squawk of the neighborhood rooster. She arrives in Pittsburgh from Birmingham, Alabama, in flight from "man trouble" (p. 15). Louise comments on the girl's involvement in Elmore's jailing for murdering Leroy Slater and anticipates that Ruby's "little fast behind" will shorten the visit (pp. 30, 58). Louise's point of view links nubile young women with eruptions of male-on-male violence, a pattern not entirely the fault of Ruby.

Wilson indicates that black males build self-esteem through sexual self-assertion. At the beginning of Act II, it is the girl's backside that builds lust in Hedley, who stares unashamedly at Ruby while singing, "Soon I be a big man someday" (p. 66). Because of his extreme need of affirmation and acceptance in Act II, Scene 5, Ruby offers him her body in a remarkable act of charity, which critics have compared to Rosasharn's offering of breast milk to a dying man in the final scene of John Steinbeck's *The Grapes of Wrath* (1939), a novel that revealed to middle America the sufferings of the poor during the Dust Bowl. Ruby's generosity contradicts Louise's surmise that her niece has caused her own discontent by glorying in the warring of jealous suitors.

Ruby's easy alliance with a variety of men associates her with promiscuity as well as the liberating influence of the women's movement. A letter from Elmore compels Ruby to explain the situation in Birmingham that caused him to kill Leroy. She strays from King Hedley's offer of marriage to bask in Floyd Barton's coaxing words, good looks, and woman-luring ways. Independent above all, Ruby rejects extreme sexual demands and possessiveness in potential mates and informs Louise of her distaste for "a man want to use you up like that" (p. 73). Despite Ruby's wish to make her own way, she has to acknowledge that she is pregnant by either Leroy or Elmore and that, since Leroy's murder, Elmore is serving a prison sentence that leaves her manless and her child fatherless. Wilson postulates that liberated women pay dearly for their freedom in much the same way that all blacks suffered after emancipation.

The sixty-one-year-old mother of the title character in *King Hedley II* (1999), Wilson's second view of Ruby depicts her as the victim of youthful sexual license and advancing age. She is too proud to admit to Tonya that she can't read. When she spies gray in her hair, she prefers a stranger's rough sex at the Ellis Hotel to the comfort of a singing career. A jaded blues singer who croons "Red Sails in the Sunset" in an elderly voice, she is older, wiser, widowed, and reduced to poverty and a tenuous relationship with Elmore, who drops in on her on rare occasions. She extends love to the strong-willed Hedley, who lives upstairs in her house, and echoes her daughter-in-law Tonya in urging him to give up get-rich-quick plots to sell stolen GE refrigerators. Hedley considers her intrusive and looks forward to her departure to a retirement high-rise. To Tonya, Ruby murmurs the mother's dilemma: "I love me but I love King more. Sometimes I might not love me but there don't never come a time I don't love him" (p. 46).

Even though his mother sent money each month from her earnings for Hedley's upkeep, he resents Ruby for the period during which she abandoned him to the care of her aunt Louise, the landlady in *Seven Guitars*, to sing with Walter Kelly's band in East St. Louis. He accuses her of arriving a month before Louise's death to claim her house. Given to quiet musings, but few apologies for her maternal shortcomings, Ruby comments, "Life's got it's own rhythm. It don't always go along with your rhythm," the credo of a self-centered individual incapable of sacrificing for family (p. 47). Her romantic waltz and joy in a stolen diamond ring reprises the old Ruby minus the sizzle, but the final scene ends in death after she shoots her son in the throat. With a maternal touch, she stoops to sing "Red Sails in the Sunset" to her dying boy. Wilson implies that motherhood, grandmotherhood, and marriage slip from her grasp.

See also **women**

- *Further Reading*

Aaron, Jan. "Royal Treat: 'King Hedley II.'" *Education Update*, June 2001.
Fisher, Philip. "King Hedley II." *British Theatre Guide*, 2002.
Gutman, Les. "King Hedley II." *CurtainUp*, 2001.
Isherwood, Charles. "King Hedley II." *Variety*, Vol. 382, No. 12, May 7, 2001, pp. 76–77.
Papatola, Dominic P. "Thunder, Lightning Pierce 'Hedley' Storm." *St. Paul Pioneer Press*, May 31, 2003, p. B6.
Rawson, Chris. "Stage Review: Wilson's Hedley a Thrilling Ride." *Pittsburgh Post-Gazette*, December 16, 1999.
Toomer, Jeanette. "'King Hedley' Conquers Broadway." *New York Amsterdam News*, Vol. 92, No. 19, May 10, 2001, pp. 21–22.

Sam

The insightful sweeper in August Wilson's one-act play *The Janitor* (1985), Sam is an underappreciated bearer of wisdom. In reference to the choice of a menial laborer as sage, the playwright lauded his character as "someone whom this society ignores and someone who may have some very valuable information, someone who has a vital contribution to make" (Charters & Charters, p. 1900). As a repository of African American philosophy, Sam precedes a long list of Wilson's humble visionaries, including Bynum Walker in *Joe Turner's Come and Gone* (1988), Toledo in *Ma Rainey's Black Bottom* (1985), Doaker Charles in *The Piano Lesson* (1990), Canewell in *Seven Guitars* (1995), Stool Pigeon in *King Hedley II* (1999), and the most profound, Aunt Ester in *Two Trains Running* (1991) and *Gem of the Ocean* (2003).

Sam's emergence as philosopher is impromptu. At the setting for the National Conference on Youth, fifty-six-year-old Sam sweeps near the lectern of the hotel ballroom. He halts his labors to deliver a spontaneous speech rich with insight into life's passages. In reference to youth, he admires physical and spiritual resilience as well as openness to new challenges. Without undue nostalgia, he proclaims, "We are all victims of the sweetness of youth and the time of its flight" (Wilson, *Short Pieces*, p. 1901).

Of human struggles to reconnect with history, Sam admits that he has forgotten his ties to African rivers and deities. He joins all people in "wrestling with Jacob's angel" (*Ibid.*, p. 1901), a reference to an epiphany in Genesis 34:24–30 in which Jacob comes to terms with his potential. Wilson concludes the scenario abruptly with one of his key themes, the brevity of opportunity and the inevitability of change. With the return of the white supervisor, Sam must relinquish the microphone and return to menial labor.

See also **opportunity**

• *Further Reading*

Charters, Ann, and Samuel Charters, ed. *Short Pieces from the New Dramatists*. Banbury, Ox.: Orangeberry Books, 1985.

Samuel, Prophet

An unseen character already dead at the opening of *Two Trains Running* (1991), the Prophet Samuel typifies the informal, rapacious evangelism of urban street preachers and religious hucksters. Holloway describes how the prophet, originally called Reverend Samuel, preached in Pittsburgh over an amplifier from the back of his truck and "[sold] barbecue on the side" (p. 25). His magnetism allowed him a free hand with female followers like Risa Thomas, the cook and waitress at Memphis Lee's cafe, who believed that he was on a mission from God to assure justice for blacks. As his influence increased, he drove his truck into white neighborhoods, where the police arrested him for preaching without a permit.

In later years, Samuel, like a self-aggrandizing televangelist, amplified the staginess of his ministry with flashy jewelry, "seven or eight women," and a white Cadillac (p. 8). Headquartered on Herron Avenue, he "went big" and traveled robed and barefoot for riverside baptisms (p. 26). In the opinion of Wolf, the numbers runner, "He be cheating and fooling the people all these years" (p. 7). Samuel's flakiness cost him the respect of devotees and possibly precipitated his death by stroke or, according to cafe owner Memphis Lee, from poisoning "by one of them old sandal-foot women" (p. 6). His passing suggests the internal collapse or external taint that false religion spreads over the black community.

Even in death, Samuel demonstrates a lurid appeal akin to a circus sideshow. At the play's opening, Samuel has been dead for two days. Local people flock to view his remains at West's funeral parlor, rub his head for luck, and gossip about his gold jewelry, diamonds, and hundred-dollar bills tucked into his hand. To extend the notoriety of his powers, they spread an urban legend about a mourner locating twenty dollars on the sidewalk after viewing the prophet. Because of his rumored wealth, West must hire guards to ward off break-ins during the night. On the day of Samuel's funeral, Risa proudly displays a card certifying that she has paid a tithe to Samuel's ministry, the First African Congregational Kingdom, and claims that he served God by helping blacks obtain justice. Memphis Lee, her employer, uses her weeping and loyalty to the prophet as proof of her gullibility.

• *Further Reading*

Shannon, Sandra G. *The Dramatic Vision of August Wilson*. Washington, D.C.: Howard
    University Press, 1996.
Wolfe, Peter. *August Wilson*. New York: Twayne, 1999.

sanctuary

A concept derived from medieval Catholicism, sanctuary refers to the power of
the church to claim custody of fugitives who shelter on religious ground and to protect them from arrest or harassment by officials of the law or crown. The motif, a
standard feature in Benedictine philosophy and traditional Gothic fiction, recurs in
Wilson's plays as a spiritual and emotional retreat from the torment of slavery and
the despair of the Jim Crow era. In *Jitney* (1982), refuge centers on the stove and
shabby furniture at the center of a brotherhood of drivers. They shelter the alcoholic
cabbie Fielding, debate their future after urban renewal takes their cab stand, and
relieve each other of grief after their manager, Jim Becker, dies unexpectedly in an
accident. Like a cozy men's club, the site is both business center and shelter.

The kitchen with its implications of nourishment and welcome is one of Wilson's favorite settings. Rose Maxson's welcome to her retarded brother-in-law Gabe
and to Troy Maxson's illegitimate daughter Raynell in *Fences* (1985) includes frequent
offers of food from Rose's kitchen. In *Joe Turner's Come and Gone* (1988), an on-stage
kitchen setting accepts Herald Loomis and his daughter Zonia at Bertha and Seth
Holly's boardinghouse after Loomis retreats north from Turner's press gang. Similar havens center Wilson's *The Piano Lesson* (1990), which receives nephew Boy Willie
Charles and his friend Lymon Jackson at uncle Doaker Charles's kitchen table, and
Seven Guitars (1995), which turns boarders, friends, and relatives into an uplifting
community accepting the ill-omened Ruby from Birmingham, Alabama, and Floyd
Barton, the scoundrel who abandoned resident Vera Dotson to take Pearl Brown with
him to Chicago. In each instance, talk of soul food implies the soul-feeding warmth
and forgiveness of the black community.

Wilson continues to establish welcoming hearths for prodigals in his more recent
plays, including Elmore and the scarred ex-con named in the title of *King Hedley II*
(1999). In *Gem of the Ocean* (2003), the playwright accords Aunt Ester's boardinghouse what critic Paul Hodgins calls a "quasi-holy status" (Hodgins, p. 1). Citizen
Barlow retreats from the South only thirty-nine years after the Civil War and makes
tracks toward refuge. In flight from the law for stealing a bucket of nails, he carries
heavy sins to Pittsburgh's Hill District and locates Ester's kitchen. Like runaways
from the plantation era, he is a bondsman in body and soul who requires redemption and soul-cleansing to enable him to claim full citizenship. In the warm reception of the aged visionary's parlor, he is able to release his burdens and find new
direction in a chancy, often violent world.

• *Further Reading*

Abarbanel, Jonathan. "Gem of the Ocean." http://ibs.theatermania.com/content/news.cfm?
    int_news_id=3441, May 1, 2003.

Hodgins, Paul. "Finding the Cost of Freedom: Slavery and Its Aftermath Are Explored in 'Gem of the Ocean,' August Wilson's Latest Play." *Orange County Register*, August 1, 2003, p. 1.
Jones, Chris, "Review: Gem of the Ocean." *Variety*, May 5, 2003, p. 39.

segregation

As demonstrated by black enclaves in the Hill District of Pittsburgh, Wilson's characters reside in a segregated milieu. Although newcomers from the South find jobs in factories in *Gem of the Ocean* (2003) and *Jitney* (1982) and in public works projects in *Joe Turner's Come and Gone* (1988), their lives spool out in tandem with whites like trains on parallel tracks. In *The Piano Lesson* (1990), privileged Pittsburghers cross the line to buy watermelons from Lymon Jackson's truck or to hire choice domestic workers like Berniece Charles. Whites breach the divide to exploit or accuse blacks of worthlessness, incompetence, irresponsibility, and criminality, for example, the false claim of rape that Susan McKnight makes against her black boyfriend Booster Becker in *Jitney*, the refusal of a contract to Hop in *King Hedley II* (1999), and the cheating of Hambone, the retarded handyman who paints Lutz's fence in *Two Trains Running* (1991). In *Seven Guitars* (1995), scam artist T. L. Hall and his accomplice Robert Gordon bilk buyers of phony insurance by taking advantage of naivete and good will of unsuspecting blacks. To assure that the law protects white interests, city authorities hire Caesar, a black constable in *Gem of the Ocean*, to keep the peace and chase down offenders like Citizen Barlow and Solly Two Kings.

For blacks who do emerge from the ghetto, nearness to whites does not assure welcome, as demonstrated by the rude exclusion of Ma Rainey from the table at a white dinner party in *Ma Rainey's Black Bottom* (1985). In *Fences* (1985), after Troy Maxson advances from garbage lifter to driver, he moves from routes in Pittsburgh's black neighborhoods to Greentree, a white community southwest of the city center. The move also segregates Troy from his pal and fellow garbage man Jim Bono, an emotional bulwark during their lengthy friendship. Troy admits to loneliness: "Ain't got nobody to talk to ... feel like you working for yourself" (p. 83).

Wilson characterizes public venues and transportation as a failed means of uniting races, as demonstrated by the blacks-only gypsy cab service in *Jitney*. Memphis Lee, the diner owner in *Two Trains Running*, dramatizes the separation of the black community from successful whites by describing his old fantasy of buying a V-8 Ford, his entree to the upper crust. He intended to drive to Henry Ford's mansion. Good-naturedly, Memphis adds, "If anybody come to the window I was gonna wave" (p. 31). Although humorous, the image of a black on the outside catching a glimpse of the Ford family through a curtained window, like the control booth that segregates whites from blacks in *Ma Rainey's Black Bottom*, intensifies the impression of separation and insularity from black concerns and activities.

See also **Mel Sturdyvant**

• *Further Reading*

Bogumil, Mary L. *Understanding August Wilson*. Columbia: University of South Carolina Press, 1998.

self-destruction

Through drama, Wilson explores the self-mutilating, self-destructive urge that stymies black Americans. The acts range from Fielding's drinking on the job in *Jitney* (1982) to the title character's sale of stolen refrigerators and daylight robbery of a jewelry store in *King Hedley II* (1999), Floyd Barton and Poochie Tillery's hold-up of a finance company in *Seven Guitars* (1995), Crawley and Boy Willie Charles's theft of wood in *The Piano Lesson* (1990), Citizen Barlow's stealing a bucket of nails in *Gem of the Ocean* (2003), and Levee Green's murderous rage in *Ma Rainey's Black Bottom* (1985). In *Fences* (1985), Troy Maxson carries on an affair with Alberta that dismays his loyal wife Rose and withers their marriage. When he confronts Rose with his paramour's pregnancy, as though speaking from the point of view of a teenager like his son Cory, Troy exults in the freedom he enjoys to laugh out loud with Alberta and not worry about home responsibilities. In his typical baseball imagery, he describes adultery as a way to "steal second [base]" (p. 70). To his credit, he admits, "I done locked myself into a pattern trying to take care of you all that I forgot about myself" (p. 69). To his shame, he discounts the value of a good wife and stable home. Rose describes her wasted investment in marriage to Troy in terms of Jesus's parable in Mark 4:1–29 of the sower who dropped seed on rocky soil, a subtext that recurs with the planting of Tonya's garden in *King Hedley II*.

Deliberate self-mutilation is a troubling element in Wilson's characters. Clarissa "Risa" Thomas, the waitress in Memphis Lee's cafe in *Two Trains Running* (1991), discourages male attention by cutting her legs with fifteen strokes of a razor. Memphis comments, "Anybody take a razor and cut up on herself ain't right" (p. 31). He surmises that, if she would mutilate herself, she might also cut a man's throat. In *Joe Turner's Come and Gone* (1988), Herald Loomis strikes out at seven years of dehumanizing imprisonment by slashing at his chest with a knife and smearing blood on his face. Unlike Risa's desperate destruction of beauty, his self-affirming act suggests a blend of two religious traditions— the blood-letting of African animism and the image of the crucified Christ.

See also **crime**

• *Further Reading*

Bloom, Harold, intro. *August Wilson*. New York: Chelsea House, 2002.

Selig, Rutherford

The modest "first-class People Finder" of *Joe Turner's Come and Gone* (1988), Rutherford Selig, in his early fifties, is a paradoxical white pragmatist who creates a rare white-instigated synergy with blacks (p. 15). A benign peddler, Selig first appears in Pittsburgh in 1904 in *Gem of the Ocean* (2003) as the pots and pans salesman and friend of Aunt Ester and her unusual household, where he is the only white visitor. After discussing the marketing of dust pans with Seth Holly in 1911, the character supplies him with sheet metal for the manufacture of domestic items, which Selig hauls away by wagon on his sales route along the Monongahela River. The only white man in the cast, a rarity in August Wilson's decade cycle, Selig, like wandering blacks, migrates north from Kentucky. As an entrepreneur, he represents the capitalist's exploitation of black laborers; as a friend, he suggests the possibilities of a peaceful alliance in an integrated world.

Selig's value lies in the ability to locate and remove people. He bears a German surname meaning "blessed" and a natural gift for organizing a customer list that informs him of the whereabouts of individuals and families. After the freeing of the slaves, Selig turned detective work into a profession and began aiding blacks in reuniting with other blacks. In an interview with Michael J. Bandler, the playwright explained: "When people were moving, Selig would provide transportation. They'd hitch a ride on his wagon. And then, when somebody'd say they were looking for [those people], he'd say, 'I know where they are — give me a dollar and I'll find them for you'" (Bandler). Thus, Selig's business demonstrates both profit motive and altruism.

Like other of Wilson's sinners, Selig bears his own load of guilt. His ancestors— a great-grandfather who was a slaver and a father, Jonas B. Selig, who captured and returned runaways to their masters— link the younger Selig to the central issues of the black diaspora. Derived from a long line of antebellum slavery enablers, he atones for his family's past by using his people-finding skills for good. He remarks, "You're in good hands, mister. Me and my daddy have found plenty Nigras. My daddy, rest his soul, used to find runaway slaves for the plantation bosses" (p. 41). Selig's admission of the crime of black bondage admits a wide ray of hope to Wilson's plays in its openness. Without rationalizing the faults of his ancestors, Selig refuses inherited guilt and makes his reputation from his own values, integrity, and upright behavior.

It is Selig who orchestrates the family reunion, a pervasive theme that Wilson repeats at a funeral in *Fences* (1985), at the cab stand in *Jitney* (1982), between Louise and her niece Ruby in *Seven Guitars* (1995), and at Doaker's apartment in *The Piano Lesson* (1990). On the peddler's weekly jaunts up and down the Monongahela River and south to Wheeling, West Virginia, Selig helps Herald Loomis reclaim identity by locating Martha Pentecost, Loomis's estranged wife. Selig receives hospitality at Bertha and Seth Holly's boarding house in the form of coffee and biscuits shared with roomers and in gifts of tomatoes and cabbages from Seth's garden. A generous giver as well as receiver, Selig graces Loomis with a new identity, as a shiny man glittering "like new money!" (p. 94).

• *Further Reading*

Bandler, Michael J. "USIA Interview with American Playwright August Wilson." http://usembassy-australia.state.gov/hyper/WF980415/epf308.htm, April 15, 1998.

Powers, Kim. "An Interview with August Wilson." *Theater*, Vol. 16, Fall/Winter 1984, pp. 50–55.

Preston, Rohan. "Oglesby Sparkles in Wilson's 'Gem.'" *Minneapolis Star Tribune*, May 4, 2003, p. 4F.

Üsekes, Ciggdem. "'We's the Leftovers': Whiteness as Economic Power and Exploitation in August Wilson's Twentieth-Century Cycle of Plays." *African American Review*, Vol. 37, No. 1, Spring 2003, pp. 115–125.

Seven Guitars

Wilson's seventh major play and perhaps the most enigmatic of his chain of ten dramas, *Seven Guitars* (1995) is both a lyric, insightful prose opera and a bawdy, elegaic murder mystery told in flashback. The drama takes place after a funeral in a backyard of Bella's three-story brick boardinghouse in Pittsburgh's Hill district shortly before Mother's Day, 1948. The cast requires seven actors to become the seven instruments— the dynamic dreamer Floyd "Schoolboy" Barton and his wronged girlfriend Vera Dotson, Floyd's drummer Red Carter, back-up harmonica-player Canewell, earth mother and whist-playing landlady Louise, and old Hedley, a childless male who intends to sire a messiah with Ruby, Louise's man-destroying niece. A pick-up music session begins with a note from Canewell's harmonica, the tuning of Floyd's guitar, and Red playing rhythms on the tabletop with drumsticks. Hedley joins with a one-wire stringed instrument he nails together with a hammer and two-by-four. As the characters sing their individual blues— longing, betrayal, abandonment, injustice — the resulting polyphony fulfills the metaphoric promise of the title.

Wilson claims that all his characterizations come from blues lyrics. He acknowledges that *Seven Guitars* contains his first effort to portray a fully realized malefemale relationship. In scenarios more complete than the flirtation of Sterling Johnson with Risa Thomas in *Two Trains Running* (1995), the playwright characterizes Floyd as a traitor to his girl Vera on the journey to Chicago in early June to cut a first disk with the Savoy Record Company. Symbolizing their sterile love match is the goldenseal plant, which produces an herb made from dried-out roots. Adding to the sobriety of Floyd's last moments, he speaks of people taking a last chance and declares, "I'm just getting started" (p. 91). His ambition ennobles a man who wastes his promise in a hasty felony.

Overhung with gloom following a burial, the story opens outside Vera's apartment in a brick house and the location of Hedley's slaughtering business and an outdoor card table, a two-sided reflection on violent death and the luck of the draw. The plot relates events of the week preceding the death of Floyd, a blues guitarist and singer whose ambitions appeared to near fruition. A montage of mystery, folksy humor, homespun philosophy, and eulogy, the text harmonizes the input of friends who express their own troubles while extolling a musician inexplicably murdered in his prime. At the heart of black discontent is their failure to prosper after relocating in the North and Floyd's faulty vision of Chicago as the promised land.

See also **Floyd Barton, Canewell, Red Carter, Vera Dotson, King Hedley, King Hedley II, Louise, rooster, Ruby**

• *Further Reading*

Jones, Chris. "Homeward Bound." *American Theatre*, Vol. 16, No. 9, November 1999.
Taylor, Regina. "That's Why They Call It the Blues." *American Theatre*, Vol. 13, No. 4, April 1996, pp. 18–23.
Weber, Bruce. "Sculpturing a Play into Existence." *New York Times*, March 24, 1996, p. H7.

Shealy

A numbers runner in *Jitney* (1982), Shealy is a parasite on his own race. He camps out at the cab stand and conducts an illegal racket in the brassy style that Wolf adopts at Memphis Lee's diner in *Two Trains Running* (1991). To his credit, Shealy maintains a personal honor code in refusing to repeat gossip, a character trait lacking in Turnbo, his foil. Shealy claims to keep his business to himself because of the volatile nature of Hill District society where "First thing you know somebody be done got killed talking about 'Shealy said....'" (p. 15). He violates his rule by announcing Booster Becker's return from the penitentiary, but keeps his own icy father-son relationship under wraps. He refuses to discuss the cost of the new Buick Riviera of his estranged son Pope, a character in *Fences* (1985) who uses a gambling windfall to buy a restaurant on Centre Avenue.

When Shealy's not supplying bets to the numbers syndicate, he sticks close to home matters. The theme of loneliness links him with other womanless men in Wilson's plays, including Canewell in *Seven Guitars* (1995), the wanderer Herald Loomis and binding man Bynum Walker in *Joe Turner's Come and Gone* (1988), Lymon Jackson, a newcomer from the South in *The Piano Lesson* (1990), Solly Two Kings, the former conductor on the Underground Railroad in *Gem of the Ocean* (2003), and the undertaker West and the ex-con Sterling Johnson in *Two Trains Running*. Shealy tries to find work for his troubled nephew, Robert Shealy, and looks for the right woman to replace his jealous girlfriend Rosie, who spurns him. Rather than a short-term relationship, he yearns for the girl who will be "the one" (p. 16). His idealism relieves the character of sleaze by ennobling his faith in love, a quality he shares with Youngblood.

• *Further Reading*

Bowen, Joseph. "Jitney." http://centerstage.net/theatre/articles/jitney.html.

shiny man

August Wilson endows his slice-of-life dramas with touches of magical realism. Like Solly Two Kings in *Gem of the Ocean* (2003), the charismatic shiny man is an agent of the black diaspora and bringer of good fortune. The promise of a shiny man links the black future to serendipity, the positive side of fate that bestows a windfall on Memphis Lee in *Two Trains Running* (1991) and on Pope in *Fences* (1985). The fact that blacks cling to good fortune as their rescue from poverty recurs in Wilson's plays in superstition and bets on lucky numbers.

In *Joe Turner's Come and Gone* (1988), the wise Bynum Walker pays the peddler Rutherford Selig a dollar to locate the "shiny man," a fellow traveler whom Bynum once met in the road outside Johnstown, Pennsylvania. Because of the magnetism of his person and the offer of "the Secret of Life," Bynum followed him (p. 9). The shiny man conferred power on his follower by rubbing Bynum's hands in blood before exuding a great light, then disappearing. The event transfigures Bynum, giving his life direction and purpose.

Bynum refers to the mystic wayfarer as John, "the One Who Goes Before and Shows the Way" (p. 10). The depiction suggests John the Baptist, the cousin and forerunner of Jesus, whom John baptized and set to work on a formal ministry in the third chapter of Matthew's gospel. Critics have also interpreted the shiny man as the risen Christ, who confronts Saul of Tarsus on the Damascus road in Acts 9:3–8. Whatever his link with scripture, the illuminated presence is a touch of deity that endows an ordinary guy with a transformative power to aid people in distress and direct them toward fulfillment.

The supernatural portrayal of the shiny man suggests a parallel to the metallic nature of the Yoruban deity Ogun, god of iron, and to his role in the black laboring class, who power Pittsburgh's steel mills. The name "John" also refers to High John the Conqueror, a mythic black hero-divine who followed black Africans across the Middle Passage and remained nearby to protect and uplift them from slavery's degradation by deceiving or outwitting slavemasters. In *Seven Guitars* (1995), Floyd Barton is so down on his luck that he calls on High John, the crafty trickster, as well as an assortment of other heroes to assure his success as a musician. The indistinct nature of the shiny man implies a heavenly guidance to seekers who despair of earthly happiness.

See also **superstition, Bynum Walker**

• *Further Reading*

Anderson, Douglas. "Saying Goodbye to the Past: Self-Empowerment and History." *CLA Journal*, Vol. 40, No. 4, June 1997, pp. 432–457.
Tidjani-Serpos, Noureini. "The Postcolonial Condition: The Archeology of African Knowledge." *Research in African Literatures*, Vol. 27, No. 1, Spring 1996, pp. 3–18.

slavery

Slavery bears a fierce historical burden in August Wilson's plays. His characters suffer rootlessness because of their ancestors' abrupt separation from an African heritage and subsequent enslavement. The playwright compared the effects of bondage on blacks and Jews: "The stigma of slavery is powerful. A few years ago, I went to a Passover service, and the first words were 'We were slaves in the land of Egypt.' They are remembering events of thousands of years ago, not just a century" (Henry, p. 77).

Emancipation did little to free African Americans from ignorance, want, oppression, and fear, thus elongating the miseries of a marginalized non-white people. In *The Piano Lesson* (1990), the extended Charles family struggles to overcome the wrongs done them in the mid–1800s by the Robert Sutter family, rural Mississippians who owned the characters' forebears. The task of carving a piano inspired the slave Willie Boy, grandsire of the Charleses, to honor his ancestors with a montage of family accomplishments, an heroic act of creativity and self-definition. In *King Hedley II* (1999), the title figure, an ex-con, compares low wages to the earnings in slave times. The subtext indicates that the post-emancipation economy retained blacks in a less obvious form of bondage.

Scattered mention of slavery crops up at unforeseen moments in Wilson's dramas, such as the Aesopic animal fable in Canewell's clever discussion of roosters in *Seven Guitars* (1995). After contrasting roosters across the South, the fablist adds that the bird refused to crow during slavery because it didn't want to arouse people from their rest, a suggestion of sympathy for the overworked black field hand. In the jubilee following the Emancipation Proclamation, which President Abraham Lincoln issued on January 1, 1863, the rooster felt left out of the celebration and launched his morning wake-up call. The tale attests to spontaneity, exuberance, and unity in blacks at the moment they grasped freedom.

With *Gem of the Ocean* (2003), set thirty-nine years after the Civil War, Wilson creates stage magic with a mystical reclamation of the past. Through a parlor seance, Aunt Ester, Pittsburgh's long-lived black seer, reclaims Citizen Barlow from mortal sin. With a paper boat she shapes from a slave bill of sale and names Gem of the Ocean, she conducts him through myth to the City of Bones, a virtual reliving of the hellish Middle Passage. By visiting the boneyard in the mid–Atlantic of those West Africans who died between capture and sale, Barlow acquires compassion for his own people and forgiveness for himself.

Additional references to slavery reflect the playwright's intent to use drama as a subtle tutorial. In a note accompanying *Joe Turner's Come and Gone* (1988), Wilson implies that blacks arrived in a strange land equipped with an African past that sustains them during the permanent separation from home and the acclimation to American life. Holloway, the philosopher in *Two Trains Running* (1991), supplies verbal images of blacks stacked in the hold of slaving vessels during the Middle Passage, which brought captive Africans to the Western Hemisphere for sale in slave markets. He claims that, for three hundred years, slaves worked for free and "didn't take no lunch hour" (p. 34). He makes his droll claim to prove that blacks are not shiftless, a charge the white world chose to believe once blacks progressed from field laborers to free hirelings and sharecroppers. He reminds his hearers, "If it wasn't for you the white man would be poor. Every little bit he got he got from standing on top of you" (p. 35). The charge holds true in the time of urban renewal, when whites discover gold in black tenements, which they purchase, raze, and replace with center-city renewal projects, which once more devalue and displace black citizens.

See also **Citizen Barlow, City of Bones, Aunt Ester, Holloway,** *The Piano Lesson,* **urbanism**

• *Further Reading*

Freedman, Samuel G. "A Voice from the Streets: August Wilson's Plays Portray the Sound and Feel of Black Poverty." *New York Times Magazine,* March 15, 1987, p. 36.

Gantt, Patricia. "Ghosts from 'Down There': The Southernness of August Wilson," in *August Wilson: A Casebook.* New York: Garland, 1994.

Henry, William A. "Exorcising the Demons of Memory: August Wilson Exults in the Blues and Etches Slavery's Legacy." *Time,* Vol. 131, No. 15, April 11, 1988, pp. 77–78.

Patterson, Orlando. *Slavery and Social Death.* Cambridge: Harvard University Press, 1982.

Slow Drag (character)

In *Ma Rainey's Black Bottom* (1985), bassist Slow Drag, a colleague of band leader and trombonist Cutler since 1905, is a multifaceted character and model of stability. He remains loyal both to music and to his rural roots, symbolized by a pair of rustic brogans and a string that ravels from his instrument. Like Cutler, Slow Drag is affable and low-key, but reveals intelligence, a tendency toward African rhythms, and respect for a good time, as exhibited by his steady pull on a bottle of bourbon. He earned his name by slow-dancing with another man's girlfriend and by disarming a potentially explosive situation on the dance floor by Slow Drag's rationalization of why he was doing the man a service in squiring his woman. The story connects him with the quick-witted Br'er Rabbit in Joel Chandler Harris's Uncle Remus fables, which depict the small creature in constant danger from larger, fiercer animals.

In contrast to his name, Slow Drag is a methodizer and regulator of the dramatic action. He tries to keep Ma's blues group on track by forcing them to rehearse to get the recording right on the first take. Given to escapism through substance abuse, Slow Drag then involves himself in demeaning pleading for some of Cutler's reefer. After jazz trumpeter Levee Green introduces a Faustian element to the plot, Slow Drag becomes an impromptu storyteller. He develops the theme of diabolism by narrating the cautionary tale of a male resident of Tuscaloosa, Alabama, with the unusual name of Eliza Cotter, who bargained his soul to the devil. The story is prophetic of Levee's brash blasphemies and his plunge from promising composer and performer to murderer.

See also **slow drag (dance)**

- *Further Reading*

Gener, Randy. "Salvation in the City of Bones: Ma Rainey and Aunt Ester Sing Their Own Songs in August Wilson's Grand Cycle of Blues Dramas." *American Theatre*, Vol. 20, No. 5, May-June 2003, pp. 20–28.
Powell, Jason. "August Wilson: The Playwright Versus the Politician." *Knox College Common Room*, Vol. 4, No. 1, May 29, 2000.

slow drag (dance)

In *Ma Rainey's Black Bottom* (1985), the character Slow Drag takes his name from performing a dance that evolved from the two-step in New Orleans in the 1890s. Dance expert Alcide Pavageau helped popularize the dance, which migrated north to New York. Scott Joplin (1835–1921) used the slow drag as an integral part of his folk opera *Treemonisha*, an unpublished suite that was not performed until the Houston Grand Opera staged it in 1975. The contrasting rhythms of the slow drag, influenced by West African and Caribbean dance, involved dragging first one foot, then the other in counterpoint to prancing, hopping, and skipping. The alterations of mode are dance metaphors for musician Slow Drag's varied moods, which range from good-natured member of the group to impromptu raconteur of a devil tale. The occasional glimpses of wisdom and Afrocentric philosophy suit August Wilson's interweaving of meaningful glimmers amid ordinary exchanges between friends and associates.

• *Further Reading*

Hazzard-Gordon, Katrina. *Jookin': The Rise of Social Dance Formations in African-American Culture*. Philadelphia: Temple University Press, 1992.

soul food

The Great Migration carried north a displaced nonwhite people unsure of their relationship to industry and urbanism. To retain their love of uncles who barbecued ribs and grandmothers who dished up chow-chow, spoonbread, corn pudding, and field peas with ham hocks, the emigres revered family domesticity, the aspect of Southern history most disrupted by slave escapes and the breeding and sale of family members as livestock. In urban surroundings, the newcomers cultivated soul food, the comfort foods that linked them to home and the ingredients raised in humble kitchen gardens, fruit and nut trees, and poultry pens or gleaned from woods, rivers, and seashores.

In *America and Americans* (1966), novelist John Steinbeck explained the salutary effect of meager foodstuffs on slave populations:

> A diet of coarse, natural foods in small quantities and a diet low in sugars and fats did for [slaves] what any doctor counsels for his weak and flabby patients. Meanwhile a complete lack of medical care sent the slaves to herbs and soothing teas as well as to the powerful and psychiatric safety of religion [p. 58].

The array of recipes for low country red beans and rice, gumbo, and seafood and for piedmont-grown peanuts, yams, okra, dried peas, turnips and mustard greens, molasses, corn meal mush, pork belly, and stewed chicken preserved a classic Southern cuisine. The standard bill of fare reached beyond the slave diet to the West African vegetable medleys, fish fries, milk puddings, oyster roasts, peanut soup, foufou, and griddle cakes of the distant past. Like worship and juba dances, feasting revived a sense of community that uplifted blacks through familiar flavors and shared recipes passed orally from cook to cook like treasured heirlooms.

August Wilson peoples his casts with characters hungry in body and soul, including Jeremy Furlow, an out-of-work street beggar in *Joe Turner's Come and Gone* (1988), the greedy Levee Green, who snatches at deli sandwiches in *Ma Rainey's Black Bottom* (1985), the peripatetic Elmore in *King Hedley II* (1999), and Boy Willie Charles in *The Piano Lesson* (1990), who migrates north from Mississippi to Pittsburgh in 1936. He immediately asks for a piece of his uncle Doaker's grilled bread, a suggestion of the spiritual nourishment offered at Christian communion by the consecrated bread of life. Boy Willie displays his Southern roots by sharing Doaker's hospitality with Lymon Jackson, an outsider to the family. Doaker sends his niece for more supplies—smoked ham hocks, turnip greens, and buttermilk for cornbread, the traditional food of Southern blacks.

To preserve a major portion of their agrarian heritage, Wilson's characters cling to familiar Southern meals of pigsfeet, short ribs, striped watermelon, and the fried chicken, grits, and biscuits which Ruby serves to welcome Elmore. The patrons of Memphis Lee's diner in *Two Trains Running* (1991) choose from a blackboard menu listing dried beans with corn muffins, meat loaf, chicken, and a choice of down-home side dishes—collard greens, mashed potatoes, green beans, macaroni & cheese, and potato salad (p. 1). Likewise, in *Seven Guitars* (1995), Vera Dotson and Louise please Floyd Barton and Hedley by feeding them home-cooked chicken, cornbread, collards, green beans and potatoes, and black-eyed peas. Canewell directs Vera on how to tear mustard and turnip greens in pieces, boil them with salt pork, and season with red pepper seed. The recipe is typical in Southern cookbooks and in the kitchens of families who still rely on fresh ingredients for traditional country cooking.

The playwright also connects meals of soul food with death, as with Rose Maxson's insistence on a hot breakfast in *Fences* (1985) before she and her children attend her husband Troy's funeral. In *Seven Guitars*, Hedley profits from the sale of boiled eggs and "plenty plenty chicken sandwiches" after George Butler's funeral (p. 20). In both plays, the characters reaffirm life through structured meals, an antidote to the disorder and disruption caused by death. With the abrupt slaughter of Miss Tillery's rooster, King Hedley warns that life is impermanent and death unforeseen and swift. After Hedley murders Floyd, mourners return from the graveyard to share sweet potato pie, a staple Southern dessert made from a lowly tuber, the food of slaves and sharecroppers. The sweetness of the after-funeral treat suggests the kindness and generosity of friends who forgive Floyd's troubled past.

Homestyle food serves Wilson as a token of emotion and a statement of camaraderie and family, for example, the chicken that Ruby fries when Elmore comes to visit in *King Hedley II*. In *Ma Rainey's Black Bottom*, Toledo summarizes the sharing of African tribes in the assembly, cooking, and eating of one stew. For Rose Maxson, meals of roast chicken and short ribs express her love of family and hospitality to Jim Bono, a long-time friend. Her ham sandwich and slice of striped watermelon welcome Gabriel, the mentally defective brother-in-law whom war has alienated from his own people. The gift of food as a token of acceptance and validation also exalts the lone female character in *Two Trains Running*, in which cook and waitress Risa Thomas negates the sharp words of her employer Memphis by treating Hambone, a retarded handyman, to free coffee and a bowl of beans. The food not only nourishes and soothes him, but also stops his repeated claims that someone has gypped him of a ham, his rightful pay for painting a fence. With these instances of food in dramatic scenarios, Wilson equates the sharing of food with integrity, welcome, and belonging.

• *Further Reading*

Harrison, Molly. *The Kitchen in History*. New York: Charles Scribner's Sons, 1972.
Jones, Evan. *American Food*. Woodstock, N.Y.: Overlook Press, 1990.
Snodgrass, Mary Ellen. *Encyclopedia of Kitchen History*. London: Fitzroy Dearborn, 2004.
Steinbeck, John. *America and Americans*. New York: Viking, 1966.

Stool Pigeon

In *King Hedley II* (1999), Stool Pigeon, a sixty-five-year-old bible quoter and mystic, offers the most comprehensive world view of the mid–1980s. Once known as Canewell in *Seven Guitars* (1995), he earned his new name after he informed police about King Hedley's murder of Floyd Barton in May 1948. Engrossed in deity, ritual, and feeding dogs from people's garbage cans, Stool Pigeon strolls in and out of the action muttering woe to sinners. He exhorts, "God say something and you come to attention right away" (p. 27). The prophecy misfires in Act II, Scene 2, when robbers in black outfits kick Stool Pigeon in the head and take his newspapers. The crime dismays Ruby, who feels that the climate of the Hill District has declined to senseless crime and victimization of the elderly.

Stool Pigeon is a receptacle of history, symbolized by his stacks of newspapers, compendia of useless data that surround him like paper insulation from the mundane world outside. His view of the order of things is deterministic, predicting that whatever happens is "all God's will, not man's will" (p. 126). Stool Pigeon reduces human involvement in history to a bit part for the middleman: "You can't play in the chord God ain't wrote. He wrote the beginning and the end. He let you play around with the middle but he got it all written down" (p. 1). The axiom applies to the downhill slide of the title character, the son of a murderer who is destined to follow his father's example.

Stool Pigeon lives in dilapidated quarters next to the residence of Ruby, Hedley II, and his new wife Tonya. A religious fanatic not unlike the original King Hedley in the earlier play, Stool Pigeon is the voice crying in the wilderness about the lost, rootless black race during the Reagan era. Stool Pigeon informs the raging ex-con King Hedley II that God is deliberately seeking Hedley's downfall. In Stool Pigeon's opinion, the only path out of the wild is history, the past eras of black life that will give black people a grasp on where they came from and what values supported their ancestors. After handing over a machete, the murder weapon the elder Hedley used to slay Floyd Barton, Stool Barton exults to the protagonist, "You got the Key to the Mountain!," an ironic mixed metaphor in a grimly realistic play (p. 122). A symbol of the younger Hedley's fate, it is his to use as he will.

In addition to commenting on family history and the tight circle of characters in the backyard setting, Stool Pigeon delivers an important message in Wilson's decalogue concerning the death of the beloved guru Aunt Ester at age 366. He regrets that she left too soon, but interprets her passing as God's way of preparing to destroy the earth by fire. Stool Pigeon honors her with flowers and an appropriate African offering of peanuts, a food plant that black slaves introduced to the New World. To restore her divine presence to the black community, he feels obligated to make a blood sacrifice, bury her black cat in Hedley's flower garden, and sprinkle ashes on top. He carries the search for a sacrificial animal to the countryside, where he hopes to acquire a "fatted calf," the biblical gift that appeased Yahweh in the Old Testament (p. 97).

See also **Canewell, Marion McClinton**

• *Further Reading*

Gener, Randy. "Salvation in the City of Bones: Ma Rainey and Aunt Ester Sing Their Own Songs in August Wilson's Grand Cycle of Blues Dramas." *American Theatre*, Vol. 20, No. 5, May-June 2003, pp. 20–28.

Keating, Douglas J. "A 'King' with Majesty Sadly Thwarted." *Philadelphia Inquirer*, January 31, 2003.

Papatola, Dominic P. "Thunder, Lightning Pierce 'Hedley' Storm." *St. Paul Pioneer Press*, May 31, 2003, p. B6.

Rawson, Chris. "Stage Review: Wilson's Hedley a Thrilling Ride." *Pittsburgh Post-Gazette*, December 16, 1999.

Stovall, Jim

A symbol of white oppression, Jim Stovall recurs in Wilson's plays in reference to shady deals. In *The Piano Lesson* (1990), set near the end of the Great Depression in 1936, Stovall is the white landowner for whom Boy Charles sharecropped in Marlin County, Mississippi. At one time, his father looked at his hands and mourned, "Best I can do is make a fifty-acre crop for Mr. Stovall" (p. 91). In the next generation, Stovall stalks Boy Willie and Lymon Jackson for their part in petty thievery of wood. Lymon explains the hold that Stovall gains over black criminals: "Mr. Stovall come and paid my hundred dollars [fine] and the judge say I got to work for him to pay him back his hundred dollars. I told them I'd rather take my thirty days but they wouldn't let me do that" (p. 37). In a display of self-actualization, Boy Willie attempts to amass two thousand dollars to buy the Sutter property to keep Stovall from adding it to his extensive holdings. The purchase becomes an emblem of the rise of the black entrepreneur farmer in a Southern state dominated by unscrupulous whites.

Thirty-three years later, Stovall's name maintains its ill savor among blacks who resettled in Pittsburgh, far from the bitter memory of hard labor for a cruel taskmaster. In 1969 in *Two Trains Running* (1991), Memphis Lee recalls how Stovall drove him out of Jackson, Mississippi, in 1931 by hiring hitmen to kill and emasculate his mule and torch his cropland. The act, a warning to uppity blacks who competed with white farmers, suggests the marauding of the Ku Klux Klan, which found ready membership among bigoted white landowners. Memphis vows to return with a 30.06 rifle and retaliate, but takes no action on his intent. Rather, he keeps Stovall as an identifiable persecutor — a name and face among the many anonymous whites who forced blacks north during the Great Migration.

See also **Boy Willie Charles, Great Migration, Memphis Lee**

• *Further Reading*

Elam, Harry J. "The Dialectics of August Wilson's 'The Piano Lesson.'" *Theatre Journal*, Vol. 52, No. 3, 2000, pp. 361–379.

Vorlicky, Robert. *Act Like a Man: Challenging Masculinities in American Drama*. Ann Arbor: University of Michigan Press, 1995.

Sturdyvant, Mel

An edgy, penny-pinching producer at Paramount Records in Chicago, Mel Sturdyvant is a pivotal white figure and symbol of segregation in *Ma Rainey's Black Bottom* (1985). In a separate world above blacks rehearsing in the basement band room and performing on the first floor, he occupies the control booth in the upper reaches of the building, where he demands a microphone check like the voice of God calling for an accounting of human failings. Driven solely by money, Sturdyvant harangues the diva's manager to supervise Ma and her band during a recording session.

Wilson depicts the set-to between Sturdyvant and Ma as a head-butting of two self-important divas. Like the overseers of plantation days, Sturdyvant insists that the session go like clockwork, as though he has the power to manipulate people like robots. He takes umbrage that the black diva previously disputed the list of songs, complained of sore throat and a cold building, and refused to re-record first takes. In a snit, he storms, "I'm not putting up with any Royal Highness ... Queen of the Blues bullshit! ... I don't care what she calls herself.... I just want to get her in here ... record those songs on that list ... and get her out" (p. 18). To save himself the headaches, he considers leaving the recording profession and getting into Irish textiles, a dark bit of humor that refers to a labor force as badly discounted and exploited as blacks. Metaphorically, while Ma's accompanists bide their time in their basement quarters, Sturdyvant paces the booth like a caged tiger and complains that she is late to the session. Wilson implies that Ma enjoys a sadistic hold on Sturdyvant, who enriches himself off her labor. He exploits both Ma, a bankable star, and jazz trumpeter Levee Green, whom he cajoles with compliments to his new dance-band trumpet riffs and a low-ball offer of five dollars for each new song he composes. Sturdyvant's betrayal of Levee produces a backlash that results in Levee's back-stabbing of Toledo, who expires on the recording room floor. The transfer of animosity from the white Simon Legree to the hapless pianist produces a grim tragedy of black-on-black violence set off in response to white racism.

• *Further Reading*

Blackburn, Regina Naasirah. "Erupting Thunder: Race and Class in the 20th Century Plays of August Wilson." *Socialism and Democracy*, Vol. 17, No. 2.
Gener, Randy. "Salvation in the City of Bones: Ma Rainey and Aunt Ester Sing Their Own Songs in August Wilson's Grand Cycle of Blues Dramas." *American Theatre*, Vol. 20, No. 5, May–June 2003, pp. 20–28.

supernatural

Influenced by the magical realism of Argentine author Jorge Luis Borges (1899–1986), August Wilson empowers and illuminates his drama cycle with the illogic of the supernatural, for example, Aunt Ester's ability to turn a paper bill of sale for a slave into a boat to waft Citizen Barlow to the City of Bones, a vision quest at the crux of *Gem of the Ocean* (2003), and Troy Maxson's wrestlings with Mr. Death in

Fences (1985). One of the playwright's most critically acclaimed supernatural scenarios, Bynum Walker's encounter with the mystic shiny man in *Joe Turner's Come and Gone* (1988), results in a reunion with the spirit of Bynum's father. Marked by oversized mouth and arms to suggest the significance of paternal words and deeds on the next generation, the elder Walker passes along "the Binding Song," an intuitive knowledge that confers blessing and reunion on scattered folk (p. 10). The spirit's revelation of an ocean imparts to Bynum "something I ain't got words to tell," a transcendent personal experience that fills him with confidence and willingness to aid others (*Ibid.*). Thus, Bynum's supernatural confers control over fate just as St. Paul's conversion offered him a binding power as well as the keys to the heavenly kingdom, a two-stage gift from Christ stated in Matthew 16:19.

Because Wilson focuses on the disruption of black lives by slavery and by the Great Migration from south to north, he invests major characters with the onus of the past and generates a cast of phantoms that dwells in the inner person. Thus, the appearance of supernatural elements in his decade cycle seems appropriate, almost expected, as with the ghost of Miss Mabel, Seth Holly's mother, that thrashes Reuben Mercer in *Joe Turner's Come and Gone;* the six black-hatted angels that Vera Dotson sees hovering at the graveside of Floyd Barton, who floats in the air above the casket in *Seven Guitars* (1995); and the phenomenally old Aunt Ester, a conductor of a vision quest in *Gem of the Ocean* (2003) and counselor and prophet in *Two Trains Running* (1991) and *King Hedley II* (1999).

Most puzzling to critics are the avenging specters in *The Piano Lesson* (1990), the Ghosts of the Yellow Dog who allegedly push the 340-pound Robert Sutter into his well and Sutter's ghost, which haunts both floors of Doaker's flat. Wilson uses the white man's rancorous spirit as a malevolent remnant of the slave past. Boy Willie Charles, who first scoffs at the idea of a poltergeist, later comes to believe that the phantom resides in the family piano and appears to Doaker, Boy Willie's sister Berniece, and her daughter Maretha. He urges that the way to drive it off is to sell the piano. With his sister's cooperation, Boy Willie ably battles the ghost to rid his family of a cycle of debilitating and demoralizing times.

The playwright's enlargement of supernatural elements in the falling action and resolution earns skepticism from literary analysts, who question how and why the slave-owner's ghost inhabits the Charles family heirloom. Critics label the device a crutch that enabled the playwright to resolve the differences between a squabbling brother and sister. Devon Boan disagrees: "[The ghosts] are mythical explanations, yet they serve to authenticate the lives of the men who died and became the Ghosts (just as Boy Willie seeks authentication through ownership of Sutter's land), and they serve to authenticate the sacredness of the piano itself—it was important enough for black men to die for, and it was important enough for white men to kill for" (Boan, p. 267).

See also **Aunt Ester, Reuben Mercer, *The Piano Lesson, Seven Guitars*, shiny man, superstition, Bynum Walker**

• *Further Reading*

Boan, Devon. "Call-and-Response: Parallel 'Slave Narrative' in August Wilson's 'The Piano Lesson.'" *African American Review*, Vol. 32, No. 2, Summer 1998, pp. 263–272.

Gantt, Patricia. "Ghosts from 'Down There': The Southernness of August Wilson," in *August Wilson: A Casebook*. New York: Garland, 1994.

King, Robert L. "World Premieres." *North American Review*, Vol. 280, No. 4, July-August 1995, pp. 44–48.

Pereira, Kim. *August Wilson and the African-American Odyssey*. Urbana: University of Illinois Press, 1995.

superstition

Wilson applies superstition to African American beliefs as evidence of power and omniscience as well as a source of solace and inner strength to those who believe in luck and the spirit world. Superstitious elements occur in *King Hedley II* (1999), in which the title character dreams he wears a halo, and permeate *Two Trains Running* (1991), in which ex-con Sterling Johnson testifies to good luck resulting from a rub on the head of the deceased Prophet Samuel. Wolf orders the cook and waitress Risa Thomas not to sweep at his feet lest he end up in jail. Holloway, a gambler and seeker of justice for the black man, ridicules folk superstitions such as fear of broken mirrors and of umbrellas opened in the house. He relates an incident in which the driver of a truck went insane after he crashed into a telephone pole and broke a load of mirrors. Holloway's tale is an ambiguous element in the play that both supports and refutes superstitions about the breaking of a looking glass.

Despite his brave talk, Holloway himself turns to the supernatural as a spiritual comfort. Both he and Risa have faith in the Prophet Samuel, who "say the truth ain't nothing to be afraid of" (p. 7). Holloway recommends that seekers of peace and consolation visit the savant Aunt Ester, the 322-year-old sage who lives behind the red door at 1839 Wylie Street, to allow her to lay her hands on their heads. Sterling looks to changes in the moon for signs of the end-time and clings to innate good fortune, which he says accompanied his birth. On Holloway's advice, he consults Aunt Ester and also views the remains of the Prophet Samuel. When Sterling's trust in dreams and the numbers game fails him, he begins counting Buicks, Cadillacs, and Fords to arrive at a winning number and accepts from Risa the number 781. These reliances on illogical sources of knowledge suit a company of characters who live in a tumble-down world that will soon fall to the wrecking ball. As though reaching back to the animism of their African ancestors, they demonstrate a lack of faith in the white world, which has brought them nothing but ill fortune and empty promises.

Other examples of superstition in Wilson's drama cycle require explanation and interpretation. In *Fences* (1985), the half-witted scavenger Gabe Maxson fantasizes about "chasing hellhounds" and anticipating the battle of Armageddon, the end-of-time conflict predicted in the biblical book of Revelation 9:16 (p. 47). In *The Piano Lesson* (1990), Wining Boy Charles summons invisible forces, "the Ghosts of the Yellow Dog," the spirits of his father Boy Charles and four hobos burned to death in a boxcar by Robert Sutter's henchmen. The ghosts hover "where the Southern [railroad] cross the Yellow Dog," a blues line recorded by W. C. Handy referring to the junction of the Yazoo Delta and Southern railroads (p. 34). Wining Boy provides a mystical interpretation to the event: "I can't say how they talk to nobody else.... I felt like the longer I stood there the bigger I got" (pp. 34–35). The experience was empowering, leaving him feeling like royalty. As analyzed by Margaret Thompson Drewel, "The crossroads is a prime spot to place sacrifices so that they will be taken to the otherworld, a practice that has been retained by both Cuban and American practitioners of Yoruba religion" (Drewel, p. 26).

At melodramatic moments in his dramas, Wilson's characters demonstrate their trust in superstition as an answer to difficulties, as with Bynum Walker's recounting of his father's healing a little white girl with a song and Bynum's transfiguration in a redemptive blood ceremony in *Joe Turner's Come and Gone* (1988). Stool Pigeon, the crazed seer in *King Hedley II*, interprets wind as "God riding through the land" and the loss of electricity as a sign that God has extinguished Aunt Ester's mystic power (p. 18). Less evocative is King Hedley's dependence on Miss Sarah Degree's root tea as a curative for tuberculosis in *Seven Guitars* (1995). He lauds her saintliness with exaggerated trust: "She got a power. She got her roots. She got her teas. She got her powders" (p. 19). The litany of her virtues declines into drollery after Hedley considers Sarah's worth as a lover. At the play's climax, when he slaughters a rooster and spills its blood in a ritual circle, Hedley displays another side of his belief in dark powers. His brash slicing of the bird's throat astounds the other characters, who have no inkling of the meaning of his actions and inchoate mutterings nor of the foreshadowing of sudden death to come.

Wilson indicates that characters often feel separation from African nature lore and spiritualism, which the diaspora left behind as blacks populated the New World. In *The Piano Lesson*, Berniece, the urbanized non-believer in the Charles family, turns away from African superstitions until the final scene, when she plays the piano and calls on ancestors to help her brother battle Robert Sutter's ghost. In a similar motif in *Joe Turner's Come and Gone*, Bynum Walker, the conjure man, reveals to protagonist Herald Loomis that his search in Pittsburgh is not for his estranged wife Martha, but for meaning and purpose for his future. In both examples, superstition becomes a bolster in a chaotic world and a handhold for people battered by post-slavery disorder and rootlessness.

See also **Jack Carper, death, Aunt Ester, gambling, King Hedley, Reuben Mercer, shiny man, Stool Pigeon, supernatural, Yoruba**

• *Further Reading*

Appiah, Kwame Anthony. *In My Father's House: Africa in the Philosophy of Culture*. New York: Oxford University Press, 1992.

Drewel, Margaret Thompson. *Yoruba Ritual*. Indianapolis: Indiana University Press, 1992.

Fleche, Anne. "The History Lesson: Authenticity and Anachronism in August Wilson's Plays," in *May All Your Fences Have Gates: Essays on the Drama of August Wilson*. Iowa City: University of Iowa Press, 1994, p. 1.

Gantt, Patricia. "Ghosts from 'Down There': The Southernness of August Wilson," in *August Wilson: A Casebook*. New York: Garland, 1994.

Shannon, Sandra G. *The Dramatic Vision of August Wilson*. Washington, D.C.: Howard University Press, 1996.

Sutter, Robert

Mississippi planter Robert Sutter, who owned a plantation in Sunflower County, was the villain in the miserable lives of the enslaved Charles family in *The Piano Lesson* (1990). To please his wife Ophelia on their anniversary, he traded Berniece Charles and her nine-year-old son, the family of plantation carpenter Willie Boy Charles, for a piano belonging to two Georgians, Joel Nolander and his brother. When Ophelia Sutter sickened and pined for Berniece, her cook and maid, Sutter set Willie Boy to carving portraits of Berniece and her boy on the piano. The implication is that Ophelia would be assuaged by masks of her former slaves and forget her wish to have them back in the flesh.

Ownership of the piano initiates a series of crimes and hauntings. The Charles brothers, twenty-two-year-old Doaker and thirty-one-year-old Wining Boy, steal the piano while whites attend a county picnic on July 4, 1911. Sutter's grandson, also named Robert, masterminds vigilante retaliation by burning the Charles house and immolating the boxcar in which Boy Charles and four vagrants are riding. Sutter mysteriously falls down a well and apparently breaks his neck, a suitable underworld death for a villain. When his brother James comes from Chicago to settle the estate, he offers the farm to Boy Willie Charles for two thousand dollars. The sale symbolizes the closure of an era of white domination of the South's agrarian economy, but the crimes remain unpunished and trickery flourishes in James Sutter's one-third increase in price of the land to a black buyer. In the form of a specter, Robert Sutter returns to Doaker's Pittsburgh flat to inhabit the piano and harry the family. As though holding his head in place with one hand, the spirit suggests the degeneration of white power over years of adversity against blacks.

See also **supernatural, superstition**

• *Further Reading*

Boan, Devon. "Call-and-Response: Parallel 'Slave Narrative' in August Wilson's 'The Piano Lesson.'" *African American Review*, Vol. 32, No. 2, Summer 1998, pp. 263–272.
Gibron, Bill. "The Piano Lesson." *Artisan*, February 12, 2003.
Leib, Mark. "Keys of History: *The Piano Lesson* Imparts Importance of Our African-American Past." *Weekly Planet*, February 12, 2003.
Zimmerman, Heather. "Keys to the Past." *Silicon Valley Metro*, April 5–11, 2001.

Thomas, Clarissa "Risa"

The beleaguered cook and waitress at Memphis Lee's cafe in *Two Trains Running* (1991), Risa Thomas forms one half of August Wilson's first multifaceted stage courtship. A soft touch in a tough part of Pittsburgh, she extends a maternal welcome to the diner's male clientele. She cooks well and willingly waits on customers, bringing a spot of hospitality and joy to an otherwise gloomy neighborhood. Unlike the weary Rose Maxson in *Fences* (1985), flirty Ruby in *Seven Guitars* (1995) and coaxing Dussie Mae in *Ma Rainey's Black Bottom* (1985), and the accusing mate Rena in *Jitney*, Risa keeps to herself and chooses celibacy and a quiet self-assurance as her means of coping with fears and inadequacies. To Sterling Johnson's comments about losing her job, she has enough confidence in her importance to the diner to declare, "I ain't worried about getting fired" (p. 18). Wilson lauds her strength of character for its relief of a progression of unemployed and hopeless people in his decade cycle.

Unlike Memphis, Risa looks for the best in people. She expresses tolerance for Hambone, the retarded handyman who comes to the cafe for coffee and food. She gives him a coat, defends his reputation, and trusts his ability to understand complex people and community events. A one-on-one person, she enjoys dancing with Sterling Johnson, but rejects his gifts of stolen gas and flowers snitched from the Prophet Samuel's viewing. Risa chooses not to view the prophet's remains or to attend the Malcolm X celebration at the Savoy Ballroom because she dislikes crowds. Her reasoning is sensible: "I don't want to go down there with them niggers. There might be a riot or something" (p. 47). Her intense self-protection and brief replies to Memphis's complaints indicate a person who is accustomed to warding off attackers.

Like the other characters, Risa battles loneliness but is too savvy to give up her independence by banking on a destructive relationship like those that burden the lives of Mama Ola and Berniece Charles in *The Piano Lesson* (1990), Ruby and Vera Dotson in *Seven Guitars*, and Rose Maxson and Troy Maxson's first wife in *Fences*. Risa speaks directly to Sterling about her fears: "I don't want to be tied up with nobody I got to be worrying is they gonna rob another bank of something.... You'll never have me sitting and worrying what you gonna do next" (pp. 100, 101). In her other relationships, she appears to flourish as a Christian fundamentalist who anticipates the end-time promised in the bible. Her longest speeches involve defense of the Prophet Samuel. Of the interest in viewers in his corpse, she declares, "If you be a hypocrite it don't count with God. He want you all the time" (pp. 86–87). Her insistance that "God sent him to help the colored people get justice" is touching for its sincerity and naivete (p. 87).

Risa's appearance is pleasing enough to make Memphis comment that "a man would be happy to have a woman like that" (p. 31). She immediately draws the eye of ex-con Sterling Johnson, who remembers her in years past as the skinny sister who cooked for her brother Rodney. Memphis puzzles over her decision to slice her own legs fifteen strokes with a razor, seven on one side and eight on the other. Critics also surmise that she is too shy to admit that she also mutilated her genitals, an act she hints at with mention of an extra scar and by her embarrassment when Sterling asks, "Where you get the one from?" (p. 49). The possibility of African-style genital mutilation and of the defeat of Western beauty standards through leg scarring combines two traditions in Risa's complex reaction to male admirers.

Holloway supplies the answer to her self-marring with his evaluation of a woman who matured too early. Because men began pursuing her at age twelve, to avoid having to "lay up with them somewhere," she ruined the beauty of her legs to force males to see her as a person rather than a sex object (*Ibid.*). Memphis's rejection of so self-destructive a person makes a commentary on Wilson's many devalued, scarred characters. Like the emotionally hampered Troy Maxson in *Fences*, wifeless wanderer Herald Loomis in *Joe Turner's Come and Gone* (1988), Tonya Hedley, the indecisive mother-to-be in *King Hedley II* (1999), grudge-bearing Black Mary in *Gem of the*

Ocean (2003), and vindictive widow Berniece Charles in *The Piano Lesson*, Risa bears permanent marks of psychic pain, even though Western Psych, a state facility, could make no definite diagnosis of mental illness.

Risa remains an enigma to males, whom she serves at the counter but holds at a distance. Holloway, Memphis, and Wolf differ in their responses to Risa's self-torment. Holloway considers her normal. Memphis fears that a self-mutilating woman like Risa might cut the throat of her mate. Wolf, who offers a purely sexual solution to Risa's anguish, believes that, after six years of loneliness, she needs romancing by "a good man" (*Ibid.*). All three fail to value her altruism and compassion toward Hambone and her devotion to the teachings of the Prophet Samuel as proof of a warm heart that suffices on expressing goodness and love to others. Wilson abandons the love interest between Risa and Sterling, causing critics to charge him with advancing subplots without bringing them to fruition.

See also **self-destruction**

• *Further Reading*

Marra, Kim. "Ma Rainey and the Boyz: Gender Ideology in August Wilson's Broadway Canon," in *August Wilson: A Casebook*. New York: Garland, 1994.
Pettengill, Richard. "The Historical Perspective: An Interview with August Wilson," in *August Wilson: A Casebook*. New York: Garland, 1994.
Weales, Gerald Clifford. "Two Trains Running." *Commonweal*, Vol. 119, June 1992, p. 18.

Toledo

The literate, philosophical pianist in *Ma Rainey's Black Bottom* (1985), Toledo recognizes the black American's low social status as the leftovers of the white man's table. He is content with the simple life and would return to farming to "smell that dirt. Be out there by yourself ... nice and peaceful," but is too old to plow behind a mule (p. 93). He considers the entertainer's life a lucky economic opportunity in contrast to people limited to hauling wood.

In creating a verbal jazz combo from the dissonant interaction of Levee, Cutler, Slow Drag, and Toledo, the playwright assigns Toledo the role of harmonizer and organizer of black efforts to redeem themselves, even after Levee insults him as a "cracker-talking nigger" (p. 31). Toledo exhorts, "It's everybody! What you think ... I'm gonna solve the colored man's problems by myself? I said, we. You understand that. We" (p. 42). To stress the importance of a unified effort, he adds, "That's every living colored man in the world got to do his share. Got to do his part (*Ibid.*). When Levee Green warns Cutler, "I ain't but two seconds off your ass no way," it's Toledo who urges, "Don't you all start nothing now" (p. 106). Unfortunately, his idealism layered against Levee's anger foreshadows a clash before the company can depart the studio.

Wilson sets Toledo apart from the other musicians by showcasing his education. Because he is the only character who can read, he wins a bet against jazz trumpeter Levee Green about spelling "music." Although Toledo respects his profession and lauds Ma for her unique blues style, he stands outside the frame of reference for uneducated blacks who have only oral stories, hymns, spirituals, and the blues as sources of culture. He is the victim of Levee during a lengthy conversation that turns into a discussion of black history. In Toledo's view, black culture is a lost cause because "We done sold Africa for the price of tomatoes.... We done sold who we are in order to become someone else" (p. 93). Wilson sets him up like Malcolm X and Dr. Martin Luther King, two literate visionaries who were martyred in the cause of black education.

Toledo recognizes that his aggressor is immature, but doesn't recognize how severely his verbal agility agitates and grates on Levee. Of Levee's brash self-promotion, Toledo jokes, "Levee think he the king of the barnyard. He think he's the only rooster know how to crow" (p. 59). After warning Levee about romancing Dussie Mae, Toledo is man enough to admit the mistakes of his own youth, when he and God vied for the same woman. Following marriage to a worthy woman, he lost her to Christianity after she joined the church and denigrated him as a heathen. When she left his house empty, he castigated himself for failing to see that "she needed something that I wasn't giving her" (p. 91). He admits, "So, yeah, Toledo been a fool about a woman. That's part of making life" (*Ibid.*). To a self-promoter like Levee, Toledo's honesty suggests weakness rather than character.

The final battle retreats from philosophy to trivia: Levee differs with Toledo on matters of status by contrasting the older man's clodhoppers to Levee's new Florsheim shoes. As pseudo-expert and provocateur, Toledo, the combo's graybeard, is unaware of the severity of Levee's emotional maladjustment or of how much venom Levee stores up against adversity. By inadvertently stepping on the costly Florsheims, Toledo incites a lethal retribution and dies on the studio floor of a stab wound in the back. Wilson sets up the knifing scene as an explanation of black-on-black violence when the younger generation fails to comprehend the dignity and self-esteem of its elders. Ironically, Toledo has adequate reason to be bitter because of the dissolution of his family, yet he is the most peace-loving, pro-black, and thoughtful member of the four-man band.

- *Further Reading*

Clark, Keith. *Black Manhood in James Baldwin, Ernest J. Gaines, and August Wilson.* Urbana: University of Illinois Press, 2002.
Gener, Randy. "Salvation in the City of Bones: Ma Rainey and Aunt Ester Sing Their Own Songs in August Wilson's Grand Cycle of Blues Dramas." *American Theatre*, Vol. 20, No. 5, May-June 2003, pp. 20–28.
Harrison, Paul Carter. "August Wilson's Blues Poetics," in *Three Plays*. Pittsburgh: University of Pittsburgh Press, 1991.

Turnbo

A nosy, sanctimonious cabbie in *Jitney* (1982), Turnbo is the playwright's mouthpiece and source of background information as well as the play's Pandora. As described by the reviewer for the *London Times*, he is "the sort of harmless-seeming chap who talks scandal, delights in others' setbacks, stirs trouble, yet takes violent offence" ("Jitney"). By releasing multiple evils among the station's cabbies, the elderly troublemaker is responsible for a pernicious imbalance among men who are essentially congenial.

Turnbo spreads the story of the theft of Sarah Bolger's television by her teenage grandson, McNeil's older boy, whom Turnbo dehumanizes as having "an old funny shaped head" (p. 20). He later maligns Shealy's nephew Robert as a rogue and thug who's served time in the workhouse for breaking into Taylor's bar, Turnbo justifies his assumptions about folly by reminding his audience that he foresaw rashness in Jasper, a suicide who jumped from the Irene Kaufman Settlement House. Turnbo intrudes on Youngblood's relationship with Rena by warning her of his interest in her sister Peaches. To return the station to peaceful working conditions, Becker skewers Turnbo as the neighborhood yenta: "You just like an old lady, always gossiping and running off at the mouth" (p. 21).

As the play develops, Turnbo plays an obvious game of compensation to free himself of criticism and to elevate his meddling to the level of useful advice. With circular logic he rationalizes, "I just live and let live, but damn if I can't talk to express an opinion same as everybody else" (p. 25). To Rena, he declares that he learned respect for others in boyhood and discovered from experience that "it come back to you double" (p. 30). He spouts a lengthy monologue to shore up his reputation while he ventures into a warning that Youngblood is two-timing her. Self-righteously, he declares, "I'm telling you this for your own good" (p. 32). After trying to take Youngblood's rightful fare, Turnbo rejects his next client so he can eavesdrop on the resulting quarrel between Youngblood and Rena. In Act I, Scene 4, during the tense reunion of Jim and Booster Becker, Turnbo repeats his skulking about to overhear an obviously private conversation.

Wilson portrays Turnbo as a man skirting the edge of disaster by goading Youngblood with successive incidents of pettiness, crepe-hanging about the destruction of the Hill District, and toying with violence. Turnbo's jaundiced view of the world sees half his contemporaries as "running on empty" (p. 29). He predicts that civic authorities "won't be satisfied until they tear the whole goddamn neighborhood down!" (p. 38). In keeping with the rise in district violence, he has a reputation for pulling a gun that he keeps in his car. He once threatened a man over a half-dollar fare and has no hesitation in drawing on Youngblood. Doub predicts that, after the four or five incidents in the past, Turnbo is actually going to fire on someone. The playwright reduces the threat of gunplay with a simple assault. As a result of Turnbo's careless nosing into private matters and spreading specious rumors about Peaches and Youngblood's car trips and telephone conversations, Youngblood punches the older man in the mouth, one source of the play's undercurrent of discontent.

• *Further Reading*

Berson, Misha. "Humor, Hope Hitch Ride on Wilson's Engrossing 'Jitney.'" *Seattle Times*, January 30, 2002.
"Jitney." *London Times*, October 16, 2001.

Turner, Joe

The name of Joseph "Joe" Turney, whom blacks call "Turner," was a red flag to the underclass during the Jim Crow era. Turner was a sheriff in Memphis, Tennessee, and the youngest brother of Peter "Pete" Turney, a Civil War hero as colonel of the First Tennessee Infantry and a successful Democrat who governed Tennessee for two terms, from 1893 to 1897. By arranging incriminating crap games and manipulating political connections, the real Turner had black men arrested, sentenced to seven-year terms, and remanded to chain gangs, which he leased as labor for his plantation. When people asked the whereabouts of a prisoner, which the sheriff spirited away during the night, the standard reply was "Joe Turner's come and gone." Ironically, Pete Turney garnered votes from the laboring class by denouncing the brutal convict lease system and by calling for the construction of more state prisons. His political climb also placed him over important legal issues as state supreme court chief justice and later as a U.S. senator.

Further confusing the issue of Joe Turner/Turney's identity are the blues shouter Big Joe Turner, who flourished in Kansas City in the late 1930s, and the repeated line from one of the earliest blues songs ever recorded, which August Wilson chooses as the title for his play. A family of blues work chants—"Old Joe Turner Blues" and "Going Down the River Before Long"— developed by Bill Big Broonzy, W. C. Handy, and Mississippi John Hurt — pictures Turner as "Joe Turney," a complex blend of personae that is both mercy man and demon, a good Samaritan to blacks and a white dominator of the underclass in the late nineteenth century who transports negro prisoners from Memphis, Tennessee, at midnight to the lockup in Nashville. In Handy's version, "Joe Turner Blues" (1915), the rapid arrival and departure of the enslaver Turner explains the failure of black fieldhands to return home to their families.

August Wilson turns the shadow of an historical figure into the fictional victimizer of Herald Loomis, former chain gang laborer and protagonist of *Joe Turner's Come and Gone* (1988). In an interview, the playwright explained that, in Tennessee, "when the men would be late coming home from the fields, someone would say, 'Haven't you heard? Joe Turner's come and gone.' Soon the women around Memphis made up this song" (Bandler). Although Loomis has never seen Turner, the terror of a sudden swooping down of kidnappers and the dehumanization of chains and forced labor become symbolic enemies that strip Loomis and other convicts of their humanity and self-worth. The dispossessed, like those who gather at Bertha and Seth Holly's rooming house, are fixed in concentric circles of misery that radiate out to their lovers, wives, and children. The separate lovers and fragmented families left behind by roving men provide August Wilson with themes just as they generated generations of classic blues lyrics.

• *Further Reading*

Bandler, Michael J. "USIA Interview with American Playwright August Wilson." http://usembassy-australia.state.gov/hyper/WF980415/epf308.htm, April 15, 1998.
Barbour, David. "August Wilson's Here to Stay." *Theater Week*, April 25, 1988, pp. 8–14.

Two Kings, Solly

One of August Wilson's obsessive characters, Solly Two Kings, in his late sixties, is a mighty and relentless agent of the black diaspora. A fellow quarry with Citizen Barlow in *Gem of the Ocean* (2003), at age sixty-seven, Solly wars against injustice. He still looks and dresses the part of a former slave and tracker for the Union Army. According to reviewer Laura Hitchcock, "He has the authority of a king in the shabby clothes of a homeless person" (Hitchcock). At his dramatic self-introduction in the play, he slams his former leg chain onto Aunt Ester Tyler's table and declares, "That's my good-luck piece. That piece of chain used to be around my ankle. They tried to chain me down but I beat them on that one. I say I'm gonna keep this to remember by. I been lucky ever since" (Phillips, p. 1).

Crotchety from frustrated ideals, Solly is a living legend, an icon of the unbowed former slave. As a conductor on the Underground Railroad, in 1857, he once aided other blacks fleeing the plantation system. He relives the flight of seven others to Canada, which he dubs "Freedom-land," and recalls: "All the time the dogs after you. All the time. You got to keep going. I done been bit nine times by dogs" ("Gem of the Ocean"). The statement resonates with warning to blacks who enter the twentieth century naively expecting fewer hounds on their trail.

Like Barlow, Solly is a cagey survivor who flees the unrelenting spite of Caesar, the inhumane lawman. Solly's courage and persistence derive from observing the extremes that slaves dared for a taste of liberty. He states as a creed, "You gotta fight to make [freedom] worth something. I saw many a man die for it, and didn't understand what he was fighting for" (Hodgins, p. 1). In a symbolic recycling system, he collects dog dung from the streets to sell for fertilizer. His elevation of "great dane pure" suggests the black man's ability to redirect the raging dogs of slave catchers into generators of a peacetime commodity (Preston, p. 4F).

As with others newly snatched from bondage, the release brought no clear view of the future. Without an aim to guide him, Solly chose to return south and free his family. By the time of the Emancipation Proclamation, which President Abraham Lincoln issued on January 1, 1863, Solly had freed sixty-two former slaves, registering each with a notch on his walking stick. To keep fresh his exploits, he points out to Barlow a portion of muscle gnawed by a dog. Solly reveres freedom, but knows that the fight for quality of life in the white world is ongoing. Without undue rancor, he is selective in his blame of whites and claims as friend the white peddler Rutherford Selig, whom Aunt Ester freely admits to the rear entrance of her home.

As a foil for Caesar, the implacable black constable and cat's paw of the white majority, Solly allies with Aunt Ester, the matriarch of the Pittsburgh boarding house, whom he longs to marry. He witnesses the disparate lives of Southern blacks fleeing north in hopes of finding a more satisfying environment. In repudiating slavery as the curse of the black race, he relives the torment of the Middle Passage. From personal experience, he declares that no misery was worse than enslavement, even the indignities of the Jim Crow era. Solly is willing to return to the South to rescue his sister from the spite of Klansmen, who target those blacks who thrive by competing with whites. At play's end, he passes his quest to Barlow, who has undergone a spiritual change in readying himself for the task.

• *Further Reading*

Hitchcock, Laura. "Gem of the Ocean." *Los Angeles Review*, July 30, 2003.
Hodgins, Paul. "Finding the Cost of Freedom: Slavery and Its Aftermath Are Explored in 'Gem of the Ocean.' August Wilson's Latest Play." *Orange County Register*, August 1, 2003, p. 1.
Philips, Michael. "Wilson's 'Gem' a Diamond in the Rough." *Chicago Tribune*, April 30, 2003, p. 1.
Preston, Rohan. "Oglesby Sparkles in Wilson's 'Gem.'" *Minneapolis Star Tribune*, May 4, 2003, p. 4F.

Two Trains Running

Set at Memphis Lee's dilapidated Pittsburgh diner over seven days in mid–May, 1969, *Two Trains Running* (1991) is the first of August Wilson's plays to picture realistic romance and to end with an identifiable victory over oppression. As director Lloyd Richards described the milieu, the story takes place "where the rivers converge, where the boats of the various rivers come and go, one behind the other. They pick up baggage, baggage and people, baggage of ideas, and it all flows into and out of this cistern" (Pettengill, p. 203). The drama, according to Minneapolis reviewer Dylan Hicks, is a "one-set, real-as-dirt, vox-humana play" (Hicks). Lacking a focal character, the text contours the community itself into a living entity, an endangered body slowly strangling from inner city decline, crime, and urban encroachment. Those characters who survive do so with nobility and courage.

The plot, moody and freighted with personal regrets, turns on the responses of regular diner customers and staff to local matters, including the jailing of Bubba Boy and the pending sale of the working-class eatery and gathering spot. The naturalistic dialogue dismays some critics, who fail to value Wilson's survey of the individual and community struggles of the times. Against the backdrop of the urban Black Power movement, one woman and six men, including Wolf the numbers runner, a retarded handyman, and an ex-con named Sterling Johnson, ponder the heritage of lives spent at hard labor for limited wages. Dreamers and idealists like Holloway pin their hopes on gambling and the promises of Nation of Islam leader Malcolm X. More experienced men like the undertaker West know that money comes from careful calculation and hard-nosed bargaining.

To show characters taking responsibility for their lives, Wilson depicts the young cook and waitress Risa Thomas, who fears the crowds at a Malcolm X rally, and Sterling, her admirer, an orphan from infancy who was on his own at age eighteen. Wilson depicts Risa deliberately slicing her legs thirteen times with a razor to define herself as something more than a bauble for men to ogle. In his notes, he observes that she wants to be known "in terms other than her genitalia" (p. 3). In a parallel to Johnson's awkward courtship of Risa, the playwright depicts negotiation between urban renewal officials and a property owner. He champions Memphis Lee as a tough-minded businessman who intends to sells his property for $25,000.

As in all Wilson's decade plays, *Two Trains Running* incorporates death as the ultimate in earthly change. The motif takes the form of a neighborhood viewing of the remains of Prophet Samuel, the return of Miss Mabel's ghost, cheap welfare caskets, Hambone's sudden death, and speculation on when Aunt Ester will die. Most obvious are the behaviors of West, the black-gloved undertaker. Memphis jokes about the mortician's guarantees on leak-proof coffins. With a pragmatist's logic he demand, "You gonna dig up the casket twenty years later to see if it's leaking and go back and tell West and get your hundred dollars back?" (p. 12). The iffiness of guarantees on funeral arrangements characterizes the impermanence of life in the Hill District, which is rapidly vanishing as more lucrative uses of the land displace small businesses in the black community.

More significant than a human death is the demise of an African American institution, in this case, an everyday diner serving soul food. The serving counter becomes a gathering spot and sounding board for the concerns, hopes, and dreams of locals. Memphis, who does battle with City Hall, demands twenty-five thousand dollars for his property, which authorities value at only sixty percent of that amount. At the play's end, Wilson retreats from frequent references to loss by portraying Memphis as a winner after he negotiates the surprising offer of thirty-five thousand for his cafe, a gain of forty percent over the asking price.

In a 1993 interview with Sandra G. Shannon, Wilson stated the quandary of *Two Trains Running*— whether blacks should abandon their culture and assimilate into American society or remain apart from mainstream America by perpetuating Afrocentric culture. He expressed his respect for ghetto residents who remain true to themselves by rejecting the changes necessary to appease and gain the respect of white culture. In his estimation, it is these abstainers who suffer socially and economically. Their reward comes from an inner satisfaction in perpetuating their African traits and in sustaining personal integrity.

See also **death, Aunt Ester, Hambone, Sterling Johnson, Memphis Lee, Malcolm X, Prophet Samuel, soul food, Clarissa "Risa" Thomas, West**

• *Further Reading*

Hicks, Dylan. "Doing What Comes Naturally." *Minneapolis City Pages,* Vol. 24, No. 1160, February 26, 2003.

Kanfer, Stefan. "Two Trains Running." *New Leader,* Vol. 75, No. 6, May 4, 1992, p. 21.

Pereira, Kim. *August Wilson and the African-American Odyssey.* Urbana: University of Illinois Press, 1995.

Pettengill, Richard. "Alternatives ... Opposites ... Convergences: An Interview with Lloyd Richards," in *August Wilson: A Casebook.* New York: Garland, 1994.

Weales, Gerald Clifford. "Two Trains Running." *Commonweal,* Vol. 119, June 1992, p. 18.

urbanism

A troubling theme in Wilson's drama points to the African American's unsuitability for big-city life, from the exploitation of hapless mill workers in *Gem of the*

Ocean (2003) to the disgruntlement of cab drivers in *Jitney* (1982) and low pay to ex-cons and the title figure's uproar in Sears over a receipt in *King Hedley II* (1999). Some clashes appear minor, yet nettling, for example, in 1948, Floyd Barton's confusion over a missing workhouse voucher and Miss Tillery's problems with a rooster and unlicensed dog in the city limits of Pittsburgh in *Seven Guitars* (1995). With a country girl's logic, Ruby remarks, "All you got to do is watch [the dog] and see where he go when he go home. You don't need no license for that" (p. 83). In *Two Trains Running* (1991), which takes place in 1969, Wilson describes the troubles of the Reverend Samuel in evangelizing in white neighborhoods. Whites have him arrested on suspicion that he wants to steal from them. Samuel's troubles worsen after he is arrested for income-tax evasion, a charge that U.S. Treasury agents effectively lodged against Chicago gangster chief Al Capone in October 1931 to end a lengthy crime spree.

Personal finances and ownership enlarge to a major issue when they involve real estate in the black community. The playwright places protagonist Memphis Lee, the diner owner in *Two Trains Running*, in conflict with city officials over the acquisition of his property for an urban development project bringing new highway to Pittsburgh's inner city. Lee bemoans the reshaping of downtown Pittsburgh and the effect on blacks of losing their neighborhood: "Ain't nothing gonna be left around here. Supermarket gone. Two drugstores. The five and ten. Doctor done moved out. Dentist done moved out. Shoe store gone" (p. 9). He predicts that disenfranchisement will lead to violence: "Ain't nothing gonna be left but these niggers killing one another" (*Ibid.*). His statement implies that ownership prevents crime by making black residents proud of their homes and protective of their businesses. On the down side, as prosperity and independence slip away, morality and respect for law are also endangered.

With the destruction of buildings come the problems of unemployment, which stymy black men who are willing to work, but are unable to find jobs. In the same play, Sterling Johnson, an unemployed dinner patron and smooth-talking ex-con, recalls the hardships faced by his foster father, Mr. Johnson, who worked thirty years at a mill and after hours as a janitor at a fish market. In token of hard labor for little reward or respect from white business owners, Sterling shies away from honest work. He complains about the inexplicable rules of city employment: "I went over to J & L Steel and they told me I got to join the union before I could work. I went down to the union and they told me I got to be working before I could join the union" (p. 20). The ping-pong effect of conflicting regulations reduces Sterling to dependence on wily street smarts rather than middle-class values.

Other characters seem similarly out of sync with urban values and behaviors. In *The Piano Lesson* (1990), which takes place in 1936, Lymon Jackson needs to protect his truckload of watermelons, stereotypical symbols of black agrarian values. To guard against pilfering on the streets of Squirrel Hill, a toney white neighborhood, he must sleep in his truck. In *Seven Guitars* (1995), characters mourn restrictions on black success. They live in the inner city, where thievery is rampant, forcing the wary to bar their doors. Vera Dotson, girlfriend of blues musician Floyd Barton, listens to his florid description of the blues scene in Chicago, but doubts the city's overblown promise to his career. She distances herself from him and his visions of fame and wealth by remaining behind. Her friend Louise rebukes another outsider, King Hedley, a Bible-crazed West Indian visionary who believes that God will punish racists and award him a plantation. Louise snorts, "Ain't no plantations in Pittsburgh, fool! This the city" (p. 24).

In *Fences* (1985), set in 1957, Wilson orchestrates the despair of the "descendents of African slaves," whom white society relegates to the low end of the caste system (p. xvii). In the introduction, he contrasts the acclimation of European immigrants with that of Southern blacks from "the Carolinas and the Virginias, Georgia, Alabama, Mississippi, and Tennessee" (*Ibid.*). He particularizes the rejection of blacks by Pittsburghers and mentions the high prices that the black grocer Bella charges in comparison to the A & P, which is ten cents cheaper per item. His essay names the humble jobs that sustain the survivors—collecting refuse, laundering clothes, cleaning houses, and shining shoes. The opportunities remain at the level of work that slaves once performed for their masters.

The setting of fifty-three-year-old Troy Maxson's house bears two oil drums as garbage cans, a reminder of his job as a Pittsburgh garbage man. He regrets furniture bought on time over a fifteen-year period because less expensive bank credit is unavailable to blacks, even those regularly employed. Although Troy stands up to the system by demanding a change in the job description to acknowledge the rights of black "lifters" to drive garbage trucks, he is still trapped in a low-end job, which fills him with distaste for his life and frequent musings on death (p. 2). Increasing his discontent is the decision of his son Lyons Maxson to pursue a catch-as-catch-can career in music rather than hoist the slops of white neighborhoods and toss them into a garbage truck.

See also **crime, Great Migration, opportunity, poverty, rooster, victimization, violence**

• *Further Reading*

Watlington, Dennis. "Hurdling Fences." *Vanity Fair*, Vol. 356, April 1989, pp. 102–113.

victimization

Wilson walks a fine line between depicting blacks as survivors and as victims, a charge leveled by the playwright's most vocal critic, Robert Brustein, long-time columnist for *New Republic*. Examples of Wilson's portrayals include the shady dealings of the title character and his partner Mister in *King Hedley II* (1999), two felons striving for a legitimate video outlet; the false incarceration of Herald Loomis on a Tennessee chain gang in *Joe Turner's Come and Gone* (1988); the exploitation of Levee Green's musical compositions in *Ma Rainey's Black Bottom* (1985); the proposed razing of a black-owned cab stand in *Jitney* (1982); and constable Caesar's terrorizing of an innocent man for petty theft in *Gem of the Ocean* (2003). On the down side of the Great Migration from the agrarian South to the industrialized North, during the 1940s, Floyd Barton and Canewell in *Seven Guitars* (1995) encounter repressive vagrancy laws that target the poor, unemployed, and homeless by declaring them worthless and, therefore, culpable. Because Canewell produces five dollars from his pocket, the Chicago police release him. However, in another incident, Floyd has no money and must serve ninety days in a Pittsburgh workhouse at the pivotal moment in his career when the Savoy Record Company wants him to make a second disk. From bitter experience with racist cops, Floyd sneers that possession of a pistol would have worsened his predicament: "They would have tried to dig a hole and put me under the jail" (p. 9). His remark is typical of the cynical, can't-win attitude that permeates black society.

In *Two Trains Running* (1991), Wilson characterizes the self-impairment of Memphis Lee, who was tricked by L. D. into buying the diner for fifty-five hundred dollars without the knowledge that L. D. owed twelve hundred in back taxes. Rather than grumble about being cheated by a dying black man, Memphis chooses to complain about the wrongs done him by grasping white urban authorities. As a balance, Wilson creates Hambone, a mentally retarded handyman in his forties and the model of the self-actualized individual who refuses to be bamboozled. For nine and a half years, the man rejects butcher Lutz's offer of a chicken in payment for painting a fence around the meat market. Because the original deal called for a ham if the paint job was well done, Hambone refuses anything less, muttering repeatedly "He gonna give me my ham. I want my ham. He gonna give me my ham" (p. 14). The rise of Hambone from fuzzy-brained derelict to example of integrity and self-respect occurs after his sudden death, which prompts residents of the Hill District to collect money to honor their departed champion. The spontaneous outpouring illustrates Wilson's contention that black people admire the individual who demands justice.

See also **Robert Brustein, cultural nationalism, urbanism, white-black relations**

• *Further Reading*

O'Mahony, John. "American Centurion." Manchester *Guardian*, December 14, 2002.

violence

Threats pump adrenaline in the males in Wilson's dramas, elucidating the causes of a disturbing pattern of random violence and self-destruction in blacks. Reviewer Jonathan Abarbanel characterized the cause as "the 900 lb. gorilla of dominant white society, proscribing black culture and pushing it inward, initiating the cycle of black-on-black exploitation and violence that permeates the series" (Abarbanel). Critic Harry Elam notes that, in an era when the self is fractured by doubt and uncertainty, homicide is a leading cause of death in young black males between ages sixteen and twenty-five, the result of carnage on city streets.

Moving beyond fists, Wilson's characters choose deadlier weapons, such as the razor in *King Hedley II* (1999) that Elmore's daddy used to kill eleven people and Pernell Sims's razor, which strikes Hedley's face in a "hot flash" and leaves it "warm and wet" with a gash that requires four hours' work and a hundred and twelve stitches to close (p. 90). In *Seven Guitars* (1995), Red Carter mentions knives, icepicks, meat cleavers, and a hatchet as possible self-protection for local blacks. The original weapon of choice is the personal blade, the raw edge that an angry rival flashes at Slow Drag in *Ma Rainey's Black Bottom* (1982), the knife that Herald Loomis lifts against obstacles in *Joe Turner's Come and Gone* (1988), and the machete, a common field tool of Caribbean islanders that King Hedley brandishes in *Seven Guitars*. Near the end of his virility and earning power, the paranoid Hedley exults in the gift of the machete, which will be his protection when whites "come to take him away" (p. 87).

Although Canewell holds on to the machete that kills Floyd Barton and carries it onstage in *King Hedley II* (1999), the generation that follows Hedley prefers the handgun, a ubiquitous weapon that requires a different style of agility and menace. When hard times force the elder Hedley's friend Red Carter to pawn his gun, he feels unsettled without the comfort of a pistol. Another friend, Floyd Barton, is a driven musician who takes an electric guitar out of pawn while contemplating hocking his .38. In reference to his need of force, he zeros in on the beautiful and appealing Vera Dotson, a "woman a man kill somebody over" (p. 12). Later, upon finding Canewell's hat in Vera's apartment, Floyd displays jealousy and possessiveness by growling, "You living dangerous" (p. 16). The threat is potentially lethal for both men, for Canewell has his own reputation for knifing enemies.

Wilson's conversants disagree about the type of weapon that is most effective. Red, who contemplates Canewell's past record with the blade, jeers that his knife is so slow that it's ancient history. When facing an adversary, Red prefers to "put four or five holes in him before he can draw back his arm" (p. 43). Floyd concurs that guns are superior. He claims that big guns and the atomic bomb are the reason for an American victory in World War II. Ironically, it is Hedley's skill with the primitive field hand's machete rather than the modern pistol that brings about Floyd's unforeseen death.

Wilson pursues the problem of inner-city gun violence in the play's sequel, *King Hedley II*, set in 1985. After Ruby gives birth to a son, he grows up to be the title figure in the latter play, where inner Pittsburgh seethes with gang warfare, random assault on the elderly, and drive-by shootings. To Stool Pigeon, the mad prophet, such violence as the shooting of Little Buddy Will lacks manly honor because its "stealing somebody's life from the back seat of a Toyota" (p. 37). In the six-character play, four are armed with guns, including the fateful pearl-handled derringer that Elmore sells Mister, who feels like the Lone Ranger. Reliance on fire power fails to improve community lives and prompts Tonya Hedley to consider aborting her child rather than bring another human being into a deadly milieu.

Wilson correlates pistols with faux masculinity and the ominous ambiguity of weaponry as a symbol of self-protection and control as well as random or unintentional killing. In *King Hedley II*, King, like his partner-in-crime Mister, sports a Glock 9mm pistol and shoves in the clip on stage; Elmore goes armed with a Smith and Wesson .38 Special because "They got too many fools out there" (p. 37). In *Jitney* (1982), set in 1977, a pistol ends Booster Becker's anticipation of a college career after he shoots Susan McKnight dead on her front porch for her trumped-up rape charge against him. Validating Booster's rash act is another hothead, Youngblood, who declares, "Served the bitch right!" (p. 41). Turnbo, an older cabbie working for Booster's father Jim, retorts, "See, that's what's wrong with you young folks" (p. 42). After Booster serves a twenty-year prison sentence, pistols are still the settlers of differences. Following a senseless workplace argument, Turnbo takes the opposite point of view by aiming his pistol at Youngblood. With the advantage over a younger, stronger man, Turnbo finds the courage to taunt and threaten to "blow your ass to kingdom come!" (p. 44). However, as is true throughout the play, it is not guns but Turnbo's mouth that causes the most damage.

Wilson depicts the ambivalence of blacks toward carrying concealed weapons. Memphis Lee, a changed man since his arrival to Pittsburgh from Mississippi in *Two Trains Running* (1991), believes Black Power advocates are fools for not carrying guns. Overawed by handguns, he recalls a time he shored up his courage with four or five hundred dollars in his pocket and "one of them big .44s" (p. 8). In a droll touch, he admits, "Used to scare me to look at it" (p. 9). To Sterling Johnson, a cafe patron released from the penitentiary a week before after serving a sentence for bank robbery, waitress Clarissa "Risa" Thomas comments on her brother Rodney, who moved from Pittsburgh to Cleveland "before he kill somebody" (p. 18). Likewise, Wolf, the numbers runner, considers arming himself after his employers, the Alberts, arousing anger in gamblers by halving the winnings on a popular number. He reconsiders because he fears that he might have to use his pistol on an angry client. The hesitance of armed males to accept the possibility of shooting someone indicates that brash he-man talk about carrying a gun covers practical concerns for the outcome of sudden violence.

Wilson offers numerous views of the role of guns in black communities, for example, West's employment of Mason and equipping him with a twelve-gauge shotgun to halt thieves from robbing the funeral home. In a discussion of human rights, Memphis Lee declares that the only way for blacks to grasp freedom, justice, and equality is with a gun. In his opinion, after urban renewal destroys the neighborhood, "Ain't nothing gonna be left but these niggers killing one another. That don't never go out of style" (p. 9). Sterling Johnson concurs by questioning Wolf about the availability of a black snub-nosed .32, which Johnson prefers over a heavy .38 or an unreliable .45. In this verbal exchange, the playwright implies that blacks have themselves to blame for high percentages of criminality.

The playwright frequently employs violence from the past or potential clashes in the present without actually committing onstage mayhem. For example, the characters in *Two Trains Running* are armed and hostile, but they refrain from firing a shot. In *The Piano Lesson* (1990), violence at the Charles residence in Pittsburgh remains verbal, but threatens to take physical form when Berniece proposes to use her dead husband Crawley's .38 to eject Boy Willie from the Pittsburgh flat. Their uncle Doaker describes the flight of blacks by train "before they kill somebody" or "to keep from getting killed" (p. 18). His brother Wining Boy, corroborating the opinion of Memphis Lee about self-protection through weapons, exonerates violence by characterizing the bigshot: "You need a pistol and pocketful of money to wear that suit" (p. 60). In contrast, Doaker, the peacemaker, urges Berniece to release her grudge against her brother, whom she charges with causing Crawley's demise.

Wilson sets up a similar three-way arrangement of peacemaker and opponents in *Fences* (1985), where Rose Maxson stands between a warring father and son. As Cory reaches for a major sports recruitment, his father Troy shoves him away from his goal by sabotaging his place on the high school football team and refusing him support for signing with a college team. Cory withholds his anger at Troy's tyranny until Troy grabs Rose in a painful hold. The sudden jolt of Cory's fist against Troy's chest surprises both men. Like Doaker, Rose stands on the middle ground to halt father and son from further assault. Wilson characterizes the military as the appropriate outlet for Cory's hostility.

See also **death, self-destruction**

* *Further Reading*

Abarbanel, Jonathan. "Gem of the Ocean." http://ibs.theatermania.com/content/news.cfm?
    int_news_id=3441, May 1, 2003.
Coleman, A. D. "Slices from the Jazz Life." *Staten Island Journal,* May 1998.
Elam, Harry J., ed. *Colored Contradictions: An Anthology of Contemporary African-American Plays.* New York: Plume, 1996.
Keating, Douglas J. "A 'King' with Majesty Sadly Thwarted." *Philadelphia Inquirer,* January 31, 2003.
McDonough, Carla J. *Staging Masculinity: Male Identity in Contemporary American Drama.* Jefferson, N.C.: McFarland, 1997.
West, Cornel. *Race Matters.* Boston: Beacon Press, 1993.

Walker, Bynum

The spiritual leader, conjurer, and "binding man" in *Joe Turner's Come and Gone* (1988), Bynum Walker counteracts the cultural fragmentation that destabilizes black Americans. A rootworker in his early sixties, he rooms at the Holly boarding house in Pittsburgh from 1908 to 1911 and echoes the wistfulness of lovers through memories of brief relationships in his own past. He is a repository of wisdom that he learned from his father, a healing man, in a male-to-male transfer of lore and experience. Like a self-contained priestly counselor, Bynum helps individuals look for appropriate mates and embrace a life's path, two essentials to members of the black diaspora.

A rover enervated by years on the road, Walker is the opposite of Seth Holly, the innkeeper and seeker of stability, land ownership, and material comfort. To Seth's pursy conservatism and lack of charity toward the downtrodden, Bynum challenges the northern status quo by purchasing pigeons from Reuben Mercer and slaughtering them to extract blood for animistic African rituals, which Seth dismisses as "that old mumbo jumbo nonsense" (p. 1). For good reason, Bynum is the appropriate voice to provide counsel and vision to Herald Loomis, who has lost his "song" to Joe Turner a white exploiter of black labor. Because Loomis lacks understanding of what he seeks and why he searches, Bynum encourages him to end his restless nomadism by reclaiming his song. In the playwright's explanation of the song to interviewer Nathan Grant, he pointed out that "understanding and knowing who you are and also having that political understanding, that political awareness, as well as the social awareness as an African, is in essence your song" (Grant).

Wilson created Bynum as a keeper of African tradition. He confounds ordinary mortals by the sprinkling of pigeon blood on the earth and the blessing of the boarding house with salt and a row of pennies placed along the threshold. Brandishing wonder-working packets, he claims the power to charm away failure. With psychic accuracy, he intones the blues lyric "They tell me Joe Turner's come and gone," an insightful glimpse of the kidnap of Herald Loomis (p. 67). From Bynum's own experience with wanderers, he correctly identifies the hollow center of Loomis, a space that Loomis himself must replenish. Just as Loomis is bound to search for redemption, Walker is driven to lead the way. The synergy of their relationship fulfills both men.

Bynum carefully selects the missing element and explains the importance of identity to Loomis, whose sense of self suffered intense battering during seven years of false imprisonment. In Bynum's words, "You bound to your song…. All you got to do is sing it. Then you be free" (p. 91). However, in an intuitive statement, Bynum acknowledges that revealing the truth comes at a price, which he describes as a piece of himself. The image summons spectors of martyred binding men — Christ, St. Paul, Socrates, Malcolm X, and Dr. Martin Luther King.

See also **Marion McClinton, shiny man, supernatural**

• *Further Reading*

Grant, Nathan L. "Men, Women, and Culture: A Conversation with August Wilson." *American Drama*, Vol. 5, No. 2, Spring 1996, pp. 100–22.

Pereira, Kim. *August Wilson and the African-American Odyssey.* Urbana: University of Illinois Press, 1995.

Richards, Sandra L. "Yoruba Gods on the American Stage: August Wilson's *Joe Turner's Come and Gone.*" *Research in African Literatures*, Vol. 30, No. 4, Winter 1999, p. 92.

Wang, Qun. *An In-Depth Study of the Major Plays of African American Playwright August Wilson: Vernacularizing the Blues on Stage.* Vol. 6 of *Black Studies.* Lewiston, Ont.: Edwin Mellen Press, 1999.

West

The ominous black-gloved undertaker in *Two Trains Running* (1991), West is the only prosperous black in the neighborhood. At the nadir of Pittsburgh Hill District history, he makes his living burying people, a foreshadowing of the play's dominant motifs. A widower in his sixties, he claims to have been a gambler, numbers runner, and bootleg liquor seller in his younger days. The high mortality rate of his contemporaries caused him to conclude "so many people was dying from that fast life I figured I could make me some money burying them and live a long life too" (p. 93). He is perpetually demanding sweetening for his coffee, a symbol of yearning in his private life since the death of his wife. He missed her so much that he visited Aunt Ester, the local prophet to ask if his wife went to heaven, but refused to waste her twenty dollar fee by tossing it into the river, as Ester directed. His unwillingness to follow through indicates a rejection of the spiritual side of life and a dependence on money to content him.

West is prominent by local standards because he owns a funeral parlor, the only business that can thrive in a decaying black economy. Outfitted in white shirt and black hat, suit, and tie, West dresses the part of a mortician and shines his black shoes, which he wears until the heels run over. He owns seven Cadillacs, operates four or five viewing rooms, and buys up condemned land to sell at inflated urban redevelopment prices. According to diner owner Memphis Lee and his friend Holloway, West profits from death by reusing burial suits and caskets, a frivolous allegation that the playwright leaves unsubstantiated as an example of street gossip. Wolf, the numbers runner, carries rumor to extremes by claiming that West has a wooden hand. In contrast to Lee's nurturing diner, West's business interests suggest a boundless hunger for slick deals on real estate, which white authorities intend to put to new uses to rejuvenate the inner city.

Despite speculation about the mortician's ethics, he maintains a high personal standing among local marginalized blacks. Wolf comments that the corpses that West embalms "look better than when they was living" (p. 12). West exploits clients by cultivating their admiration for his services, by promising to bury Aunt Ester for free, and by offering the Prophet Samuel's corpse for extensive viewing before burial, a macabre exhibition that takes on the trappings of a freak show. As evidence of community esteem for West's courtesy and spiffy appearance and for making corpses "look natural," Memphis hurries the waitress Risa Thomas to fetch pie and coffee for their honored patron (p. 11). For all their adulation of West and his business acumen, he is bound to a dying neighborhood. His profiteering from black misery and his residence in quarters above the funeral parlor suggest the ghoulishness of a man who makes money every time a black citizen dies.

West's greed is his compensation for the lack of a well-rounded family life. He maintains professional standards, hires people to keep his cars washed, and protects bodies from pilfering of rings and watches. He cultivates business by catering to the whims of grieving clients. He allows them to bury familiar and comforting articles with the dead — "Bibles, canes, crutches, guitars, radios, baby dolls, … tomatoes" (p. 37). At the viewing of the Prophet Samuel, West exerts his authority by banning a gate fee and battling rowdiness from people trying to break in line. Having risen from hard work and investments, West is too proud to board up the window that viewers break while pushing and shoving to see the prophet's remains. West boasts, "I spent twelve years putting up board. I worked hard not to put up board. Let [the builder] cut a piece of glass and bring it out and bill me" (p. 70). West's rise from a lesser location on Centre Street to a new structure and his loss of two buildings that burn down prove his experience in surviving the ups and downs of business.

August Wilson gives West a speech derived from one of the playwright's conversations with the graybeards of the Hill District. To the materialistic aims of ex-con Sterling Johnson, West advises him to reduce his unrealistic expectations from a ten-gallon bucket to a cup. In West's pragmatic view, "That ten-gallon bucket ain't never gonna be full" (p. 94). Like Lyons Maxson in *Fences* (1985) and Doaker Charles in *The Piano Lesson* (1990), West clings to the advice his father gave him to acquire property and wait for the right woman to come along. To Risa Thomas's fantasy of burying Hambone in a gold casket, West patiently explains to her the high cost of embalming fluid and caskets and the obligation of individuals to buy insurance to cover their funeral expenses. His reasoning is logical, but devoid of the humanism that Risa extends to those she loves.

West's experience with money and profit enables him to evaluate Memphis's asking price for the diner. After buying Philmore's property down the street, West counters the city's offers with his own bid of fifteen thousand dollars cash, which he later ups to twenty thousand. He warns about eminent domain, the right of city authorities to seize property for the public good and to offer a set price for it. In his estimation, the city is likely to pay Memphis no more than twelve hundred dollars for the cafe. The playwright heightens the irony of the rapacious undertaker castigating urban renewal as a form of profiteering in a period of hard times for blacks of the Hill District.

- *Further Reading*

Pereira, Kim. *August Wilson and the African-American Odyssey.* Urbana: University of Illinois Press, 1995.

Rocha, Mark William. "American History as 'Loud Talking' in *Two Trains Running*," in *May All Your Fences Have Gates: Essays on the Drama of August Wilson.* Iowa City: University of Iowa Press, 1994, pp. 116–132.

Wang, Qun. *An In-Depth Study of the Major Plays of African American Playwright August Wilson: Vernacularizing the Blues on Stage.* Vol. 6 of *Black Studies.* Lewiston, Ont.: Edwin Mellen Press, 1999.

white-black relations

August Wilson emphasizes the inequities of a white-controlled world that destroy white-black relations. In *Jitney* (1982), Youngblood charges that whites "think of all kind of ways to get your money" (p. 32). Turnbo dismisses Booster Becker's scholarship to the University of Pittsburgh in the Sputnik era as the white world's attempt to "catch up to the Russians and they didn't care if he was colored or not" (pp. 40–41). From childhood memories, Booster recalls his father Jim's refusal to retort to Rand, the landlord, for berating him on the family's front porch. Becker's failure to take up for his family causes his son to abandon hero workshop and see Becker as "just another man in the barbershop" (p. 57). To overcome the loss of his hero, Booster inflates his ego by romancing Susan McKnight, daughter of the vice president of Gulf Oil. The pursuit of a rich white girl leads to Booster's downfall from her false charge of rape.

In other dramas by Wilson, whites and blacks manage tentative and occasionally satisfying relationships with each other, for example, Jim Becker's cooperation with a white manager of J & S Steel in *Jitney* and Maretha's free education at the Irene Kaufman settlement house and a white buyer's straightforward purchase of musical instruments from blacks in *The Piano Lesson* (1990). Seth Holly does business with the peddler Rutherford Selig in *Joe Turner's Come and Gone* (1988) but is unable to convince Cohen or Sam Green to underwrite a small shop employing five more pot makers. More successful in dealings with whites is Troy Maxson in *Fences* (1985). He negotiates a promotion from garbage collector to driver with Mr. Rand, the white manager, and secures the release of Troy's mentally impaired brother Gabe from police custody with a fifty-dollar bribe. These one-on-one exchanges are less lethal than the exploitation of black factory workers by white managers in *Gem of the Ocean* (2003), the title figure's shouting match with a Sears photographer in *King Hedley II* (1999), and the payday arrest of Jeremy Furlow and Roper Lee in *Joe Turner's Come and Gone*, in which "Piney's boys" seize the men's money and put them in jail overnight without food (p. 13).

Imperative to the black evaluation of white-black dealings is a sense of proportion and self-worth, which bigots constantly undermine. In *Ma Rainey's Black Bottom* (1985), Toledo catechizes the band with a brief homily expressing the black man's need to set his own criteria. If he relies on whites for approval, "He's just gonna be about what white folks want him to be about" (p. 37). Levee Green, a representative of the younger generation, chooses to placate white with obsequious groveling, a demeaning behavior that dates to plantation times. He claims to study whites as a means of self-protection: "The first time one fixes on me wrong, I'm gonna let him know how much I studies" (p. 67). Veiling his threat with imprecise promises of action, Levee ends up muttering, "You let one of them mess with me, I'll show you how spooked up I am" (*Ibid.*). To his sorrow, he takes as his model Ma Rainey, whom he misperceives as controlling her own destiny. His misreading of the studio situation leads to an untimely explosion, Levee's murder of Toledo, and the end of Levee's career. As summarized by critic Qun Wang, Levee is trapped because he "senses the ending of the world once his dreams are taken away" (Wang, p. 60).

- *Further Reading*

Ambush, Benny Sato. "Culture Wars." *African American Review*, Vol. 31, No. 4, Winter 1997, pp. 579–586.

Wang, Qun. *An In-Depth Study of the Major Plays of African American Playwright August Wilson: Vernacularizing the Blues on Stage*. Vol. 6 of *Black Studies*. Lewiston, Ont.: Edwin Mellen Press, 1999.

Wilson, August

One of America's dynamic, inventive, and lyrical stage crafters, August Wilson achieved a height of monetary and critical acclaim by the stage production and publication of his first three plays, *Ma Rainey's Black Bottom* (1985), *Fences* (1985), and *Joe Turner's Come and Gone* (1988). Wilson earned two Pulitzer Prizes, a Tony, major fellowships, and best play awards for his bold macroscopic view of African Americans and the issues and shared suffering that impact the lives of common folk. From boyhood, Wilson was able to master composition and thrilled to his ability to concretize thoughts as words, a craft he learned in seventh grade while scribbling notes to girls he wanted to impress. Interviewer Sharon Fitzgerald accounted for Wilson's success as a result of his major strengths—detailed memories and skillful storytelling: "He remembers people, places and attitudes, where he stood, how he felt, and what he learned about human nature. Some of his life's stories are told as one-man narratives; others are fully cast, but he enacts all of the parts" (Fitzgerald, p. 14). Fitzgerald also saluted his ability to recreate time, place, and dialogue: "The rhythms and nuances of language are adhesives for his memories, and he uses them, as he always has, with delight and abandon" (*Ibid.*).

The playwright's ongoing saga of the black experience preserves challenges and successes as well as the long-term effects of discrimination, bitter loss, and failure in an ever-shifting historic continuum. Surprisingly, except for sampling the music of each era, he does no background research for his scenarios. To prepare himself for writing, he performs a ritual hand-washing. Of its importance, he told Paul Grondahl, "It's a symbolic cleansing because I consider writing a mystical and spiritual experience" (Grondahl). With immaculate hands, he moves on to pacing the neighborhood and ordering coffee at a diner. Holding notebook and pen for ideas, he waits for voices from the past to talk to him: "Sometimes, nobody wants to talk to me. That's cool. I'll wait awhile and if it's no good, I'll move on to the next coffee shop. Like fishing. Eventually, something starts to happen" (*Ibid.*). Bluesy notes from characters begin to percolate, setting the playwright to work. Of his ability to create verisimilitude, actor Kwame Kwei-Armah exalts Wilson's loyalty to his vision as "the man that he was when he entered into manhood. August is unapologetic for the politics that he has now, which are the same politics that he had when he first listened to Malcolm X, to Martin Luther King, and when he first spoke with James Baldwin" (O'Mahony).

Wilson's themes derive from his black grandparents, who established a worthy creed and lived by family values while sharecropping in Spear, North Carolina. Of them he said, "Every conceivable facet of life was mapped out and handed to us and we got the maps stored in the closet" (Ards). Commenting on the more recent past, in 1984, he divulged that his parents concealed the wrongs and indignities they suffered in their early years. He characterized their deliberate cover-up as a means of shielding their six unsuspecting children. To save the current generation of youth from ignorance of black history, he crafts plays from universal themes. In an interview, he summarized, "Ultimately the plays are about love, honor, duty, betrayal. They're about the big things in life" ("Interview").

Wilson's structural method has sparked some controversy among critics. Playwright David Copelin observed in *The Writer* that the plays *Fences, The Piano Lesson,* and *Seven Guitars* display "a loose, open architecture and a lot of rambling discourse that can seem repetitive and verbose" (Copelin, p. 23). Copelin exonerates Wilson for "fits and starts and blind alleys" because the character interactions dramatize aspects of black culture that suit his purpose of revealing idiosyncratic dialogue (*Ibid.*). Copelin concludes: "The rough edges of Wilson's writing, the meandering and curlicues, become attributes of an identifiable individual style of playwriting" (*Ibid.*). Without them, the plays would seem generic and predictable.

To justify his method, Wilson has stated that his task is to portray the long hidden black history, along with individual aspirations, social cohesion, creativity, folklore, and myths, all of which contribute to minority culture. In reference to contemporary issues, he warned that the demise of affirmative action has produced complacency: "You have to look at the Reconstruction era to understand the sort of assault that is going on now. It's the same as then" (Goodale). Amid the community and family conflicts in his plays are glimpses of admirable character, personal fulfillment, and a profound morality that bolsters individuals who must establish satisfying lives in a nation where white citizens thrive at the expense of people of color. Critic Judith Green summarized, "He creates people and lets the story come out of their journeys. As their paths cross, they may collide, or abrade, or explode, or melt and merge. They don't live by anyone's rules except their own — least of all those imposed by a playwright" (Green, p. R4).

Wilson does not perform on stage, but he influences actors' performances by helping to select directors whom he considers the interpreters of his art. When they begin work on his scripts, he attends actor auditions and advises on cast selection, involves himself in staging and costuming, monitors rehearsals, and rewrites dialogue overnight for use the next day. Leslie Uggams, the actor who debuted the part of Aunt Ester in *Gem of the Ocean* (2003), remarked on Wilson's organic method: "August likes to watch his actors. He'll see or hear something in rehearsal and he'll incorporate it" (Rawson). The performance-by-performance refinement is nerve-wracking, but beneficial to smooth pacing and a verbal lightning that reviewer Elysa Gardner calls "searing poetry with uncompromising realism" (Gardner).

By applying considerable energy and verbal agility as a poet and scenarist, Wilson began retrieving the African American past as a means of educating his generation about their roots. He chose truth as his curriculum, whether in the account of the rise of black baseball star Jackie Robinson to major league play in *Fences* (1985), a recipe for mustard greens in *Seven Guitars* (1995), the high price of slavery in *Gem of the Ocean*, the search for the soul's song in *Joe Turner's Come and Gone* (1988), or Wilson's satiric view of the Black Power movement in *Two Trains Running* (1991), in which Hambone parrots to ex-con Sterling Johnson word by word the phrase "Black is beautiful" (p. 57). As Wilson states in the introduction to *Seven Guitars*, rather than history, his focus is culture and a recreation of "so many things that threaten to pull [characters] asunder" (n.p.).

Wilson creates characters who act out plots that place black experience in viewable context. In the body of his plays are compelling, realistic, often ambiguous figures rather than the caricatures common to movies and television in stereotypical scenarios at ghetto street corners, homes, pool halls, diners, and barber shops. They survive via the dodge-and-weave of boxers, athletes whom Wilson has long admired. Each bears a unique combination of elements drawn from the ongoing hardships that blacks face in a white-controlled urban society. Rather than bemoan failures and inequities, the playwright imbues his characters with perseverence, glimmers of wisdom, glints of wicked humor, and a modicum of joy gained from the uplifting black milieu in which they live.

A loner given to workaholism, Wilson set out to explore the black experience in works of dramatic art rather than in plays that would entertain audiences. According to interviewer Charles Whitaker, the playwright drew on material he "collected and mentally codified" in Pittsburgh during a twenty-year apprenticeship (Whitaker, p. 80). While living in a mostly white milieu in St. Paul, he heard the echoes of Pittsburgh's black neighborhoods in his memories of boyhood. Composing in longhand, he began with a single line of dialogue and gradually added character names and setting before deciding how the plot would end. The finished plays easily captured conversations, family confrontations, and nuances that transcend race to reveal the universal elements in black society. Wilson noted, "I find that white audiences are surprised to discover the humanity," a failing that reveals the low expectations of whites (*Ibid.*). As a result of the connection between viewer and actors, Wilson has earned the second most honors in American drama, just behind Neil Simon.

Wilson's plays lean toward dynamic build-up of character and action from the trivial and commonplace rather than from any religious movement or grand political stance. Sandra G. Shannon, an expert on his writing, quoted him in an interview for *African American Review* concerning the factors he considers essential: "I try to keep all of the elements of the culture alive in my work, and myth is certainly a part of it. Mythology, history, social organizations, economics—all of these things are part of the culture" (Shannon). By incorporating the basics of humanism, he creates the impression of a microcosm of everyday black life freighted with a pervasive reminder that human life is brief and change inevitable. The resulting black situations and philosophies are so universal that Londoners applauded *Joe Turner's Come and Gone*, *Ma Rainey's Black Bottom*, and *King Hedley II* and Ugandans embraced *The Piano Lesson*, *Fences*, and *Jitney*.

See also **Chronology of Life and Works, Marion McClinton, Ben Mordecai, Lloyd Richards**

• *Further Reading*

Ards, Angela. "The Diaspora Comes to Dartmouth." *American Theatre*, Vol. 15, No. 5, May-June 1998, pp. 50–52.
Blackburn, Regina Naasirah. "Erupting Thunder: Race and Class in the 20th Century Plays of August Wilson." *Socialism and Democracy*, Vol. 17, No. 2.
Brock, Wendell. "Q&A: August Wilson, Pulitzer Prize-winning Playwright: Wilson Sees 'Light at End of Tunnel' for Play Cycle." *Atlanta Journal-Constitution*, September 29, 2003, p. E1.
Copelin, David. "Transforming Story into Plot." *The Writer*, Vol. 112, No. 9, September 1999, pp. 21–23, 45.
Fitzgerald, Sharon. "August Wilson: The People's Playwright." *American Visions*, Vol. 15, No. 14, August 2000, p. 14.
Freedman, Samuel G. "August Wilson, Defining an Era." *New York Times*, February 5, 2003.
Gardner, Elysa. "It's Good to Be Wilson's 'King.'" *USA Today*, May 3, 2001.
Goodale, Gloria. "Playwright August Wilson on Race Relations and the Theater." *Christian Science Monitor*, May 15, 1998.
Green, Judith. "Despite Bumps, 'Jitney' a Pleasure Ride." *Atlanta Journal-Constitution*, October 15, 1999, p. R4.
Grondahl, Paul. "August Wilson: Hearing His Characters All Over Town." *Albany Magazine*, Fall 1996.
"Interview with August Wilson." *EGG the Arts Show*. http://www.pbs.org/wnet/egg/233/wilson/interview_content_1.html.
O'Mahony, John. "American Centurion." Manchester *Guardian*, December 14, 2002.
Rawson, Chris. "Many Pittsburghers Turn Out to Celebrate August Wilson's Latest Opening." *Pittsburgh Post-Gazette*, May 1, 2001.

Saltzman, Simon, and Nicole Plett. "'Jitney' at Crossroads." *U.S. 1 Newspaper*, April 16, 1997.

Shannon, Sandra G. "Blues, History, and Dramaturgy." *African American Review*, Vol. 27, No. 4, Winter 1993, pp. 539–559.

Whitaker, Charles. "Is August Wilson America's Greatest Playwright?" *Ebony*, Vol. 56, No. 11, September 2001, p. 80.

wisdom

August Wilson peppers his texts with the adages common to black thinking, for example, the rueful statement in the introduction to *Two Trains Running* (1991) "If the train don't hurry there's gonna be some walking done" (p. ix). Some of the more upbeat advice comes from Bynum Walker, the genial binding man in *Joe Turner's Come and Gone* (1988), who urges Jeremy Furlow to risk another raid at Seefus's place by joining his customers in music and fun. In Bynum's opinion, "Some things is worth taking the chance going to jail about" (p. 18). In the same play, three women counter the male perspective with female views. Bertha Holly negotiates in the world with laughter and generous servings of soul food; Mattie Campbell travels a less hospitable road while seeking the wisdom to allay her self-blame for her children's deaths in infancy. More interested in survival than in physical allure, boarder Molly Cunningham attests that "Beauty wanna come in and sit down at your table asking to be fed" (p. 65).

Gender inequities are a source of spirited debate and commentary. In a jaundiced reference to male-female relationships in *Jitney* (1982), Fielding declares that "Women and money will get a preacher killed." Jim Becker's belief is more moderate: "One can pull and the other can pull … as long as it's in the same direction" (pp. 63, 78). Bynum's wisdom refutes the type of negativity that Fielding espouses by concurring with Becker. Bynum perceives women as wives, mothers, and companions who socialize and nurture men and impart "what to do with yourself when you get lonesome" (p. 46). His view concurs with the black myth of saintly motherhood.

Much of black wisdom is the everyday knowledge gained from experience. The theme empowers *The Janitor* (1985), a four-minute one-act play in which Sam, a hotel janitor, challenges young people to embrace the sweetness of youth. Without revealing too much about her foster son's past in *King Hedley II* (1999), Louise reminds him, "Be yourself. That's enough" (p. 95). In *Seven Guitars* (1995), good-timer Red Carter's humor proves that "the hand is quicker than the eye" as he snatches a piece of sweet potato pie before Canewell can take it. Later in the play, Floyd Barton reflects on the loss of his mother and states an old truism that "you don't miss your water till your well run dry" (p. 50). An even more common bromide is King Hedley's statement of reciprocity as "one hand wash the other," his version of black people doing business with their own race (p. 86). Toledo, the philosopher in *Ma Rainey's Black Bottom* (1985), moves into more serious territory with his observation that "The more niggers get killed having a good time, the more good times niggers wanna have" (p. 41).

More caustic is Rose's accusation that her adulterous husband is "a day late and a dollar short" in *Fences* (1985), a play about the personal and marital shortcomings of Troy Maxson (p. 68). From a survivor's viewpoint, he advises his son Cory to accept hard knocks and "take the crookeds with the straights" (p. 37). As proof of Troy's influence on his sons, the adage returns twice in the final scene to Cory as Lyons explains how he followed his father's advice and weathered a sentence of three years in a Pittsburgh workhouse for cashing other people's checks. In a paean to Troy's friendship, his confidante Jim Bono states what he learned from observing Troy and how "to take life as it comes along and keep putting one foot in front of the other" (p. 62). As the two men progress in their discussion of fidelity and family responsibility, Bono speaks for the playwright the importance of being "responsible for what you do" (p. 63).

Less trite and packaged is the direct advice of Aunt Ester, the 322-year-old sage in *Two Trains Running* (1991) and *Gem of the Ocean* (2003). A Hill District phenomenon known for a serene, sweet nature, she receives visitors and gives them simple guidance on how to lay aside hatred and vengeance to cleanse the spirit of negative energy. To Sterling Johnson, a troubled ex-con in *Two Trains Running* who chooses the easy way out rather than work for his living, Aunt Ester advises, "Make better what you have and you have best" (p. 98). Her simple advice is valuable counsel to blacks of the 1960s who struggle toward an African American ideal.

See also **Jim Becker, Canewell, Cutler, Aunt Ester, Louise, Sam, Stool Pigeon, Toledo, Bynum Walker**

• *Further Reading*

Charters, Ann, and Samuel Charters, ed. *Short Pieces from the New Dramatists*. Banbury, Ox.: Orangeberry Books, 1985.

Wolf

The self-important numbers runner in *Two Trains Running* (1991), Wolf is a hard worker lacking in character. He is given to standing on the street observing the actions of others, a habit that the playwright uses as a source of background material as he does with the nosy Turnbo in *Jitney* (1982). Wolf dresses the part of two-bit gambler and diligently pursues his trade over the telephone in Memphis Lee's cafe. Wolf's outlook is colored by his false arrest for colliding with a fleeing criminal on the sidewalk. He considers the black man's life as always under attack and chooses not to sire children, a hint at his negative attitude toward the future. His pessimism suits the era, when urban reclamation threatens the viability and ethnic integrity of the Hill District's black community.

In his private life, Wolf's name is misleading. He makes no headway in impressing women. He makes idle boasts about having two women in Atlanta and claims that one is always available: "All I got to do is call. All she got to do is hear my voice" (p. 81). He later exults, "When I die every woman in Pittsburgh gonna cry," a claim he repeats for effect (p. 105). Because of his jaded view of women as collectible items, he overrates the importance of sex in solving human problems like waitress Risa Thomas's depression and rigid celibacy, which he secretly would love to correct.

Because he makes no overt effort to win her, Wilson suggests that Wolf's outward behavior is only one projection from a large iceberg.

Overall, Wolf's attitude is defeatist and anti-humanistic. He excuses his own three-month jail term for obstructing justice with hyperbole: "Every nigger you see done been to jail one time or another" (p. 54). He exaggerates the black man's situation in a white-controlled world: "You always under attack" (*Ibid.*). To exalt his manhood, he tiptoes carefully around Sterling Johnson while explaining why the Alberts family chose to halve returns on the day's winning number, but, in Sterling's absence, Wolf makes big talk about going to the pawnshop to retrieve his pistol. He redeems himself before the audience by grieving for Hambone, whom he views at West's funeral parlor, by giving Risa some stockings and English Leather cologne for Memphis, and by empathizing with the plight of Bubba Boy, who goes to jail for stealing a dress in which to bury his woman. By presenting multiple sides of Wolf's personality, Wilson rescues him from ignominy.

- *Further Reading*

Gelhaus, Anne. "'Two Trains' on Track." *MetroActive*, March 14–20, 1996.
Shaw, Kristen. "Closely-watched Trains: Penumbra Does Good with Wilson." *Mac Weekly*, Vol. 96, No. 3, February 21, 2003.
Sincere, Rick. "Two Trains Running: A Marvelous Ride." *Metro Herald*, February 1996.

women

Critics have chastised August Wilson for muting the female point of view and for failing to sustain significant roles for strong, independent female characters, a fault he remedied with the riveting appearance of the mythic Aunt Ester in *Gem of the Ocean* (2003). In reference to the value of women, he acknowledged the tendency of men to take them for granted. In his essay "Where to Begin" (1991), he describes missed moments in terms of a man's failure to embrace love "only after we have kissed the woman for the last time unknowingly, or have left her final nakedness and been marked by the unsurety and the bruise" (Wilson, pp. 2234–2235). Critics have explained his diminution of female characters as the result of his concentration on the transformative spiritual journeys of men. By default, the resulting elevation of male epiphanies overrides women's needs and ambitions, but does not preclude the strength of character in Bertha Holly and Martha Pentecost in *Joe Turner's Come and Gone* (1988), the resilience of the title character in *Ma Rainey's Black Bottom* (1985) and of Rena in *Jitney* (1982), the gentle heart and altruism of Risa Thomas in *Two Trains Running* (1991), the loyalty of Black Mary in *Gem of the Ocean* (2003), or the endurance of Bonnie and Rose Maxson in *Fences* (1988), Ruby and Tonya Hedley in *King Hedley II* (1999), Louise and Vera Dotson in *Seven Guitars* (1995), and Mama Ola and Berniece Charles in *The Piano Lesson* (1990).

Overall, Wilson's plays situate women in limited and limiting spheres of influence under the burden of a single character flaw or weakness. He places in Rose's long monologue about loyalty her admission of faulty logic: "I took all my feelings, my wants and needs, my dreams … and I buried them inside you" (p. 71). His other female characters are similarly self-limiting:

woman	mate(s)	sphere of influence	fault or weakness
Gem of the Ocean			
Aunt Ester	husbands	black history; counseling	withdrawal from the outside world
Black Mary	—	home; job	limited interaction; distrust of men; grudge against an evil brother
Joe Turner's Come and Gone			
Mattie Campbell	Jack Carper	marriage	future home; loving a drifter
Molly Cunningham	Jeremy Furlow	brief relationships	egocentrism; conceit
Jeremy Furlow's woman	Jeremy	lover	disloyalty
Bertha Holly	Seth Holly	husband; home; roomers	commitment to work and profits
Zonia Loomis	—	father	lack of mothering; dread of separation from her father
Martha Pentecost	Herald Loomis	evangelism; her daughter	religious fanaticism; impatience
Selig's wife	Rutherford Selig	home; self	lack of commitment
Ma Rainey's Black Bottom			
Levee Green's mother	Levee's father	home; family	devaluation through rape by white men
Dussie Mae	Ma Rainey	sexual relationship	limited interaction; greed; lack of commitment
Ma Rainey	Dussie Mae Sylvester Brown	blues; fans	fear of loss of audience; self-importance
Toledo's wife	Toledo	home; husband	religious fanaticism
The Piano Lesson			
Berniece Charles	Crawley	daughter; job; memories	bitterness; bossiness; grudge against her brother
Cleotha Charles	Wining Boy Charles	self	loving a drifter

woman	mate(s)	sphere of influence	fault or weakness
Coreen Charles	Doaker Charles	self; escapism	lack of faith in husband
Mama Ola Charles	Boy Charles	home; family	obsessive grief; repetitive labors
Dolly	Lymon Jackson	sexual relationship	insincerity; manipulation of dates
Grace	Leroy; Boy Willie Charles	sexual relationships	lack of commitment; impatience
Lymon Jackson's mother	L. D. Jackson	family; honor	willingness to supply sex as payment for a favor
Maretha	—	home; school; mother	lack of autonomy
Seven Guitars			
Maude Avery Barton	—	home; son	limited interaction
Pearl Brown	Floyd Barton	sexual relationship	lack of commitment
Vera Dotson	Floyd Barton; Canewell	small circle of friends; lover	loving a drifter
Louise	Henry	boardinghouse; friends; Ruby	distrust of males; judging others
Ruby	Leroy Slater; Elmore; King Hedley	sexual relationships; fun	lack of commitment; independence
WillaMae	Red Carter	lover; son	loving a drifter
Fences			
Alberta	Troy Maxson	lover; unborn child	loving a married man; choosing laughter over responsibility
Bella	—	store; customers	overcharging
Lucille Bono	Jim Bono	home; husband	limited interaction
Bonnie Maxson	Lyons Maxson	home; job	loving a poor provider
Raynell Maxson	—	home; mother; brothers	loss of birth parents; disobedience
Rose Lee Maxson	Troy Maxson	home; church; family	undeveloped potential; regret
Troy's mother	Troy's father	self; escapism	fleeing a brutal husband and leaving her children behind

woman	mate(s)	sphere of influence	fault or weakness
Two Trains Running			
Petey Brown's woman	Petey	lovers	infidelity
Bubba Boy's lover	Bubba	lover; drugs	lack of self-control
Memphis Lee's wife	Memphis	home; self	lack of commitment
Risa Thomas	unnamed	cafe kitchen; counter	retreat from men
West's wife	West	home; husband	early death
Wolf's woman	Wolf	sexual relationship	greed
Jitney			
Cigar Annie	clients	home; security	promiscuity
Coreen Becker	Jim Becker	home; son	loss of faith in husband; defeatism; excessive grief
Lucille Becker	Jim Becker	home; husband	limited interaction
Sarah Bolger	—	home; family	isolation; gullability
Susan McKnight	Booster Becker	sexual relationship; fun	independence; racism; perjury
Peaches	—	friendship; sister	secrecy
Philmore's wife	Philmore	home	sanctimony
Rena	Youngblood	home; son	limited interaction; distrust; unfounded suspicion
Rosie	Shealy	sexual relationship	greed
King Hedley II			
Deanna	Mister	self; furniture	expecting a husband to change
Tonya Hedley	J. C.; King Hedley	home; daughter; child and grandchild	loving a criminal; loss of faith in the future
Mama Louise	Henry	foster son	lack of a husband; grudge against men
Natasha	—	self; son	immaturity; materialism
Ruby	Elmore; Leroy Slater; King Hedley	singing career; son; lover	disinterest in son; loving a criminal
Edna Stewart	lover	self; lover	neglecting to mourn her lover

Wilson's two-dimensional treatment of women includes depictions of decorative temptresses like the love-wrecker Pearl Brown in *Seven Guitars*, the singer's insecure kept girl Dussie Mae in *Ma Rainey's Black Bottom*, the citified jezebels who lure Floyd Barton back to Chicago in *Seven Guitars*, the jealous, money-hungry Rosie, Shealy's ex-girlfriend in *Jitney*, the grasping Deanna, who steals Mister's furniture in *King Hedley II*, and Grace, Boy Willie's whining date and Lymon Jackson's companion in *The Piano Lesson*. In a milieu dominated by male grifters, has-beens, ex-cons, and knockabouts, Wilson tends to reduce women to saint-or-sinner extremes: either the beloved dead wife of West, the mortician, in *Two Trains Running* (1991) and dead mothers Mama Ola and Maude Avery Barton in *The Piano Lesson* and *Seven Guitars* or their foils, the disgruntled survivors, drones, or trollops like Susan Mc-Knight in *Jitney*, a spoiled white girl who "didn't want her daddy to know she was fooling around with no colored boy" (p. 41). As Barbara Christian explains in *Black Feminist Criticism, Perspectives on Black Women Writers* (1985), black stereotyping tends to denigrate promiscuous women and sanctify mothers, a perspective demonstrated by Southern "mother of the year" contests. Other of Wilson's women fall into the handmaiden/dray category, such as the cheerful cook and hostess Bertha Holly in *Joe Turner's Come and Gone*; the self-scarred, love-scorched cook and waitress Clarissa "Risa" Thomas in *Two Trains Running*; and the faithful, discounted wife Lucille Bono and the loyal Rose Maxson, a tyrannized drudge and devout church choir member in *Fences* who hangs up the wash without complaint, cooks soul food for her scattered family, and acknowledges the loss of self in loving her husband Troy.

By reducing some of his women to ciphers of extreme female type-casting, Wilson's plays contrast a string of dutiful, pious women with their polar opposites, notably, Rose, the sustainer of the self-pleasuring Troy, vs. the fleshy, good-timing Alberta from Tallahassee, the adulteress who makes him laugh in *Fences*; Jeremy Furlow's experience with desperate flirts as opposed to the sweet-natured Mattie Campbell in *Joe Turner's Come and Gone*; the selfish Natasha opposite the grieving mother of Little Buddy Will in *King Hedley II*, and Floyd Barton's beloved, ego-affirming lover Vera Dotson vs. Ruby, a siren and casual despoiler of men, in *Seven Guitars*. In characterizing the latter play, Wilson dramatizes an overpowering sex drive in men that defines their responses to beauty and carnal appeal, as Jeremy Furlow expresses in his statement that "It's hard to ignore a woman got legs like [Mattie Campbell] got" (p. 46). The male reaction to Ruby in *Seven Guitars* is visceral and instantaneous. When she appears dressed in red for an evening at the Blue Goose, three males halt and gaze without moving. Their fractiousness in her presence suggests rutting male animals who would fight to the death to possess the most promising female as though she were a trophy for manhood.

Like Troy Maxson's mistress Alberta in *Fences* and Memphis Lee's departed wife and Wolf's money-hungry woman in Atlanta in *Two Trains Running*, some of the significant females in Wilson's plays are present in name only. Examples include Jim Becker's first and second wives Coreen and Lucille and Philmore's disapproving, but hospitable mother in *Jitney*, Jim Bono's wife Lucille and Lyons Maxson's neglected ex-wife Bonnie in *Fences*, and Wining Boy's deceased wife Cleotha Holman and Doaker's former wife Coreen, who fled to New York in *The Piano Lesson*. Even less substantial than Canewell's "old gal" on Clark Street and Red Carter's unseen Willa-Mae, mother of Mister, in *Seven Guitars* are the idealized sylphs that Red dredges up from his memories of Opelika, Alabama, "where the women as soft as cotton and sweet as watermelon" (pp. 28, 34).

Wilson portrays the casual attitude of men toward commitment and their ill-defined needs as the causes of break-ups. Mister, a clownish robber in *King Hedley II*, reduces a relationship with two women to sex: "With one of them I can get it any-time I want. I'm working on the other one" (p. 87). In the same play, a stranger enjoys a rough-handed sexual dalliance with Ruby at the Ellis Hotel and wanders out of her life, leaving her to contemplate her gray hair in the mirror. Memphis, the clueless husband in *Two Trains Running*, whose unseen mate left him after twenty-two years of marriage, assesses his worth as a husband by the gifts of a Cadillac, dishwasher, and color TV to his nameless woman. He oversimplifies that she had nothing to do but stay home and keep house and that she moved out after he asked her to bake bread. He states his bewilderment at complex female behaviors in a summation of Risa's self-mutilation: "Somebody that's all confused about herself and don't want nobody ... I can't figure out where to put her" (pp. 31–32). Even less palpable is Canewell's idealized mate in *Seven Guitars*, where he summarizes his needs as "three rooms and a woman know how to sit with me in the dark" (p. 28). His reduction of a female to a mere presence suggests a phantom rather than a real lover.

Instead of improving themselves or their relationships with the opposite sex, male characters tend to reflect on the shortcomings of the female gender, as displayed in criticism of the loveless and unloving widow and mother Berniece Charles in *The Piano Lesson* and innuendo against Peaches, the falsely accused run-about in *Jitney* who helps Youngblood select a home for her sister Rena and nephew Jesse. In reference to Vera Dotson's strict standards, Canewell declares, "Some women make their bed up so high don't nobody know how to get to it" (p. 98). In *Joe Turner's Come and Gone*, Rutherford Selig has more respect for his horse Sally than for a woman. In his experience with a wife who locked him out of the house, he finds horses more obedient: "I say giddup and she go. Say whoa and she stop" (p. 40). Wilson is obviously going for laughs in Selig's portrayal of the docile wife.

As Memphis implies in *Two Trains Running*, women can endanger the male, both in ego and body. As Haki Madhubuti states in *Black Men: Obsolete, Single, Dangerous?: Afrikan American Families in Transition* (1990), gynephobia is a deep fear derived from black culture. The black male has reason to fear a woman as complicated and handy with a razor as Risa Thomas. Later, Wolf, the numbers runner, sums up the black man's mistrust of women in terms of danger to the man: "See, when you lay down with her, you trusting her with your life" (p. 106). Because he can't commit himself to one mate, he visits numerous women around Pittsburgh and a few more in Atlanta, but makes no permanent attachment to any female. By keeping a trunk packed and his options open, Canewell justifies a temporary situation. He trivializes his rootlessness with a light-hearted jest, "When it come to the end of our understanding I'm gonna drink a toast and keep on stepping" (p. 29). Such irresponsible attitudes toward loyalty prompt Vera, Floyd's wronged love whom he left for eighteen months, to reflect on the era's disdain for long-term commitment: "Everybody keep their trunk packed up" (p. 28). The image suggests impermanence as well as a constriction of self within tight inner spaces that admit no glimpses of true emotion.

Wilson depicts some males as possessive and incapable of fidelity to one woman, the cause of the contretemps between Floyd and Vera in *Seven Guitars* and Ruby and Elmore in *King Hedley II*. In *Fences*, the adulterous Troy Maxson states his womanizing philosophy: "I eye all the women. I don't miss nothing" (p. 3). In the opening scene, he contrasts Lucille's dinner of pigfeet with Rose's menu of chicken and collard greens. As though dismissing a hireling, he commands, "Go on back in the house and let me and Bono finish what we was talking about. This is man talk" (p. 6). He concludes his demeaning statement with a veiled promise of sexual intercourse and crudely orders, "You go on and powder it up" (*Ibid.*). He demands that Rose come when called and, like a deer in rut, be immediately available for copulation. Later, when there are no witnesses to a heartfelt admission, Troy declares, "You the only decent thing that ever happened to me" (p. 39). The relationship with so deceitful a man is taxing. Rose realizes too late that "to keep up his strength I had to give up little pieces of mine" (p. 98). When her willingness to submit and forgive fail her, the marriage crumbles.

By portraying Risa and Vera, Wilson moves away from male-dominant scenarios to a fuller, more realistic appreciation of women. He dramatizes the hesitance of Risa to trust a sweet-talker like ex-con Sterling Johnson and honors her award of a kiss and embrace as the two listen to blues on the cafe jukebox. Their intimacy gives Sterling the change to play the macho rescuer if a riot breaks out at the Malcolm X celebration. He promises: "You just get behind me. I won't let nobody hurt you. Not when you with me" (p. 47). Wilson assigns to Vera a speech that expresses the woman's point of view of faithless love. After offering all her womanliness to "know where you was bruised at," she regrets eighteen months of nights spent in an empty bed (p. 13). She demands of the betrayer Floyd, "Where? Someplace special? Someplace where you had been? The same room you walked out of?" (*Ibid.*). In her logic, no man as selfish as Floyd deserves having everything he wants while leaving a woman with nothing. In a stronger demand for accounting, Berniece Charles, the evolving matriarch in *The Piano Lesson*, upbraids her willful brother Boy Willie for a series of male crimes: "You always talking about your daddy but you ain't never stopped to look at what his foolishness cost your mama" (p. 52). Her view of violence as a male phenomenon reduces family crimes to a cycle: "All this thieving and killing and thieving and killing. And what it ever lead to? more killing and thieving. I ain't never seen it come to nothing" (*Ibid.*). Her despair precipitates a distrust of emotion that remands her to self-defeating grudges and an empty bed.

In the rising action of *Seven Guitars*, Wilson caps Vera's frustration with his most explosive female flashpoint: "He ain't here he ain't here he ain't here quit looking for him because he ain't here he's there! there! there! there!" (p. 14). Shoring up subsequent doubts about Floyd's commitment, she buys a one-way ticket from Chicago to Pittsburgh and intends to keep it in her shoe as a fail-safe against a second betrayal. As a counterweight to female disillusion and disappointment with men, in the falling action, the playwright constructs Floyd's reply in a description of his short-term love, Pearl Brown. More daring and less cautious than Vera, Pearl agreed to accompany Barton to Chicago for his initial recording session because, in his words, she was "willing to believe" (p. 92). A boost to his self-esteem, her risk-taking, even though it was based on materialistic hopes of success and wealth, buoyed his spirits because she offered him "a chance to try" (*Ibid.*). Of her support, Wilson told interviewer Bill Moyers, "The men need support and nourishment, and in the black community, there are always women who can supply that for them" (Moyers, p. 175).

See also **promiscuity, wisdom**

• *Further Reading*

Christian, Barbara. *Black Feminist Criticism, Perspectives on Black Women Writers.* New York: Pergamon, 1985.

Clark, Keith. *Black Manhood in James Baldwin, Ernest J. Gaines, and August Wilson.* Urbana: University of Illinois Press, 2002.

Elam, Harry J. "*Ma Rainey's Black Bottom:* Singing Wilson's Blues." *American Drama,* Vol. 5, No. 2, Spring 1996, pp. 76–99.

Haki Madhubuti. *Black Men: Obsolete, Single, Dangerous?: Afrikan American Families in Transition.* Chicago: Third World Press, 1990.

McDonough, Carla J. *Staging Masculinity: Male Identity in Contemporary American Drama.* Jefferson, N.C.: McFarland, 1997.

Moyers, Bill. "August Wilson's America: A Conversation with Bill Moyers." *American Theater,* Vol. 7, No. 6, 1989, p. 14.

_____. *A World of Ideas.* New York: Doubleday, 1989.

Sklar, Kathryn Kish. *Women's Rights Emerges Within the Antislavery Movement 1830–1870.* Boston: Bedford, 2000.

Vorlicky, Robert. *Act Like a Man: Challenging Masculinities in American Drama.* Ann Arbor: University of Michigan Press, 1995.

Wang, Qun. *An In-Depth Study of the Major Plays of African American Playwright August Wilson: Vernacularizing the Blues on Stage.* Vol. 6 of *Black Studies.* Lewiston, Ont.: Edwin Mellen Press, 1999.

Wilson, August. "Where to Begin," in *Short Pieces from the New Dramatists.* Banbury, Ox.: Orangeberry Books, 1985, pp. 2033–2037.

Yoruba

The Yoruba people of Benin, Nigeria, and Togo influenced August Wilson's plays with their farming culture, skilled metalworking and woodcraft, and folklore that formed the basis of Santería, a folk religion common to Brazil and Cuba. In other parts of the African diaspora, Yoruban theology imparted a unique ethical code, a paradigm for character development, and oral traditions intended to inform the author's study of African scripture and ritual. Yoruban forecasting offered a method of divination based on analysis of oral mythology and the sacred forces of nature, which order human birth, growth, death, and rebirth, all significant themes in August Wilson's decade cycle. The fact that strands of Yoruban philosophy survived black assimilation to American life impressed him for their resilience and value to blacks.

The playwright grounded *Joe Turner's Come and Gone* (1988) and *King Hedley II* (1999) in Yoruba myth and the Ifa religion with reference to Ogun, a deity who suffered destruction by the winds and reintegrated himself once more. A blacksmith's deity like the Greek Hephaestus and the Roman Vulcan, Ogun is the god of iron and manly pursuits, including warfare, hunting, farming and herding, butchering game, fishing, shoeing horses, shaping wrought metal, barbering, driving cars and trains, and repairing vehicles, all of which involve skill with metal tools. Ogun meets humankind at the crossroads of their lives and promotes the individual's search for a life "song," an image suggesting unique talents, capabilities, and self-actualization.

Wilson's references to iron serve an allegorical purpose in his dramas, as with Boy Willie's adept attachment of wheels to a dolly in *The Piano Lesson* (1990), King Hedley's skill with a machete in *Seven Guitars* (1995), Jim Becker's retirement from work at J & S Steel and Youngblood's survival of the Vietnam War and his repair of a cab in *Jitney* (1982), and the length of chain that Solly Two Kings carries with him in *Gem of the Ocean* (2003) to remind himself of his enslavement and his dedication to freeing others by conducting runaways on the Underground Railroad. Symbolically, in *Joe Turner's Come and Gone*, the wanderer Herald Loomis, like Ogun, battles emotional fragmentation and seeks fulfillment of his "song." Suitably, Loomis fits the Ogun myth of imprisoning iron for his seven years on Joe Turner's chain gang. In *King Hedley II* (1999), the title character acknowledges Ogun by wrapping his frail garden in a circlet of barbed wire, an image suggesting the tiara of thorns that crowned Jesus before his crucifixion and the prickly exterior that Hedley uses as a shield against racial injustice. According to one analysis of the image as a promise of possibilities, the playwright uses Hedley's encircling iron to "create a new legend, a new fable, a new mythological figure, a Messiah of the 20th century" ("Sharing"). Adjacent to the seeds that Hedley plants is the grave of Aunt Ester's black cat, which the shaman Stool Pigeon interred with Yoruban honors, a ritual that establishes hope for her return.

See also **superstition**

- *Further Reading*

Appiah, Kwame Anthony. *In My Father's House: Africa in the Philosophy of Culture*. New York: Oxford University Press, 1992.

Drewel, Margaret Thompson. *Yoruba Ritual*. Indianapolis: Indiana University Press, 1992.

Harrison, Paul Carter, Victor Leo Walker, and Gus Edwards, eds. *Black Theatre: Ritual Performance in the African Diaspora*. Philadelphia: Temple University Press, 2002.

Richards, Sandra L. "Yoruba Gods on the American Stage: August Wilson's *Joe Turner's Come and Gone*." *Research in African Literatures*, Vol. 30, No. 4, Winter 1999, p. 92.

"Sharing the Stage with August Wilson." http://www.donshewey.com/theater_articles/marion_mcclinton.htm, April 29, 2001.

Youngblood

A cabbie in *Jitney* (1982), Darnell "Youngblood" Williams wears well the pride of an up-and-coming family man, which Wilson features as a model of hope for a declining black community. He bears a nickname that August Wilson himself acquired from old men in the Hill District in 1963. The name may refer to a time when the character ran around with women, drank, and partied too much. When the play opens, Youngblood is a Vietnam veteran in his latter twenties and the do-right father of his girlfriend Rena's two-year-old son Jesse. After the death of Ace, the fictional Youngblood spurns work in a mill and gets a job with Jim Becker's jitney station driving a gypsy cab. Youngblood's decision suits a risk-taker who envisions embracing the future as solid employee, husband, father, and homeowner.

The ups and downs of dialogue present Youngblood in a shifting interpersonal *chiaroscuro*, beginning with the opening scene, in which he competes against his nemesis, Turnbo. At first, Youngblood loses audience respect by claiming to be "the checker champ of 'Nam'," by boasting, "I'm like Muhammad Ali. I'm the greatest!" and by rejecting business that requires him to haul groceries that might soil his car (p. 12). Because Turnbo contributes to a negative view of his quarry with malicious gossip, Youngblood appears to betray Rena by driving around the neighborhood in the company her sister Peaches. At the nadir of his portrayal, he steals eighty dollars of Rena's food money but refuses to reveal where he spent it. The playwright allows questions to hang unanswered as an example of the need of black men to prove themselves and their aspirations.

On the up side, Wilson presents Youngblood as a friend who buys coffee for Turnbo, a cautious earner who keeps track of his expenses, and a capable mechanic who uses his expertise to clean a flywheel and replace a belt on Doub's car. Youngblood schemes to buy a house in Penn Hills under the GI Bill by working an early morning shift for UPS and earning fifty dollars a day tax free by supplying car service in the Hill District. When he confesses in Act Two his search for a house to get Rena and Jesse out of the projects, he sulks that she sees no change in his behavior — that he no longer keeps late hours, chases women, drinks, or plays cards. His reason presents a mature point of view: "I don't want to make no more mistakes in life. I don't want to do nothing to mess this up" (p. 76). The comment softens Youngblood with its admission of vulnerability.

One of August Wilson's most promising family men, Youngblood models the hope of the rising generation. He admits to Rena, "You already my pride. I want you to be my joy" (p. 77). As prospects for the jitney station dim, Youngblood refuses to be defeated by an economic turndown. He develops into one of Wilson's most admirable young males with his declaration to "find a job somewhere. Go to school. Raise my family. Do whatever I have to" (p. 95). His willingness contrasts the self-limiting aspirations of Sterling Johnson in *Two Trains Running* (1991) to drive a Cadillac but not to haul bricks. Less demanding than Boy Willie Charles in *The Piano Lesson* (1990), more ethnical than Mister, Elmore, and the title character in *King Hedley II* (1999), less money hungry than Seth Holly in *Joe Turner's Come and Gone* (1988), and more pragmatic than Floyd Barton in *Seven Guitars* (1995), Lyons Maxson in *Fences* (1985), and Levee Green in *Ma Rainey's Black Bottom* (1985), Youngblood appears to be Wilson's sure bet for success.

• *Further Reading*

Berson, Misha. "Humor, Hope Hitch Ride on Wilson's Engrossing 'Jitney.'" *Seattle Times*, January 30, 2002.

Lichtenstein, Gene. "An Evening with August Wilson." *Jewish Journal of Greater Los Angeles*, February 11, 2000.

Sobelsohn, David. "Ridin' All Over." *CenterStage*, January 8-February 14, 1999.

Appendix A:
Time Line of Hill District Residents and Events

The following time line incorporates references to actual history (in **boldface** type) with the fictional characters and events from August Wilson's plays.

1617	**Slavery begins in colonial North America.**
1619	Aunt Ester is born.
1631	Aunt Ester is sold into slavery.
January 1, 1863	Abraham Lincoln signs the Emancipation Proclamation.
1886	Seth Holly marries Bertha.
1896	Bynum Walker hears women in Memphis, Tennessee, singing "Joe Turner's Come and Gone."
1899	**The Toner Institute and Seraphic Home for Boys is established in Derry township.**
ca. 1900	Pittsburgh welcomes European immigrants, but rejects the blacks who flee the South.
1901	Shortly after the birth of Zonia Loomis, Herald Loomis falls into the hands of Joe Turner in Memphis, Tennessee. Two months later, Martha Loomis is evicted from the farm. She and her infant daughter Zonia move to Martha's mother's house.
1902	**Pittsburgh native Andrew Mellon becomes president of the Mellon National Bank.**
ca. 1903	Levee Green watches helplessly as eight or nine white men rape his mother in Jefferson County, Tennessee.
1904	Solly Two Kings reminisces about rescuing blacks on the Underground Railroad.
	Aunt Ester celebrates her 287th birthday.

1906	Martha Loomis leaves her child with her mother and flees north with Reverend Tolliver's evangelist church.
1908	Herald Loomis is freed from Joe Turner's chain gang.
	Loomis reunites with his daughter Zonia and sets out with her to the North to find his wife Martha.
	Bynum Walker comes to live at the Hollys' boardinghouse and causes Hiram to leave out of fear of Bynum's magic.
	Martha Loomis Pentecost rooms at the Holly boardinghouse and mourns the loss of her daughter Zonia.
1911	While Pittsburgh expands with steel mills, tunnels, roads, and bridges, Jeremy Furlow joins the dispossessed living under bridge spans.
	In August, Herald Loomis and his daughter Zonia arrive at Bertha and Seth Holly's boardinghouse in search of Martha.
1912	Troy Maxson's mother abandons her family when he is eight years old and his brother Gabriel is a year old.
1915	**The Great Migration from South to North begins.**
1918	Troy Maxson's father whips him for abandoning Greyboy to romance Joe Canewell's daughter. Troy walks to Mobile, Alabama, and hitches a ride to Pittsburgh.
1919	Louise stops going to church.
ca. 1923	Troy Maxson goes to prison for manslaughter, leaving his son Lyons without a father.
ca. 1925	Troy Maxson and Jim Bono become friends.
1928	**The boogie woogie develops popularity on the dance floor.**
Easter 1929	Ruby stops going to church.
July 19, 1930	Wining Boy Charles stands at the crossing of the Yazoo Delta and Southern railroads and calls out the names of the Ghosts of the Yellow Dog.
1931	Memphis Lee leaves Jackson, Mississippi, for Natchez.
	Sterling Johnson witnesses the suicide of Eddie Langston at Toner Institute.
1932	**Charley Burley, a Pittsburgh resident, begins a fifteen-year boxing career.**
1933	After the shooting death of Crawley, Berniece Charles comes north with her eight-year-old daughter Maretha to live with Uncle Doaker.
	Wining Boy Charles completes a three-year streak of good luck.
1934	Troy Maxson gets out of prison.
1936	Boy Willie Charles visits his sister Berniece and Uncle Doaker a few weeks after Robert Sutter's ghost inhabits the family piano.
	Avery Brown rents a building from Cohen to establish the Good Shepherd Church of God in Christ.
	Memphis Lee leaves Natchez and opens a cafe in the Hill District of Pittsburgh.
1939	Rose Lee marries Troy Maxson; Jim Bono marries Lucille.
1940	Troy Maxson fails to play major league baseball.
1941	After Rose Maxson gives birth to Cory, Troy vows that his son won't involve himself in sports.

mid–July 1941	Troy wrestles with Mr. Death for three days and nights at Mercy Hospital.
1942	Troy buys furniture from Glickman.
mid–1940s	Gabriel Maxson returns from military service in the Pacific with severe brain damage. Troy takes his brother's three thousand-dollar disability settlement to buy a house.
April 27, 1945	**August Wilson is born. He grows up in a two-room house behind Bella's grocery store at 1727 Bedford Avenue.** **Pittsburgh flourishes as home to Negro League baseball teams and prize-fighter Charley Burley and as the source of music by Billy Eckstine, Erroll Garner, Earl "Fatha" Hines, and Lena Horne, who performed regularly at the Crawford Grill.**
1945	At age seven, Booster Becker rides an imaginary red bicycle, which later vanishes.
August 1946	Floyd Barton scores a hit with his first record, "That's All Right." He two-times Vera by leaving for Chicago with Pearl Brown.
1947	West goes to Aunt Ester to ask if his wife is in heaven.
1948	After serving ninety days in the workhouse for vagrancy, Floyd tries to win Vera back after leaving her alone for eighteen months. Louise's niece Ruby leaves home in Birmingham, Alabama, to live in Pittsburgh with her aunt for a while. Red Carter claims that more blacks live in Chicago than in Pittsburgh because Highway 61, the world's longest stretch, runs straight from the South to Chicago. The poor fill the pauper section of Greenwood cemetery.
February 1948	Floyd Barton buries his mother, Maude Avery Barton, among paupers in Greenwood cemetery.
spring 1948	Louise urges Hedley to seek treatment for tuberculosis at the recently opened black sanitarium on Bedford Street.
May 1948	Friends gather for the funeral of Floyd, who had an appointment on June 10 to make another disk with the Savoy Record Company in Chicago.
ca. 1949	Ruby gives birth to King Hedley II.
1949	Holloway claims that Pittsburgh officials begin planning to tear down a whole block of the Hill District.
1950	**Pittsburgh's Hill District grows to 53,648.**
1950	Doub is drafted into the military and serves in the Korean War for nine months with the corpse detail as a retriever of combat casualties.
1951	King Hedley dies.
March 5, 1952	Holloway's grandfather dies at home because the hospital won't admit him without insurance.
1954	Bubba Boy falls in love and builds a fifteen-year relationship. Memphis Lee's mother dies, setting him free of responsibility.
1955	Fielding separates from his wife.
ca. 1957	King Hedley II kicks Miss Biggs when she inquires why he has to go to the bathroom.

October 10, 1957	The Milwaukee Braves win the World Series by beating the New York Yankees at Yankee Stadium.
1957	Booster Becker goes to the Western State Penitentiary death row for murdering Susan McKnight, daughter of an executive at Gulf Oil. Booster's mother, Coreen Becker, grieves herself to death twenty-three days later. Jim Becker estranges himself from his son and gives up on God.
	At age eighteen, Sterling Johnson leaves Toner Institute and lives on his own.
	Troy Maxson is promoted to garbage truck driver.
	West leaves his mortuary on Centre Street and builds a new place across from Memphis Lee's diner.
1958	**August Wilson's family moves to the Hazelwood section of town.**
1958	Troy Maxson signs away his brother Gabriel's freedom in exchange for half his government check.
	Alberta dies while giving birth to a daughter sired by Troy.
	Cory Maxson graduates from high school and flees home.
1959	Jim Becker begins driving cabs.
	Cory Maxson joins the marines.
	Zanelli's jukebox breaks in Memphis Lee's diner.
ca. 1959	Lutz promises Hambone a ham for painting a fence down the side and across the back of Lutz's Meat Market.
	The fifth-grade teacher of King Hedley II predicts he will grow up to be a janitor.
1960	Troy Maxson retires.
1960 or 1961	Memphis Lee hits the numbers and can change clothes daily.
	Jim Becker marries Lucille, his second wife.
1961	**August Wilson quits school and takes up residence at the Carnegie Library in Oakland.**
1961	Memphis uses $5,500 of his cash to buy a diner from L. D. and rejects an offer of $8,000 from West, the mortician across the street.
	Lyons and Bonnie Maxson divorce.
1963	**Wilson hangs out at Pat's Place and acquires the nickname Youngblood.**
1963	Risa Thomas makes fifteen razor slashes on her legs and enters a six-year period of loneliness.
	Lyons Maxson goes to the workhouse for cashing other people's checks.
1964	Sterling Johnson goes to prison for five years for driving the getaway car during a robbery.
1965	**August Wilson hears recordings by black singing star Bessie Smith.**
February 21, 1965	**Three black Muslims shoot Malcolm X to death in a Harlem ballroom.**
1965	Troy Maxson dies from heart disease.
	Doub begins driving a cab for Jim Becker's station.
1967	**Wilson listens to jazz saxophonist John Coltrane outside the Crawford Grill.**
1968	**Wilson and drama teacher Rob Penny co-found the Black Horizons Theatre Company.**
	Tonya is happy to give birth to Natasha.

1969	The Prophet Samuel, founder of the First African Congregational Kingdom, dies.
	Aunt Ester counsels seekers at her home at 1839 Wylie Avenue.
	When urban renewal threatens Memphis Lee's cafe, he accepts the city's offer of $35,000 for the property. His sale occurs after West buys Philmore's property.
	Fielding begins driving a cab for Jim Becker.
1971	On May 16, Philmore gets a job as doorman at the William Penn Hotel.
1972	After fifteen years in the Western State Penitentiary for murder, Booster Becker refuses parole.
1975	Cigar Annie's residence is condemned.
	Rena gives birth to Jesse, sired by Youngblood.
	Pernell Sims's cousin is run out of Pittsburgh for shooting two brothers over a football game.
1977–1982	**Edward deLuca directs Pittsburgh's Department of City Development.**
1977	Pittsburgh tears down part of the Irene Kaufman Settlement House and fails to replace it.
	Cigar Annie stops traffic on Robert Street by cussing and raising her dress at passing cars to protest eviction from a residence marked for the wrecking ball.
	Pope hits the numbers big and buys a Buick Riviera, but loses his restaurant to urban renewal.
	Cab stand manager Jim Becker dies in a freak mill accident at J & L Steel.
	McNeil's teenage boy pawns a television that he stole from Sarah Bolger, his elderly grandmother.
	Jim Bono is dying of cancer.
1978	**On September 28, Carletta Washington files a class-action suit demanding desegregation of Pittsburgh city schools.**
1978	Pernell Sims cuts the face of King Hedley II. Hedley reciprocates two weeks later by killing Pernell, for which Hedley serves a seven-year prison sentence in Western Penn.
1982	**August Wilson produces *Jitney* at the Allegheny Repertory Theater.**
1983	Stoller dies on the street from heart attack brought on by obesity.
1985	The son of the original King Hedley shoots craps with his father's murderer.
	Tonya Hedley anticipates the birth of a child.
	Ruby's aunt Louise, King Hedley's foster mother, dies.
	Aunt Ester dies.
	Pernell Sims's cousin returns to Pittsburgh after Pernell's mother dies.
1989	**The Pittsburgh Public Theater produces *Fences*.**
1990s	An attorney educated at Harvard retrieves the corpse of Aunt Ester in a *pro bono* court case.
1992	**August Wilson receives an honorary doctorate from the University of Pittsburgh.**
1999	**In December, *King Hedley II* debuts at the launching of the Pittsburgh Public Theater.**

2000	Looting and population decline reduce the Hill District to around 22 percent its size in 1950.
2003	In August, the Carnegie Museum exhibits three hundred photos shot by Charles "Teenie" Harris, an amateur shutterbug. The collected prints shown in "Documenting Our Past: The Teenie Harris Archive Project" record Hill District life over a forty-year period in eighty thousand images.
	August Wilson writes his first Hollywood screenplay, an adaptation of *Fences*, which contains a speaking part for Alberta, the unseen mistress of Troy Maxson.

Appendix B:
Writing and Research Topics

[Note: At the time of this work's publication, two of August Wilson's nine decade plays were not yet in print — *King Hedley II* and *Gem of the Ocean*. Researchers will have to rely on second-hand reports of characters, actions, and themes until these dramas are published.]

1. With a flow chart, contrast the contributions and awards of Maya Angelou, William Armstrong, James Baldwin, Toni Cade Bambara, Edward R. Braithwaite, W. E. B. Du Bois, Mari Evans, Ernest Gaines, Nikki Giovanni, Virginia Hamilton, Langston Hughes, Zora Neale Hurston, Toni Morrison, Ann Petry, Paul Robeson, and Alice Walker to black arts with those of playwrights Amiri Baraka, Ntozake Shange, Wole Soyinka, and August Wilson.

2. Discuss reasons for August Wilson's focus on male heroes and protagonists, including John the Baptist, Saint John the Revelator, Lazarus, the Lion of Judea, Toussaint L'Ouverture, Marcus Garvey, the folk figure Stagger Lee, the mythic High John the Conqueror, Br'er Rabbit, John Coltrane, Muddy Waters, Buddy Bolden, Jackie Robinson, Joe "the Brown Bomber" Louis, Billy Conn, Ezzard Charles, Archie Moore, Muhammad Ali, Josh Gibson, Satchel Page, Malcolm X, Dr. Martin Luther King, Jr., and movies about King Kong and Mighty Joe Young, both male gorillas.

3. Characterize elements of black dialect and slang in *Fences, Two Trains Running, Jitney,* and *Joe Turner's Come and Gone.* Note the difference between dialect in daily conversation and folk expressions in wise adages, as with "Carry you a little cup through life and you'll never be disappointed" *(Two Trains Running,* p. 94).

4. Explain the value of composing a ten-play cycle to express black issues and conflicts in successive decades of the twentieth century. Outline controversies that Wilson's male-dominated drama may have omitted or overlooked, particularly women's right to vote and seek office, domestic violence, equal pay and union membership for women, child labor, inaccessible health care for the poor, equal opportunities for blacks and gays in the military, heavy penalties for drug trafficking, health care for the elderly, planned parenthood and birth control, and abortion rights.

5. Suggest topics for a play about the 2000s that would elucidate the role of law

enforcement in black urban problems, profiling black drivers and suspects, especially imprisonment of underage felons and possessors of small amounts of controlled substances, entrapment and Miranda rights, police violence against minorities, federal wiretapping, investigation of Black Muslims for complicity with Arab terrorists, and the three strikes law that requires lengthy prison time for criminals found guilty a third time.

6. Compose a letter to *New Republic* either supporting August Wilson's call for a black national theater or corroborating critic Robert Brustein's charge that Wilson's views are divisive and separatist. Use examples from your own community of the absence or presence of opportunities for black artists and writers.

7. Summarize August Wilson's "The Ground on Which I Stand" and Robert Brustein's column rebutting Wilson's arguments for a separate black national theater. Outline your own opinion.

8. Identify and explain opposing elements suggested by the title *Two Trains Running*. Consider examples of property ownership, peace-keeping, neighborhood reclamation, opportunity, self-respect, gender differences, love, good fortune, loss, and death.

9. Account for the image of Stagger Lee in dialect songs and in Wining Boy's reference to him in *The Piano Lesson*.

10. Contrast the parenting in several of Wilson's plays. Include the following models:

- Jim and Coreen Becker's loyalty to Booster Becker in *Jitney*
- Berniece Charles's rearing and refinement of Maretha in *The Piano Lesson*
- Tonya Hedley and the title character with their unborn child in *King Hedley II*
- Floyd Barton's idealization of Maude Avery Barton and Ruby's concern for her unborn child in *Seven Guitars*
- Aunt Ester's naming of her star children in *Gem of the Ocean*

- Ma Rainey's concern for her nephew Sylvester Brown in *Ma Rainey's Black Bottom*
- Martha Pentecost and Herald Loomis's treatment of Zonia in *Joe Turner's Come and Gone*
- Rose and Troy Maxson's responses to Lyons, Cory, and Raynell in *Fences*. Include a summary of the community's parenting of Gabe Maxson in *Fences* and of Hambone, the retarded handyman in *Two Trains Running*.

11. Select blues lyrics from each decade represented by Wilson's plays. Analyze emotions, ambitions, losses, and frustrations that weigh heavily on black people, for example, petty ghetto crime, imprisonment and service on chain gangs, declining income from sharecropping, bewilderment at the social and economic challenges of living in an industrialized city, the white-dominated justice and penal systems, anti-black unions and mill management, disproportionate drafting of black males to fight wars, endangerment of male self-esteem, indifference to God and worship, and the dissolution of the black family.

12. Outline the history of American baseball, beginning with informal rules and pick-up games and continuing through the rise of the Negro League, Satchel Paige, Josh Gibson, Jackie Robinson, Hank Aaron, and Wes Covington. Explain why Troy Maxson is bitter that his own career plans failed and why he believes a football scholarship will disappoint Cory.

13. Compare the strengths of the nuclear family in two of August Wilson's plays, for example:

- the remains of the Charles family in *The Piano Lesson*
- Herald and Zonia Loomis, a father and daughter in search of the mother, Martha Pentecost, in *Joe Turner's Come and Gone*
- the members of Troy Maxson's three combined families in *Fences*. Ma and her nephew Sylvester Brown in *Ma Rainey's Black Bottom*

- West and his former wife in *Two Trains Running*
- the title character, Tonya Hedley, and their unborn child in *King Hedley II*
- Ruby's deception of King Hedley about her unborn child in *Seven Guitars*
- Jim, Coreen, Booster, and Lucille Becker or Youngblood, Rena, and Jesse in *Jitney*.

14. Compare the source of anger and mistrust of whites in Toni Cade Bambara's story "Blues Ain't No Mockin' Bird," James Baldwin's "Sonny's Blues," Terry McMillan's *Mama*, Dick Gregory's *Nigger*, Toni Morrison's *Beloved*, Margaret Walker's *Jubilee*, Richard Wright's *Black Boy*, or Ernest Gaines's *A Lesson Before Dying* to a similar discontent in *Fences*, *The Piano Lesson*, *Ma Rainey's Black Bottom*, *Jitney*, *King Hedley II*, *Gem of the Ocean*, *Seven Guitars*, *Joe Turner's Come and Gone*, or *Two Trains Running*.

15. Compare the ambitions and yearnings in Richard Wright's story "Almos' a Man" with those of Troy, Lyons, and Cory Maxson in *Fences*, Sterling Johnson and Hambone in *Two Trains Running*, Ruby, Floyd Barton, Vera Dotson, King Hedley, and Canewell in *Seven Guitars*, Levee Green and Dussie Mae in *Ma Rainey's Black Bottom*, Youngblood, Rena, and Booster Becker in *Jitney*, Jeremy Furlow, Molly Cunningham, Mattie Campbell, and Herald Loomis in *Joe Turner's Come and Gone*, or Lymon Jackson, Berniece Charles, and Avery Brown in *The Piano Lesson*.

16. Compare losses in James Agee's *A Death in the Family*, Olive Ann Burns's *Cold Sassy Tree*, William Faulkner's *As I Lay Dying*, Kay Gibbons's *Ellen Foster*, Lillian Hellman's *The Little Foxes*, Arthur Miller's *Death of a Salesman*, John van Druten's *I Remember Mama*, or Thornton Wilder's *Our Town* with either *Two Trains Running*, *Jitney*, *King Hedley II*, or *Fences*. Note what remains of deceased characters' lives as their families and friends grieve their passing.

17. Compile a brochure to accompany a walking tour of Pittsburgh, noting locales that August Wilson mentions in his plays,

particularly Squirrel Hill, North Side, Little Haiti, Greentree, East Liberty, Shadyside, Logan Street, Herron Avenue, Irene Kaufman Settlement House, Henry Buhl Planetarium and Observatory, Homestead Field, Wylie Avenue, Workingmen's Club, Mercy Hospital, Monongahela River, Brady Street Bridge, courthouse and the Brass Rail, Crawford Grill, the 88, Penn Hills, Savoy Ballroom, Ellis Hotel, Rankin, Little Washington, Braddock, Scotchbottom, Clairton, Blawknox, and the Hill District, a locus of black community life.

18. Summarize the rites for Floyd Barton in *Seven Guitars*, the pre-funeral gathering of the Maxsons in *Fences*, memories of Jim Becker in *Jitney*, grief for Leroy Slater, Little Buddy Will, and Aunt Ester in *King Hedley II* and for Mama Ola and Boy Charles in *The Piano Lesson*, and the numerous funerals that West conducts in *Two Trains Running*. Note details of community and family response and number and behavior of mourners at the rites and memorials for Little Buddy Will, Boy Charles, Aunt Ester, Hambone, Troy Maxson, Floyd Barton, Neesi, Mama Ola Charles, Leroy Slater, Pernell Sims, the Prophet Samuel, Patchneck Red, Jim Becker, and Begaboo, a victim of police brutality.

19. Contrast the title character in *The Autobiography of Miss Jane Pittman* with King Hedley in *Seven Guitars* and Stool Pigeon in *King Hedley II* in terms of their longing for a great black leader such as Toussaint L'Ouverture to retrieve blacks from the tyranny of whites. Include names of people whose aims and careers disappointed the hopeful, particularly Marcus Garvey, Malcolm X, Shirley Chisholm, Louis Farrakhan, Barbara Jordan, Elijah Muhammad, Carol Moseley Braun, Condoleezza Rice, Clarence Thomas, Colin Powell, and Jesse Jackson.

20. Select contrasting scenes and describe their pictorial qualities, for example:
- Sam moving toward the lectern and speaking into the microphone in *The Janitor*
- Cory striking at the rag ball with his bat

or Rose Maxson singing hymns and hanging up clothes in *Fences*
- Levee Green romancing Dussie Mae or Ma arguing with a police officer in *Ma Rainey's Black Bottom*
- Louise dealing cards for whist or Canewell and Red Carter offering to carry Ruby's suitcase in *Seven Guitars*
- Doaker Charles ironing a uniform and cooking or Boy Willie protecting Maretha from a ghost in *The Piano Lesson*
- Turnbo spreading gossip about Youngblood to Rena, Booster Becker striking Doub, or Fielding hiding an empty liquor bottle from other cabbies in *Jitney*
- Aunt Ester's creasing of her bill of sale into a paper boat or Black Mary washing Ester's feet in *Gem of the Ocean*
- Martha Pentecost reuniting with her husband or Bynum Walker blessing Herald Loomis in *Joe Turner's Come and Gone*
- Tonya threatening to abort her child, Stool Pigeon honoring a dead black cat, or King Hedley shooting dice with Elmore in *King Hedley II*
- Risa Thomas offering sugar for West's coffee or dancing with Sterling Johnson to jukebox music in *Two Trains Running*.

21. Discuss sports, career advancement, and sex as sources of macho attitudes in Troy Maxson in *Fences*, land ownership and sex as stimuli to Boy Willie Charles in *The Piano Lesson*, guns and sex as compensations to Sterling Johnson in *Two Trains Running*, home ownership and sex as elements of Youngblood's relationship with Rena in *Jitney*, family line and sex as driving forces in the title character of *King Hedley II*, and music and promiscuous sex as the founts of Floyd Barton's overblown ego in *Seven Guitars*, the title character's self-esteem in *Ma Rainey's Come and Gone*, and Jeremy Furlow's crude credo in *Joe Turner's Come and Gone*.

22. Compare Citizen Barlow's failings and constable Caesar's regrets in *Gem of the Ocean*, Boy Charles's murder in *The Piano Lesson*, Levee Green's self-incrimination in *Ma Rainey's Black Bottom*, Floyd Barton's demise in *Seven Guitars*, Jeremy Furlow's arrest on payday in *Joe Turner's Come and Gone*, and Troy Maxson's downfall in *Fences* with similar themes in Percy Bysshe Shelley's "Ozymandias," Lord Byron's "The Prisoner of Chillon," Alfred Lord Tennyson's "Ulysses," Thomas Hardy's "The Man He Killed," Christina Rossetti's "The Goblin Market," Gwendolyn Brooks's "Annie Allen," Marge Piercy's "The Grey-Flannel Sexual Harassment Suit," Adrienne Rich's "Snapshots of a Daughter-in-law," or Robert Frost's "Death of the Hired Man."

23. Write an extended definition of *legend* using High John the Conqueror, the Ghosts of the Yellow Dog, and Robert Sutter's ghost as models or compose an extended definition of *myth* using as an example a former slave woman who outlives death or a visit to the City of Bones, its location, history, inhabitants, and purpose.

24. Compare the skill of binding man Bynum Walker in *Joe Turner's Come and Gone* or of Aunt Ester at spiritual healing in *Gem of the Ocean* and *Two Trains Running* to that of the mother in William Armstrong's *Sounder*, the title character in Ernest Gaines's *The Autobiography of Miss Jane Pittman*, the title character in Gary Paulsen's *Nightjohn*, or Grandma Baby in Toni Morrison's *Beloved*. Describe rhythmic, physical, and vocal methods of releasing the hurt of slave times.

25. Compare family dynamics in *The Piano Lesson*, *Fences*, Margaret Walker's *Jubilee*, Toni Morrison's *The Bluest Eye*, Isabel Allende's *The House of the Spirits*, Laura Esquivel's *Like Water for Chocolate*, Amy Tan's *The Kitchen God's Wife*, Alice Walker's *The Color Purple*, or Lorraine Hansberry's *A Raisin in the Sun* in terms of the male's need to override matriarchy and satisfy personal needs.

26. Improvise a conference of Caesar, Aunt Ester, Tonya Hedley, Martha Pentecost, West, Wolf, King Hedley, King Hedley II, Boy Willie Charles, Louise, Rena, Cutler, Rutherford Selig, Canewell/Stool Pigeon, Seth Holly, Eli, and the Prophet Samuel about the nature of human happiness as

regards to money. As a model, explain through dialogue how Aunt Ester changed the Reverend Samuel into the Prophet Samuel, why Boy Willie decides not to sell the Charles family's piano, why Turnbo threatened a poor man over a fifty-cent fare, and why Memphis Lee refused West's lucrative offer to buy the diner.

27. Contrast the use of vision quests in *Black Elk Speaks*, the biography of Black Elk, with Aunt Ester's seance that redeems Citizen Barlow in *Gem of the Ocean* and Herald Loomis's trance and glossolalia in *Joe Turner's Come and Gone.*

28. List and describe a variety of narrative forms and styles in August Wilson's plays, including call-and-response, dialogue, anecdote, history lecture, satire, genealogy, scripture, eulogy, testimony, animal fable, quip, witticism, adage, song, elegy, boast, lament, *double entendre*, homily, fool tale, and debate.

29. Compare Toledo, Canewell/Stool Pigeon, Louise, Cutler, Doaker, Jim Becker, Bynum Walker, Tonya Hedley, Bertha Holly, and Aunt Ester as advisers and bearers of wisdom with the roles of Marcus Aurelius, Isaiah, the Cumaean Sibyl, Mother Teresa, Confucius, Marian Wright Edelman, Cesar Chavez, Solomon, Dr. Elie Wiesel, Barbara Jordan, Malcolm X, Ann Landers, Jeremiah, Dr. Martin Luther King, Eleanor Roosevelt, Dr. Ruth Westheimer, the Dalai Lama, Pope John XXIII, and Black Elk.

30. Choose two characters to compare in terms of religious beliefs, for example, King Hedley's visions of catastrophe and Vera Dotson's insistence that death is unpredictable in *Seven Guitars*, Cutler's religiosity and Levee Green's blasphemy in *Ma Rainey's Black Bottom*, Hedley's condemnation of murderers and Stool Pigeon's anticipation of a messiah in *King Hedley II*, Martha Pentecost's immersion in fundamentalism or Bynum Walker's African mysticism in *Joe Turner's Come and Gone*, Risa's faith in the Prophet Samuel and Memphis Lee's skepticism in *Two Trains Running*, and Rose Max-

son's religiosity and Gabriel Maxson's hope of a glorious reception in heaven for his brother Troy in *Fences.*

31. Hypothesize the predicaments and points of view of the black women in Wilson's plays who are only mentioned. Include these:

- the love-wrecker Pearl Brown, Grandma Ruby, WillaMae, and Floyd's beloved mother Maude Avery Barton in *Seven Guitars*
- Levee Green and Sylvester Brown's mothers in *Ma Rainey's Black Bottom*
- the jealous, money-hungry Rosie, Shealy's ex-girlfriend, the liar Susan McKnight, Lucille and Coreen Becker, and Rena's helpful sister Peaches in *Jitney*
- Wining Boy's Cleotha, Mama Ola Charles, Ophelia Sutter, and Doaker's former wife Coreen in *The Piano Lesson*
- the grasping Deanna, the grieving mother of Little Buddy Will, and the traitorous Neesi in *King Hedley II*
- the beloved dead wife of West and Wolf's money-grabbing Atlanta woman in *Two Trains Running*
- West's deceased wife and Memphis Lee's unfaithful wife in *Two Trains Running*
- the ghost of Miss Mabel Holly and the women who abandon Bynum Walker and Jeremy Furlow in *Joe Turner's Come and Gone*
- the faithful, but discounted wife Lucille Bono and Lyons Maxson's ex-wife Bonnie in *Fences.*

For example, present Alberta's side of her romance with Troy Maxson and the conception of their daughter Raynell in *Fences*, the hurt of Miss Sarah Bolger, the grandmother robbed of a television by her grandson in *Jitney*, WillaMae's attitude toward Mister, the son sired by Red Carter in *Seven Guitars*, the sister whom Solly Two Kings rescues from the Klan in *Gem of the Ocean*, the reason for Miss Mabel Holly's haunting in *Joe Turner's Come and Gone*, or Mama Ola Charles's perpetual care of the carved piano in *The Piano Lesson.*

32. Characterize the importance of character placement in Wilson's dramas. For

example, note the stance of Sam at the microphone in *The Janitor*, the circling of the dinner table by juba dancers in *Joe Turner's Come and Gone*, the clustering of mourners in the backyard of a rooming house in *Seven Guitars*, the spacing of cabbies around a stove in *Jitney*, the cluster of diners at the counter in *Two Trains Running*, the gathering of mourners at the front porch in *Fences*, the welcome of Elmore in *King Hedley II,* ghost appearances in *The Piano Lesson*, or the relegation of band members to a basement room and Ma Rainey one floor up in the studio in *Ma Rainey's Black Bottom* while whites occupy the control room farther up the building.

33. Summarize the pragmatic values of Seth Holly, the innkeeper in *Joe Turner's Come and Gone*. Explain the benefits of a vocational educational program by which he proposes to elevate road worker Jeremy Furlow to a stable position as pot maker. Include the educational philosophies of Maya Angelou, Booker T. Washington, Mary McLeod Bethune, W. E. B. DuBois, Marian Wright Edelman, Walter Hines Page, and George Washington Carver.

34. Contrast characters in terms of their analyses of their fathers, a recurrent motif in August Wilson's plays and an autobiographical clue to his own boyhood. Include Booster Becker, Canewell, Doaker Charles, Molly Cunningham, Levee Green, King Hedley, King Hedley II, Seth Holly, Zonia Loomis, Cory Maxson, Lyons Maxson, Troy Maxson, Bynum Walker, and West.

35. Locate examples of shoes in August Wilson's plays as symbols of ambition and persistence, as with Toledo's muddy clodhoppers and Levee Green's Florsheims in *Ma Rainey's Black Bottom*, Raynell's tight dress shoes and Cory Maxson's football shoes in *Fences*, the title character's removal of shoes in *Ma Rainey's Black Bottom*, and Herald Loomis's worn-out traveling shoes in *Joe Turner's Come and Gone.*

36. Collect wisdom lore and adages from August Wilson's plays. Match them with similar statements in compendia of world quotations from native Americans, Africa, Australia, and China.

37. Compare Bynum Walker's concept of a personal song in *Joe Turner's Come and Gone* with the songs that empower John Steinbeck's novella *The Pearl.*

38. Compare Ralph Ellison's unnamed title character in *Invisible Man* with these downtrodden figures in Wilson's plays:

- Sam in *The Janitor*
- Citizen Barlow in *Gem of the Ocean*
- Herald Loomis, Jeremy Furlow, Mattie Campbell, and Martha Pentecost in *Joe Turner's Come and Gone*
- Troy Maxson in *Fences*
- Risa Thomas, Hambone, and Sterling Johnson in *Two Trains Running*
- King Hedley, Vera Dotson, and Floyd Barton in *Seven Guitars*
- Levee Green in *Ma Rainey's Black Bottom*
- Jim Becker and Fielding in *Jitney*
- Wining Boy Charles in *The Piano Lesson*
- Tonya Hedley, Ruby, Elmore, and the title character in *King Hedley II.*

39. List and discuss the effectiveness of Gothic elements from *The Piano Lesson, Seven Guitars, King Hedley II,* and *Joe Turner's Come and Gone*, including melodrama, superstition, violence, prophecy, *chiaroscuro*, and the supernatural. Explain how Gothic conventions function in realistic drama.

40. Compare the vision of a nurturing, supportive community in August Wilson's decade cycle to that of Dubose Heyward and George Gershwin's *Porgy and Bess* (1935), the first American opera. Include superstitions, faith, shared labors, ritual, fears, betrayal, love, and trust.

Bibliography

Primary Sources

"Bessie." *Black Lines*, Vol. 1, Summer 1971, p. 68.

Fences. New York: Plume, 1986.

"For Malcolm X and Others." *Negro Digest*, Vol. 18, September 1971, p. 58.

"The Ground on Which I Stand." *American Theatre*, Vol. 13, September 1996, pp. 14–15, 71–74.

"I Want a Black Director." *New York Times*, September 26, 1990.

The Janitor in *Short Pieces from the New Dramatists*. Banbury, Ox.: Orangeberry Books, 1985.

Jitney. Woodstock, N.Y.: Overlook Press, 2001.

Joe Turner's Come and Gone. New York: Penguin, 1988.

King Hedley II. Unpublished manuscript, 2001.

"The Legacy of Malcolm X." *Life*, December 1992, pp. 84–94.

Ma Rainey's Black Bottom. New York: Plume, 1988.

"Morning Song." *Black Lines*, Vol. 1, Summer 1971, p. 68.

"Muhammad Ali." *Black World*, Vol. 1, September 1972, pp. 60–61.

The Piano Lesson. New York: Plume, 1990.

Seven Guitars. New York: Dutton, 1996.

Testimonies. *Antaeus*, No. 66, Spring 1991.

"Theme One: The Variations," in *The Poetry of Black America: Anthology of the Twentieth Century*. New York: Harper & Row, 1973.

Two Trains Running. New York: Plume, 1992.

Secondary Sources

Aaron, Jan. "Royal Treat: 'King Hedley II.'" *Education Update*, June 2001.

Abarbanel, Jonathan. "Gem of the Ocean." http://ibs.theatermania.com/content/news.cfm?int_news_id=3441, May 1, 2003.

Adcock, Joe. "A Moment with August Wilson, Playwright." *Seattle Post-Intelligencer*, May 20, 2003.

_____. "Wilson's 'What I Learned' Droll, Thoughtful, Packed with Surprises." *Seattle Post-Intelligencer*, May 27, 2003, p. F5.

Adell, Sandra. "Speaking of Ma Rainey/Talking about the Blues," in *May All Your Fences Have Gates: Essays on the Drama of August Wilson*. Iowa City: University of Iowa Press, 1994.

Ambush, Benny Sato. "Culture Wars." *African American Review*, Vol. 31, No. 4, Winter 1997, pp. 579–586.

Anderson, Douglas. "Saying Goodbye to the Past: Self-Empowerment and History." *CLA Journal*, Vol. 40, No. 4, June 1997, pp. 432–457.

Appiah, Kwame Anthony. *In My Father's House: Africa in the Philosophy of Culture*. New York: Oxford University Press, 1992.

_____, and Henry Louis Gates, Jr., eds. *Africana*. New York: Perseus Books, 1999.

Ards, Angela. "The Diaspora Comes to Dartmouth." *American Theatre*, Vol. 15, No. 5, May-June 1998, pp. 50–52.

Arthur, Thomas H. "Looking for My Relatives: The Political Implications of 'Family' in Selected Works of Athol Fugard and August Wilson." *South African Theatre Journal*, Vol. 6, No. 2, 1992, pp. 5–16.

Auerbach, Nina. *Our Vampires, Ourselves.* Chicago: University of Chicago Press, 1995.

August Wilson (video). California Newsreel, 1992.

"August Wilson." http://www.cee.umn.edu/ufv/catalog/data/659.html.

"August Wilson: A Maverick Playwright with Unadulterated Wisdom." *New York Amsterdam News*, May 17, 1997.

"August Wilson's Sacred Book." http://soundprint.brnadywine.American.edu/~soundprt/more_info/August_Wilson.

Austin, April. "'Seven Guitars' Makes Sweet, Sweet Music." *Christian Science Monitor*, Vol. 87, Issue 205, September 18, 1995, p. 13.

Awkward, Michael. "'The Crookeds with the Straights': *Fences*, Race, and the Politics of Adaptation," in *May All Your Fences Have Gates: Essays on the Drama of August Wilson.* Iowa City: University of Iowa Press, 1994, pp. 205–229.

Backalenick, Irene. "A Lesson from Lloyd Richards." *Theater Week*, April 15, 1990, pp. 16–19.

Baker, Houston A. *Blues, Ideology, and Afro-American Literature.* Chicago: University of Chicago Press, 1984.

Bandler, Michael J. "USIA Interview with American Playwright August Wilson." http://usembassy-australia.state.gov/hyper/WF980415/epf308.htm, April 15, 1998.

Barbour, David. "August Wilson's Here to Stay." *Theater Week*, April 18-25, 1988, pp. 8–14.

_____. "The Mysteries of Pittsburgh." *Entertainment Design*, Vol. 34, No. 7, July 2000.

Barnett, Douglas O. "Up for the Challenge." *American Theater*, Vol. 13, No. 10, 1996, pp. 60.

Bellamy, Lou. "The Colonization of Black Theatre." *African American Review*, Vol. 31, No. 4, Winter 1997, pp. 587–590.

Bennett, Weyman. "Hill District Blues." *Socialist Review*, January 2003.

Berkowitz, Gerald M. *American Drama of the Twentieth Century.* London: Longman, 1992.

Berson, Misha. "August Wilson Makes Leap from Playwright to Thespian." *Seattle Times*, May 18, 2003, p. K3.

_____. "August Wilson's Solo Show Deftly Catches Life's Contradictions." *Seattle Times*, May 27, 2003.

_____. "Humor, Hope Hitch Ride on Wilson's Engrossing 'Jitney.'" *Seattle Times*, January 30, 2002.

_____. "Seattle Playwright Wilson Awarded Humanities Medal." *Seattle Times*, September 22, 1999, p. E1.

"The Best of 1995 Theater." *Time*, Vol. 146, No. 26, December 25, 1995, p. 152.

Bigsby, C. W. E. *Modern American Drama, 1945–1990.* Cambridge: Cambridge University Press, 1992.

Billington, Michael. "King Hedley II." *Guardian Unlimited*, December 12, 2002.

"Biography of August Wilson." http://www.dartmouth.edu/~awilson/bio.html.

Birdwell, Christine. "Death as a Fastball on the Outside Corner: *Fences*' Troy Maxson and the American Dream." *Aethlon: The Journal of Sport Literature*, No. 1, Fall 1990, pp. 87–96.

Bissiri, Amadou. "Aspects of Africanness in August Wilson's Drama: Reading *The Piano Lesson* through Wole Soyinka's Drama." *African American Review*, Vol. 30, No. 1, 1996, pp. 99–113.

"Black Empowerment: Playwright August Wilson Less Known by Blacks." *New Pittsburgh Courier*, March 5, 1997.

Blackburn, Regina Naasirah. "Erupting Thunder: Race and Class in the 20th Century Plays of August Wilson." *Socialism and Democracy*, Vol. 17, No. 2.

Blanchard, Jayne M. "An August Tradition." *St. Paul Pioneer Press*, May 4, 1993, p. 10F.

_____. "This 'Piano' Found the Key for Great Theater." *St. Paul Pioneer Press*, May 4, 1992, p. 5C.

Bloom, Harold, intro. *August Wilson.* New York: Chelsea House, 2002.

Blumenthal, Anna S. "More Stories Than the Devil Got Sinners: Troy's Stories in August Wilson's *Fences*." *American Drama*, Vol. 9, No. 2, Spring 2000, pp. 74–96.

Boan, Devon. "Call-and-Response: Parallel 'Slave Narrative' in August Wilson's 'The Piano Lesson.'" *African American Review*,

Vol. 32, No. 2, Summer 1998, pp. 263–272.

Bogumil, Mary L. *Understanding August Wilson*. Columbia: University of South Carolina Press, 1998.

Bommer, Lawrence. "August Wilson's Ride into the Past." *Chicago Tribune*, June 25, 1999, p.5.

_____. "A Keeper of Dreams." *Chicago Tribune*, January 15, 1995, pp. 16, 21.

Bouthiller, Russell. "King Hedley II." *Broadway Snap-Shot*, May 13, 2001.

Bowen, Joseph. "Jitney." http://centerstage.net/theatre/articles/jitney.html.

_____. "Ma Rainey's Black Bottom." http://www.pathfinder.com/people/960513/features/wilson.html.

Brantley, Ben. "'King Hedley II': The Agonized Arias of Everyman in Poverty and Pain." *New York Times*, May 2, 2001.

_____. "The World That Created August Wilson." *New York Times*, Vol. 144, February 5, 1995, p. H1.

Brenner, Robert. "Playwright's Heart Is in Pittsburgh." *Pittsburgh Post-Gazette*, July 19, 1982, p. 17.

Breslauer, Jan. "Theater Lifting an Embargo on the Past Writing About His Native Cuba Did Not Come Easily to Playwright Nilo Cruz, But Once He Started, He Quickly Found Familiar Territory." *Los Angeles Times*, April 25, 1999, p. 42.

Brock, Wendell. "Q&A: August Wilson, Pulitzer Prize–winning Playwright: Wilson Sees 'Light at End of Tunnel' for Play Cycle." *Atlanta Journal-Constitution*, September 29, 2003, p. E1.

Brustein, Robert. "The Lesson of 'The Piano Lesson.'" *New Republic*, Vol. 202, No. 21, May 21, 1990, pp. 28–30.

_____. "On Cultural Power." *New Republic*, Vol. 216, No. 9, March 3, 1997, pp. 31–34.

_____. "The Piano Lesson." *New Republic*, Vol. 202, No. 21, May 21, 1990, pp. 28–30.

_____. *Reimagining American Theater*. New York: Wang, 1991.

_____. "Subsidized Separatism." *New Republic*, Vol. 215, No. 8–9, August 19, 1996, pp. 39–42.

Buford, John. "Plight of 1920s Blacks— Superbly Portrayed in New Wilson Drama."

Christian Science Monitor, October 16, 1984.

Burrison, John A., ed. *Storytellers: Folktales & Legends from the South*. Athens: University of Georgia Press, 1989.

Carey, Lynn. "Playwright Lets His Characters Do the Work." *Time Out*, October 6, 1991, p. 9.

Charters, Ann, and Samuel Charters, eds. *Short Pieces from the New Dramatists*. Banbury, Ox.: Orangeberry Books, 1985.

Ching, Mei-Ling. "Wrestling Against History." *Theater*, Vol. 20, Summer-Fall 1988, pp. 70–71.

Christian, Barbara. *Black Feminist Criticism: Perspectives on Black Women Writers*. New York: Pergamon, 1985.

Christiansen, Richard. "Artist of the Year: August Wilson's Plays Reveal What It Means to Be Black in This Country." *Chicago Tribune*, December 27, 1987, pp. F9–F10.

_____. "August Wilson: A Powerful Playwright Probes the Meaning of Black Life." *Chicago Tribune*, February 5, 1988, pp. 12–13.

_____. "August Wilson Stays True to His Artistic Vision." *Chicago Tribune*, February 9, 2000, p. 1.

_____. "Epic Dream Eludes Wilson 'King Hedley' Continues Playwright's American Odyssey." *Chicago Tribune*, December 12, 2000, p. 2.

_____. "Mother of All Plays Wilson's 'Ma Rainey' Sets Stage for Next Works." *Chicago Tribune*, July 1, 1997, p. 2.

Clark, Keith. *Black Manhood in James Baldwin, Ernest J. Gaines, and August Wilson*. Urbana: University of Illinois Press, 2002.

Cohen, Robert. "In Los Angeles." http://drama.arts.uci.edu/cohen/jitney.htm.

Clover, Ben. "King Hedley II." *London Review*, December 12, 2002.

Coleman, A. D. "Slices from the Jazz Life." *Staten Island Journal*, May 1998.

Copelin, David. "Transforming Story into Plot." *The Writer*, Vol. 112, No. 9, September 1999, pp. 21–23, 45.

Crawford, Eileen. "The B Burden: The Invisibility of Ma Rainey's Black Bottom," in *August Wilson: A Casebook*. New York: Garland, 1994.

Cummings, Scott. "King Hedley II." *Boston Phoenix*, May 18–25, 2000.

Davidson, Jim. "A Playwright Who Stirs the Imagination: A Dropout from the Hill District, August Wilson Is Now a Hit on Broadway." *Pittsburgh Press*, November 4, 1984, p. F1.

DeVries, Hilary. "Drama Lesson." *Boston Globe Magazine*, June 23, 1990, p. 20, 46.

_____. "A Song in Search of Itself." *American Theatre*, January 1987, pp. 22–25.

DiGaetani, John L. "August Wilson," in *A Search for a Postmodern Theater: Interviews with Contemporary Playwrights*. Westport, Conn.: Greenwood, 1991.

Dobelis, Inge N., project ed. *Magic and Medicine of Plants*. Pleasantville, N.Y.: Readers Digest Association, 1986.

Drewel, Margaret Thompson. *Yoruba Ritual*. Indianapolis: Indiana University Press, 1992.

D'Souza, Karen. "Playwrights Dig for Lost History of Blacks." *San Jose Mercury News*, March 17, 2002.

Dwyer, Victor. "Two Trains Running." *Maclean's*, Vol. 105, No. 20, May 18, 1992, pp. 56–57.

Elam, Harry J., ed. *Colored Contradictions: An Anthology of Contemporary African-American Plays*. New York: Plume, 1996.

_____. "The Dialectics of August Wilson's 'The Piano Lesson.'" *Theatre Journal*, Vol. 52, No. 3, 2000, pp. 361–379.

_____. "*Ma Rainey's Black Bottom*: Singing Wilson's Blues." *American Drama*, Vol. 5, No. 2, Spring 1996, pp. 76–99.

_____. "Signifyin(g) on African American Theatre: *The Colored Museum* by George C. Wolfe." *Theatre Journal*, Vol. 44, No. 3, 1992, pp. 291–303.

_____, and David Krasner, eds. *African American Performance and Theater History: A Critical Reader*. New York: Oxford University Press, 2001.

Elkins, Marilyn, ed. *August Wilson: A Casebook*. New York: Garland, 1994.

Englehart, Mark. "Seven Guitars." http://seattle.sidewalk.com/detail/32177.

Euell, Kim. "Wilson's Worlds through African Eyes." *American Theatre*, Vol. 20, No. 1, May/June 2003, pp. 22–23.

Evans, Greg. "On Cultural Power: The Wilson-Brustein Discussion." *Variety*, February 3, 1997.

Fanger, Iris. "King Hedley II." *TheaterMania*, June 12, 2000.

Fisher, Philip. "King Hedley II." *British Theatre Guide*, 2002.

Fishman, Joan. "Developing His Song: August Wilson's *Fences*," in *August Wilson: A Casebook*. New York: Garland, 1994.

Fitzgerald, Sharon. "August Wilson: The People's Playwright." *American Visions*, Vol. 15, No. 14, August 2000, p. 14.

_____. " Lloyd Richards: The Griot Wears a Watch." *American Visions*, Vol. 13, No. 4, August-September 1998.

Fleche, Anne. "The History Lesson: Authenticity and Anachronism in August Wilson's Plays," in *May All Your Fences Have Gates: Essays on the Drama of August Wilson*. Iowa City: University of Iowa Press, 1994, p. 1.

Fleming, John. "A Casting Call." *St. Petersburg Times*, March 7, 1997, pp. D1–D2.

Foner, Eric. *Reconstruction: America's Unfinished Revolution*. New York: Harper & Row, 1988.

Foreman, Rebecca. "Portrait of life in 1904 Mesmerizes Audience: 'Gem of the Ocean': Poetic Dialogue Lifts This Play About Pittsburgh's African-Americans." *Riverside Press-Enterprise*, August 1, 2003.

Frascella, Lawrence. "Fakin' Whoopi." *Entertainment Weekly*, February 14, 2003, p. 78.

_____. "Fine Tuning: 'The Piano Lesson.'" *New York Times Magazine*, September 10, 1989, p. 19.

_____. "'King' of the Hill." *Entertainment Weekly*, May 11, 2001, p. 70.

Freedman, Samuel G. "August Wilson, Defining an Era." *New York Times*, February 5, 2003.

_____. "Leaving His Imprint on Broadway." *New York Times*, November 22, 1987.

_____. "A Voice from the Streets: August Wilson's Plays Portray the Sound and Feel of Black Poverty." *New York Times Magazine*, March 15, 1987, p. 36.

_____. "Wilson's New Fences Nurtures a Partnership." *New York Times*, May 5, 1985, p. 80.

Fulani, Lenora B. "Black Empowerment:

Playwright August Wilson Less Known by Blacks." *New Pittsburgh Courier*, March 5, 1997.

Fuoco, Michael A. "Hill District Determined to Regain Lost Greatness." *Pittsburgh Post-Gazette*, April 11, 1999.

Gamer, Michael. *Romanticism and the Gothic: Genre, Reception, and Canon Formation*. Cambridge: Cambridge University Press, 2000.

Gantt, Patricia. "Ghosts from 'Down There': The Southernness of August Wilson," in *August Wilson: A Casebook*. New York: Garland, 1994.

Gardner, Elysa. "'Bottom' Sings Blues with Bounce, Charm." *USA Today*, February 10, 2003, p. 5D.

_____. 'It's Good to Be Wilson's 'King.'" *USA Today*, May 3, 2001.

Gates, Henry Louis. "The Chitlin Circuit." *New Yorker*, Vol. 72, No. 45, February 3, 1997, pp. 44–55.

Gelhaus, Anne. "'Two Trains' on Track." *MetroActive*, March 14–20, 1996.

"Gem of the Ocean." *New York Times*, April 27, 2003, p. 2.6.

Gener, Randy. "Salvation in the City of Bones: Ma Rainey and Aunt Ester Sing Their Own Songs in August Wilson's Grand Cycle of Blues Dramas." *American Theatre*, Vol. 20, No. 5, May-June 2003, pp. 20–28.

Genovese, Eugene D. *Roll, Jordan, Roll*. New York: Vintage, 1976.

Gibron, Bill. "The Piano Lesson." *Artisan*, February 12, 2003.

Gill, Brendan. "Hard Times." *New Yorker*, October 22, 1984.

Glover, Margaret E. "Two Notes on August Wilson: The Songs of a Marked Man." *Theater*, Vol. 19, No. 3, Summer-Fall, 1988, pp. 69–70.

Goddu, Teresa A. "Blood Daggers and Lonesome Graveyards: The Gothic and Country Music." *South Atlantic Quarterly*, Vol. 94, No. 1, 1995, pp. 57–80.

Goodale, Gloria. "Playwright August Wilson on Race Relations and the Theater." *Christian Science Monitor*, May 15, 1998.

Grant, Nathan L. "Men, Women, and Culture: A Conversation with August Wilson." *American Drama*, Vol. 5, No. 2, Spring 1996, pp. 100–22.

Graves, Jen. "Playwright August Wilson Born to Perform." *Tacoma News Tribune*, May 26, 2003, p. D1.

Green, Judith. "Despite Bumps, 'Jitney' a Pleasure Ride." *Atlanta Journal-Constitution*, October 15, 1999, p. R4.

Greenberg, James. "Did Hollywood Sit on 'Fences'?" *New York Times*, January 27, 1991.

Grondahl, Paul. "August Wilson: Hearing His Characters All Over Town." *Albany Magazine*, Fall 1996.

Gussow, Adam. "'Making My Getaway': The Blues Lives of Black Minstrels in W. C. Handy's Father of the Blues." *African American Review*, Spring 2001.

Gutman, Les. "King Hedley II." *CurtainUp*, 2001.

Haki Madhubuti. *Black Men: Obsolete, Single, Dangerous?: Afrikan American Families in Transition*. Chicaco: Third World Press, 1990.

Harris, J. William. *Deep Souths: Delta, Piedmont, and Sea Island Society in the Age of Segregation*. Baltimore: Johns Hopkins University Press, 2001.

Harris, Trudier. "August Wilson's Folk Traditions," in *August Wilson: A Casebook*. New York: Garland, 1994.

Harrison, Molly. *The Kitchen in History*. New York: Charles Scribner's Sons, 1972.

Harrison, Paul Carter. "August Wilson's Blues Poetics," in *Three Plays*. Pittsburgh: University of Pittsburgh Press, 1991.

_____. "The Crisis of Black Theatre Identity." *African American Review*, Vol. 31, No. 4, 1997, p. 576.

_____, Victor Leo Walker, and Gus Edwards, eds. *Black Theatre: Ritual Performance in the African Diaspora*. Philadelphia: Temple University Press, 2002.

Hartigan, Karelisa V. *Within the Dramatic Spectrum*. Lanham, Md.: University Press of America, 1986.

Hazzard-Gordon, Katrina. *Jookin': The Rise of Social Dance Formations in African-American Culture*. Philadelphia: Temple University Press, 1992.

Heard, Elisabeth J. "August Wilson on Playwriting." *African American Review*, Vol. 35, No. 1, Spring 2001, p. 93.

Heilbrunn, Jacob. "Bus Boy." *New Republic*, Vol. 217, No. 17, October 27, 1997, p. 42.

Henerson, Evan. "A 'Gem' to Behold." *Los Angeles Daily News*, August 1, 2003.

_____. "Rashad, Chisholm Excel in August Wilson Play in L. A." *Houston Chronicle*, August 5, 2003.

_____. "Rashad Discovers a 'Gem.'" *Long Beach Press-Telegram*, August 1, 2003.

Henry, William A. "Exorcising the Demons of Memory: August Wilson Exults in the Blues and Etches Slavery's Legacy." *Time*, Vol. 131, No. 15, April 11, 1988, pp. 77–78.

Herrington, Joan. *I Ain't Sorry for Nothin' I Done: August Wilson's Process of Playwrighting*. New York: Limelight Editions, 1998.

Hicks, Dylan. "Doing What Comes Naturally." *Minneapolis City Pages*, Vol. 24, No. 1160, February 26, 2003.

"The Hill District: August Wilson." http://www.clpgh.org/exhibit/neighborhoods/hill/hill_n102.html.

Hine, Darlene Clark, et al., eds. *Black Women in America: An Historical Encyclopedia*. Bloomington: Indiana University Press, 1993.

Hirschhorn, Joel. "Review: Gem of the Ocean." *Variety*, August 11, 2003, p. 30.

Hitchcock, Laura. "Gem of the Ocean." *Los Angeles Review*, July 30, 2003.

_____. "King Hedley II." *CurtainUp*, 2000.

Hobsbawm, Eric, and Terence Ranger. *The Invention of Tradition*. New York: Cambridge University Press, 1983.

Hodgins, Paul. "Finding the Cost of Freedom: Slavery and Its Aftermath Are Explored in 'Gem of the Ocean.' August Wilson's Latest Play." *Orange County Register*, August 1, 2003, p. 1.

_____. "A Lesson in Theatrical Greatness: This Ghost Story Will Haunt You with Its Beauty Long After the Lights Go Up." *Orange County Register*, October 25, 1999, p. F3.

Hoover, Bob. "Bedford Avenue to Broadway: Childhood in Hill Leads to a Pulitzer for August Wilson." *Pittsburgh Post-Gazette*, June 1, 1987, p. 15.

Ifill, Gwen. "American Shakespeare." *PBS News*, April 6, 2001.

"In Black and White." http://www.newsreel.org/films/inblack.htm.

"Interview with August Wilson." *EGG the Arts Show*. http://www.pbs.org/wnet/egg/233/wilson/interview_content_1.html.

Isherwood, Charles. "King Hedley II." *Variety*, Vol. 382, No. 12, May 7, 2001, pp. 76–77.

Jackson, Kerry. "Industrialist Andrew W. Mellon His Focus Helped Him Become One of History's Most Prosperous." *Investor's Business Daily*, March 8, 2001.

Jaques, Damien. "Dialogue Drives Another Wilson Gem." *Milwaukee Journal Sentinel*, May 1, 2003.

"Jitney." *London Times*, October 16, 2001.

Johnson, Javon. "A Dialogue Between August Wilson and Javon Johnson." *USA Weekend*, December 17, 2002.

Jones, Chris. "Homeward Bound." *American Theatre*, Vol. 16, No. 9, November 1999, pp. 14–19.

_____. "Review: Gem of the Ocean." *Variety*, May 5, 2003, p. 39.

_____. "This Man Can't Be Serious." *Chicago Tribune*, April 24, 3002, p. 3.

Jones, Evan. *American Food*. Woodstock, N.Y.: Overlook Press, 1990.

Jones, James Earl. "August Wilson." *Time*, Vol. 158, No. 1, July 9, 2001, p. 84.

Jones, Kenneth. "Bill Irwin, Paula Vogel and August Wilson Selected for Off-Bway Signature's Next Three Seasons." *Playbill*, March 7, 2003.

Joseph, May. "Alliances across the Margins." *African American Review*, Vol. 31, No. 4, Winter 1997, pp. 595–599.

Kanfer, Stefan. "Kings and Commoners." *New Leader*, Vol. 84, No. 4, July 2001, p. 45.

_____. "Seven Guitars." *New Leader*, Vol. 79, No. 3, June 3, 1996, p. 23.

_____. "Two Trains Running." *New Leader*, Vol. 75, No. 6, May 4, 1992, p. 21.

Kaufman, Ed. "Review: Gem of the Ocean." *Hollywood Reporter*, August 5, 2003, p. 13.

Keating, Douglas J. "A 'King' with Majesty Sadly Thwarted." *Philadelphia Inquirer*, January 31, 2003.

Keller, James R. "The Shaman's Apprentice: Ecstasy and Economy in Wilson's Joe Turner." *African American Review*, Vol. 35, No. 3, Fall 2001, p. 471.

Keller, Julia. "Through Words August Wilson Finds His Sense of History 'People Need to Know the Story.'" *Chicago Tribune*, December 10, 2000, p. 1.

Kelly, Jack. "The Genius of Romare Bearden." *American Legacy: Celebrating African-American History & Culture*, Vol. 7, No. 1, Spring 2001, pp. 66–73.

Kendt, Rob. "Review: Gem of the Ocean." *Back Stage West*, August 7, 2003, pp. 19, 20.

Kester, Gunilla Theander. "Approaches to Africa: The Poetics of Memory and the Body in Two August Wilson Plays," in *August Wilson: A Casebook*. New York: Garland, 1994.

King, Robert L. "World Premieres." *North American Review*, Vol. 280, No. 4, July-August 1995, pp. 44–48.

Kinzer, Stephen. "A Playwright Casts Himself to Tell His Angry Story." *New York Times*, May 26, 2003, p. E5.

Kolin, Philip C. *American Playwrights Since 1945: A Guide to Scholarship, Criticism, and Performance*. Westport, Conn.: Greenwood, 1989.

Kramer, Mimi. "Traveling Man and Hesitating Woman." *New Yorker*, April 30, 1990, pp. 82–83.

Kroll, Jack. "And in This Corner." *Newsweek*, Vol. 129, No. 6, Feb 10, 1997, p. 65.

_____. "August Wilson's Come to Stay." *Newsweek*, April 11, 1988, p. 82.

_____. "Seven Guitars." *Newsweek*, Vol. 125, No. 6, February 6, 1995, p. 60.

Kubitschek, Missy Dehn. "August Wilson's Gender Lesson," in *May All Your Fences Have Gates: Essays on the Drama of August Wilson*. Iowa City: University of Iowa Press, 1994.

Lahr, John. "Black and Blues: *Seven Guitars*, a New Chapter in August Wilson's Ten-Play Cycle." *New Yorker*, April 15, 1996, p. 100.

Launer, Pat. "'Two Trains Running' at the Old Globe Theatre." *KPBS Radio*, March 21, 1991.

Leib, Mark. "Keys of History: *The Piano Lesson* Imparts Importance of Our African-American Past." *Weekly Planet*, February 12, 2003.

Levine, Lawrence W. *Black Culture and Black Consciousness: Afro-American Folk Thought from Slavery to Freedom*. New York: Oxford University Press, 1977.

Lichtenstein, Gene. "An Evening with August Wilson." *Jewish Journal of Greater Los Angeles*, February 11, 2000.

Lorant, Stefan, et al. *Pittsburgh: The Story of an American City*. Pittsburgh: Esselmont Books, 1999.

Lowe, John. "Wake-up Call from Watts." *World & I*, Vol. 13, No. 5, May 1998, p. 250.

Lowry, Mark. "Still Tasty after All These Years: The 'Chitlin Circuit,' Born in the Era of Segregation, Continues to Tap into African-Americans' Need for a Theater of Their Own." *Fort Worth Star-Telegram*, June 29, 2003, p. 1.

Lyons, Bonnie. "An Interview with August Wilson." *Contemporary Literature*, Vol. 40, No. 1, Spring 1999, p. 1.

Majors, Richard, and Janet Mancini Billson. *Cool Pose: The Dilemmas of Black Manhood in America*. New York: Lexington Books, 1992.

Margolis, Lynn. "Black Artists Who Defied Stereotypes." *Christian Science Monitor*, October 3, 2003, p. 19.

Marra, Kim. "Ma Rainey and the Boyz: Gender Ideology in August Wilson's Broadway Canon," in *August Wilson: A Casebook*. New York: Garland, 1994.

Marshall, Michael. "Spiritual Odyssey: August Wilson's *Joe Turner's Come and Gone*." *World and I*, December 1987.

Maufort, Marc, ed. *Staging Difference: Cultural Pluralism in American Theatre and Drama*. New York: Peter Lang, 1995.

"May All Your Fences Have Gates." http://lime.weeg.uiowa.edu/~uipress/newbooks nadel-ma.html.

McCord, Keryl E. "The Challenge of Change." *African American Review*, Vol. 31, No. 4, Winter 1997, pp. 601–609.

McCracken, Nancy. "When the YA Authors Are the Students: Learning from Cissy Lacks." *ALAN Review*, Vol. 23, No. 2, Winter 1996.

McDonough, Carla J. *Staging Masculinity: Male Identity in Contemporary American Drama*. Jefferson, N. C.: McFarland, 1997.

Mckanic, Arlene. "Wilson's 'Jitney' Drives Home." *New York Amsterdam News*, pp. 21, 22.

McKelly, James C. "Hymns of Sedition: Portraits of the Artist in Contemporary African-American Drama." *Arizona Quar-*

terly, Vol. 48, No. 1, Spring 1992, pp. 87–107.

Metzger, Linda, et al., eds. *Black Writers: A Selection of Sketches from Contemporary Authors*. Detroit: Gale Research, 1989.

Migler, Raphael. "An Elegant Duet." *Gentleman's Quarterly*, April 1990, p. 114.

Mills, Alice. "The Walking Blues: An Anthropological Approach to the Theater of August Wilson." *Black Scholar*, Vol. 25, No. 2, 1995, pp. 30–35.

Monaco, Pamela Jean. "Father, Son, and Holy Ghost: From the Local to the Mythical in August Wilson," in *August Wilson: A Casebook*. New York: Garland, 1994.

Morales, Michael. "Ghosts on the Piano: August Wilson and the Representation of Black American History," in *May All Your Fences Have Gates: Essays on the Drama of August Wilson*. Iowa City: University of Iowa Press, 1994.

Morehouse, Ward. "Powerful 'King' Traces the Black Experience." *Christian Science Monitor*, Vol. 93, No. 127, May 25, 2001, p. 16.

Morley, Sheridan. "High Society and Slumming It: Sheridan Morley on Conflicts of Colour in Noel Coward and August Wilson." *New Statesman*, January 6, 2003.

Moyers, Bill. "August Wilson's America: A Conversation with Bill Moyers." *American Theater*, Vol. 7, No. 6, 1989, p. 14.

_____. *A World of Ideas*. New York: Doubleday, 1989.

Nadel, Alan, ed. *May All Your Fences Have Gates: Essays on the Drama of August Wilson*. Iowa City: University of Iowa Press, 1994, pp. 116–132.

Nesmith, Eugene. "What's Race Got to Do with It?" *American Theatre*, Vol. 13, No. 3, March 1996, pp. 12–17.

Norman, Tony. "Demolition Leaves Artist Scavenging for Answers." *Pittsburgh Post-Gazette*, September 24, 2002.

Nunns, Stephen. "Wilson, Brustein & the Press." *American Theatre*, Vol. 14, No. 3, March 1997, pp. 17–19.

Oliver, Edith. "Interlude 1987: 'Fences.'" *New Yorker*, May 31, 1993, p. 136.

O'Mahony, John. "American Centurion." Manchester *Guardian*, December 14, 2002.

Papageorge, John. "Train He Rides." *MetroActive*, 1995.

Papatola, Dominic P. "Thunder, Lightning Pierce 'Hedley' Storm." *St. Paul Pioneer Press*, May 31, 2003, p. B6.

Patterson, Orlando. *Slavery and Social Death*. Cambridge: Harvard University Press, 1982.

Pender, Rick. "Speaking the Truth." *New Orleans CityBeat*, Vol. 9, No. 23, April 16–22, 2003.

Pereira, Kim. *August Wilson and the African-American Odyssey*. Urbana: University of Illinois Press, 1995.

_____. *Reference Guide to American Literature*. New York: St. James Press, 1994.

Pettengill, Richard. "Alternatives ... Opposites ... Convergences: An Interview with Lloyd Richards," in *August Wilson: A Casebook*. New York: Garland, 1994.

_____. "The Historical Perspective: An Interview with August Wilson," in *August Wilson: A Casebook*. New York: Garland, 1994.

Philips, Michael. "Wilson's 'Gem' a Diamond in the Rough." *Chicago Tribune*, April 30, 2003, p. 1.

"'Piano Lesson' Gets Top Emmy Nominations." *Jet*, Vol. 88, No. 13, August 7, 1995, p. 61.

Plum, Jay. "Blues, History, and the Dramaturgy of August Wilson." *African American Review*, Vol. 27, No. 4, Winter 1993, pp. 561–567.

Plummer, William, and Toby Kahn. "Street Talk." *People Weekly*, Vol. 45, No. 19, May 13, 1996, pp. 63–65.

Powell, Jason. "August Wilson: The Playwright Versus the Politician." *Knox College Common Room*, Vol. 4, No. 1, May 29, 2000.

Power, Edward M. "Our Wonder of the Hill District." *Greater Pittsburgh* [a publication of the Chamber of Commerce], February 1932.

Powers, Kim. "An Interview with August Wilson." *Theatre*, Vol. 16, No. 1, 1984, pp. 50–55.

Pressley, Nelson. "D.C. Theater's Uncast Role, Lack of African American Troupe Leaves Nagging Question: Why?" *Washington Post*, October 3, 1999, p. G1.

Preston, Rohan. "Cast Gives Lift to Heavy 'King Hedley.'" *Minneapolis Star Tribune*, May 31, 2003, p. 5B.

_____. "Hudson Returns in 'King'-size Role." *Minneapolis Star Tribune*, June 1, 2003.

_____. "Oglesby Sparkles in Wilson's 'Gem.'" *Minneapolis Star Tribune*, May 4, 2003, p. 4F.

"The Public Stages an Emotionally Explosive 'Seven Guitars.'" *Pittsburgh Post-Gazette*, June 14, 1997.

"Pulitzer Deadline Looms." *Variety*, February 26, 2001.

Rawson, Chris. "August Wilson — A Timeline." *Pittsburgh Post-Gazette*, December 16, 1999.

_____. "Many Pittsburghers Turn Out to Celebrate August Wilson's Latest Opening." *Pittsburgh Post-Gazette*, May 1, 2001.

_____. "O'Reilly Theater: Charting 20th Century Black America." *Pittsburgh Post-Gazette*, December 5, 1999.

_____. "O'Reilly Theater: Wilson Again Proves Home Is Where the Art Is." *Pittsburgh Post-Gazette*, December 5, 1999.

_____. "Playwright August Wilson Still Has Miles to Go." *Pittsburgh Post-Gazette*, July 5, 2001.

_____. "The Power Behind the Plays." *Pittsburgh Post-Gazette* Special Report, 1999.

_____. "Stage Review: Wilson Polishes 'Jitney' in Richer, Longer Production." *Pittsburgh Post-Gazette*, November 22, 1998.

_____. "Stage Review: Wilson's Hedley a Thrilling Ride." *Pittsburgh Post-Gazette*, December 16, 1999.

_____. "Stage Reviews: Wilson's 'Jitney,' 'King Hedley II' Have Become Clearer, Tighter Since Leaving Pittsburgh." *Pittsburgh Post-Gazette*, June 25, 2000.

Reed, Ishmael. "A Shy Genius Transforms the American Theater." *Connoisseur*, Vol. 127, 1987, pp. 92–97.

Reich, Howard. "The Real Ma Rainey the Mother of the Blues Was More Than a Flashy Character." *Chicago Tribune*, June 30, 1997, p. 1.

Renner, Pamela. "Black Theaters in a Fight for Survival." *Variety*, July 10, 2000, p. 35.

_____. "'King' Takes Royal Road to Broadway." *Variety*, April 30, 2001, p. 67.

Reynolds, Christopher. "Mr. Wilson's Neighborhood: Playwright August Wilson No Longer Lives in Pittsburgh's Hill District, but It Is Consistently at Home in His Work." *Los Angeles Times*, July 27, 2002, p. E1.

Rich, Frank. "A Family Confronts Its History in August Wilson's 'Piano Lesson.'" *New York Times*, April 17, 1990, pp. C13, C15.

_____. *Hot Seat: Theater Criticism for the New York Times, 1980–1993*. New York: Random House, 1998.

_____. "Theater: 'Ma Rainey's Black Bottom.'" *New York Times*, April 11, 1984.

Richards, Sandra L. "Yoruba Gods on the American Stage: August Wilson's *Joe Turner's Come and Gone*." *Research in African Literatures*, Vol. 30, No. 4, Winter 1999, p. 92.

Robb, J. Cooper. "August Tidings." *Philadelphia Weekly*, January 22, 2003.

Robinson, Beverly J. "Africanisms and the Study of Folklore," in *Africanisms in American Culture*. Bloomington: Indiana University Press, 1990.

Rocha, Mark William. "American History as 'Loud Talking' in *Two Trains Running*," in *May All Your Fences Have Gates: Essays on the Drama of August Wilson*. Iowa City: University of Iowa Press, 1994, pp. 116–132.

_____. "A Conversation with August Wilson." *Diversity: A Journal of Multicultural Issues*, Vol. 1, Fall 1992, pp. 24–42.

_____. "August Wilson and the Four B's: Influences," in *August Wilson: A Casebook*. New York: Garland, 1994.

Rothstein, Mervyn. "Round Five for a Theatrical Heavyweight." *New York Times*, April 15, 1990, pp. 1, 8.

Rotundo, E. Anthony. *American Manhood*. Chicago: Perseus Books, 1990.

Rousuck, J. Wynn. "Everyone Wants to Get into the Act." *Baltimore Sun*, May 2, 1997, p. 1E.

_____. "People with Vision." *Baltimore Sun*, April 27, 1997, p. 1E.

"The Roving Editor." *The Writer*, Vol. 110, No. 6, June 1997, p. 4.

"The Roving Editor." *The Writer*, Vol. 112, No. 5, May 1999, p. 4.

Saltzman, Simon, and Nicole Plett. "August Wilson vs. Robert Brustein." *U.S. 1 Newspaper*, January 22, 1997.

_____. "'Jitney' at Crossroads." *U.S. 1 Newspaper*, April 16, 1997.

Savran, David. *In Their Own Words: Contemporary American Playwrights.* New York: Theatre Communications Group, 1988.

Scott, Daniel M. "August Wilson and the African-American Odyssey." *MELUS*, Vol. 24, No. 3, Fall, p. 163.

Shafer, Yvonne. *August Wilson: A Research and Production Sourcebook.* Westport, Conn.: Greenwood, 1998.

Shannon, Sandra G. "Blues, History, and Dramaturgy." *African American Review*, Vol. 27, No. 4, Winter 1993, pp. 539–559.

_____. "Conversing with the Past: *Joe Turner's Come and Gone* and *The Piano Lesson*." *CEA Magazine*, Vol. 4, No. 1, 1991, pp. 33–42.

_____. *The Dramatic Vision of August Wilson.* Washington, D.C.: Howard University Press, 1996.

_____. "From Lorraine Hansberry to August Wilson: An Interview with Lloyd Richards." *Callaloo*, Vol. 14, No. 1, 1991, pp. 124–135.

_____. "The Good Christian's Come and Gone: The Shifting Role of Christianity in August Wilson's Plays." *MELUS*, Vol. 16, No. 3, 1989, pp. 127–142.

_____. "Subtle Imposition: The Lloyd Richards–August Wilson Formula," in *August Wilson: A Casebook.* New York: Garland, 1994.

_____. "A Transplant That Did Not Take: August Wilson's Views on the Great Migration." *African American Review*, Vol. 31, No. 4, 1997, pp. 659–666.

"Sharing the Stage with August Wilson." http://www.donshewey.com/theater_articles/marion_mcclinton.htm, April 29, 2001.

Shaw, Kristen. "Closely-watched Trains: Penumbra Does Good with Wilson." *Mac Weekly*, Vol. 96, No. 3, February 21, 2003.

Sheward, David. "Seven Guitars." *Back Stage*, Vol. 37, No. 14, April 5, 1996, p. 5.

Shirley, Don. "Queen of the Hill: August Wilson's Potent But Ungainly 'Gem of the Ocean' Opens at the Taper." *Los Angeles Times*, August 1, 2003, p. E1.

Simon John. "King Hedley II." *New York Magazine*, May 14, 2001.

_____. "Two Trains Running." *New York Times*, April 27, 1992.

Sincere, Rick. "Two Trains Running: A Marvelous Ride." *Metro Herald*, February 1996.

Sklar, Kathryn Kish. *Women's Rights Emerges within the Antislavery Movement 1830–1870.* Boston: Bedford, 2000.

Smiley, Tavis. "Profile: August Wilson's 'Gem of the Ocean.' Starring Phylicia Rashad." *National Public Radio*, August 29, 2003.

Smith, Philip E. "Ma Rainey's Black Bottom: Playing the Blues as Equipment for Living," in *Within the Dramatic Spectrum.* New York: University Press of America, 1986, pp. 177–186.

Snodgrass, Mary Ellen. *Encyclopedia of Kitchen History.* London: Fitzroy Dearborn, 2003.

Sobelsohn, David. "Ridin' All Over." *CenterStage*, January 8–February 14, 1999.

Staples, Brent. "August Wilson." *Essence*, Vol. 18, August 1987, pp. 51, 111, 113.

Stearns, David Patrick. "'The Piano Lesson,' Heavy on Drills." *USA Today*, April 17, 1990.

Stearns, Marshall. *The Story of Jazz.* New York: Oxford University Press, 1956.

Steinbeck, John. *America and Americans.* New York: Viking, 1966.

Stern, Gary. "Playwrights Agree That the Workshops Process Is a Major Aid in Rewriting." *Backstage*, June 8, 1984, pp. 18A–19A.

Stuckey, Sterling. *Slave Culture: Nationalist Theory and the Foundations of Black America.* New York: Oxford University Press, 1987.

Swanson, Carl. "Theater Wars: A Live Report from the Brustein vs. Wilson 10-Rounder." http://salonmagazine.com/media/media970129.html.

Tallmer, Jerry. "Fences: Anguish of Wasted Talent." *New York Post*, March 26, 1987, p. 28.

Taylor, Regina. "That's Why They Call It the Blues." *American Theatre*, Vol. 13, No. 4, April 1996, pp. 18–23.

"Theater Critics Name Finalists for $15,000 New Play Award." *Business Wire*, February 15, 2001.

Thompson, Maxine. "Writer's Watershed." *The Writer*, Vol. 110, No. 11, November 1997, pp. 5–6.

Tidjani-Serpos, Noureini. "The Postcolonial Condition: The Archeology of African Knowledge." *Research in African Literatures*, Vol. 27, No. 1, Spring 1996, pp. 3–18.

Timpane, John. "Filling the Time: Reading History in the Drama of August Wilson," in *May All Your Fences Have Gates: Essays on the Drama of August Wilson*. Iowa City: University of Iowa Press, 1994.

Tolnay, Stewart E., and E. M. Beck. *A Festival of Violence: An Analysis of Southern Lynchings, 1882–1930*. Urbana: University of Illinois, 1995.

Toomer, Jeanette. "'King Hedley' Conquers Broadway." *New York Amsterdam News*, Vol. 92, No. 19, May 10, 2001, pp. 21–22.

Torrens, James S. "Seven Guitars." *America*, Vol. 174, No. 19, June 8, 1996, p. 22.

Tu, Janet I-Chin. "Story to Tell — Playwright August Wilson, Now Settled in Seattle's Misty Nest, Writes About the Black Experience Like No Other Storyteller." *Seattle Times*, January 18, 1998.

Tynan, William. "Death and the Blues." *Time*, Vol. 145, No. 5, February 6, 1995, p. 71.

Üsekes, Ciggdem. "'We's the Leftovers': Whiteness as Economic Power and Exploitation in August Wilson's Twentieth-Century Cycle of Plays." *African American Review*, Vol. 37, No. 1, Spring 2003, pp. 115–125.

Vaughan, Peter. "Mending 'Fences.'" *Minneapolis Star Tribune*, May 11, 1997, p. 1F.

———. "Questions Linger about 'Fences' Project.'" *Minneapolis Star Tribune*, January 25, 1997, p. 1B.

Vaughn, Michael. "On the Right Track." *Palo Alto Weekly*, March 15, 1996.

Vorlicky, Robert. *Act Like a Man: Challenging Masculinities in American Drama*. Ann Arbor: University of Michigan Press, 1995.

Wang, Qun. *An In-Depth Study of the Major Plays of African American Playwright August Wilson: Vernacularizing the Blues on Stage*. Vol. 6 of *Black Studies*. Lewiston, Ont.: Edwin Mellen Press, 1999.

Watlington, Dennis. "Hurdling Fences." *Vanity Fair*, Vol. 356, April 1989, pp. 102–113.

Weales, Gerald Clifford. "Two Trains Running." *Commonweal*, Vol. 119, June 1992, p. 18.

Weber, Bruce. "Sculpturing a Play into Existence." *New York Times*, March 24, 1996, p. H7.

Weisenburger, Steven. "The Shudder and the Silence: James Baldwin on White Terror." *ANQ*, Vol. 15, No. 3, Summer 2002, pp. 3–13.

Weiss, Hey. "'Ocean' Voyage Proves Rough but Rewarding." *Chicago Sun-Times*, April 29, 2003, p. 34.

Werner, Craig Hansen. *Playing the Changes: From Afro-Modernism to the Jazz Impulse*. Urbana: University of Illinois Press, 1994.

Wertheimer, Linda, and Noah Adams. "August Wilson's New Play, 'King Hedley II.'" *NPR: All Things Considered*, March 13, 2000.

Wessling, Joseph H. "Wilson's *Fences*." *Explicator*, Vol. 57, No. 2, Winter 1999, pp. 123–127.

West, Cornel. *Race Matters*. Boston: Beacon Press, 1993.

Whitaker, Charles. "Is August Wilson America's Greatest Playwright?" *Ebony*, Vol. 56, No. 11, September 2001, p. 80.

Wilde, Lisa. "Reclaiming the Past: Narrative and Memory in August Wilson's *Two Trains Running*." *Theater*, Vol. 22, No. 1, Fall/winter 1990-1991, pp. 73–74.

Willis, John C. *Forgotten Time: The Yazoo-Mississippi Delta after the Civil War*. Charlottesville: University Press of Virginia, 2000.

Willis, Susan. *Specifying: Black Women Writing the American Experience*. Racine: University of Wisconsin Press, 1989.

Wilson, August. "Feed Your Mind, the Rest Will Follow." Pittsburgh *Post-Gazette*, March 28, 1999.

———. "How to Write a Play Like August Wilson." *New York Times*, March 10, 1991, Sect. 2, p. 5.

———. "I Want a Black, Director." *New York Times*, September 26, 1990.

———. "Living on Mother's Prayer." *New York Times*, May 12, 1996, p. 13.

———. "Sailing the Black Stream of Culture." *New York Times*, April 23, 2000.

———. "Where to Begin," in *Short Pieces from the New Dramatists*. Banbury, Ox.: Orangeberry Books, 1985, pp. 2033–2037.

———, and Elizabeth J. Heard, interviewer.

"August Wilson on Playwriting." *African American Review*, Vol. 35, No. 1, 2001, pp. 93–102.

_____, and Sandra G. Shannon, interviewer. "Blues, History, and Dramaturgy." *African American Review*, Vol. 27, No. 4, 1993, pp. 539–559.

Wilson, Charles Reagan, and William Ferris, eds. *Encyclopedia of Southern Culture.* Chapel Hill: University of North Carolina Press, 1989.

Winn, Steven. "50 for the Ages: A Critic's List of Great 20th Century American Plays." *San Francisco Chronicle*, May 30, 1999, p. 37.

Wolfe, Peter. *August Wilson.* New York: Twayne, 1999.

Yardley, Jonathan. "In the Fields of Despair." *Washington Post*, March 31, 1996.

Zimmerman, Heather. "Keys to the Past." *Silicon Valley Metro*, April 5–11, 2001.

Index

Main entries are in **boldface**.

255

Shall We Dance?

HIP-HOP DANCE

by Wendy Hinote Lanier

FOCUS READERS

FOCUS READERS

www.focusreaders.com

Focus Readers is distributed by North Star Editions:
sales@northstareditions.com | 888-417-0195

Produced for Focus Readers by Red Line Editorial.

Photographs ©: Mlenny/iStockphoto, cover, 1; ginosphotos/iStockphoto, 4–5; PYMCAUIG Universal Images Group/Newscom, 7; Creatista/iStockphoto, 9; ra2studio/Shutterstock Images, 10–11; oneinchpunch/iStockphoto, 13; blanaru/iStockphoto, 14–15, 29; jonya/iStockphoto, 17; Benis Arapovic/iStockphoto, 18; szefei/Shutterstock Images, 21; LarsZahnerPhotography/iStockphoto, 22–23; Polka Dot Images/iStockphoto, 25; Pavel L Photo and Video/Shutterstock Images, 26

ISBN
978-1-63517-274-4 (hardcover)
978-1-63517-339-0 (paperback)
978-1-63517-469-4 (ebook pdf)
978-1-63517-404-5 (hosted ebook)

Library of Congress Control Number: 2017935122

Printed in the United States of America
Mankato, MN
June, 2017

About the Author

Wendy Hinote Lanier is a native Texan and former elementary teacher who writes and speaks for children and adults on a variety of topics. She is the author of more than 20 books for children and young people. Some of her favorite people are dogs.

TABLE OF CONTENTS

WHAT IS HIP-HOP DANCE?

The street party begins. It's time to dance. Hip-hop is an athletic style of street dance. Dancers might pop or lock. They might spin on their heads or backs. Break dancing moves are common, too.

Hip-hop dancers are known for their fun, energetic styles.

Hip-hop dance is part of hip-hop culture. The culture includes music and art, too. Hip-hop began in the 1970s. It started in the Bronx in New York City. Neighborhoods there hosted block parties. Usually a **DJ** hosted the event. Clive Campbell was one of them. He and his sister

DANCE TIP

You need good upper-body strength to break-dance. Increase upper-body strength by doing push-ups or working with a weighted ball.

Clive Campbell was nicknamed DJ Kool Herc.

hosted a block party in the summer of 1973. Their goal was to raise money to buy new school clothes.

Clive was only 16 years old. But his style caught on. Clive began **isolating** drum breaks in popular music. This involved two **turntables**. He switched back and forth between them. These breaks could be repeated. This gave dancers plenty of time to show off their moves.

DANCE TIP

Keep your arms and hands relaxed and loose at your sides.

> Breaking is often done in groups.

Clive's party was the birth of hip-hop. Clive was the first to call the dancers break boys, or b-boys. Their style of dancing soon became known as breaking, or break dancing.

CHAPTER 2

WHAT TO WEAR

Hip-hop dancers create their own style. Clothes usually reflect **urban** street wear. Many dancers wear sweatpants or cargo pants. Oversized T-shirts or hoodies are common. Others prefer tank tops.

A hip-hop dancer shows off her style.

The key is to dress in layers. You can cool off by removing a layer when needed.

Busting a big move can be dangerous. Safety gear helps prevent injuries. Dancers sometimes wear wrist pads, elbow pads, and knee pads.

DANCE TIP

Dance shoes should allow you to slip and spin. If the soles grip too hard, you could fall or injure yourself.

 Hip-hop dancers dress to look good and move freely.

Sneakers or soft-soled shoes work great for hip-hop. High-top sneakers are a popular choice, too. For **competitions** or **exhibitions**, you might want a special pair for dancing.

CHAPTER 3

POP AND LOCK IT

Creativity is key in hip-hop dancing. Dancers bring their own moves or style. But there are a few basic moves you'll want to master. One is called popping. First you **contract** a muscle.

Hip-hop dancers combine many different types of movements.

Then you quickly release it. Doing so causes a jerk or pop. Popping is usually combined with other moves and poses.

Locking is also common. It starts when a dancer makes a quick move. Then the dancer locks into position for a few seconds. Locking is often done to make viewers laugh.

The boogaloo is another basic move. It uses mostly the hips and legs. Dancers try to make it appear as if they have no bones.

 Break-dancers often use their hands in their moves.

Breaking is one of the best-known parts of hip-hop dance. It features fun, **acrobatic** moves. Head spins are common. So are back spins.

 A break-dancer practices a head spin.

Watch other dancers to find fresh ideas. You can try to copy their moves.

Some moves are unique to hip-hop dance. Hip-hop dancers also borrow moves from other **social** dances. They might use jazz or funk moves. Sometimes they even look to gymnastics or martial arts. These moves are combined with basic hip-hop **choreography**. This is often seen in music videos.

THE CRADLE

Any good dance needs a killer ending. A freeze move called the cradle does the trick.

1. Start by sitting with your feet tucked under your bottom. Your knees should be spread apart.
2. Press your arms together. They should touch from the wrist to the elbow.
3. Keep your elbows firmly against your stomach. Lean forward. Open your arms and place your hands on the floor.
4. Now lift yourself up onto your hands. Turn your head to the side. Now freeze!

A dancer cradles in style.

CHAPTER 4

SHOW OFF WITH YOUR CREW

By the 1980s, hip-hop dance was becoming popular. It was featured in movies. Some television shows had hip-hop dancers, too. And the style continued to gain popularity.

High-energy moves make hip-hop dance fun to watch.

By the 1990s, hip-hop dance was in many music videos.

Today's hip-hop dancers often perform without a set plan. They can be creative. This is called hip-hop freestyling. It includes classic hip-hop moves. But the best freestyling includes some original moves, too.

Dance groups are called crews. Sometimes they challenge each other to friendly competitions. The competitions are called battles.

▷ **Break-dancers must be strong to show off their most acrobatic moves.**

Dance battles allow dancers to show off their best moves. Freestyling, dance crews, and battles are the main ingredients of the hip-hop style.

▷ **Hip-hop crews practice hard to make sure their moves match when they get to competition.**

Hip-hop competitions can be more than just neighborhood dance-offs. Some are featured on TV. Competitions are held all over the world. They give dance crews a chance to win money and recognition. Judges look for creative routines and flawless moves. They give each crew a score. A 10 is a perfect score.

Hip-hop dance is a great way to have fun and make new friends. And with a little practice, you could bust a move with the best of them.

DANCE TIP

Relax and have fun. Don't worry about how you look to others.

FOCUS ON
HIP-HOP DANCE

Write your answers on a separate piece of paper.

1. Write a letter to a friend explaining how hip-hop began.

2. What is your favorite hip-hop dance move? Why?

3. How does the boogaloo make dancers appear?
   - **A.** as though they are playing a trumpet
   - **B.** as though they have no bones
   - **C.** as though they are made of a stiff material

4. Why would someone want to participate in a hip-hop battle?
   - **A.** to earn the praise and respect of his or her friends
   - **B.** to convince others to dance hip-hop
   - **C.** to hear new music

5. What does **culture** mean in this book?

*Hip-hop dance is part of hip-hop **culture**. The culture includes music and art, too.*

    A. manners appropriate for a formal party

    B. a famous museum in New York City

    C. the actions and beliefs of a
       particular group

6. What does **freestyling** mean in this book?

*Today's hip-hop dancers often perform without a set plan. They can be creative. This is called hip-hop **freestyling**.*

    A. dance routines with
       no planned set
       of moves

    B. dance routines you
       need to memorize

    C. dance routines with
       all the basic moves

Answer key on page 32.

GLOSSARY

acrobatic
Showing skillful control of one's body.

choreography
The arrangement of steps and movements for a dance.

competitions
Events in which teams try to beat each other.

contract
To bring a muscle together and make it shorter.

DJ
A person who plays music for dances and parties.

exhibitions
Displays or demonstrations for the public.

isolating
Setting something apart from the rest.

social
Having to do with activities involving other people.

turntables
Machines that spin records.

urban
Relating to a city environment.

TO LEARN MORE

BOOKS

Fuhrer, Margaret. *American Dance: The Complete Illustrated History*. Minneapolis: Voyageur Press, 2014.

Garofoli, Wendy. *Hip-Hop Dancing: The Basics*. Mankato, MN: Capstone Press, 2011.

Royston, Angela. *Hip-Hop*. Chicago: Heinemann-Raintree, 2013.

NOTE TO EDUCATORS

Visit **www.focusreaders.com** to find lesson plans, activities, links, and other resources related to this title.

INDEX

Answer Key: 1. Answers will vary; **2.** Answers will vary; **3.** B; **4.** A; **5.** C; **6.** A